Kingdoms in Peril

Volume 4

Kingdoms in Peril

Volume 4

The Assassins Strike

Feng Menglong

Translated by Olivia Milburn

UNIVERSITY OF CALIFORNIA PRESS

University of California Press
Oakland, California

© 2023 by Olivia Milburn

Cataloging-in-Publication Data is on file at the Library of
Congress.

ISBN 978-0-520-38109-4 (cloth : alk. paper)
ISBN 978-0-520-38110-0 (pbk. : alk. paper)
ISBN 978-0-520-38111-7 (ebook)

Manufactured in the United States of America

32 31 30 29 28 27 26 25 24 23
10 9 8 7 6 5 4 3 2 1

Contents

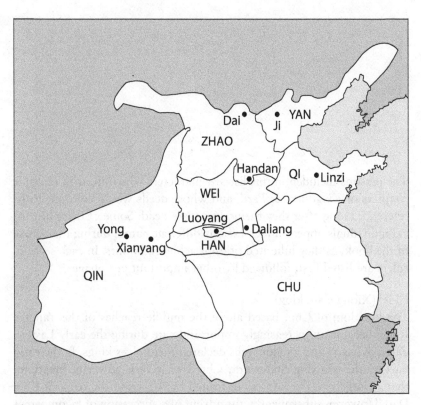

The Kingdoms of the Warring States Period circa 260 B.C.E. Adapted from *The Warring States of China c. 260 BCE* by Philg88, CC-BY-SA 3.0.

List of Main Characters

Volume Four

The persons included in this list are characters who appear in multiple chapters of *Kingdoms in Peril*, and whose deeds would continue to be referenced long after they themselves were dead. Some of these historical individuals appear under various different names during the course of the book, as they inherited titles or achieved honors. In each section, rulers are listed first, followed by other important personages.

CHU (Xiong clan; king)
The kingdom of Chu, based along the middle reaches of the Yangtze River, became an increasingly important state during the early Eastern Zhou dynasty, and its monarchs declared themselves kings. In the early part of the Warring States era, Chu was a very powerful kingdom, thanks largely to the reforms instituted by Wu Qi in the reign of King Dao. However, subsequently, the advent of a succession of incompetent or minor rulers under whose auspices corruption flourished meant that Chu was unable to resist increasing pressure from Qin.

King Dao (r. 401–381 B.C.E.), personal name Yi: the final patron of the great general and administrator Wu Qi, whose reforms angered the aristocracy of Chu.
King Wei (r. 339–329 B.C.E.), personal name Shang: a highly competent monarch under whose reign Chu underwent a significant expansion of territory.
King Huai (r. 328–299 B.C.E.), personal name Xionghui: a very stupid man dominated by his favorites, who was eventually tricked into coming to Qin by King Zhaoxiang and held hostage there until his death in 296 B.C.E.

King Qingxiang (r. 298–263 B.C.E.), personal name Heng: came to power while a hostage in Qi upon the imprisonment of his father and was engaged in constant struggles against the growing power of Qin.

King Kaolie (r. 262–238 B.C.E.), personal name Xiongwan: presided over important government reforms and a significant expansion of territory, ably assisted by the Lord of Chunshen.

King You (r. 237–228 B.C.E.), personal name Han: succeeded King Kaolie as a small child, though in actual fact he was the son of the queen and the Lord of Chunshen. The controversial circumstances of his accession threw the kingdom of Chu into chaos, from which it proved impossible to recover.

Lord of Chunshen, Huang Xie (d. 238 B.C.E.): one of the Four Great Lords of the Warring States, a senior government minister in Chu, companion to the future King Kaolie during his time as a hostage in Qin, ultimately murdered by the family of King Kaolie's queen, with whom he had earlier had a sexual relationship.

Zhao Yang, a powerful government minister under King Huai of Chu, and at one time owner of the greatest treasure of ancient China: Bian He's jade disc.

HAN (Han clan; marquis, then king)

The ruling house of Han was descended from a junior branch of the Jin marquesses. Over time, this family accumulated more power until they were able to formally partition Jin with other senior ministerial families in 403 B.C.E., a division recognized by the Zhou king. Subsequently, Han (as with the other two states that had formerly been part of Jin) struggled to remain independent in the face of the growing dominance of Qin. Ultimately, Han would be the first of the Warring States–era kingdoms to fall to Qin, collapsing in 230 B.C.E.

Lord Kang (r. 453–425 B.C.E.), personal name Hu: played a key role in the partition of Jin and the establishment of Han as an independent state.

Lord Xuanhui (r. 332–312 B.C.E.), personal name unknown: the first ruler of Han to declare himself a king in 323 B.C.E.

King Li (r. 295–273 B.C.E.), personal name Jiu: suffered constant pressure and depredations from Qin, which he proved powerless to resist.

QI (Tian clan; marquis, then king)

The Tian ruling family of Qi were descended from one of Lord Huan of Qi's ministers. Over time, this family gradually established their authority in Qi, becoming increasingly powerful, until they were ultimately able to usurp the marquisate and then crown themselves as kings of Qi. This state, often allied with Qin, would be the last to be destroyed by the First Emperor of China.

Lord Tai (r. 404–348 B.C.E.), personal name He: exiled the last ruler of Qi from the Jiang family and established himself as the first ruler from the Tian house with the title of marquis.

King Wei (r. 356–320 B.C.E.), personal name Yinqi: a very competent ruler, whose excellent choice of officials and resolute determination to resist the wiles of sycophants brought him great admiration.

King Xuan (r. 319–301 B.C.E.), personal name Bijiang: like his father, a highly successful ruler, noted for his efforts to recruit clever ministers and generals.

King Min (r. 300–284 B.C.E.), personal name Di: an increasingly unstable ruler who managed to alienate a succession of wise and sensible advisors through his cruelty and capriciousness, before finally being murdered.

King Xiang (r. 283–265 B.C.E.), personal name Fazhang: installed in power following his father's murder and a series of invasions by Yan, who temporarily stabilized the political situation.

King of Qi (r. 264–221 B.C.E.), personal name Jian: the final monarch of this kingdom, eventually deposed by the First Emperor, and thus left without posthumous title or honors.

Sun Bin (d. 316 B.C.E.): a direct descendant of Sun Wu who served King Wei of Qi as a general, and defeated his archrival, Pang Juan, in the Battle of Maling in 342 B.C.E.

Lord of Mengchang (d. 279 B.C.E.), Tian Wen, Duke of Xue: a member of a junior branch of the Tian ruling family of Qi and one of the Four Great Lords of the Warring States, noted for their intelligence and recruitment of competent advisors for the state.

QIN (Ying clan; earl, then king.)

The origins of the Ying ruling family of Qin remain highly obscure and very controversial. During the course of the Warring States period, Qin gradually became more and more powerful, until it was clear to all that unification was merely a matter of time. The enormously powerful Qin army, the highly attractive meritocratic system instituted within the kingdom, and the resolute insistence of a succession of kings on establishing the rule of law ensured that unification by Qin was increasingly regarded as inevitable and was welcomed by many as a respite from constant warfare and social collapse.

Lord Xiao (r. 361–338 B.C.E.), personal name Quliang: employed Shang Yang to reform the government, bringing Qin great wealth and power.

Lord Huiwen (r. 337–311 B.C.E.), personal name Si: executed Shang Yang for offending him when he was crown prince, was the first ruler of Qin to crown himself as king in 325 B.C.E.

King Wu (r. 310–301 B.C.E.), personal name Dang: began Qin's warfare against Han, only to die young following a weight-lifting accident.

King Zhaoxiang (r. 306–251 B.C.E.), personal name Ji: came to the throne after his brother's sudden death and proceeded to make Qin extraordinarily powerful, holding King Huai of Chu hostage, and presiding over the appalling massacre at the Battle of Changping in 260 B.C.E., in which many hundreds of thousands of Zhao soldiers died. A key figure in the early stages of the unification of China, which would ultimately be completed by his great-grandson, the First Emperor.

King Xiaowen (r. 250 B.C.E.), personal name Zhu: better known as Lord of Anguo during his tenure as crown prince during his father's long reign.

King Zhuangxiang (r. 250–247 B.C.E.), personal name Yiren, later also known as Prince Chu: held hostage in Zhao until released through the machinations of Lü Buwei, who ultimately provided him with a crown and a wife.

The First Emperor (r. 247–221 B.C.E. as king; 221–210 B.C.E. as emperor), personal name Zheng: officially the son of King Zhuangxiang of Qin and Queen Zhao Ji, here described as the illegitimate offspring of the queen and her first husband Lü Buwei. A highly competent and intelligent man, he survived many rebellions and assassination attempts by family members and foreign powers to unify China under his own rule, bringing an end to the Warring States era.

Bai Qi (d. 257 B.C.E.): the great Qin general who fought a series of successful campaigns during the reign of King Zhaoxiang, and commanded at the notoriously bloody Battle of Changping.

Fan Ju (d. 255 B.C.E.): originally from Wei, served King Zhaoxiang of Qin as a senior minister for many years, steering government policy as the process of unification intensified.

Fan Wuqi (d. 227 B.C.E.): a senior military commander who incited the Lord of Chang'an's rebellion, only to flee to the kingdom of Yan when it failed.

Lao Ai (d. 238 B.C.E.): lover of Zhao Ji, Queen Zhuangxiang of Qin, and father of two of her children, who died after plotting to place his offspring on the throne.

Lord of Chang'an, Ying Chengjiao (256–239 B.C.E.): the younger brother of the First Emperor who rose against him in a badly planned and badly executed rebellion.

Lü Buwei (d. 235 B.C.E.): originally a merchant in Zhao, a key supporter of King Zhuangxiang of Qin, first husband of his queen, Zhao Ji, and the real father of the First Emperor of China, a senior government official in Qin under a succession of monarchs.

Zhao Ji, Queen Zhuangxiang of Qin (d. 228 B.C.E.): mother of the First Emperor of China, first married to Lü Buwei, then to King Zhuangxiang of Qin, and finally the lover of Lao Ai, with whom she produced two further children. She was involved in a very stupid plot by Lao Ai to place his offspring on the Qin throne.

Shang Yang (d. 338 B.C.E.): the earliest Legalist thinker, who reformed the government of Qin in the reign of Lord Xiao, setting in place the necessary state apparatus for this kingdom's rise to preeminence.

WEI (Wei clan; marquis, then king)

The ruling family of Wei was ultimately descended from a junior branch of the Zhou royal family, and this state was created by the partition of

Jin. The early rulers of Wei were highly effective, intelligent men, under whose government this state flourished. Initially Wei was able to make significant inroads on Qin territory; however, after their defeat at the Battle of Maling in 341 B.C.E., they proved unable to resist Qin aggression and were continuously at war with them, ultimately falling in 225 B.C.E.

Lord Huan (d. 446 B.C.E.), personal name Ju: presided over the division of Jin, and successfully eliminated various rivals to partition their lands into three.

Lord Wen (r. 445–396 B.C.E.), personal name Si: a competent ruler, noted for his recruitment of excellent ministers, during whose reign Wei expanded significantly.

Lord Wu (r. 396–370 B.C.E.), personal name Ji: like his father, an intelligent and successful ruler, who continued the expansion of Wei.

Lord Hui (r. 369–319 B.C.E.), personal name Ying: took power after a controversial succession battle and declared himself king in 344 B.C.E.

King Xiang (r. 318–296 B.C.E.), personal name Si: caught up in endless fighting with Qin, and thus a major figure in attempting to preserve the Vertical Alliance.

King Zhao (r. 296–277 B.C.E.), personal name Chi: as during the reign of his father, conflict with Qin was the major political issue that he struggled to deal with.

King Anli (r. 276–243 B.C.E.), personal name Yu: suffered significant incursions from Qin, resulting in appalling casualties, but was assisted by his ongoing alliance with Zhao.

Lord of Xinling, Prince Wuji of Wei (d. 243 B.C.E.): one of the Four Great Lords of the Warring States, and a senior minister in the kingdom of Wei.

Pang Juan (d. 342 B.C.E.): an important general serving under King Hui of Wei, whose rivalry with Sun Bin of Qi proved extraordinarily violent and resulted ultimately in defeat at the Battle of Maling.

YAN (Ji clan; king)

The ruling family of Yan was descended from a younger brother of King Wu of Zhou (r. 1049/45–1043 B.C.E.). As the northernmost state of the Zhou confederacy, attacks by tribal peoples were a major concern, and they played little role in the affairs of the Central States. During the Warring States era, Yan became a powerful kingdom, but remained largely remote from much of the conflict at this time.

King Yi (r. 332–321 B.C.E.), personal name unknown: the first ruler of Yan to crown himself as king, suffered enormous losses in defeats to Qi, but employed Su Qin successfully to restore some of the damage.

King of Yan (r. 320–318 B.C.E.), personal name Kuai: attempted to abdicate the throne and thus threw the government into chaos, resulting in a prolonged period of warfare in Yan.

King Zhao (r. 311–279 B.C.E.), personal name Ping: came to the throne following the invasion by Qi, and was determined to restore the independence of
Yan and take his revenge.

King Hui (r. 278–272 B.C.E.), personal name Yuezi: succeeded following his
father's death by elixir poisoning, whose incompetent rule and personal ani-
mosities endangered Yan.

King of Yan (r. 255–222 B.C.E.), personal name Xi: a stupid and incompetent
ruler, dominated by his son, Crown Prince Dan.

Crown Prince Dan (d. 226 B.C.E.): a reckless and silly man, whose ill-conceived
assassination attempt on the future First Emperor of Qin ultimately brought
about the unnecessary deaths of many people.

Gao Jianli: a musician friend of Jing Ke, who died trying to avenge him.

Jing Ke (d. 227 B.C.E.): the assassin recruited by Crown Prince Dan, who gave
his life in what turned out to be a suicide mission to kill the future First
Emperor of Qin.

ZHAO (Zhao clan; marquis, then king)

The Zhao kings were descended from a powerful aristocratic clan in
Jin, which repeatedly intermarried with the ruling house. After Jin was
partitioned, Zhao was not initially one of the strongest states, but the
reforms of King Wuling brought about a significant change in its fortunes. By the late Warring States era, Zhao was the only kingdom strong
enough to resist Qin, though their morale was crushed at the Battle of
Changping in 260 B.C.E.

Lord Xiang (r. 458–425 B.C.E.), personal name Wuxu: born to a slave mother
but early recognized as exceptionally talented, he was chosen to inherit the
headship of the house of Zhao, and went on to preside over the partition of
Jin, eliminating major rivals.

Lord Su (r. 349–326 B.C.E.), personal name Yu: launched a series of military
campaigns when angered at being left out of the process by which other rulers crowned themselves as kings.

King Wuling (r. 325–299 B.C.E.), personal name Yong: transformed the Zhao
army through his reforms, crowned himself as king, eventually abdicated in
favor of his son, only to be murdered by his supporters.

King Huiwen (r. 298–266 B.C.E.), personal name He: was engaged in significant
conflict with Qin, mitigated by his greatest diplomat, Lin Xiangru.

King Xiaocheng (r. 265–245 B.C.E.), personal name Dan: his reign was dominated
by his catastrophic decision to dismiss Lian Po, just before the terrible Battle of
Changping, in which Zhao took more than four hundred thousand casualties.

Lian Po (d. 253 B.C.E.): a great general who commanded in numerous important campaigns for Zhao during his long career, with particular emphasis on
defensive warfare; his dismissal was a key factor in Zhao's defeat at the
Battle of Changping in 260 B.C.E.

Lin Xiangru: a famous diplomat, who cleverly engaged with King Zhaoxiang of Qin on behalf of the kingdom of Zhao without offending this powerful monarch.

Lord of Pingyuan, Zhao Sheng (d. 251 B.C.E.): a member of the Zhao royal family and one of the Four Great Lords of the Warring States, noted for his generous treatment of the knights and scholars in his household.

TRANSNATIONAL FIGURES

It is one of the characteristics of the Warring States era that there was an international market for talented men, who often traveled vast distances to serve at a variety of different courts, seeking kings who would appreciate their talents and reward them with high office and great wealth. This being the case, it is often very difficult to assign them to a single state, even if they were originally born into the ruling house of a particular country, since their allegiances were fluid and their careers international. The most important of these men are therefore here listed as transnational figures.

Su Dai: younger brother and disciple of Su Qin, and after his death one of the key diplomats involved in maintaining the Vertical Alliance of states opposed to the rise of Qin.

Su Li: younger brother and disciple of Su Qin, like Su Dai a key figure in maintaining the Vertical Alliance after Su Qin's death.

Su Qin (d. 284 B.C.E.): with Zhang Yi, Pang Juan, and Sun Bin a student of the Master of Ghost Valley, and the architect of the Vertical Alliance, designed to unite the six kingdoms of the Warring States against Qin.

Wu Qi (d. 381 B.C.E.): a military genius who served in various different countries, whose corruption and disloyalty consistently caused serious political problems whenever he was not in the field.

Zhang Yi (d. 309 B.C.E.): with Su Qin a student of the Master of Ghost Valley, and architect of the Horizontal Alliance, which sought to create a diplomatic framework through which Qin could ally with other countries (usually Qi) to disrupt the endeavors of the Vertical Alliance members.

Chapter Eighty-four

*The Earl of Zhi diverts the water supply to
flood the city of Jinyang.*

*Yu Rang stabs a garment in order to take
revenge on Lord Xiang.*

The personal name of the Earl of Zhi was Yao; he was the grandson of
Le, Lord Wu of Zhi, and the son of Xuwu, Lord Xuan of Zhi. When
Xuwu was deciding the succession, he discussed the matter with a member
of his own clan, Zhi Luo: "I want to make Yao my heir, what do you
think?"

"He does not match up to Xiao!" Zhi Luo replied.

"Xiao is neither as intelligent nor as talented as Yao," Xuwu said. "I
think I had better appoint him."

"Yao is in many ways a fine man, but he has one shortcoming. He is
much handsomer than other men; he is a better archer and charioteer;
he is a fine musician and artist; he is very strong and powerful; and he
is exceptionally clever. However, he is unpleasantly greedy: that is his
one shortcoming. His outstanding points will allow him to control others,
but they are all balanced out by the fact that he is not benevolent.
Who will put up with that? If you do indeed establish Yao as your heir,
the house of Zhi will be destroyed!"

Xuwu did not agree with him, and in the end he decided to establish
Yao as his heir. Zhi Luo sighed and said: "I belong to the same family,
and I am afraid that I will drown in the backwash!" He secretly contacted
the Grand Historian and requested that he should be given
another clan name. From this time on he used the surname Fu.

When Zhi Xuwu died, Yao was established in his turn and took sole
control of the government of the state of Jin. On the one hand he was

I

supported by his closest relatives, men like Zhi Kai and Zhi Guo, while on the other he had the services of loyal advisors like Chi Ci and Yu Rang. Given that he was both powerful and greatly respected, he decided that the time had come to usurp the marquisate of Jin. He summoned his men to discuss this matter in secret.

His advisor, Chi Ci, came forward and said: "At the moment the four great ministerial families hold each other in check; if one family were to make its move first, the other three would prevent it. If you want to usurp the marquisate of Jin, you will first have to reduce the power of the other three clans."

"How do I do that?" the Earl of Zhi asked.

"At the moment," Chi Ci replied, "the kingdom of Yue is the most powerful and Jin has lost the position of Master of Covenants. If you were to make the excuse of raising an army in order to dispute hegemony with Yue, pretending that it is done by order of the Marquis of Jin, you could order the three families of Han, Wei, and Zhao to each present one hundred *li* of land, the taxes to be dedicated to paying the expenses of the army. If the three families obey this command and partition off a piece of land, our territory will expand to the tune of three hundred *li*. The Zhi family will benefit greatly, and the other three ministerial clans will become weaker day by day. If anyone refuses to obey your orders, they are guilty of disregarding an express command from the Marquis of Jin, whereby you can lead your army to destroy them before they have a chance to mobilize. This is the way you eat the fruit and throw away the peel."

"That's a wonderful plan!" the Earl of Zhi declared. "But which of the three should we ask to hand over land first?"

"We are on good terms with both the Han and the Wei clans," Chi Ci said, "but we have our differences with the Zhao family. Let us begin with Han and then Wei. If they both agree to our demands, Zhao will not be able to refuse!"

The Earl of Zhi then sent Zhi Kai to Han Hu's mansion. Han Hu slowly made his way to the main hall and asked why he had come.

"My brother, the Earl of Zhi, has received an order from the Marquis of Jin to take his army to attack Yue," Zhi Kai explained. "He has further commanded that each of the three ministerial clans should partition off one hundred *li* of land and make it over to the ruling house, so the taxes can be devoted to the public good. My brother commanded me to take this message to you. Please give me the land and I will leave."

"You can go back now," Han Hu said. "I will send a messenger along with the land tomorrow."

When he had departed, Han Hu—otherwise known by his posthumous title of Lord Kang of Han—summoned his subordinates to discuss the situation: "Zhi Yao is trying to weaken the other three ministerial clans by threatening us with the Marquis of Jin, so that he can force us to hand over this land. I want to raise an army to get rid of this bandit. What do you think?"

His advisor, Duan Gui, said: "The Earl of Zhi is insatiably greedy. He has forged an edict from His Lordship in order to steal our land. If we use troops against him, we will be disobeying an order from the marquis and he can punish us for it. We had better give him what he wants. If he gets our land, he will go on to demand more from Zhao and Wei. If Zhao and Wei do not agree, there will be war. We can simply sit tight and wait to see who wins." Han Hu thought that this was good advice.

The following day, he ordered Duan Gui to draw a map showing the one hundred *li* of land in question and went in person to present it to the Earl of Zhi. His Lordship was delighted and held a banquet on top of the Lan Tower, to show his respect for Han Hu. As the wine was being circulated, the Earl of Zhi ordered his entourage to unroll a painting and place it on top of the table, so he could inspect it with Han Hu. It was a painting showing Bian Zhuangzi of Lu stabbing three tigers. There was an inscription along the top, which read:

> When three tigers each bite the same sheep, the situation will inevitably end in fighting. If you wait until they have finished, you can take advantage of their exhaustion. It was Bian Zhuangzi who realized that he could get all at one stroke.

The Earl of Zhi spoke jokingly to Han Hu: "I often read history books, and I have discovered many individuals with the same name as you in different countries. There was Gao Hu in the state of Qi and Hanh Hu in the state of Zheng. You make a third!"

At this time Duan Gui was standing just to one side. Now he came forward and said, "According to the rules of ritual propriety, it is rude to mention someone else's personal name. If we were to let you get away with this, would you not be even ruder to His Lordship?"

Duan Gui was a very short man. When he stood next to the Earl of Zhi, he only came up to his chest. His Lordship patted him on the head and said, "What would you know about it, kid? There is no point in your saying anything. After all, if three tigers were to bite down on you, there would be nothing left." When he had finished speaking, he clapped his hands together and laughed heartily.

Duan Gui did not dare to answer back, but he glanced over at Han Hu. His Lordship pretended to be drunk. He said with eyes shut, "You are absolutely right, my lord!" He immediately said goodbye and left.

When Zhi Luo heard about what had happened, he remonstrated: "You have made fun of their lord and humiliated their vassal—the Han family is sure to be furious with you for this! If you do not make some preparations, disaster is sure to follow!"

The Earl of Zhi glared at him and shouted, "They are very lucky that I do not kill them. Who would dare to try and kill me?"

"A wasp or a bee can kill a human being, not to mention the ruler of a state!" Zhi Luo retorted. "If you make no preparations now, when you realize your mistake in the future, will it not be too late?"

"I am going to be like Bian Zhuangzi and kill three tigers with a single stroke!" the Earl of Zhi declared. "What can a wasp or a bee do to me?"

Zhi Luo sighed and went away.

A historian wrote a poem:

> The Earl of Zhi was as narrow-minded as a frog in a well,
> He cared no more about reestablishing the royal family.
> Heroes in his clan in vain presented plans to ensure the survival of the
>   country,
> How many others were as lucky as Zhi Luo in escaping disaster?

The following day, the Earl of Zhi again sent Zhi Kai to demand land from Wei Ju—better known as Lord Huan of Wei. Wei Ju wanted to refuse, but his advisor, Ren Zhang, said: "If they want the land, give it to them. The person who loses the land will be frightened, but the person who gains it will become arrogant. If you are arrogant, then you will underestimate the enemy. If you are frightened, you will try and make friends. Once you have gained the support of your people, you can turn against your arrogant enemy. That way, the fall of the house of Zhi is guaranteed!"

"Good to know!" Wei Ju said. He presented a parcel of land, inhabited by ten thousand households, to the Earl of Zhi.

The Earl of Zhi now sent his older brother, Zhi Xiao, to demand the lands of Cai and Gaolang from the Zhao family. Zhao Wuxu—also known as Lord Xiang of Zhao—was already furious with them, and now he said angrily: "This land was inherited from my ancestors; how can I simply give it up? Han and Wei may have land to give you, but I do not!"

When Zhi Xiao returned to report this, the Earl of Zhi was furious and mobilized his entire army. He also sent messengers to ask the Han and Wei families to contribute troops for a joint attack on the Zhao clan. On the day that the Zhao were destroyed, their territory would be divided into three. Han Hu and Wei Ju were terrified of the Earl of Zhi's military might and they were tempted by the lands of Zhao, so they each brought an army and joined in the attack. The Earl of Zhi commanded the central army, while the Han army was the right wing and the Wei army formed the left wing. They marched on the Zhao mansion, hoping to be able to catch Zhao Wuxu alive.

Zhang Mengtan, an advisor to the Zhao clan, guessed that troops would soon arrive, so he hurried to inform Zhao Wuxu: "The few cannot defeat the many. You had better run away, my lord, as quickly as you can!"

"Where should I go?"

"You had better go to Jinyang," Zhang Mengtan suggested. "In the past, Dong Anyu built a palace inside the city walls there, and furthermore, it was managed by Yin Duo for a while. The people there were subject to Yin Duo's excellent regime for several decades, and so they will certainly be loyal to the death. When His Late Lordship was dying, he said that if at any time in the future the country was faced with a crisis, you should go to Jinyang! Go now, my lord, as quickly as you can. You must not delay!"

Zhao Wuxu immediately took his staff, including Zhang Mengtan and Gao He, and fled in the direction of Jinyang. The Earl of Zhi chased after him, dragging the other two armies in his wake.

• • •

One of Zhao Wuxu's servants was a man named Yuan Guo. On the retreat he fell behind, and on the road he encountered a divine being, composed of cloud and mist: the only thing he could see clearly was that he was wearing a golden crown and was dressed in a brocade robe. His face was vague and indistinct, but he handed over a piece of green bamboo and said, "Give this to Zhao Wuxu on my behalf." When Yuan Guo caught up with Zhao Wuxu, he reported what he had seen and presented him with the section of bamboo. Wuxu cut it open, and inside there were two lines of red writing, which read:

> To Zhao Wuxu: I am the Spirit of Mount Huo, and I have received an order from God on High. In the third month, on Bingwu day, I will allow you to destroy the Zhi clan.

Zhao Wuxu ordered that this matter be kept secret.

When he arrived in Jinyang, the people there—remembering the virtuous and benevolent rule of Yin Duo—came out of the city to meet him, bringing their old and young with them. He took up residence in the palace. Zhao Wuxu noted how supportive the people were, how high and strong the walls and fortifications of Jinyang were, not to mention the plenitude of resources in the granaries and storehouses, so he began to feel more confident. He immediately reported the situation to the populace and then climbed onto the walls to inspect the city. When he counted the stocks of weapons, he discovered that the spears and halberds were all rusty and blunt, while there were fewer than one thousand arrows in the place. This was very worrying indeed.

"When you are defending a city," Zhao Wuxu said to Zhang Mengtan, "the best weapons are bows and arrows. We have only a couple of hundred arrows here: it is not worth even handing them out. What should I do?"

"I have heard that when Dong Anyu was in charge of Jinyang," Mengtan replied, "he built the walls of the palace out of the same kind of bamboo that is used for making the shafts of arrows. Why don't you try and pull down one of the walls to see if this is true?"

Zhao Wuxu ordered a man to tear down one of the walls, and sure enough it was made out of arrow bamboo. "Now we have enough arrow shafts," he said, "but where are we going to get the metal to make the tips and other weapons?"

"I have heard that when Dong Anyu built the palace," Zhang Mengtan replied, "he had all the supporting pillars made of the finest bronze. We could take them out and use them, for then we would have more than enough metal for weapons."

Zhao Wuxu gave orders to have one of the pillars taken down, and it was made of nothing but the finest bronze. Straightaway, he set his workmen to smelting down the pillars and turning out swords and halberds, sabers and spears, all of the highest quality. People now began to feel much more secure.

"How lucky I am to have had such excellent advisors!" Zhao Wuxu said with a sigh. "Dong Anyu prepared weapons for me to use, and Yin Duo made sure that the people support me. Heaven is on the side of the Zhao family! Who can bring us low?"

. . .

The three armies of Zhi, Han, and Wei arrived and split into three camps, which were sited in easy reach of one another. Jinyang was now under siege. There were many ordinary people in Jinyang who would have been happy to go out and fight them; they rushed to the palace and asked permission from His Lordship. Zhao Wuxu discussed this with Zhang Mengtan.

"They are many and we are few," he said, "so if we do battle we will not necessarily be victorious. We had better take advantage of the deep moat and high walls to sit tight, waiting until the situation changes. Han and Wei have no quarrel with Zhao; they have been forced to come here by the Earl of Zhi. They did not want to partition off their land and give it to him, so even though they have joined in this campaign, they are not united. Within a couple of months, they will have started to fight among themselves. Once that has happened, will they be able to keep up the siege for long?"

Zhao Wuxu took this advice and went in person to speak to his people, instructing them to save their strength for the defense of the city, so that they would support his army's efforts. Even women and children were willing to die for his cause. Whenever the enemy soldiers approached the walls, they were immediately met with a volley of arrows. Even after the three armies had laid siege to the city for many months, they were not able to defeat them. The Earl of Zhi rode in a chariot around the city walls. He sighed and said, "These ramparts might as well be made of iron. How are we going to break them down?" Just as he was at his most depressed, he arrived at a little mountain, where he noticed a spring flowing east in a myriad rivulets. He grabbed hold of a local man and asked him where he was.

"This is Mount Long," he replied. "Halfway up there is a great rock shaped like a pitcher, so it is also called Mount Xuanweng, meaning 'Hanging Pitcher.' The Jin River flows to the east, where it joins with the Fen River. This mountain is the source."

"How far are we from the city?" the Earl of Zhi asked.

"We are about ten *li* from the West Gate."

The Earl of Zhi climbed the mountain in order to look at the Jin River, curling around the northeast corner of the city. He thought for a while, and then suddenly the realization struck him: "I know how to break through the walls!" He immediately went back to the camp and summoned the other commanders for a discussion, because he wanted to use water to flood the city.

"The Jin River flows east," Han Hu pointed out. "How can we get it to flow west?"

"I am not proposing to divert the Jin River," the Earl of Zhi explained. "The Jin River starts from a spring at Mount Long, and the flow there is very powerful. If we dig a great canal from the north slopes of that mountain towards the city and prepare a dam there, we can prevent the waters flowing towards the Jin River. Since the waters cannot join the Jin River, when the dam is breached they will have to flow along the newly constructed canal. If we wait until the spring rains start to fall, the waters will come pouring off the mountains. We can breach the dike and flood the city on the day that the waters are at their height. The people inside Jinyang will be sent to feed the fishes!"

Han Hu and Wei Ju both praised him at the tops of their voices: "This is a wonderful plan!"

"Today we had better organize who does what," the earl said, "so that each can be responsible for one task. The Lord of Han will guard the east and the Lord of Wei will guard the south—you much be very careful day and night to prevent anyone from breaking through the siege. My main camp will move to Mount Long, whereby we will be responsible for both guarding the northern and western sides of the city and building the dam and digging the canal." The lords of Han and Wei accepted their orders and said goodbye.

The Earl of Zhi issued his commands, and his soldiers were armed with shovels and set to digging. They cut a canal running north from the Jin River, while other men were responsible for blocking the routes of the waters from the spring. They built huge dams to the left and right of the canal, so that all the waters that flowed down the mountain would be gathered behind these embankments and dikes. As the waters bubbled up in the spring, there was no outlet other than to the north, so the entire flow was channeled into this new canal. There it met a stoppage in the form of wooden logs that were piled ever higher to prevent the waters from escaping. Since there was nowhere for the water to go, it backed up past this blockage.

Now the northern tributary of the Jin River is called the Earl of Zhi's Canal, and it was dug at that time.

One month later, just as anticipated, the spring rains began and the waters poured off the mountains, rising to the same height as the embankments. The Earl of Zhi sent someone to breach the dike on the northern side, and the waters came rushing out, flooding the city of Jinyang.

There is a poem that testifies to this:

If you have ever seen the floodwaters pour over a dike,
You have experienced the spring engulfing the city of Jinyang.
Who could have imagined that the lord of these waters would be so
    daring,
As to try and change the work of the great sage-king and flood-
    controller Yu?

. . .

At this time, even though the city was under siege, the people were still living perfectly comfortably, suffering neither hunger nor cold. Furthermore, since the city walls were both high and thick, even though the floodwaters beat against them, they were not able to break through. However, after a couple of days, as the power of the waters continued to grow, they gradually seeped into the city. No house could withstand this, and they were flooded. The people were left with nowhere to lay their heads and no fires by which to warm their bodies. They had to live in huts built on the roofs of their houses, cooking in pots suspended in the air. Even though the palace was constructed on top of a pounded-earth platform, Zhao Wuxu did not dare to stay there. He spent his entire time out on a bamboo raft with Zhang Mengtan, patrolling the city walls. He could hear the waters beating against the ramparts and, looking out, he could see that everywhere was flooded. The force of the waters was such that it could topple a mountain. Given another four or five feet, it would be coming over the tops of the city walls.

Zhao Wuxu was terrified. He was lucky that the soldiers and ordinary people guarding the walls were on patrol day and night, without the slightest sign of disaffection, and his people had sworn to fight to the death without any disloyalty. He sighed and said, "Now I realize quite what Yin Duo has done for me!" He spoke in private with Zhang Mengtan: "Even though the people are still loyal to me, the flooding shows no sign of abating. If the amount of water coming off the mountain continues to increase, this entire city will be joining the fish and turtles. What should we do? The Spirit of Mount Huo lied to me!"

"Han and Wei did not offer land willingly," Zhang Mengtan reminded him. "They have sent their armies here because they have no choice. I am going to sneak out of the city tonight and talk to the lords of Han and Wei. If we join together in an attack on the Earl of Zhi, we can escape this disaster."

"Their armies have us under siege and the waters pin us down here. Even if we were to grow wings, we would not be able to escape!"

"I have a plan. Do not worry, my lord. You should order your men to make as many rafts as possible and prepare their weapons. If Heaven is indeed on our side and I can persuade them, we will take the Earl of Zhi's head any day now!" Zhao Wuxu agreed to this.

Zhang Mengtan knew that Han Hu's army was camped by the East Gate, so he dressed up as one of the Earl of Zhi's soldiers and let himself down from the top of the city wall under cover of darkness. He headed straight for the main camp of the Han clan. Once there, he said, "The Earl of Zhi has sent me with a secret message, which I am to deliver in person." Han Hu was sitting in the middle of the tent, and he ordered them to let him in. At this time, discipline in the army was very strict. If you wished to have an audience with one of the commanders, you would be thoroughly searched before being allowed to proceed. Zhang Mengtan was dressed as an ordinary officer and he was not carrying a sword, so he did not arouse any suspicions. When he went in to have an audience with Han Hu, he requested that he send away his entourage. Han Hu ordered his people to leave. When he asked the reason for this, Zhang Mengtan explained: "I am not a soldier. My name is Zhang Mengtan, and I work for the Zhao family. My master has now been under siege for many days, and any moment now the city will fall. He is afraid that once he is dead and his family destroyed, there will be no way to express what is in his heart, so he specially ordered me to dress up like this and come here secretly under cover of darkness to seek an audience with you, sir. He has something to say to you. If you agree to let me speak, I will say my piece. If not, then I will die right here in front of you."

"If you have something to say, then do. If what you say is reasonable, I am prepared to take your advice."

"In the past the six ministerial families lived in harmony, sharing the government of the state of Jin between them. However, the Fan and the Zhonghang families were not able to maintain popular support and ended up getting themselves killed; ever since, there have just been the Zhi, Han, Wei, and Zhao families. The Earl of Zhi wanted to extort the lands of Cai and Gaolang from the Zhao clan, but my lord, bearing in mind that this was part of the territory he had inherited from his ancestors, was not prepared to give them. That is why he has angered the Earl of Zhi. The earl is proud of his military prowess, and so he joined with Han and Wei to destroy the Zhao clan. But once the Zhao clan has gone, Han and Wei will be next!"

Han Hu sat there in silence, so Zhang Mengtan continued: "Now, the reason why Han and Wei have joined with the Earl of Zhi in this attack on Zhao is because you imagine that on the day that the city falls, you will divide the lands of Zhao into three. But did not Han and Wei hand over two cities of ten thousand households to the Earl of Zhi? These were lands that you had inherited from your ancestors, and yet when he licked his lips and announced that he was taking them, did either of you dare to say a word of complaint? What will happen when it is not your land but someone else's? Once Zhao is destroyed, the Zhi clan will be greatly strengthened. Will you be able to demand from him the proper rewards for your hard work today? And even supposing that he does divide the lands of Zhao into three in the first place, what is to prevent him from turning around and taking them back at some point in the future? I hope that you will think carefully about this!"

"What do you want me to do?" Han Hu asked.

"In my humble opinion," Zhang Mengtan said, "you had better secretly make peace with my master and launch a joint attack on the Earl of Zhi with him. He will divide the land equitably with you, and the lands of Zhi are many times larger than those of Zhao! Furthermore, you will have no worries about the future. If you three lords are united in this, you will be at peace for many generations. Would that not be wonderful?"

"What you say is absolutely correct," Han Hu declared. "You had better wait until I have discussed the matter with Wei Ju. You should go now, and come back in three days to hear our answer."

"I have risked my life to come here," Zhang Mengtan said. "It was extremely difficult to arrive in one piece. With so many eyes and ears in the army, it would be hard to keep my comings and goings secret. Let me stay here for the next three days; I will await your further instructions."

Han Hu ordered someone to summon Duan Gui in secret and told him what Zhang Mengtan had said. Duan Gui had been so deeply insulted by the Earl of Zhi that he had never forgiven it. He expressed great approval of this plan. Han Hu arranged for Duan Gui and Zhang Mengtan to meet. The two men got along very well and stayed overnight in the same tent.

The following day, in accordance with Han Hu's order, Duan Gui went in person to Wei Ju's camp and secretly reported that they had received a messenger from the Zhao clan and what he had said: "My lord would not dare to make a decision on this matter without consulting you. Please tell us what you think."

"That bastard has behaved with unbelievable arrogance," Wei Ju said, "and I hate him too! However, I am afraid that if we mess this up, he will turn around and destroy us instead."

"The Earl of Zhi has no intention of letting us escape his clutches," Duan Gui said. "As soon as he has the power, he will turn on us. Rather than leaving it as a source of regret for the future, why don't you solve the problem today? The Zhao clan is about to be destroyed; if the Han and Wei families were to save them, they would be very grateful to us. Surely you cannot want to carry on serving that horrible man."

"I need to think about this very carefully," Wei Ju declared. "I don't want to rush into anything." Duan Gui said farewell and left.

. . .

On the following day, the Earl of Zhi personally inspected the waters and held a banquet at Mount Long. He invited the leaders of the Han and Wei clans to attend and view the flooding with him. As the wine was circulating, the Earl of Zhi pointed at the city of Jinyang and said happily to Han Hu and Wei Ju: "The only thing that is still not drowned is the city wall. Today I have finally come to understand that water can destroy a country. The prosperity of the state of Jin rests on its mountains and rivers; the Fen, the Hui, the Jin, the Jiang—these are all our great rivers. The way I see it, water is something to beware of—it does speed collapse."

Wei Ju secretly nudged Han Hu, and he kicked the other's foot. The two men looked at each other, and both were clearly very frightened. A short time later, the banquet broke up and everyone said goodbye and departed. Chi Ci spoke to the Earl of Zhi: "Han and Wei are going to rebel."

"How do you know?"

"I have not spoken to them," Chi Ci said, "but I have seen their faces. You agreed with them that on the day Zhao is destroyed, you will divide their lands into three parts. Now Zhao will fall at any moment. The pair of them showed no signs of happiness about the land that they will receive, but they looked worried and thoughtful—that is how I knew that they are planning to rebel!"

"We have all been working together perfectly happily," the earl said. "What on earth are they worried about?"

"You said that water was something to beware of, since it could be used to hasten the destruction of a country. Just as the Jin River can be used to flood Jinyang, the Fen River could be used to flood Wei's Anyi, and the Jiang River could be used to flood Han's Pingyang. You may have been talking about the waters around Jinyang, but how could they not be concerned?"

On the third day, Han Hu and Wei Ju sent wine to the Earl of Zhi's camp, to thank him for his invitation the previous day. The earl raised his cup, but before he drank, he said to the pair of them: "I am a very straightforward kind of person, and I would always rather speak out than keep things bottled up inside me. Yesterday someone suggested to me that the two of you are planning to rebel. Is this true?"

Han Hu and Wei Ju both spoke in unison: "Do you believe it, my lord?"

"If I believed it, would I be willing to mention it to the two of you?"

"I have heard that the Zhao family have offered great quantities of gold and silk in the hope of creating a breach between the three of us," Han Hu said. "This rumor must have been put about by some wicked man who has taken the bribes offered by the Zhao clan and is hoping to make you suspect us. No doubt he imagines that we will cease to lay siege so strictly and hence they may be able to escape from danger for a while."

"You are absolutely right," Wei Ju declared. "After all, the city will fall at any moment. Who would be willing to forego a parcel of their land? Why would we pass up the benefits that we are going to gain any day now, and instead run the risk of bringing down appalling disaster on our heads?"

The Earl of Zhi laughed: "I knew that the two of you would never do anything like that. Chi Ci is so suspicious!"

"Even if today you don't believe this gossip," Han Hu said, "I am afraid that sooner or later there will be someone else who accuses us of something, where we have much greater trouble in demonstrating our loyalty. What can we do to prevent ourselves from falling into the traps laid by wicked men?"

The earl poured his wine on the ground as a libation. "Let this wine bear witness that in the future we will not suspect each other," he said.

Han Hu and Wei Ju made a respectful gesture with their hands, thanking him for his magnanimity. That day they circulated the wine many times, and hence it was very late when the party finally broke up.

Afterwards, Chi Ci came forward and had an audience with the Earl of Zhi. "Why did you tell the two lords what I said to you?" he demanded.

"How do you know I did that?"

"Just now," Chi Ci explained, "I met their lordships leaving by the main gate to the camp. They looked at me askance and quickened their paces. That means that they are scared of me because I know what they are up to. That is why they were in such a hurry."

The Earl of Zhi laughed and said: "I swore an oath with the other two gentlemen that we would not suspect each other in future. I don't want you to say another thing, because if you do I will get cross."

Chi Ci withdrew. He sighed and said: "The Zhi clan will not last much longer." Pretending that he had become stricken with a serious illness and needed to find a doctor, he fled into exile in the state of Qin.

An old man wrote a poem commemorating Chi Ci:

> The signs were already clear that the alliance with Han and Wei had
>   broken.
> How could they conceal this from such a clever man as Chi Ci?
> One morning he announced that he was sick and fled like the wind;
> The bright moon and gentle breeze can be found in every part of the
>   world.

Han Hu and Wei Ju left the Earl of Zhi's camp. On the way back, the two lords settled their plan, and swore a blood covenant with Zhang Mengtan to the following effect: "Tomorrow at midnight, we will take down the dikes and let the water return to its original channels. The lowering of water levels is to be your sign. You must lead the forces inside the city out on the attack, and between us, we will take the Earl of Zhi prisoner."

Zhang Mengtan took this order and went back to the city, where he reported to Zhao Wuxu. His Lordship was delighted and secretly gave orders that everything should be arranged in advance, so that his men could wait until they were needed. At the appointed time, Han Hu and Wei Ju quietly arranged for their men to make a surprise attack and kill the soldiers guarding the embankments. They made a breach in the dams to the west. The waters started flowing in that direction, flooding the Earl of Zhi's camp. The army was terrified and a great shout rose up on all sides. The earl was wrenched from his dreams, the waters lapping around his bed, his clothes and bedding soaked. He still imagined that some mistake must have been made, which resulted in an accidental breach in the dam, so he quickly ordered his entourage to go and shore up the embankments. A short time later, the waters were flowing with even greater strength. Now Zhi Guo and Yu Rang arrived on rafts, leading the rest of the earl's waterborne forces with them, and they helped him to get onto one of the boats. Looking back at his camp, he saw it engulfed by the waves, the defensive walls gone, his food and weapons floating away. His officers and men were all swimming for their lives.

Just as the Earl of Zhi was caught in the midst of this horror, suddenly he heard the sound of drums as the armies of Han and Wei, riding in small boats, attacked them. The Zhi army was cut to pieces. The shout was passed from mouth to mouth: "Whoever captures Zhi Yao will be generously rewarded!"

The Earl of Zhi sighed and said: "I did not believe what Chi Ci told me and so I have fallen into their trap!"

"The situation is critical!" Yu Rang shouted. "If you go around the back of these mountains, you can escape. Go to Qin and ask them for troops! I will prevent the enemy from following you, even if it kills me."

The Earl of Zhi followed his advice; he and Zhi Guo sailed around the back of this mountain range on a small boat. Who could have imagined that Zhao Xuwu would calculate that the Earl of Zhi would try to escape to the state of Qin? He sent Zhang Mengtan to assist Han and Wei in chasing down the remnants of the Zhi army, while he himself was lying in ambush at the back of Mount Long. It was there that they ran into one another. Zhao Wuxu took the Earl of Zhi prisoner and, after enumerating his crimes, beheaded him. Zhi Guo threw himself into the water and drowned. Yu Rang encouraged the remnants of the Zhi army to carry on fighting, but he could do nothing about the fact that they were hopelessly outnumbered. His men gradually started to desert. When they heard that the Earl of Zhi had been taken prisoner, they took off any garments that marked them out as his soldiers and fled for Mount Shishi. The earl's army had now completely collapsed. Zhao Wuxu checked the day. It was Bingxu day in the third month. The bamboo text that the spirit had given him had turned out to be completely true.

. . .

The three clans assembled their armies in one place. They destroyed the embankments and dams completely so that the waters could flow eastward as before, returning to the channel of the Jin River. The waters covering the city of Jinyang now gradually receded. When Zhao Wuxu had finished reassuring his people, he said to Han Hu and Wei Ju: "Thanks to your help, I have been able to keep my city safe. I would never have imagined a result like this. However, even though the Earl of Zhi is dead, his family is still with us. We had better get rid of them, to prevent further disaster."

Han Hu and Wei Ju agreed: "Let us execute his entire clan, to assuage our anger."

Zhao Wuxu returned to Jiangzhou with the leaders of the Han and Wei clans, whereupon they slandered the Zhi family with accusations that they were plotting treason. The mansion was surrounded and all the people inside, male and female, old and young, were butchered. *The only person who was able to escape was Zhi Luo, who had earlier changed his surname to Fu. From this you can see how farsighted he was.*

The Han and Wei clans took back the land that they had earlier presented to the Earl of Zhi, and his territories were divided into three. Not a single person or foot of land was given to the Marquis of Jin. This happened in the sixteenth year of the reign of King Zhending of Zhou.

When Zhao Wuxu discussed who should receive rewards for their success at Jinyang, his entourage all recommended Zhang Mengtan to be the first. Zhao Wuxu was the only person who wanted to give the highest-level rewards to Gao He.

"When Gao He was living in the city under siege," Zhang Mengtan said, "he did not offer a single plan, or suffer any exceptional hardship, so why should he be the first to receive an award and be given the highest rank of any of us? I really don't understand."

"When I was in danger," Zhao Wuxu explained, "everyone else was completely petrified by fright. Gao He was the only person to behave with proper respect from start to finish, without once failing to treat me as he should. Any success is temporary, but proper respect is something that endures for ten thousand generations. Is it not right that he should receive the highest reward?"

Zhang Mengtan was shamed into agreeing. Zhao Wuxu was also grateful for the help he had received from the mountain spirit, so he established a shrine at Mount Huo and commanded that Yuan Guo and his descendants should be responsible for maintaining sacrifices there from one generation to the next. Since his hatred of the Earl of Zhi had hardly been assuaged, he lacquered his skull and used it as a chamber pot.

• • •

Yu Rang heard about this from his place of refuge at Mount Shishi. He wept and said: "A knight should die for the man who understands him. I received so many kindnesses from the Zhi clan. Now their lands have gone and the family is dead—even their bones are subject to humiliation. How can I bear to remain alive like this?"

He changed his name, dressed up as a prisoner assigned to menial duties, and, clutching a dagger in his hand, lay in ambush in the privy attached to the Zhao mansion. He was hoping to hide there until Zhao Wuxu entered the privy, at which point he could take advantage of the situation to stab him. When Xuwu went to the privy, he suddenly felt a sense of panic. He asked his entourage to search the building, and they dragged Yu Rang out before Wuxu.

"You have a weapon concealed about your person," he said. "Were you hoping to stab me?"

Yu Rang answered without any sign of fear: "I used to work for the Zhi family. I want to avenge the Earl of Zhi."

"This man is a dangerous rebel and deserves to be executed," his entourage declared, but Zhao Wuxu stopped them with the words: "The Earl of Zhi is dead and he has left no descendants. If Yu Rang wants to avenge him, it proves that he is a loyal knight. It would not be auspicious to murder such a good man." He ordered them to release Yu Rang and allow him to go home.

When he was about to leave, Zhao Wuxu summoned him back and asked him another question: "I have released you today. Is that enough to write off the enmity between us?"

"Releasing me is a private kindness on Your Lordship's part," Yu Rang said. "Revenge is still my duty."

"This man is so rude," his entourage said. "Releasing him will bring about disaster in the future."

"I have already given my word," Zhao Wuxu declared. "Do you want me to break it? I will just have to be extra careful from now on."

He immediately returned to Jinyang, where he instituted a series of excellent policies, in order to avoid further trouble from Yu Rang.

When Yu Rang returned home, he thought day and night of ways to avenge his lord, but without coming up with any plan. His wife encouraged him to take office with either the Han or the Wei families, in the hope that he would become rich and honored. Yu Rang was furious at this and left the house. He wanted to go back to Jinyang, but he was afraid of being recognized, which would get him into trouble. Therefore he shaved off his beard and reshaped his eyebrows, painting lacquer on his body so that he would look as though he had contracted leprosy. He went out to beg in the marketplace. His wife went there to look for him, and when she heard his voice begging for alms, she said in shock: "That is my husband's voice!" She rushed over to have a look, but when she saw Yu Rang, she said, "The voice is right, but the appearance is not at all the same." Then she turned away.

Yu Rang realized that he was still handicapped by his voice, so he swallowed charcoal until his throat was raw. The next time he went and begged in the marketplace, even though his wife heard his voice, she did not recognize it. One of his friends knew what Yu Rang was planning, and when he saw the beggar moving about, he wondered whether it might not be he. Having called him by name, he discovered it was indeed Yu Rang. He invited him into his house for a meal, and said: "You have made up your mind to take revenge, but you do not yet have the necessary skills to be able to do so. With your abilities, if you were to pretend to throw in your lot with the Zhao family, you would certainly be given a trusted position. In that case, you would be able to find a good opportunity to strike and your attack would certainly succeed. Why have you put yourself through such pain? What good do you think it will do?"

Yu Rang thanked him: "If I were to serve the Zhao clan and then carry out my assassination, I would be condemned as disloyal. I have painted my skin with lacquer and swallowed charcoal in order to be able to take revenge for the Earl of Zhi so that in the future those wicked men who serve their lords while harboring disloyal thoughts will be ashamed when they hear what I have done. Let us say goodbye now. We will not meet again."

Yu Rang went to the city of Jinyang, begging like before, but this time there was nobody to recognize him. Zhao Wuxu went out to inspect the new canal that the Earl of Zhi had dug near Jinyang. Realizing that the work had already been carried out and it would be impractical to try and destroy it, he ordered his men to build a bridge over the canal to facilitate access. It was called the Vermilion Bridge. Red is the color of fire, and in the theory of the Five Elements, Fire can conquer Water. Having suffered disaster from the Jin River, he wanted to use the Vermilion Bridge to control it. When the building work was completed, Zhao Wuxu drove out in his chariot to inspect it. Yu Rang was informed in advance that Wuxu wanted to look at the bridge, so he again hid a sharpened sword about his person and lay under the bridge, pretending to be dead. As Zhao Wuxu approached the Vermilion Bridge in his chariot, his horses suddenly started to neigh and stepped backwards. The charioteer tried to whip up the horses, but they refused to advance.

Zhang Mengtan came forward and said: "I have heard the saying that a good horse will not put his master in danger. These horses are refusing to cross the Vermilion Bridge, which means that there must be a wicked man lying in ambush there. You had better investigate what is going on."

Zhao Xuwu stopped his chariot and ordered his entourage to go and search the place. They reported back: "There are no spies anywhere around the bridge. There is just a dead body lying there."

"This bridge has only just been built," Zhao Wuxu said. "How can there be any dead bodies lying around? This must be Yu Rang!"

He ordered them to bring him forward. Even though his appearance had changed greatly, Zhao Wuxu was still able to recognize him. He cursed the man and said: "I have already bent the law in your favor once and pardoned you; why have you tried to assassinate me a second time? Surely Heaven is not on your side." He ordered his servants to drag him away and behead him. Yu Rang screamed up at the sky, tears of blood rolling down his cheeks.

"Are you afraid to die?" the servants asked him.

"I am not afraid of death," Yu Rang declared. "I am sad that after I die, there will be nobody to take revenge for His Lordship."

Zhao Wuxu summoned him back and demanded: "You served the Fan clan first of all, and the Fan family was killed by the Earl of Zhi. You were prepared to bear that humiliation and carry on living; you even went on to serve the Earl of Zhi! You did not think of trying to avenge the Fan family! Now the earl is dead and you are determined to avenge him at all costs. Why is this?"

"When a ruler and a vassal meet on righteous terms, the ruler treats his vassals as if they were his own hands or feet, and the vassal thinks of the lord as his own heart," Yu Rang explained. "If the lord were to treat his vassal as he does his horses or his dogs, the vassal would think of his lord as a stranger. When I worked for the Fan clan, they treated me just like everybody else. That is why I repaid them in this fashion. When I worked for the Earl of Zhi, he made sure that I lived like a prince, and hence I repay him as a gentleman should. Surely you cannot expect to have one rule that suits all eventualities?"

"You have made up your mind and are not prepared to change it," Zhao Wuxu said. "I cannot pardon you again." He drew his sword and ordered him to commit suicide.

"I have heard it said a loyal subject does not worry about his own death and an enlightened ruler does not hide the achievements of others," Yu Rang proclaimed. "By pardoning me, you have already done enough. How could I possibly expect to survive today? I have tried to assassinate you twice and failed both times—my anger is unappeased. Please take off your robe and let me stab it, that I may have the satisfaction of avenging His Lordship. Then I can rest in peace!"

Zhao Wuxu felt sorry for him and took off his brocade robe, ordering his entourage to give it to Yu Rang. The latter drew his sword and glared at the robe, as if it were really Zhao Wuxu that was wearing it. He lunged three times and stabbed the robe three times, saying: "Now I can go and report to the Earl of Zhi in the Underworld!" He committed suicide by falling on his sword.

The bridge is still in existence today. Later generations called it Yu Rang's Bridge.

Master Hu Zeng wrote a "Poem on History," which reads:

> Yu Rang repaid all the kindness he received;
> That is why he is still remembered today.
> Every year since then, people have crossed this bridge,
> But who still feels the same way?

When Zhao Wuxu saw that Yu Rang had killed himself, he felt very sorry for him. He gave orders that the body should be collected for burial. His officers picked up the brocade robe and gave it back to Zhao Wuxu, who noticed that fresh blood was dripping from each of the holes in his robe. This was a sign of the sincerity of Yu Rang's actions. Zhao Wuxu was horrified and became very sick.

Do you know whether he survived or not? READ ON.

Chapter Eighty-five

Le Yang angrily eats the stew provided by Zhongshan.

Ximen Bao proudly escorts a bride for the River God.

When Zhao Wuxu allowed Yu Rang to stab his clothes three times, he sneezed three times in a row. After Yu Rang was dead, Zhao Wuxu looked at the holes in his clothes and saw they were stained with blood. After this he became sick, and by the end of the year he was dying.

Zhao Wuxu had five sons, but since his older brother, Bolu, had been crippled trying to save his life, he wanted Bolu's son, Zhou, to succeed to his title. When Zhou died young, he appointed his son, Huan, as his heir. When Zhao Wuxu was dying, he said to his heir, Zhao Huan: "Ever since we three ministerial houses destroyed the Zhi clan, our lands have been broad and rich, our people happy and submissive. You should take advantage of this opportunity to unite with the Han and Wei families to partition the state of Jin, each one of you setting up your own ancestral shrines and handing your territory on to your sons and grandsons. If you wait many more years, it may perhaps be that Jin has an enlightened ruler who takes power and regains control of the government, capturing his people's hearts. In that case, the ancestral sacrifices to the Zhao clan will cease!" After he had finished speaking, he closed his eyes forever.

Having completed the funeral ceremonies, Zhao Huan reported his great-uncle's dying words to Han Hu. This occurred in the fourth year of the reign of King Kao of Zhou. When Lord Ai of Jin died, his son, the Honorable Liu, was established as Lord You. Han Hu plotted with the Wei and Zhao families to give the two cities of Jiangzhou and Quwo to

Lord You as his fief, while the remainder of the state was partitioned among the three of them, to be known as the Three Jins. Lord You was a weak young man who went to pay court to the three ministerial clans. In this way, the proper places of lord and vassal were reversed.

When the prime minister of Qi, Tian Pan, heard that the Three Jins had partitioned their lord's territory, he appointed all his brothers and cousins to be grandees in the capital and the other major cities of Qi. He also sent an ambassador to congratulate the Three Jins and make an alliance with them. From this time onwards, the four families of Tian, Zhao, Wei, and Han were in constant communication—the rulers of Jin and Qi were reduced to the status of puppets. It was at around this time that King Kao of Zhou enfeoffed his younger brother, Prince Jie, with the Royal City of Henan, in order to continue the work of the Duke of Zhou. Prince Jie's young son, Ban, was enfeoffed with the city of Gong. Since Gong was located east of the Royal City, he was given the title Duke of Eastern Zhou; his father was the Duke of Western Zhou. This was the beginning of the division of the Zhou realm. When King Kao died, his son, Prince Wu, was established as King Weilie. In the time of King Weilie of Zhou, Zhao Huan died and his son, Zhao Ji, succeeded him. Likewise Han Qian took charge of the Han clan, and Wei Si took over the Wei family. The Tian clan was headed by Tian He. The alliance between these four houses was very strong and they had agreed on a mutual security pact, in the hope that they would thus be able to establish their own regimes.

In the twenty-third year of the reign of King Weilie, a bolt of lightning hit the nine sacred bronze *ding*-cauldrons of the Zhou royal house, causing them to tremble. When the lords of the Three Jins heard this, they discussed the matter in private: "Those nine bronze vessels have been royal regalia handed down through three dynasties; now they have been shaken. This means that the luck of the Zhou dynasty has finally run out. We have already established our own regimes a long time ago; it is just that we have not made a formal declaration of this fact. Let us take advantage of the fact that the Zhou ruling house is in terminal decline to each send an ambassador to the king, requesting that we be recognized as lords of our own states. He will be too terrified of the military might at our command to dare to refuse. That way we will have the name that we deserve to add to the wealth and nobility we already own, without having to bear the odium of having usurped the title. Would that not be wonderful?"

Each of them sent a trusted ambassador—Tian Wen in the case of Wei, Gong Zhonglian in the case of Zhao, and Xia Lei in the case of

Han—armed with gold and silk, as well as local produce, and presented it to King Weilie, requesting a royal mandate.

King Weilie asked the ambassadors: "Do the three ministerial families control all the lands of Jin?"

The Wei ambassador, Tian Wen, replied: "Jin lost control of the government, and hence they have no support abroad and are faced with internal dissent. We three families used our military might to put down the rebels, in return for which we took possession of their land—we did not snatch it from the Marquis of Jin!"

"The Three Jins all want to become ranked as lords," King Weilie noted. "Why don't you establish yourselves rather than reporting to me?"

The Zhao ambassador, Gong Zhonglian, spoke up: "The Three Jins have been powerful for many generations now: they could easily establish themselves. The reason why they have determined to ask for a royal mandate is because they have never dared to forget the respect that they owe to the Zhou kings. If you invest them with this land, they will treat you with even greater loyalty and sincerity in generations to come, protecting Your Majesty's domain. Would that not be beneficial to the royal house?"

King Weilie was very pleased. He immediately ordered his palace scribe to write out a document of command, giving Ji the title of Marquis of Zhao, Qian the title of Marquis of Han, and Si the title of Marquis of Wei. Each was given a formal robe and ceremonial hat, not to mention the jade staff of office and other regalia. Tian Wen and the others returned to report this. The three families of Zhao, Wei, and Han now announced His Majesty's command to all the Central States. Zhao made its capital at Zhongmou; Han at Pingyang; and Wei at Anyi. They established their own ancestral shrines and altars of soil and grain. Again, they sent ambassadors to announce this development to each court, and many of the lords congratulated them. One exception was Qin, which had conducted no dealings with the Central States since they broke off their alliance with Jin and became subordinate to Chu. The Central States treated these people as barbarians, so there was no question of sending congratulations. Not long afterwards, the three families had Lord Jing of Jin degraded to the status of a commoner, moving him to live in Chunliu and dividing the remainder of his lands between them. From the founding of the state of Jin under Ji Tangshu to Lord Jing, twenty-nine generations had passed, but now their sacrifices came to an end.

An old man wrote a poem bewailing these events:

The six ministerial clans were reduced to four, then four were cut to
  three,
Now they faced south and crowned themselves without a sign of shame.
When dealing with sharp weapons you must hold tight to their handles;
So many stupid rulers have brought disaster down upon themselves.

There is also a poem criticizing the king of Zhou, who should not
have done what the Three Jins wanted him to do, which simply encouraged people to rebel. This poem reads:

The Zhou royal house, weak and isolated, found its power sapped;
How could they prevent the Three Jins from declaring themselves lords?
If they had not given them a royal command and just let them get on
  with it,
People could only have blamed them and not the Zhou.

Of the three new lords, Si, Marquis Wen of Wei, was by far the cleverest, able to make common cause with his knights. At this time one of
Confucius' chief disciples, Zixia, otherwise known as Bu Shang, was
teaching in the Xihe area—Lord Wen received instruction from him.
Wei Cheng also recommended a man named Tian Zifang as being of
exceptional intelligence, and Lord Wen became his friend. Wei Cheng
also happened to mention: "There is a man named Duan Ganmu who
lives in Xihe. He is a most remarkable man, but he lives in seclusion and
refuses to take office." Lord Wen immediately ordered his chariot to
take him to see this man. When Duan Ganmu heard the chariot pull up
at his gate, he jumped over the back wall to avoid them. Lord Wen
sighed and said, "He really is a man of sterling character!" He remained
at Xihe for one month, going every day to the gate to ask to be allowed
to meet him. Whenever he approached the man's hut, he would stand
leaning against the railing of his chariot, since he did not dare to sit
down. When Duan Ganmu realized his sincerity, he had no choice but
to meet him. Lord Wen took him to his residence in a comfortable carriage, and he was ranked as a senior advisor with Tian Zifang. Knights
and scholars from all four corners of the country heard of what had
happened and came to join his service. Lord Wen also acquired the services of Li Ke, Zhai Huang, and Tian Wen, making them his senior advisors who came to court every day. At this time the western regions of
Wei were by far the wealthiest and most populous area, so Qin repeatedly tried to invade, but being scared of the numerous brilliant strate-
gists at their command, in the end they desisted.

Lord Wen once made an appointment with one of his officials to go hunting outside the suburbs at noon. On that day he held morning court, and since it was very cold and rainy, he drank hot wine with his ministers. When they were all tipping the wine down their throats, Lord Wen asked one of his entourage, "Is it noon yet?"

"It is," the man replied.

Lord Wen immediately gave orders to remove the wine and ordered his charioteer to take him out to the wilds as quickly as possible. His entourage said, "It is raining. You cannot possibly go hunting in this weather. Why do you have to go all that way for nothing?"

"I made an appointment with one of my officials," Lord Wen explained, "and he is certainly going to be waiting for me out in the suburbs. Even though we are not going to be going hunting, I see no reason to break my promise to be present."

When the people of the capital saw Lord Wen rushing out in spite of the pelting rain, they all thought it was most peculiar. However, when they heard that it was because he had an appointment with a junior official, they looked at each other and said, "His Lordship is clearly quite determined to keep his word in all circumstances." From this time onwards, the government was well-ordered and laws were obeyed; nobody dared to refute his authority.

...

East of the lands of Jin there was a state called Zhongshan, ruled by the Ji family with the title of viscount. The populace was a branch of the Bai Di nomadic peoples, also known as the Xianyu. From the time of Lord Zhao of Jin, they changed their alliances many times and hence were repeatedly invaded—Lord Jian of Zhao led his army to besiege them, forcing them to sue for peace and offer tribute to his court. After the Three Jins were formally divided into separate countries, Zhongshan did not offer allegiance to anyone. Ji Qu, Viscount of Zhonghan, liked to drink late into the night. He would turn night into day and day into night. He was estranged from his most important ministers, keeping company instead with a host of vulgar boors. His people suffered greatly under his regime, and a series of natural disasters and inauspicious omens struck his country. Marquis Wen of Wei wanted to attack him, whereupon Wei Cheng came forward and said: "Zhongshan is close to Zhao in the west, but it is located far from Wei to the south. If you were to attack and take this state, it would not be easy to hold it."

"But if Zhao were to get Zhongshan, their power in the north would be much strengthened," Lord Wen pointed out.

Zhai Huang presented his opinion: "May I recommend a man? His name is Le Yang, and he is a native of Guqiu in this country. He is a brilliant scholar and an excellent warrior—he would make an ideal choice of general."

"Can I meet him?" Lord Wen asked.

"There was one time when Le Yang was walking along the road," Zhai Huang replied, "and happened to pick up some gold that had been dropped there. He took it home and his wife spat at him, saying: 'A knight with true ambitions would not drink water from the Robber's Stream; a virtuous man would not eat food that he has gained by begging. Who knows where this gold comes from! How can you possibly take it? Why are you bringing this humiliation on yourself?' Le Yang was moved by his wife's words and promptly threw the gold into the weeds before saying goodbye to his wife and setting out in search of fame and fortune. He traveled through Lu and Wey, studying in both countries, before coming back one year later. His wife was sitting at her loom. She asked her husband, 'Have you finished your studies?' Le Yang said: 'Not yet.' His wife picked up a knife and hacked through the threads on her loom. Le Yang was startled and asked her why she had done this. His wife said: 'Once you have completed your studies you can do great things, once you have woven your cloth you can wear it. Now you have come home in the middle, having failed to complete your studies—what is the difference between that and me cutting the threads on my loom?' Le Yang came to his senses and went back to resume his studies, not returning for seven years. Now he has come back to his own country and is waiting to be offered a suitably senior post, since he will not demean himself by taking office as a minor functionary. Why don't you give him a job?"

Lord Wen ordered Zhai Huang to go in a large chariot to collect Le Yang, but one of his entourage stopped him with the words: "I have heard that Le Yang's oldest son, Le Shu, holds government office in Zhongshan. How can you possibly employ him?"

"Le Yang is a famous knight," Zhai Huang replied. "His son is in Zhongshan, but when he summoned Le Yang on his lord's behalf, Le Yang refused to go on the grounds that the Viscount of Zhongshan is a wicked man. If you entrust him with the position of general, I am sure that you will have nothing to worry about!" Lord Wen followed his advice.

Le Yang arrived at court and had an audience with Lord Wen in company with Zhai Huang.

"I want to appoint you to deal with the matter of Zhongshan," Lord Wen explained, "but what am I to do about the fact that your son is serving there?"

"Each man chooses his own master," Le Yang replied. "How could I possibly allow my own private feelings to affect me when I am working for the government? If I cannot destroy the state of Zhongshan, I will accept due punishment under military law!"

Lord Wen said happily: "If you have such confidence in yourself, how can I not trust you?" He appointed him as commander-in-chief, with Ximen Bao leading the advance guard of five thousand men, and ordered them to attack Zhongshan. Ji Qu, Viscount of Zhongshan, sent his senior general Guxu to camp at Mount Qiu, where he was to intercept the Wei army. Le Yang made camp at Mount Wen, after which a stalemate ensued that lasted for more than a month. It was unclear at this stage who would win and who would lose.

Le Yang said to Ximen Bao: "I accepted this command in front of His Lordship. Now we have been here for more than a month and we have not achieved anything. How can we not feel ashamed? I have noticed that Mount Qiu is covered with dense forests. If we had but one brave knight prepared to infiltrate enemy lines and set fire to the forest, they would be thrown into panic and we could take advantage of the chaos. Then we would be sure to win!"

Ximen Bao announced that he was willing to go himself. It was the eighth month, and the Viscount of Zhongshan had ordered his servants to lay out a banquet of lamb and wine on Mount Qiu, with Guxu as the guest of honor. Guxu lifted his cup in the moonlight, forgetting all his duties in the pleasure of the moment. Just after midnight, Ximen Bao led his soldiers in a silent surprise attack; each man held a long brand made from dry twigs soaked in oil and other flammable material. In an instant the trees were on fire on all sides. When Guxu saw that his army had been engulfed in flames, he rushed back to the camp, trying to mobilize his drunken soldiers into putting out the fires. There was crackling and burning on all sides, the entire mountain was on fire—he could not save a single thing. The army was in complete chaos! Guxu knew that the Wei army was camped in front of him, so he had no choice but to escape over the rear side of the mountain. He ran straight into Le Yang, in personal command of his troops, who launched a surprise attack on them at the back of the mountain. The Zhongshan soldiers suffered a terrible defeat, but Guxu was able to wrench them out of the jaws of death. He fled to Baiyang Pass. With the Wei army in hot pursuit immediately behind them, Guxu had no choice but to abandon the pass and keep on running.

Le Yang pushed his advance deeper and deeper into enemy territory; anyone who crossed his path was defeated. Guxu led the remnants of his army back to have an audience with the Viscount of Zhongshan, at which he explained how he had failed to counter Le Yang's intelligence and bravery. A short time later, Le Yang moved his army to lay siege to the capital. The viscount was furious.

Grandee Noble Grandson Jiao came forward and said: "Le Yang is the father of Le Shu, who holds office in this country. Why don't you order him to go to the top of the city walls and talk his father's troops into withdrawing? That would be the very best plan!"

The viscount took his advice and said to Le Shu: "Your father, in his capacity as a Wei general, has attacked our city. If you can talk him into withdrawing, I will reward you with a large city as your fief!"

"In the past, my father refused to accept office in Zhongshan and went to serve the Wei instead," Le Shu said. "We are each serving our own lord. Surely nothing that I can say would change his mind."

The viscount forced him to go. Le Shu now had no choice; he had to climb to the top of the city walls and shout out to them, asking to see his father. Le Yang got dressed in his formal robes and climbed into a battle chariot. The moment he caught sight of Le Shu, without even waiting for him to open his mouth, he started shouting at his son: "A gentleman should not stay in a doomed country, nor should he serve a wicked lord. You have been blinded by wealth and power to the point where you do not realize it is time to leave. I have received an order from His Lordship to put an end to the suffering of the wretched people in this place and punish their evil ruler. Why don't you persuade the viscount to surrender as quickly as possible? That way, we may yet meet again!"

"The decision about whether to surrender or not is up to His Lordship," Le Shu retorted. "I cannot decide it for him. I would just request that you hold off your attack for a bit, Father, so that he has time to discuss your proposal with his ministers!"

"I will rest my troops for one month," Le Yang said. "That is all I can do for you, my son. Your lord had better make his decision as soon as possible and stop holding us all up!"

Le Yang did indeed give the order to keep the city under siege, but did not attack them again. The Viscount of Zhongshan realized that thanks to Le Yang's affection for his son, he was not prepared to attack the city immediately. He was hoping that if he drew the whole thing out for long enough the danger would eventually vanish; he had no other plan. One month later, Le Yang sent an envoy to ask for their surrender. His Lordship asked Le Shu to beg for more time, and Le Yang gave them another month. This happened three times.

Ximen Bao now came forward and said, "Do you not want to capture Zhongshan, sir? Is that why you are delaying the attack?"

"The Viscount of Zhongshan shows no concern for his people," Le Yang replied. "That is why we have attacked him. If we pressed the attack too strongly now, we would kill many innocent civilians. The reason why I have agreed to his requests three times is not purely out of affection for my son, it is also to make sure that we gain popular support."

• • •

Lord Wen of Wei's entourage felt it to be very unfair that just after Le Yang had joined his service, he had immediately been appointed to such an important position. When they heard that he had delayed the attack three times, they slandered him to Lord Wen, saying: "Le Yang could have taken advantage of his repeated victories to crush the enemy, but thanks to what Le Shu said, he has delayed three months without making a move. From this we can see how strong the affection is between father and son, but if you don't recall him, we are afraid that you will have wasted your men and provisions, without gaining anything to the point."

Lord Wen did not respond, but asked Zhai Huang about this. "He must have a plan," Zhai Huang declared. "Do not worry, my lord."

After this, his ministers wrote a whole series of letters to him. Some said that the ruler of Zhongshan was going to give half his country to Le Yang, others said that Le Yang was plotting a joint attack on Wei with the Lord of Zhongshan. Lord Wen locked all of these letters in a box. However, at the same time he sent an envoy to feast the army, while also building a mansion in the capital, which would become Le Yang's residence when he came back. He was very appreciative of all that His Lordship was doing for him and, seeing that Zhongshan showed no sign of surrendering, he led all his troops on the attack. Given that the walls of Zhongshan were very solid and thick and that they had ample provisions, not to mention that Guxu and Noble Grandson Jiao were patrolling day and night and they had gathered all the wood and rocks inside the city to aid with their defenses, even though he attacked for several months, he could not break in. This was so annoying that Le Yang started to become desperate; he ordered a joint attack on all four city gates at once, which he personally commanded with Ximen Bao, braving a hail of missiles. At this time Guxu was directing the defense of the city; he was shot dead by an arrow through the head. There was not a single house left undamaged within the city walls.

Noble Grandson Jiao said to His Lordship, "The situation is now critical! There is only one thing that we can do now to make the Wei army leave!"

"What is that?" the viscount asked.

"Le Shu has three times requested an extension of our ceasefire," Noble Grandson Jiao said, "and Le Yang granted it every time. This is proof of how much he loves his son. Since his attack is now pressing us hard, let us tie Le Shu up and hang him from the top of a pole. If he does not withdraw his army, we will kill his son. There is no way that Le Yang can attack us in the face of his son screaming and begging for his life."

The viscount followed this advice. Dangling from the end of a pole, Le Shu shouted: "Save me, Father!"

When Le Yang saw this, he cursed and said: "Useless child! You took up office in this country and you have not been able to come up with a single good plan to make their lord successful in battle, while on the other hand you have also not been able to see the danger threatening you and make His Lordship do the sensible thing. How dare you beg for mercy like some mewling infant?"

When he had finished speaking, he grabbed a bow and nocked an arrow to the string, intending to shoot Le Shu, who screamed and begged to be allowed off the walls. Catching sight of the Viscount of Zhongshan, he said: "My father is determined to take this city for Wei; he does not care about me in the slightest. If you are planning to fight to save it, let me die now. Punish me for having failed to make the enemy withdraw."

"Since it is his father who is attacking our city," Noble Grandson Jiao said, "he is guilty by association. You ought to put him to death."

"This is not Le Shu's fault," His Lordship declared.

"Once Le Shu is dead," Noble Grandson Jiao said, "I have a better plan to make the enemy withdraw."

The viscount drew his sword and handed it to Le Shu, who cut his own throat. Then Noble Grandson Jiao said: "The closest of all human relationships is that between a parent and a child. Why don't you have Le Shu cooked up to make a stew and send it to Le Yang? When Le Yang sees the stew he will be completely devastated. While he is still at the height of his anguish, he will have no wish to do battle. You can then lead your army out and attack him. If we are lucky enough to win, we can then make further plans."

The Viscount of Zhongshan had no choice but to follow this advice. He ordered Le Shu to be butchered and cooked up into a stew, which he sent to Le Yang along with the head and the following message: "Since the junior general was not able to make your army withdraw, His Lordship has killed him and cooked him into a stew. I now make you a present of it. Your son's wife and children are still in the city. If you attack again, they will all be executed."

Le Yang realized that this was his son's head. "Unfilial child!" he cursed. "You have been killed because you chose to serve a wicked and unprincipled man!" He took the stew and ate it in front of the Zhongshan envoy. When he had finished the whole bowl, he said: "Tell His Lordship I appreciated the stew, and I will give my thanks in person on the day that the city is taken. We have a large cooking pot here that will be waiting for your lord." The envoy returned to report this.

The Viscount of Zhongshan realized that Le Yang was completely unaffected by his son's death and that his attacks on the city were increasing in severity. Being afraid that the city would fall and that he would suffer torture and humiliation, he went to the palace harem and hanged himself. Noble Grandson Jiao opened the gates of the city and surrendered. Le Yang listed the crimes he had committed in slandering and misinforming his ruler resulting in the destruction of the whole country and beheaded him. Having pacified the populace, he left Ximen Bao in charge of guarding the city with five thousand troops. He took all the gold and jade out of the Zhongshan treasury, stood down the army, and returned to Wei.

A historian wrote a poem about Le Yang eating his son:

These great city walls, one hundred cubits high, just collapsed,
All because he was prepared to eat his son's meat.
This general was not utterly heartless:
He thought the public good more important than his own feelings.

An old man wrote a poem:

The ruler of Zhongshan was so evil, no wonder his regime fell;
A good general and a fine army brought him low.

He avenged the death of his son as well as repaying his lord's kindness,
But why did he force himself to eat a bowl of stew?

When Lord Wen of Wei heard that Le Yang had achieved victory, he came out of the city in person to welcome him and feast his troops.

"You lost your son for the sake of the country," he said. "That is my fault."

Le Yang kowtowed and responded: "In the interests of justice, I could not possibly consider my personal feelings. That would have betrayed Your Lordship's trust in me when you gave me the axe of office."

When Le Yang had finished his formal court audience, he presented His Lordship with a map of the lands of Zhongshan and a list of its treasures. All the ministers congratulated him. Lord Wen held a banquet at the tower in his palace, personally pouring wine for Le Yang to drink. Le Yang raised his goblet and drained the draught, looking very proud and pleased with himself. When the banquet was over, Lord Wen ordered his servants to carry in two boxes, heavily sealed. He had them transported to Le Yang's mansion. The entourage handed the boxes over, and Le Yang thought: "These boxes must contain pearls or jade or gold or something of that kind. His Lordship is afraid that the other ministers will be jealous, and that is why he has sealed them before giving it to me."

He ordered his servants to lift them into the main hall. He opened the boxes and looked inside. They were filled with the memorials of other ministers, all accusing him of treason. Le Yang was deeply shocked and said: "I had no idea what a malicious and unpleasant place the court is! If it were not for the fact that His Lordship trusted me deeply and was not misled by these slanders, could I have enjoyed my current success?"

The next day, he went to court to thank His Lordship for his kindness. Lord Wen was discussing whether to give him any further rewards. Le Yang bowed twice and refused: "The destruction of Zhongshan was entirely made possible by Your Lordship's support at court. All that I did was to carry out your orders. I made no contribution myself."

"The problem is not that I cannot employ good ministers, it is that the ministers don't do what I tell them," Lord Wen replied. "Since you have worked so hard, General, how can I not give you a city as your fief?" He granted Lingshou as Le Yang's fief and he received the title of Lord of Lingshou, though at the same time, he lost his military command.

Zhai Huang stepped forward and said: "Since you know how capable Le Yang is, my lord, who don't you send him to guard the borders? Why should he be kept in idleness?"

Lord Wen laughed and did not reply. When Zhai Huang left the court, he asked Li Ke about it, who replied: "Le Yang did not care about his own son, let alone other people. That is the very reason that Guan Zhong was so suspicious of Yi Ya." Zhai Huang now realized exactly what the problem was.

. . .

Lord Wen was worried that Zhongshan was so far away. He needed someone whom he trusted to guard it, so that he would not have to be on tenterhooks the entire time. For this reason, he decided to make Scion Ji the Lord of Zhongshan. When Ji had accepted the order, he left. He happened to encounter Tian Zifang riding on a cart. Scion Ji immediately got down from his chariot and respectfully stood to one side of the road to let the other man pass. Tian Zifang drove straight past without even turning his head. Scion Ji was unhappy about the other man's rudeness, so he sent someone to grab hold of the reins of his horses. Then he came forward and said, "I have a question that I would like to ask you. Is it the rich and noble who are arrogant? Or the humble and poor?"

Tian Zifang laughed and said: "Ever since antiquity it has only been the humble and poor who have behaved with arrogance, never the rich and noble. If the lord of a state were to treat other people badly, how could he preserve the altars of soil and grain? If a grandee were to behave arrogantly, would the sacrifices at his ancestral temples continue? King Ling of Chu lost his country due to arrogance; Yao, Earl of Zhi, destroyed his clan the same way. Being rich and noble does not mean that you are clever! If you are a poor knight of low birth, you will never get to eat anything other than porridge and greens, you will dress in hemp and other coarse clothes, but you ask nothing of any other man and hope for nothing from your times. A lord who enjoys the company of such knights must take his pleasures as they do, speaking carefully and listening with attention, doing everything he can to make them stay, otherwise one fine morning they will pack their bags and go! Who can prevent them? King Wu of the Zhou dynasty was able to execute his enemy who held an army of ten thousand chariots, yet he was not able to bend the two knights of Shouyang to his will—that shows you what valuable things poverty and humble background are!"

Scion Ji was very ashamed of himself and apologized before he withdrew. When Lord Wen heard that Tian Zifang had refused to truckle to the scion, he treated him with redoubled courtesy.

• • •

At this time there was nobody appointed to guard the city of Yedu. Zhai Huang said, "Yedu is located between Shangdang and Handan, on the border with Han and Zhao. We need a knight of strength and intelligence to guard it for us. No one but Ximen Bao will do." Lord Wen immediately appointed Ximen Bao to guard Yedu.

On his arrival, he saw the villages and towns overgrown with weeds and noted the scarcity of the population. Summoning the local elders into his presence, he asked them what the problem was. They all said, "We are suffering because of the brides offered to the River God."

"How odd!" Ximen Bao remarked. "That really is most strange! How can the River God take a bride? Please explain what you are talking about."

"The Zhang River springs from Mount Zhanling," the elders explained, "and once it reaches the city of Shacheng, it turns east, skirting Yedu. The River God is the spirit that lives in the Zhang River. This god loves beautiful women, and every year it takes a wife. We have to select a woman for it, in order to guarantee a good harvest every year with proper rainfall. Otherwise the god will be angry and cause the waters to flood, drowning everybody."

"Who says so?" Ximen Bao asked.

"That is what the shamans say," the elders explained. "Since we are so frightened of floods, we would not dare to disobey their instructions. Every year gentry families and local officials get together with the shamans to discuss the matter. They tax us tens of thousands of cash and use two or three hundred thousand to pay for the expenses of the River God's bride. The rest they divide among themselves."

"Do people just put up with this?" Ximen Bao asked in horror. "Why don't they complain?"

"The shamans take charge of all our religious ceremonies," the elders replied, "while the officials work hard on our behalf; we are happy for them to take some public money for this! What is much worse is the fact that at planting time every spring, the shamans visit each family to inspect their daughters. If there is a pretty one, they say, 'This girl ought to be the River God's wife.' There are many who do not want this, so they use money or silk to buy their daughter out, so that the shamans go and find another girl. But there are poor families that cannot afford to buy their daughters out, in which case they have to hand the girl over. The shamans build a purification chamber up on the riverbank with everything new—curtains, bed, and bedding—and then the girl is made to wash and change her clothing, after which she lives in the chamber. They divine an auspicious day and construct a reed boat. They put the girl on board and float her down the river. It may sail for perhaps thirty or forty *li*, but in the end it sinks. The people here suffer from the taxation and then those with daughters are afraid that she may be selected as a bride for the River God, so they take their girls and hide in caves far away. That is the reason why the city is increasingly empty."

"Does the city often suffer flooding?" Ximen Bao asked.

"Thanks to the fact that the River God gets a wife every year," the elders replied, "we do not provoke his wrath. However, even if we escape flooding, given the height of the hill on which the city is built and the distance we are from the river, it is very difficult to get enough water. As a result, it is lack of water, even outright drought, that is the problem."

"Since this River God is so powerful, when he marries his next bride, I will escort her myself," Ximen Bao announced. "Furthermore, I will pray to the River God on your behalf."

On the appointed day, the elders came to inform him. Ximen Bao put on his official robe and hat and walked to the riverbank, where he found the local officials, representatives of the gentry families, village chiefs and elders all assembled. The ordinary people were also present, whether they lived far away or near at hand. There must have been several thousand people there. The local officials and village chiefs led the senior shaman forward, looking very arrogant. Ximen Bao looked carefully at this old woman. There were also a couple of dozen young female shamans and disciples present, very finely dressed, each holding a towel and comb or an incense burner or something of that kind in her hands. They walked in a procession behind her.

"Can I trouble you, Senior Shaman," Ximen Bao said, "to call the bride of the River God here, so that I can have a look at her?"

The old woman nodded to one of her disciples, who went off to call her. Ximen Bao looked at the girl, who was dressed in fine new clothes but only of middling looks. Ximen Bao said to the shaman and the local officials present: "The River God is a powerful deity, so his bride should be outstandingly beautiful. This woman is simply not good enough. May I trouble the shaman to go and say to the River God on my behalf, 'We are going to have to find a better girl and we will send her to you on another occasion . . .'?"

He ordered a couple of his soldiers to grab the old shaman and throw her into the river. Those present were so shocked that they blenched. Ximen Bao sat quietly and waited. After a long time he said, "That old hag is really good for nothing. She has spent ages in the river and still has not come back to report. Her disciples had better be sent to hurry her up."

He ordered his soldiers to grab one of the women and throw her into the river. A short time later he asked: "How long as the disciple been gone?" He had yet another of the disciples thrown in. Complaining that the first two had taken too long, he threw in yet another until three disciples had been drowned in the river. Ximen Bao said, "They are all women, so of course they cannot give a message accurately. How about sending the local officials, because they will speak more clearly?"

The men wanted to refuse, but Ximen Bao shouted: "Off you go. The sooner you go, the sooner you get back." The soldiers dragged one and pushed the other, not giving them a moment to speak, and then threw them into the river, where they were quickly washed away. The bystanders all stuck their tongues out in shock. Ximen Bao waited patiently, standing next to the river in a respectful attitude. After nearly an hour, he said, "The local officials were all too old, that is why they have not come back. We need to send the representatives of the gentry families and the village chiefs to report."

The representatives and the chiefs were now as white as chalk. Cold sweat rolled down their backs. As one they fell to their knees and started kowtowing, begging for mercy. Even when blood flowed down their foreheads, they were not willing to stop. Ximen Bao said, "Let us wait a little bit longer."

They were all terrified, but after a while, Ximen Bao said, "The waters of this river keep rolling past; they go and do not come back. Where is the River God? How dare you murder the daughters of the peasantry? You are going to pay for this crime with your lives!"

Everyone kowtowed again and apologized: "We were tricked by that wicked witch. We are innocent!"

"The witch is already dead," he said, "but if in the future there is anyone who talks about sending the River God a bride, they will have to go on ahead as a matchmaker, to make a formal announcement to the River God."

The money that the gentry families, the local officials, and the village chiefs had appropriated was all divided up and returned to the people. He also ordered the elders to seek unmarried men among the populace, whereby they were married to the remaining disciples. This put an end to shamanism here. The people who had run away returned to their original homes.

There is a poem that testifies to this:

Since when has a River God taken a bride?
In their ignorance these stupid people were preyed upon by shamans.
But the moment that a good official loosened the web of superstition,
The girls of this city could sleep safe and sound, untouched by misery.

Ximen Bao took account of the lay of the land, observing the route cut by the Zhang River. He sent people to cut twelve canals, diverting the course of the Zhang River, in order to reduce the power of the waters. The fields in the region were now irrigated by the waters of the canals, so there was no more worry about drought. What is more, the harvests doubled and the people were very happy.

To this day in Linzhang County, there is a Ximen Canal, which was dug by Ximen Bao.

Lord Wen said to Zhai Huang: "Thanks to your advice, I sent Le Yang to attack Zhongshan and I sent Ximen Bao to govern Yedu. Both of them have been very successful at their jobs and I have benefited greatly. Now Hexi is the western border of Wei, and it is the route that the Qin people take when attacking us. Whom do you think I should send to guard it?"

Huang Di was sunk in thought for a long time, then he replied: "I can recommend a man named Wu Qi. He is a great general who has fled to Wei from Lu. You must summon him immediately and give him the job, because if you delay someone else will snap him up!"

"Isn't Wu Qi the man who killed his wife in order to become a general in Lu?" Lord Wen asked. "I have heard that this man is corrupt and vicious, as well as cruel in character. How can I possibly give him such an important position?"

"I recommend people who will be able to help you achieve great things, my lord," Zhai Huang declared. "I do not care about their day-to-day behavior!"

"Well, summon him and let me have a look at him!" Lord Wen said.

Do you know what Wu Qi did for the state of Wei? READ ON.

Chapter Eighty-six

Wu Qi kills his wife in order to be appointed a general.

Zou Ji plays the qin so as to become prime minister.

Wu Qi originally came from the state of Wey. When he was young he lived in a little village, where he went swaggering around with a sword surrounded by other would-be young blades. His mother complained about his behavior, so he bit his arm until it bled and then used that blood to swear a solemn oath: "Today I will say goodbye to my mother and go abroad to study. If I do not become a senior minister, entitled to a personal standard and riding in a great chariot, I will never come back to Wey and see my mother again." His mother cried and tried to make him stay, but Wu Qi walked out of the North Gate without even turning his head. He went to the state of Lu, where he studied with one of Confucius' most senior disciples, Zeng Can. He worked day and night, without ever complaining of the hardship. Grandee Tian Ju of the state of Qi happened to visit Lu. Admiring Wu Qi's love of learning, he discussed all sorts of subjects with him. He was amazed by the breadth of his knowledge. For this reason, he decided that Wu Qi should marry his daughter.

Wu Qi had by this time been part of Zeng Can's household for more than a year, and Zeng Can was aware that he had an aged mother back home. One day he asked: "You have been away studying for six years now without ever going home to see your family. As a son, how can you bear it?"

"I swore an oath in front of my mother that I would not go back to Wey except as a senior minister," Wu Qi replied.

"You could swear such an oath to another person," Zeng Can said, "but how could you swear it to your mother?"

As a result of this conversation, Zeng Can was very unimpressed with Wu Qi. Not long afterwards, a letter arrived from the state of Wey to say that his mother was dead. Wu Qi looked up towards the sky and shouted three times, beat his breast, and wept; then he stopped crying and carried on studying just like before. Zeng Can said angrily: "Wu Qi is not even proposing to go home for his mother's funeral; he has completely forgotten where he came from! Water that has lost its source will soon run dry, while a tree that has lost its roots will soon wither. If a person forgets where he came from, how can he prosper? This man can no longer be my disciple!" He ordered his other students to break off their relationship with Wu Qi, telling them that they would not be allowed to see him again. Wu Qi decided to abandon studying Confucianism in favor of military strategy. After three years, he had completed his studies and applied for an official position in Lu.

The prime minister of Lu, Gongyi Xiu, often discussed military matters with him and thus became aware of quite how brilliant he was. He mentioned his name to Lord Mu, which got him a position as a grandee. Since Wu Qi was now earning a lot of money, he bought himself many concubines and maids with which to enjoy himself. At this time Tian He, as prime minister of Qi, was planning to usurp the marquisate, but he was afraid that he might be punished by Lu, which had a long-standing marriage alliance with his state. He was also determined to avenge the humiliation inflicted on him by his defeat at the battle of Ailing. Therefore, he raised an army and attacked Lu, hoping to threaten them into submission. The prime minister of Lu, Gongyi Xiu, came forward and said, "If you want to defeat the Qi army, you need Wu Qi."

Lord Mu agreed, but in the end he refused to give him the appointment. When he heard that the Qi army had already razed the city of Cheng to the ground, Gongyi Xiu repeated his request: "I have told you that you should give the job to Wu Qi. Why do you not employ him?"

"I know that Wu Qi is a talented general," Lord Mu replied, "but he is married to Tian Ju's daughter. There is no greater love than that between a husband and wife. How can you guarantee that he will not turn to her side? That is the reason why I have been hesitating over this appointment."

Gongyi Xiu left the court, to find that Wu Qi was already waiting for him at his residence. "The Qi invaders have already penetrated deep into our territory," he said. "Has His Lordship appointed a good general yet or not? I do not want to praise myself, but if you were to appoint me as commander-in-chief, I would cut the Qi army to pieces."

"I have said exactly that over and over again," Gongyi Xiu replied, "but His Lordship cannot make his mind up, because he is worried about the fact that you are married to a daughter of the Tian family."

"It is easy enough to assuage His Lordship's concerns!" Wu Qi declared. He went home and asked his wife, Lady Tian: "Why do people pay so much respect to men who are married?"

"Everyone has both a private life and a public persona," she responded. "The family is the first thing to be established. The reason why married men are respected is because they have a family."

"For a man to have office as a minister or indeed as prime minister, to enjoy a salary of tens of thousands of bushels of grain, to have his successes recorded on bamboo and silk and his name handed down to posterity—is this not much more important than setting up a family? Isn't that what every wife would like for her husband?"

"Of course," Lady Tian answered.

"I have a request to make," Wu Qi said. "Will you grant it?"

"Is there anything that I can do to help you become famous?"

"The Qi army has invaded Lu and the Marquis of Lu would like to appoint me as general," he explained. "However, because I am married to a daughter of the Tian family, he hesitates to make the appointment. If I take your head and present it to the Marquis of Lu, his suspicions will be assuaged. Then my fame is assured!"

Lady Tian was horrified, but just as she was about to open her mouth to reply, Wu Qi drew his sword and beheaded her.

A historian wrote a poem:

One night as a husband and wife leads to one hundred days of affection.
How could you bear to turn an innocent woman into a vengeful ghost?
But if you did not even care about your mother's funeral, you are so
   inhuman
That we cannot be surprised at the way you treated your wretched wife!

He wrapped Lady Tian's head in a silk cloth and went to have an audience with Lord Mu, at which he presented his opinion: "It is my ambition to serve the country, but Your Lordship's suspicions were aroused by my wife. I have now beheaded her, in order to demonstrate that my loyalty is given to Lu and not to Qi!"

Lord Mu was very shocked and unhappy. "Please wait a while, sir," he said. A short time later, Gongyi Xiu came to the palace to have an audience with His Lordship. Lord Mu said: "Wu Qi has murdered his wife in order to be appointed general; he really is a wicked man. I have no idea what he will be up to next!"

"Wu Qi does not love his wife," Gongyi Xiu pointed out. "He only cares about becoming famous. If you were to refuse to give him office, my lord, you would just be helping the state of Qi!"

Lord Mu followed Gongyi Xiu's advice and appointed Wu Qi to be his commander-in-chief. He ordered Xie Liu and Shen Xiang to assist him. They set off in command of twenty thousand men to intercept the Qi army. After Wu Qi had been given his orders, he wore the same clothes as his soldiers and ate the same food, never once sleeping in a bed or riding in a chariot. When he saw a soldier collapsing under the weight of a bag of grain, he would take it and carry it himself; when his soldiers were sick, Wu Qi would doctor them himself, even going so far as to suck the pus from an infected wound. The troops were deeply impressed by Wu Qi's concern for them and felt that he was like a member of their own family, that they would live or die together. For this reason, they were happy to fight for him.

. . .

Tian He led his senior generals—Tian Ji and Duan Peng—deep into enemy territory, straight through the southern borderlands of Lu. When he heard that Wu Qi had been appointed as the Lu commander-in-chief, he laughed and said, "That son-in-law of the Tian family cares about nothing but women. How could he possibly lead an army out on campaign? If Lu is defeated, it is because they have appointed him!"

When the two armies made camp opposite each other, Wu Qi did not go out to provoke battle. Tian He secretly sent people to spy on what they were up to. They saw Wu Qi sitting on the ground with the very humblest of his soldiers, eating porridge out of the same pot. When the spies returned to report this, Tian He laughed and said: "If the general is respected, his soldiers fear him. If the soldiers fear him, they will fight to the death. If Wu Qi behaves like this, how can he possibly expect to command his men? I have nothing to worry about here!"

He sent his favorite general, Zhang Chou, on a special mission to the Lu army, pretending to be willing to enter peace negotiations. In fact, he was to sound Wu Qi out on whether he planned to fight or simply to defend. Wu Qi had all his best troops hidden with the baggage train, leaving only the old and the weak on display for his guest. He made a point of being very respectful and attentive, treating his visitor with the utmost courtesy.

"We have heard rumors that you killed your wife in order to be appointed general," Zhang Chou asked. "Is that true?"

Wu Qi looked appalled and replied: "Although I am an unworthy man, I have had the honor of studying with a disciple of the Sage himself. How could I dare to do such a wicked thing? My wife became sick and died around the same time as I received military command. What you have heard is nothing but malicious gossip."

"If you are prepared to maintain good relations with the Tian family," Zhang Chou responded, "I would be happy to hold a blood covenant and swear a peace treaty."

"I am just a scholar," Wu Qi declared. "I could not possibly fight against the Tian family! If a peaceful outcome were possible, I would be delighted!"

Wu Qi kept Zhang Chou in his camp for three days, feasting him. The whole time that he was present, he did not so much as mention military matters. When Zhang Chou was about to depart, he kept saying over and over again that he should convey his best wishes to the Tian family. Zhang Chou said goodbye and left, whereupon Wu Qi secretly gave orders to mobilize his men, dividing them into three groups to follow on behind him.

. . .

When Tian He received Zhang Chou's report that Wu Qi's troops were in very poor condition and had no intention of doing battle, his mind was put absolutely at ease. Just at that moment, the sound of great battle drums could be heard outside the gates to the camp as the Lu army began their surprise attack. Tian He was horrified. None of his horses were ready; none of his chariots were hitched up. The army was in chaos. Tian Ji led the infantry out to do battle while Duan Peng hurriedly gave orders that his men were to get the chariots ready to join in as soon as possible. He was completely unprepared for Xie Liu and Shen Xiang to attack in unison, one on either side. They took advantage of the disorder in the army to catch them in a pincer movement. The Qi troops suffered a terrible defeat, leaving dead bodies all over the place. Wu Qi chased them past Pinglu and then returned. Lord Mu of Lu was delighted and appointed him as a senior minister.

Tian He was determined to punish Zhang Chou for giving him misleading information.

"I told you exactly what I saw," Zhang Chou said. "How could I know that it was all part of Wu Qi's plan?"

Tian He sighed and said, "Wu Qi is as great a military strategist as Sun Wu or Tian Rangju; as long as he is employed by Lu, we will not know a moment's peace! I am going to have to send someone to Lu to make a peace treaty in secret, whereby we both agree not to attack each other. Would you be prepared to go?"

"I will risk my life on this mission," Zhang Chou declared, "to atone for my previous failure."

Tian He paid good money for a couple of beautiful slaves and added one thousand ingots of gold. He ordered Zhang Chou to dress up as a merchant and make his way to Lu, where he was to offer this bribe to Wu Qi. Since Wu Qi was a greedy and lascivious man, he took the bribe the moment it was offered. He said to Zhang Chou, "Tell the prime minister of Qi that if he does not attack Lu, we certainly would not dare to fight him."

As Zhang Chou left the Lu capital, he deliberately made these facts known to some other people, who then gossiped about the matter to everyone they came across. The rumors that Wu Qi had accepted bribes from the enemy spread far and wide. Lord Mu said, "I knew Wu Qi was not to be trusted!" He planned to strip him of his titles and punish him to the letter of the law. When Wu Qi heard this he became frightened and fled to the state of Wei, abandoning his family. He took up residence in Zhai Huang's house. Thus it happened that when Lord Wen was discussing who should go and guard the Xihe region with Zhai Huang, the latter recommended Wu Qi.

Lord Wen summoned Wu Qi and had an audience with him, at which he said: "I have heard that you did very well in Lu, sir, so why have you come here to suffer in obscurity?"

"The Marquis of Lu listened to malicious gossip and developed unreasonable suspicions," Wu Qi explained. "I escaped here simply in order to survive. I have long admired the way that Your Lordship treats gentlemen in difficulty, which has caused so many brave knights to give their allegiance to you. I am willing to hold a whip and walk in front of your horses, like the humblest of your grooms. If I were to die doing this, I would have no regrets."

Lord Wen appointed him to guard Xihe. When Wu Qi arrived there, he repaired the walls of the fortress and deepened the moat, training the soldiers in the garrison. His love and sympathy for his men was in no way inferior to that which he had shown when he was a general in Lu.

The fortifications that he built to prevent further incursions by Qi were known as the Wu Walls.

. . .

At this time Lord Hui of Qin died and his scion, Chuzi, was established. Lord Hui was the son of Lord Jian, who was himself the youngest uncle of Lord Ling. When Lord Ling of Qin died, his son the Honorable Shixian was still very young, so the ministers appointed Lord Jian in his place. The title had now reached Chuzi, three generations later. The Honorable Shixian was already an old man, and he said to the senior ministers, "This country once belonged to my father. What crime have I committed, that I was dispossessed in this way?" The senior ministers found nothing to say. They joined forces to kill Chuzi and established the Honorable Shixian as Lord Xian of Qin. Wu Qi took advantage of the many problems faced by the Qin court to raise an army and make a surprise attack on Qin, capturing five cities to add to the domain of Hexi; Han and Zhao both sent ambassadors to congratulate him. Lord Wen was very pleased that Zhai Huang had recommended a good man for office, and so he wanted to appoint him as prime minister. He discussed this idea with Li Ke, who said, "Wei Cheng would be better." Lord Wen nodded his head.

When Li Ke went to early morning court, Zhai Huang met him and asked, "I have heard that His Lordship is considering whom to appoint as prime minister and that he asked your advice before making the final decision. Who is the man?"

"His Lordship has decided on Wei Cheng," Li Ke replied.

Zhai Huang said angrily: "When His Lordship wanted to attack Zhongshan, I recommended Le Yang; when His Lordship was worried about the situation in Yedu, I suggested Ximen Bao; when His Lordship needed someone to guard Xihe, I put forward Wu Qi. In what way am I inferior to Wei Cheng?"

"Wei Cheng has recommended Bu Zixia, Tian Zifang, and Duan Ganmu; these men are either His Lordship's instructors or his close friends," Li Ke retorted. "The people whom you have recommended are His Lordship's vassals. Wei Cheng gets a salary of one thousand bushels of grain, ninety percent of which goes to support scholars and knights. You spend your salary on yourself. How can you possibly be compared with Wei Cheng?"

Zhai Huang bowed twice and said, "I was wrong about what I said. Please instruct me further."

From this time onwards, the state of Wei had the greatest civil officials and military men of the time in their employ, resulting in peace along the borders for many years. Of the Three Jins, Wei was by far the most powerful. There is a poem that testifies to this:

Each kingdom fought to be the most powerful;
The advice of clever men allowed them to ride the whirlwind.
Just look at whom Lord Wen of Wei treated as his friends:
Of course he deserved to succeed!

When the prime minister of the state of Qi, Tian He, realized how strong Wei was and how Lord Wen's reputation as a wise ruler had spread throughout the world, the alliance between them became even more important. He moved Lord Kang of Qi to the seaside, giving him the tax revenues of a single town, taking the rest himself. Afterwards he sent someone to visit Lord Wen of Wei, requesting that he take a message to the king of Zhou, asking to be recognized as one of the lords of the Central States, following the precedent set by the Three Jins. King Weilie of Zhou was dead by this time and his son, Prince Jiao, had been established as King An. He was in a much weaker position even than his father. In the thirteenth year of the reign of King An, he accepted Lord Wen's request and appointed Tian He as the Marquis of Qi with the title of Lord Tai. It had been ten generations since the Honorable Wan of Chen moved to Qi, giving up his chance to become ruler in order to serve Lord Huan of Qi as a grandee. Now Tian He took over the state of Qi, putting an end to the sacrifices to the Jiang family. No more of this now.

. . .

At this time, the Three Jins were all busily engaged in selecting suitable prime ministers and recruiting men of talent—the prime ministerial position being of particular importance since it was the most powerful. Zhao gave this position to Gongzhong Lian and Han to Xia Lei. For the moment we are going to follow the story of Xia Lei, who as a young man became very good friends with Yan Sui from Puyang. Xia Lei was poor, but Yan Sui was rich; he gave him all the money that he needed and later on advanced him one thousand pieces of gold to help pay his traveling expenses. It was thanks to this money that Xia Lei was able to go to Han, where he was appointed prime minister. Once Xia Lei was in control of the government, he took his position very seriously and refused to receive private guests. When Yan Sui arrived in Han, he wanted to visit Xia Lei because he hoped he would recommend him, but having waited more than a month he was still unable to clap eyes on him. Yan Sui used his private wealth to bribe some of His Lordship's entourage and hence was able to have an audience with the marquis. Lord Lie was delighted to meet him and wanted to reward him generously. However, Xia Lei made much of Yan Sui's shortcomings in conversation with Lord Lie, thus preventing him from receiving an official post. When Yan Sui discovered what had happened, he was furious. He left Han and traveled around a number of other countries, hoping to find some bravo who would be prepared to kill Xia Lei and avenge this insult.

When he arrived in the state of Qi, Yan Sui happened to meet a butcher who raised an enormous axe with which to kill his beef. When the axe descended it cleaved bone and sinew, without any noticeable expenditure of energy. Looking at his axe, he realized that it must weigh at least thirty pounds. Yan Sui was amazed at this. Inspecting the man more closely, he noticed how tall he was, with protuberant eyes and a curly beard, not to mention exceptionally prominent cheekbones. From his accent, he did not appear to be a local.

Going over to him and making his acquaintance, Yan Sui asked his name and where he had come from.

"My name is Nie Zheng and I come from the state of Wei," he answered. "My home is at Shenjing Village in the outskirts of the city of Zhi. Thanks to my aggressive and uncompromising personality, I got into trouble with some people in my village, so I had to move here with my mother and sister. I am now making a living as a butcher."

He asked Yan Sui's name in return, and after he had given it, he quickly said goodbye and left. The following morning, Yan Sui put on his finest hat and robe and went to visit him, carrying wine. Having performed the proper ceremonies due to an honored guest, the wine was circulated three times. Yan Sui gave him one hundred ingots of gold as a gift, and Nie Zheng was amazed at his generosity.

"I have heard that you have an aged mother living with you," Yan Sui explained. "Even though I cannot offer you much, I can at least provide the means to let her live comfortably for a day or two."

"If you are concerned about my mother," Nie Zheng replied, "it must be because you have a job for me. If you do not tell me what it is that you want me to do, I cannot possibly accept this gift!"

Yan Sui explained exactly how Xia Lei had ignored all his kindness and what he wanted to do about it.

"There is an old saying: 'As long as your parents are alive, you cannot risk your life for anyone else,'" Nie Zheng said. "You had better find some other bravo, for I would not dare to take your presents when I can do nothing for you in return."

"I have the greatest respect for you and would like to swear blood-brotherhood. I would not dare to prevent you from doing your duty as a good son by asking you to carry out a private mission for me."

Nie Zheng was now placed in a position where he had no choice but to take the present. He used one half of the money as a dowry for his sister, Nie Ying, while the remaining money was used to make sure that his mother ate well every day. A few years later when Nie Zheng's mother got sick and died, Yan Sui came again to condole; what is more, he took charge of all the funeral arrangements. When the funeral was over, Nie Zheng said: "My life is yours to do with as you will. I am happy to be of service, for I have no regrets in this life!"

Yan Sui asked him his plan for revenge, and wanted to give him chariots and soldiers, but Nie Zheng said: "The prime minister occupies an exceptionally important position and therefore he will be surrounded by a host of guards wherever he goes. This kind of man can be attacked with surprise and skill; he cannot be overwhelmed by superior forces. I will go to him armed with a dagger and wait for an opportunity to strike. I will say goodbye to you today, for we will not meet again. You should not ask me any questions about what I mean to do."

When Nie Zheng arrived in Han, he found somewhere to stay in the suburbs of the capital, where he rested for three days. Then he got up early and entered the city, just in time to see Xia Lei leaving the court after the early morning audience. He was riding in a large carriage drawn by a team of four horses. His bodyguards, dressed in full armor and carrying halberds, walked in front and behind. They moved past extremely quickly. Nie Zheng tailed them to the prime minister's official residence, where Xia Lei got out of his carriage and entered his mansion, where he was going to make a series of administrational decisions. From the front gate all the way to the main hall, there were soldiers on guard at every step. Nie Zheng looked at Xia Lei, sitting far away in the main hall, leaning against an armrest. There was a vast crowd standing around holding documents and waiting for a decision. After what seemed like an age, business had been completed and he was about to withdraw.

Nie Zheng took advantage of this to catch him off guard. Shouting "I have an urgent report to make to the prime minister!" he came rushing in from outside the gate, waving his arms, bumping aside those guards who tried to stop him. When Nie Zheng reached the seat of honor, he drew his dagger and stabbed Xia Lei. Although Xia Lei got up in alarm, he was dead before he had even managed to find his feet. The place was thrown into complete chaos. The guards shouted: "Get the assassin!" They shut the gate and set about trying to capture Nie Zheng. He succeeded in killing a couple of soldiers but then, having estimated that his chances of being able to escape were zero and being afraid that someone might recognize him, he disfigured his face with his dagger and gouged out his eyes before drawing the blade across his throat.

By this time someone had reported the news to Lord Lie of Han. "Who is the assassin?" His Lordship asked, but nobody recognized him. They exposed his body in the marketplace, offering a reward of one thousand pieces of gold for anyone who came forward with information about the name or the antecedents of the assassin, in the hope that they would be able to avenge the prime minister's murder. After seven days, even though hordes of people had been past, nobody had recognized him. Word of this matter reached the city of Zhi in the state of Wei, where Nie Zheng's older sister heard it. She wept bitterly and said, "This must be my younger brother." Dressed in plain clothes, she made her way to the state of Han, and when she saw Zheng's body exposed in the marketplace she threw herself across the corpse and burst into floods of tears.

The official in charge of the marketplace arrested her and questioned her: "Who is this dead man to you?"

"He is my younger brother, Nie Zheng," she replied. "My name is Nie Ying. Our home is Shenjing Village, near the city of Zhi, and he is famous there for his bravery. Since he knew how serious the penalties for murdering the prime minister would be, he was afraid that I would be punished too, hence he gouged out his eyes and mutilated his face in order that his name should not be known. But how could I survive if that were at the cost of letting my brother go unrecognized?"

"If the dead man is indeed your brother," the official said, "you must know the motive for the crime. Who hired him? If you tell me the truth, I will report to His Lordship and request that the death penalty be commuted."

"If I were afraid of death," Nie Ying retorted, "I would not have come here in the first place. My brother got killed taking revenge for his master by assassinating the prime minister of a state of one thousand chariots. I am happy to tell you my brother's name in order that his memory should be preserved. However, if I were to tell you the motive, I would ruin his reputation!"

She dashed her head against the stone pillar by the well in the marketplace, cracking her skull open.

A historian wrote a poem about this:

How sad that both brother and sister ended up dead;
Having become famous, they did not mind dying.
If you fail to be kind, vengeance will follow;
Which is better: making friends or making enemies?

The official reported these events to Lord Lie of Han. He sighed deeply and gave orders that her body should be collected and buried properly. He appointed Han Shanjian to the position of prime minister, taking over from Xia Lei.

When Lord Lie of Han died, his son, Lord Wen, inherited. When Lord Wen died, his son, Lord Ai, inherited. Han Shijian did not get along well at all with Lord Ai, to the point where he eventually took his opportunity and assassinated him. The other senior ministers executed Han Shijian for this crime. Afterwards they established Lord Ai's son, the Honorable Ruoshan, as their new ruler, and he assumed the title of Lord Yi. It was Lord Yi's son and heir, Lord Zhao, who appointed Shen Buhai as his prime minister. Shen Buhai was a distinguished Legalist philosopher who administered the state excellently. This part of the story we will return to later on.

. . .

In the fifteenth year of the reign of King An of Zhou, Lord Wen of Wei became terminally ill. He summoned Scion Ji from Zhongshan. When Zhao heard that the scion had left Zhongshan, they took their army on a surprise attack and conquered this territory. This brought about a serious breach between the states of Zhao and Wei. By the time that Scion Ji arrived back home, Lord Wen of Wei was already dead. He presided over the funeral and succeeded to the title under the name of Lord Wu. He appointed Tian Wen as prime minister. Wu Qi came from Xihe to pay court, full of hope that he might be appointed prime minister himself on the grounds of his great achievements. When he discovered that Tian Wen was already in office, he was furious and walked out of the court. He happened to run into Tian Wen at the gate.

"Do you know what I have done for this country?" he demanded. "I would like to recite the list for you."

Tian Wen made a respectful gesture and said, "I am happy to listen."

"I command all three armies in Wei," Wu Qi said, "and I have trained them to the point where they forget about the possibility that they might die when they hear the sound of the battle drums. I have done great things for this country. How do you compare?"

"I don't."

"When it comes to giving orders to the bureaucracy and doing the best for our people, making sure that the treasuries and storehouses are full, how do you compare?"

"I don't."

"In guarding Xihe and making sure that the Qin army does not dare to put one foot over the border, while forcing Han and Zhao to submit to our authority, how do you compare to me?"

"I don't."

"If you are inferior in all these three points, why do you have a position superior to mine?" Wu Qi demanded.

"I feel myself very unworthy for the high office that I hold," Tian Wen said. "However, today we have a new lord who has just succeeded to the title. His Lordship is very young and the country is restive, the populace does not respect him and senior ministers do not yet obey his authority—this is particularly true of those who accomplished great things under His Late Lordship's rule. What he needs right now are people whom he can trust. This is not the moment to be making a parade of your past achievements."

Wu Qi looked at his feet and thought deeply. After a long pause, he said, "You are right. But I think eventually this position will be mine."

One of the palace eunuchs overheard the conversation between the two men and reported it to Lord Wu. His Lordship was concerned that Wu Qi might be bearing a grudge and hence kept him at court, because he intended to send someone else to guard Xihe. Wu Qi was afraid that he might be killed by Lord Wu, so he fled to the kingdom of Chu.

King Dao of Chu had heard much of Wu Qi's talents, and so the moment he saw him, he gave him the seals of office as prime minister. Wu Qi was enormously pleased and grateful for this, because he now found himself in charge of a country of enormous wealth and with a huge army. He said to King Dao: "The kingdom of Chu has territories that extend for thousands of *li*, and you have millions of soldiers—not only are you the premier ruler of our time, but Chu has held the position of Master of Covenants for many generations. The reason that you have not been able to extend your dominance over the Central States is because you have forgotten how to train troops properly. When you are training up an army, you have to build up their strength; then you can make use of them. The court is packed with unnecessary officials and there are a huge number of remote relations of the royal house frittering away the grants they receive from the public purse. Your soldiers only receive a couple of handfuls of rice a day—how can you expect them to risk their lives in the service of the country? If you follow my plan, Your Majesty, you will prune the bureaucracy and eliminate grants to your most distant relations, using the savings to encourage your army to fight for you. If this does not bring about a renaissance in the power of your kingdom, I am prepared to be executed for my temerity!"

King Dao followed his advice. In spite of the fact that many of his ministers warned him not to pay any attention to what Wu Qi said, King Dao did not listen. He put Wu Qi in charge of reorganizing the structure in government, as a result of which he got rid of hundreds of officials surplus to requirements. Junior members of hereditary ministerial families no longer found themselves in receipt of unearned emoluments. Anyone related to the royal family at a greater remove than five generations was henceforward required to earn their own living, just like an ordinary person. The salaries given to those within five generations were measured according to the closeness of the relationship and were reduced one grade with every generation. This saved the state granaries tens of thousands of bushels of grain every year. Wu Qi selected the finest warriors in the country and drilled them morning and evening, discovering their special talents. The salary they received was dependent on their grade, and some received many times that of their colleagues. This created strong competition among the troops and a noticeable strengthening in Chu's army. Once again, they began to threaten the security of other countries. The Three Jins, Qi, and Qin were all terrified; as long as King Dao was alive, they did not dare to fight him. However, when His Majesty died, before his body had even been placed in its coffin, riots broke out, instigated by those nobles in Chu who had lost their titles and emoluments, in the hope of killing Wu Qi. He fled to the royal palace, pursued by armed men. Wu Qi knew that he could not possibly defeat them, so he lay down holding His Majesty's body. The men drew their bows and shot Wu Qi, driving many of the arrows through the king's corpse.

"I do not care about my own death," Wu Qi shouted, "but how dare you mutilate His Majesty's corpse! That is a most heinous crime, and you will pay for it according to the laws of the kingdom of Chu!" He died as soon as he had finished speaking.

When the rioters heard what Wu Qi said, they all ran away. Crown Prince Xiongzang now came to the throne, with the title of King Su. A couple of months later, he got around to punishing people for mutilating his father's body. He ordered his younger brother, Prince Xiongliang, to take charge of the troops, who arrested those guilty of inciting the riots and punished them. Some seventy households were executed to the last man.

An old man wrote a poem bewailing this:

He always hoped that in the end he would become a senior minister;
He killed his wife and neglected his mother, in defiance of all norms.
Who could have imagined that once Lu and Wei lay behind him,
He would end up dying in the kingdom of Chu?

There is also a poem about how Wu Qi ensured that his enemies would be punished by taking hold of His Majesty's dead body. Even in the last extremity, he never lost his native intelligence. This poem reads:

He was prepared to risk his life in the service of his adopted country,
And arranged that the rebels' arrows also found a home in the king's
    corpse.
Since the law guaranteed that this crime would be punished,
His private vengeance came wrapped up with the public good.

. . .

Let us now turn to another part of the story. Two years after he made himself Marquis of Qi, Tian He died. The title passed to his son, the Honorable Wu. When Wu died, the title passed to his son, the Honorable Yinqi, who succeeded to the marquisate in the twenty-second year of the reign of King An of Zhou. He was very proud of the wealth and military might of his state, and when he thought about how Wu and Yue had both declared themselves to be kings and used that title in diplomatic exchanges, he did not like to be behindhand. He declared that henceforward Qi would be a monarchy and took the title of King Wei of Qi. When the Marquis of Wei heard that Qi had declared itself a monarchy, he said, "How can we be considered inferior?" He announced that he was now the king of Wei.

This is the King Hui that Mencius met.

Now, when King Wei of Qi was established, he spent every day drinking wine and enjoying the company of his wives, listening to music and ignoring the business of government. In the space of nine years, the states of Han, Wei, Lu, and Zhao all raised armies to attack him, and his generals defending the border were defeated over and over again. Suddenly one day, a gentleman came to the palace gates and requested an audience. He introduced himself as follows: "My name is Zou Ji and I am a native of this country. I am a *qin* player and, having heard that Your Majesty is fond of music, I came here specially to request an audience with you."

King Wei summoned him and, after allowing him to sit down, he ordered his servants to bring in a table and place a *qin* on top of it. Zou Ji laid his hands upon the strings but did not begin to play. "I have heard you say that you are a fine *qin* player and I would be happy to listen to you perform," King Wei said. "However, you are just sitting there with your hands touching the strings. Is this instrument not good enough? Or is there some other problem?"

Zou Ji took his hands off the instrument and replied with a serious face: "I have studied the principles of the *qin*; if you are only interested in the sound of silk strings plucked against a paulownia-wood backing-board, all you need is a journeyman player. However, I do not think my studies will be of interest to Your Majesty."

"What do you mean by the principles of the *qin*?" King Wei asked. "Can you explain them to me?"

"The *qin* is subject to serious prohibitions," Zou Ji explained. "That is the reason why it is said to expel evil and lewdness and allow its listeners to return to rectitude. In ancient times when Fuxi first created this instrument, it was three *chi*, six *cun* and six *fen* long, to correspond to the three hundred and sixty-six days of the year. It was six *cun* wide, to correspond to the four points of the compass and the directions of up and down. It was broad in front and narrow behind, to show the difference between the noble and the base. It was round on top and square underneath, in order to represent Heaven and Earth. Its five strings corresponded to the Five Elements. The fat string represented the ruler; the thin strings represented his ministers. The sound uses tempo in order to clarify the difference between the pure and the turbid; the turbid is expansive and relaxed—this is the way of the ruler. The pure is restrained and ordered—this is the way of the subject. The first string was tuned to the note *gong*, the second to *shang*, the third to *jiao*, the fourth to *zheng* and the fifth to *yu*. King Wen and King Wu, the founders of the Zhou dynasty, each added a string; King Wen's string was *gong* minor and King Wu's string was *shang* minor. These represent gifts made by the ruler to his subjects. When ruler and subjects trust each other, the orders issued by the government are obeyed. This is the way to obtain good order."

"Wonderful!" King Wei exclaimed. "Since you are so knowledgeable about the principles of the *qin*, sir, you must be an excellent musician. Please play me a song."

"Music is my profession," Zou Ji responded, "so you can test me by asking me to play the *qin*. The country is your business, Your Majesty, but you refuse to have anything to do with it. Your Majesty sits there and refuses to govern; what is the difference between that and me sitting here and refusing to play the *qin*? If I sit here and refuse to play, I have no means to fulfill Your Majesty's expectations; if Your Majesty sits there and refuses to govern, you have no means to fulfill the expectations of the people!"

King Wei was shocked and said, "You have managed to use your *qin*-playing to remonstrate with me! I would be very happy to listen to your advice!"

He asked Zou Ji to stay in one of the guestrooms of the palace. The following morning, when His Majesty had made his ablutions, he summoned him into his presence, and they discussed the government of the kingdom. Zou Ji encouraged His Majesty to stop drinking and keep away from his womenfolk, concentrating instead on establishing the facts, investigating whether his advisors were loyal or just flattering him. His Majesty was also encouraged to care for his people, to make sure that his army was well-instructed and prepare for an attempt to take hegemony. King Wei was very pleased and appointed Zou Ji as prime minister.

• • •

At this time there was a certain traveling knight named Chunyu Kun, who was very unhappy when he realized that Zou Ji had apparently been made prime minister on the basis of an afternoon's conversation. He took his students and went to see Zou Ji. Zou Ji treated him with great respect, and Chunyu Kun behaved with considerable arrogance. He went straight in and sat in the seat of honor, then said to Zou Ji: "I have a plan that I would like to tell you about. I do not know if you are interested."

"I am happy to listen."

"A baby does not leave its mother; a wife does not leave her husband."

"I agree with you," Zou Ji replied. "I will not leave His Majesty's side."

Chunyu Kun continued: "A wheel of jujube wood that has been greased with lard ought to turn smoothly, but when the socket is square, it cannot be used for long."

"Of course. One has to take other people's feelings into account."

"Once the bow is ready it can be strung, but nevertheless it must occasionally be relaxed. All rivers flow to the sea and hence naturally converge."

"I agree with you," Zou Ji assured him. "I will make sure that I have the support of the people."

"Even if your fox-fur cloak is worn out," Chunyu Kun continued, "you should not patch it with dog fur."

"Absolutely. I will be sure to select wise men as my advisors and not allow anyone of poor character to infiltrate the ranks."

"If the axle and pole do not fit, you cannot make your chariot. If the qin is not played now fast, now slow, the music will not please."

"I assure you," Zou Ji said, "that I will conduct a thorough overhaul of the legal code and make sure that evil officials are properly punished."

Chunyu Kun sat for a while in silence, then bowed twice and withdrew. Just as they were going out of the gate, one of his disciples said: "When you began the audience with the prime minister, you were very arrogant, sir. But now you leave having bowed twice to him. Why were you so humble?"

"I tested him with five riddles," Chunyu Kun replied, "and he answered me immediately in each case. He knew exactly what I meant. He really is a most remarkable man, and I am certainly not in the same league."

After this, Zou Ji's name became famous among the knights who roamed from place to place seeking employment, and none of them dared to go to Qi.

Zou Ji paid careful attention to the advice that he had received from Chunyu Kun and did his very best to ensure the good government of the kingdom. He would often make visits to outlying districts and ask, "Is there anyone here of exceptional wisdom? Or someone who has done wicked deeds?"

Many of his colleagues praised the Grandee of E to the skies while disparaging the Grandee of Jimo. Zou Ji reported this to King Wei, who wasn't paying attention. However, he mentioned to his entourage from time to time that he wanted to do something about the matter, and secretly sent people to make inquiries in the two cities. When the reports came in, he summoned the officials from E and Jimo to court. The Grandee of Jimo was the first to arrive, and he had an audience with King Wei, at which neither of them said a word. His servants were surprised and did not understand what the reason could be. A short time later, the Grandee of E also arrived, and King Wei now summoned all his officials, with the intention of issuing rewards and punishments. His entourage now understood exactly what was going on and said: "The Grandee of E is now going to be given generous rewards, and the Grandee of Jimo will be lucky if he is not executed!"

When the usual ceremonies had been completed on the arrival of the civil and military officials, King Wei summoned the Grandee of Jimo into his presence and said: "Since you became Grandee of Jimo, you have been slandered to me virtually every single day. I have sent someone to Jimo to make secret investigations. He reports to me that the fields are full of grain and new land is being put under the plough, the people are rich and the local officials have nothing to do, leaving the eastern part of my country at peace. Ever since you were appointed, you have concentrated on bringing your area of administration into fine form. However, because you were unwilling to bribe my servants, they have done their best to keep me from discovering your excellent work. You are indeed a very fine official." He gave him a fief of ten thousand households.

Next His Majesty summoned the Grandee of E and said: "Ever since you were appointed to administer E I have heard nothing but praise for you. I sent someone to investigate the situation on the ground and I have discovered that the fields there are uncultivated and people are dying of hunger and cold. In the past when troops from Zhao approached the border, you did not go to the rescue, but instead gave lavish bribes of silk and gold to my servants to make them say nice things about you. It is your fault that the administration of this city is in such a parlous condition."

The Grandee of E kowtowed and apologized for his crimes, promising to reform his ways. King Wei did not listen. Instead, he yelled for his guards to bring in a huge cauldron. A short time later, when the fire was hot and the liquid inside was bubbling, he had the Grandee of E tied up and thrown in. Now he summoned his servants who had spent so much time praising the Grandee of E and slandering the Grandee of Jimo, a total of a couple of dozen people, and upbraided them: "You are members of my personal staff, my eyes and ears. You have taken bribes to distort the truth, trying to mislead me. What is the point of keeping people like you? You all deserve to be boiled with him!"

They wept and bowed and begged for mercy. King Wei had still not calmed down, so he selected a dozen or so of his most trusted members of staff and had them boiled too. Everyone was absolutely petrified.

There is a poem that testifies to this:

When power rests in the hands of servants, the ruler has to rely on
  them,
But they never tell the truth in their praise and blame.
How many others would have boiled the one and enfeoffed the other?
It was King Wei of Qi who actually made the right decision.

It was now time for His Majesty to select the officials who would guard the border regions. He sent Tan Zizuan to guard Nancheng in order to prevent attacks from Chu and Tian Xi to Gaotang to prevent attacks from Zhao; Qian Fu went to Xuzhou to prevent attacks from Yan, while Zhong Shou was appointed as minister of justice, with Tian Ji as the marshal. This brought the internal administration of the country into good order, and the other kings were afraid of his military might. King Wei of Qi enfeoffed Zou Ji with the lands of Xiapi, saying: "You have made it possible for me to achieve my ambitions." He gave him the title of Marquis of Cheng.

When Zou Ji had thanked His Majesty, he presented his opinion: "The reason why Lord Huan of Qi and Lord Wen of Jin were the most respected of the hegemons was because they honored the Zhou royal house. Even though the Zhou kings are in decline, they still possess the nine bronze *ding*-cauldrons that are our royal regalia. Why do you not go to Zhou, Your Majesty, and perform all the ceremonies of a formal audience with the king? That way you can use His Majesty's favor to manage the other rulers. Will you not then surpass the hegemony of Lord Huan of Qi and Lord Wen of Jin?"

"I have already crowned myself king," His Majesty replied. "Can I go to pay court to His Majesty as a monarch myself?"

"Kings are merely the most powerful of the rulers of the day," Zou Ji responded. "Being a king does not make you the Son of Heaven. If you go to pay court to His Majesty, you should temporarily refer to yourself as the Marquis of Qi. The Zhou Son of Heaven will be so delighted with your behavior that he will favor you even more!"

King Wei was delighted. He immediately gave orders to prepare his chariot for the journey to Chengzhou, where he had an audience with the Zhou king. This happened in the sixth year of the reign of King Lie of Zhou. By this time the royal house was so weak that it was a very long time since they had last seen a lord come to court; now that the Marquis of Qi came, everyone danced and sang in congratulation. King Lie presented him with many treasures. When King Wei returned to Qi from Zhou, all along the road he heard the people singing songs in praise of his wisdom, and henceforth he considered himself a hegemon-king.

A historian wrote a poem about this:

As a king himself, how could he respect the Zhou king?
What is the point of this parade of empty ritual?
By now the Eastern Zhou dynasty was fading fast,
A faint echo resounding through the empty valleys.

At that time there were seven great countries in the world: Qi, Chu, Wei, Zhao, Han, Yan, and Qin. These seven countries commanded vast territories and strong armies; there was little to choose between them. Other countries like Yue, though they claimed to be kings as well, were in fact growing weaker day by day. There is no need to even mention states like Song, Lu, Wey, and Zheng. After King Wei of Qi declared himself an independent monarch, the five countries of Chu, Wei, Han, Zhao, and Yan all got together and recommended that King Wei should also be the Master of Covenants.

The state of Qin, located among the Western Rong people, was completely isolated, having abandoned all contacts with the Central States. Nevertheless, in the time of Lord Xian of Qin, it rained gold for three days. In Zhou, the Grand Astrologer Zhan sighed to himself and said: "The lands of Qin were originally part of the Zhou domain. Having been separated for five hundred years, it is time that they return. A great ruler will be born there, and his golden virtue will shine throughout the entire world. If it is now raining gold in Qin, this is a very auspicious omen!"

When Lord Xian died, he was succeeded by his son, Lord Xiao. The latter felt humiliated that he was not included among the ranks of the lords of the Central States, so he gave orders to recruit new men into government service. The order said: "Any visiting scholar or official who can come up with a good plan for strengthening Qin will receive a senior government position and be enfeoffed with a large city."

Do you know if any remarkable men responded to this advertisement? READ ON.

Chapter Eighty-seven

*Having persuaded the ruler of Qin, Shang
Yang changes the legal code.*

*Having said goodbye to the Master of Ghost
Valley, Sun Bin descends the mountain.*

Shang Yang of the state of Wey was descended from a son of one of the
marquises of Wey, born to a concubine. He was very interested in Legalist studies, and when he realized how weak the state of Wey had become,
he decided that it would not be a suitable arena for developing his talents. For this reason he traveled to the kingdom of Wei, where he
decided to look for a job with the prime minister, Tian Wen. By this time
Tian Wen had died and been replaced by Gongshu Cuo—hence Shang
Yang joined his household. Gongshu Cuo was impressed by Shang
Yang's intelligence and recommended him for office as an advisor to the
crown prince. Any time a serious matter cropped up, he would discuss
it with him. Shang Yang's recommendations were always excellent and
Gongshu Cuo became very fond of him. He decided that he should be
promoted to high office. However, not long after he came to this decision, Gongshu Cuo became ill. King Hui visited him in person to inquire
after his health. When he saw how very sick Zuo was, he sighed deeply.
In tears, he asked: "If you are so unlucky as to break down under this
complaint, to whom should I entrust the country?"

"Even though Shang Yang is still very young," Gongshu Cuo replied,
"he is one of the most remarkable men of our age. If you put him in charge
and listen to his advice, you will find him ten times better than I ever was."

King Hui was silent.

"If you cannot give this position to Shang Yang, you must kill him,"
Gongshu Cuo told him. "Whatever you do, you must prevent him from

leaving the country. I am afraid that if he obtains high office in some other state, he will bring disaster down upon Wei."

"I understand," King Hui said, but as he was getting into his chariot, he sighed and remarked: "Gongshu Cuo is terribly ill. First he wanted me to give Shang Yang a job here and then he told me to kill him. What threat could Shang Yang possibly pose to me? I am afraid that these were the mere ramblings of a deluded mind."

When King Hui left, Gongshu Cuo summoned Shang Yang to his bedside. He said: "I told His Majesty that he ought to employ you but he did not agree. Then I said that if he could not give you a job, he ought to kill you, and he said, 'I understand.' It is my duty to put His Majesty first; that is why I told him this before mentioning it to you. You had better leave as quickly as you can, before His Majesty kills you!"

"His Majesty has refused to give me a job in spite of your recommendation," Shang Yang replied. "Is it likely that he will now kill me on your say-so?" He did not go. The Honorable Ang of Wei was also a close friend of Shang Yang's and repeatedly recommended him to King Hui, but His Majesty did not give him a job.

At around this time, Lord Xiao of Qin issued an order summoning clever men into government service, and so Shang Yang left Wei and went to Qin. He asked for an audience with Lord Xiao's favorite minister, Jing Jian, to discuss matters of state with him. Jing Jian realized what a brilliant man his interlocutor was and recommended him to Lord Xiao. His Lordship summoned Shang Yang for an audience and asked him about the way to govern a country well. Shang Yang spoke of the brilliance of the administration of the sage-kings Fuxi, Shennong, Yao, and Shun, but before he had even finished his exposition, Lord Xiao had gone to sleep.

The following day, Jing Jian went into the palace to see His Lordship. "Your visitor is a madman!" Lord Xiao said. "I grant you that he is glib, but his ideas are completely impractical! Why on earth did you recommend him?"

Jing Jian withdrew from the court and said to Shang Yang, "I gave you the opportunity to speak to His Lordship because I thought you wanted to throw your lot in with ours. What were you thinking of—to bore His Lordship so with your theories?"

"I hoped that His Lordship would be able to enact the same kind of government as the sage-kings," Shang Yang said, "but he did not understand my meaning. Let me talk to him again."

"His Lordship is still very unhappy about last time," Jing Jian replied. "You had better give him five days to recover before you speak to him again."

Five days later, Jing Jian did indeed raise the subject with Lord Xiao: "My visitor still has more to say. He has requested another audience with you. I hope that you will grant it, my lord."

Lord Xiao summoned Shang Yang back to the palace, whereupon he gave an exposition on the great sage-king Yu's division of the land and tax regulations and the way in which the founders of the Shang and Zhou dynasties obtained the support of the people and obeyed the will of Heaven.

"You are certainly a very learned man," Lord Xiao said, "but that was then and this is now. I do not think that the kind of policies that you are talking about could be practical in implementation."

He waved him away, intending that he should withdraw. Jing Jian was waiting at the gate, and when he saw Shang Yang leaving the palace, he went forward and asked, "How did it go today?"

"His Lordship understands what he ought to do to govern like a sage-king," Shang Yang replied, "but he does not intend to do anything of the kind."

Jing Jian said crossly: "When a ruler obtains land he will employ good men, just like the archer will pull back the string of the bow, hoping to shoot down his prey. What ruler would be prepared to abandon the models of history and deliberately fail to become a sage-king? Please stop your nonsense!"

"Before I came here," Shang Yang returned, "I had no idea of what His Lordship intends to do, but I wondered whether he might not have great plans for the future. Thus I used a deliberately vulgar form of words in order to sound him out. Now I have found out what I need to know. If you can enable me to have an audience with His Lordship again, I am sure I will gain a suitable appointment."

"You have spoken to him twice and irritated him both times," Jing Jian retorted. "Do you think I would dare to annoy him a third time?"

The following day, Jing Jian went into the palace to apologize, not daring to mention Shang Yang again. When he went home, Shang Yang said, "Did you speak to His Lordship about me?"

"Not yet."

"How sad!" Shang Yang sighed. "His Lordship has given orders to encourage clever men to seek service in his government, but he does not actually know how to employ the people he has gathered together. I had better leave."

"Where are you going, sir?" Jing Jian asked.

"There are the six kings—surely one of them will prove a better master than the ruler of Qin. Even if that is not the case, perhaps there will be someone who is more patient than you in recommending competent men for government office! I have merely to find such a person."

"Give me another five days," Jing Jian declared, "and I will speak to him again."

Another five days passed, and Jing Jian found himself in attendance on Lord Xiao. His Lordship was drinking wine when suddenly he caught sight of a wild swan flying overhead. He put down his cup and sighed. Jing Jian came forward and said, "Why did you sigh, my lord, when you caught sight of the flying swan?"

"Lord Huan of Qi once said: 'When I recruited Guan Zhong into my employment, it was like the wild swan gaining its wings.' I have given orders to summon clever men into my service but even though several months have passed, not a single man of talent has arrived. I am like a wild swan; I have the ambition to fly high into the sky but without the support of my wings, I can go nowhere. That is why I sighed."

"My visitor, Shang Yang, says he has the skills to make you a sage-king, a great ruler, or a hegemon," Jing Jian responded. "He spoke to you about the way in which first the sage-kings and then the great rulers governed the country, and you complained that these were difficult and impractical. Today he would like to talk to you about becoming hegemon. If you will give him a moment of your free time, my lord, you can let him finish what he has to say."

When Lord Xiao heard mention of the word "hegemon," he became deeply interested and ordered Jing Jian to bring Shang Yang into his presence. When he came in, Lord Xiao asked: "I have been told that you know the secret to becoming hegemon. Why didn't you mention this before?"

"I wanted to," Shang Yang replied, "but the way of the sage-king or the great ruler is completely different from that of the hegemon. Sage-kings have to accord with the people, but hegemons go against them."

Lord Xiao put his hand on the pommel of his sword and said angrily, "How can the way of the hegemon be against the will of the people?"

"If the sounds of the zither and *qin* do not harmonize, you change the strings and retune the instrument," Shang Yang said. "If the government is not periodically retuned, it cannot be considered good. Ordinary people are only interested in their present peace and do not think about what will benefit later generations; they enjoy the results, but do not consider how to bring these about. When Guan Zhong became prime minister in Qi, he reformed the government and took control of the army, reorganizing the distribution of land into twenty-five counties and ensuring that the people kept to their hereditary professions. This resulted in a root-and-branch reform of the traditional government of Qi. This is surely not something that an ordinary person would be happy to see! It was only when the government had been successfully reformed, when enemy powers submitted to his authority, when the ruler praised his name, when the people benefited from his new laws that they realized what a truly great man Guan Zhong was."

"If you really have the same level of abilities as Guan Zhong," Lord Xiao said, "how could I refuse to entrust the country to your control and listen to your advice? The only problem is that I am not yet convinced of your powers."

"If a country is not rich, it cannot employ its army," Shang Yang told him. "If the army is not strong, it cannot resist the enemy. If you want to enrich your country, you must pay attention to agriculture. If you want to strengthen your forces, you must implement policies that encourage people to fight. If you offer generous rewards, people will understand what it is you want them to do. If you discourage them with heavy punishments, people will understand what they should fear. If rewards and punishments are regularly implemented, then government orders will be enacted. In that case, the country will indeed become rich and powerful."

"Good!" Lord Xiao said. "This is something that I can do!"

"If you want your country to be rich and powerful, you need talented men. If you succeed in recruiting them, but do not use them properly, you will fail. If you give them the right jobs but believe in other people's slanderous gossip, resulting in delay and suspicion, you will also fail."

"Good!" His Lordship said again, and Shang Yang requested permission to leave.

"I want to follow your advice; why are you leaving?"

"I want to give you three days to think it over," Shang Yang replied, "and make your decision. After that, I will tell you what you have to do."

He withdrew from the court, and Jing Jian complained to him: "His Lordship repeatedly praised your suggestions, and you could have taken advantage of that to explain exactly what it is that you have in mind to do. Instead you announced that he needed three days to think things over carefully—what do you mean by that?"

"His Lordship has not yet made up his mind," Shang Yang explained. "I am concerned that he might give the whole thing up midway if not given proper time to reflect."

The following day, Lord Xiao sent someone to summon Shang Yang, but he refused to go, with the words: "I have already explained my position to His Lordship. I will not go to court until three days have passed."

Jing Jian encouraged him to go on the grounds that a direct order should not be disobeyed. "I have already agreed on the matter with His Lordship, and I am not going to break my word," Shang Yang said. "If I were to do so, how could His Lordship trust me in the future?" Jing Jian had to agree.

When the three days were up, Lord Xiao sent a servant to collect Shang Yang in a chariot. Again he had an audience with His Lordship. Lord Xiao told him to sit down and asked for further instruction. His mind was clearly made up. Shang Yang explained which precise areas of the government of the state of Qin required a thorough overhaul. They asked each other questions—a process that lasted for three days and three nights. Lord Xiao showed no sign of exhaustion. He appointed Shang Yang as Militia General of the Left and bestowed a mansion upon him, together with five hundred gold ingots. He informed his ministers: "Henceforward, the Militia General of the Left is to be entrusted with ultimate authority in all government matters. Anyone who disobeys him will be treated as a traitor!" His officials showed every sign of respect.

There is a poem that testifies to this:

After three meetings, the king of Qin began to understand,
Wealth and power was all that he wanted to know about.
Now old ways were set aside in favor of new laws,
And the people of Qin suffered day and night.

Shang Yang now prepared a new law code, which he presented to Lord Xiao. There was a lot of discussion about it, and before it had even been promulgated, Shang Yang became worried that the people would not accept it, so he delayed implementation. Instead he took a piece of wood three yards long and had it placed at the South Gate to the city of Xianyang, ordering the local officials to guard it. He issued a command: "Anyone who moves this piece of wood to the North Gate will be rewarded with ten pieces of gold." Lots of people came to look at this order, but they did not believe it could possibly be true. Since they were not sure what it meant, they did not dare to move the wood.

"Nobody has moved the piece of wood," Shang Yang mused. "Maybe the reward is not big enough?"

He gave orders to change the terms of the notice, making the reward fifty pieces of gold. This made the populace even more suspicious. One person stepped forward and said, "Such rewards have never been offered in the history of the state of Qin. Now we suddenly see an order like this . . . there must be some trick. However, even if I don't get the full fifty pieces of gold, surely they will give me something!"

He picked up the piece of wood and took it around to the North Gate. People followed him to see what happened. The official rushed off to report this development to Shang Yang, who summoned the man and praised him: "What a good person you are! You have obeyed my order."

He gave him fifty pieces of gold. "I will never let you down!" the man declared. Everyone in the city was talking about this, and they all decided that the orders of the Militia General would have to be obeyed, since they believed that he was trustworthy. The following day, he had a new series of commands posted up. When the people of the city gathered to read them, they were amazed. This occurred in the tenth year of the reign of King Xian of Zhou.

Shang Yang's new orders were as follows:

1. Establishing the Capital. The finest lands of Qin are to be found in the Xianyang area. This city has its back to the mountains and it is cradled by the Yellow River—it is a fine city of magnificent proportions. The capital is to be moved to Xianyang, which is to be the heart of our country in perpetuity.

2. Establishing Counties. All the villages and hamlets within the borders of our country must be grouped into counties. Each county will have one administrator to oversee the implementation of the new laws. Anyone who fails in their duties will be punished in accordance with the severity of the crime.

3. Increasing Farmland. Outside the suburbs there are large areas of land situated far from any road. These areas should be laid out as fields separated by raised paths, and the local people should put them under cultivation. Once the harvest is ripe, they will be surveyed, and that figure will be used to calculate taxes. Six feet will form a standard *bu*, and two hundred and forty *bu* will form

one *mu*. If any attempt is made to fiddle with these figures, the whole field concerned will be made over to the government.

4. Establishing Taxes. In future all taxes will be calculated according to the number of *mu* under cultivation and not the number of fields. All fields are to be held by the government and no person is to be in private possession of land.

5. Enriching the People. Men should plough the fields and women should weave—those who produce a great deal of grain or cloth will be raised to the rank of squire, and the whole family will henceforth be exempt from military service. The lazy and greedy will be reduced to the status of government slaves. Anyone who so much as leaves some charcoal by the side of the road will be punished for neglecting their agricultural labors. Artisans and merchants will be taxed at double the rate of farmers. If a family has two sons, they are required to divide the property and establish separate residences with the proceeds. Anyone who refuses to divide the property will have to pay double taxes.

6. Encouraging Warfare. Official rank will be determined by success in battle. Anyone who beheads an enemy soldier will be rewarded by having their rank increased by one grade; anyone who retreats a single step will be beheaded. The highest ranks will be open to those who have achieved great things in battle, and their chariots and clothes will be suitably lavish. Those who have achieved nothing in battle, though they may be members of the aristocracy, will be reduced to wearing coarse cloth and riding on an ox. Members of noble families will find their status within the clan entirely dependent on their achievements in battle; those who fight without killing any of the enemy will find themselves struck off the clan register and reduced to commoner status. Anyone engaging in private vendettas will be executed, regardless of the rights and wrongs of the matter.

7. Punishing Crime. Five households will form a Security Group and ten households will form an Aggregation. They will be responsible for checking up on each other. If one family commits a crime, the other nine in the Aggregation should inform on them. If they do not do so, all ten families will be regarded as equally guilty, and they will all be cut in half at the waist. Anyone who hands a criminal over to the authorities will be rewarded as if they had cut the head off an enemy soldier. Anyone who reports a crime

will be rewarded by an increase of one grade in rank. Anyone who hides a criminal will be punished to the same degree as the guilty individual. Anyone who owns a hostel at which persons stay overnight is required to see their credentials; if they cannot produce them, they are not allowed to stay. If one person is guilty of a crime, his whole family will be punished with him.

8. Respecting the Law. Once government orders have been issued, they must be respected by everyone, regardless of social status. Anyone who does not obey will be executed as a warning to others.

When these new commands were promulgated, they were much discussed by the populace, some of whom approved and some of whom did not. Shang Yang gave orders that everyone be arrested and brought to his office, where he upbraided them: "When you are given an order, it is your duty to obey it implicitly. Those who disapproved are too harsh; while those who approved are guilty of flattery. None of these are good things!" He made a note of their names and places of origin and had them dispatched to the border to serve a term of military service. Grandees Gan Long and Du Zhi were also guilty of discussing the new laws in private, and they were both demoted to commoner status. It got to the point where people merely looked at each other as they passed on the streets, not daring to speak. Shang Yang ordered a large number of soldiers to construct a new palace inside the walls of the city of Xianyang, selecting an auspicious day to formally move the capital there. Scion Si did not like the idea of moving and complained that changing the laws was a bad idea.

Shang Yang said angrily: "When laws are not properly enacted, it is because men of superior status refuse to obey them. Since the scion is His Lordship's heir, it is not possible to punish him properly. But if we were to excuse him, it would suggest that it is all right for him to flout the law."

He spoke about this to Lord Xiao, who agreed that the punishment should be meted out to the Grand Tutor. Thus, the Grand Tutor, the Honorable Qian, had his nose cut off and the Grand Preceptor, Noble Grandson Jia, had his face tattooed. The ordinary people said to one another: "The scion flouted the law, and so his Grand Tutor ended up being punished—can we expect to escape?"

Shang Yang understood that the people had now accepted the situation and he could select an auspicious day to move the capital. Several thousand great families from Yongzhou moved to Xianyang. The lands of the state of Qin were divided into thirty-one counties and a network of boundaries was established to open up new land for cultivation. Tax revenues now increased to over one million pieces of gold per annum. Shang Yang often went in person to the Wei River to inspect the prison there, and in one day he executed more than seven thousand men. The Wei River ran red with blood, and the sound of weeping could be heard throughout the land. When people lay down to sleep at night, their dreams were all of warfare. As a result of this, nobody dared to pick up anything that had been dropped on the road, the country had no thieves, the storehouses and granaries were packed to the rafters, and the entire populace was focused on military expansion rather than their own private quarrels. The state of Qin became the richest and most powerful in the world. It was at this point that Shang Yang decided to raise an army to attack Chu. He captured the lands of Shangyu beyond the Wu Pass, expanding the territory of Qin by more than six hundred *li*. King Xian of Zhou sent an ambassador to appoint Qin as the regional hegemon, and all the other aristocrats offered their congratulations.

. . .

At this time, of the Three Jins, Wei was the only one to have declared itself a kingdom, and it harbored ambitions to conquer both Han and Zhao. When the king of Wei heard that Shang Yang had found a government position in the state of Qin, he sighed and said, "I wish I had listened to Gongshu Zuo's advice!" By this time Bu Zixia, Tian Zifang, Wei Cheng, and Li Ke were all dead, so he issued lavish rewards to encourage gentlemen from all four corners of the world to work in his administration. There was a certain man named Meng Ke or Mencius, styled Ziyu, who came from the state of Zou, who was a senior disciple of Master Zisi. Master Zisi was better known as Kong Ji; he was the oldest grandson in the direct line of Confucius himself. Mencius had received training in the teachings of the Sage from Zisi, and it was his ambition to be able to help his generation by bringing peace to the world. When he heard that King Hui of Wei was a man who loved the company of intelligent and learned men, he left Zou to travel to Wei. King Hui went out to the suburbs to meet him and treated him with all the ceremonies due to an honored guest. Afterwards, he asked him about the way to benefit his kingdom.

"I have been trained in the teachings of the sage," Mencius replied, "so I know all about kindness and benevolence, but nothing about benefits."

King Hui was offended by his words and did not offer him a government position. Mencius went to Qi instead.

Master Qian Yuan wrote a poem:

> Kindness and justice are nothing to do with constant scheming for
>   profit;
> If competition is everything, why would anyone study Confucianism?
> Mencius explained the teachings of the sage to no purpose:
> No matter what he said to the king, he was not prepared to listen.

In the vicinity of Yangcheng in the Zhou Royal Domain, there was a place known as Ghost Valley. The mountains were very high and the forest very dense, sunlight never penetrated, and you might imagine that no one could possibly live there—that is why it was called Ghost Valley. However, it was the abode of a recluse who called himself the Master of Ghost Valley. According to tradition, his real name was Wang Xu. He was a contemporary of Lord Ping of Jin, and he had studied medicine and cultivated the Way in the Yunmeng Mountains in company with Mo Di from the state of Song. In the end, Mo Di abandoned his family and announced that he wanted to travel around the world helping people and saving them from danger. Wang Xu stayed behind, living in hiding in Ghost Valley; over time people started to talk about the Master of Ghost Valley, who was supposed to be incredibly wise, trained in many different branches of learning, so that no mere mortal could compare. What did he know? He was learned in mathematics and in astronomy; furthermore, he could divine the future with uncanny accuracy. He was also trained in the military arts, in the Six Strategies and Three Plans, whereby he could respond to any emergency and array his troops so that not even a god could find a way to break through his lines. He had also studied the arts of rhetoric and was learned in many different things, so he could speak of underlying principles and taking advantage of situations. When he spoke, his logic and arguments were impeccable. He had also learned medicine, so that he could cultivate his own body and nourish it with the right foods, preventing disease and extending his own lifespan to the point of becoming an immortal.

Since the Master of Ghost Valley could indeed have become an immortal, why did he stay on this earth? It was because he wanted to recruit a number of brilliant disciples so that they could become immortals at the same time—that is the reason why he stayed at Ghost Valley. To begin with, he would occasionally go to the city and perform divinations for people: the accuracy of his predictions of good luck and bad was uncanny. As a result, gradually people began to want to study with him. The Master would consider the personality of his would-be disciples and then instruct them in the branch of study that was most suitable. This would train them in learning that would be of great use to the country and would also allow them to develop the qualities that could allow them to become immortals. Nobody knew how many years he had spent in Ghost Valley or how many disciples he had. The Master never turned anyone away who wanted to study with him, but if they decided to leave, he would not try to keep them. The story goes that a couple of his most famous disciples were there at the same time: Sun Bin from Qi, Pang Juan and Zhang Yi from the kingdom of Wei, and Su Qin from the city of Luoyang. Sun Bin and Pang Juan were sworn blood brothers, and they both studied military arts; Su Qin and Zhang Yi were sworn blood brothers, and they both studied diplomacy. Each was required to train in a single discipline.

Sun Bin and Pang Juan were sworn blood brothers, and they both studied military arts. Having spent some three years familiarizing himself with the arts of war, Pang Juan thought that he had made great advances. It so happened that one day he went to draw water and happened to go down to the foot of the mountain, where he heard some travelers discussing how the kingdom of Wei was offering large rewards to recruit men of talent, since they were hoping to hire new senior ministers and generals. Pang Juan decided to cash in on this. He resolved to say goodbye to the Master and go down the mountain to seek his fortune in the kingdom of Wei. However, on reflection he was worried that the Master would not let him leave. He vacillated, unable to decide whether to speak or not. The Master knew exactly what was going on from just one look at his face. He said laughingly, "Your time here is up. Why don't you go down the mountain to seek fame and fortune?"

When Pang Juan heard the Master's words, his feelings were assuaged. Falling to his knees, he said, "That is exactly what I was thinking, but I am not sure whether I will achieve my ambitions."

"Pick a wildflower for me," the Master said, "and I will perform a divination on your behalf."

Pang Juan went down the mountain and looked for wildflowers. This was in the dog days of the sixth month, so while the trees were growing well, the wildflowers that bloom in the mountains were nowhere to be seen. Pang Juan hunted high and low, spending ages to try and find one of these plants, but all he found was a vine. He ripped it out of the ground, roots and all, thinking that he had found what he was looking for and could present it to the Master. Then suddenly the thought struck him: "This plant is weak and weedy—it would not be auspicious." He threw it on the ground and kept on looking. The strange thing is that there was not a single other plant to be seen for miles around, so in the end he had to go back and put the one that he had found earlier into his sleeve. He returned and told the Master: "There are no flowers on the mountain."

"In that case, what is that you have in your sleeve?"

Pang Juan could not conceal it; he had to hand it over. Having been ripped from the ground, it had wilted in the sun, as a result of which it was now half-dead.

"Do you know the name of this plant?" the Master said. "This is the 'Horse-bell' flower. It puts out twelve flowers in each floret; that is the number of years that you will enjoy success. You picked it in Ghost Valley, and now it is wilted in the sun. If you combine the character for 'ghost' with that for 'wilting,' it makes the word 'Wei.' You will find success in the kingdom of Wei."

Pang Juan was silent, but he was marveling inwardly. The Master continued: "You had better be careful about bullying. If you make someone else suffer, they will punish you for it; you are warned! Let me give you a message to remember: 'Success will come with a Ram. Death will come with a Horse.'"

Pang Juan bowed twice and said, "I will keep your teachings in mind at all times, Master!"

When he was about to leave, Sun Bin escorted him down the mountain. "We are sworn blood brothers," Pang Juan declared, "and have promised that we will share wealth and honor with one another. If this journey brings me success, I will recommend you for office too. That way the two of us will be able to work together as colleagues."

"Is this true?" Sun Bin asked.

"If I am lying, may I die under the hail of ten thousand arrows!" Pang Juan said.

"Many thanks for your generous intention. There was no need for you to swear such an oath." The two of them said goodbye in tears.

When Sun Bin returned to the mountain, the Master noticed his tear-stained face. "Are you sad that Pang Juan has gone?" he asked.

"How could I fail to be sad," Sun Bin replied. "He is my classmate!"

"Do you think that Pang Juan will make a great general?" the Master asked.

"He has received your teaching for so long, Master, how could he fail?"

"Not at all! Not at all!" the Master said.

Sun Bin was shocked and asked what he meant. The Master of Ghost Valley was silent. A couple of days later, he said to his disciples: "Last night I was disturbed by the sounds of rats—do you think you could all take it in turns to guard my room and chase these vermin away for me?" His disciples obeyed.

One night when it was Sun Bin's turn, the Master took a scroll out from under his pillow and said: "These are the thirteen chapters of *The Art of War*, written by your grandfather, Sun Wu. He presented them to King Helü of Wu, and His Majesty used these stratagems to defeat the Chu army. King Helü was very fond of this book, but he did not want it to become known to everyone, so he had an iron casket made and hid what he thought was the only copy of this book inside one of the roof beams at the Gusu Tower. That copy was destroyed when the Yue army burned the tower. However, I was a great friend of your grandfather, and he gave me another copy of his book. which I have annotated personally. All the secrets of military strategy are recorded here, but I have never taught them to anyone. Since you have impressed me as a kind and generous person, I have decided to give this book to you."

"My parents died when I was still a small child," Sun Bin said, "and thanks to the many political problems of recent years, my family has become dispersed. I knew that my grandfather had written a book, but nothing more. Since you know this book so well, Master, why did you not teach it to Pang Juan rather than leaving it for me alone?"

"A good person who obtains a copy of this book can use it to help others," the Master of Ghost Valley said. "A bad person who obtains this book could bring disaster down upon humanity. Pang Juan is not a good man, and I am not going to give it to him!"

Sun Bin carried the book back to his own room and studied it day and night. Three days later, the Master asked for the original text back. Sun Bin took it from his sleeve and handed it over to the Master. The Master asked him questions about particular chapters, and Sun Bin replied without the slightest hesitation. In reciting the text, he did not leave out a single word. The Master said happily, "Your intelligence and powers of concentration remind me very much of your grandfather."

. . .

To turn now to another part of the story: After Pang Juan said goodbye to Sun Bin, he went directly to the kingdom of Wei. He used his knowledge of military strategy to seek service with the prime minister, Wang

Cuo, who recommended him to King Hui. At the moment that Pang Juan entered the court, a cook was serving King Hui from a dish of braised lamb. As His Majesty raised his chopsticks, Pang Juan said happily to himself: "There you are! 'Success will come with a Ram'!"

King Hui was impressed by Pang Juan's appearance and put his chopsticks down. Getting up to meet him, he welcomed him politely. Pang Juan bowed twice, whereupon King Hui helped him up, asking him about the nature of his studies. Pang Juan replied: "I am one of the Master of Ghost Valley's disciples. I have learned a great deal to do with military strategy." He pointed to the map as he launched into his exposition, going into great detail.

"My country has Qi to the east, Qin to the west, Chu to the south, and Han, Zhao, and Yan to the north," King Hui said. "All are of about equal strength. Now Zhao has just stolen Zhongshan off us, and we have not yet avenged this insult; what plan can you suggest?"

"If you do not appoint me as a general, Your Majesty," Pang Juan said, "there is nothing to be done. However, if you put me in charge of the army, I will train them so well that they are guaranteed to win every battle they fight and achieve success in every attack. You will unite the whole world under your own control, not just these six kingdoms!"

"That sounds very fine," King Hui said, "but surely it will be difficult to achieve."

"I have recommended myself for this position because I can control these other countries on the palm of my hand," Pang Juan assured him. "If I fail, you can execute me!"

King Hui was delighted and appointed him as commander-in-chief, combined with the position of military advisor. Pang Juan's son, Pang Ying, and his nephews, Pang Cong and Pang Mao, were all appointed as junior generals. Pang Juan trained his troops and then invaded the two small states of Wey and Song, obtaining repeated victories in both cases. The rulers of Song, Lu, Wey, and Zheng all agreed to pay court to Wei in rotation. When the Qi army invaded, Pang Juan succeeded in stopping their advance. He thought he was the finest general alive and could not stop himself from becoming haughty and proud.

. . .

At this time Mo Di was traveling around various famous mountains, and he happened to pass by Ghost Valley to visit his old friend. He met Sun Bin and the two of them got into conversation, getting along extremely well with one another.

"You have already completed your studies," he said to Sun Bin, "so why don't you leave here and make a name for yourself? Why should you waste your time hidden away here?"

"I have a friend and fellow student named Pang Juan who went to take up office in Wei," Sun Bin explained. "We agreed that when he got a job, he would recommend me too. That is why I am waiting."

"Pang Juan has already been appointed as a general," Mo Di said. "Let me go to Wei and find out what he is up to."

He then said goodbye and left, heading straight for the kingdom of Wei. He quickly discovered that Pang Juan was a very arrogant man, who made the most extravagant claims about his own abilities without the slightest blush, and it was quite clear that he had absolutely no intention of recommending Sun Bin for office. Therefore, Mo Di put on rustic clothing and sought a personal interview with King Hui of Wei.

King Hui knew Master Mo by reputation, and so he came down the steps of the palace to welcome him, asking him about military strategy. Mo Di spoke of the underlying principles of any military campaign, and His Majesty was extremely impressed. He hoped to be able to recruit him into his service. Mo Di firmly refused: "I am used to living in the mountains and would not be happy in an official robe and hat. However, I am acquainted with the grandson of the great Sun Wu. His name is Sun Bin, and he would make a truly fine general. I simply cannot even begin to compare with him. At present he is living in seclusion in Ghost Valley. Why don't you summon him, Your Majesty?"

"If this Sun Bin studied at Ghost Valley, then he must have had the same master as Pang Juan," King Hui remarked. "Which of the two is better?"

"Even though Sun Bin and Pang Juan studied together," Mo Di replied, "Sun Bin is the sole inheritor of his grandfather's *Art of War*. There is nobody in the whole world who can match him—Pang Juan is nothing!" After this, Master Mo said goodbye and left.

King Hui immediately summoned Pang Juan and asked him, "I have been told that you have a fellow student named Sun Bin who is the only person to have inherited Sun Wu's secret teachings, and that he is a man of the most remarkable talents. Why have you not recommended him to me?"

"I am perfectly aware of Sun Bin's abilities," Pang Juan replied, "but he is a man of Qi, and his family has been based there for many generations. If he were to take office in Wei, you can be sure that he would still put Qi's interests first. For that very reason I did not dare to mention him."

"A knight will die for the man who understands him," King Hui declared. "Surely it cannot be right that we only employ people from our own kingdom?"

"If you want to summon Sun Bin, Your Majesty," Pang Juan replied, "I will write to him immediately."

Although he did not say so, he was very unhappy about this development: "Control of the Wei army is at present entirely in my hands," he said to himself. "If Sun Bin comes here, he will steal my thunder. However, since the king of Wei has given me a direct order, I would not dare to openly disobey him. I will have to wait until he arrives and then come up with some plan to get rid of him, to stop him from being promoted to a senior position. That would also work!"

He drafted a letter, which he showed to King Hui. His Majesty sent an ambassador directly to Ghost Valley to present Pang Juan's letter to Sun Bin, riding in a fine chariot drawn by four horses and laden with gifts of gold and white jade.

When Sun Bin opened the letter, this is what he read:

> I have been lucky enough to have had an audience with the king of Wei, and he has appointed me to a senior government position. I have never forgotten the agreement we made when we said goodbye. Today I have specially recommended you to the king of Wei, and so he has sent this chariot to collect you. Let us join forces in making the country great!

Sun Bin showed this letter to the Master of Ghost Valley. The Master realized that Pang Juan must have already held high office for some time, and yet it was only now that he wrote to suggest that he would recommend Sun Bin for office. Furthermore, there was no mention in the letter of any good wishes being extended to his former teacher. This proved that he was a complete good-for-nothing, but the Master could not be bothered to get angry about it. However, he was concerned: with Pang Juan's arrogant and jealous character, if Sun Bin went to join him, would he not cause trouble for him? He did not want to allow him to go. On the other hand, he realized that it would be difficult to resist the express command of the king of Wei, and Sun Bin himself was desperate to go. That being the case. it would be hard to stop him. He decided to send Sun Bin to pick a flower on the mountain, which would function as a divination of whether he should proceed. At this time it was the ninth month, and Sun Bin noticed that there was a vase on the Master's table with a single yellow chrysanthemum in it. He took it out of the vase and presented it to the Master, before putting it straight back in the vase.

The Master made his pronouncement: "This flower was cut before you picked it, so it is already damaged. It is a characteristic of this kind of flower that they can endure the cold and will not wither even when struck by frost—even though this plant has been damaged, it is not a particularly bad omen. Furthermore, it has been placed in a vase to allow people to enjoy it. This vase is made of gilded metal, of the same kind as would be used for a bell or sacrificial vessel—in other words, having braved cold winds and frost, it has finally been appreciated. This flower has experienced two pluckings, which means that you are unlikely to achieve your ambitions in the short term, but you returned it to its vase, which means that you will finally make your name once you have returned to the home of your ancestors. I am going to change your name, in the hope that it may improve your luck."

He decided that he would change the character "Bin" in Sun Bin's personal name, from the character that means "Guest" to the one that dictionaries tell us is the name of a form of punishment—to have the kneecaps cut off. The Master of Ghost Valley changed his name because he knew that one day he would suffer this punishment, but he could not tell his disciple that. Was he not a truly remarkable man?

An old man wrote a poem:

A flower was plucked to determine his fortune.
This proved to be more efficacious than any oracle-bone divination.
Though you may laugh at modern fortune-tellers,
That is simply because they do not have the Master of Ghost Valley's skills.

When he was about to set out, the Master of Ghost Valley gave him a silk brocade bag with the words: "If you ever find yourself caught in a terrible crisis, you can open this and have a look."

Sun Bin bowed and said goodbye to the master, then followed the king of Wei's messenger down the mountain, where he got into the waiting chariot.

• • •

Su Qin and Zhang Yi were both present on this occasion, and they were looking on in admiration and envy. Afterwards they discussed getting an official position themselves, for they too wanted to leave and seek fame and fortune elsewhere.

"The most difficult thing to find in this world is an intelligent man," the Master said. "Both of you offer good basic material, so if you were prepared to work really hard, you might even end up as immortals. Why put yourselves through having to endure endless vicissitudes in pursuit of a vain reputation and pointless honors?"

Su Qin and Zhang Yi replied as with one voice: "A fine tree should not be left to rot on a remote mountainside, nor should a precious sword remain forever hidden in its scabbard. Time is slipping away, and it will never return. We have received your teachings, and we would now like to take advantage of our opportunities to achieve great things, for that way our fame will be handed down to later generations."

"Would one of you be prepared to stay behind and keep me company?" the Master asked.

Both Sun Qin and Zhang Yi insisted that they wanted to leave. Neither of them was prepared to stay behind. The Master could not remain insistent, and so he sighed and said: "How difficult it is to find anyone with the potential to become an immortal!"

He performed a divination for each of them and said: "Sun Qin will be lucky at first and unlucky later in his career; Zhang Yi will be unlucky at first, but his career will be crowned by success in the end. Su Qin should be the first to leave, while Zhang Yi should set off later. I can see that Sun Bin and Pang Juan will sooner or later find themselves in conflict, and one day one will kill the other. In the future the two of you should give way for each other, for that is how you will become famous. Do not harm the friendship that enriched your lives when you were students together!"

The two young men kowtowed and accepted his advice. The Master now took out two books and gave each of them one. When Su Qin and Zhang Yi looked at them, they found they had each been given a copy of the Grand Duke's *Secret Tallies*. "We learned that book off by heart a long time ago. Why do you give us a copy today?"

"Although you can recite this text off by heart," the Master told them, "you have not yet understood its inner meaning. If you leave now, you may not be able to achieve your ambitions, but if you continue your researches into this book, you may yet find it helpful. I am planning to leave myself and travel overseas, so I will not be staying in this valley."

Su Qin and Zhang Yi then said goodbye and left. A few days later, the Master of Ghost Valley also set off on his journey to the Penglai Islands, or as some would have it, he became an immortal.

If you do not know what happened when Sun Bin set off down the mountain, READ ON.

Chapter Eighty-eight

*Sun Bin pretends to have gone mad in order
to escape from disaster.*

Pang Juan finds his army defeated at Guiling.

The story goes that when Sun Bin arrived in the kingdom of Wei, he took up lodgings in Pang Juan's mansion. Sun Bin thanked Pang Juan for his kindness in recommending him for government service, which seemed to please him. Sun Bin then recounted how the Master of Ghost Valley had changed his name.

"That is a horrible meaning!" Juan said in a shocked tone of voice. "Why did you change it?"

"I would not dare to disobey the Master's orders," Sun Bin declared.

The following day, the pair went to court together and had an audience with King Hui. His Majesty walked down the steps to greet them and treated them with the greatest respect. Sun Bin bowed twice and presented his opinion: "I am just a peasant, and yet Your Majesty has treated me with such excessive kindness; I am overwhelmed!"

"Master Mo informed me that you are the only person to have received of Sun Wu's secret teachings," King Hui said. "I have been awaiting your arrival as a thirsty man longs for drink. Now you are here, and it is time for you to bring peace to the world!" He turned to ask Pang Juan: "I wish to appoint Sun Bin as my deputy military strategist, with the same powers as you to command the army. What do you think?"

"Sun Bin and I are not only fellow students but also close friends," Pang Juan replied. "He is my sworn older brother. Surely it is not acceptable that he should be appointed as my deputy. Why don't you

make him a minister without portfolio? When he has made some contribution to this country I will resign my position in his favor and happily accept office under his command."

King Hui agreed to this and appointed Sun Bin as minister without
portfolio, rewarding him with exactly the same emoluments as Pang
Juan received.

*The position of minister without portfolio served to sideline Sun Bin,
while also ensuring that he did not have to be treated with the same
ceremony as an honored guest. While it seemed to show Pang Juan's
respect, in fact he suggested this because he did not want to have his
military command shared with Sun Bin.*

From this time on, the two men had little to do with one another.

Pang Juan thought to himself, "Sun Bin has received this special
instruction, but I have not yet seen any sign of it. I must find a way to
force him to show his hand."

He had tables set out for a banquet, and as the wine circulated, he
turned the conversation to the subject of military strategy. Sun Bin
answered every question without the slightest difficulty, but when it was
the turn of Sun Bin to challenge Pang Juan to cite the chapter and verse
of his sources, Pang Juan had no idea where they had come from. He
asked deviously: "Are they by any chance from Sun Wu's *Art of War*?"

Sun Bin was completely unsuspicious and said, "Of course."

"Although I was lucky enough to have received instruction from the
Master of Ghost Valley, I simply did not study hard enough and have
forgotten much of what I did learn. If you would let me read your book,
I will pay you back in the future."

"The version I studied includes the Master's annotations and explanations, so it is somewhat different from the original text. The Master
allowed me three days to learn it and then took it away again. I do not
actually possess a physical copy."

"Do you still remember every word?"

"It is all there in my memory."

Pang Juan was even more determined to study this text, but at that
moment, he had no idea how he was going to set about it.

. . .

A couple of days later, King Hui decided to test Sun Bin's abilities, so he
held a demonstration of martial arts at the training ground. He wanted
Sun Bin and Pang Juan to demonstrate battle formations. Pang Juan put
his troops in position, and then Sun Bin took one look, after which he

could name the formation and explain how to defeat it. Afterwards Sun Bin arranged the troops in a formation that Pang Juan simply could not identify. He privately consulted Sun Bin on the subject.

"This is the 'Reversible Eight Gates' formation," Sun Bin explained.

"Is there a further move?" Pang Juan asked.

"If it is attacked, you can easily move into 'Snake' formation," Sun Bin replied.

Pang Juan thought about this and then went back to report to King Hui: "Sun Bin has arranged the 'Reversible Eight Gates' formation; it can be transformed into the 'Snake' position."

When the demonstration was over, King Hui asked Sun Bin what he had done, and it was exactly as Juan had said. King Hui was now under the impression that Pang Juan was every bit as brilliant as Sun Bin, and he was delighted by this.

Pang Juan returned to his mansion and thought, "Sun Bin is a much more brilliant man than I. If I do not get rid of him, I will end up being surpassed by him." He came up with a plan. So, one day when he met Sun Bin, he happened to mention to him privately: "All your family are back in the state of Qi. Since you have now accepted government office in the kingdom of Wei, why don't you send someone to bring them here so that they too can enjoy your present prosperity?"

Sun Bin burst into tears and said: "Even though we studied together, you really don't understand my position. My mother died when I was four and my father died when I was nine. After that, I was brought up by my uncle, Sun Qiao, who served Lord Kang of Qi as a grandee. When Lord Kang had his position usurped by the Tian family and he was forced into exile by the sea, all his ministers were either transported or executed. My family ended up being scattered to the four winds. My uncle and cousins, Sun Ping and Sun Zhuo, fled to the Zhou Royal Domain, taking me with them. There we encountered a famine year, and they sent me to work as a servant for a family living at the North Gate of the Zhou capital; I do not know where they went. When I grew up, I happened to overhear one of the neighbors talking about the brilliance of the Master of Ghost Valley, and I came to admire him very much. That is why I went off all by myself to study with him. Through these years I have received no communication from any member of my family. What relatives could I bring here to live with me?"

"Surely you still care about your hometown and the ancestral tombs?" Pang Juan said.

"Men are not animals—how could I forget where I came from? When we were saying goodbye, the Master said, 'You will finally make your name once you have returned to the home of your ancestors.' However, now I am working for the Wei government, so it would not be suitable to mention such an ambition again."

Pang Juan sighed and pretended to agree: "You are absolutely right. A real man makes his reputation where he can. Why should he have to stay at home?"

Things started to happen about six months later, by which time Sun Bin had completely forgotten this earlier conversation. One day on his way home after attending court, he suddenly bumped into a man with a thick Shandong accent, who asked him, "Are you Sun Bin, the minister without portfolio?"

Sun Bin invited him into his mansion and asked who he was.

"My name is Ding Yi," the man said, "and I come from Linzi. I was on a business trip to the Zhou Royal Domain, so your cousin asked me to take a letter to you at Ghost Valley. When I got there, I heard that you had accepted government office in the kingdom of Wei, so I came here to find you." When he had finished speaking, he handed over the letter. Sun Bin picked it up in his hands. He broke open the seal and read the contents:

> This letter is addressed to Sun Bin by his cousins Ping and Zhuo. It is now three years since our family was overtaken by disaster and we found ourselves forced into exile. We went to work as tenant farmers in the state of Song, where our father became ill and died. We have suffered so much far from home and all by ourselves. Luckily, His Majesty has now decided to offer an amnesty for all earlier offenses and informed us that we can go back, and we would like you to go with us. Let us reestablish our clan! We have heard that you have been studying in Ghost Valley and are sure that you will have done well. You have a great future ahead of you. We write this letter to inform you of our news and will entrust it to someone to take to you. Please make your plans to return home as soon as possible! We hope to see you again soon.

When Sun Bin got this letter he thought that it was true and burst into tears.

"Your cousins told me that I should encourage you to return home as soon as possible," Ding Yi said. "It is not right that relatives should be parted."

"I hold a government position in Wei," Sun Bin explained. "I can't just leave."

He treated Ding Yi to a banquet and served him wine, while he wrote his reply. He began by expressing his wish to return home and then he continued: "Since I have taken up a position in the government of Wei, I cannot return right now. Let me wait until my position here is secure, and then I will try and find a way to go home."

He gave Ding Yi a gold ingot to cover his travel expenses. He took the reply and left after saying goodbye. What Sun Bin did not know was that this man was no Ding Yi. Instead, he was one of Pang Juan's most trusted subordinates, Xu Jia. Once Pang Juan had discovered Sun Bin's background and the names of his relatives, he had been able to forge this letter purporting to be from Sun Ping and Sun Zhuo. He instructed his subordinate, Xu Jia, to pretend to be a merchant from Qi named Ding Yi and sent him to see Sun Bin. Since Sun Bin had become separated from the rest of his family at a very young age, he did not even know what their handwriting looked like. That is why he thought this letter was real.

Having obtained a reply by trickery, Pang Juan imitated Sun Bin's handwriting and forged an additional couple of lines at the end:

Although I am at present serving in the government of the kingdom of Wei, I have never forgotten where I come from. Every day I think of ways to get home. If the king of Qi were to give me a job, I would do my very best to repay his kindness.

There is a poem that testifies to this:

Although they were once classmates, he used his subordinate to get rid of him.
Who would have guessed that his trickery would have such terrible consequences?
A forged letter set a dreadful trap:
Sun Bin's life hung by a thread!

Pang Juan went to court and sought a private audience with King Hui. Having sent away His Majesty's entourage, he presented the forged letter and said: "Sun Bin is intending to betray Wei to Qi, and he has recently been in secret communication with an envoy from that country. I was able to obtain part of their correspondence by having my men intercept and search the messenger outside the suburbs."

When King Hui had finished reading the letter, he said: "Sun Bin is still greatly attached to his own country, but surely that does not mean that I cannot give him a senior government position here. Why should I not make use of his talents?"

"Sun Bin's grandfather was a great general who served the king of Wu," Pang Juan replied, "but he went home to Qi in the end. Who can forget where his family comes from? Even if you give Sun Bin a senior appointment, he will care most about Qi and will not be capable of doing his best for Wei. Besides which, Sun Bin is not inferior to me—if he were to be appointed as a general by Qi, sooner or later they would end up in competition with Wei. Were that to happen, it would be a disaster for Your Majesty. You had better kill him."

"Sun Bin came here in answer to my summons," King Hui said, "and he has not done anything wrong. If I were to kill him now, I am afraid people would accuse me of being a bad ruler."

"You are absolutely right, Your Majesty," Pang Juan replied. "I will go and talk to Sun Bin. If he is willing to stay in the kingdom of Wei, let him be appointed to a senior position. If not, then you can send him to me for punishment. I will deal with him myself."

When Pang Juan had said farewell to King Hui, he went to see Sun Bin, and asked, "I have heard that you have recently received a letter from your family, is that true?"

Sun Bin was a very straightforward kind of person, and so he was not suspicious at all of this. He simply answered, "I have." He explained how the letter called for him to go back to his old hometown.

"It has been such a long time since you saw any member of your family . . . you must be desperate for a reunion. Why don't you go to the king of Wei and ask for leave for two or three months, so that you can go home and visit your ancestral tombs? Once that is done, you can come back again."

"I am afraid that His Majesty will be suspicious of my intentions and refuse my request."

"Why don't you ask him?" Pang Juan suggested. "I will be there to support you."

"I would appreciate that very much," Sun Bin assured him.

That night, Pang Juan returned to the palace to have a second audience with King Hui, and presented his opinion: "In accordance with Your Majesty's orders, I went to see Sun Bin. He is simply not willing to stay in this country and was angry at the mere suggestion. If he sends in a request for leave in the near future, you should punish him for the crime of secretly communicating with the Qi ambassador." King Hui nodded his head.

The following day, Sun Bin did indeed present a memorial in which he requested a month's leave in order to go to Qi and visit his ancestral tombs. King Hui was furious when he saw this document and wrote across the top: "Sun Bin has already engaged in treasonous commerce with the Qi ambassador, and that is why he now asks to go home. He is clearly intending to betray the kingdom of Wei, turning his back on the trust that I have always shown him. He is hereby stripped of his official rank with immediate effect. Let him be taken to the office of my military advisor for punishment."

The military officials, having received this order, arrested Sun Bin and took him to the military advisor's office to see Pang Juan. When he caught sight of him, Pang Juan pretended to be shocked: "What are you doing here?" The officials reported King Hui's orders. When Pang Juan received them, he said to Sun Bin, "I will go and speak to His Majesty on your behalf. I will not let you suffer such a terrible injustice."

When he had finished speaking, he gave orders for his charioteer to whip up the horses and go and see King Hui. He presented his opinion as follows: "Although Sun Bin is guilty of secret communication with the Qi ambassador, this is not a crime that merits the death penalty. In my humble opinion, he should be punished with penal tattooing and having his kneecaps cut away. In that case he will never be able to return to his old hometown. He will be kept alive, but it will prevent him from causing trouble in the future. Surely that would be best? However, I would not dare to make such a decision on my own authority, so I have come to you to ask for directions!"

"I think that is an excellent suggestion," King Hui said.

Pang Juan said goodbye and drove back to his office. "The king of Wei is absolutely furious and he was quite determined to have you executed," he told Sun Bin. "I begged and pleaded with him, which has at least served to save your life. However, you will have your kneecaps cut away and your face tattooed—this is the law of the kingdom of Wei, and I am afraid that there is nothing that I can do about it."

Sun Bin sighed and said: "The Master of Ghost Valley said, 'Even though it has been damaged, it is not a particularly bad omen.' Today, at least I will keep my head on my shoulders! This is all thanks to your efforts and I will never forget what I owe you!"

Pang Juan called in the executioner, who tied Sun Bin down and then cut away his bony kneecaps. Sun Bin screamed and fainted away. It was a very long time before he recovered consciousness. Afterwards, his face was pierced with needles as they pricked out the words 'Secret Communication with an Enemy Country' and rubbed ink into the wounds. Pang Juan pretended to be crying as he packed medicinal herbs onto

Sun Bin's knees and wrapped them with bandages. He ordered people carry him into the archives building where he said what he could to cheer the man up, giving him good food and encouraging him to rest. After about a month the wounds on Sun Bin's knees had pretty much healed but without his kneecaps he could not move his legs properly—naturally he would never be able to walk again. He could only sit with his legs stretched out in front of him.

An old man wrote a poem:

When he changed his name, he knew that disaster would strike.
Why did he wait until Pang Juan tried to destroy him?
How stupid of Sun Bin to be so naively loyal:
Just because he survived, he felt thankful to Pang Juan!

Sun Bin was now a cripple and was very unhappy to think that he was entirely dependent upon Pang Juan for receiving three meals a day. Pang Juan begged for the text of Sun Wu's *Art of War* with the Master of Ghost Valley's commentary and explanations, and Sun Bin naturally agreed. Pang Juan provided him with wooden strips and asked him to write it out, but Sun Bin had so far only managed to get down one tenth of the whole text. At this point, Pang Juan ordered a slave named Cheng'er to look after Sun Bin. This Cheng'er saw how much the innocent Sun Bin had suffered and felt deeply sorry for him. Now Pang Juan summoned the slave into his presence and asked him how many lines Sun Bin could write in a day.

"General Sun's two legs are crippled, and so he spends most of his time resting," the slave explained. "It is difficult for him to sit for long. He can only write two or three paragraphs a day."

"If it is that slow, when will he ever finish?" Pang Juan said angrily. "I want you to make him hurry up."

Cheng'er withdrew and asked one of Pang Juan's personal servants about this: "The general wants Mr. Sun to write this text out for him, but why does he have to keep harassing him on the subject?"

"You don't understand," the servant replied. "Although the general appears to be very fond of Mr. Sun on the surface, in fact he is deeply jealous of him. The only reason he kept him alive was because he was hoping to obtain this book from him. Once he has written it all out, he won't be getting any more food or water, but don't tell anyone about this!"

When Cheng'er heard this news he secretly informed Sun Bin. The latter was dreadfully shocked: "How heartless Pang Juan has turned out to be! How can I possibly let him get his hands on the *Art of War*?"

Then he thought to himself: "If I don't carry on writing it out, he is sure to be furious with me. My life is really hanging by a thread!"

He thought and thought, trying to come up with some way to get himself out of this predicament. Suddenly the idea struck him: "When the Master of Ghost Valley said goodbye to me, he gave me a silk brocade bag and said, 'If you are ever in real danger, you can open it up and have a look.' Now is the time!" He opened up the silk bag and took out a piece of yellow silk. On it were written the words: "Pretend to be mad."

"So that is the answer," Sun Bin said.

That very evening, when his meal was set out, Sun Bin was just about to pick up his chopsticks when suddenly he buckled up and made as if to vomit. After some time he went into fits. Glaring around him, he shouted, "Why are you trying to poison me?"

He swept all the crockery onto the floor and then picked up the wooden strips he had been writing and threw them into the fire. Rolling around on the floor, he cursed and screamed. Cheng'er did not realize that this was all pretend, so he rushed off to report this to Pang Juan. The next day, Pang Juan came to see for himself. Sun Bin was lying on the floor laughing heartily, his face covered with spittle, and then all of a sudden he burst into tears. Pang Juan asked him, "Why were you laughing? Why did you then cry?"

"I was laughing at the idea of the king of Wei wanting to kill me when I have a hundred thousand soldiers at my disposal," Sun Bin cackled. "What can he do to me? I was crying because without me, the kingdom of Wei has no competent generals!" When he had finished speaking, he again opened his eyes wide and stared at Pang Juan. Kowtowing over and over again, he shouted, "Master of the Ghost Valley, save me!"

"It is me, Pang Juan!" he shouted. "Don't you recognize me?"

Sun Bin grabbed hold of Pang Juan's robe and would not let go. He was shouting: "Save me, Master!" Pang Juan ordered his entourage to pull him free. He spoke privately to Cheng'er: "When did General Sun get so sick?"

"Last night," Cheng'er said.

Pang Juan got back into his chariot, his mind churning with suspicion. Since he was afraid that he might be pretending to be mad, he decided to test him: he ordered his servants to drag Sun Bin into a pigpen full of shit. Sun Bin lay there in the muck, his hair down over his face. Afterwards, Pang Juan sent a servant with wine and food to trick him into revealing himself: "I am so sorry to see you suffer the punishment of having your kneecaps removed when you are innocent of any crime. I bring you this wine as a token of my respect. Pang Juan does not know anything about it."

Sun Bin knew that this was another of his little schemes, so he looked at the servant with furious eyes and cursed him. "Are you here to poison me too?" he screamed, upsetting the wine and food all over the ground. The servant then threw some dogshit and lumps of mud into the pen, and that Sun Bin did eat. Afterwards he went back to report to Pang Juan, who said: "If he really is mad, there is nothing to be worried about."

After this he relaxed his surveillance of Sun Bin, allowing him to go in and out. Sometimes he would leave in the morning and come back at night, sleeping in the pigpen. Sometimes he would go out and simply not return, spending the night in the marketplace. Sometimes he seemed really cheerful and full of laughter, and other times he would wail and scream. The people in the marketplace knew that this was Sun Bin, the minister without portfolio, and they were very sorry to see him so crippled and sick, so there were many who gave him food and drink. Sometimes he would eat it and sometimes not, but he kept on saying crazy things all the time. There was nobody who realized that he was actually pretending to be insane. Pang Juan told the local officials that they should report Sun Bin's position every day just before dawn, because he was still checking up on him.

An old man wrote a poem to bewail this:

Seven great kingdoms were embroiled in constant warfare;
Heroes took advantage of the situation, not realizing that they were
    facing ruin.
How dreadful that thanks to the jealousy of a wicked minister,
This fine man and former friend was reduced to shamming madness.

At this time, Master Mo Di was traveling in Qi and stayed at the house of Tian Ji. His disciple, Li Hua, arrived from Wei and Mo Di asked him, "Has Sun Bin done well in Wei?"

Li Hua reported how Sun Bin had ended up having his kneecaps cut off. Master Mo Di sighed and said, "I originally wanted to help Sun Bin by recommending him for office, but all I have done is harm him!" He told Tian Ji all about how talented Sun Bin was and how Pang Juan had been jealous of him. Tian Ji went on to mention this to King Wei of Qi: "This man has remarkable talents, and he has suffered a great deal in government service abroad—it is such a shame!"

"Why don't I send some troops to bring Master Sun home?" King Wei suggested.

"Pang Juan would not allow Sun Bin to serve in the government of Wei," Tian Ji replied. "Do you think it is likely that he would let him take office in Qi? If you want Sun Bin to come here, there are certain things that you have to do to keep his travels a secret, for that is the only way he will get here alive."

King Wei accepted his suggestions and ordered his minister without portfolio, Chunyu Kun, to go to Wei to find Sun Bin while pretending to be taking a present of tea to their king. Chunyu Kun accepted the mission and arranged for a cartload of tea to be prepared. Armed with his official credentials, he arrived in the kingdom of Wei. Li Hua accompanied him, disguised as a servant.

On arrival in the Wei capital, Chunyu Kun had an audience with King Hui in accordance with the orders he had received from the king of Qi. King Hui was delighted and allowed Chenyu Kun to stay in an official guesthouse. When Li Hua saw that Sun Bin was acting crazy, he did not attempt to speak to him. Instead, he went back secretly in the middle of the night to talk to him. Sun Bin was sitting with his back resting against a wellhead. When he caught sight of Li Hua he opened his eyes wide, though he remained silent. Li Hua said with tears in his eyes: "How much you have suffered! I am Li Hua, a disciple of Master Mo Di. My master has told the king of Qi all about you, and His Majesty has expressed the greatest admiration. Chunyu Kun is here, not to present a tribute offering of tea, but to get you back to Qi. We will avenge the punishment they inflicted on you!"

Sun Bin was now in floods of tears. After a long time, he replied: "I have been anticipating that I would end up dead in a ditch—I could never have imagined that I would have the opportunity that you offered me today! However, Pang Juan is a very suspicious man, and I am afraid that it will not be easy to wrest me from his clutches. What shall we do?"

"I have a plan," Li Hua replied. "Do not worry, sir. On the day we are due to leave, someone will come to collect you."

They agreed that this was the only time that they would meet, so as not to arouse suspicion.

• • •

The following day, the king of Wei held a banquet in Chunyu Kun's honor. Discovering that he was a very learned man, he gave him generous gifts of gold and silk. Afterwards Chunyu Kun said goodbye to the king and was about to set off, when Pang Juan invited him to another farewell banquet at Changting. The night before, Li Hua had concealed Sun Bin inside a covered carriage, while his servant, Wang Yi, put on his clothes. With tousled hair and mud plastered all over his face, he looked just like Sun Bin. The guards made their usual report and Pang Juan was completely unsuspicious. Chunyu Kun went out to Changting and enjoyed his banquet with Pang Juan. Afterwards he said goodbye and set off: Li Hua sped on ahead with the covered carriage, and Chunyu Kun himself brought up the rear. After a couple of days, Wang Yi made his escape and joined them. By the time that the guards discovered Sun Bin's filthy clothes lying in a heap on the ground, he was already long gone. They immediately reported this to Pang Juan, who wondered whether he might not have fallen into the well and drowned. When the people he sent to drag the well found no body there, they searched everywhere but without discovering any trace of him. Being afraid that the king of Wei would blame him for this, he ordered his entourage to send in a report saying that Sun Bin had drowned. He had no idea that he was safe and sound in Qi.

Once Chenyu Kun had carried Sun Bin across the border, he arranged for him to be given a bath. When they approached Linzi, Tian Ji himself came ten *li* out of the city to welcome them. He mentioned his arrival to King Wei, who had a comfortable carriage sent to collect him and bring him to court. The two men discussed military matters, and King Wei wanted to appoint him to an official position. Sun Bin refused: "I have achieved nothing, so it would not be appropriate to receive a title. If Pang Juan hears that I have been given an official appointment in Qi, it will provoke his jealousy. It would be better to keep my presence here a secret for the time being and wait until there is something for me to do. Then I can show my mettle."

King Wei agreed and sent him to live in Tian Ji's household, where he was treated as an honored guest. Sun Bin wanted Li Hua to convey his thanks to Master Mo Di, but the two of them disappeared without even saying goodbye. Sun Bin was very upset about this. He also sent someone to try and find Sun Ping and Sun Zhuo, but all the information that had been given in the letter was wrong. Then he realized that this too was part of Pang Juan's trickery.

King Wei of Qi amused himself in his free time by gambling with other members of the royal family over horseback archery. Tian Ji did not own any particularly strong horses, so he repeatedly lost money.

One day, Tian Ji invited Sun Bin to go with him to the archery ground to watch the shooting. Sun Bin realized at once that the horses were simply not strong enough to be able to get far, and Tian Ji did indeed lose three ends. Afterwards, he spoke privately to Tian Ji: "When you go back to shoot tomorrow, I can guarantee that you will win."

"If you can indeed guarantee victory for me," Tian Ji said, "I will ask His Majesty to put up a stake of one thousand pieces of gold."

"Do so, sir."

Tian Ji said to King Wei: "I lost in today's shooting, but tomorrow I am prepared to beggar myself over a single competition. Let the stake be one thousand pieces of gold on each end." King Wei agreed with a laugh.

The next day, all the members of the royal family arrived at the archery ground in fancy ornamented carriages. There were also a couple of thousand ordinary people present as spectators.

"What are you going to do to guarantee my victory?" Tian Ji asked. "One thousand pieces of gold is riding on each end, and that is a lot of money!"

"His Majesty owns the very finest horses in the kingdom of Qi," Sun Bin explained, "so if you want to beat him with the second-rate, that will be very difficult. However, there is a strategem to counter this. You both have to change horses for each end. I want you to use your worst horse in competition against his best horse. Use your best horse in competition against his second-best horse and your second-best horse against his worst horse. Although you will lose one end, there are two that you will win."

"That is very clever!" Tian Ji declared. He had his gold saddle and silk brocade caparison put on his worst horse, pretending that it was in fact his best. He and King Wei then went out to shoot their first end. The horse proved to be very poor, and Tian Ji lost one thousand pieces of gold. King Wei laughed heartily.

"There are two more ends to go," Tian Ji reminded him. "If I lose them too, you can laugh at me then."

In the second and third ends, Tian Ji's horses won, just as had been anticipated. Thus he gained back all that he had lost and another thousand pieces of gold besides. Tian Ji presented his opinion: "The victory that I obtained today is not thanks to my horses. It was made possible by Master Sun's advice." He explained just what had happened.

King Wei sighed and said, "Even in this little matter, you can see just how clever Master Sun is!" He redoubled the respect with which he treated him and gave him countless presents. No more of this now.

. . .

Having crippled Sun Bin, King Hui of Wei tasked Pang Juan with reconquering Zhongshan. Pang Juan presented his opinion: "Zhongshan is far from Wei but close to Zhao. Rather than competing with them for lands far away, we would do better to capture territory located near to us. Let me attack Handan for you, Your Majesty, and thus avenge the loss of Zhongshan."

King Hui agreed to this. Pang Juan led an army of five hundred chariots out of the city and attacked Zhao, laying siege to Handan. The official in charge of the city, Pi Xuan, was defeated in one battle after the other and sent a report to this effect to Lord Cheng of Zhao. He sent an envoy to present the lands of Zhongshan to Qi in return for assistance. King Wei of Qi was aware of how brilliant Sun Bin was, so he appointed him as commander-in-chief. However, Sun Bin refused: "I have suffered a crippling punishment, so if you were to employ me to take charge of your army, it would look as if the kingdom of Qi is lacking in men of real ability, thus making us a laughingstock to the enemy. Please appoint Tian Ji as general."

King Wei did indeed appoint Tian Ji as the commander-in-chief. Sun Bin became chief military advisor instead. He spent his time sitting inside a battle chariot, thinking up their next move, and his name was not made public.

Tian Ji wanted to lead his army to rescue Handan, but Sun Bin stopped him: "The generals in Zhao cannot possibly defeat Pang Juan—before we have even reached Handan, the city will already have fallen. You had better station your troops mid-route and announce your intention of attacking Xiangling. That will force Pang Juan to turn back, and then you can attack him. Victory is certain!"

Tian Ji followed his advice. At this time, since the help that the people of Handan were waiting for had not arrived, Pi Xuan had to surrender the city to Pang Juan. The general sent a messenger to report his victory to the king of Wei. However, just as he was about to advance his troops, he was suddenly informed that Qi had sent Tian Ji to take advantage of his absence to attack Xiangling.

"If Xiangling falls, the capital is in danger!" he said in alarm. "I must go back to rescue my base." He immediately stood down the army.

When they were twenty *li* from Guiling, they encountered the Qi army. Sun Bin had already discovered which route the Wei army would use and made his own preparations. He opened by sending the junior general, Yuan Da, to throw three thousand soldiers in their way to provoke battle. One of Pang Juan's nephews, Pang Cong, was in command of the vanguard—he launched himself into the fray. Having crossed swords about twenty times, Yuan Da pretended to be defeated and started to flee. Pang Cong was afraid that there might be some kind of ambush ahead, so he did not dare to chase him. He returned and reported this to Pang Juan. The latter shouted at him: "If you are so scared of a junior general that you do not dare to try and capture him alive, how are you going to deal with Tian Ji?" He ordered the main body of the army to set off in pursuit.

When they arrived at Guiling, they could see that the Qi troops ahead of them were already in battle formation. Pang Juan leaned on the railing of his chariot and inspected it—this was the "Reversible Eight Gates" formation that Sun Bin had used all that time ago in the kingdom of Wei. Pang Juan was now suspicious and thought to himself, "How does Tian Ji know this battle formation? Can it be that Sun Bin has managed to make his way home to Qi?"

He gave orders for his own men to go into formation. Now they saw the battle standard of General Tian fluttering above the Qi army, as a battle chariot pulled out from the line. Tian Ji, in full armor and holding a painted spear in one hand, was standing on top of it. Tian Ying, holding a halberd, was in place on his right.

"Can a responsible Wei general come forward to speak?" Tian Ji shouted.

Pang Juan drove his own chariot forward and responded: "Qi and Wei have always been allies, while Wei and Zhao are enemies. What has that to do with Qi? I think it is a very bad idea for you to abandon the alliance between us to team up with our enemies."

"Zhao has presented the lands of Zhongshan to His Majesty, and so our king ordered me to come and rescue them," Tian Ji replied. "If you would be prepared to hand over a couple of commanderies to us, our army will withdraw immediately."

Pang Juan was furious. "This battle formation is called 'Reversible Eight Gates,'" he shouted. "I studied under the Master of Ghost Valley and there is nothing you can do to baffle me! Even small children in my country could recognize that!"

"Since you recognize it," Tian Ji retorted, "would you dare to attack it?"

Pang Juan was now starting to sweat, but if he said that he would not attack, it would make him look bad. Hence, he replied in a loud voice, "Since I know what it is, why shouldn't I be able to attack it?"

Pang Juan now instructed Pang Ying, Pang Cong, and Pang Mao as follows: "I remember Sun Bin talking about this battle formation, and I think I know how to defeat it. However, this particular formation is easy to move into 'Snake' position: if you attack the head, then the tail fights back; if you attack the tail, then the head fights back; and if you attack the middle, you get caught in a pincer movement—the attacker is immediately in trouble. I am now going to go and fight this formation. Each of you is in command of your own army, and I want you to watch as it changes. You must then move forward in a simultaneous attack. This will ensure that the head and tail cannot help each other and the formation can be broken."

When Pang Juan had given his instructions, he led his own vanguard of five thousand men forward to attack the initial formation. However, once he had burst through their lines, he was only able to orientate himself according to the eight flags marking direction. This being the case, the enemy kept moving them around, until he was completely confused and had no idea where he was. He attacked this way and that, but encountered a forest of weapons in all directions and simply could not find a way out. He could hear the sound of drumming and bells chiming, and there was shouting on all sides. Standing in among all the other generals' flags was one bearing the name "Sun." Pang Juan was appalled: "The cripple has indeed managed to make his way to Qi. I have fallen into his trap!"

It was just at this critical moment that Pang Ying and Pang Cong fought their way in and rescued Pang Juan. Every single one of the five thousand men he had led into battle was dead. When he asked after Pang Mao, he was informed that he had been killed by Tian Ying. All in all, they had lost more than twenty thousand men. Pang Juan was deeply shocked.

This particular battle formation, based on the eight trigrams, corresponds to the eight directions; together with the central position, it is formed by nine divisions of troops. This formation sees the troops arranged in a square. When Pang Juan attacked, two of these divisions split off to prevent anyone outside from trying to rescue him. The remaining seven divisions moved into a circular formation. It was this which confused Pang Juan. Later on in the Tang dynasty, Li Jing, Duke of Wey, used this particular formation as the basis for his "Snowflake" formation, whereby the troops started off in a circle.

There is a poem that testifies to this:

This particular battle formation can undergo remarkable transformations;
Although the Master of the Ghost Valley knew this, he taught it to few.
Pang Juan knew that it could transform into "Snake,"
But he did not know the subtle changes between "Square" and "Round."

Today southeast of Tangyi County there is a place called "Ancient Battlefield." This is where Sun Bin and Pang Juan fought.

When Pang Juan realized that Sun Bin was over with the Qi army, he became very frightened. He discussed this development with Pang Ying and Pan Cong. They decided to abandon their camp and flee. That very night they made their way back to the kingdom of Wei. Tian Ji and Sun Bin discovered that the enemy camp was empty and went home to Qi in triumph. This happened in the seventeenth year of the reign of King Xian of Zhou. King Hui of Wei decided that Pang Juan's success in the capture of Handan cancelled out his defeat in the battle of Guiling. Meanwhile, King Wei of Qi had been so impressed by Tian Ji and Sun Bin that he entrusted them with absolute power over his army. Zou Ji was afraid that in the future one or the other of them would replace him as prime minister, so he secretly discussed what to do with one of his clients, Gongsun Yue. He was determined to replace Tian Ji and Sun Bin in His Majesty's favor. By coincidence, it was just at this moment that Pang Juan sent someone to Zou Ji's house with a bribe of one thousand pieces of gold, wanting him to get rid of Sun Bin. Since this was exactly what Zou Ji wanted himself, he ordered Gongsun Yue to pretend to be a member of Tian Ji's household, and sent him to knock on the door of a fortune-teller in the middle of the night, armed with ten pieces of gold. "General Tian Ji has ordered me to request a divination from you," he announced.

When the hexagram had been laid out, the diviner asked, "What do you want to know?"

"My master is a member of the Tian royal family," Gongsun Yue said. "He has control over the army, and his power strikes awe into enemy countries. He is plotting a coup and wants to know if it will be successful."

The diviner was horrified and said, "That is treason! I would not dare to perform such a divination!"

"If you do not want to perform the divination, that is quite all right," Gongsun Yue said, "but if you know what is good for you, you must not tell anyone about this!"

Once he had gone, Zou Ji's men arrived and arrested the fortune-teller. They accused him of performing a divination for the traitor, Tian Ji. "Even though someone did come to me," the diviner said, "I did not perform a divination for them."

Zou Ji rushed to court and informed King Wei of what Tian Ji had wished to have a divination about—he brought the fortune-teller along to prove it. King Wei now became suspicious and had his people watching Tian Ji's movements every day. When Tian Ji found out what had happened, he immediately resigned on the grounds of ill health. This assuaged King Wei's animosity. Sun Bin also resigned his position as military advisor. The following year, King Wei of Qi died. Prince Bijiang inherited the throne, taking the title of King Xuan. Since King Xuan was aware of Tian Ji's innocence and Sun Bin's abilities, he restored both of them to their old positions.

. . .

Going back a little now, when Pang Juan heard that Tian Ji and Sun Bin had been stripped of their offices by the kingdom of Qi, he said happily: "Now I can take over the whole world!" It was around this time that Lord Zhao of Han destroyed the state of Zheng and made his capital there. The prime minister of Zhao went to Han to offer congratulations and invited them to take part in a joint campaign against Wei, whereby they would partition their territory equally between them after their final victory. Lord Zhao of Han agreed to this, sending back the following message: "Unfortunately, we have just suffered a famine. We will have to wait until next year before we can take our army out on campaign."

When Pang Juan heard this news, he said to King Hui: "I have discovered that Han is plotting to assist Zhao in an attack on us. We should take advantage of the fact that their alliance has not yet stabilized to attack Han. That will put an end to their conspiracy."

King Hui agreed to this. He appointed Crown Prince Shen as the commander-in-chief and Pang Juan as senior general, and they advanced on the state of Han in a truly massive show of force.

If you do not know whether they won or lost, READ ON.

Chapter Eighty-nine

On the road to Maling, Pang Juan is shot to
bits by crossbow bolts.

In the marketplace of Xianyang, Shang Yang
is torn to pieces by five oxen.

Pang Juan and Crown Prince Shen raised an army to attack Han. When
they were traveling through Waihuang, a commoner named Xu Sheng
requested an audience with the crown prince.

"Since you have asked to see me, sir, what do you have to say?" the
crown prince asked.

"You are here today, Your Highness, in order to attack Han," Xu
Sheng said. "I have a method that will ensure you victory every time
you fight. Would you like to hear it?"

"I would be delighted!" Crown Prince Shen replied.

"Do you think anywhere in the world is richer than Wei? Do you
think your position is more important than that of a king?"

"I do not," Crown Prince Shen replied.

"Now, you have made yourself general, Your Highness, and attacked
Han. If you succeed, you will not be any richer and your position will
still not be as important as that of His Majesty the king. On the other
hand, if you lose, what will happen then? You are lucky enough to be in
a situation where one day you will enjoy the honors of a king without
ever having to go to war—that is my method for ensuring your ultimate
victory."

"Excellent!" the crown prince declared. "I will follow your advice
and stand down my army immediately."

"Even though you think that my advice is good," Xu Sheng replied,
"you are not going to be able to put it into practice. When one man

cooks a pot of food, many people get to taste the soup. There are a huge number of people who are hoping to get a mouthful of Your Royal Highness's soup. You may want to go home, but will they let you?" He said goodbye and left, whereupon the crown prince issued an order to stand down the army.

"His Majesty has entrusted the command of three armies to you," Pang Juan said. "If you stand down your troops before you have even fought a single battle, what is the difference between that and being defeated?"

The other generals were also unwilling to return empty-handed. Crown Prince Shen could not make up his mind what to do, so he led the army forward until they arrived at the Han capital.

• • •

Lord Ai of Han sent someone to report this emergency to Qi, begging them to send an army to help him. King Xuan of Qi assembled all his ministers and asked them, "Should I assist Han? Would this be a good idea?"

The prime minister, Zou Ji, said: "If Han and Wei are fighting, that is good for their neighbors. We should not try and help them."

Tian Ji and Tian Ying said: "If Wei defeats Han, then Qi will suffer disaster next. We ought to assist them."

Sun Bin was the only person present to remain completely silent. "You have not said a word, military advisor," King Xuan remarked. "Surely it cannot be that both options are wrong?"

"That is in fact the case," Sun Bin replied. "The kingdom of Wei makes much play of their military might. Last year they attacked Zhao, and this year they have invaded Han. Surely Qi will not escape their attention forever! If we do not go to the rescue, we will be abandoning Han to enrich Wei—therefore those who have spoken out against assistance are wrong. Wei is now attacking Han, and if we save them before they have been seriously weakened, we are going to get our troops killed in order to spare theirs. Han will suffer little and we will suffer much— that is why those who have spoken in favor of going to the rescue are also wrong."

"If that is so, what should I do?" King Xuan asked.

"My advice, Your Majesty, is that you begin by promising assistance to Han in order to improve their morale," Sun Bin replied. "Once Han knows that help from Qi is on the way, they will resist Wei with all their might. Similarly, Wei will attack Han with everything that they have got. We will wait until Wei is exhausted and then lead our army out to attack them in order to rescue Han. That way, we can achieve a great result with little expenditure of effort. Surely this is better than the two suggestions previously on offer."

King Xuan clapped his hands and said, "Good." He made his promise to the Han ambassador: "The Qi army will be on its way to help you immediately."

Lord Zhao of Han was delighted and resisted the incursion by the Wei army with all the forces at his command. They fought some five or six battles and Han did not win a single one. Again he sent an ambassador to Qi to hurry up their relief troops. Yet again Qi appointed Tian Ji as commander-in-chief and Tian Ying as his deputy. Sun Bin was the military advisor. They took an army of five hundred chariots to rescue Han. As before, Tian Ji was planning to advance straight to Han, when Sun Bin said: "No! No! When we went to rescue Zhao, we did not set foot inside their territory. Now we are going to rescue Han, what on earth do we want to go there for?"

"What do you think we should do?" Tian Ji asked.

"If you want to put an end to all of this, we are going to have to attack something that Wei cannot afford to lose," Sun Bin replied. "Right now, our target is the Wei capital."

Tian Ji followed his advice. He gave orders to the three armies to march on Wei. Meanwhile Pang Juan, having defeated the Han army in one engagement after the other, was now pressing close on the new capital. Now suddenly he received an urgent dispatch from home. This read: "Qi has invaded us again. You must return immediately!" Pang Juan was horrified and gave orders to leave Han and return to Wei. The Han army did not go in pursuit of them.

Sun Bin knew that Pang Juan would soon arrive. He said to Tian Ji: "The armies of the Three Jins are very brave and tough—they despise Qi. Since the Qi army has a reputation for cowardice, a good general would make use of this to maneuver the enemy into a disadvantageous position. *The Art of War* says, 'If you race one hundred *li* after profit, the general will get himself killed; if you race fifty *li* after profit, half the army will not make it.' Our army has now penetrated deep into Wei territory, so we should pretend to be weak to trick them."

"How exactly do we trick them?" Tian Ji asked.

"Today we will light one hundred thousand cooking fires," Sun Bin explained. "Starting tomorrow, we will gradually reduce the number. They will see the number of fires decreasing and so they will imagine that our troops are afraid of having to do battle and so many of them have deserted. They will chase after us, trying to take advantage of that. They will be rendered more arrogant, but they will also be exhausted. We can then use my plan to defeat them." Tian Ji followed his advice.

Pang Juan's army was moving southwest. The general knew that the Han troops had been defeated time and time again, and he had been looking forward to the next stage of the advance. Now, since Wei had been invaded by Qi, he had been robbed of his victory and was furious about this. When he arrived at the Wei border, he discovered that the Qi army had already retreated. He gave orders to have their campsite cleaned up and noticed that it had been laid out on the most massive scale. He tasked someone with counting up the number of cooking fires, and there were one hundred thousand of them in total. He said in amazement: "I had no idea there were so many of them. We should not underestimate the enemy!"

The following day they arrived at the site of their next camp. On checking the number of fires, they discovered that there were more than fifty thousand. The following day, they only counted thirty thousand. Pang Juan clapped his hand against his forehead: "How lucky the king of Wei is!"

"We have not even engaged the enemy yet," Crown Prince Shen said. "Why are you so happy?"

"I've always known that the people of Qi are cowards," Pang Juan replied, "but it appears that having entered Wei territory, more than half of their army has deserted in the space of just the last three days. How could they dare to fight us?"

"People from Qi are full of tricks," the crown prince said. "You need to be very careful."

"Tian Ji has met his match today!" Pang Juan declared. "Although I am not a talented man, I reckon I can go and capture him alive. That will wipe out the humiliation I suffered at Guiling."

He gave the following orders: twenty thousand picked troops, together with the two divisions under the command of Crown Prince Shen, were to march off on the double. The infantry was all to remain behind, with Pang Cong, advancing at their own pace.

Sun Bin immediately sent someone to spy on what Pang Juan was up to. The report came back: "The Wei army has already passed Mount Shalu and they are pressing forward, traveling day and night." He traced out their journey with his finger on a map and realized that they would reach Maling at dusk. The road there passed between two mountains, traveling through a very deep valley with extremely steep sides. This was perfect for an ambush. The woods growing along the sides of the road were very dense. Sun Bin indicated one huge tree to be spared and then had all the others felled. They were laid across the road to block it. A piece of bark was stripped off the one remaining tree on the east side, and here he wrote with a piece of charcoal the six words: "Pang Juan died below this tree." Then he signed this message: "The military advisor, Sun Bin." He ordered generals Yuan Da and Dugu Chen to take five thousand archers each and lie in ambush to the left and right of the road. He instructed them: "When you see a fire lit below that tree, you are to open fire in unison." He also gave orders that Tian Ying should take ten thousand men and lie in ambush three *li* from Maling, He was to wait until the Wei army had passed and then attack them from behind. Once everyone knew what they had to do, he and Tian Ji took the main body of the army and made camp a considerable distance away. They would respond to the situation as it developed.

. . .

When Pang Juan heard that the Qi army was not far ahead, he was furious that he could not overtake them in a single bound. However, he restricted himself to hurrying his men along. When they arrived at Maling, the sun was setting over the western mountain. It was the last week in the tenth month and there was no moon. His advance guard reported: "There are cut trees blocking the road, so it will be difficult for us to proceed."

"The Qi army must have been terrified that we would be coming up behind them," Pang Juan shouted, "so that is why they have done this."

He ordered his troops to move the trees out of the way. Suddenly, raising his head, he noticed that a piece of bark had been stripped off the one remaining tree. He could make out some writing but it was simply too dark to read. He ordered his soldiers to light a torch to illuminate it. As his officers all came forward with lighted torches. Pang Juan could now read exactly what it said. He exclaimed: "I have fallen into that crippled bastard's trap!"

Immediately he shouted at his men: "Retreat as quickly as you can!" Before he had even finished speaking, Yuan Da and Gudu Chen's troops, who had been lying in ambush, saw the flames and ten thousand crossbows fired in unison. The bolts fell like rain, and the army was thrown into utter confusion. Pang Juan was so severely injured he knew that he would not survive this encounter. He sighed and said: "How much I

regret not killing that cripple. All I have done is make the brute famous!"
He then drew his sword and committed suicide by cutting his throat.
Pang Ying was also shot dead by a single bolt in this encounter. The
number of Wei soldiers killed was truly incalculable.

A historian wrote a poem:

> In the past it seemed such a cunning scheme to forge the letter;
> Today, a further crafty plan saw ten thousand crossbows fired.
> In your dealings with your friends, you should be loyal and just;
> Do not imitate Pang Juan, whose evil ways brought about his own
>   death!

. . .

In the past, when Pang Juan was about to leave Ghost Valley, the Master
had told him: "If you make someone else suffer, they will punish you for
it." Pang Juan forged a letter to get Sun Bin into trouble: that resulted in
Sun Bin's kneecaps being cut off. Now he was in turn tricked by Sun Bin,
thanks to his scheme of reducing the number of cooking fires. The Master of Ghost Valley had also said, "Death will come with a Horse." In
the end he died at Maling, which means "Horse Hill." Pang Juan held
office in Wei for twelve years, right up until the moment of his death—
this corresponds to the twelve flowers. From this we can see how mirac-
ulously accurate the Master of Ghost Valley's divinations were.

At this time, Crown Prince Shen was with the rearguard troops.
When he heard that the vanguard had run into trouble, he rushed to set
up some kind of protective palisade since they were not going to be able
to advance. He was hence completely unprepared for Tian Ying's army
to come up behind him and attack. The Wei army's morale had utterly
collapsed, and nobody dared to fight—they just ran away in all directions. Crown Prince Shen, isolated with only a handful of remaining
troops, was captured alive by Tian Ying and placed, tied up, upon a
wagon. Tian Ji and Sun Bin now moved on the offensive with the main
body of the army, slaughtering the Wei forces until bodies and chariots
lay strewn across the field of battle. All the heavy equipment and military supplies were captured by Qi. Tian Ying presented his captive,
Crown Prince Shen, while Yuan Da and Gudu Chen presented the bodies of Pang Juan and his sons. Sun Bin cut off Pang Juan's head with his
own hands and hung it above his chariot. Having won such a great
victory, the Qi army went home singing songs of triumph. That night,
overcome by a sense of shame and humiliation, Crown Prince Shen committed suicide by cutting his own throat. This upset Sun Bin very much.

The main body of the Qi army had advanced as far as Mount Shalu when they met Pang Cong's infantry division. Sun Bin ordered someone to take Pang Juan's head and show it to him. The infantry division simply crumbled without a fight. Pang Cong got down from his chariot and kowtowed, begging that his life be spared. Tian Ji wanted to execute him too, but Sun Bin said: "The fault is that of Pang Juan alone—his son is innocent, not to mention his nephew!" He handed the bodies of Crown Prince Shen and Pang Ying over to Pang Cong and told him to go back and take the following message to the king of Wei: "You had better quickly present tribute to the court of the king of Qi. Otherwise, when we come back again, your kingdom may not survive!" Pang Cong agreed politely and left. This occurred in the twenty-eighth year of the reign of King Xian of Zhou.

Tian Ji and the other generals now stood down the army and went home. King Xuan of Qi was delighted and held a great banquet in their honor, at which he personally poured cups of wine for Tian Ji, Tian Ying and Sun Bin. The prime minister, Zou Ji, was worried about the fact that he had taken bribes from the kingdom of Wei in the past, not to mention that he had attempted to slander Tian Ji as a traitor, so he felt his position to be extremely precarious. Therefore, he announced that he had become ill and sent someone to return his seals of office. King Xuan of Qi responded by appointing Tian Ji as the prime minister. Tian Ying became commander-in-chief of the army and Sun Bin retained his position as military advisor, though he was offered a large fief as a reward. Sun Bin resolutely refused this. He presented a copy of his grandfather's *Art of War* in thirteen chapters to King Xuan with the following words: "Although I am a cripple, I have been entrusted with high office. Today I am happy to say that I have both repaid Your Majesty's trust in me and taken revenge against my enemies—enough is enough. Everything that I have learned is contained in this book. There is no point in keeping me anymore, so I would like to retire to some remote place and spend the rest of my life there!"

Since King Xuan was not able to keep him, he enfeoffed him with Mount Shilü. Sun Bin spent a number of years living at this mountain, and then suddenly one night he disappeared. Some say that he died just as the Master of Ghost Valley had predicted. This happened somewhat later on.

Wucheng Wangmiao wrote a poem titled "In Praise of Sun Bin":

Master Sun Bin understood the arts of war,
And yet he was slandered as a traitor.
Although he suffered the punishment of having his kneecaps cut off,

This did not affect his remarkable abilities in the slightest.
He saved Han and invaded the kingdom of Wei,
Expunging the humiliation inflicted upon him.
In spite of his success, he refused all rewards,
Retiring to live a life of seclusion.
Comparing his skills with those of his grandfather,
He may be said to have lived up to his example!

King Xuan of Qi ordered that Pang Juan's head should be hung from the gate to the capital in order that everyone should know of his country's might. He sent ambassadors to announce his victory to the other rulers, all of whom were deeply impressed. The two rulers of Han and Zhao were mindful of how much they owed to the timely assistance of Qi, so they came in person to congratulate His Majesty and pay court to him. King Xuan wanted to organize a joint attack on Wei with Han and Zhao. King Hui of Wei was now terrified and sent an ambassador to Qi to offer a peace treaty and request permission to be allowed to pay court to Qi. King Xuan of Qi announced that he wanted to hold an interstate meeting with the rulers of the Three Jins at the city of Bowang; the rulers of Han, Zhao, and Wei did not dare to refuse. The three rulers had audience with His Majesty simultaneously, which brought him great glory.

King Xuan was extremely proud of his military might, but he abandoned himself to the pleasures of wine and women. He had the Snow Palace built inside the walls of the capital as a site for banquets and other entertainments. An area of forty *li* outside the suburbs was converted into a park for hunting. He also enjoyed listening to the speeches of traveling advisors and he had members of the Jixia Academy fill his court, collecting several thousand people of this kind. There were seventy-six of them whom His Majesty particularly favored, including Zou Yan, Tian Pian, Jie Yu, and Huan Yuan. They were all given grand mansions and appointed as senior grandees. His Majesty spent all his time chatting and debating with these men, not bothering to deal with the business of government. Tian Ji repeatedly remonstrated with His Majesty, but finding himself ignored, he became depressed, and shortly afterwards he died.

. . .

One day, King Xuan was holding a banquet at the Snow Palace, at which he was entertained by women musicians. Suddenly a woman appeared at the gate and said, "I would like to have an audience with the king of Qi."

She had broad cheekbones and deeply set eyes, a large nose, and her head was set almost on her shoulders. She had a hunchback and a goiter, her hands and feet were both huge, her hair looked like hay, and her skin was extremely dark. Her clothes were practically rags. The guards at the gate stopped her and said, "How can someone as ugly as you dare to ask for an audience with His Majesty?"

"I come from Wuyan in the kingdom of Qi," the woman said. "My name is Zhongli Chun, and I am over forty years of age and still unmarried. I have heard that His Majesty is holding a banquet at this palace, and so I have come here specially to seek an audience with him. I would like to join His Majesty's harem and give the place a thorough clean-out."

Everyone around hid their laughter behind their hands: "This is one shameless woman!" They reported this to His Majesty, and King Xuan announced that he would like to see her.

When the ministers attending this banquet saw how ugly she was, they too were hard put to conceal their amusement. King Xuan asked her: "I have many concubines and maids in my palace already. Now it seems to me that a woman as ugly as you who refuses to stay at home in your village and comes here asking to see a great king like me must have some special talent."

"I have no special talent," Zhongli Chun replied, "though I am good at mime."

"I would like to see you perform a mime and let me guess the subject," King Xuan said. "However, if I do not like it, I will have you beheaded."

Zhongli Chun opened her eyes wide and gritted her teeth, punched the air a couple of times, and finally slapped her knees. She shouted: "Disaster! Disaster!" King Xuan had no idea what this all meant. He asked his ministers, and none of them had any clue either.

"Come forward and explain it to me," His Majesty said.

Zhongli Chun kowtowed: "You must exempt me from any punishment, Your Majesty, for only then will I dare to speak."

"You will not be punished," the king promised her.

"I opened my eyes wide in order that Your Majesty might see the beacon fires indicating an invasion of the country," Zhongli Chun declared. "I gritted my teeth, in order that you might realize the stupidity of refusing to listen to remonstrance. I punched the air that I might get rid of the flattering sycophants who surround you. Then I dusted off my knees to tell you to stop holding all these banquets."

King Xuan was furious. "Are you telling me that I have committed four serious mistakes? How dare a peasant woman criticize me like this!" He shouted an order for her to be beheaded.

"Please let me explain the four things that you have done wrong, Your Majesty, and then you can punish me," the woman said. "I have heard that since the kingdom of Qin employed Shang Yang, that country has become rich and powerful. Any day now they are going to send their army through the Hangu Pass to fight Qi, in which case you are going to be in serious trouble. You do not have any good generals at your disposal, and the border defenses have gradually fallen into disrepair; that is why I opened my eyes wide to warn you of this problem. There is a common saying: 'A ruler whose ministers are prepared to speak out does not lose his country; a father whose sons are prepared to criticize him will have a well-ordered household.' You spend too much time with women, Your Majesty, and ignore the business of government—you have failed to pay attention to men offering you loyal remonstrance. I gritted my teeth in order to encourage Your Majesty to listen to them. Men like Tian Pian flatter and fawn on you, but by doing so they are preventing men of real ability from joining your service. People like Zou Ji seem to be very learned, but it is all empty, for they waste their time speculating on far-fetched scenarios. Your Majesty trusts and employs these men, but I am afraid they will lead the country to ruin, and so I cleared them away with a couple of punches. You have exhausted the people and emptied the treasury in order to build your palaces and hunting parks, with their belvederes and pavilions, artificial hills and ponds; that is the reason I dusted off my knees in order to represent getting rid of them. Having made these four mistakes, Your Majesty, your position is as precarious as a stack of eggs—you are enjoying your present security without a thought for coming disaster. I have risked my life to speak to you. If you have learned anything from what I have told you, my death will not be in vain!"

King Xuan sighed and said, "If it were not for Zhongli Chun, I would never have heard of my mistakes!" He immediately called a halt to the banquet. Calling for a chariot, he rode with her back to the palace, where he declared his intention to appoint her as queen.

Zhongli Chun refused: "If you don't listen to my advice, what is the point of having my body?"

King Xuan issued a general summons for men of ability and turned flattering sycophants out of office. He sent away the people from the Jixia Academy and the men he had recruited from among the wandering knights. He appointed Tian Ying as his prime minister and made Mencius a senior advisor. Thus the kingdom of Qi entered a period of good government. He gave the Zhongli family the lands of Wuyan as their fief and appointed Zhongli Chun Lady of the Manor of Wuyan. This happened somewhat later on.

. . .

Let us now turn to another part of the story. When Shang Yang, the prime minister of Qin, heard that Pang Juan was dead, he said to Lord Xiao: "Qin and Wei are neighbors. In relation to us, Wei can be compared to a disease of the vitals; as long as Wei is there, we cannot flourish, nor can they. It is clear that only one of us can survive. Wei has now suffered a serious defeat at the hands of Qi, and their allies have turned against them. We could take advantage of this opportunity to attack them. Wei will not be able to withstand this assault, so we should be able to force them to move their capital eastward. Since Qin occupies an area protected by mountains and rivers, we will be able to exert our authority over the other rulers and you will become a king!"

Lord Xiao thought that this was a good idea. He appointed Shang Yang as senior general, with the Honorable Shaoguan as his deputy, and they took fifty thousand troops to attack Wei. The army left the city of Xianyang and headed east. Warning messages had by this time already reached Xihe, and Zhu Cang, the man in charge there, sent three emergency calls for assistance in the space of a single day. King Hui of Wei held a meeting with all his ministers to discuss the situation, asking them for a plan to resist the Qin invasion.

Prince Ang came forward and said: "When Shang Yang was still living in Wei, we were good friends. I once recommended him to your service, Your Majesty, but you did not listen to me. Let me go and attempt to get a peace treaty with him. If that does not work, we can retreat behind the city walls and request aid from Han and Zhao."

The other ministers present all expressed their support for this plan. King Hui promptly appointed Prince Ang as senior general and gave him command of fifty thousand troops. Their mission was to rescue Xihe. They advanced and made camp at the Wu fortress. *This fortress had been built by Wu Qi when he was guarding Xihe, in order to prevent attacks by Qin. It was very strong and easy to defend.*

Prince Ang prepared a letter and sent someone to the Qin encampment to see Shang Yang and request that he cease the attack. The officer in command of the fortress said, "Someone has already come from the Qin prime minister with a letter. They are waiting at the foot of the city wall." Prince Ang gave orders that the letter be hauled over the wall. He opened it and read the following:

> You and I used to be good friends, Your Royal Highness—as close as brothers. However, now each of us serves our own master and we have ended up as generals in two different countries. How can we bear to fight each other? I would like to propose peace talks whereby we send away our armies and take off our armor, turning up in civilian garb. Let us meet at Mount Yuquan, where we can both enjoy each other's company and prevent our two countries from butchering each other. Let future generations praise our friendship in the same terms as Guan Zhong and Bao Shuya! If you agree to this plan, please let me know what date you would like to meet.

When Prince Ang read this letter he was very pleased: "That is just what I was hoping for." He issued lavish rewards to the man who had brought the letter and replied as follows:

> I am delighted to discover that you, Prime Minister, still remember our old friendship and mention the events of the rule of Lord Huan of Qi. It is my ambition to prevent warfare and bring peace to the people of Qin and Wei, while emulating the friendship that existed between Guan Zhong and Bao Shuya. Let us meet in three days' time. I am delighted to follow your suggestion.

When Shang Yang received this reply, he said happily: "My plan has succeeded!" He sent an envoy back to the city again to confirm the date and give the following message: "The Qin army have already abandoned their advance camp and are heading home. Once the commander-in-chief has held this meeting with you, the main camp will also be dismantled." The envoy also handed over a gift of dried lotus root and musk. He said: "These two items are specialties from Qin. Dried lotus root has nourishing properties, while musk dispels noxious miasmas. The prime minister is deeply aware of the old friendship between you, which he hopes will continue forever."

Prince Ang thought that Shang Yang must be very fond of him and was quite sure he harbored no evil intentions, so he wrote a letter back to thank him. Shang Yang issued a deceptive order to abandon the advance camp, whereupon the Honorable Shaoguan led these troops away. They had secret instructions that they were to announce that they were going hunting in order to supplement their food supply, but when they reached Mount Huqi and Mount Baique, they were to fan out and wait in ambush. At noon on the day of the meeting, they were to assemble at the foot of Mount Yuquan. When they heard the signal of a siege engine being fired, they were to attack. They had orders to arrest everyone present and not allow anyone to escape.

Just before dawn on the appointed day, Shang Yang began by sending an envoy to the city to report: "The prime minister has already set out for Mount Yuquan, where he will await your arrival. He is accompanied by just three hundred men."

Prince Ang believed every word of this, and so he loaded food and wine onto one cart, together with musical instruments, and set off for the meeting, accompanied by the same number of men as Shang Yang. Shang Yang was waiting for him at the foot of the mountain. When Prince Ang realized that he did indeed only have a few people in attendance and they were unarmed, he was completely unsuspicious. When the two of them met, they talked about their old friendship and laid out the outlines of a peace treaty between their two countries. The people on the Wei side were delighted with this turn of events. Both sides had brought food and drink, but since this was taking place on Prince Ang's home turf, it was he who poured the first drink for Shang Yang. Three rounds of toasts were drunk and three songs performed. When one of his officers approached to make a report, Shang Yang had him remove all the dishes from Wei and use only food and wine from Qin. The two men serving wine were both famous warriors from the state of Qin: one was called Wu Huo, and he could lift a one-thousand-pound weight; the other was called Ren Bi, and he could rend tigers and leopards with his bare hands. As Shang Yang raised his cup to offer his first toast, he glanced at his entourage, and they went to the top of the mountain and fired a signal. Soon the mountain reverberated with the firing of siege engines, and a deafening sound filled the valley.

Prince Ang was deeply alarmed. "Where did these siege engines come from? Are you trying to pull some kind of trick on me?"

Shang Yang grinned and said, "It's just a bit of fun. I do hope you don't mind!"

Prince Ang was now becoming frightened and tried to run away, only to be held fast by Wu Huo so he could not move. Ren Bi directed his men to arrest the others present. The Honorable Shaoguan now led his troops forward and captured all the remaining chariots and men—not a single one of whom was able to escape.

Shang Yang gave orders that Prince Ang should be placed in a prison cart and sent back to Qin with the report of their victory. He had the bonds on the other people removed and gave them wine to help them

overcome the shock that they had sustained. He told them: "The commander-in-chief is going to have to go back in a hurry. If you get the city
gate opened, you will all receive rich rewards. However, if you refuse to
help, you will immediately be beheaded."

The men whom Prince Ang had brought with him were all very young
and naive; they were afraid to die and so agreed to do as he said. Shang
Yang instructed Wu Huo to dress up like Prince Ang and sit in his carriage, with Ren Bi as an escorting ambassador following along behind
him in a single chariot. The people on top of the wall recognized their
own people in the escort and immediately opened the gate. The two
brave warriors struck at once. With a punch and a kick, they disabled
the mechanism so that the gate could not be closed again. The guards
who tried to tackle them were all wrestled to the ground. Shang Yang
was right behind them in command of the main body of the Qin army,
and he now rushed forward as fast as he could. The soldiers and people
inside the fortress panicked. After a short and brutal battle, Shang Yang
took possession of the Wu Fortress.

Zhu Cang realized that Prince Ang must have been taken prisoner
and calculated that it would be virtually impossible to retain hold of
Hexi, so he abandoned the city and fled. Shang Yang marched deep into
Wei territory and was soon pressing hard on Anyi. King Hui was absolutely terrified and ordered Grandee Long Jia to go to the Qin army and
make peace.

"The king of Wei was unable to find employment for me, so I ended
up serving the state of Qin," Shang Yang said. "Thanks to His Lordship, I have been appointed prime minister of that country, and I enjoy
a salary of ten thousand bushels of grain. Since I have now been given
command over the army, if I do not destroy the kingdom of Wei, I will
feel that I will have let His Lordship down."

"I have heard it said that a good bird remembers its former forest
home; a good man respects the lord he used to serve," Long Jia said.
"Even though the king of Wei did not employ you in his government,
this is still the home of your parents. How can you be so heartless?"

Shang Yang thought deeply for a moment and then said to Long Jia:
"I cannot stand down my army unless you agree to hand over the lands
of Hexi to Qin."

Long Jia had to agree to this. He returned and reported to King Hui.
His Majesty accepted the deal and ordered Long Jia to present a map of
the lands of Hexi to Qin in order to make peace. Shang Yang took the
map as a sign of possession, and the army returned home singing songs

of triumph. Prince Ang surrendered to Qin. King Hui of Wei decided that Anyi was now too close to the Qin border and hence difficult to defend, so he moved the capital to Daliang, which was henceforth known as Liangguo.

Lord Xiao of Qin was so delighted at Shang Yang's success that he appointed him as a lord of the manor and gave him a fief of fifteen cities from the lands of Shangyu that he had earlier captured from the kingdom of Wei. Thus he took the title of Lord Shang.

To later generations, he was best known by the name of Shang Yang.

Shang Yang thanked His Lordship for his kindness and returned to his mansion, where he told his staff: "I was originally just a member of a junior branch of the Wey ruling house, but since coming to Qin I have reformed the government here and made the country rich and powerful. Now I have captured seven hundred *li* of land from Wei and been given a grant of fifteen cities—I have achieved my ambition. Is that not a wonderful thing?"

His household all offered their congratulations. However, there was one man who stepped forward and shouted: "Everyone is just nodding sycophantically; there is no one to speak out! You are all members of Lord Shang's household, so why are you just flattering him when that is going to cause disaster?"

Everyone turned around to stare. The speaker was one of Shang Yang's senior advisors: Zhao Liang. "You have just said that everyone is flattering me," Shang Yang said. "How about you tell me which is better, my methods of government or the administration of Baili Xi?"

"Baili Xi was prime minister in the time of Lord Mu of Qin," Zhao Liang replied. "He established three rulers in Jin, conquered twenty countries, and made his master the hegemon of the Western Rong nomads. However, when he was in office he did not relax in the shade no matter how hot the day was, nor did he sit down in His Lordship's presence even when he was exhausted. On the day that he died, the people of Qin wept as if they were mourning for their own parents. You have been prime minister of Qin for eight years—although your laws are enacted, the punishments involved are too harsh, so people obey them because they are afraid, not because they think they are right. Likewise, they encourage people to think about their own personal benefit rather than the interests of justice. The scion loathes you down to the very marrow of his bones for your role in punishing his Grand Tutor, and the people have swallowed their hatred for a long time. When the ruler of Qin dies, your position will be precarious indeed!

How can you be so greedy for the wealth and honors that have come from Shangyu, not to mention crowing over your successes? Why don't you recommend other wise men for office and resign all your positions? If you decline your emoluments and leave office, moving to live somewhere remote in retirement, perhaps you may yet escape with your life." Shang Yang was silent and displeased.

Five months later, Lord Xiao of Qin became sick and died. The ministers assisted Scion Si to succeed to the title, and he became Lord Huiwen. Since Shang Yang had achieved great things in the previous administration, he felt justified in behaving with considerable arrogance. The Honorable Qian was still furious that he had earlier had his nose cut off on Shang Yang's orders, and now he and Noble Grandson Jia both petitioned Lord Huiwen as follows: "There is a saying that when a senior minister is too powerful, the country is in danger; when a servant is too powerful, your position is imperiled. Shang Yang has reformed the laws and achieved good government in Qin, but even though the country is well-ordered, mere women and children speak of Shang Yang's laws and not the laws of Qin. He has a fief consisting of fifteen cities; he holds an honorable position that is invested with great power; sooner or later he is going to rebel."

"I have loathed that bastard for years!" Lord Huiwen shouted. "However, he served as a minister in my father's administration and he hasn't done anything openly wrong, so I have had to let things go until now."

He sent an envoy to collect the prime ministerial seal of office from Shang Yang and order him to return to his estate at Shangyu. Shang Yang bade a formal farewell to His Lordship at court and then drove out of the city, accompanied by an honor guard just like the ruler of a country. So many officials went to see him off that the court was denuded. The Honorable Qian and Noble Grandson Jia reported privately to Lord Huiwen: "Shang Yang is showing no sign of repentance—he is conducting himself like an independent monarch. When he gets back to Shangyu, he is sure to plot a rebellion."

Gan Long and Du Zhi also testified to the truth of this. Lord Huiwen was now furious, and he immediately ordered Noble Grandson Jia to take three thousand crack troops and head out in pursuit of Shang Yang. They were to execute him and bring his head back. Noble Grandson Jia accepted this order and left the court.

By this time the entire populace hated Lord Shang. When they heard that Noble Grandson Jia had taken troops in pursuit of him, thousands excitedly waved their arms and set off after him. By this time Shang Yang's carriage was already more than a hundred *li* from the capital, but hearing the shouting behind him, he sent someone to find out what was going on. This man returned to report: "The court has sent soldiers after you." Shang Yang was horrified. He knew that he had lost the new lord's support and was afraid he was in very serious trouble. He quickly changed his hat and gown to look like an ordinary soldier and ran away.

When he arrived at the Hangu Pass, dusk was already falling. He went to a guesthouse and asked to stay the night. The manager asked him for his documentation, and Shang Yang had to admit he had none. "According to the laws of Shang Yang," the manager said, "I cannot let anyone stay here without the proper documentation. If I were to disobey the law, I would be beheaded! I do not dare to let you reside here."

"I made this law," Shang Yang sighed, "and now it comes back to bite me!"

During the night he managed to smuggle himself out through the pass, fleeing to the kingdom of Wei. King Hui of Wei was angry with Shang Yang for the trick by which he had captured Prince Ang and taken his territory in Hexi, so he decided to imprison him and extradite him back to Qin. Shang Yang was able to escape this fate and make his way to Shangyu, where he plotted an uprising and attack on Qin. However, Noble Grandson Jia finally caught up with him and took him prisoner. Lord Huiwen listed the crimes that he had committed and ordered that he be taken to the marketplace to be ripped to pieces by five oxen. The people competed to gnaw his flesh, and in a trice it was gone. This punishment was followed by the execution of his entire family.

How sad that Shang Yang, having established a new law code and made the state of Qin rich and powerful, now ended up being ripped to pieces. Surely this was an overreaction to the things he had done wrong.

These events occurred in the thirty-first year of the reign of King Xian of Zhou.

An old man wrote a poem:

Having enjoyed his fief at Shangyu for less than a year,
How sad that his body was ripped to pieces in five directions.
Cruelty has always resulted in harsh revenge;
It is best for rulers to keep a close eye on the punishments on the statute
books.

When Shang Yang died, the people danced and sang in the streets, as if they had been released from some heavy burden. When the six other countries heard the news, they all congratulated each other. Gan Long and Du Zhi, who had lost their jobs because of him, now both returned to office. Gongsun Yan was appointed as the new prime minister. Gongsun Yan persuaded Lord Huiwen that he should conquer Ba and Shu to the west and announce to the world that henceforth he would assume the title of king. He demanded that every other country follow the example of Wei and give him some land. If anyone refused, he would raise an army and attack them. Lord Huiwen now took the title of king and sent ambassadors to announce this to the other countries, demanding that all of them should present him with a congratulatory gift of land. They all hesitated, unable to make up their minds. At this time King Wei of Chu employed Zhao Yang, and he defeated the Yue army, killing King Wujiang of Yue and conquering their country. Their army being powerful and their lands extensive, they were in a position to match Qin militarily. When the Qin ambassador arrived in Chu, he was shouted down by the Chu king. It was after this that Su Qin used the "Vertical Alliance" policy to persuade the king of Qin.

If you do not know what Su Qin said to the king of Qin, READ ON.

Chapter Ninety

*Su Qin creates the Vertical Alliance and
becomes prime minister of six countries.*

*Zhang Yi is forced into going to the kingdom
of Qin.*

When Su Qin and Zhang Yi said goodbye to the Master of Ghost Valley
and went down the mountain, Zhang Yi went to the kingdom of Wei
while Su Qin returned to his old home in Luoyang. His mother was at
home; of his brothers, his older brother had died, leaving a widowed
wife. His two younger brothers were Su Dai and Su Li. Having been
separated for so many years, it is not necessary to say that their reunion
on this day was deeply joyful. A couple of days later, Su Qin decided
that he wanted to leave for a journey around the various kingdoms and
states, so he asked permission from his mother to sell the family property to pay for the journey. His mother, sister-in-law, and wife opposed
this with all their might: "If you did not want to plough the fields and
became a merchant or artisan instead, you might still make a bit of
profit. Do you really think that you can get rich and powerful simply by
talking to people? Why are you giving up on a perfectly good inherit-
ance in order to seek a goal that you may never attain? If things go
badly for you, will you not regret it?"

"If you are indeed so good at this," his brothers said, "why don't you
go and talk to the Zhou king? That way you can become famous in
your own home country and do not need to travel far away."

Su Qin found himself opposed by his family on every front, so he
decided to seek an audience with King Xian of Zhou, at which he spoke
of the ways in which the country could become strong. King Xian had
him stay in an official guesthouse. His Majesty's entourage was well

aware of the fact that Su Qin came from a farming family, and so they worried that his advice would be bad. They were not willing to recommend him to King Xian.

Su Qin stayed at the guesthouse for more than a year. Realizing that he had no means to advance his career at court, he went home angrily. This time he sold up all the property and obtained a sum of one hundred gold ingots. He bought a coat of black sable fur and a carriage with horses and servants, with which he set off on a tour of the various other states, learning the geography of mountains and rivers, the customs of the people, and how to survive in the bitter warfare of the times. However, after a couple of years of this, he had yet to find his own master. When he heard that Shang Yang had been appointed as Lord of Shang and that he was much trusted by Lord Xiao of Qin, he went west to Xianyang. By the time he arrived, Lord Xiao was dead and Shang Yang had been executed. Nevertheless, he sought an audience with King Huiwen.

When His Majesty summoned Su Qin into the main hall of the palace, he asked: "You, sir, have come to my humble abode after a journey of a thousand *li*. What do you have to teach me?"

Su Qin presented his opinion: "I have heard that Your Majesty has demanded a present of land from the other rulers. Does this mean that you are planning to just sit quietly on your throne and unite the world under your own rule?"

"That is so," King Huiwen replied.

"Your Majesty's kingdom is marked by the Hangu Pass and the Yellow River to the east, Hanzhong to the west, Ba and Shu to the south, and the Hu nomadic people to the north," Su Qin said. "You have thousands of *li* of rich land and a massive army. With your wisdom, Your Majesty, and your huge population, I have a plan that will allow you to defeat the other rulers and swallow up the Zhou royal house, uniting the world under your own control. It will all be as easy as waving your hand, but I am afraid that you cannot do it while sitting quietly on your throne."

One of the reasons for King Huiwen's decision to execute Shang Yang was his dislike of foreign advisors. He now sent Su Qin away with the words: "I have heard it said that until your feathers are grown it is difficult to fly. I am interested in what you have to say, but the time is not yet ripe. You will have to wait a few years until I have made my army stronger. Then we will discuss it."

Su Qin withdrew and wrote a book about the techniques used by the three sage-kings of antiquity and the five hegemons of more recent times to obtain authority over the world. This book amounted to over one hundred thousand words. He presented it to the king of Qin, who read it but refused to give Su Qin any kind of official position. He went to see the prime minister of Qin, Gongsun Yan, but he was jealous and would not help him.

Su Qin lived for a couple of years in Qin, but in the end he had spent his one hundred ingots of gold and his coat of black sable fur had become threadbare. There was nowhere to utilize his talents, so he sold his carriage, horses, and servants to pay for his journey home. He went back on foot, carrying his remaining belongings in a sack on his back. When his parents saw the prodigal, they cursed him with humiliating words. His wife was weaving, and when she saw that Su Qin had returned, she did not even bother to get up from the loom to greet him. Su Qin was hungry and begged his sister-in-law for a bite to eat, but she refused on the grounds that they had run out of firewood—she was not willing to cook for him.

There is a poem that testifies to this:

> If you are rich, even passing strangers treat you like their own flesh and
>   blood;
> If you are poor, your own family will walk by on the other side of the
>   road.
> Just look at Su Qin coming home with his fur coat in tatters:
> In a blink of an eye, his relatives started to treat him heartlessly.

Su Qin burst into tears. He sighed and said: "When you are poor, you wife doesn't want you as a husband, your sister-in-law doesn't want you as a brother-in-law, and your parents don't want you as their child. This is all my fault!"

He happened to take from his box of books the copy of the Great Lord of Qi's *Secret Tallies*. Suddenly he realized what this was: "The Master of Ghost Valley told me: 'If on your travels you run into difficulty, you must go back and study this book again, after which you will know what you have to do.'"

He shut his door and settled down to study it, getting to the bottom of every phrase, not resting day or night. When it got dark and he became sleepy, he would stab himself in the thigh with an awl until the blood ran down his legs. When he understood every nuance of the *Secret Tallies*, he thought about the geography and terrain of each of the countries he had traveled through. By the end of the year, he understood the most important principles and was ready to use them. He consoled himself with the following thought: "Now that I understand this, I can persuade the rulers of the world to my way of thinking. Will they not heap gifts of gold and jade, silk and brocade on me, and offer me the position of a prime minister or senior official?"

He spoke to his younger brothers, Su Dai and Su Li: "I have now completed my studies and it will be easy for me to gain fame and fortune. If you will help me by subsidizing my journey, letting me go and persuade the rulers of the Central States, I will recommend you for office once I have established myself." He explained the contents of the *Secret Tallies* to his brothers. Su Dai and Su Li now also understood the situation, and they each gave him some gold ingots to pay for his travel expenses.

Su Qin said goodbye to his wife and parents and headed off back to the kingdom of Qin. He thought to himself: "Of the seven great states in the world, Qin is by far the most powerful. I could have helped them to unify the entire country and establish an empire, but His Majesty the king of Qin was not prepared to employ me. What could I do? Now I am going to go back again. If the same thing happens to me, how on earth am I going to face going home?" At this point he came up with a plan of resistance, whereby the other countries would unite and isolate Qin. This would be a means to bring him to fame and fortune!

He turned east to head for the state of Zhao. At this time, Marquis Su of Zhao was in power there, with his younger brother, the Honorable Cheng, as prime minister, holding the title of Lord of Fengyang. Su Qin went first to speak to the Lord of Fengyang, who was not at all pleased. Su Qin left Zhao and headed north to the state of Yan. He sought an audience with Lord Wen of Yan, but none of his entourage were prepared to help to arrange this. By this time, more than a year had passed and his funds were exhausted; Su Qin was left starving in a hostel. The owner of the hostel felt sorry for him and gave him a hundred cash. Thanks to his timely assistance, Su Qin was able to go to where Lord Wen of Yan was hunting and prostrate himself by the side of the road. Lord Wen of Yan asked him his name, and when he discovered that this was Su Qin, he said happily: "I have heard that you gave a book of one hundred thousand words to the king of Qin a few years back—I have the greatest admiration for you! I would love to be able to read your book. Now I am lucky enough to meet you in person; this is indeed a blessing for the state of Yan!" He turned his chariot around and headed back to court, whereupon he bowed deeply and asked for instruction.

Su Qin presented his opinion: "You are the ruler of one of the great states of the world, Your Lordship, and you govern a territory of two thousand *li*, with an army of over one hundred thousand men, six hundred chariots, and six thousand cavalry. This is not even half the army that you would see in one of the great states on the Central Plains, but you have not heard the scrape of weapons launched in anger or the rattle of armored horsemen, nor have you seen the terrible sight of chariots being overturned and generals slain. You have been completely safe from all harm. Do you know why this is, Your Lordship?"

"I don't," Lord Wen of Yan replied.

"The reason why Yan has never been attacked is because you are protected by Zhao," Su Qin explained. "You have paid no attention to the importance of affirming your alliance with Zhao, but instead have handed over land in submission to bullying from Qin—is this not really stupid?"

"What should I do?" Lord Wen of Yan asked.

"In my humble opinion, you had better seek a marriage alliance with Zhao, followed by further peace treaties with the other states," Su Qin replied. "When the entire country is united, you can join in defending against Qin. This will keep your people at peace for generations to come."

"You are proposing a Vertical Alliance to protect the state of Yan. I am happy with this idea, but I am afraid that the other rulers will not necessarily be willing to join."

Su Qin spoke up again: "Although I am not a man of any notable talents, I am prepared to go to seek an audience with the Marquis of Zhao and get him to agree to this Vertical Alliance."

Lord Wen of Yan was delighted and gave him gold and silk to pay for the expenses of his journey. He also presented him with a grand chariot and team of four horses, and provided a guard of knights to escort Su Qin to Zhao.

. . .

By this time, the Lord of Fengyang was dead. When Lord Su of Zhao heard that the state of Yan had sent an ambassador, he went down the palace steps to meet him. "You have come from so far away," he said, "what do you have to tell me?"

Su Qin presented his opinion: "I have heard that the knights and wise men of the world all admire Your Majesty's sense of honor and justice and they would love to enter your service, but they have been prevented by the

Lord of Fengyang's jealousy and suspicion of other men's abilities. Thus, they have found themselves with no means to make Your Lordship's acquaintance and have been prevented from even speaking to you. Now that the Lord of Fengyang has passed away, it is possible for me to explain the stupidity of his brand of loyalty. I have heard it said that when you want to keep your country safe, you need to bring peace to its people; when you want to bring peace to your people, you need to consider your choice of allies carefully. Of the countries east of the mountains, Zhao is by far the most powerful—you have more than two thousand *li* of land and one hundred thousand soldiers, one thousand chariots, and ten thousand cavalry. With your grain resources, you could feed this army for many years. The country that Qin is most anxious to see come to harm is Zhao. The only reason that they do not dare to raise an army and attack you is because they are afraid that Wei or Han might make a surprise attack on their rear. Zhao is protected by Han and Wei. However, Han and Wei do not have the natural defenses of huge mountains or great rivers—should the Qin army attack them, they would be swallowed up. If these two countries are forced to surrender, Zhao will certainly be next. I have often studied the map, considering the lands of the various rulers, and I have traveled through the ten thousand *li* of Qin's territory. If the armies of the other countries are all added together, they are ten times the forces that Qin has at its disposal. If the six countries were prepared to unite against a common enemy and send all their forces west, would it be difficult to defeat Qin? Their diplomats and advisors have used Qin as a bugbear with which to frighten other rulers, tricking them into feeling that they have to offer gifts of land in order to make peace. If you simply hand over the land without making a fight, you will be destroying yourselves. Which is better: defeating them or watching them butcher you? In my humble opinion, you should summon the other rulers to a meeting at the Huan River at which you swear a blood covenant and establish a solemn oath, uniting as brothers to face the enemy together. If Qin were to attack one country, the other five would unite to rescue it. If anyone betrayed this alliance, the others would jointly attack him. Even though Qin is a powerful country, surely they cannot fight everyone else alone!"

"I am but a young man," Lord Su of Zhao said, "and I have not been in power for long—I have never heard such sensible advice! Since you have told me that I should unite the other rulers in an alliance against Qin, how could I refuse?"

He presented Su Qin with the seals of the prime minister and bestowed a large mansion upon him. He was also given one hundred chariots and one thousand ingots of gold, as well as one hundred pairs of matched white jade discs and one thousand lengths of fine silk. He was named "Leader of the Vertical Alliance."

Su Qin sent an envoy with one hundred ingots of gold back to Yan, with instructions to give it to the innkeeper as a reward for having given him one hundred cash. Then he selected an auspicious day to set out on the next phase of his journey, to visit the kingdoms of Han and Wei. Suddenly Lord Su of Zhao summoned Su Qin to court because he had an urgent matter to discuss. Su Qin rushed to the court to have an audience with the Marquis of Zhao, who said, "An official at the border just reported: 'The prime minister of the kingdom of Qin, Gongsun Yan, has attacked Wei, taking prisoner their commander-in-chief, Long Jia, and killing forty-five thousand soldiers. The king of Wei has presented them with ten cities north of the Yellow River in order to make peace. Gongsun Yan is now going to turn his forces against Zhao.' What should I do?"

When Su Qin heard this, he was silent. He thought to himself with horror: "If the Qin army does come to Zhao, the ruler of Zhao is going to follow Wei's example in suing for peace. In that case the Vertical Alliance will fail." This was a real crisis, and he decided to buy himself some time. Assuming a peaceful and unconcerned expression, he waved his hands lightly and replied: "By my reckoning the Qin army will be exhausted, and it is far from certain that they are going to be capable of an attack on Zhao. If they do come, I have a plan to make them withdraw."

"You had better stay here temporarily, sir," the Marquis of Zhao said. "If the Qin army does indeed fail to turn up, then you can proceed on your way." This was exactly what Su Qin had been hoping for. He expressed his agreement and left the court.

When he returned to his mansion, he summoned one of his most trusted servants, a man named Bi Cheng, and took him into a secret room. There he issued the following instructions: "I have an old friend and fellow student whose name is Zhang Yi, styled Yuzi; he comes from Daliang in the kingdom of Wei. I am going to give you one thousand pieces of gold, and you are to dress up as a merchant, changing your name to Jia Sheren. I want you to go to Wei and find Zhang Yi. When you meet him, you are to repeat my words exactly. If he comes to Zhao, you are to do the following. You must be very careful." He accepted these orders and set off that very night for Daliang.

There is a poem that testifies to this:

Of the six kingdoms, he had persuaded the rulers of two,
When beacon fires flared because of the powerful state of Qin.
To establish the Vertical Alliance he needed to buy himself some time,
So he summoned the clever "Jia Sheren" to his side.

• • •

Let us now turn to another part of the story. When Zhang Yi left Ghost Valley and returned to Wei, he tried to get a job with King Hui of Wei, but it was impossible—his family was too poor. Later on, the Wei army suffered repeated defeats, and so he and his wife packed up and went to Chu. He joined the household of Zhao Yang, Grand Vizier of Chu, as one of his advisors. Zhao Yang was later appointed to command troops in an attack on Wei, at which he inflicted a terrible defeat on the enemy, capturing Xiangling and a further six cities. King Wei of Chu was delighted at his success and presented him with the jade disc of Master He.

What is this item, the jade disc of Master He? In the last years of the reign of King Li of Chu, a Chu person named Bian He found a rough jade stone on Mount Jing, which he presented to His Majesty. The king asked his jade workers to inspect the stone, and they said: "It is a rock." King Li was furious and thought that Bian He was making fun of him, so he had his left foot cut off in punishment. When King Wu of Chu was established, Bian He presented his rough stone again. The jade workers yet again pronounced it to be an ordinary rock. This king of Chu was also furious and cut off his right foot. When King Wen of Chu came to the throne, Bian He decided to present his stone again. However, his two feet had both been cut off and he could not move. Carrying his rough stone against his breast, he wept at the foot of Mount Jing for three days and three nights, until his tears ran with blood.

A friend of Bian He's asked him: "You have presented it twice and had both feet cut off. Surely that is enough. Are you hoping for some kind of reward? Why do you cry so sadly?"

"I am not hoping for any reward," he replied. "It is dreadful that this fine piece of jade has been repeatedly condemned as a rock, just as I, an honest gentleman, have been set down again and again as a fraudster. Right and wrong have been turned on their heads and nothing has been done to resolve the problem; that is the real tragedy!"

King Wen of Chu heard Bian He crying and picked up his stone. He had a jade worker cleave it, and it was indeed a piece of the most beautiful and flawless jade. This was fashioned into a circle: Master He's jade disc. Today at the summit of Mount Jing in Nanzhang County,

Xiangyang City, there is a pool, and beside it there is a stone hut—this place is called Cherishing Jade Cliff, and it is supposed to be where Bian He lived when he wept over his stone. The king of Chu was deeply impressed by his sincerity and gave him the salary of a senior grandee, enabling him to live comfortably for the rest of his days. This jade disc was indeed a priceless treasure. It was only because Zhao Yang had achieved so much in his conquest of the kingdom of Yue and his victories over Wei that he was worthy of receiving such a munificent reward.

Zhao Yang kept the jade disc on his person at all times, hanging from his belt. One day he went out to visit Mount Chi in the company of some one hundred members of his household gathered from all four corners of the world. There was a deep pool at the foot of Mount Chi, and according to legend the Great Lord of Qi once went fishing there. A high belvedere had been constructed to one side of the pond and the company ascended to the top to eat, drink, and make merry. When they had all become a bit drunk, the company announced that they had heard so much of the beauty of Master He's jade disc and they asked Zhao Yang whether he would be prepared to let them have a look at it. Zhao Yang gave orders to his treasurer to bring in the chest of valuables from his chariot and place it before the company, after which he unlocked it himself. Having folded back the three layers of silk brocade wrappings around it, the jade shone out like a beacon, lighting up the faces of those present. The guests took it in turns to inspect it and they all praised it to the skies.

Just as they were enjoying this, someone said, "There is a huge fish leaping about in the pond." Zhao Yang got up and leaned out over the balustrade to have a look; he was followed by the rest of the company. The fish, fully a yard long, kept jumping up, and a large number of other fish were following in its wake. Just at that moment, clouds began to gather in the northeast and a downpour followed. Zhao Yang gave instructions to pack up and go back. The treasurer went to pack the jade disc back into its chest, but he had no idea who had it; the jade had vanished. After a short panic Zhao Yang returned to his mansion, and his staff was put through a fine-tooth comb in the hope of discovering who had stolen the jade disc. They all said, "Zhang Yi is really poor and has often behaved badly. He is the only person who would steal the jade."

Zhao Yang was also suspicious. He sent someone to arrest and beat Zhang Yi in the hope of forcing him to confess. Zhang Yi was in fact not the thief, and there was no way that he was willing to take the blame for a crime he had not committed. They beat him several hundred strokes until his body was a mass of wounds, then they paused for a breather. Zhao Yang realized that at any moment now they would have succeeded in beating Zhang Yi to death, so he had no choice but to set him free. One of the onlookers felt sorry for Zhang Yi and made arrangements to have him taken home. When his wife saw Zhang Yi's battered appearance, she wept and said, "You have suffered such pain and humiliation because of your determination to study and become a traveling persuader. If you had stayed at home and ploughed the fields, would this disaster have happened to you?"

Zhang Yi opened his mouth and asked his wife to look inside. "Is my tongue still there?" he asked.

She laughed and said, "It is."

"My tongue is my capital," Zhang Yi said. "I do not have to worry about being poor for the rest of my life." He rested until he had more or less recovered from his injuries and then returned to the kingdom of Wei.

. . .

When "Jia Sheren" arrived in the kingdom of Wei, Zhang Yi had already been back for about six months. He had heard much of Su Qin's success in Zhao, and was thinking about going there himself, when he happened to open his gate and bumped straight into Jia Sheren, who had stopped his cart outside. Talking to him, he discovered that he had come from Zhao, and so he inquired: "Is it true that Su Qin is now the prime minister in Zhao?"

"Who are you?" Jia Sheren inquired. "I guess you must be some old friend of the prime minister, otherwise why would you ask?"

Zhang Yi explained that they were indeed old friends and had studied together. "If that is so, why don't you go and see him?" Jia Sheren suggested. "The prime minister is sure to recommend you for office. I have already finished my business here, and I am going to set off back home to Zhao. If you don't mind, you could come with me . . ."

Zhang Yi was delighted to agree. When they arrived at the suburbs of the Zhao capital, Jia Sheren said: "My home is located here outside the city walls. I have business to conclude, so I am afraid that I am going to have to say goodbye for now. If you enter the gates you will find plenty of guesthouses there, where any passing visitor can find good accommodation. I will come and find you in a couple of days."

Zhang Yi said goodbye to Jia Sheren and got down from the cart, entering the city to find somewhere to stay. The following day, Zhang

Yi prepared a letter in which he asked for an audience with Su Qin, but the latter had already warned his gatekeepers and none of them were prepared to take a message in. He waited for five days and then finally got his name included on the list of callers. Su Qin refused to see him on the grounds that he was too busy—he suggested that they meet some other time. Zhang Yi waited for a couple more days but still was not able to catch even a glimpse of Su Qin; angry, he decided to leave.

The owner of the hostel in which he was staying grabbed hold of him and said, "You have already sent a message to the prime minister's mansion and have not had a response. If the prime minister summons you, what am I going to say? Even if you have to wait six months or a year, you must not give up!"

Zhang Yi was extremely depressed and tried to track down Jia Sheren, but nobody had ever heard of the man.

Another couple of days later, he sent a further message to the prime minister's mansion. This time Su Qin sent back the following command: "I will see you the day after tomorrow."

Zhang Yi went to the hostel keeper and borrowed a gown and shoes so that he might look respectable. The following day, he went off at dawn to await his summons. Su Qin had ordered his guards to line up in a most awe-inspiring array; the main gates were closed, and he gave orders that his guests should enter by the side gate. Zhang Yi wanted to climb the steps to the main hall directly, but the others stopped him, saying, "The prime minister is still in audience. Please wait a moment." Zhang Yi had to wait in the corridor, fuming with irritation, while a huge number of officials went in and greeted Su Qin. There also seemed to be hosts of people who had already finished their reports. After an age, when the sun was already high in the sky, he heard someone shout from the hall: "Where is the visitor?"

"The master is calling for you!" the servants said.

Zhang Yi straightened his clothing and went up the steps, where he could see Su Qin waiting for him in his seat. He was not expecting that Su Qin would not even show him the courtesy of getting up. Zhang Yi controlled his anger and bowed respectfully, at which point Su Qin did rise from his seat and make a small gesture with his hands in return. "How've you been?" he asked in an offhand tone.

Zhang Yi was now too furious to speak. It was at this point that one of the servants reported that lunch was served. Su Qin said, "I had a great deal of official business to attend to, and so I had to make you wait. I am afraid that you must be starving. Let us have a simple meal;

we can talk afterwards." He ordered his servants to set a table in the
lower hall, while he himself ate in the upper, with every sort of delicacy
piled on his plate. Zhang Yi, on the other hand, was served only one
meat dish and one vegetable dish, together with coarse rice. At first,
Zhang Yi was inclined not to eat a single mouthful, but he was absolutely starving. Besides which, the money that the hostel keeper had
given him had pretty much been used up by this time. He had staked
everything on today's meeting with Su Qin; even if he was not prepared
to recommend him for an official position, he might at least give him
some money. He was not expecting the treatment that he had in fact
received. As the saying goes: "Under someone else's low eaves, do you
dare to refuse to bow your head?"

Having no other choice, Zhang Yi swallowed his shame and picked
up his chopsticks. Even at that distance, he could see that Su Qin had
been presented with a vast number of different plates and bowls. He
was doling out the remains of his meal to his servants, and it was clear
he had been served a much more lavish lunch than Zhang Yi, who was
now feeling both angry and humiliated. When the eating was over, Su
Qin gave orders: "Please bring my guest up to the main hall." Zhang Yi
looked up at him, and he could see that Su Qin was back in his high seat
and showed no sign of getting up. He was now so furious he could no
longer contain himself. Walking forward a couple of steps, he shouted:
"Hey, you! I thought that you were still my friend—that is why I came
all this way to throw in my lot with you. What do you mean by humiliating me like this? Is this how you treat an old friend?"

Su Qin replied with a drawl: "With your abilities, I was expecting
you to have achieved great things already. I was not expecting to find
you reduced to such poverty! I could recommend you to the Marquis of
Zhao and make you rich and noble. However, I am afraid that you are
no longer as ambitious and brilliant as you once were and you would
not be able to make a go of things, in which case all that would happen
is that you get the person who recommended you into trouble!"

"I can make myself rich and famous, thank you very much," Zhang
Yi snarled. "I don't need you!"

"If you can make yourself rich and famous, what are you doing here
talking to me?" Su Qin retorted. "Remembering that we used to be
friends, I am going to give you one gold bar. You can spend it as you
like!" He ordered his servants to hand the gold over to Zhang Yi. The
latter was now in such a rage that he hurled it onto the floor before
rushing out, and Su Qin made no efforts to restrain him.

Zhang Yi marched straight back to the inn, where he could see that all his belongings had been moved out onto the street. Zhang Yi asked the reason. The innkeeper said: "You got to see the prime minister today. He must have arranged that you live somewhere more suitable. That is why I am getting your things together to move them."

Zhang Yi shook his head, muttering over and over again: "Bastard! Bastard!" He ripped off the clothes and shoes that he had borrowed and gave them back to the innkeeper.

"I thought you were friends and fellow students," the innkeeper said. "Are you not being a little unreasonable?"

Zhang Yi grabbed hold of the man and told him about their old friendship and how he had been treated that day.

"The prime minister is arrogant," the innkeeper said, "but he occupies a high position and is very powerful and important—it is right that you should treat him with greater politeness than in the past. It was very kind of him to give you a gold bar. With that money you could have paid your outstanding obligations here and still had enough to go home. Why did you refuse it?"

"I was in a foul mood, so I dashed it to the ground," Zhang Yi said. "Right now, I don't have a single copper to my name. What am I going to do?"

It was just at this moment that Zhang Yi caught sight of his old acquaintance, Jia Sheren, walking along outside the inn. When the two men met, he said: "I do apologize for not coming to see you the last few days. Have you been able to have an audience with the prime minister?"

Zhang Yi's anger came bubbling up again, and he hit the table with a thump of his fist. "What a heartless, selfish bastard!" he cursed. "Don't mention his name to me again!"

"That is a terrible thing to say, sir!" Jia Sheren said. "What can have happened that you are so upset?"

The innkeeper told him about the disastrous audience in Zhang Yi's stead: "Not only does he owe money here that he can't repay, he also has no way of getting home. No wonder he is so worried!"

"Well, it was my idea in the first place that you should come here," Jia Sheren said. "Whatever happens here is in some measure my fault. I would be happy to refund the money that you owe, sir, and I will prepare a horse and carriage to take you back to Wei. What do you think?"

"I cannot face going back to Wei like this," Zhang Yi declared. "I would like to go to Qin, but I simply don't have the money!"

"Why do you want to go to Qin?" Jia Sheren asked. "Do you have friends there too?"

"No, but Qin is the strongest of the seven states, and they are the only people powerful enough to attack Zhao. If I go to Qin and am lucky enough to gain office there, I will be able to take revenge on Su Qin!"

"If you wanted to go to some other country, I would not be able to help you," Jia Sheren said. "But if you want to go to Qin, I have long been wanting to go and visit my family there. Why not travel with me as we did before? That way, we will have each other's companionship. Wouldn't that be nice?"

"That really is most kind of you," Zhang Yi said happily. "You put Su Qin to shame!"

He formally swore an oath of brotherhood with Jia Sheren. His friend paid Zhang Yi's bill at the inn, and since his carriage had by that time pulled up at the gate, the two men got in it and headed west to Qin. On the way he sold off his servants in order to pay for new clothes and equipment for Zhang Yi. If there was something that Zhang Yi needed, he did not stint. When they arrived in the kingdom of Qin, he again disbursed large sums of cash, bribing King Huiwen of Qin's servants to speak well of Zhang Yi.

At this time, King Huiwen was feeling regret at having lost Su Qin. When he heard his servants' praise, he immediately summoned Zhang Yi for an audience. He appointed him to a ministerial position and began plotting an attack on the other states. Jia Sheren now prepared to leave. Zhang Yi wept and said: "I was in a terrible situation, and it is all thanks to your help that I have been able to achieve my current eminence in the kingdom of Qin. Just as I was thinking of being able to pay back some part of your kindness, you tell me that you are going!"

Jia Sheren laughed and said: "I am not your friend. Your real friend is Su Qin."

Zhang Yi was surprised into a long silence. Then he asked, "You have been subsidizing me. Why did you mention him?"

"The prime minister is at present trying to construct a Vertical Alliance, and he was worried that if Qin attacked Zhao it might bring all his plans to naught," Jia Sheren explained. "He decided that the only person with a hope of taking control of matters here in Qin was you. For that reason he sent me, dressed as a merchant, to bring you back to Zhao. He was afraid that you might get stuck there, so he deliberately treated you in a humiliating way so that you would become angry. Just as he intended, you decided that you wanted to go to Qin. He told me to spend as much of his money as was necessary to help you to get a job, because he was sure that you would sooner or later find your feet here. Now that you have accomplished this, it is time for me to go back and report to the prime minister."

Zhang Yi sighed and said: "Ah! It was all a trap on Su Qin's part, and I fell into it without noticing a thing! He really is a much cleverer man than I! I will trouble you to present my compliments to the prime minister and tell him that as long as he is alive, we will not dare to attack Zhao. That is my way of repaying all that he has done for me!"

An old man wrote a poem, which says:

Once he was furious at the treatment meted out by an old friend,
Now he is only grateful to this Jia Sheren.
Only when everything was explained did he begin to understand
Just how much he owed to Su Qin.

Jia Sheren returned and reported this to Su Qin, who presented his opinion to Lord Su of Zhao: "The Qin army will not be coming."

. . .

Su Qin said goodbye and traveled to Han, where he had an audience with Lord Xuanhui, at which he said: "Han has lands stretching more than nine hundred *li* and several hundred thousand soldiers. The finest bows and crossbows in the world are made in this country. However, since you are allied with Qin, sooner or later they will demand land off you. And then next year, they are going to demand more land. There is a limit to the lands of Han, but there is no limit to Qin's greed. With one exaction after another, one day the lands of Han will all be gone! As the saying goes: 'I would rather be in front of a chicken than walk after an ox!' Given the benevolence of Your Lordship's rule and the strength of your army, why do you agree to walk after this particular ox? I find it humiliating on your behalf!"

Lord Xuanhui said firmly: "For the sake of the country, I will listen to your advice. I will join the Marquis of Zhao's alliance." He presented Su Qin with one hundred ingots of gold.

Afterwards, Su Qin traveled to Wei, where he said to King Hui: "The territory of Wei is a thousand *li* square. However, when it comes to the size of population or the number of your horses and chariots, there is no other country that can compare with you. You have all that is needed to resist the encroachments of Qin. I do not understand why you pay any attention, Your Majesty, to those ministers who advise you to hand over land and serve Qin as a vassal. Supposing that Qin makes demands of you and you just ignore them, what can they do about it? I would recommend that you join the Vertical Alliance with the other six countries and unite against Qin—that way you can prevent them from ever doing you any harm. I am here with the Marquis of Zhao's command to make a treaty with you to this effect."

"I am a useless and stupid man," King Hui of Wei said. "I have brought these humiliations upon myself. Since you have told me of this excellent plan, sir, how could I dare to refuse your commands?" He too presented him with gold, silk, and a chariot.

Su Qin now traveled back to the kingdom of Qi. He persuaded King Xuan of Qi with the following words: "I have heard that on the streets of Linzi, chariots and carriages follow each other in an endless chain and people rub shoulders with each other constantly—this is the wealthiest city in the world. Don't you feel humiliated by the idea that you might have to serve Qin to the west? The kingdom of Qi is located so far from the borders of Qin; how could their army possibly threaten you? What do you think you are doing allying with them? Let me recommend an alliance with Zhao to you, Your Majesty, that six nations may be joined together in peace and harmony, helping each other in times of crisis."

"I will follow your advice," King Xuan of Qi assured him.

Su Qin got back in his chariot and headed south. He persuaded King Wei of Chu with the following words: "Chu has more than five thousand *li* of land—you are the strongest country in the entire world. Qin understands that you are their greatest enemy. If Chu is strong then Qin is weak; if Qin is strong then Chu is weak. The rulers of the world are now going to be gathered into an alliance with one or the other of you. If they are allied with you, they can be forced to hand over land to Chu; if they are allied with Qin, you are going to have to hand over land to Qin too. Which one of these plans is better for you?"

"It is indeed a blessing to the kingdom of Chu to receive the benefit of your advice!" King Wei of Chu said.

Su Qin went north to report all of this to Lord Su of Zhao.

• • •

When Su Qin passed through Luoyang, the other rulers all sent ambassadors to escort him. A magnificent procession of banners preceded him, and he was followed by a train of heavy wagons that stretched unbroken for twenty *li*. His entourage was in no whit inferior to that of a king. All along the route he took, the road was lined by bowing officials. When King Xian of Zhou heard that Su Qin had arrived, he ordered his servants to sweep the roads through which he would pass and had a tent erected outside the suburbs where he could greet him. Su Qin's mother observed all this, propped up on her stick and muttering exclamations of shock and regret; his two younger brothers, his wife, and his sister-in-law dared only take occasional peeks at the procession. When they met, they prostrated themselves.

Su Qin, still sitting in his carriage, said to his sister-in-law: "In the past you wouldn't cook a meal for me, so why are you treating me with such respect now?"

"Your position is so important and you have so much money," she replied. "I wouldn't dare behave rudely, sir!"

Su Qin heaved a sigh and said: "Weather is appreciated according to whether it is hot or cold; people are valued depending on their social status. Today I realize quite what money and a noble title can do!"

He loaded his family into carriages and went back with them to his old hometown. There he built a huge mansion in which his entire clan could live. He disbursed one thousand pieces of gold as gifts to clan members.

Today in the city of Henanfu, there stand the remains of Su Qin's mansion. There is a story that someone once dug up the ruins and found one hundred ingots of gold—they must have been buried at this time.

Su Qin's younger brothers Su Dai and Su Li were very envious of their older brother's success, so they applied themselves again to studying the *Secret Tallies* and learning the skills necessary to become diplomats.

Su Qin spent a couple of days at home, and then he got into his chariot and returned to Zhao. Lord Su of Zhao enfeoffed him as Lord of Wu'an. He sent ambassadors to the rulers of Qi, Chu, Wei, Han, and Yan, proposing that they all meet at the Huan River. Su Qin and Lord Su of Zhao went off to make preparations on site; they constructed a sacrificial platform and arranged placement, waiting for the arrival of the other kings. Lord Wen of Yan was the first to arrive, followed by Lord Xuanhui of Han. Over the course of the next couple of days King Hui of Wei, King Xuan of Qi, and King Wei of Chu arrived one after the other. Su Qin held a preliminary meeting with the senior ministers of these states, and they privately discussed the order of precedence. This was a tricky issue. Chu and Yan were ancient states, with Qi, Han, Zhao, and Wei being founded in more recent times. However, this was a time of much warfare, and if you went by size of the country, Chu was the most important, followed by Qi, Wei, Zhao, Yan, and Han. Of these countries, Chu, Qi, and Wei were monarchies governed by a king, while Zhao, Yan, and Han were marquisates, but it seemed awkward to give certain countries precedence over others on the basis of the title they claimed. For this reason Su Qin suggested that all six monarchs should take the title of "king" and that the king of Zhao should be regarded as the convener of the meeting and hence take the chair, while the king of Chu and the others should take second place as guests. This was all arranged with the respective countries in advance.

When the appointed time came, each king ascended to the ceremonial platform and took his place. Su Qin walked up the steps and announced to their majesties: "You all rule great countries and are ranked as kings—with your broad acres and powerful armies, any one of you could take control. The ruling house of Qin is descended from a peasant horse-breeder, and they live amid the mountain fastness of Xianyang. They have swallowed up many countries; are you prepared to surrender your position and serve Qin as subjects?"

"We do not want to serve Qin," the kings declared. "Please tell us what we should do, sir!"

"I have already explained to each of you my plan to unite in a Vertical Alliance to isolate Qin," Su Qin replied. "Now let us sacrifice a beast that you may smear your lips with blood, calling upon the Bright Spirits to witness your oath that henceforth you will be as brothers, helping each other in times of trouble."

The six kings all clenched their fists and said: "We accept this oath."

Su Qin lifted up the basin and invited each monarch in turn to smear his lips with blood. They bowed and reported their new covenant to Heaven, Earth, and their own ancestral spirits: "If one country betrays this oath, the other five will all attack it!" Six copies were made of the text of the covenant so that each country could receive one.

After this a banquet was held. The king of Zhao said: "Su Qin is the author of this great plan to bring peace to our six countries, and hence he should be given a noble title, in recognition of all his hard work in coming and going between our countries in order to create this Vertical Alliance."

The five other kings said: "You are quite right, Your Majesty."

The six kings appointed Su Qin as "Founder of the Vertical Alliance" and presented him with the prime ministerial seals of each country, together with a gold pass and precious sword that would give him authority over the populace. In addition to that, each monarch presented him with one hundred ingots of gold and ten teams of blood horses. Su Qin thanked their majesties for their kindness, and the six kings each returned to their own countries. Su Qin himself went back to Zhao with King Su. This happened in the thirty-sixth year of the reign of King Xian of Zhou.

A historian wrote a poem:

To bolster the treaty sworn at the Huan River, they invoked the Bright
    Spirits;
Knowing the disaster that might overtake them, enmity was set aside.
Supposing that the Vertical Alliance had not failed,
How easy it would have been to destroy an isolated Qin!

In this same year, King Hui of Wei and King Wen of Yan both died. King Xiang of Wei and King Yi of Yan succeeded to the throne. If you don't know what happened after that, READ ON.

Chapter Ninety-one

Although he intended to abdicate, King Kuai
of Yan actually brings about a war.

By pretending to offer a gift of land, Zhang
Yi succeeds in tricking Chu.

When Su Qin created the Vertical Alliance of six countries, he wrote out a copy of the treaty and had it sent to the Qin border, where an ambassador collected it and took it to King Huiwen of Qin to read. His Majesty was deeply shocked and said to his prime minister, Gongsun Yan, "If these six countries are united, I can no longer hope for any significant gains. We must come up with a plan to disrupt this Vertical Alliance and then move on to greater things."

"The leader of the Vertical Alliance is Zhao," Gongsun Yan replied. "You must raise an army and attack Zhao, Your Majesty, and see who is the first to go to their rescue; then you can attack them. In that way, the other rulers will come to fear you and the alliance will fall apart."

At this time Zhang Yi was present, and he had no intention of allowing an attack on Zhao, which would be a betrayal of all that Su Qin had done for him. He now came forward and said: "These six countries have only just allied, and it is too soon to be trying to break them apart. If you were to attack Zhao, you would find that Han's army stationed at Yiyang, Chu's stationed at the Wu Pass, Wei's at the Yellow River, Qi's at the Qing River, and Yan's at Xirui would all pitch in to help. The Qin army would find it impossible even to put their noses out beyond the Hangu Pass, let alone try and go and attack anyone else! Wei is by far the most powerful of the countries located close to Qin, and Yan is the furthest away to the north. Why don't you send an ambassador loaded with bribes to seek a peace treaty with Wei, thereby sowing the seeds of suspicion in the minds of their alliance partners? You could also offer a marriage alliance to the crown prince of Yan. Under such pressure, the Vertical Alliance will simply collapse of its own accord."

King Huiwen thought that this was an excellent idea. He agreed to return to the kingdom of Wei Xiangling and the other six cities that he had captured in order to assure the success of the peace treaty. Wei sent an ambassador back to pay court to Qin, and a princess was promised in marriage to the crown prince of Qin.

When the king of Zhao heard this, he summoned Su Qin and upbraided him: "You promised me that with this Vertical Alliance, we six nations would be united against Qin. Now in less than a year the two kingdoms of Wei and Yan have both been in communication with them, and it is clear that we can no longer depend upon our allies. If the Qin army were to launch an assault on us, do you think those two countries would come to rescue us?"

Su Qin was horrified and apologized: "Let me go as your ambassador to the kingdom of Yan. I am sure that I can find a means to bring Wei back into the fold."

He left and headed straight for Yan. When he arrived, King Yi of Yan treated him with the ceremony due to a prime minister. At this time, King Yi had only just come to the throne. King Xuan of Qi had taken advantage of the period of national mourning to attack them, taking ten cities. King Yi now said to Su Qin: "My late father listened to your advice, imagining that it was the best thing for the country that our six nations be united in a mutual defense pact. Now, before the late king's bones have even had time to grow cold, the Qi army has crossed our borders, taking ten of our cities. Is this what the covenant at the Huan River has brought us?"

"Let me go to Qi and make representations on your behalf, Your Majesty," Su Qin replied. "I am sure that I can get these ten cities returned to Yan."

King Yi of Yan accepted his offer and Su Qin set off for an audience with King Xuan of Qi, at which he said: "The king of Yan is not only your ally; he is also the favorite son-in-law of the king of Qin. You now have possession of ten of their cities. This will ensure that Yan hates you, but it will also ensure that Qin is your enemy too. It is not a good idea to make two powerful enemies merely for the sake of ten cities. If you will listen to my advice, I would encourage you to return these cities to Yan, putting yourself in the good books not only of them, but also of Qin. If you have Yan and Qin on your side, your position in the world will be unassailable!" King Xuan was delighted and returned the ten cities to Yan.

King Yi's mother, Dowager Queen Wen, had heard a great deal about how brilliant Su Qin was, and so she ordered her servants to summon him to the palace and they began having an affair. King Yi knew about this, but he did not say anything. Su Qin was alarmed at the possible implications of this, so he made friends with the prime minister of Yan, Prince Zhi, agreeing that the son of one should marry the daughter of the other. He also told his younger brothers, Su Dai and Su Li, to make sure that they maintained good relations with Prince Zhi, for he hoped by these means to make his position unassailable. The Dowager Queen of Yan repeatedly summoned Su Qin to her palace, and he was becoming more and more uncomfortable about the whole thing, to the point where he did not dare to go. He said to King Yi: "The position of Qi and Yan is at the moment approximately equal. Let me go to Qi, Your Majesty, and act as a mole."

"What do you mean by 'act as a mole'?" King Yi inquired.

"I will pretend to have committed some crime in Yan and hence fled to Qi," Su Qin explained. "The king of Qi is sure to appoint me to high office. I can disrupt the government of Qi, and you can take advantage of this to conquer their territory."

King Yi agreed to this. He took back Su Qin's prime ministerial seals, and afterwards he fled to Qi. King Xuan of Qi had long respected and admired him, so he appointed him as minister without portfolio. Su Qin spent much time talking to King Xuan of the joys of hunting and listening to music. Since King Xuan was a greedy man, he also persuaded him that he should raise taxes. His Majesty's appetite for sex also made it easy to encourage him to select more beautiful girls for his harem. It was his intention to wait until Qi was in real trouble and then strike on Yan's behalf—King Xuan was naturally completely unaware of this. The prime minister, Tian Ying, and one of the other ministers without portfolio, Mencius, remonstrated severely, but he did not listen to either of them. When King Xuan died, his son succeeded to the throne, taking the title of King Min. In the first years of his reign, he did try to reform the government. He married a Qin princess as his queen and enfeoffed Tian Ying as Duke of Xue, though he was better known by his other title of Lord of Jingguo. However, Su Qin retained his old position as minister without portfolio.

• • •

Let us now turn to another part of the story. When Zhang Yi heard that Su Qin had departed from Zhao, he knew that the Vertical Alliance would not hold water. He therefore refused to give the city of Xiangling back to Wei, along with the other six that he had promised. King Xiang of Wei was furious and sent someone to demand them from Qin. King Hui of Qin appointed Prince Hua as the senior general with Zhang Yi as his assistant, and they led the army to attack Wei, capturing the city of Puyang. Zhang Yi requested the king of Qin's permission to return Puyang to Wei. Furthermore, he sent Prince Yao as a hostage to Wei, in order to make peace between the two countries. Zhang Yi escorted the prince on his journey. King Xiang of Wei was deeply appreciative of the king of Qin's gesture, so Zhang Yi advised him: "His Majesty the king of Qin has treated Wei with great generosity; they have captured one of your cities but refused to take possession of it, and they have also offered you a hostage. Wei cannot be seen as being rude to Qin. You must consider giving them some suitable present to thank them."

"How should I thank them?" King Xiang asked.

"Qin is not interested in anything other than land," Zhang Yi replied. "If you would give a parcel of land to Qin, they will be very grateful to Wei. If Qin and Wei were to join forces in an attack on some other country, Your Majesty would be able to conquer lands far in excess of what you have had to give away today."

King Xiang was bewitched by Zhang Yi's dulcet tones; he decided to present the lands of Shaoliang as a thank-offering to Qin. He also announced that he did not dare to demand a hostage from them. The king of Qin was delighted and promptly removed Gongsun Yan from office, appointing Zhang Yi as prime minister in his stead.

At this time King Wei of Chu died and was succeeded by Prince Xiongkui, who took the title of King Huai. Zhang Yi sent an envoy to King Huai with a letter requesting the return of his wife and mentioning the false accusation that he had once stolen the jade disc. King Huai of Chu upbraided Zhao Yang to his face: "Zhang Yi is a wonderful man— why didn't you recommend him for office under the late king? Why did you force him to go and seek office in Qin?"

Zhao Yang mumbled something and felt very ashamed of himself; when he got home, he fell ill and died. King Huai was afraid that Zhang Yi might yet rise to the heights in the Qin administration, so he communicated with Su Qin about the prospect of restoring the Vertical Alliance and bringing the various rulers together. By this time Su Qin had already been forced to leave Yan and seek sanctuary in Qi. Zhang Yi had an audience with the king of Qin, at which he refused the office of prime minister and asked permission to be allowed to go to Wei.

"Why do you want to leave Qin and go to Wei?" King Huiwen asked.

"The six nations have been deluded by Su Qin's persuasions, and they have not been able to free themselves from his spell," Zhang Yi replied. "If I can get control of Wei, I can bring them to seek an alliance with Qin of their own accord, and they will cause the other rulers to change their minds."

King Huiwen granted him permission and Zhang Yi went to throw in his lot with Wei, whereupon King Xiang did indeed appoint him as prime minister. Zhang Yi persuaded him: "Your country borders on Chu to the south, Zhao to the north, Qi to the east, and Han to the west; you have no natural barricade in the form of a mountain range or great river. Sooner or later, you will find yourself being torn to pieces. Unless you seek an alliance with Qin, your country will know no peace."

King Xiang could not make up his mind what to do. Zhang Yi secretly sent someone to incite Qin into attacking Wei, whereby they inflicted a great defeat on the Wei army and captured the city of Quwo.

An old man wrote a poem:

One sought office in Qi at the behest of the kingdom of Yan,
The other was prime minister in Wei in order to serve the interests of
    Qin.
Even though the Vertical and Horizontal Alliances were opposed to each
    other,
They rested on the machinations of a couple of remarkable men.

King Xiang was now angry and increasingly determined not to do Qin's bidding. He decided to revive the Vertical Alliance and recommended that King Huai of Chu should serve as its head. From this time onwards, Su Qin was increasingly important to Qi.

• • •

At around this time the prime minister of Qi, Tian Ying, became sick and died. His son, Tian Wen, succeeded to his honors as Duke of Xue, though he was better known as the Lord of Mengchang.

Tian Ying had more than forty sons, and Tian Wen was the child of one of his most minor concubines. Furthermore, he was born on the unlucky day of the fifth day of the fifth month. When the baby was born, Tian Ying ordered his concubine to abandon the child. The concubine was unwilling to give up her baby, and so she raised him in secret. When the child was five years old, she brought him to see Tian Ying, who was furious that his orders had been disobeyed.

Tian Wen kowtowed and asked: "Father, why did you want to abandon me?"

"It has been handed down from our ancestors that the fifth of the fifth is unlucky and that any child born on that day will kill his parents when he grows as tall as the lintel on the door," Tian Ying replied.

"The destiny of men is determined by Heaven; how can it be up to the door?" Tian Wen inquired. "If destiny is to be decided by the door, why don't you simply raise the lintel?"

Tian Ying couldn't answer that. Although he did not say anything, he was deeply impressed. When Tian Wen was in his teens, he began to make many friends among his father's clients. They were all happy to go out traveling with him, and, because of this, his reputation began to spread. When an ambassador arrived in Qi from a foreign country, he would be sure to ask to meet Tian Wen. This again made Tian Ying realize how clever his son was, and he decided to make him his heir. Thus it came about that he inherited the dukedom of Xue and the title of Lord of Mengchang.

When the Lord of Mengchang had succeeded to his father's titles and emoluments, he had huge hostels built and summoned men of talent from all over the world to join his household. Everyone who came to join him was accepted, with no inquiry made into their qualifications. Many wanted criminals and murderers also came to give allegiance to him. Even though the Lord of Mengchang was a nobleman, he ate and drank the same as his clients. One day when he was dining with his clients, there was someone who could not see properly because of the glare from the fires, who decided that he must be eating better quality food than they were having. He threw down his chopsticks and walked out. Tian Wen got up from his seat and made a point of comparing his own food with what they had been served; it was identical. The man sighed and said: "The Lord of Mengchang is so generous to his guests, and yet I have suspected him of duplicity. I really am a mean person! How can I possibly remain as part of this household?"

He drew his sword and committed suicide by cutting his throat. The Lord of Mengchang wept and presided over his funeral with great sadness, moving all his many clients to tears. Now even more people came to seek service with him, until the number of his guests swelled to several thousand men. The other rulers heard of how wise the Lord of

Mengchang was and how many clients he had, which made them respect Qi even more. Nobody now dared to encroach upon their borders. As the poem says:

Birds and beasts stay far away from the mountain where the tiger
  dwells;
No fish are to be found in the waters where dragons lurk.
When three thousand men had joined his household as clients,
The whole world stood in awe of the Lord of Mengchang.

Three years after Zhang Yi became prime minister in Wei, King Xiang died and his son was crowned as King Ai. King Huai of Chu sent an ambassador to offer official condolences and suggest a joint attack on Qin. King Ai agreed. King Xuanhui of Han, King Wuling of Zhao, and King Kuai of Yan happily followed suit. When the Chu ambassador arrived in Qi, King Min discussed the matter with his assembled ministers. They all said: "You are joined by a marriage alliance and there is no enmity between you; you cannot attack them."

Su Qin, as the architect of the Vertical Alliance, was insistent that he could join the campaign. The Lord of Mengchang was the only one to make the following point: "It would be wrong either way. If you join the attack, then you will make an enemy of Qin; if you do not join the attack, you will be the sole focus of the hatred of five other countries. In my humble opinion, you had better send troops, but give them orders to delay. If the troops are sent, there will be no break with the other five countries in the alliance. If they go slowly, you can withdraw them at the appropriate moment."

King Min thought that this was excellent advice and placed the Lord of Mengchang in command of twenty thousand men. The Lord of Mengchang exited the suburbs of the Qi capital but then announced that he was sick and in need of medical treatment, as a result of which the entire campaign ground to a halt.

. . .

Let us now turn our attention to the four kings of Han, Zhao, Wei, and Yan, who had met with King Huai of Chu outside the Hangu Pass and were now awaiting the right moment to advance and attack. Even though King Huai of Chu was officially the head of the Vertical Alliance, each of the other four kings was in charge of his own army, and they were not united. The general in command of guarding the pass was Chuli Ji. He threw open the gates and put his troops in battle formation.

The five nations jockeyed for position, but no one was prepared to be the first to advance. Having maintained this deadlock for a couple of days, Chuli Ji sent out his sappers, and they cut the road by which Chu's food supply reached them. Once the Chu army started to feel the pinch, the officers and men were all murmuring revolt. Chuli Ji took advantage of this to launch a surprise attack on them, in which the Chu army was defeated and put to flight. The other four countries took their armies home too. Before the Lord of Mengchang had even arrived at the Qin border, the armies of the other five nations had all been stood down.

This was an excellent plan on the part of Lord Mengchang.

When he went back to Qi, King Min sighed and said, "I almost made the mistake of listening to Su Qin's advice!" He presented the Lord of Mengchang with one hundred *jin* of gold, which he used to maintain the expenses of his household, and valued him even more than before. Su Qin was ashamed for having failed to match up to the other man. King Huai of Chu was now worried about the prospect of an alliance between Qin and Qi, so he sent an ambassador to offer rich gifts to the Lord of Mengchang, which served to cement the alliance with Qi. A constant stream of gifts and envoys now came and went between these two countries.

When King Xuan of Qi was alive, Su Qin held sway in the government and monopolized His Majesty's favor. There were many noblemen and relatives of the royal house who were deeply jealous of him. Now King Min had come to the throne, and Su Qin remained in favor. However, His Majesty had refused to follow Su Qin's advice and relied upon the Lord of Mengchang instead, as a result of which the attack on Qin had failed and the Lord Mengchang had been rewarded with great wealth. His Majesty's courtiers suspected that King Min was no longer enamored of Su Qin, so they arranged for an assassin, lying in wait with a dagger, to stab him as he went to court. Although the dagger did indeed penetrate Su Qin's stomach, he was able to report this outrage to King Min, clutching his vitals. His Majesty gave orders that the assassin be taken alive, but by that time he had made good his escape and nobody could catch up with him.

"After I am dead," Su Qin instructed, "you must cut off my head and announce: 'Su Qin was engaged in treasonous communications with Yan while working for Qi—today he has paid the penalty for his crimes. Anyone who knows who killed him and comes forward with this information will be rewarded with one thousand pieces of gold!' If you do this, you will find the assassin."

When he had finished speaking he pulled the dagger out of his wound. He died as the blood poured out across the floor. King Min did exactly as he had suggested and gave orders that Su Qin's head should be exhibited in the marketplace. A short time later someone walked past the head and, seeing that a reward was offered, announced to those present: "I am the man who killed Su Qin." The officials there promptly arrested him and took him to see King Min, who ordered that the minister of justice supervise his torture until they had the names of everyone involved. Several families were completely wiped out.

Later historians commented that even though Su Qin was dead, he was still able to avenge what was done to him, which shows his great intelligence! However, the assassination could also be regarded as punishment for his lack of loyalty to his adopted country.

After Su Qin died, his clients gradually revealed what he had really been plotting, and how he was still working for Yan while holding office in Qi. King Min now realized how Su Qin had tricked him, and from this time onwards, he entertained no friendly feelings towards the kingdom of Yan. In fact, he wanted the Lord of Mengchang to raise an army and attack them. Su Dai persuaded the king of Yan that he should offer one of his sons as a hostage to guarantee the peace treaty with Qi. The king of Yan followed this advice, and so Su Li accompanied the hostage on his journey and had an audience with King Min. His Majesty was no longer able to lay his hands on Su Qin, but he wanted to imprison Su Li instead.

"The king of Yan thought that he ought to seek an alliance with Qin, but my brother persuaded him that you, Your Majesty, were a most awe-inspiring and virtuous monarch and hence he had better make a peace treaty with Qi instead," Su Li shouted. "That is the reason I have been sent to you with a hostage. Why do you suspect the good intentions of a dead man and punish an innocent living one?"

King Min was pleased with what he said and treated him generously. Su Li accepted a position as a grandee of Qi, while Su Dai remained behind, working in the government of the kingdom of Yan.

A historian wrote "In Praise of Su Qin":

Su Qin was a man of Zhou, the student of the Master of Ghost Valley.
He measured up his opponents thanks to his reading of the *Secret Tallies*.
Having created the Vertical Alliance, he wore the seals of office of six nations,
Yet his final years ended in disaster because he served the interests of Yan!

When Zhang Yi saw that the six-nation attack on Qin had failed, he was quietly delighted. When he heard that Su Qin was dead, he was even happier and said, "Now it is time for me to get busy with my tongue!" He took advantage of this opportunity to persuade King Ai of Wei: "Qin is more than strong enough to resist five other countries; from this it is clear that it is fatal to fight them! Su Qin went on and on about the Vertical Alliance but he could not even protect himself, let alone the entire country! Sometimes it happens that a family rips itself to pieces over a squabble about money—if blood relatives behave like that, how can you expect it to be any different for foreign countries? If Your Majesty insists on holding to the advice you received from Su Qin and refuses an alliance with Qin, they will unite with the first country that joins them to attack Wei, and you will then be in serious danger!"

"I am happy to follow your advice, Prime Minister, and seek an alliance with Qin," King Ai declared. "However, I am afraid that they will not agree to this. What am I to do?"

"I will apologize to the kingdom of Qin on your behalf," said Zhang Yi. "I am sure that I can make a peace treaty between your two countries."

King Ai presented him with a fancy carriage and outriders, sending Zhang Yi on his way to Qin to ask for a peace treaty. Once the treaty between Qin and Wei had been concluded, Zhang Yi remained behind in Qin to take up the office of prime minister.

. . .

The prime minister of the kingdom of Yan, Prince Zhi, was a tall man running to fat, with a broad, square face. Nevertheless, he was dexterous enough to be able to catch a bird in flight and could run as fast as a galloping horse. Even in the time of King Yi, he already held the reins of power within the country. When King Kuai succeeded to the throne, it was soon apparent that he was an alcoholic lecher whose only interest was his own pleasures; he had no intention of going to court and dealing with matters of state. This gave Prince Zhi the idea of usurping the throne. Since Su Dai and Su Li were both close friends of the prince, they made a point of stressing to the other rulers how kind and wise His Royal Highness was. King Kuai ordered Su Dai to go to Qi and visit their hostage there. When this was over and he returned to Yan, King Kuai asked: "The Lord of Mengchang is living in Qi and he is famous throughout the world for his great wisdom. Given that the king of Qi has such a brilliant minister, will they be able to take control of the world?"

"No."

"Why not?" asked King Kuai.

"His Majesty may know that the Lord of Mengchang is a very clever man but he does not let him act freely with respect to the government," Su Dai replied. "How is it possible that they can take control of anything like that?"

"If I had a minister like the Lord of Mengchang, I would let him do whatever he wanted," the king said.

"But you have the prime minister, Prince Zhi. He is a remarkable servant of the government. In fact, you could say that he is the Lord of Mengchang in the kingdom of Yan . . ." Afterwards, King Kuai gave Prince Zhi sole responsibility for the government of the country.

Suddenly one day, King Kuai asked Grandee Lu Maoshou: "There were lots of rulers in ancient times, but why do we only ever hear of Yao and Shun?"

Lu Maoshou was a member of Prince Zhi's faction, and so he answered: "The reason why Yao and Shun are called sage-kings is because Yao abdicated the throne in favor of Shun and Shun abdicated the throne in favor of Yu."

"If that is so, why was Yu the only person to have handed on the throne to his son?"

"Yu was intending to abdicate in favor of Boyi, who had replaced him as the head of the government," Lu Maoshou explained, "but he had not managed to get around to stripping his son, the crown prince, of his title. That is why, when King Yu died, Crown Prince Qi stole the country from Boyi. Right up to the present day people speak of the failures of Yu's government and how he did not match up to Yao and Shun—that is the reason."

"I would like to abdicate in favor of Prince Zhi," the king of Yan said. "Do you think that would be possible?"

"If Your Majesty could indeed do this, you would be fully the equal of Yao and Shun!"

King Kuai convened a grand assembly of his ministers and announced that Crown Prince Ping was stripped of his title because he was proposing to abdicate in order to allow Prince Zhi to ascend the throne. The prince pretended to demur, but after refusing a couple of times, he finally agreed to accept. He presided over a sacrifice to Heaven and Earth, after which he put on royal robes and crown and took the scepter in his hands, sitting facing south as befitted a monarch. He did not show the slightest sign of embarrassment or shame. The ex-king Kuai faced north and took his place among the ministers; after the ceremony, he left to take up residence in a traveling palace. Su Dai and Lu Maoshou were both appointed senior ministers. General Shi Bei was not at all happy at this development and led his own troops to attack Prince Zhi. Many ordinary people inscribed themselves under his banner. The two sides fought for more than ten days with casualties of tens of thousands of men. In the end, Shi Bei's attack collapsed and he was killed by Prince Zhi. Lu Maoshou told His Royal Highness: "The reason why Shi Bei rebelled is because the ex–crown prince Ping is still alive." The prince wanted to kill Prince Ping, but he fled in plain clothes with Grand Tutor Guo Huai to Mount Wuzhong for safety. Prince Ping's younger half-brother, Prince Te, fled to the kingdom of Han. The people of the capital were in uproar over this.

• • •

When King Min of Qi heard that Yan had become engulfed in civil war, he appointed Kuang Zhang as the senior general and gave him command of one hundred thousand soldiers, with instructions to cross the Gulf of Bohai. The people of Yan loathed Prince Zhi down to the very marrow of their bones, and so they welcomed the Qi army with food and drink—there was not a single person willing to take up arms and fight on his behalf. Fifty days after Kuang Zhang and his army set out, they arrived at the Yan capital. There the people opened the gates and allowed them into the city.

When Prince Zhi's faction heard that the Qi army had arrived in force, marching directly on the city, they all panicked and started to flee. Prince Zhi was very proud of his own prowess, so he and Lu Maoshou marched his army out to fight at Daqu. His officers and men gradually deserted him, and Lu Maoshou was killed in battle. In spite of the fact that Prince Zhi received severe injuries, he was still able to kill more than a hundred enemy soldiers before his strength gave out and he was taken prisoner. The former King Kuai hanged himself in his traveling palace, and Su Dai fled to Zhou. Kuang Zhang destroyed the ancestral temples of the Yan royal family, packed up all the treasures he found in their storehouses, and retreated back to Linzi together with Prince Zhi, whom he kept in a prison cart.

Of the more than three thousand *li* of land in the kingdom of Yan, half was appropriated by Qi. Kuang Zhang left a garrison in the Yan capital while he himself went on a tour of inspection of nearby areas. This happened in the first year of the reign of King Nan of Zhou. King

Min of Qi personally recited the list of Prince Zhi's crimes to him and sentenced him to death. His flesh was pickled and distributed among the various ministers.

Prince Zhi ruled as king for little more than a year before his greed and arrogance got him killed. Is that not stupid?

A historian wrote a poem:

Ever since antiquity abdications have been rare,
Why should King Kuai suddenly adopt this practice?
The country was thrown into chaos and Qi invaded,
So ever since people have mocked Prince Zhi.

Although the people of Yan hated Prince Zhi, when they realized that the king of Qi intended to destroy their kingdom they were very unhappy about it. They put in great efforts to locate the former crown prince Ping, who was discovered living at Mount Wuzhong. He was now crowned as their new monarch and took the title of King Zhao. Guo Huai became prime minister. Since King Wuling of Zhao did not want to see Qi take over Yan entirely, he sent the commander-in-chief Le Chi to find Prince Te, who was at that point residing in the kingdom of Han. It was his intention to make this prince the new king of Yan. However, when he heard that Crown Prince Ping had already been established, he gave up on this idea. Guo Huai had placards circulated in the capital announcing the restoration of the monarchy. In an instant, the counties that had surrendered to Qi all threw out their new masters and returned to Yan. Since Kuang Zhang could do nothing to prevent this, he stood down his army and returned to Qi.

King Zhao now took up residence in the Yan capital, reconstructing the ancestral shrines. He was determined to take revenge for what Qi had inflicted upon them. To this end, he humbled himself and gave generous rewards to recruit clever men into his service. He announced to the prime minister, Guo Huai: "I remember the humiliation suffered by our former kings day and night. If I had brilliant men in my administration, I might find someone who could help me in my plans to deal with Qi. I would be willing to do whatever is necessary to bring this about. Please help me to find someone suitable."

"In olden times, there was a ruler who gave his servant one thousand pieces of gold and told him to get him a horse that could run a thousand *li* a day," Guo Huai said. "On the road, he came across a dead horse with people standing around it in a circle, sighing. The servant asked the reason, and they said, 'When this horse was alive, it could run a thousand *li* a day. But it is dead, and that is why we are sad.' The serv-ant bought the bones for five hundred pieces of gold, packed them into a sack, and carried them home on his back. The lord was absolutely furious and shouted: 'What do you want these bones for? How much money did you waste on this?' The servant said: 'The reason why I spent five hundred pieces of gold on this is that these are the bones of a horse that could gallop a thousand *li* a day. People are going to be amazed and gossip about it. The following point is sure to strike them: if a dead horse is worth that much, how much more will they pay for a live one? The horses that you want will be turning up any moment now.' As a result, the ruler was able to get his hands on three of these remarkable animals. If you want to recruit knights into your service from abroad, you had better treat me like the horse's bones. Men who are cleverer than I am are sure to want to come and join you!"

King Zhao constructed a palace especially for Guo Huai to reside in; he treated him with the same ceremony as a close family member; and he would face north when listening to his advice. The two men would eat and drink together, and, at all times, His Majesty behaved with the utmost decorum and respect. He constructed a high tower overlooking the Yi River and gold was collected in the room at the top, which was to be disbursed among the knights who came from other countries to enter his service.

Some people called this the Summoning Wise Men Tower, while to others it was the Golden Tower.

The news that the king of Yan was recruiting men spread far and wide. Ju Xin came from Zhao, Su Dai came from Zhou, Zou Yan came from Qi, and Qu Jing came from Wey. King Zhao gave them all office as ministers without portfolio and employed them in planning govern-ment policy.

During the Yuan dynasty, Liu Yin wrote "A Poem on the Golden Tower":

> The mountains of Yan are as green as in olden times,
> The Yi River still sings its song.
> Who would have imagined that one little tower
> Would be hymned through ages long?
> The inferior men of modern times
> Still love the magic word "gold."
> What is this thing called "gold,"
> That has been so valued since ancient times?
> As the sun gradually rises in the east,
> Two old men slowly totter west.

If you care about your people and recruit clever men,
You will be a great king one day!

. . .

Let us now turn to another part of the story. King Min of Qi's victory over Yan, in which he succeeded in killing both King Kuai and Prince Zhi, resulted in his striking awe into the entire world. This did not please King Huiwen of Qin one little bit. At this time King Huai of Chu was the leader of the Vertical Alliance and had a strong relationship with the kingdom of Qi, their correspondence guaranteed by a tally. The king of Qin was determined to break the association between Chu and Qi. To this end, he summoned Zhang Yi and requested him to think up a plan. Zhang Yi presented his opinion: "I have a fine tongue in my head, and I think I will go south to Chu and wait for the right moment to talk to His Majesty. I am sure that I can persuade the king of Chu to break off his alliance with Qi and make a new treaty with Qin."

"Do as you think best," King Huiwen told him.

Zhang Yi then resigned his position as prime minister and traveled to Chu. He was well aware that King Huai had a favorite minister called Jin Shang. He was a member of His Majesty's entourage, and the king always did what he said. He gave lavish bribes to establish a good relationship with Jin Shang and afterwards requested an audience with King Huai. His Majesty had already heard much of Zhang Yi, so he courteously welcomed him outside the suburbs and permitted him to be seated in his presence. He asked: "Since you have come to visit my humble home, sir, do you have any advice for me?"

"I am here to make peace between Qin and Chu!" Zhang Yi said.

"I would be perfectly happy to see my country allied with Qin," King Huai of Chu returned. "However, Qin invades us constantly, and this has prevented me from seeking any agreement with them."

"Although there are seven countries in the world at the moment, Chu, Qi, and Qin are the most powerful," Zhang Yi responded. "If Qin makes an alliance with Qi to the east, Qi is the most important. If Qin makes an alliance with Chu to the south, Chu is the most significant. However, His Majesty currently seems to be more interested in Chu than in Qi. Why is this? In spite of the fact that a marriage alliance exists between these two countries, Qi has seriously betrayed Qin. His Majesty would like to help you here, just as I would be happy to serve as the lowest of your gatekeepers. However, it is your long-standing agreement with Qi that stands in the way. If you would be prepared to close your borders and break off your alliance with them, the king of Qin will return to you the six hundred *li* of land in Shangyu conquered by Shang Yang, which will henceforth be governed by Chu as before. He will also give you a Qin princess as your wife. With Qin and Chu as allies, our royal houses intermarried, we can stand united against the other lords. The final decision rests with Your Majesty!"

King Huai of Chu was delighted and said: "If Qin would be willing to return the lands they have captured from us in the past, why should I stick to the alliance with Qi?"

His ministers all congratulated His Majesty on the return of the land. However, one person presented a contrary opinion: "You must not do this! Your Majesty, say no! In my opinion, this is more a matter for condolence than it is for congratulation!"

King Huai of Chu looked at the speaker; it was the minister without portfolio Chen Zhen. "I am going to get back six hundred *li* of land without losing the life of even a single soldier," the king said. "All the other ministers are congratulating me, but you tell me that it is a matter for condolences. Why is this?"

"Do you think that Zhang Yi is to be trusted?" Chen Zhen asked.

King Huai laughed and asked, "Why not?"

"The only reason that Qin shows us any respect at all is because of our alliance with Qi," Chen Zhen said. "If we now break off that alliance, Chu will be isolated. Why should Qin show any respect to an isolated country? Why should they give us six hundred *li* of land? This is all a trick by Zhang Yi. If you break off the alliance with Qi and Zhang Yi betrays you, refusing to give you the land, Qi will still be furious with you, and that will take them closer to Qin's camp. If Qi and Qin were to unite in an attack on Chu, we would be in very serious trouble! That is the reason why I said this is a matter for condolences. Why do you not send an ambassador to follow Zhang Yi back to Qin, Your Majesty, and collect the land from them? Once the land is ours, you can still break off the treaty with Qi if you like."

Grandee Qu Yuan came forward and said: "Chen Zhen is right. Zhang Yi is a crooked little bastard and you should not trust him!"

Jin Shang, His Majesty's favorite minister, said: "If the alliance with Qi is not ended, why should Qin give us the land?"

King Huai nodded his head and said: "Zhang Yi would not let me down. Shut your mouth, Chen Zhen! Your job is to stand back and watch while I collect the land."

He bestowed the seals of the prime minister on Zhang Yi, together with a gift of one hundred ingots of gold and ten teams of blood-horses. He gave orders that the guards at the North Gate should refuse entry to ambassadors arriving from Qi, and commanded Pang Houchou to follow Zhang Yi back to Qin to collect the land.

The whole way back, Zhang Yi and Pang Houchou were chatting, eating, and drinking to their hearts' content. The two men got along really well together. When they got close to Xianyang, Zhang Yi pretended to be drunk and slipped and fell from the chariot. His servants rushed forward to assist him back to his feet.

"I have hurt my ankle," Zhang Yi screamed. "I need a doctor right now!"

He got into an upholstered carriage and had himself conveyed into the city, where he reported to the king of Qin what had happened. Pang Houchou was left behind in a guesthouse. Zhang Yi shut his doors and announced that he was not going to go to court until he had recovered; Pang Houchou could not have an audience with His Majesty without him, so he was reduced to waiting for Zhang Yi, who dragged the whole thing out by saying that he was still not better. When things had gone on like this for three months, Pang Houchou wrote a letter to the king of Qin explaining that Zhang Yi had promised to give him the land. King Huiwen returned the following reply:

> If Zhang Yi has made this promise, I will honor it. However, I have been informed that the alliance between Qi and Chu has not yet been broken off. I am afraid that this may all be a ruse on your part to cause trouble. Until Zhang Yi recovers and reports in person, I am not in a position to believe your assertions.

Pang Houchou went back to Zhang Yi's house, but he still did not appear. He decided to forward the king of Qin's letter to King Huai by a trusted messenger.

"From the looks of things," His Majesty said, "the only problem is that we have not made our break with Qi clear enough!"

He sent the knight Song Yi to request permission from the state of Song to allow passage through their territory. With the necessary tallies he made it all the way to the Qi border, where he shouted insults at King Min. The king of Qi was extremely angered by this and sent a messenger west to Qin to propose a joint attack upon the kingdom of Chu. When Zhang Yi heard the news of the arrival of the envoy from Qi, he knew that his plan had worked. He announced that he had recovered from his accident and returned to court. When he bumped into Pang Houchou at the gates of the palace, he pretended to be surprised and said, "What are you doing here? Why haven't you collected the land, General?"

"The king of Qin has been waiting until he can talk to you to make the final announcement," Pang Houchou explained. "Now that you have fully recovered, Prime Minister, please go and speak to His Majesty to decide precisely where the border will run. Then I can go back home to report to the king."

"Why do we need to bother His Majesty?" Zhang Yi asked. "I have been talking about six *li* of land adjoining my own estates; I am happy to make those over to the king of Chu myself."

"When His Majesty ordered me to go with you," Pang Houchou said, "he spoke of six hundred *li* of land in Shangyu. It was definitely much more than just six *li*."

"His Majesty must be deaf," Zhang Yi laughed. "These are lands that Qin conquered after many battles; how could we just hand them over to someone else? Besides this is six hundred *li* of land!"

Pang Houchou returned to report this conversation to King Huai. The king of Chu was furious. He shouted: "Zhang Yi is indeed a right crooked little bastard! If I catch up with him, I am going to skin him alive!" He gave orders to raise an army to attack Qin.

The minister without portfolio Chen Zhen stepped forward and said: "Can I open my mouth now?"

"I should have listened to your advice," the king said. "I would never have fallen into that bastard's trap! Do you have a plan, sir, to deal with this?"

"You have already lost the support of Qi, Your Majesty, and you are proposing an attack on Qin that may not succeed," Chen Zheng replied. "Why don't you give two cities as a bribe to Qin and launch a joint attack on Qi with them? You may have lost land to Qin, but you can recoup it with your gains in Qi."

"Qin is the villain here," King Huai said. "What has Qi done? If I join forces with them and attack Qi, people will laugh at me!"

He immediately appointed Qu Gai as commander-in-chief and ordered Pang Houchou to assist him. They were given command of one hundred thousand troops. They advanced northwest past Mount Tianzhu, making a surprise attack on Lantian. The king of Qin appointed Wei Zhang as commander-in-chief and Gao Mao as his deputy. They raised an army of one hundred thousand men. Their orders were to resist this invasion, while asking for reinforcements from Qi. The Qi general, Kuang Zhang, was put in charge of these troops. Even though Qu Gai was very brave, he could not resist the onslaught of two armies in a pincer movement. He was defeated in one engagement after another. The Qin and Qi armies harried him as far as Danyang, where Qu Gai gathered up the scattered remnants of his battered forces and did battle again. Gan Mao succeeded in cutting his head off. The Chu casualties in this campaign numbered more than eighty thousand men, with more than seventy famous generals—including Pang Houchou—being killed. They captured six hundred *li* of land in Hanzhong. These events shook the kingdom of Chu to its very foundations.

When Han and Wei heard of this defeat, they too began to plot surprise attacks on Chu. King Huai of Chu was terrified. He sent Qu Yuan as an ambassador to Qi with orders to apologize. At the same time, he sent Chen Zhen to the Qin army with a present of two cities to beg for a peace treaty. Wei Zhang sent someone to request instructions from the king of Qin. "I would be happy to exchange Qianzhong for the lands of Shangyu," King Huiwen said. "If His Majesty agrees, I will stand down my troops."

Wei Zhang arranged to have the king of Qin's message conveyed to King Huai.

"I don't want the land," His Majesty replied. "Give me Zhang Yi and I will be happy! If you would be willing to hand over Zhang Yi, I will simply give you the territory of Qianzhong!"

Do you know if the king of Qin was prepared to let Zhang Yi go to Chu? READ ON.

Chapter Ninety-two

In a bronze ding-lifting competition, King
Wu of Qin breaks his leg.

In rushing to a meeting, King Huai of Chu
falls into Qin's trap.

King Huai of Chu was so enraged at Zhang Yi's trickery that he announced he would be willing to exchange the lands of Qianzhong for him. There were many among the king of Qin's entourage who were jealous of Zhang Yi, and they all said: "You will get several hundred *li* of land merely for handing over a single individual—what could be better than that?"

"Zhang Yi is the cornerstone of my administration," King Huiwen of Qin replied. "I would rather not have the land than be forced to give him up!"

Zhang Yi himself said: "I want to go!"

"But the king of Chu hates you down to the very marrow of his bones. If you go he will certainly kill you! That is why I cannot bear to send you."

Zhang Yi presented his opinion: "If by my death you obtain the lands of Qianzhong for Qin, it is worth it! Besides which, I am not convinced this will necessarily result in my death."

"Do you have some plan to escape?" the king asked. "Please tell me."

"The queen of Chu, Zheng Xiu, is a beautiful and extremely intelligent woman," Zhang Yi said thoughtfully. "She has been much favored by His Majesty. When I was in Chu before, I heard that the king had recently acquired a new beauty. Zheng Xiu told this woman: 'The king of Chu dislikes feeling of other people's breath upon him. When you are in his presence, you must cover your nose.' The concubine believed every word of this. The king of Chu asked Zheng Xiu, 'My concubine covers her nose immediately every time she sees me, why is this?' Zheng You replied: 'She finds your body odor disgusting.' The king of Chu was furious and gave orders that the beauty should have her nose lopped off. Afterwards, the queen monopolized favor again. His Majesty also has a favorite minister, Jin Shang, who is in cahoots with Zheng Xiu; between the two of them, they dominate the administration. I am a good friend of Jin Shang, and I think that he can protect me—at the very least, I should be able to escape with my life. If Your Majesty would order Wei Zhang to keep his troops stationed in Hanzhong, so he can advance if required, Chu will certainly not dare to kill me."

The king of Qin sent Zhang Yi on his way.

. . .

When Zhang Yi arrived in the kingdom of Chu, King Hai immediately ordered that he be arrested and thrown into prison. He selected a day to make a report to the ancestral temple, after which he would be executed. Zhang Yi secretly sent someone to explain the situation to Jin Shang, who went to speak to Zheng Xiu: "You will not retain His Majesty's favor for much longer. What will you do then?"

"What are you talking about?"

"Qin did not realize how angry the king of Chu was with Zhang Yi, and that is why they sent him here," Jin Shang explained. "Now I have been informed that the king of Chu wants to execute him. However, in order to ransom Zhang Yi, Qin is going to return the lands that they have captured from Chu and their king will marry his own daughter to His Majesty. She will arrive with a train of beautiful junior wives and female musicians. Once the Qin princess arrives, His Majesty will be sure to respect her and treat her with great ceremony. Once that happens, do you think you will be able to monopolize his favors as you have so far?"

Zheng Xiu was horrified and said: "Do you have a plan to prevent this?"

"If you would talk to His Majesty about where his best interests lie, as a disinterested party, you might be able to get him to return Zhang Yi to Qin," Jin Sheng said. "Then we should be able to put a stop to all of this."

In the middle of the night, Zheng Xiu cried all over King Huai of Chu as she said, "You wanted to exchange some land for Zhang Yi;

however, he has arrived before the transfer was made. This shows how much Qin respects you. The Qin army has been mobilized and stationed in Hanzhong—they could easily conquer us. If you were to enrage them by executing Zhang Yi, they will send their troops to attack us. I feel as though my heart has been pierced with thorns when I think of how much danger you will be in . . . I have not been able to eat or sleep for many days now. Besides which, every man has the right to work for his own master. Zhang Yi is a man of remarkable ability and he has been prime minister of Qin for many years now. Can you really blame him for working in Qin's best interests? If you were to treat Zhang Yi with generosity, he would be as beholden to Chu as he is to Qin."

"Do not worry," King Huai reassured her. "I will be thinking about the long-term situation when I make my decision."

Jin Shang again took advantage of a private moment to say: "What damage will Qin suffer if we kill Zhang Yi? However, we will lose a couple of hundred *li* of territory in Qianzhong. Why don't you keep Zhang Yi to hand, that you may make a peace treaty with Qin?"

King Huai was regretting the lands of Qianzhong that he did not want to have to hand over to Qin, so he let Zhang Yi out of prison and treated him with lavish ceremony. Yi then spoke of the benefits that would accrue to King Huai if he entered an alliance with Qin. King Huai sent Zhang Yi back to Qin with a peace treaty between the two countries. When Qu Ping returned from his embassy to Qi, he heard that Zhang Yi had already left and remonstrated as follows: "In the past you were tricked by Zhang Yi, and when he came here, I imagined that you were going to have him cooked and eaten. Instead you have pardoned him. Furthermore, you have followed his duplicitous advice and agreed to a peace treaty with Qin. An ordinary man never forgets his enemy, but what have you done? Without any special concessions from the kingdom of Qi, you have laid yourself open to general contempt. This is a very bad idea."

King Huai regretted his decision and sent someone in a fast chariot to pursue Zhang Yi, but he had left the city two days earlier under cover of darkness. When Zhang Yi returned to Qin, Wei Zhang stood down his army and went home.

A historian wrote a poem:

Zhang Yi could turn a disaster into a triumph for Qin,
In the morning a prisoner, by evening an honored guest.
It is laughable to think of how he pulled King Huai of Chu's strings;
His Majesty refused loyal advice and listened to flatterers instead.

Zhang Yi said to the king of Qin: "I risked near-certain death, and yet I am able to see Your Majesty again. The king of Chu is indeed very frightened of Qin. However, you must not let me break faith with them. You must give them half of the Hanzhong region and conclude a marriage alliance to confirm the peace treaty with Chu. I will use this to persuade the other six nations into doing Qin's bidding."

The king of Qin agreed to his plan. He partitioned off five counties in Hanzhong and gave them to Chu in accordance with the terms of their treaty. He accepted King Huai's daughter as the wife of Crown Prince Tang, while a princess of Qin was married off to King Huai of Chu's youngest son, Prince Lan. King Huai was delighted by these developments and decided that Zhang Yi had done very well by Chu. Mindful of all that Zhang Yi had achieved, the king of Qin enfeoffed him with five towns, granting him the title of Lord of Wuxin. Armed with gold and jade, riding a fine chariot drawn by a team of four horses, Zhang Yi set off on a round of diplomatic visits to persuade other rulers to join the Horizontal Alliance.

Zhang Yi had an audience with King Min of Qi, at which he said: "Your Majesty! Would you say you have more land than Qin? Or that your soldiers are better than theirs? When you joined the Vertical Alliance, you were persuaded by men telling you that Qi is located far from Qin and therefore it could not hurt you. You have been misled by a specious argument, which has blinded you to coming disaster. Qin and Chu have now concluded a marriage alliance that establishes peace between them; this has resulted in the Three Jins being terrified into presenting Qin with land and seeking to serve them. You are now Qin's only remaining enemy. If they attack your southern border through either Han or Wei, or supposing that the entire Zhao army crosses the Yellow River and pushes forward to Linzi or Jimo; if you then seek an alliance with Qin, will you be in time? Your safest policy right now is to join an alliance with Qin. Resisting them is too dangerous!"

"For the sake of the country," King Min of Qi said, "I will have to follow your advice, sir." He rewarded Zhang Yi generously.

From there, Zhang Yi went west to speak to the king of Zhao: "His Majesty the king of Qin has a few weak troops at his disposal and is proposing to fight at the foot of the walls of Handan. He sent me on ahead to see what is going on here. You are relying on the Vertical Alliance to protect you. However, Su Qin betrayed Yan and fled to Qi, resulting in his execution. He could not save himself and yet people still trust him; this is wrong! Qin and Chu are now joined by marriage, Qi has presented the lands of Wuyan, Han and Wei refer to themselves as the guardians of His Majesty's eastern border: these five countries are united! Do you really believe that you can fight five countries on your own? You will be crushed! In my opinion, your best interests would be served by throwing in your lot with Qin."

The king of Zhao agreed.

Now Zhang Yi turned north and traveled to Yan, where he persuaded King Zhao of Yan: "Your Majesty's closest ally is the kingdom of Zhao. In the past Lord Xiang of Zhao gave his older sister in marriage to the king of Dai, but when he wanted to annex these lands, he simply arranged for a friendly meeting with the king and ordered his guards to act as a military escort. At the banquet, when the servants were presenting the soup, his guards turned their weapons on the king of Dai, killing him with a spear thrust through the chest. They followed this with a surprise attack in which they captured Dai. When his sister heard this, she wept and screamed before committing suicide by stabbing herself to death with her hairpin. Even today, people call the place where she is buried Hairpin Hill. If he is prepared to torment his own sister in the pursuit of profit, what do you think he will do to others? The king of Zhao has already presented land to Qin in apology, and he will shortly go to pay court to their king at Shengchi. If one day the Qin army were to strike through Zhao and attack Yan, the northern defensive walls and the Yi River would not remain in Your Majesty's possession!"

King Zhao of Yan was thoroughly frightened and decided to present five cities east of Mount Heng in order to make peace with Qin.

Zhang Yi returned to Qin to report that he had succeeded in constructing the Horizontal Alliance. Before he even arrived in Xianyang, King Huiwen of Qin got sick and died. Crown Prince Tang succeeded to the throne, taking the title of King Wu.

• • •

When King Min of Qi first listened to Zhang Yi's persuasion, he was under the impression that the Three Jins had already given land to Qin so that they could join the alliance: that is why he did not dare to stand alone. When he discovered that after speaking to him, Zhang Yi set off for Zhao, he realized that he had been tricked and was absolutely furious. When he subsequently heard that King Huiwen of Qin had died, he sent the Lord of Mengchang with suitable diplomatic credentials to all the various courts, seeking to restore the Vertical Alliance in opposition to Qin. Since he suspected that Chu had indeed entered a marriage alliance with Qin, he was afraid that they would not agree, so he decided to attack them. King Huai of Chu sent Crown Prince Heng as a hostage to Qi, whereupon the invasion was called off. King Min declared himself "Head of the Vertical Alliance," and he declared to his fellow rulers that if any one of them was able to lay hands on Zhang Yi, he would reward them with ten cities.

. . .

King Wu of Qin's nature was coarse and direct; right from the time that he was still crown prince, he had always loathed Zhang Yi's trickery. There were many ministers who were jealous of the favor shown to Zhang Yi, and they all slandered him with accusations of various crimes. Zhang Yi was afraid that disaster would overtake him, so he went to court and said to King Wu: "I have a plan that I would like to present to you."

"What plan?" King Wu asked.

"I am told that the king of Qi hates me to such an inordinate degree that he will raise an army and attack any country that I reside in," Zhang Yi explained. "I would like to resign my post, Your Majesty, and move east to Daliang. Qi will then be certain to attack Daliang. While the armies of Qi and Wei are locked in conflict, you can take advantage of this opportunity to attack Han, crossing the three rivers and demonstrating your might to the Zhou royal house. Then you will be king indeed."

King Wu thought this was a good idea. He sent Zhang Yi to Daliang with an escort of thirty chariots. King Ai of Wei appointed him as prime minister, replacing Gongsun Yan. Gongsun Yan responded by leaving Wei and moving to Qin. When King Min of Qi heard that Zhang Yi had become prime minister in Wei, he was indeed absolutely furious and raised an army to attack them. King Ai of Wei was shocked and requested advice from Zhang Yi. Zhang Yi sent his majordomo, Feng Xi, disguised as a Chu person, to seek an audience with King Min and say: "I have heard that Your Majesty really hates Zhang Yi. Is this true?"

"It is," King Min said.

"If you do indeed hate Zhang Yi," Feng Xi said, "you had better not attack Wei. I have just been in Xianyang, and I am told that when Zhang Yi left Qin, he made an agreement with the king. He said: 'The king of Qi hates me and will attack any country in which I reside.' The king of Qin sent Zhang Yi to Wei with a military escort; he was hoping to provoke a war between your two countries. When the armies of Qi and Wei are locked in combat, Qin will take advantage of this opportunity to control matters in the north. If you attack Wei, you will simply be falling into Zhang Yi's trap. You had better not attack anyone, Your Majesty, thereby sowing the seeds of doubt in Qin's mind about Zhang Yi's veracity. As long as Zhang Yi stays in Wei, he will be powerless."

King Min stopped his army's attack on Wei. King Ai of Wei treated Zhang Yi with ever-increasing generosity. A few years after these events, Zhang Yi got sick and died in Wei.

A historian wrote a poem in praise of Zhang Yi:

> His studies over, he began his travels;
> As long as his tongue survived, he had no worries.
> In danger and humiliation,
> His ambitions drove him onward.
> As Su Qin established the Vertical Alliance,
> He persuaded everyone to join the Horizontal Alliance.
> He tricked everyone with a paper tiger,
> Terrifying all the other kings.
> Twisting and turning at every juncture,
> So that none could plumb his deep stratagems.
> He stayed rich and noble his entire life,
> A model for other persuaders!

That same year, Queen Wuyan of Qi also died.

. . .

It is said that King Wu of Qin was a very strong man, and he enjoyed competing with other knights. Wu Huo and Ren Bi had become generals of Qin in the previous reign, but King Wu favored them even more, increasing their salary and emoluments. There was also at this time a certain Meng Ben, styled Yue, who was famous for his strength—he could swim like a dragon and did not bother to get out of the way when tigers and wolves crossed his path. When angry he would bellow with rage, the sound reverberating through the skies. One time, he noticed two bulls fighting out in the wilds. Meng Ben pushed them apart with his bare hands. One bull fell to the ground, but the other was determined not to stop. Meng Ben got angry and, placing his left hand on the animal's head, with his right hand he grabbed one of its horns. When the horn came out, the bull died. People were so terrified of him that nobody dared to annoy him. When he heard that the king of Qin was summoning brave and strong knights from all over the world into his service, he crossed the Yellow River to the west. There were a great many people waiting on the bank of the river for their chance to sail;

normally, they would get on the boats in order. Meng Ben was the last to arrive, but he insisted on being the first onto the boat to cross the river. The boatman was angry at his bad manners and hit him on the head with an oar, saying, "How dare you behave like that? Who do you think you are: Meng Ben?" Meng Ben glared at him, his hair standing on end. He shouted out, causing a mini tidal wave. The people on the boat were so frightened that they fell over, tipping themselves into the river. Meng Ben grabbed the tiller and stamped his foot, whereupon the boat lurched forward a dozen feet. A short time later he had crossed to the far bank. When he arrived in Xianyang, he had an audience with King Wu. When the latter had tested his strength, he appointed him as a high official and he was as favored as Wu Huo or Ren Bi. This happened in the sixth year of the reign of King Nan of Zhou, which was the second year of the reign of King Wu of Qin.

Since all the other six kingdoms had the same title of prime minister, Qin decided to go one better by using a different nomenclature. For this reason they established the position of chancellor. Furthermore, two men held this office, the Left and the Right. His Majesty appointed Gan Mao as the Chancellor of the Left, and Chuli Ji became Chancellor of the Right. Wei Zhang was angry that he had not been appointed to the position of prime minister, so he fled to Daliang.

King Wu remembered what Zhang Yi had told him, and said to Chuli Ji: "I have lived my entire life among the Western Rong nomads, and I have never seen the glories of the Central Plain. If I could cross the three rivers and travel between Gong and Luo . . . even if I died, I would have no regrets! Which of the two of you can attack the kingdom of Han for me?"

"If you want to attack Han, Your Majesty, you need to capture Yiyang in order to open up the route past the three rivers," Chuli Ji explained. "Yiyang is located far from here, along a dangerous route—this is going to be expensive and challenging for our armies. It would be easy for Wei and Zhao to send troops to rescue them. I am afraid that it is impossible."

King Wu asked the same question of Gan Mao, who said: "Let me go as an ambassador to Wei and persuade them to join us in a joint attack on Zhao."

King Wu was delighted and sent Gan Mao to speak to the king of Wei, who agreed to assist Qin with their troops. Of the two chancellors, Gan Mao was superior to Chuli Ji, but he was afraid that the latter might yet put a spoke in his wheel. He sent one of the junior men on his mission, Xiang Shou, back to report to the king of Qin: "Wei has already agreed. Even so, I would urge Your Majesty not to attack Han."

King Wu was most surprised at these words and set off in person to meet him. When he arrived at Xirang, he ran into Gan Mao. "You promised me that you would go to Wei and make a treaty with them for a joint attack on Han," King Wu said. "Now the Wei people have already agreed to this, and yet you tell me not to attack Han. Why is this?"

"To cross one thousand *li* of dangerous mountain tracks and then attack one of Han's great cities is not something that one can undertake lightly," Gan Mao explained. "In the past a man named Zeng Can was living in Fei, and there was a man with an identical name who came from Lu who committed a murder. Someone ran to tell his mother: 'Zeng Can has killed someone!' His mother was weaving at the time and she replied: 'My son would not kill anyone.' Then she carried on weaving like before. A short time later someone else ran in and said: 'Zeng Can has committed murder!' His mother stopped her shuttle and thought for a moment, after which she said: 'My son would not do that kind of thing.' Again, she carried on weaving like before. A short time later, yet another person ran in and shouted: 'The killer is indeed Zeng Can!' This time his mother threw down her shuttle, and, getting down from the loom, she climbed over a wall and ran off to hide. Zeng Can was a good man and his mother knew it, but when three people told her that he had killed someone, even she began to believe it. Now, I am far from being as wise a man as Zeng Can, but I am also not sure that Your Majesty trusts me as much as Zeng Can's mother did her son. If some slandering official announced that I had killed someone, I am afraid that Your Majesty would throw down your shuttle long before three people had repeated it!"

"I am not going to listen to what anyone else says," King Wu assured him. "Let us swear a blood covenant!" The two of them smeared their mouths with blood and buried the text of their covenant at Xirang.

The king of Qin now issued fifty thousand troops, with Gan Mao in command as the senior general and Xiang Shou as his deputy. When the army arrived at Yiyang, they laid siege to the city for five months, but the officials defending it were so resolute, they could not capture it. The Chancellor of the Right, Chuli Ji, spoke to King Wu. "The Qin army is becoming exhausted. If you do not recall them, I am afraid it may result in a mutiny." King Wu ordered Gan Mao to stand down the army. Gan Mao wrote a letter to His Majesty, refusing to accept the order. When King Wu opened the letter, it contained just the word "Xirang." King

Wu realized immediately what he meant: "Gan Mao told me about this before. It is my mistake." He gave him another fifty thousand troops and sent Wu Huo to assist him.

The king of Han sent his senior general, Prince Ying, in command of an army to go and rescue Yiyang. A great battle was fought below the walls of the city. Wu Huo charged the Han army alone, wielding two great iron spears weighing one hundred and eighty pounds each. The Han soldiers in his way were all knocked to pieces, and nobody dared to attempt resistance. Gan Mao and Xiang Shou took advantage of this to advance their own forces. The Han army suffered a terrible defeat, losing more than seventy thousand men. Wu Huo leapt up onto the bastion and started destroying the battlements. As one of the battlements collapsed, Wu Huo fell in a hail of stones, breaking his legs badly. He died of this injury. The Qin army followed up his assault and took the city of Yiyang. The king of Han was petrified and sent his prime minister, Gongzhong Yi, armed with great treasure to try and make peace with Qin. King Wu was delighted and agreed. He ordered Gan Mao to stand down the army and left Xiang Shou behind to take control of Yiyang and the surrounding area. He ordered the Chancellor of the Right, Chuli Ji, to go on ahead and open the route through the three rivers, after which His Majesty set off himself with Ren Bi, Meng Ben, and his other knights, heading straight for Luoyang.

King Nan of Zhou sent an ambassador to greet him in the suburbs, announcing that he was prepared to personally conduct all the ceremonies due to an honored guest. King Wu of Qin thanked His Majesty but said that he would not dare to seek an audience with him; however, having been told that the nine *ding*-cauldrons were stored in the side chamber of the great ancestral shrine, he would like to go and inspect them. When he saw these vessels, they were lined up in a row: a truly magnificent sight!

The nine ding *-cauldrons were each minted from the finest metal of the nine regions of the country by the great King Yu, and the designs represented the mountains and rivers, people, and important products of that place. The feet and lugs of each* ding *were in the form of dragons, and hence they were also known as the "Nine Dragon Dings." From the Xia dynasty they had been handed down to the Shang, functioning as royal regalia. When King Wu of Zhou defeated the Shang dynasty, he moved these bronze vessels to Luoyang. At that time, he had his troops push and pull them, loading them onto barges and then carts, but from the weight you would have thought that they were moving nine small mountains—who knows how heavy they actually were!*

When King Wu inspected them, he sighed with admiration. Each *ding* was marked with the name of a different region: Jing, Liang, Yong, Yu, Xu, Yang, Qing, Yan, and Ji.

King Wu pointed to the *ding* marked "Yong" and said with a sigh, "That is the one for the Yong region. That is the Qin *ding*! I would like to take it home to Xianyang." He asked the official in charge of the care of the vessels, "Has anyone ever lifted it?"

The official kowtowed and answered: "This *ding* has never been moved since it first came here. I have heard the story that each of these bronzes weighs one thousand pounds: can any mortal man lift such a weight?"

King Wu asked Ren Bi and Meng Ben: "You are both very strong; do you think you can lift this *ding*?"

Ren Bi knew that King Wu was very proud of his own strength and also liked to win. He declined. "I can lift a hundred pounds, but this vessel is ten times heavier. I cannot possibly do it!"

Meng Ben came forward, waving his arms. "I will have a go. But if it turns out I can't lift it, you mustn't punish me!"

He ordered the servants to make an enormous silk rope, which he threaded through the lugs on the *ding*. He tightened his belt and rolled up his sleeves. He picked up the rope with two arms like steel cables and bellowed: "Lift!" The *ding* did indeed rise about half a foot before sinking back to the ground. He used so much force in this lift that his eyes were practically starting from his head and they became completely bloodshot.

King Wu smiled and said, "That was a great effort. However, if you can lift this bronze vessel, I can certainly do so too!"

"Your Majesty is the ruler of a country with ten thousand chariots," Ren Bi remonstrated. "How can you possibly compete like this?"

King Wu did not listen to him. He immediately removed his brocade robe and jade belt, tying a sash around his waist and using a string to tie back his sleeves. Ren Bi remonstrated sternly against His Majesty's decision.

"Since you couldn't do it yourself," King Wu said teasingly, "are you jealous of me?"

Ren Bi did not dare to say another word. King Wu strode forward and took hold of the silk rope with both hands. He thought to himself, "Meng Ben just lifted this *ding*. If I lift it and walk a couple of steps, I will have definitely beaten him." He summoned all the strength at his disposal and, breathing out in a rush, he shouted: "Lift!" The bronze vessel did indeed lift about half a foot above the ground, but as he shifted, he lost his grip. The *ding* crashed to the ground, falling right on His Majesty's right foot. There was a horrible crunch as his leg broke. "Aaahh!" King Wu screamed, as he fainted away on the spot. His entourage carried him back to the guesthouse as quickly as they could. Blood soaked through the bed and the pain was unbearable. During the night, His Majesty died.

King Wu had said: "If I can travel around Gong and Luoyang, even if it kills me, I would have no regrets!" This day he did indeed die in Luoyang—were his words perhaps a curse?

When King Nan of Zhou heard about these dreadful events, he was deeply shocked. He rushed to prepare a fine coffin and personally attended the ceremony that saw the king of Qin placed within it. He performed all the ceremonies of wailing and mourning. Chuli Ji escorted the coffin home. Since King Wu had no sons, he was succeeded by his younger half-brother, Prince Ji, who now became King Zhaoxiang. When Chuli Ji came to punish those involved in the *ding*-lifting competition, he executed Meng Ben and all his family. Since Ren Bi had tried to remonstrate with His Majesty, he was rewarded with the office of magistrate of Hanzhong. Chuli Ji also announced to the court: "This whole idea of crossing the three rivers was all Gan Mao's doing!" Since Gan Mao was afraid he might be executed, he fled into exile in Wei, where eventually he died.

A historian wrote a poem about King Wu of Qin:

> All of this martial might went for nothing,
> A *ding*-lifting competition is just stupid.
> Having crushed his leg, the king of Qin died,
> In a reckless crossing of the three rivers.

. . .

When King Zhaoxiang of Qin heard that Chu had sent a prince as a hostage to Qi, he suspected that they were planning to betray him. He appointed Chuli Ji as general and raised an army with which to attack Chu. The kingdom of Chu sent its general, Jing Yang, to join battle, but his troops were defeated and a massacre ensued. King Huai of Chu was terrified. King Zhaoxiang sent an ambassador with a letter to the king of Chu, which read as follows:

> We are long-standing allies united by marriage alliances. However, you have betrayed me and sent a hostage to Qi, which made me extremely angry. This is the reason why I have invaded your country, something I would otherwise

be loath to do. There are two great kingdoms in the world today: Chu and Qin. If we two are not in agreement, how can we expect other rulers to obey our commands? I would like to meet you at Wu Pass, that we may discuss the future of our alliance face-to-face. When we have sworn a blood covenant, we can all go back home. I will return the territory that I have conquered from Your Majesty and we will go back to the old friendly relations between our two countries. It is up to you to see that this happens. If you do not make an appearance, I will take it that you are determined to break off the agreement between us. In that case, I will not withdraw my troops!

When King Huai read this letter, he immediately summoned his ministers to discuss the matter. "I do not want to go, but I am afraid of provoking Qin's anger. If I do go, I am afraid that I will be bullied by Qin. What is the best option?"

Qu Yuan stepped forward and said: "Qin is a country of tigers and wolves. They have kicked us around many times. If you go, Your Majesty, you will not come back!"

The Grand Vizier, Zhao Sui, said: "These are loyal words indeed! Do not go, Your Majesty! You must send out your army to defend us, to prevent the advance of the Qin army."

"No," Jin Shang said. "Chu alone stands no chance of resisting Qin: our soldiers have been defeated, our generals killed, and our territory has gradually been nibbled away. Now they want to reaffirm the alliance between us. If you refuse, the king of Qin will be really furious and he will send yet more troops to attack Chu. What will we do then?"

King Huai of Chu's youngest son, Prince Lan, who had married a princess of the Qin royal house, thought that this marriage alliance could be relied upon. He strongly urged the king to go: "Qin and Chu have married their princesses to each other—no friendship could be closer than this! They have brought their army here, but they are still willing to consider a peace treaty—why else would they be encouraging Your Majesty to attend this meeting? Jin Shang is absolutely correct. You must listen to him, Your Majesty."

King Huai of Chu was frightened of Qin, given that his armies had so recently been defeated by them. However, he was put under such pressure by Jin Shang and Prince Lan that he felt he had no choice but to agree to the meeting with the king of Qin. He selected an auspicious day for the journey, and only Jin Shang would follow in his suite.

. . .

King Zhaoxiang of Qin sent his younger brother, the Lord of Jingyang, to go to the Wu Pass. He rode in the royal chariot with its pennants of feathers, with a full guard and all the accoutrements, pretending to be the king of Qin. He ordered General Bai Qi to take ten thousand men and lie in ambush inside the pass, with instructions to take the king of Chu prisoner. He sent General Meng Ao with a further ten thousand men to lie in ambush outside the pass, in case of some mischance. Furthermore, he ordered a series of ambassadors to go on ahead and welcome the king of Chu with fine words. This constant coming and going meant that King Huai of Chu's mind was completely put at rest, so he advanced straight up to the Wu Pass. He saw that the great gates had been flung open, and the Qin ambassador came forward to greet him: "The king of Qin has been waiting for Your Majesty inside the pass for three days. I would not dare to humiliate you by suggesting that you remain in this wild and lonely spot; please come to the guesthouse, where the proper ceremonies can be performed."

King Huai was already in Qin territory, so it was impossible for him to refuse. He followed the ambassador through the pass. Just as King Huai went through the gates, with a thunderous clang, they were pulled shut. His Majesty was suspicious and asked the ambassador: "Why have you been so quick to shut the gates?"

"This is the law of the kingdom of Qin," he explained. "In times of war, this is always done."

"Where is your king?"

"He is waiting with horse and chariot at the guesthouse up ahead." The ambassador shouted at the charioteers to whip up their horses.

When they had advanced about two *li*, they could see the king of Qin's honor guard in the distance, lined up in front of the entrance to the guesthouse. The ambassador gave orders to halt. A man came out of the guesthouse to greet them. King Huai could see that he was wearing a silk brocade gown and a jade belt, but his manner was quite different from that of the king of Qin. King Huai was now very nervous, and he refused to get down from the chariot.

The man bowed and said, "Do not be afraid, Your Majesty. I am not the king of Qin, but his younger brother, the Lord of Jingyang. Please come into the guesthouse and I will explain everything."

King Huai had no choice but to follow him into the building. The Lord of Jingyang and the king exchanged formal greetings, but just as he was about to sit down, he heard shouting outside. Ten thousand Qin soldiers had just surrounded the guesthouse.

"I am here in accordance with the king of Qin's invitation," King Huai screamed. "Why have you put me under guard?"

"We are not going to hurt you," the Lord of Jinyang replied. "His Majesty is unwell at present and cannot leave the palace. However, he was afraid of being seen to break faith with you, so he sent me to greet you. You are going to be coming with us to Xianyang, to see His Majesty there. These soldiers are your honor guard. Please do not refuse them."

The king of Chu had now completely lost control of the situation, and he was bundled onto a chariot. Meng Ao and his army stayed behind to guard the pass as the Lord of Jingyang climbed into the same chariot. With Bai Qi's soldiers pressed close on all sides, they turned westward in the direction of Xianyang. Jin Shang escaped and fled for his life back to the kingdom of Chu. King Huai sighed and said, "I regret not listening to Zhao Sui and Qu Yuan's advice—Jin Shang has gotten me into terrible trouble!" He cried without stopping.

Later on, someone wrote a poem:

Prince Lan was young and ignorant,
Jin Shang was an incompetent sycophant.
Trapped in the lair of tigers and wolves,
It was too late to remember loyal remonstrance.

When King Huai arrived in Xianyang, King Zhaoxiang of Qin held a great meeting for all his ministers and foreign ambassadors on top of the Zhao Tower. The king of Qin sat facing south, while the king of Chu was forced to sit facing north as if he were a subject. King Huai was furious at this insult and refused at the top of his voice: "I trusted in the marriage alliance between our two countries and so I agreed to humble myself, attending this meeting at your behest. Now you have pretended to be sick, Your Majesty, and tricked me into coming all the way to Xianyang. What do you mean by not treating me with proper respect?"

"In the past you promised to hand over the lands of Qianzhong and then failed to do so," King Zhaoxiang retorted. "Your sufferings today are entirely because you went back on that earlier agreement! If you agree to give me the land, I will send you home to Chu immediately."

"If all you wanted was the land, why didn't you ask for it?" King Huai demanded. "Why did you have to resort to all these little schemes?"

"If I didn't," King Zhaoxiang pointed out, "you wouldn't have come."

"I hereby agree to give you the lands of Qianzhong," the king of Chu said. "Let us swear a blood covenant to that effect. You can send a general back with me to take command of this territory. How would that be?"

"I don't believe in blood covenants," King Zhaoxiang replied. "You must first send an ambassador back to Chu, and the land must be clearly given into my possession. Then I will hold a banquet to send you back in style."

The ministers of the kingdom of Qin all came forward to encourage King Huai to agree. He was now even angrier and shouted: "You tricked me into coming here, and now you are trying to extort land from me. If I die, so be it. I will not accept blackmail!"

King Zhaoxiang kept King Huai prisoner within the city of Xianyang, not allowing him to go home.

As mentioned above, Jin Shang fled home and informed Zhao Sui what had happened: "The king of Qin wants to obtain the lands of Qianzhong from His Majesty, so he has imprisoned him."

"His Majesty is now held in Qin, and the crown prince is a hostage in Qi," Zhao Sui moaned. "If the people of Qi are in league with Qin in this matter and they retain hold of the crown prince, we are going to be left leaderless!"

"Prince Lan is here," Jin Shang suggested. "Why don't we establish him as the new monarch?"

"The crown prince was appointed a long time ago," Zhao Sui reminded him. "Although His Majesty is now a prisoner in Qin, how could we ignore his express order and strip the crown prince of his title, appointing a younger son—born to a concubine to boot—in his place? If His Majesty is ever lucky enough to be able to return, how could we explain? I am going to write to Qi, requesting the return of the crown prince on some pretext. Hopefully Qi will believe it."

"I was not able to save His Majesty from danger," Jin Shang said. "Let me be entrusted with this mission that I may do something to help!"

Zhao Sui sent Jin Shang on an embassy to Qi, where he announced that His Majesty had died. The crown prince was required to come home and take charge of the funeral, to be crowned as the new king. King Min of Qi said to his prime minister, Tian Wen, the Lord of Mengchang: "The kingdom of Chu finds itself without a ruler. I want to keep the crown prince and force them to hand over the lands of Huaibei to obtain his release. What do you think?"

"You cannot do that," the Lord of Mengchang replied. "The king of Chu has many sons. If we had imprisoned the crown prince and they ransomed him with some land—that would be one thing. But in the current circumstances, if they simply establish another prince as the new king, we will get nothing and be criticized for behaving unjustly. What's the point of that?"

King Min thought that this was good advice and sent Crown Prince Heng home to Chu, attended with every ceremony.

Crown Prince Heng now ascended the throne, taking the title of King Qingxiang. Prince Lan and Jin Shang retained their old government positions. They sent a message to Qin: "Thanks to the beneficence of the state altars, the gods and the spirits, Chu has a king again!" The king of Qin now realized that his capture of King Huai was pointless; he had gained not even a foot of land. In his anger and humiliation, he appointed Bai Qi as general and Meng Ao as his deputy and sent them to attack Chu with a force of one hundred thousand men. They captured fifteen cities before returning home.

As time went by, the guards appointed by Qin to keep King Huai of Chu in custody became more and more lax. King Huai disguised himself and fled from Xianyang, hoping to be able to make his way eastward, back to the kingdom of Chu. The king of Qin sent soldiers after him. King Huai did not dare proceed, so he changed direction, heading for Zhao to the north.

If you do not know whether the kingdom of Zhao was willing to help King Huai return home, READ ON.

Chapter Ninety-three

*The Royal Father of Zhao starves to death at
the Shaqiu Palace.*

*The Lord of Mengchang sneaks through the
Hangu Pass.*

King Wuling of Zhao was a man of great height and a broad chest to
match, with a face like a dragon and a sharp mouth. His square jaw was
covered by a thick and curling beard, and his skin was dark. He was
highly bellicose, and it was his ambition to unite the lands within the
four seas. Five years after he came to the throne, he married a princess
from the kingdom of Han as his queen. Their son, Prince Zhang, was
installed as crown prince. When he had been sixteen years in power, he
dreamed one night of a beautiful woman playing a *qin*, and he became
desperate to see her like again. The following day, he told his ministers
of this. Grandee Hu Guang happened to mention that his daughter,
Mengyao, was a very fine *qin* player, so His Majesty summoned her to
the Daling Tower. She looked just like the woman he had seen in his
dream. When she played the *qin*, he was utterly delighted. He had her
brought to his palace and renamed her Wuwa. She gave birth to a son:
Prince He. After Queen Han died, he installed Wuwa as the new queen
and deposed Zhang, making Prince He the crown prince.

King Wuling was very conscious of the position of Zhao, with the
kingdom of Yan on their northern border, the Hu nomads to the east,
and Linhu and Loufan to the west as his neighbors. Furthermore, Qin
was just over on the other side of the Yellow River. Given that they were
faced with hostile neighbors on all four sides, he was afraid that their
position would weaken over time, so he took up wearing nomadic clothing, with narrow sleeves and the fastening on the left, not to mention

their leather belts and fur boots. This was done to make it easier to ride and shoot. Everyone in the country, from aristocrats down to peasants, took up wearing Hu garb.

His Majesty also got rid of his chariots and went everywhere on horseback, taking his troops out hunting every day until their skills improved markedly. King Wuling of Zhao led his army to Mount Chang to survey the terrain; there was a vast plain from Yunzhong in the west to Yanmen in the north, stretching several hundred *li*. Since it was his ambition to conquer Qin, he was hoping to be able to take his army through Yunzhong and then turn south at Jiuyuan, making a surprise attack on Xianyang. However, he did not dare entrust such a task to his generals, so he left his son behind to govern the country and took command himself. This being the case, he had his ministers attend a grand ceremony at the East Palace at which he abdicated in favor of Crown Prince He, who became King Hui. King Wuling now took the title of Royal Father.

The title of Royal Father is similar to that used by abdicated emperors in later times.

Fei Yi was appointed as prime minister, Li Dui became the Grand Tutor, and Prince Cheng became the marshal. He enfeoffed his older son, Prince Zhang, with the lands of Anyang; henceforward he was known as the Lord of Anyang, and Tian Buli was his chancellor. This happened in the seventeenth year of the reign of King Nan of Zhou.

The Royal Father was determined to discover the lay of the land in Qin and investigate the personality of their king. To this end, he took over the name and identity of Zhao Shao, an ambassador from that kingdom. He took his credentials and went to report the enthronement of a new king to the kingdom of Qin. He took with him a number of cartographers in his train, whose job was to map the territory they passed through. When he arrived in Xianyang, he went to have an audience with the king of Qin.

"How old was your monarch?" King Zhaoxiang inquired.

"In the prime of life."

"If he was still in the prime of life, why did he abdicate the throne in favor of his son?"

"His Majesty was concerned that so many people, on inheriting such a title, find themselves unable to cope with the burden of office. He wanted to let his son take over when he was still there to help to train him. Even though His Majesty is known by the title 'Royal Father,' there are still many matters of state in which he takes the ultimate decision."

"Is your country afraid of Qin?" King Zhaoxiang asked.

"If His Majesty had not been afraid of Qin, he would not have taken up wearing Hu clothing or practicing horseback archery. Now he has ten times the number of mounted archers that he did before, so he can defend against Qin, or perhaps finally agree to a peace treaty with you."

When King Zhaoxiang saw how confidently the man replied, he was deeply impressed. The "ambassador" then said goodbye and returned to the official guesthouse.

King Zhaoxiang woke up in the middle of the night, thinking about the remarkable appearance and authority shown by this ambassador from Zhao—he really did not seem like anybody's subordinate. He found the whole thing so concerning that he tossed and turned for the rest of the night. At dawn, he asked someone to summon Zhao Shao for another audience. His servant said, "The ambassador is unwell and cannot possibly go to court right now. I hope that you will accept a slight delay." After three days, the ambassador still had not appeared. King Zhaoxiang was now furious and sent someone to fetch him. On entering the guesthouse, he did not see the ambassador and ended up arresting his servant. This person said that he was the real Zhao Shao, and he was brought before King Zhaoxiang.

"If you are Zhao Shao," His Majesty asked, "who was the ambassador that I met?"

"That was our king's father," he replied. "He wanted to see Your Majesty's awe-inspiring might for himself, so he pretended to be the ambassador. He left Xianyang three days ago. He ordered me to stay behind and take any punishment that you might care to mete out."

King Zhaoxiang was enraged by this. Stamping his foot, he shouted: "The Royal Father has tried me too far!"

He ordered the Lord of Jingyang and Bai Qi to take an army of three thousand crack troops and pursue him day and night. When they arrived at the Hangu Pass, the soldiers guarding it informed them: "The ambassador from the kingdom of Zhao left three days ago." Lord Jingyang and his company returned to report this to the king of Qin. His Majesty was tense and jumpy for many days. He did, however, send the real Zhao Shao home with every courtesy.

An old man wrote a poem:

Given that a vicious tiger lurked in Xianyang,
Who would want to spy out the land around the Hangu Pass?
In spite of the remarkable appearance of the Royal Father of Zhao,
Those present only had eyes for the king of Qin.

The following year, the Royal Father left Yunzhong on campaign, turning west once he reached Dai, collecting troops from Loufan. He built a city at Lingshou to guard Mount Zhong, which was named the King of Zhao's City. Queen Wuwa also built her own city at Feixiang, which was known as the Queen's City. At this time Zhao was by far the strongest of any of the Three Jins.

. . .

It was this year that King Huai of Chu escaped from captivity in Qin. King Hui of Zhao discussed the situation with his ministers, but they were frightened of causing trouble with Qin. The Royal Father was far away in the territory of Dai, and His Majesty did not dare to make such an important decision himself, so he shut the border and did not allow the king of Chu to enter. King Huai was at his wits' ends, but he decided to turn south and seek sanctuary in Wei. The Qin army chased after him and recaptured him, forcing him to return to Xianyang in the custody of the Lord of Jingyang. King Huai was so deeply angered by this that he vomited blood and collapsed. A short time later, he died. The kingdom of Qin returned his body to Chu for burial. The people of Chu were deeply upset by the way in which King Huai had been tormented by Qin, dying far from home. They flocked to see the cortege return home, weeping bitterly, as if they were mourning the death of a family member. The other aristocrats were appalled by how Qin had behaved in this matter, and so the Vertical Alliance was restored to defend against them.

Grandee Qu Yuan of Chu blamed King Huai's death on the mistakes made by Prince Lan and Jin Shang, in spite of which the two men were still in charge of government matters as before. The two of them seemed to be determined to maintain peace at any price. They clearly had no intention of taking revenge on Qin for what they had done. He offered remonstrance over and over again, encouraging King Qingxiang to employ clever men and keep vile flatterers at a distance, while selecting good generals to train the troops to expunge the shame of the humiliation inflicted on King Huai. Prince Lan realized what he was up to and sent Jin Shang to speak to King Qingxiang: "Qu Yuan is angry that he has not received a senior government appointment. Furthermore, he is going around telling everyone that you are unfilial, Your Majesty, in failing to take revenge upon the kingdom of Qin, while Prince Lan and the others are disloyal because they are refusing to attack."

King Qingxiang was furious and dismissed Qu Yuan from his position, ordering him to go home and plow the fields. Qu Yuan's older sister, Xu, had married into a family living some distance away, but when she heard that he had been dismissed, she visited him at their old home in Kui. On seeing Qu Yuan with his hair unbound and dirty, his whole face worn and aged, walking along the bank of the river reciting a poem, she tried to cheer him up by saying: "The king of Chu does not listen to you, but you have done your best! What is the point of worrying any more about it? Luckily, your lands have been left to you, so you can always support yourself on the produce of your own fields. Why should you not live out your days like that?"

Qu Yuan had a great deal of respect for his sister's opinion, so he took up the plow and began to cultivate his land. All the villagers were happy to help, out of respect for his great loyalty. About a month later, his sister left. Qu Yuan sighed and said: "The kingdom of Chu is indeed in a parlous condition. It is unbearable to think that my family may be ruined by this!" One day he got up early in the morning and threw himself into the Miluo River, clutching a stone. This occurred on the fifth day of the fifth month. When the local people heard that Qu Yuan had drowned himself, they rushed to their little boats and went out on the river to try and save him, but it was already too late. They threw little pyramids of rice wrapped up in a leaf and tied with colored string into the river as a sacrifice to him. This was done lest the body should be eaten by the water dragons.

The dragon-boat races arose to commemorate the attempts of the local people to rescue Qu Yuan. Nowadays, this is celebrated all the way from Chu to Wu. The lands plowed by Qu Yuan yielded rice whose grains were as white as jade, so they became known as the Jade Fields. The local people built a private shrine to the memory of Qu Yuan and renamed their village Sister's Return. Today in the department of Jingzhou, there is a county known as Gui or "Return," which takes its name from this village. In the Yuanfeng reign–era of the Song dynasty, Qu Yuan was given the title of Honored and Meritorious Duke and a temple was built to the memory of him and his sister. This was known as the Sister's Return Temple. Later on, Qu Yuan's title was increased, making him the Loyal and Meritorious King.

An old man wrote a poem titled "Verse on the Temple of the Loyal and Meritorious King":

This magnificent temple dominates the river bank on which it stands;
Incense has been burnt in perpetuity to the Loyal and Meritorious King.
The bones of vile flatterers are left to rot in unknown tombs,
As dragon boats ply the waves year after year in memory of Qu Yuan.

. . .

As mentioned above, at this time the Royal Father of Zhao was on a tour of Yunzhong. When he returned to Handan, he issued rewards to those who had done well in his service. He awarded the people of the capital wine and food for five days. That day, the ministers of state all assembled to offer their congratulations. The Royal Father ordered King Hui to hold court in his presence while he took a seat off to one side, observing his behavior. When he saw how young his son was and yet he was sitting facing south in royal robes while his older son, Prince Zhang, was a grown man and had to face north and kowtow to him, he felt very sorry for his older son, for he had made the elder truckle to a younger. When the court was dismissed, the Royal Father caught sight of Prince Sheng standing to one side, and he mentioned to him: "Did you notice the Lord of Anyang? Even though he went through the motions, he seems to be unhappy. I am going to divide the lands of Zhao into two portions. That way, Zhang can be king of Dai and on an equal footing with Zhao. What do you think?"

"You made a mistake when you demoted the crown prince in the first place," Prince Sheng replied. "However, everyone has gotten used to it now. If you are going to start changing things, I am afraid it will cause a civil war!"

"It is my right to change things how I want them," the Royal Father declared. "What more is there to say?"

When the Royal Father returned to the palace, Queen Wuwa noticed something unusual in his expression and asked, "Did something happen at court today?"

"I saw the former crown prince Zhang," the Royal Father told her. "It is not right to make an older brother pay court to a younger one. I wanted to establish him as king of Dai, but Prince Sheng says that would not be a good idea. I simply cannot make up my mind what would be the right thing to do."

"In the past Lord Mu of Jin had two sons: the older was called Chou and the younger was called Chengshi," Wuwa said. "When Lord Mu died, his son Chou inherited the marquisate and established the capital of his country at Yi. He enfeoffed his younger brother Chengshi with Quwo. Later on, Quwo became more and more powerful and they ended up by destroying the family line of Chou, taking over Yi. You know all this. Chengshi was the younger of the two, but he still ended up being stronger than his brother. What do you think will happen if you keep putting Zhang in a position of power and allow him to bully his brother? My son and I would be left defenseless!"

The Royal Father was moved by her words and decided to do nothing.

A servant secretly reported to Prince Zhang the burden of his father's discussions. This man had previously been in service with him at the East Palace. Prince Zhang and Tian Buli now came up with a plan.

"His Former Majesty would like to divide the country into two parts, which shows his sense of fairness, but he was prevented from doing anything by the machinations of that woman," Tian Buli said. "His Majesty is still a child and doesn't understand what is going on. If you were to find an opportunity to assassinate him, there would be nothing that the Royal Father could do."

"I want you to find the right moment for me to strike," Prince Zhang said. "I will share all my future honors with you!"

Grand Tutor Li Dui was a close friend of Fei Yi's, and he secretly reported: "The Lord of Anyang is a powerful and arrogant man with a large following in the country. Furthermore, he is known to be angry about being dispossessed. Tian Buli is a nasty piece of work, who often bites off more than he can chew. If these two men have gotten together there will be trouble, and it will strike sooner rather than later. You are in a position of great importance and trust, so you too will be in danger when they act. Why don't you announce that you are ill and resign your position in favor of Prince Cheng? That way you will escape."

"The Royal Father has entrusted His Majesty to my care, appointing me to the honorable position of prime minister," Fei Yi replied. "Now you tell me that I need to take immediate action to survive. I have not yet seen the slightest sign of danger, but you are already telling me to run away and hide. If I did so, would I not be the object of Xun Xi's scorn?"

Li Dui sighed and said: "You may be a loyal minister, but you certainly cannot be described as intelligent." He burst into tears and eventually said goodbye and left.

Fei Yi was so worried by what Li Dui had told him that he could not sleep that night, nor could he swallow any food. He kept pacing up and down, but could not come up with a good plan. He said to his servant, Gao Xin: "In the future, if someone wants to see His Majesty, report to me first."

"I will," Gao Xin said.

It so happened one day that the Royal Father and the king were out traveling at Shaqiu, with the Lord of Anyang in attendance. There was a tower at Shaqiu that had been built by the last king of the Shang dynasty. There were also two traveling palaces; the Royal Father and the king were staying in different palaces, located some five or six *li* apart. The guesthouse where the Lord of Anyang was accommodated was placed between the two. Tian Buli said to the Lord of Anyang: "Since His Majesty has gone out traveling, he has not brought a full complement of attendants and guards. If you were to tell the king that the Royal Father has summoned him, he would have to go. I will have soldiers lying in ambush en route, and we can kill him. As long as we have the Royal Father under our control, we can use him to placate the rest. Who would dare to disobey us?"

"That is a wonderful plan!" Prince Zhang exclaimed. He ordered one of his trusted personal servants to pretend to be a messenger sent by the Royal Father. That night, he summoned King Hui with the words: "The Royal Father has become unwell and he would like to see you. Please come quickly!"

Gao Xin immediately reported this to the prime minister, Fei Yi, who said: "The Royal Father is not sick at all. This is very suspicious." He suggested to His Majesty: "Let me go on ahead. If there is nothing wrong, Your Majesty can follow." Fei Yi gave final instructions to Gao Xin: "Close the gates to the palace and remain vigilant!"

The prime minister set off with a cavalry escort. En route they were mistaken for the royal party by the soldiers lying in ambush, who rose up and slaughtered all of them. When Tian Buli lit a torch and checked the bodies, he discovered Fei Yi's corpse. Horrified, he said: "Things are now critical! Before anyone finds out what is going on, we need to mobilize all our forces for an attack on His Majesty tonight. If we are lucky, we may yet succeed."

He and the Lord of Anyang went to attack the king. However, since Gao Xin had already been warned about this possibility by Fei Yi, he had made preparations. Tian Buli attacked the royal palace but was not able to force his way in. At dawn, Gao Xin ordered his troops to climb up onto the rooftops and shoot down at them, killing and injuring many of the attackers. When their arrows were used up, they threw down roof tiles. Tian Buli gave orders for the construction of a stone and wood battering ram, which they turned on the palace gates with a hideous rending sound. Just as it seemed as though nothing could save King Hui, the sound of shouting could be heard outside the palace walls. Two divisions of cavalry attacked, defeating the attackers utterly and putting them to flight. As it transpired, back at the capital both Prince Cheng and Li Dui had debated whether the Lord of Anyang would take advantage of this opportunity to rebel, so they each led an army division out to help. They arrived just as the rebels were laying siege to the royal palace, and they rescued His Majesty from his plight.

Once the Lord of Anyang's troops had been defeated, he asked Tian Buli, "What do I do now?"

"You must go to the Royal Father as soon as possible to cry and beg for mercy," Tian Buli said. "The Royal Father will protect you. I will do my best to prevent any soldiers from coming after you."

Prince Zhang followed his advice and rode alone to the Royal Father's palace. Just as anticipated, the Royal Father had the gates opened to let him in and hid him without making any trouble about it. Tian Buli gathered up his scattered forces and fought Prince Cheng and Li Dui again, but they were faced with overwhelming numbers of ene-mies. Tian Buli was beheaded by Li Dui, who calculated that the Lord of Anyang would not have been able to escape, so he must have gone to throw in his lot with the Royal Father. He led his troops to lay siege to the Royal Father's palace. When they opened the palace gates, Li Dui walked ahead with his sword drawn; Prince Cheng followed behind him. When they encountered the Royal Father, they kowtowed and said: "The Lord of Anyang has rebelled. Let the law take its course. You must hand him over to justice."

"He has never been to my palace," the Royal Father declared. "You are going to have to look for him elsewhere."

Li Dui and Prince Cheng repeated their request three or four times, but the Royal Father stuck to his story.

"Things have already reached this pass," Li Dui said. "Let us search the palace. If we do not find the traitor, we can still go back and apolo-gize for our mistake."

"You are right," Prince Cheng said. He shouted for his personal guard to assemble—a couple of hundred soldiers—and they searched the entire palace. They found the Lord of Anyang in a hole behind a false wall and dragged him out. Li Dui drew his sword and prepared to cut his head off.

"Why are you in such a hurry?" the prince asked.

"The Royal Father may turn up at any moment and object," Li Dui replied, "and if we disobey a direct command, we will be guilty of lèse-majesté. However, if we follow his wishes, we will be guilty of letting a traitor go free. Let's just kill him!"

Prince Cheng agreed.

Li Dui picked up the Lord of Anyang's head, but as he walked out of the inner chambers of the palace, he could hear the sound of the Royal

Father's sobbing. He spoke again to Prince Cheng: "The Royal Father opened the gates to the palace and allowed Prince Zhang to enter, which means he still sympathizes with him. Because of Prince Zhang we have laid siege to the Royal Father's palace, searched the place for him, and killed him—how can that have failed to wound the Royal Father deeply? Once everything has calmed down, he will punish us for our assault on the palace and our families will be killed to the last man! His Majesty is still just a child, and we cannot count on him. We had better make our own arrangements to deal with this situation."

Thus he instructed his soldiers: "You are not to lift the siege." He sent someone in with an order purporting to be from King Hui: "Those palace servants who leave immediately will be assumed to be innocent. Anyone who stays behind will be treated as a member of the rebel faction and executed with his family!"

When the eunuchs and courtiers heard the king's command, they all rushed out of the palace as fast as they could. The only person left behind was the Royal Father. When he called for his attendants, nobody answered; when he tried to leave, he discovered that the gates were locked. The siege lasted for several days, during which time the Royal Father starved inside the palace, unable to find anything to eat. There was a sparrow nest in a tree in the courtyard, so he grabbed the eggs and swallowed them raw. A month later, he finally died of starvation.

An old man wrote a poem bewailing this:

As he rode the borders in barbarian costume, he brought these areas
    peace;
His ambitions extended to the conquest of Qin to the west.
Wuwa was the root of all the evil that overtook him,
The sound of the *qin* in his dreams just served to mislead him.

The Royal Father was now dead, but nobody knew. Li Dui and his cohort still did not dare to enter the palace. They waited for three whole months before unlocking the gates and entering, by which time the Royal Father's body had rotted away. Prince Cheng told King Hui to move into the Shaqiu Palace and preside over the funeral. The former king was buried in Dai.

Lingqiu County nowadays takes its name from the fact that it is the site of the tomb of King Wuling of Zhao.

When King Hui returned to his capital, he appointed Prince Cheng to be the new prime minister, and Li Dui became the minister of justice. A short time later, Prince Cheng died. King Hui was mindful of the fact that Prince Sheng had prevented the Royal Father from carrying on with his harebrained idea of partitioning the country, so he appointed him to be prime minister and enfeoffed him with the lands of Pingyuan. Henceforward he was known as the Lord of Pingyuan.

. . .

The Lord of Pingyuan was very fond of the company of knights, somewhat like the Lord of Mengchang. He used his honorable position to summon many clients into his service, and there were often a couple of thousand men to sit down to eat with him. The Lord of Pingyuan's mansion was graced by the presence of a belvedere, which was the residence of one of his concubines. This belvedere looked down on a neighboring house whose owner was a cripple. He would get up early in the morning and stumble out to draw water. The concubine looked down from her point of vantage and laughed heartily. A short time later, the cripple made his way to the Lord of Pingyuan's gate and asked for an audience. Prince Sheng respectfully invited him in.

"I have heard that you are fond of the company of knights," the cripple said. "The reason why they travel great distances to seek service in your household is that you care more about them than about your womenfolk. I am so unfortunate as to have suffered great ill health, and hence I find it difficult to walk—now one of your concubines has laughed at the sight of me. I cannot accept being humiliated by a woman! I hope that you will behead the woman who laughed at me!"

Prince Sheng smiled and said, "Of course."

The cripple departed. Now the Lord of Pingyuan laughed and said, "What a stupid man! He wanted to kill my concubine over a single laugh!"

It was the rule in the Lord of Pingyuan's household that the majordomo would take a register of the clients present every month, in which he would note the number of men and then calculate the expenditure in money and grain. Prior to this, the number of clients had been growing steadily, but now there was a gradual decrease day after day until by the end of the year half of them had gone.

Prince Sheng was most surprised at this and had the bell rung to convene a grand assembling of his clients. "In my treatment of you, I have never dared to behave without proper ceremony, and yet men have left my service in droves," he said. "What is the reason for this?"

One of his clients explained: "You did not kill the concubine when she laughed at the cripple. We are angry that you care more for your sex life than you do for knights. That is the reason why so many of us have left. I am planning to leave myself any day now!"

The Lord of Pingyuan was deeply shocked and immediately apologized: "This is my mistake!" He drew the sword by his side and ordered his servants to behead the concubine who lived in the belvedere. He took the head around to the cripple's house in person and knelt down in apology. The cripple was pleased with his attentions. His household all praised the Lord of Pingyuan's wisdom, and gradually his clients returned to their former number.

At the time there was a ditty in circulation about this:

Who will feed me?
Who will clothe me?
Who will house me?
Who will employ me?
Lord Mengchang of Qi,
Lord Pingyuan of Zhao
Are princes of the royal blood
And the wisest of masters.

King Zhaoxiang of Qin heard the story of the Lord of Pingyuan cutting off his concubine's head in order to apologize to an offended cripple. One day he was discussing this with Xiang Tao, sighing over the man's wisdom.

"He is far from being as great as the Lord of Mengchang!" Xiang Tao said.

"What is the Lord of Mengchang like?"

"Even when his father, Tian Ying, was alive, the Lord of Mengchang was already in charge of the administration of the household and gathering clients into his service," Xiang Tao explained. "So many men have joined his household that the other aristocrats all respected him enormously—that is why they petitioned Tian Ying that he should be appointed his heir. Once he inherited the dukedom of Xue, he recruited even more knights into his service, giving them food and clothing in no wit inferior to his own: the expense bankrupted him. The knights who have come from Qi all say that the Lord of Mengchang treated them like members of his own family and spoke to them without reserve. The Lord of Pingyuan allowed his concubine to laugh at the cripple and did not punish her. He waited until his staff showed signs of great dissatisfaction and then cut her head off in order to apologize to the offended man. Is that not all too late?"

"I would like to meet this Lord of Mengchang," His Majesty remarked. "Perhaps I can recruit him into my administration."

"If you want to meet the Lord of Mengchang," Xiang Tao suggested, "why don't you invite him to come here?"

"He is the prime minister of Qi. If I asked him, would he be willing to come?"

"If you were to send one of your brothers as a hostage to Qi and request the Lord of Mengchang in return, Qi would not dare to refuse, given the alliance between you. Once you have obtained the Lord of Mengchang, Your Majesty, you could appoint him as the prime minister, and Qi would then make your brother their prime minister too. If Qin and Qi swapped prime ministers, the alliance between you would become even more secure. You could then safely turn your attention to the other kingdoms."

"Good!" the king of Qin said.

He sent the Lord of Jingyang to Qi as a hostage: "I would like the Lord of Mengchang to come to Qin so I may have an audience with him. Such has long been my heartfelt wish." When his clients heard of the summons from Qin, they all urged the Lord of Mengchang to go.

At this time, Su Dai held an appointment as ambassador to Qi from the kingdom of Yan. He said to the Lord of Mengchang: "I was traveling outside the suburbs today and I saw a wooden doll and a clay doll arguing. The wooden doll said to the clay doll, 'It is raining! You are going to be destroyed! What are you going to do?' The clay doll laughed and said, 'I was made from earth and to the earth I shall return. If you get caught in a thunderstorm you will simply float away. Who knows where you will end up?' Qin is a country of tigers and wolves—even King Huai of Chu was not able to leave, so how will you escape? If when the time comes they refuse to let you leave, I cannot imagine what will happen to you!"

The Lord of Mengchang refused Qin's offer and declined to leave. Kuang Zhang spoke to King Min: "Qin has offered a hostage in exchange for the Lord of Mengchang, so they are trying to befriend Qi. If he refuses to go, you will lose their support! Of course, if we were to keep the hostage offered by Qin, it would suggest that we did not trust them. You had better allow the Lord of Jingyang to return to Qin with full diplomatic honors and then send the Lord of Mengchang on a mission to return their initial visit. If you do that, the king of Qin will trust the Lord of Mengchang and treat the kingdom of Qi with generosity."

King Min thought that this was a good idea. He said to the Lord of Jingyang: "I am going to send the prime minister on a diplomatic mission to your country in accordance with the wishes of the king of Qin. How could I possibly expect you to remain behind as a hostage?"

He had a chariot prepared to convey the Lord of Jingyang back to Qin and sent the Lord of Mengchang on a mission to Qin.

• • •

The Lord of Mengchang went west to Xianyang with more than one thousand of his clients in his train and a cavalry escort of more than one hundred chariots. He sought an audience with the king of Qin. His Majesty went down the steps to greet him, shaking his hand as a sign of welcome, and saying how very pleased he was to meet him. The Lord of Mengchang possessed a cloak of fox fur, two inches thick and as white as snow, worth one thousand pieces of gold and without an equal in the world. This he presented as a private gift to the king of Qin. His Majesty wore the cloak back to the palace and vaunted it in front of his favorite, Lady Ji of Yan.

"That is a perfectly ordinary cloak," she said. "What is so valuable about it?"

"A fox's fur only turns white when it is several thousand years old," His Majesty explained. "This white fox-fur cloak is made from the skin found under the fox's belly, which has been stitched together. This fur is the purest in color and it is very, very expensive—it really is a priceless treasure! Qi is a great state located on the Shandong peninsula, and so they are able to lay hands on such a fabulous garment."

Since at that time the weather was still warm, His Majesty handed the cloak over to the official in charge of his treasury with instructions to store it away carefully until he called for it. He selected a suitable day to confirm the Lord of Mengchang as chancellor. Chuli Ji was envious of the fact that the Lord of Mengchang was to be given such an important position, and he was worried that his own power would be compromised. Therefore, he sent his client, Gongsun Shi, to speak to the king of Qin: "Tian Wen is a member of the Qi royal family. If you make him chancellor, he will put Qi first and Qin second. The Lord of Mengchang is a very intelligent man, and his plans are sure to be excellent—what is more, he has a huge number of clients. If he were to use his position in Qin to plot for the benefit of Qi, we would be in great danger!"

The king of Qin reported what he had said to Chuli Ji, who told him: "Gongsun Shi is quite right."

"If that is so, should I send him home?" the king asked.

"Lord Mengchang has been in Qin for more than a month, and he arrived with a staff of one thousand men," Chuli Ji replied. "By now he must be aware of every aspect of life in Qin. If you allow him to return to Qi, he will cause disaster for us sooner or later."

The king of Qin was misled by this advice and gave orders to keep the Lord of Mengchang under arrest in the official guesthouse.

When the Lord of Jingyang was in Qi, the Lord of Mengchang had treated him with great generosity, holding banquets daily in his honor. When he was about to depart, he gave him many valuable presents. The Lord of Jingyang had been very impressed by him. Now, hearing the king of Qin's plan, he went in private to discuss the matter with the Lord of Mengchang. His Lordship was frightened and asked what he should do.

"His Majesty has still not yet made up his mind what to do," the Lord of Jingyang said. "There is a certain Lady Ji of Yan in the palace who is His Majesty's favorite, and he always does what she says. If you select some valuable items, I will present them to her in your name and ask her to speak up on your behalf, so you can go home. Perhaps you can still avoid disaster . . ."

The Lord of Mengchang gave the Lord of Jingyang two white jade discs to be presented to Lady Ji of Yan with a request for help.

"I would really like a white fox-fur cloak such as what I have heard is available in the kingdom of Qi," she said. "If I were to receive such a cloak, I would be happy to speak, but I do not want these jade discs."

The Lord of Jingyang reported this conversation back to the Lord of Mengchang.

"I only have one cloak," His Lordship said, "which I have already presented to the king of Qin. Where do I get another one?" He asked his clients: "Is there anyone who can get me another white fox-fur cloak?"

They all sat still and nobody replied. Now the man seated in the very lowest position spoke up: "I can get one."

"What plan do you have to lay hands on such a cloak?" the Lord of Mengchang asked.

"I can steal like a dog," the man explained.

The Lord of Mengchang laughed and sent him on his way.

. . .

That night the man crouched down and dug a hole, which gave him entry into the treasury of the Qin palace. He made a barking sound, just like a dog, and the official in charge thought it was one of the guard dogs woofing and did not pay any attention. He waited until the treasury official was fast asleep and then abstracted the key from his person. Opening the trunks, he found the white fox-fur cloak and stole it. He handed it over to the Lord of Mengchang, who gave it to the Lord of Jingyang to present to Lady Ji of Yan. She was absolutely thrilled. When she was drinking that night with His Majesty and he was in a good mood, she spoke: "I have heard that Lord Mengchang of Qi is one of the wisest men in the world! Since he was the prime minister of Qi, he did not want to come to Qin, but you insisted. It is already bad enough that you have not given him a senior government post—do you really have to kill him? First you invite the prime minister of another country to come here and then execute him for no reason—are you quite determined to have the reputation of a man who butchers sages? I am afraid that the wise men of the world will be giving Qin a wide berth in future!"

"You are right," the king of Qin said.

The next day at court, he gave orders to prepare chariots and horses and issued chits to allow him to change his horses at post stations. Then he gave the Lord of Mengchang permission to return home to Qi.

"Thanks to Lady Ji of Yan speaking up for me," the lord said, "I have been able to extract myself from the tiger's jaws. If the king of Qin regrets his decision immediately, I am still going to die."

One of his clients was good at forgery, so he changed the name given on the chits issued to the Lord of Mengchang, and they set out that very night. When they arrived at the Hangu Pass, it was still the middle of the night. There was still a long time to wait before the gate would be opened. The Lord of Mengchang was worried that pursuers might arrive at any moment, and so he was in a hurry to get out through the pass. There was a set time each day for the gate to be opened and closed—the time of closing was decided by the guards, but the gate was opened each day at cockcrow. The Lord of Mengchang and all his staff were gathered inside the pass, getting more and more nervous. Suddenly the sound of crowing rose up from among them. The Lord of Mengchang was surprised and looked around him; it was one of his junior clients who could imitate the sound of a cockerel. This caused all the rest of the cocks to crow. The officials in charge of the Hangu Pass imagined that it must be getting light, so they started checking their documentation and then opened the gate. Lord Mengchang's people carried on their journey, speeding through the night. He said to his clients: "I have been able to escape from danger thanks to someone who could steal like a dog and another person who could crow like a cock!" The remainder of his clients felt deeply ashamed of how little they had been able to help, and after this they did not dare to behave arrogantly to the junior clients.

An old man wrote a poem of praise:

Do not use a pearl to shoot a sparrow when a clay pellet works just as
well.
A white jade disc will not relieve your hunger, for that you want a bowl
of rice.
A thief who could bark like a dog recovered the fox-fur cloak,
A man who could crow like a cock got the border pass opened at once.
Even a sage does not match up to these criminals.
Just as fine streams may serve to fill up an ocean,
Piled-up earth may conceal a layer of iron;
Do not despise the Lord of Mengchang for his choice of servants.

When Chuli Ji heard that the Lord of Mengchang had been released and allowed to return home, he rushed to court. He had an audience with King Zhaoxiang, at which he said: "If you were not going to kill Tian Wen, you could still have kept him as a hostage. Why have you set him free?"

The king of Qin deeply regretted his actions and sent someone to pursue the Lord of Mengchang at all possible speed. When he arrived at the Hangu Pass, he inspected the records of travelers but did not find the name of the ambassador from the kingdom of Qi, Tian Wen. "He cannot have taken this route," he said, "or perhaps he has not yet arrived?"

He waited for half a day without any sign of his arrival. Now he described the appearance of the Lord of Mengchang and the number of his clients, horses, and chariots. The official in charge of the pass said, "He went through early this morning."

"Do you think I could still catch up with him?"

"He was going really fast," the official said. "I imagine that he is already more than a hundred *li* away. You will not be able to catch up."

The envoy reported this to the king of Qin. His Majesty sighed and said: "The Lord of Mengchang is a really remarkable man. I will not see his like again!"

Later on, the king of Qin wanted to collect his white fox-fur cloak from the official in charge of his treasury, only to find it missing. When he saw Lady Ji of Yan wearing an identical cloak, he asked about it and thus discovered that it had been stolen by one of the Lord of Mengchang's clients. Again he sighed and said: "Meeting the Lord of Mengchang's clients is like taking a walk through the marketplace of a great city; all human life is there. We in the kingdom of Qin are no match for him!"

He gave Lady Ji of Yan the cloak and did not punish the official in charge of his treasury for the loss.

If you do not know whether the Lord of Mengchang returned home safely, READ ON.

Chapter Ninety-four

Feng Huan dances with his sword to gain a
position with the Lord of Mengchang.

The king of Qi raises an army to attack the
Wicked King of Song.

When the Lord of Mengchang fled homeward from Qin, his journey took him through Zhao. Zhao Sheng, the Lord of Pingyuan, met him thirty *li* outside the capital and treated him with the greatest respect. The people of Zhao had often heard tell of the Lord of Mengchang, but they had never seen him. They rushed out to catch a glimpse of the man. The Lord of Mengchang was extremely short, being well below average in height. One of the onlookers laughed and said, "When we heard such glowing things of the Lord of Mengchang, we imagined that he would look like a god. Now we see him, and he is just like a little doll." A number of people laughed along with him. By the evening, the joker and those who had laughed at the Lord of Mengchang had all lost their heads. The Lord of Pingyuan knew perfectly well that this was the work of the Lord of Mengchang's men, but he did not dare make inquiries into the matter.

When King Min of Qi sent the Lord of Mengchang to Qin, he felt as though he had lost his right and his left hands—he was also afraid that he would be appointed to senior office by Qin, and this prospect worried him deeply. When he heard that the Lord of Mengchang had run away and was on his way home, he was very pleased and appointed him to the office of prime minister. Even more men now sought service in his household. The Lord of Mengchang set up three levels of guesthouse for his people: the finest was called the Placement Hostel; the second was the Lucky Hostel; and the third was the Traditional Hostel. The name of the Placement Hostel came from the fact that the people who lived there were expected to hold high office—his senior clients resided there, and they ate meat and rode around in fine carriages. The Lucky Hostel's name indicated that its residents would be able to hold some kind of official position—his middle-ranking clients lived there, and they ate meat but were not provided with carriages. At the Traditional Hostel, the residents were given food so that they would not starve, and they came and went as they chose—his lowest-ranking clients lived here. The people who could crow like a cock, steal like a dog, or counterfeit documents originally lived here, but had now been moved into the Placement Hostel. The taxes that the Lord of Mengchang received from his fief at Xue were not enough to cover all the expenses of his guests, so he had begun lending money to the people of Xue and claiming the interest, which helped to cover his daily expenses.

One day a man asked for an audience with the Lord of Mengchang. This man was very strong and powerful in appearance, though he was dressed in coarse clothing and wore only straw sandals on his feet. He said that his name was Feng Huan and he came from the kingdom of Qi. The Lord of Mengchang bowed and asked him to sit down: "What do you have to say, sir?"

"Nothing," Feng Huan replied. "I have heard that you like the company of knights and do not distinguish them according to the rank into which they were born; that is why I have come to join you."

The Lord of Mengchang gave orders that he should be accommodated in the Traditional Hostel. Ten days later, the Lord of Mengchang asked the head of the hostel, "How is my new client getting along?"

"Mr. Feng is extremely poor," he replied. "He owns only one item: his sword. He does not even possess a scabbard; he has tied his sword to his waist with a hemp rope. When he has finished eating, he takes his sword out and dances with it, singing: 'Long Sword, let's go back! They don't give me fish to eat . . .'"

The Lord of Mengchang laughed and said, "He is annoyed because of the poor quality of the food I am offering." He had him moved to the Lucky Hostel, where he would be given meat and fish to eat. He told the head of the hostel to watch what he was up to: "Come and report to me in five days' time."

Five days later, the warden of the Lucky Hostel reported: "Mr. Feng dances with his sword and sings just like he did before, but the words are not the same. Now he sings: 'Long Sword, let's go back! They don't give me a carriage to ride . . .'"

The Lord of Mengchang was shocked and said, "Does that man want to be one of my senior clients? He must have some hidden capacities."

Now he ordered that Feng Huan be moved into the Placement Hostel. Again he commanded that the head keep an eye on what he was singing. Feng Huan would ride out in a carriage in the morning and come back late at night. Now he sang: "Long Sword, let's go back! This is no home for us . . ."

The head of the Placement Hostel reported this to the Lord of Mengchang. His Lordship wrinkled his forehead and said, "Is he really so impossible to satisfy?" He ordered his people to keep an eye on the man, but after this, Feng Huan did not sing again.

About a year later, the majordomo reported to the Lord of Mengchang: "We only have enough grain for another month!"

The Lord of Mengchang inspected his promissory notes and discovered that many people had defaulted on their loans. He asked his entourage, "Who can go to Xue and collect these debts?"

The head of the Placement Hostel suggested: "I have no idea what Mr. Feng can really do, but he seems very loyal to you and I think he could be given this job. Since he has insisted on being ranked among your top clients, it is time for Your Lordship to test him."

The Lord of Mengchang invited Feng Huan to meet him and discussed the issue of recovering the bad debts. Feng Huan did not say a word but got straight into a carriage and headed for Xue, where he took up residence in the ducal mansion. There were many wealthy men among the ten thousand households living in Xue. When they heard that the Duke of Xue had sent a senior client to demand interest payments from them, they immediately clubbed together to come up with some money, producing one hundred thousand cash. Feng Huan spent this money in buying beef and wine, then he posted the following message: "Anyone who owes the Lord of Mengchang money, regardless of whether they can afford to pay it back or not, should come to the mansion tomorrow to have their documentation checked."

When people heard that there was going to be beef and wine on offer, they all came on the appointed day. Feng Huan made sure that everyone got something to eat and drink, and he encouraged them to get their fill. Standing back and observing what was going on, he worked out who was rich and who was poor, without any mistakes. When the meal was over, he began checking the documentation and calculating a scale of repayments. In the case of those who could not afford to pay back right away, but who would be able to repay the debt in the future, he arranged a new date for the return of the money, and this was written down on the promissory note. Those who were so poor that they simply could not afford to pay back their loans bowed and begged for more time. Feng Huan ordered his servants to light a fire. Having collected their documents, he threw them all into the fire, announcing to the assembled multitude: "The reason that the Lord of Mengchang lent you this money in the first place was that he was afraid that you might otherwise not have the means to survive; he is not practicing extortion. His Lordship has several thousand clients and cannot afford to keep them—that is why he started lending out money at interest in the first place. Now those who can pay back have been given a new schedule for doing so, while those who cannot pay back have had their debts forgiven. His Lordship has treated the people of Xue with great generosity!"

The people all kowtowed and shouted happily: "Long live the Lord of Mengchang!"

By this time someone had already informed the Lord of Mengchang that the promissory notes had been burned, and he was absolutely furious. He sent someone to summon Feng Huan as quickly as he could. When Feng Huan arrived back empty-handed, the Lord of Mengchang pretended not to know what was going on and asked, "I am sure that this has been a difficult journey for you! Have you finished collecting the debts?"

"Not only have I collected your debts," he replied, "I have gained you a wonderful reputation!"

The Lord of Mengchang looked cross and said complainingly: "I have three thousand clients but not enough money to feed them; that is the reason why I have been lending out money at interest in Xue. From this I have been receiving some profit, which has been helping me with my expenses. I have been informed that you collected some of these payments and used them to buy meat and wine, with which you feasted the people. After that you burned one half of the outstanding promissory notes. However, now you tell me that I have 'gained a wonderful reputation'! How can this be?"

"Please do not be angry," Feng Huan replied. "Let me explain. There were many people there who had defaulted on their payments. If I did not hold the feast for them, they would have been very suspicious and unwilling to appear. In that case it would have been impossible for me to distinguish those who cannot pay from those who won't pay. In the case of those who can pay, I have arranged a new schedule of repayment; in the case of those who simply cannot pay, it does not matter how much you press them, you will never get your money back. Over time, as the amount of money that they owe you increases: all that will happen is that you force them into running away. Xue may not be a very big fief, but it has been handed down to you from your ancestors and its people have supported your family for generations. Today I have burned the useless promissory notes in order to demonstrate that you love your people and care little for money. Your reputation as a benevolent and just lord will spread to the ends of the earth. That is why I said that I had gained you a wonderful reputation."

The Lord of Mengchang was hard pressed to pay the expenses of his guests, and he was still very unhappy about the situation. However, the promissory notes had already been burned and there was nothing that could be done about it. He felt he had no choice but to relax his frown and bow in thanks.

A historian wrote a poem, which says:

> Having been told about the money, he insisted on being treated well;
> Burning promissory notes, he ignored his lord's complaints.
> He came back empty-handed, but with justice and benevolence,
> Thus we know that Feng Huan was indeed a great man!

King Zhaoxiang of Qin regretted having lost the Lord of Mengchang, and when he realized what an amazing man he had let slip through his fingers, he thought to himself: "If this man is given high office in the kingdom of Qi, it will be a disaster for Qin!" He spread rumors throughout the kingdom of Qi to the following effect: "The Lord of Mengchang is admired by one and all—everyone has heard of him and nobody cares about the king of Qi. One of these days it will be the Lord of Mengchang who sits on the throne!"

He also sent someone to say to King Qingxiang of Chu: "In the past, when the six kingdoms attacked Qin, Qi was the last to arrive. Although you are the head of the Vertical Alliance, the Lord of Mengchang does not accept your authority; that is why he was not willing to send troops. When King Huai was living in Qin, I wanted to send him home, but the Lord of Mengchang sent an ambassador to request me not to do so. At that time, you were still the crown prince and being held hostage in Qi. The Lord of Mengchang was hoping that we would kill King Huai and they would be able to keep you to extort land from Chu. As a result of these machinations, you were very nearly prevented from returning to Chu and King Huai ended up dying in Qin. I know that I have committed a crime against you, but this is all the fault of the Lord of Mengchang. It was for your sake that I was hoping to lay hands on the Lord of Mengchang and kill him, but he escaped home and I failed to capture him. Now he monopolizes power as the prime minister of Qi, and day and night he schemes to usurp the throne there. I am afraid that from here on in, Chu and Qin are going to be in a lot of trouble! I regret the mistakes that I made in the past and would be happy to make a peace treaty with Chu—a princess of Qin will become your wife. Let us prevent the Lord of Mengchang from causing any further disasters. I am waiting with bated breath for Your Majesty's decision."

The king of Chu was deluded by this into agreeing to a peace treaty with Qin. He took a Qin princess as his queen and also sent people to spread vicious rumors in Qi. King Min of Qi became suspicious and demanded the prime ministerial seals from the Lord of Mengchang, sending him back to live in Xue.

When the Lord of Mengchang's clients realized he had fallen from grace, they gradually dispersed. The only person who stayed was Feng Huan, who acted as the Lord of Mengchang's charioteer. Long before they arrived in Xue, the entire population—young and old—had come out to meet him. They presented him with wine and food and asked what he intended to do. The Lord of Mengchang said to Feng Huan: "This is what you meant when you said that you were getting me a wonderful reputation!"

"That is not all. If you will lend me a chariot, I will make sure that you are even more respected in this country than ever before and that your fief is even larger."

"Whatever you want," the Lord of Mengchang assured him.

Over the course of the next couple of days, the Lord of Mengchang had horses, carriages, gold, and silk prepared. He said to Feng Huan, "You may act as you see fit." Feng Huan got into his carriage and traveled west to Xianyang. There he requested an audience with King Zhaoxiang and launched into his persuasion: "The knights who travel to Qin all want to strengthen you and weaken Qi; the knights who come to Qi all want the opposite. Qi and Qin are very closely balanced rivals; whoever takes control of this situation will eventually take command of the whole world."

"What plan do you have to offer, sir, to guarantee that it is I who take control?" the king of Qin asked.

"Do you know, Your Majesty, that Qi has demoted the Lord of Mengchang?"

"I have been told so," the king answered, "but I did not believe it."

"The reason why the kingdom of Qi has the respect that it does," Feng Huan pronounced, "is entirely due to the Lord of Mengchang's wisdom. Now the king of Qi has been deluded by malicious gossip and stripped him of his seals as prime minister; he who has achieved so much in the service of his country has been treated as a common criminal. The Lord of Mengchang has been deeply upset by this. Why don't you take advantage of his anger and employ him in the government of Qin? In that way, whatever nasty little tricks Qi gets up to, Qin can defeat them. If you have his advice in your campaigns against the kingdom of Qi, you can conquer them. Surely your victories will not simply end there! You must send an ambassador at once, Your Majesty, loaded with rich gifts, to meet the Lord of Mengchang secretly in Xue. This opportunity must not be lost! If the king of Qi changes his mind and restores him to power, who knows what will happen?"

By this time Chuli Ji was dead, and the king of Qin was desperate to appoint a good prime minister. He was delighted with what Feng Huan had told him, and so he prepared ten magnificent carriages drawn by fine horses and a gift of one hundred ingots of gold, as well as an escort worthy of a chancellor of the kingdom of Qin, and sent them to the Lord of Mengchang.

"Let me go on ahead, Your Majesty," Feng Huan said. "I will report what has happened to the Lord of Mengchang and make sure that he is ready."

. . .

Feng Huan sped back to Qi. He did not even have time to go and see the Lord of Mengchang, but went straight to have an audience with the king of Qi. "As you know," he said, "the kingdoms of Qi and Qin are vying for supremacy. The ruler who obtains good advisors will win and the ruler who loses them will be crushed. I have just been told that the king of Qin is delighted that the Lord of Mengchang has been stripped of office and he is planning to send lavish gifts to him in the hope of recruiting him as the new prime minister! If the Lord of Mengchang were to go west and take up office in Qin, the person who has been helping you to greatness would instead be assisting them. Qin would reign supreme, and Linzi and Jimo would be in terrible danger!"

King Min went completely white and asked, "What should I do?"

"The envoy from Qin will arrive at Xue at any moment. You must take advantage of the fact that he has not yet turned up to restore the

Lord of Mengchang to his position as prime minister. While you are at it, you should also increase the size of his fief. The Lord of Mengchang will be delighted by this. The envoy from Qin may be representing a powerful country, but he can hardly kidnap our prime minister and force him to go to Qin without a word to you!"

"Good!" said King Min. Even as he made the promise, he did not really believe any of this. However, His Majesty sent people to the border to find out what was going on. They spotted a man with a magnificent train of carriages in attendance. Inquiring more closely, they were able to identify him as an ambassador from Qin. A messenger traveled back to report this news to King Min under cover of darkness. King Min now ordered Feng Huan to take a tally back to Lord Mengchang and restore him to office. He also increased the size of His Lordship's fief by one thousand households. When the Qin envoy arrived in Xue, he was informed that the Lord of Mengchang was already back at work. He turned his chariot around and went home.

When the Lord of Mengchang returned to office, his former clients also went back to him. His Lordship said to Feng Huan: "I am very fond of the company of knights and would never dare to treat any of them with less than proper ceremony. The moment I lost power, they all left me. Now thanks to all your hard work, sir, I have been restored to office. How do they have the gall to come back to me?"

"It is normal that what has waxed must later on wane," Feng Huan replied. "Have you never observed, my lord, that a great market is packed with people fighting to get in at dawn, but deserted by dusk? It is deserted because there is nothing there that anyone wants. It is equally normal that a rich and powerful man has crowds of hangers-on, while a poor man has but a handful of friends. Why do you blame them for this?"

"You are right," the Lord of Mengchang said with a bow, and he carried on treating his guests as he had before any of this happened.

An old man wrote a poem bewailing this:

The rich have friends that the poor lack;
Since time immemorial, people have fawned on the noble.
When you understand the ways of the world you cease to care:
Let them just get on with it!

It was at this point that King Zhao of Wei and King Li of Han were ordered by the king of Zhou to join the Vertical Alliance and attack Qin. Qin sent their general Bai Qi to intercept the invading forces, and they fought a great battle at Yique in which some two hundred and forty thousand soldiers lost their lives. Bai Qi took prisoner the Han general, Gongsun Xi, as well as capturing two hundred *li* of land in Wusui. Next he attacked Wei and captured four hundred *li* of land east of the Yellow River. King Zhaoxiang of Qin was delighted. Since the rulers of the other seven countries all called themselves kings, it was no longer sufficiently distinguished; he now wanted to become emperor to show that he was more important. However, he was concerned about the implications of going this route alone. He sent an envoy to take the following message to King Min of Qi: "Since all the rulers in the world go around calling themselves kings, the people do not know whom they should give their allegiance to. I would like to assume the title of Western Emperor, and I will govern that corner of the realm. I would suggest that you assume the title of Eastern Emperor and take charge there. If we divide the world in half between the two of us, would that suit you?"

King Min could not make up his mind and asked the Lord of Mengchang for advice. The Lord of Mengchang said: "Qin is a dictatorial country with a terrible reputation; do not follow their lead."

About a month later, Qin sent a second envoy to Qi, proposing a joint attack on Zhao. At this time Su Dai had just returned from Yan, and King Min mentioned to him the idea proposed some time earlier of becoming a joint emperor.

"Qin is not offering to share the empire with any other ruler, but with you," Su Dai remarked. "That is a sign of their respect for Qi. If you refuse, you will be seen as showing contempt for Qin. However, if you accept, you will be the focus of the enmity of all other rulers. I think that you should agree but not actually assume the title. Let Qin go first. If they can get the rulers in the west to accept it, it will not be too late for Your Majesty to assume the title of Eastern Emperor then. If Qin takes this title and the other rulers cause trouble over it, you can join them in punishing Qin."

"I will do as you suggest," King Min replied. Then he asked: "Qin has proposed a joint attack on Zhao. What do you think I should do?"

"A war without a just cause will not work out well," Su Dai replied. "If you attack Zhao when they have done nothing wrong, any land that you capture will go to benefit Qin and you will get nothing. On the other hand, Song has behaved appallingly; everyone calls their monarch the 'Wicked King.' Why should you attack Zhao when it would be so much better to wage war against Song? If you capture their lands you can keep them, and their people can become your subjects. Furthermore, you will enjoy the glorious reputation of one who has punished a tyrant. This is the work of a sage-king!"

King Min was thrilled at the idea. Afterwards he did agree to take the title of emperor, but never used it. He treated the Qin ambassador with the utmost generosity while refusing the proposed joint attack upon Zhao. King Zhaoxiang of Qin did actually use the title of emperor for two months, but when he found out that the ruler of Qi was still calling himself a king, he did not dare to continue using the grander title.

. . .

Let us now turn to another part of the story. King Kang of Song was the son of Pibing, Lord Pi of Song, and the younger brother of Ticheng. Before he was born, his mother dreamed that King Yan of Xu entrusted the baby to her care, so he was given the personal name of Yan. Right from the time that he was born, he was a remarkable-looking baby; when he grew up, he was extremely tall with a broad face, eyes that flashed like stars, an expression of great intelligence, and such enormous strength that he could pull an iron hook straight. In the forty-first year of the reign of King Xian of Zhou, he deposed his older brother, Ticheng, and took the title of duke himself. In the eleventh year of his reign, someone in the capital reported a remarkable omen, in which he had found a snake's egg, but that it had hatched out into a sparrow-hawk. He summoned the Grand Astrologer to perform a divination about it. The Grand Astrologer laid out the hexagrams and presented his opinion: "When something small gives birth to something big, this represents the weak becoming strong. It is an omen of the birth of a great king."

"Song is a very weak country," Lord Yan said happily. "If I do not put it back on its feet, who will?"

He selected a number of strong knights and trained them himself, eventually building up a fine army of one hundred thousand men. With this he attacked Qi to the east, taking five cities. Next, he defeated Chu to the south, conquering more than three hundred *li* of land. To the west, he defeated the Wei army and captured two cities. He destroyed the state of Teng and seized their land. After that, he sent an ambassador to Qin seeking a peace treaty with them. Qin responded by sending an embassy to them. From this point on, Song was a powerful country, quite on a par with Qi, Chu, and the Three Jins. Lord Yan now took the title of king of Song and proclaimed himself a nonpareil hero—he hoped to establish hegemony over the world. Every day when he held court in the morning, he would order his ministers to shout out in unison: "Long life to His Majesty!" The men assembled in the upper chamber would shout this, and the men lined up in the lower chamber would re-echo it. Even the guards outside the gates had to repeat this message. The sound could be heard for miles around.

One time he hung a leather bag filled with ox blood from the top of a long pole. He drew his bow and shot at the bag. When the arrow hit the bag, the blood rained down from the sky. He had his men circulate the following statement through the city: "His Majesty has shot at Heaven and won." He wanted to strike fear into others. When drinking through the night, he would force his ministers to take cup after cup, while he had secretly instructed his servants to give him only warm water to drink. Even those of his ministers with a fine capacity for wine would eventually end up dead drunk. Only King Kang of Song would remain clear-headed on these occasions. His servants would flatter him: "Your Majesty really is an amazing man; you can drink so much and yet remain sober." He debauched vast numbers of women as well—sometimes in one night he would have sex with dozens of different women. He had people circulate the rumor: "The king of Song is a sex god with the capacity of one hundred men. He never gets tired." It was by these means that he sought to make his reputation.

One day, when he was traveling around the ruins of the ancient city of Fengfu, the king of Song happened to catch sight of a superlatively beautiful young woman picking mulberry leaves. He had the Qingling Tower constructed in order that he might watch her. He inquired into her family and discovered that she was the wife of his majordomo, Han Ping, and that her surname was Xi. His Majesty sent someone to speak to Han Ping about handing over his wife. Han Ping discussed the matter with her, to find out her opinion. Lady Xi replied with a poem:

> There is a bird on the South Mountain,
> While nets are spread on the North Mountain.
> If the bird keeps on flying high,
> What good are the nets to you?

Since the king of Song could not stop thinking about Lady Xi, he sent some people around to her house to kidnap her. Han Ping saw her being bundled into a carriage and was so upset that he committed suicide. His Majesty had her brought to the Qingling Tower, where he said: "I am the king of Song. I can make you rich and noble beyond your wildest dreams, or I could kill you. Your husband is dead now and you have nowhere else to go. If you stay with me, I will make you my queen."

Lady Xi responded with a poem:

A cock or a hen
Does not expect a phoenix as its mate.
I am just an ordinary person,
What pleasure can I bring the king of Song?

"The situation is what it is," the king of Song said. "Even though you don't want to obey me, you don't have a choice!"

"Let me have a bath and change my clothes," she said. "After that I would like to pray for the soul of my deceased husband. Once that is done, I will become your wife."

His Majesty agreed to this. When she had washed and changed her dress, she looked into the distance and bowed twice. Then she jumped to her death from the tower. The king of Song had given orders for someone to grab her the moment he realized what she was about to do, but they were too late. By the time they found her, she had already passed away. When her body was laid out, they discovered a letter tied to her belt, which read: "Once I am dead, please bury me in the same tomb as my husband. Even in the Yellow Springs, I will feel grateful to you!"

The king of Song was angry and deliberately ordered that two graves should be dug for them to be buried separately. That way they would be in sight of each other, but would not be together. Three days after the burial, the king of Song returned to the capital. Suddenly one night a catalpa sprouted between the two tombs, and within the course of a couple of weeks it was already three feet tall. The branches intertwined with one another, creating a dense shade. A pair of mandarin ducks came to nest in its branches; stretching their necks, they sang sadly. The local people said, "These are the souls of Han Ping and his wife transformed!" They named this "The Tree of Remembrance."

An old man wrote a poem:

Two mandarin ducks roost on the Tree of Remembrance.
How many people have suffered from love in the course of history!
Although the powerful and strong may try and take advantage,
A woman can resist the will of a king.

There were many officials who criticized the violence and lawlessness of the king of Song. Since the king of Song could not answer his detractors, he took to placing a bow and arrows next to his seat. If someone tried to remonstrate with him, he would immediately pick up the bow and shoot at him. In the space of a single day, he succeeded in killing Jing Cheng, Dai Wu, and Prince Bo. After that, nobody dared to so much as open their mouths. Everyone called him the "Wicked King."

. . .

At this time, King Min of Qi decided to make use of Su Dai's advice and sent ambassadors to Chu and Wei, agreeing on a joint attack on Song after which they would split its territory three ways. When King Zhaoxiang of Qin discovered this, he said angrily: "Song has just entered into an alliance with us, and now Qi attacks it. I am going to rescue Song . . . I really have no choice."

King Min of Qi was afraid that the Qin army would go to the rescue of Song, so he asked Su Dai for help.

"Let me go west to stop the Qin army," Su Dai said. "I would not want Your Majesty to forgo the glory of defeating Song."

Accordingly, he went west, where he had an audience with the king of Qin: "Qi is attacking Song even as we speak. May I be so bold as to congratulate Your Majesty?"

"Qi is attacking Song. Why is that a matter of congratulation for me?"

"The king of Qi is just as violent and arrogant as the king of Song," he explained. "He has assembled an alliance with Chu and Wei for this attack, and he is certain to throw his weight around among his allies. If he tries to bully them, they will naturally look west for help from Qin. You could say that Qin has sacrificed Song as bait for Qi, but in the process you will gain the support of Chu and Wei at no cost to yourself. This would be very advantageous to you. Why should I not offer congratulations?"

"What will happen if I go to rescue Song?" His Majesty asked.

"The appalling violence unleashed by the Wicked King has been the subject of universal condemnation," Su Dai said. "Everyone would be delighted to see him dead. If Qin were to go to his rescue, people would condemn you too."

The king of Qin decided to stand down his army. He would not be going to rescue Song.

. . .

The Qi army was the first to arrive in the suburbs of the Song capital. The armies sent by Chu and Wei joined them shortly afterwards.

General Han Nie of Qi, General Tang Mei of Chu, and General Mang Mao of Wei assembled to discuss their next move.

"The king of Song is enormously arrogant and ferociously ambitious," Tang Mei said. "We ought to decoy him into an unfavorable position by pretending to be weak."

"The king of Song is a licentious and cruel man," Mang Mao said. "His people have turned against him. Our countries have all suffered the death of our soldiers and the loss of territory at his hands. We could circulate placards listing his crimes and encourage our conquered peoples to rise up in rebellion against Song."

"You are both right, gentlemen," Han Nie agreed. He had placards written listing the ten great crimes committed by the Wicked King:

1. Obtaining the throne by violence, having dispossessed his older brother.
2. Conquering territory with great brutality, making people suffer huge hardships.
3. Taking enjoyment from battle and invading other countries.
4. Offending against the gods and spirits by "shooting at Heaven."
5. Drinking day in and day out, showing no interest in government matters.
6. Taking other men's wives and raping them.
7. Shooting at loyal ministers and silencing just remonstrance.
8. Usurping the title of king and engaging in relentless aggrandizement.
9. Flattering and fawning on Qin while treating other nations as enemies.
10. Being a bad ruler, with no compassion for his people.

When these placards were circulated, the local populace was terrified. The people in the conquered territory did not want to belong to Song, so they threw the occupiers out and climbed up the walls to take charge themselves, waiting for the arrival of troops from their old country. The attacking troops were confident of victory and they pressed hard on Suiyang. King Kang of Song held a great muster of men and chariots, after which he took personal command of the Central Army and set off to make camp some ten *li* outside the city, in order to prevent any sudden attack. Han Nie sent General Lüqiu Jian, one of his subordinates, out in command of five thousand men, with instructions to provoke battle. The Song army did not leave their encampment. Lüqiu Jian sent a couple of soldiers with unusually loud voices to climb up a siege engine and recite the ten great crimes of the Wicked King of Song. King Kang of Song was furious and ordered General Lu Man to go out and engage the enemy. After crossing swords a couple of times, Lüqiu Jian was defeated and fled. Lu Man chased after him. Lüqiu Jian abandoned his chariot and other impedimenta, fleeing in complete disarray. King Kang of Song had climbed the battlements; seeing that the Qi army had already been defeated, he said happily: "That is one down. Chu and Wei will be scared by that!" He sent all his army out to fight, and they marched straight on the Qi encampment. Han Nie moved his battle lines back. He withdrew some twenty *li* and then made camp again. Meanwhile Tang Mei and Mang Mao had instructions to outflank the enemy, taking the main camp.

The following day, under the impression that the Qi army could not fight anymore, King Kang of Song struck camp and advanced straight at the Qi encampment. Lüqiu Jian fought as he had been directed by Han Nie, where the two armies supported each other. In the space of a couple of hours, they fought more than thirty engagements. King Kang of Song was a brave and valiant warrior; with his own hands he killed several dozens of the most important officers in the Qi army, as well as more than one hundred ordinary soldiers. The Song general, Lu Man, was killed in this engagement. Lüqiu Jian suffered a second terrible defeat and fled, abandoning countless chariots and other weaponry. The Song soldiers fought among themselves over the spoils. Suddenly a spy reported: "The enemy has made a surprise attack on Suiyang and the battle is raging! These are the armies of Chu and Wei."

The king of Song was furious and immediately gave orders for his troops to assemble and prepare to return. Before they had even gone five *li*, yet another army appeared to intercept them. The shout went up: "This is the commander-in-chief of the Qi army, Han Nie. Why don't you surrender immediately?" The king of Song's generals, Dai Zhi and Qu Zhigao, drove their chariots forward. Han Nie drew up his forces in an awe-inspiring display: the general in command of the vanguard, Qu Zhigao, fell from his chariot dead. Dai Zhi did not dare to continue driving his forces forward. He had to protect the king of Song, fighting every step of the way. When they arrived back at Suiyang, the general defending the city, Gongsun Ba, recognized that these were his own troops and opened the gates of the city to allow them in. The allied forces attacked, and battle raged day and night. Suddenly, a plume of dust could be seen rising in the distance as yet another huge army arrived. King Min of Qi had become worried that Han Nie would not be able to obtain victory on his own, so he had come in person together with the senior general, Wang Zhu, and Grand Astrologer Jiao, at the head of a new army of thirty thousand men. This provided important reinforcements for their army.

When the Song troops discovered that the king of Qi had come in person at the head of his army, they were all terrified and nobody wanted to fight any more. To add to this, the king of Song showed no compassion for his troops; he had the entire population of the city, male and female, conscripted into providing a twenty-four hour guard on the walls without any rewards or even any kind words—resentment was close to boiling over.

Dai Zhi said to the king of Song: "The enemy is very strong and the populace is increasingly mutinous. Why do you not abandon the city, Your Majesty, and flee south of the Yellow River? From there you can plan how to recover from this."

The king of Song had by this time entirely given up on his wild ambitions. He sighed heavily. In the middle of the night, the king and Dai Zhi escaped from the city. Gongsun Ba first raised and then lowered the battle standards, surrendering the city to King Min of Qi. His Majesty comforted the local people while sending his armies out to hunt down the king of Song. His Majesty fled to Wenyi, but there his pursuers caught up with him, capturing Dai Zhi alive and executing him. The king of Song threw himself into the Shennong Canal, but he did not succeed in drowning himself. He was fished out of the waters by the soldiers and then beheaded—his remains being returned to Suiyang. Qi, Chu, and Wei now formally destroyed the kingdom of Song, dividing its territory into three parts.

Chu and Wei stood down their armies and went home. King Min said, "My armies played the most important role in this attack on Song. Why should Chu and Wei have any of their land?" He ordered his soldiers to advance in silence behind Tang Mei, launching a successful surprise attack on the Chu army as they passed Zhongqiu. Taking advantage of this first victory, the Qi army pursued the defeated army northward, capturing all the lands north of the Sui River. Next he moved his forces west to invade the Three Jins, repeatedly defeating their armies. Chu and Wei were furious with King Min for reneging on their agreement, and they did indeed throw in their lot with

Qin; meanwhile, Qin ascribed this turn of events to the brilliance of Su Dai.

Having managed to incorporate all of Song into his own lands, King Min became increasingly short-tempered and arrogant. He sent one of his own favorite courtiers, Yi Wei, to visit the rulers of Wey, Lu, and Zou, demanding that henceforth they should call themselves vassals and come to pay court to him. These three countries were terrified lest they be attacked and did not dare to refuse.

"By crippling Yan and destroying Song," King Min crowed, "I have opened up one thousand *li* of new land. Having defeated Wei and Chu, my name strikes awe into the other kings! Lu and Wey both consider themselves my subjects; all the states along the Si River tremble with fear at my frown! Any moment now I will set out on campaign, conquer the two Zhou kings, and move the nine *ding*-cauldrons of the sage-king Yu to Linzi, proclaiming myself Son of Heaven and inaugurating a new dynasty. Who would dare to resist my might?"

The Lord of Mengchang remonstrated with him: "The king of Song was arrogant, which is why you were able to defeat him. I hope that you will take a warning from what happened to Song. Even though the kings of Zhou are weak, they are still our monarchs. The seven kings may attack each other, but they would not dare to attack Zhou: they are afraid for their reputations. In the past you assumed the title of emperor, Your Majesty, but you did not actually use it—this impressed many people. Now you suddenly seem to have decided that it is your ambition to replace the Zhou royal house. I am afraid that this will not be good for Qi."

"The sage-king Tang attacked the evil King Jie of the Xia dynasty; King Wu destroyed the wicked King Zhou of the Shang dynasty," King Min retorted. "Were not Jie and Zhou the rulers of the men who destroyed them? I am afraid that you do not understand that your role is to support me in this!"

He made the Lord of Mengchang hand back his seals of office. The Lord of Mengchang was afraid of being killed, so he and his household moved to Daliang with the help of Prince Wuji.

. . .

Prince Wuji was the youngest son of King Zhao of Wei. He greatly enjoyed the company of men of talent. In his treatment of others, his only fear was that he would not be polite and respectful enough. It so happened that one day as he was eating breakfast, he happened to notice a pigeon being chased by a harrier hawk. It quickly hid itself under the table and Prince Wuji protected it. When he saw that the harrier hawk had gone, he let the pigeon go. Who would have imagined that all the hawk had done was to go and hide on the far side of the roof ridge? When it saw the pigeon fluttering past, it chased and ate it. Prince Wuji felt very ashamed of himself: "This pigeon came to me when it was trying to escape disaster, but in the end it was still killed by the harrier hawk. I have betrayed the pigeon!" He did not eat anything for the whole of the rest of the day. He ordered his servants to go out and catch these harriers; they captured more than one hundred of these birds and presented them to the prince in a cage. Prince Wuji said, "Only one bird was guilty of killing the pigeon. Why should I take it out on others of the same species?" He drew his sword and rested it on top of one of the cages. He announced: "If you did not kill the pigeon, then sing sadly for me. I will set you free." The birds all sang sadly. Finally, he came to a cage where the harrier hawk hung its head and did not dare to look up. He took this bird and killed it. Afterwards he opened up the other cages and set the birds free. Those who heard about this sighed and said, "If the prince of Wei could not bear to kill even an innocent bird, how could he possibly kill an innocent human being?" From this point onwards there were many men who came to join his household, both clever and stupid, until he ended up paying the salaries of more than three thousand men. He was quite the equal of the Lord of Mengchang or the Lord of Pingyuan.

There was a recluse living in the kingdom of Wei, a man named Hou Ying, who was more than seventy years of age. His family was poor and he made a living by guarding the Yi Gate to the capital city, Daliang. Prince Wuji heard of the modest and humble way in which this man behaved and yet how he was full of brilliant ideas, so that all the people in his ward of the city admired and respected him. He was known locally as Scholar Hou. This convinced His Royal Highness to have his chariot harnessed and to go and visit the man, with twenty ingots of gold as his first meeting present.

Scholar Hou declined the gift, saying: "I may be poor, but I have enough for my simple wants. I would not dare take a penny from anyone that I do not feel I have earned. Although I am now an old man, I do not see any reason to change the principles of a lifetime just because you happen to be a prince!"

His Royal Highness did not dare to try and force him. However, since he wanted to show his respect and encourage this man to join his household, he decided to hold a great banquet in his honor. On the day in question, the main hall of his mansion was packed with members of the Wei royal house, ministers and generals, not to mention honored guests. When everyone had sat down, they discovered that the place by His Royal Highness's left hand was empty. Prince Wuji gave orders to have his chariot prepared and went in person to the Yi Gate to bring Hou Ying to the banquet. Hou Ying got onto the chariot, and the prince respectfully indicated that he should take the seat of honor. Hou Ying did so without the slightest demur. Prince Wuji took the reins and stood to one side, treating the old man with every sign of respect. Hou Ying asked him: "I have a friend, Zhu Gai, who is one of the butchers working in the marketplace, and I would like to go and see him. I don't know if you would be prepared to go too."

Prince Wuji replied, "I would be delighted."

He gave orders for his chariot to make a detour through the market. When they arrived at the butcher's house, Hou Ying said, "Please wait here for a moment. I am going to go and see my friend."

Scholar Hou got down from the chariot and went into Zhu Gai's house. He sat down opposite Zhu Gai at his meat counter and spun out what it was he had to say. From time to time Hou Ying sneaked a look at the prince, who remained perfectly calm throughout and did not seem in the least bit bored or cross. There were a couple of dozen mounted cavalry officers who had followed His Royal Highness, and when they saw Hou Ying chatting away happily with no sign of an end, they became angry and some of them started cursing. Hou Ying made a note of that too. The only person who showed no sign of impatience from start to finish was the prince. When he had finished his conversation with Zhu Gai, he said goodbye and got back onto the chariot, taking the place of honor again. Prince Wuji left his house at lunchtime, but by the time he got back, it was late afternoon!

When the nobles and grandees assembled at the prince's mansion saw His Royal Highness set off in person to collect the guest of honor for whom the seat had been left empty, they really could not imagine what famous traveling diplomat or ambassador from a great state was expected. They all settled down to wait respectfully. However, as time went on and nobody arrived, they all became increasingly irritable. Suddenly the message arrived: "His Royal Highness is here with his guest!" They were all expecting someone really impressive and got up from their seats to welcome the visitor, straining their eyes to catch sight of him. When he arrived, they saw that he was an old man dressed in very simple coarse clothes. They were all amazed. Prince Wuji introduced his visitor to the other guests. When they heard that he was the guard at the Yi Gate, they simply could not believe their ears. His Royal Highness bowed and indicated to Hou Ying that he should take the seat of honor. He again made no sign of demurring. Wine was circulated until they were all tipsy. Prince Wuji lifted up a gold cup and came forward to toast Hou Ying. He too picked up his cup and said to the prince: "I am just the guard at the Yi Gate! Not only were you prepared to make the detour I suggested, you humiliated yourself by appearing in the market-place at my request and yet you never turned a hair. Now you have given me the seat of honor before all your other guests; this is too much! Since you have done so much, I would be willing to join your household even at the lowest rank." The nobles and grandees present were all laughing to themselves. When the banquet was over, Hou Ying did indeed become a senior advisor in Prince Wuji's household. Hou Ying also recommended Zhu Gai for service. The prince went to visit him several times, but Zhu Gai resolutely refused to join him. His Royal Highness never uttered a word of complaint, since he was uniformly polite to every person he came across.

When the Lord of Mengchang arrived in Wei, the only person who was prepared to help him was Prince Wuji. Just as the old saying has it: "Birds of a feather flock together," and the two men got along really well. The Lord of Mengchang had long been a close friend of the Lord of Pingyuan in the kingdom of Zhao, but now Prince Wuji was much more important to him. As it happened, Prince Wuji's older sister was the Lord of Pingyuan's principal wife. The relationship between Wei and Zhao was a close one as a result of this, and the presence of the Lord of Mengchang was an important factor.

. . .

After the Lord of Mengchang departed, King Min of Qi became even more arrogant and difficult to deal with. He was determined to get rid of the Zhou dynasty and declare himself emperor. At this time two strange signs were observed in the kingdom of Qi: the heavens rained down blood for several hundred *li*, staining the clothes of the people and creating an unbearable stench. After that the ground cracked wide open and a spring came bubbling forth. Elsewhere at one of the border passes, someone could be heard crying and wailing. Nobody could be seen; the sound was all there was. This caused panic among the people, who worried that death might overtake them at any moment. Grandee

Hu Xuan and Chen Ju went to remonstrate with His Majesty, recommending that he recall the Lord of Mengchang. King Min was angry and killed them, displaying their bodies at the crossroads as a warning to anyone else who felt like criticizing his actions. Wang Zhu, Grand Astrologer Jiao, and a number of other officials announced that they were ill and had to resign their offices, moving back to their hometowns to live in obscurity.

If you do not know what happened to King Min of Qi in the end, READ ON.

Chapter Ninety-five

Having persuaded four countries to this effect, Le Yi destroys Qi.

Stampeding cattle with their tails aflame allows Tian Dan to defeat Yan.

After King Zhao of Yan succeeded to the throne, he thought day and night of how he was to avenge himself upon Qi. He offered condolences and assisted orphaned children; he showed his support for his officers and ordinary soldiers. He encouraged intelligent men to join his administration by treating them with great respect so that vast numbers of knights flocked to his banner. There was a certain Le Yi from the kingdom of Zhao, the grandson of Le Yang, who from a very young age had been interested in military matters. When Le Yang received a fief in Lingshou, his descendants moved there to live. After the death of the Royal Father at Shaqiu, Le Yi left Lingshou with all his family and fled to Daliang, where he sought office with King Zhao of Wei. However, he did not gain His Majesty's trust. When he heard that the king of Yan had built the Golden Tower and was summoning knights from all four corners of the world into his service, he decided to go and throw in his lot with him. He attached himself to an ambassadorial mission and traveled to Yan, where he sought an audience with King Zhao. He gave a disquisition on matters of military strategy and His Majesty was impressed by his intelligence, treating him as an honored guest.

Le Yi protested modestly, but the king of Yan said: "You were born in Zhao and at present are working in the government of Wei. It is only right that I should treat you as an honored guest in Yan."

"I sought office in Wei in order to avoid becoming caught up in a civil war," Le Yi replied. "If Your Majesty would be prepared to take me in, I would be delighted to serve as your vassal."

The king of Yan was delighted and immediately appointed him as a junior minister. His rank was above that of Ju Xin and his ilk. Le Yi immediately summoned his family and they settled down in Yan.

. . .

At this time the kingdom of Qi was very powerful, and they repeatedly invaded and attacked other countries. King Zhao of Yan kept his future intentions to himself, training his troops and succoring his people—he was biding his time. After King Min of Qi threw the Lord of Mengchang out of the country, his actions became even more violent and uncontrolled, resulting in his people becoming very disaffected. The kingdom of Yan had been preparing for many years; the country was rich and its people numerous, furthermore, their army was ready for battle. King Zhao now summoned Le Yi and said to him: "I have endured the humiliation inflicted on our former ruler for twenty-eight years now. My only fear was that death might have removed the king of Qi from the scene before my axe descended on his flesh and my desire for revenge would forever have gone unfulfilled. Such a fear has given me many a sleepless night. Now the king of Qi is arrogant and believes himself to be invincible—he has lost the support of his people. Heaven wants to destroy him! It is my intention to raise the largest army that I possibly can and fight with Qi. Do you have any advice for me?"

"The kingdom of Qi is a huge country with a large population," Le Yi answered. "Furthermore, their army is well-trained. I do not think that you are yet in a position where you can defeat them on your own. If you are determined to attack them, you must plan your campaign with others. Of all your neighbors, you have the best relations with the kingdom of Zhao. You must begin by making an alliance with Zhao, and then Han will be sure to follow suit. The Lord of Mengchang is now prime minister in Wei and he is deeply resentful of his treatment at the hands of Qi. He will definitely join you. That way, your attack on Qi will succeed!"

"Excellent!" the king of Yan said. He prepared the necessary documents and sent Le Yi to persuade Zhao on this matter as his accredited representative.

The Lord of Pingyuan, Zhao Sheng, spoke to King Huiwen on his behalf, and His Majesty agreed to the alliance. Purely by chance, an ambassador from the kingdom of Qin happened to be visiting Zhao at the same time, and Le Yi spoke to him too about the benefits that would accrue from an attack on Qi; the ambassador returned to report this to the king of Qin. His Majesty was unhappy about their growing power, and he was afraid that the other kings might abandon him and throw in their lot with Qi. For these reasons he sent another ambassador back to Zhao announcing that he was happy to join in the campaign against Qi. Meanwhile, Ju Xin went to persuade the king of Wei. He had an audience with the Lord of Mengchang, who took charge of raising an army. After that he agreed to a treaty with the kingdom of Han concerning their role in this campaign. A date was set with all parties for the commencement of hostilities. The king of Yan mobilized all the finest warriors at his disposal and placed Le Yi in command. General Bai Qi of Qin, General Lian Po of Zhao, General Bao Yuan of Han, and General Jin Bi of Wei all arrived on the appointed day with their armies. The king of Yan ordered that Le Yi should be given supreme command of all five armies, with the title of commander-in-chief, and then this huge force marched on the kingdom of Qi.

King Min of Qi took personal command of the Central Army and went out to intercept the enemy west of the Ji River, in the company of his senior general Han Nie. Le Yi marched forward in the vanguard with his own troops, whereupon the armies of the four other kingdoms fought with redoubled bravery. They slaughtered the Qi army and bodies lay everywhere in the wilds, the blood flowing in thick streams. General Han Nie was killed by Le Yi's younger brother, Le Cheng. The allied armies took advantage of their victory to pursue the defeated Qi forces northward. Having suffered a terrible defeat, King Min fled back to Linzi. That very night he sent an ambassador to Chu begging for help, promising that in return he would receive all the lands north of the Huai River. At the same time His Majesty issued commands to muster all soldiers and able-bodied men to guard the city walls. Pressing forward, the armies of Qin, Wei, Han, and Zhao each advanced by different routes, taking control of border cities. Le Yi, on the other hand, took the Yan army deep into enemy territory, striking terror into all the lands through which he passed. The defense in one Qi city after another simply crumbled at his approach. Like an avalanche, the army marched directly on Linzi.

King Min was horrified by these developments. Together with a couple of dozen civil and military officials, he secretly opened the North Gate to the city and fled. When he arrived at the state of Wey, the lord went out to meet him in the suburbs and proclaimed himself a vassal. When His Majesty entered the city, the Lord of Wey gave him his own palace as his residence, treating him with the greatest respect. However, King Min was so arrogant that he felt entitled to treat the Lord of Wey rudely. This deeply upset his ministers, who that very night launched a raid on his baggage trains. King Min was furious, and he intended to make a complaint when next the Lord of Wey came to have audience with him, demanding the arrest of the thieves. That day, His Lordship did not come to have an audience, but nor was the food allowance paid over. King Min now started to regret his behavior. By the time the sun began to set, he was really hungry, and he was also afraid that the Lord of Wey was plotting against him. Hence, together with Yi Wei, he fled the city under cover of darkness. His followers, abandoned by their monarch, scattered in all directions.

Within less than a day's travel, King Min had arrived at the border with Lu. The officials in charge of the border pass informed the Lord of Lu, who then sent an ambassador to meet His Majesty. Yi Wei asked, "What arrangements have been made for the reception of His Majesty?"

"His Lordship is prepared to offer a feast of thirty beasts for your king."

"His Majesty is the Son of Heaven," Yi Wei snorted. "When the Son of Heaven goes out on a royal progress or hunt, lesser lords are required to vacate their palaces for him. Furthermore, their personal attendance is required at his morning and evening meal. Once the Son of Heaven has finished eating, then His Lordship can withdraw and attend court. How can a mere banquet with thirty beasts meet our requirements?"

The ambassador reported this to the Lord of Lu, who was furious and gave orders to close the border passes. King Min traveled to the state of Zou instead. The Lord of Zou had recently died, and His Majesty wanted to enter the capital and condole with the bereaved. Yi Wei informed the people of Zou: "When the Son of Heaven decides to pay a visit of condolence, the family must stand with their backs to the coffin, lined up on the west side of the hall. When they wail, they must face north. The Son of Heaven can then enter along the east side, face south, and offer his condolences."

"This is just a small country" they replied. "We would not dare to put the Son of Heaven to the trouble of paying a visit of condolence." Accordingly, they refused to allow him anywhere near the city.

King Min was now at the end of his tether, but Yi Wei suggested: "I have heard that Juzhou is unmolested; why don't we go there?"

They fled for Juzhou, where they levied troops and prepared to defend the city, ever on the lookout for the Yan army. By this time, Le Yi had broken through the walls of Linzi and captured all the treasures of Qi. He made a special search for precious objects from the kingdom of Yan that had been stolen by Qi in former times—these he had loaded onto carts and returned to their former home. King Zhao of Yan was absolutely delighted. He went in person to the Ji River, where he held a great feast for the three armies and enfeoffed Le Yi with the lands of Chang. Henceforth he was known as the Lord of Changguo. King Zhao of Yan returned home and left Le Yi behind in Qi, to capture their last remaining cities.

. . .

Tian Dan was a distant relative of the Qi royal family: a most learned man with an excellent knowledge of military matters. King Min was not able to employ him in the kind of position that his abilities warranted, but he appointed him as a supervisor of the markets in Linzi. When the king of Yan entered Linzi, the people caught inside the city walls tried to find a place of sanctuary anywhere that they could. Tian Dan and his family sought refuge in Anping. There he had the protruding axle ends on all his carriages cut off, so that the hubcap sat tight on the wheel. Furthermore, he had each axle reinforced with iron cladding to make them even more secure. Everyone laughed at him for this. Not long afterwards, the Yan army arrived and attacked Anping. When the city walls were breached, the people of Anping fought each other to get away. A huge scrum of chariots and carts blocked the road, and in many cases the protruding axle ends became locked with those of other vehicles, making it impossible to move forward at any speed. In some cases, the axles actually broke and the carriages overturned, so the occupants were taken prisoner by the Yan army. The Tian family, on the other hand, was able to escape, since the iron cladding on their carriages held firm and did not break. Thus they were able to make their way to safety in Jimo.

Le Yi now divided his forces and sent them out to take control of every corner of the kingdom. When he arrived at Huayi, he was informed that the former Grand Tutor, Wang Zhu, lived there. He gave orders to his troops that nobody was allowed to go within a thirty- *li* radius of Huayi. In addition to that, he sent gifts of gold and silk to Wang Zhu, for he was hoping to recruit him into the service of the king of Yan. Wang Zhu refused this offer on the grounds that he was too old and ill. Since he was obviously unwilling to go, the envoy said, "The commander-in-chief has issued the following order: 'If you join us, you will be appointed to the office of a general and given a fief of ten thousand households. If you do not join us, our forces will put Huayi to the sword.'"

Wang Zhu raised his face to the heavens, sighed, and said: "A loyal subject does not serve two lords, and a virtuous wife does not marry two husbands. The king of Qi was deaf to loyal remonstrance, so I resigned my position and came here to plough the fields. Now my country has been destroyed and my king is dead ... I have no reason to survive! You have come here to threaten me with your soldiers, and it seems to me that it is better to die with my honor intact than to drag out a mean existence as a disloyal subject!"

He wedged his neck into the fork of a tree branch, and with a sudden wrenching movement he succeeded in breaking his own neck. When Le Yi was informed of this, he sighed and gave orders that he should be buried with full honors. The inscription on his tomb read: "Here lies Wang Zhu, a loyal minister of the kingdom of Qi."

A historian wrote a poem:

> All of Qi lay at the mercy of the Yan troops;
> Who cared what happened to the country?
> Seventy-two cities had been captured,
> But a single scholar still remained loyal.

In the first six months of Le Yi's campaign, he succeeded in capturing more than seventy cities. These were all now incorporated into the commanderies and counties of the kingdom of Yan. The only two places still holding out were Juzhou and Jimo. Le Yi now ordered his troops to rest and recover while he reorganized the ranks of his officers; he struck off all the emergency legislation he had introduced for wartime conditions, remitting taxes and military service in the newly conquered lands. He constructed shrines dedicated to Lord Huan of Qi and Guan Zhong, holding sacrifices in their memory, and did what he could to relieve the plight of refugees and bring them home. The people of Qi were delighted with these measures. Le Yi's idea was that the remaining two cities were surrounded by territory under his control, so they would not be able to cause much trouble. He was hoping that his lenient policies would lead the people there to surrender of their own accord, making it unnecessary for him to use force. This occurred in the thirty-first year of the reign of King Nan of Zhou.

• • •

As mentioned previously, King Min of Qi sent an ambassador to King Qingxiang of Chu, promising that he would be given all the lands north of the Huai River if he sent troops to rescue him. He ordered his senior general, Zhuo Chi, to take an army of two hundred thousand men and collect this land from them in the name of rescuing Qi: "The king of Qi has asked me for help in an emergency; when you get there you can act according to the situation on the ground. My only interest is what will benefit the kingdom of Chu, and I give you a free hand in all other respects."

Zhuo Chi thanked His Majesty and left. He led his army to Juzhou, where he joined forces with King Min. His Majesty was most impressed by Zhuo Chi and appointed him as prime minister, so the Chu general held absolute power. Zhuo Chi quickly realized how strong the Yan army was, and he was afraid that his mission to rescue Qi would not be successful; indeed, he might end up antagonizing two countries. He secretly communicated with Le Yi, suggesting that he assassinate the king of Qi, after which Chu and Yan would divide the lands of Qi between them, providing that the people of Yan appointed him as their new king. Le Yi responded: "If you wish to kill that wicked man, General, you are following in the footsteps of the great Lord Huan of Qi or Lord Wen of Jin: you do not need to discuss this with us. We will accept your commands!"

Zhuo Chi was thrilled. He held a military parade at Gu Village and invited King Min to inspect the troops. When King Min arrived, he was arrested and his crimes formally listed: "There have been three warnings of disaster in Qi. When the skies rained blood, it was a warning from Heaven. When the land split, it was a warning from Earth. When a human voice could be heard wailing outside the pass, it was a warning from Man. Your Majesty did not realize that you should heed these omens; instead, you executed loyal ministers and stripped able men of their office, hoping that you might achieve the status of Son of Heaven. Today Qi is in enemy hands, and you yourself are surviving by the skin of your teeth. What can you possibly hope to gain?"

King Min bowed his head, unable to reply. Yi Wei wept, holding tight to the king. Zhuo Chi killed him first and then had King Min hamstrung and suspended from a beam. He died three days later.

The evil that King Min did brought him a bitter harvest!

Zhuo Chi went back to Juzhou with the intention of seeking out the crown prince and killing him, but he was unsuccessful. Zhuo Chi reported these events to the king of Yan, writing a memorial in which he proclaimed his own merits. He ordered someone to take this to Le Yi, asking him to have it forwarded to His Majesty. From this time onwards, there was a constant stream of secret communications coming and going between Juzhou and Linzi.

. . .

Grandee Royal Grandson Jia lost his father at the age of twelve, leaving him with only his mother. King Min felt sorry for the child and hence gave him this official position. When King Min fled the capital, Royal Grandson Jia was in his train. The two of them became separated in Wey, and after that, not knowing King Min's whereabouts, he managed to make his way home in secret. When his mother saw him, she asked, "Where is the king of Qi?"

"I followed His Majesty to Wey," Jia replied, "but he fled in the middle of the night and I don't know where he has gone."

His mother was furious: "You leave the house early and come back late at night; I lean against the doorframe watching for your return. If you go out at night and don't come back, I go to the gate to our village to wait for you. You should be looking out for your king just as I look out for you! You are a subject of the king of Qi. If His Majesty left one night and you don't know where he went, why did you come home?"

Royal Grandson Jia was very ashamed. He said goodbye to his mother and went back to search for the king of Qi. When he heard that he was in Juzhou, he hastened to join him. On his arrival in Juzhou, he was informed that the king of Qi had already been murdered by Zhuo Chi. Royal Grandson Jia tore the clothes from his shoulders and wailed in the marketplace: "Zhuo Chi was prime minister of Qi and yet he assassinated his king—he has shown his vicious nature! Anyone who is willing to join me in punishing his crime should follow me in tearing his clothes."

The people in the marketplace looked at one another and said: "This child is still very young, but he is motivated by a sense of loyalty and justice. That is a wonderful thing and we should join his cause." In a trice more than four hundred men had torn their garments.

At this point the Chu army—which was extremely strong—was all camped outside the city walls, while Zhuo Chi was living in the king of Qi's palace. He was spending his time drinking and enjoying the performances of women musicians. He had several hundred troops posted outside the palace. Royal Grandson Jia now led four hundred men on the attack, stealing weapons off the regular troops. They fought their way into the palace, and, having captured Zhuo Chi alive, they cut him to pieces. The Chu army was left leaderless. One half of them ran away; the other half surrendered to the kingdom of Yan.

. . .

When Crown Prince Fazhang of Qi heard of the disaster that had overtaken his father, he quickly disguised himself as a poor man. He took the name Wang Li and claimed to be an ordinary inhabitant of Linzi who had fled the city during the troubles. In this guise he obtained a job as a gardener in the household of Grand Astrologer Ji. He worked very hard, and nobody had a clue that he was a nobleman. Grand Astrologer Ji had a daughter of marriageable age. She happened to catch sight of Fazhang when she was walking around the garden, and said in amazement: "This is no ordinary man! What can have happened to him that he should be reduced to such dire straits?" She sent one of her serving maids to find out who he was.

Crown Prince Fazhang was afraid that he might bring disaster down upon himself, so he was not willing to say anything. The Grand Astrologer's daughter said, "A dragon may occasionally masquerade as a fish—when it is frightened it hides itself away. In the future he will be rich and noble indeed!" From time to time she would send one of her maids to give him food and clothing. As time went by, the two of them became increasingly close. Crown Prince Fazhang eventually revealed his true identity to the girl, and they agreed that in the future they would become man and wife. They even began sleeping together, but no one in the Grand Astrologer's household was aware of this.

At this time, the official in charge of the defense of the city of Jimo became ill and died. The army there was left without anyone to take charge, so they decided they needed to appoint a knowledgeable person to become their general. This, however, was easier said than done. Someone who knew of Tian Dan's success in getting away on his reinforced carriages suggested that he would make a good general, and he was indeed appointed by them. Tian Dan picked up a shovel and went out to rebuild the city walls with his men. The women of his family were all sent to the walls to reinforce the garrisons there. The people in the city were awestruck at this.

. . .

Let us now go back to an earlier stage of this story. At the fall of the Qi capital, the ministers of state had scattered in all four directions, seeking sanctuary where they could. When they heard that Wang Zhu had died in such an honorable way, they sighed and said: "He had already resigned his office but he was still totally loyal. We kept our positions in the Qi court, standing by while our country was destroyed and our ruler killed. We have done nothing about ensuring a restoration. What have we been thinking?" They all now fled to Juzhou, where they threw in their lot with Royal Grandson Jia. They were determined to find the present whereabouts of the crown prince. After more than a year, Fazhang came to realize that they were sincere, and so he revealed his identity: "I am indeed the crown prince." Grand Astrologer Ji reported this to Royal Grandson Jia, and he prepared a carriage as prescribed by ritual and welcomed him, crowning him as King Xiang. When this information reached Jimo, they agreed to function in concert, resisting any further attacks by the Yan army.

Le Yi laid siege to them for three years but was not able to conquer them. Thus he decided to lift the siege and retreat nine *li*. There he constructed an army camp and gave the following orders: "If anyone comes out of the city looking for firewood, you are not allowed to arrest them. If there is anyone starving, you are to give them food. If there is anyone cold, you should give them clothing." He was hoping that by showing the people of Qi kindness he could bring them over to his side. No more of this now.

. . .

Grandee Qi Jie of Yan was a very brave and strong man, and he enjoyed talking about military matters. Thanks to this, he had become a close friend of Crown Prince Yuezi of Yan—a relationship that he was hoping would result in a senior military command. He said to the crown prince: "The king of Qi is dead now, and there are only two cities that have not yet fallen to us: Juzhou and Jimo. Le Yi was able to capture more than seventy cities in Qi in the space of just six months . . . what is so difficult about these two? The only reason he is not willing to take these cities is because the people of Qi have not yet gone over to his side. He is hoping that by a combination of kindness and shows of strength he can win them over. Any moment now he will be crowning himself the new king of Qi!"

Crown Prince Yuezi reported these words to King Zhao, who said crossly: "Without the Lord of Changguo we could not possibly have avenged the insult inflicted upon our ancestors! If he really wants to make himself king of Qi, he has every right to do so!"

He had Crown Prince Yuezi caned twenty strokes and sent an ambassador to Linzi with orders to appoint Le Yi as the new king of Qi. Le Yi was so touched by His Majesty's gesture that he burst into tears. However, he swore on his own life that he would never accept the title. "I know Le Yi," the king said. "He would never let me down."

King Zhao of Yan was very interested in techniques of immortality and had an alchemist make him an elixir that contained cinnabar. He took this potion, and not long afterwards he became sick and died. Crown Prince Yuezi came to the throne and took the title of King Hui.

. . .

Tian Dan regularly sent spies to Yan to keep an eye on events. When he was informed that Qi Jie had plotted to replace Le Yi and the crown prince had been caned, he sighed: "Will the restoration of Qi have to wait until the reign of the next king of Yan?" When King Hui of Yan came to the throne, he sent someone to spread the following rumor in the Yan capital: "Le Yi has long been planning to make himself the king of Qi. The only thing preventing him was that he could not bear to betray the great generosity with which he was treated by the late king of Yan. That is why he has been spinning out the attack on the last two cities; he is waiting for his opportunity. Now that a new king has come to the throne, he is trying to do a deal with the people in Jimo. The people of Qi are worried in case some new general is appointed, in which case Jimo is going to find itself put to the sword."

King Hui of Yan had long been suspicious of Le Yi, and the rumor corresponded exactly to what Qi Jie had told him. Naturally, he believed every word to be true. He ordered Qi Jie to go and take over Le Yi's command, while he summoned the latter back to Yan. Le Yi was afraid of being executed. "I am actually from Zhao," he reminded himself, abandoning his family and fleeing west back to that kingdom. There, the king of Zhao enfeoffed him with the lands of Guanjin and granted him the title of Lord of Wangzhu.

When Qi Jie took over as general, he changed all of Le Yi's orders. The Yan army was furious and on the verge of mutiny. Three days after Qi Jie arrived in the encampments, he led the army to attack Jimo, surrounding their city with several concentric lines of troops. The city held firm. Tian Dan got up early in the morning and informed the people of the city: "Last night I dreamed that God on High told me, 'Qi will be restored and Yan will be defeated.' Any moment now the gods will send us a military advisor, and then there is no battle that we cannot win!"

There was a soldier who understood exactly what Tian Dan was driving at, and rushing forward, he said in a low voice: "Can I be the military advisor?" When he had finished speaking, he rushed away.

Tian Dan stopped him, shouting so everyone could hear: "This is the god that I saw in my dream—he is the one!" He had the soldier change into a formal robe and hat and placed him in the command tent while he himself faced north, treating him as if he were indeed an oracle.

"I don't know what to do," the soldier muttered.

"Just shut up!" Tian Dan said. He gave him the title of "Sacred Advisor," and every time he gave an order, it was reported first to him before it was put into practice.

Tian Dan informed the people of the city: "The Sacred Advisor has ordered that anyone making a meal must first perform a sacrifice out-of-doors to their ancestors, in order that we may receive the help of the gods and spirits."

The residents of the city followed this instruction. When birds flying past spotted the food laid out, they all flapped their wings in slow circles as they descended to eat. This was happening twice a day, at dawn and dusk, and the Yan army watching this from outside the walls decided this was some kind of omen. When they heard that the defenders of the city were being instructed by the gods, the rumor of this development spread like wildfire among the troops. "Qi has received help from Heaven," they declared. "We cannot fight them! If we do, we will be going against the will of Heaven!" The army had no will to carry on fighting.

Tian Dan also encouraged his spies to talk about Le Yi's shortcomings. "The Lord of Changguo was too lenient: when he captured Qi people, he did not kill them. That is why the people here are not afraid. If he had cut the noses off his captives and sent them back to the front lines, the people of Jimo would have been terrified!"

Qi Jie believed this, and so he had the noses cut off all the surrendered troops he could lay his hands on. When the people inside the walls saw that these men had been treated with such brutality, they were deeply shocked. They now guarded the city with redoubled energy, since they were terrified lest they be captured by the Yan army. Tian Dan then spread a further rumor via his spies: "The tombs of every family in the city are located in cemeteries outside the walls. If they are desecrated by the Yan army, what are we to do?"

Qi Jie again sent his soldiers out to dig up the graves outside the city walls and burn the corpses found within. The remaining bones were left exposed to wind and rain. The people of Jimo could see this from the tops of the city walls and they wept bitter tears, swearing a terrible revenge on the Yan army. They went to the gates and requested permission to leave the city to fight, to avenge the insult inflicted on their ancestors. Tian Dan knew that the time had come to use his army. Selecting five thousand of his best troops, he concealed them among the people. He had the old and weak, as well as women, defend the city walls in rotation. He sent an envoy to the Yan army announcing that the city had run out of food and that they wanted to surrender on a particular day.

Qi Jie said to his generals: "How do I compare to Le Yi?"

"You are many times greater than he!" they answered. The army all jumped for joy and shouted acclamations.

Meanwhile, Tian Dan collected a thousand ingots of gold from the people and had a rich man to give it to one of the Yan generals in secret, to ensure the security of his family on the day that the city surrendered. The general was delighted and took the bribe. He gave the man a little flag and told him to put it on top of the city wall as a sign. The Yan army made no preparations of any kind; they just sat and waited for Tian Dan to come out of the city and surrender. Tian Dan ordered his men to collect every head of cattle inside the city walls, which amounted to more than one thousand beasts. He had earlier had a number of coats made and painted with multicolored spirals; these were now strapped to the bodies of these cattle. In addition, he had a sharp knife lashed to their horns. Lengths of hemp rope and brushwood that had been dipped in oil were tied to each of their tails, so that they looked as if they were trailing giant brooms. This was all done the night before the date of the surrender. The inhabitants of the city had no idea what he was doing. Tian Dan gave each ox a cup of wine, and then he waited until the sun had gone down and dusk was falling. Now he summoned his five thousand soldiers, all of whom had made a good meal. They were given paint to daub their faces, and each was equipped with weapons. They were told to follow in the wake of the cattle. He ordered the populace to breach the walls in a dozen or so places and then force the oxen out through the holes. As they left the city, the "brooms" attached to their tails were set on fire. As the flames licked closer to the animals' tails, they panicked and headed straight for the Yan army. The five thousand soldiers followed them in silence.

The Yan forces were under the impression that the city was going to surrender the following day, so they were all fast asleep: by this time it was the middle of the night. Suddenly they heard the sound of bellowing and were wrenched from their dreams in alarm. More than one thousand burning brooms, the flames glittering brightly, now lit up the darkness. What they could see were bizarre multicolored things coming straight at them at terrifying speed. When the knives lashed to the animals' horns connected with human flesh, they killed and injured many. The army was thrown into complete disarray. Now a division of troops advanced in total silence, swords and axes at the ready, and attacked. Even though the defenders could only muster five thousand men, in the darkness and confusion, there might as well have been ten thousand of them. Furthermore, the Yan army had been told that the Qi forces were being instructed by the Sacred Advisor, and now they saw these weird apparitions—who knew what manner of creatures they were? Tian Dan now personally led the residents of the city out to join the fight, banging on drums and shouting. The old and the sick, women and children, were all making as much noise as they could, banging bronze objects against each other. The earth seemed to shake with the racket. The Yan army was terrified, and their legs seemed to buckle beneath them. Who could withstand such an onslaught? It was now every man for himself as they ran for their lives. As they fought to get away, a countless number were killed! Qi Jie got into his chariot and fled in a complete panic: he ran straight into Tian Dan, who killed him with a single thrust of his spear. The Yan army suffered a terrible defeat. This occurred in the thirty-sixth year of the reign of King Nan of Zhou.

A historian wrote a poem:

> A trick like that of the burning cattle had never been tried before;
> They took advantage of the situation and showed up Qi Jie's stupidity.
> If the Golden Tower had brought forth no fine military talents,
> Could the kingdom of Yan have defeated Qi with quite such ease?

Tian Dan regrouped his forces and advanced, winning every battle that he fought. When the cities that he passed heard that the Qi army had been victorious and the Yan commander-in-chief was dead, they rebelled and returned their allegiance to Qi. Tian Dan's army grew bigger by the day. By now he had recaptured all their lands as far as the Yellow River and taken control of the northern border of Qi. The seventy cities that Yan had conquered all returned to Qi. The generals were so impressed by what Tian Dan had achieved that they suggested he should be crowned as king.

"Crown Prince Fazhang is at present living in Juzhou," he said, "while I am merely a distant relative of the royal house. How could I possibly take the throne?"

He went to collect Crown Prince Fazhang from Juzhou, with Royal Grandson Jia acting as his charioteer. When they arrived at Linzi, they collected King Min's body and buried it, after which an auspicious day was selected to report what had happened to the ancestral temples and hold the first court of the new reign.

"It is all thanks to you that the kingdom of Qi has recovered from the very brink of disaster!" King Xiang told Tian Dan. "Since you first became famous in Anping, henceforth you will be known as the Lord of Anping. I hereby grant you a fief of ten thousand households."

Royal Grandson Jia was rewarded with a ministerial appointment. His Majesty married the daughter of Grand Astrologer Ji and made her his queen—she was known as Queen Junwang. It was only now that the Grand Astrologer discovered that his daughter had been having an affair with Prince Fazhang, and he said angrily: "You are no daughter of mine! How dare you decide your husband for yourself!" He swore that he would never see his daughter again. King Xiang of Qi sent envoys offering to give him a senior official post or a higher salary, but he refused all these offers. Queen Junwang regularly sent servants to ask after her father and consistently treated him with the utmost ceremony. This all happened later on.

. . .

At this point the Lord of Mengchang decided to resign his position as prime minister in favor of Prince Wuji; the kingdom of Wei therefore enfeoffed His Royal Highness as Lord of Xinling. The Lord of Mengchang went home to live in Xue, in a style comparable to any monarch. He remained on good terms throughout with the Lords of Pingyuan and Xinling. King Xiang of Qi was afraid of him and sent an envoy to restore the seals of office of the prime minister to him, but the Lord of Mengchang refused to accept them. Instead, he kept shuttling between Qi and Wei, acting as a kind of supernumerary ambassador. Eventually, when the Lord of Mengchang died without an heir, the other princelings fought to succeed him. Qi and Wei launched a joint attack on Xue and destroyed it, dividing its territory equally between them.

An old man once traveled through the region where the Lord of Mengchang trained his troops and wrote a poem about it:

Here are massed chariots and horses, and crowds of men,
You could almost imagine you were back in the days of yore.
There are still plenty of people who could steal like a dog or crow
    like a cock,
But who is as generous to them as the Lord of Mengchang?

After the defeat of Qi Jie's army, King Hui of Yan realized just how vital Le Yi had been to the campaign, and he suffered boundless regrets. He sent someone with a letter in which he expressed his regrets and summoned him back to Yan. Le Yi answered the letter but was not willing to return. The king of Yan was frightened lest Zhao make use of Le Yi to plot against Yan, so he decided to make his son, Le Jianxi, the new Lord of Changguo. Meanwhile his cousin, Le Cheng, was appointed a general, and both were treated with great respect. Le Yi was very happy to work for improved relations between the kingdoms of Yan and Zhao, so he came and went regularly between the two of them, and both countries appointed him to the position of minister without portfolio. In the end Le Yi died in Zhao. At this time, Lian Po was the commander-in-chief of Zhao forces. He was personally brave and a fine commander, so all the other kings were afraid of him. The Qin army repeatedly raided the Zhao border regions, but Lian Po offered such stiff resistance that they were not able to penetrate deeply. Qin and Zhao ended up making a peace treaty.

Do you know what happened next? If not, READ ON.

Chapter Ninety-six

Lin Xiangru bends the king of Qin to his will not once but twice.

The Lord of Mafu singlehandedly lifts the siege on the Han capital.

King Huiwen of Zhao was particularly fond of one of his eunuchs, a man named Miao Xian, and as a result he was given the position of director of the palace staff and interfered much in the business of government. Suddenly one day it happened that a visitor from abroad offered Miao Xian a white jade disc for purchase. Impressed by the beautiful color of the jade and its flawless quality, he bought it for the price of five hundred gold pieces. Afterwards, he showed it to a jade worker. The jade worker was amazed and said: "This is Bian He's jade disc. It was lost at a party held by Zhao Yang, the Grand Vizier of the kingdom of Chu, and everyone thought that Zhang Yi had stolen it. He was beaten to within an inch of his life and ended up seeking office in Qin because of this. Later on, Zhao Yang offered a reward of one thousand pieces of gold for this jade, but whoever stole it did not dare to come forward. In the end, he never saw it again. Today by pure chance it has fallen into your hands. This is indeed a priceless treasure, and you must guard it carefully. Do not show it to anyone else unless you are quite sure they are trustworthy."

"I can see this is a fine jade," Miao Xian said. "Why do you say that it is priceless?"

"If you put this jade in a dark place, it will glow naturally," he replied. "It can remove impurities as well as warding off evil influences, hence its other name: 'Night-Shining Jade.' If you put it by your seat you will find it warm in winter months, just like a stove, while in the summer it is cool. No noxious insects will come within one hundred paces of it. With such remarkable properties, is it surprising that no other jade can match it? This is the greatest of treasures."

Miao Xian tested it, and all the man's words proved to be true. He had a box made for it and hid it in his clothes chest. By this time someone had already reported to the king of Zhao: "Miao Xian has laid hands on Bian He's jade disc."

The king of Zhao asked Miao Xian to give it to him, but the latter loved it too much to hand it over. This made the king of Zhao angry. Taking advantage of a hunting trip, he arrived at Miao Xian's house unexpectedly and searched the place. When he discovered the box containing the treasure, he simply removed it.

Miao Xian was afraid that His Majesty might punish him and decided to flee. One of his servants, Lin Xiangru, grabbed hold of his clothing and demanded: "Where are you going?"

"I am going to flee to Yan," Miao Xian replied.

"Are you particularly close to the king of Yan?" Lin Xiangru asked. "Why are you throwing in your lot with him so lightly?"

"A few years ago, I attended the meeting between His Majesty and the king of Yan at the border. The king of Yan took me by the hand and said, 'I would like to be friends with you.' Given the good relationship between us, why should I not go there?"

"You are wrong, sir," Lin Xiangru remonstrated. "At that time Zhao was strong and Yan was weak; that is why His Majesty wanted to be your friend. He did not particularly think much of you, but he wanted to use you to get to the king of Zhao. Now you have offended His Majesty and you are fleeing for your life to Yan. Yan may well be worried about being attacked by the king of Zhao, in which case they will simply arrest you and hand you over to please him. In that case you will indeed be in great danger!"

"What should I do?" Miao Xian asked.

"You have not committed a serious crime . . . the problem is that you were not quick enough about presenting the jade disc to the king. If you were to make a gesture of submission, kowtowing and apologizing, His Majesty would surely pardon you."

Miao Xian followed his advice, and the king of Zhao did indeed forgive him. Miao Xian had been most impressed by Lin Xiangru's intelligence and now promoted him to be one of his senior advisors.

The aforementioned jade worker happened to go to the kingdom of Qin, where King Zhaoxiang set him to polishing jades. He mentioned that the jade disc of Bian He had recently turned up in Zhao. "What's so special about this jade?" His Majesty inquired. The jade worker cited all its miraculous properties like before. Having heard so much about it, the king of Qin was desperate to obtain it for himself. At this time King Zhaoxiang's maternal uncle, Wei Ran, was chancellor of the kingdom of Qin. He came forward and said, "If you want to see this jade, Your Majesty, why don't you offer the fifteen cities of Xiyang in exchange?"

The king of Qin was shocked: "I want to keep those fifteen cities, thank you very much. Why should I exchange them for a single jade disc?"

"Zhao has been terrified of Qin for a long time now," Wei Ran said. "If Your Majesty were to offer those cities in exchange for the jade, Zhao would not dare to refuse. Once the jade is here, you just keep it. Offering the cities in exchange is just an excuse to lay your hands on it—do you really think we would lose anything?"

The king of Qin was delighted and promptly wrote a letter to the king of Zhao, which was conveyed to him by the minister without portfolio, Hu Shang. It read:

> I have long heard tell of Bian He's jade disc but I have never seen it. Having heard that Your Majesty had obtained it, I feel I should offer something in fair exchange. I am willing to hand over fifteen cities in Xiyang to you in return. Please let me know your decision.

When the king of Zhao received this letter he summoned his senior ministers, Liao Po and others, to discuss the situation. He wanted to give it to Qin but was afraid there was some trickery involved: having handed over the jade, the cities would prove entirely illusory. On the other hand, he was worried that if he did not give it to them, Qin would be angry. Some of his ministers spoke in favor of handing it over and others spoke against it, without any consensus.

"What we should do is to send an intelligent and brave knight with the jade disc," Li Ke suggested. "If he gets the cities, he can hand over the jade to Qin. If not, he should bring it back to Zhao. In that case we do not lose either way."

The king of Zhao stared at Liao Po, who hung his head in silence. The director of the palace staff, Miao Xian, stepped forward and said: "There is a man who is a member of my household—his name is Lin Xiangru. He is a brave knight and a man of considerable intelligence. If you want an ambassador to send to Qin, you could not find a better candidate."

The king of Zhao immediately ordered Miao Xian to summon Lin Xiangru. When he had finished offering formal greetings, His Majesty asked him: "The king of Qin has promised me fifteen cities in exchange for my jade disc. Do you think I should agree?"

"Qin is strong and Zhao is weak," Xiangru replied. "You have to agree."

"What do I do if I hand over the jade disc but they do not give me the cities?" His Majesty asked.

"By offering you fifteen cities in return for your jade disc, they have set a generous price. If Zhao does not agree to the deal, it puts us in the wrong. If you present them with the disc before you have taken control of the cities, it shows that you are treating Qin with great respect. If Qin then refuses to give you what they have promised, they have put themselves in the wrong."

"I need someone to go to Qin to protect this jade," the king said. "Do you think you can do this for me?"

"If you really cannot find anyone better, then I will take the jade for you. If they give you the cities, I will hand over the jade to Qin; if they do not, I will bring the jade back to Zhao safe and sound."

The king of Zhao was delighted and appointed Lin Xiangru to the position of a grandee, after which he took possession of the jade. Accordingly, Lin Xiangru set off westward in the direction of Xianyang.

. . .

When King Zhaoxiang of Qin heard that the jade disc had arrived, he was very pleased. Taking his seat on top of the Zhang Tower, he ordered all his ministers to assemble and then summoned Lin Xiangru into his presence. Xiangru removed the jade disc from its box. With his hands raised high, he bowed twice and presented the jade in its silk brocade wrappings to the king of Qin. His Majesty peeled back the layers of silk and looked at it; he saw that the jade was pure white and flawless, glowing with a gentle light. The places where the design had been incised were so beautifully done that you might imagine it was entirely natural. This really was a rare treasure! The king of Qin looked his fill, heaving a deep sigh. Then he showed it to all the ministers present. When they too had inspected it, they all bowed and said: "Congratulations, Your Majesty!" The king of Qin gave orders that his eunuchs should wrap it up again and take it into the harem for his womenfolk to enjoy. After a long time, they brought it back and placed it on the table in front of the king of Qin.

Lin Xiangru was standing to one side during all of this, waiting. Naturally, he noticed that nobody had even mentioned the cities that were supposed to be given in return. He now came up with a plan. Stepping forward, he presented his opinion: "This jade disc has a slight flaw. Let me show it to you!" The king of Qin ordered his servants to pass the jade to Lin Xiangru. Once he had the jade in his hand, he took a couple of steps backward until he fetched up against one of the pillars in the great hall, whereupon he glared at the assembled company. He was by now too angry to keep his mouth shut.

"Bian He's jade disc is one of the greatest treasures in the world!" he shouted at the king of Qin. "You wanted to lay hands on it, and so you wrote to Zhao. His Majesty summoned all his ministers to discuss your offer, and they said: 'Qin will take advantage of their military might; their promises when trying to get possession of this jade are worthless! We are afraid that once it has left your control, you will not be given the cities. You cannot agree!' I thought to myself, 'Ordinary people don't go around cheating one another—let alone rulers of great states! Would it not be terrible if by doubting Your Majesty's good faith we were to annoy you with our intransigence?' So His Majesty fasted for five days, and afterwards he ordered me to take the jade with every gesture of respect, bowing as he escorted me out of the palace. When you gave me an audience, Your Majesty, you behaved with scant ceremony, starting with the fact that you received the jade sitting down! You showed it to your cronies and afterwards sent it in to the harem for your ladies to finger—this is indeed a vile pollution! Now, to add to all of that, I discover that you have no intention of handing over the cities you promised us, so I am taking back this jade! If you try and force me to hand it over, I will break my head open on this pillar at the same time as I crush this jade to bits! I would rather die than leave this treasure in your possession!"

Clutching the disc, he eyed the pillar as if he were just about to dash it to pieces. The king of Qin was afraid that the jade he wanted to keep would indeed be broken, so he apologized: "There is no need for all of this! How could I fail to keep my promise to Zhao?" He ordered his officials to bring out the map. The king of Qin indicated exactly which areas would constitute the fifteen cities to be given to Zhao.

Lin Xiangru thought to himself, "His Majesty is still hoping to get possession of the jade by trickery. None of this is real." Accordingly, he said to the king: "His Majesty, the king of Zhao, would not dare to keep possession of this rare treasure if by doing so he would arouse your ire. Before sending me on this mission, he fasted for five days. Afterwards, he summoned all his officials and bowed as he sent me on my way. Now Your Majesty should fast for five days too, and arrange for a fine carriage and an awe-inspiring parade—then I will hand over the jade disc."

"Fine," the king of Qin said. He gave orders for five days of fasting and escorted Lin Xiangru to an official guesthouse where he would be staying. Lin Xiangru took the jade into the guesthouse. Then he thought to himself, "I promised the king of Zhao: 'If they give you the cities, I will hand over the jade to Qin; if not, I will bring the jade back to Zhao safe and sound.' Right now the king of Qin is fasting, but if he does not hand over the cities after I have given him the jade, how can I possibly go back and face His Majesty?"

He ordered his servant to dress up in coarse clothes and make himself look as poor and humble as possible. He was entrusted with Bian He's jade disc, hidden in a cloth bag hanging from his waist. He traveled back to Zhao by circuitous, minor roads. He reported Lin Xiangru's words to the king of Zhao: "I am afraid that Qin has been lying and they have no intention of handing over the cities as promised. I have instructed my servant to bring the jade back to you. I will be punished by Qin, but even if they kill me, I will not have failed in my mission."

"Xiangru has not let me down!" the king of Zhao said happily.

. . .

The king of Qin may have promised to fast, but in fact he did nothing of the kind. Five days later he went to the main hall of the palace, where a magnificent ceremony was planned. He had ordered all the ambassadors from different countries to be present when he received the jade disc, because he was hoping for a good opportunity to show off. In particular, he made a fine display of welcoming the ambassador from the kingdom of Zhao. Lin Xiangru walked forward in a relaxed and unhurried manner, just as he had before. When the formalities of thanking His Majesty for allowing him this audience had been completed, the king of Qin noticed that Lin Xiangru was not holding the jade.

"I have already fasted for five days," he said, "in order to make a suitably respectful gesture when receiving Bian He's jade disc. Why do you not have it with you?"

Lin Xiangru presented his opinion: "There have been more than twenty rulers in Qin since the time of the great Lord Mu, and each one has been more devious than the last. Let us just call to mind what the Viscount of Qi did to Zheng and what Baili Shi did to Jin; or indeed in more recent times we can think of how Shang Yang behaved with respect to Wei, or Zhang Yi in the case of Chu. There has been quite sufficient evidence that you are not to be trusted an inch. I was afraid that you might be planning to deceive me and hence cause me to lose faith with His Majesty, so I took the liberty of sending one of my servants to take the jade disc back to Zhao. You can execute me if you like."

"You complained that I did not show a properly respectful attitude, and hence I fasted for five days before taking possession of this jade," the king of Qin said angrily. "Now you tell me that you have sent it back to Zhao! Clearly you think I am someone you can just push around!"

He shouted at his servants to arrest Xiangru and tie him up. Lin Xiangru did not move a muscle. "Please be calm, Your Majesty!" he said. "I have something to say. At the moment Qin is strong and Zhao is weak, so you can bully us—how could we possibly hope to push you around? If you really want to gain possession of this jade, first you have to hand over the fifteen cities to Zhao, and then you can appoint a senior ambassador to go back with me and collect it. Zhao cannot possibly keep it once you have paid for it! They do not want to have a reputation for being untrustworthy, nor would they willingly annoy Your Majesty. I accept that I have behaved badly towards you and my crime merits the death penalty; I have already told the king of Zhao that I did not expect to come back from this mission alive! Why don't you have me boiled alive in a huge cauldron and let the other rulers know that Qin killed an envoy from Zhao because you wanted to lay hands on a jade disc? Let them see the rights and wrongs of the matter!"

The king of Qin and his ministers looked at one another, unable to think of anything to say. The foreign ambassadors who were watching this were all terrified on Lin Xiangru's behalf. The king of Qin's servants were just about to drag him out when His Majesty shouted at them to stop. He said to his ministers, "If I kill this Lin Xiangru, I won't get the jade and I will be thought completely untrustworthy, not to mention ruining the alliance between Qin and Zhao." He treated him with generosity and sent him home with full honors.

An old man, reading the history books on the subject of these events, said that Qin attacked and conquered many cities and the other kingdoms were not able to do anything about it at all. Was a jade disc really that important? Lin Xiangru was afraid that if the king of Qin succeeded in forcing Zhao to hand over the jade disc, it would make them despise it even more and in the future it would be much more difficult to maintain their integrity. If they demanded land or tribute, they would not be able to refuse. That is why he made so much fuss. He wanted the king of Qin to know that there were people in Zhao who could stand up to him.

There is a poem that reads:

> This flawless jade disc was truly priceless,
> The king of Qin was determined to possess it.
> How could a servant simply remove it?
> What were the warriors in the Qin court thinking?

. . .

When Lin Xiangru returned, the king of Zhao decided to appoint him as a senior grandee on account of his brilliant success. In fact, Qin never gave them the cities, but then Zhao did not hand over the jade disc either. The king of Qin decided in the end that he was not prepared to let this go. Therefore, he sent another ambassador to invite the king of Zhao to a meeting at Mianchi on the west bank of the Yellow River to reaffirm the alliance between their two countries.

"At the meeting with King Huai of Chu, Qin took him prisoner and held him captive in Xianyang," the king of Zhao said, "and this is still a source of great distress to the people of Chu. Now he wants to invite me to a meeting. Is he planning to treat me in the same way?"

Lian Po and Lin Xiangru discussed the matter: "If you do not go, Your Majesty, you will be showing weakness to Qin." They presented their joint opinion: "Xiangru should go with Your Majesty while Lian Po can stay behind helping the crown prince to guard the capital."

"You were able to bring my jade back safe and sound," His Majesty said cheerfully. "I will pose you no trouble!"

Zhao Sheng, the Lord of Pingyuan, presented his opinion: "In the past, Lord Xiang of Song rushed off alone to attend a meeting and ended up being taken prisoner by Chu; when the Lord of Lu met Qi at Jiagu, he was attended by the minister of war. We now have agreed that Lin Xiangru will go with you to protect Your Majesty, but I would like to have five thousand picked men accompany you, in case of unexpected developments. In addition to that, I think that the main army should be encamped thirty *li* away. That way, we should have nothing to worry about."

"Who will command these five thousand men?" the king asked.

"I understand that Li Mu, the agricultural official, would make a really fine general!" the Lord of Pingyuan replied.

"Why do you think that?"

"As I said, Li Mu is an agricultural official," the Lord of Pingyuan explained. "He went out to collect taxes, and there were a number of families that did not pay on time. As a result, he punished them according to the law. He ended up executing nine of my subordinates. I was angry and complained about this. Li Mu said to me: 'The law underpins everything in the country. If I were to let these people who work for you go, I would be failing in my duty to the public, which would do irreparable damage to the law. If the law is damaged, the country is weak. When other countries attack us, Zhao would not be able to save itself. In that case, what do you think you will gain from your high position? You should be putting the public good over all other considerations and supporting the implementation of the law, for if that happens the country will be strong and you will keep your wealth and honors for a long time. Wouldn't that be great?' He has a most unusual perspective on things, and so I am sure he would make a good general!"

The king of Zhao appointed Li Mu as grandee and general in command of the Central Army, ordering him to lead the five thousand picked men who would form his escort. The Lord of Pingyuan brought up the rear with the main body of the army. Lian Po escorted them as far as the border, where he said to the king of Zhao: "You are now entering Qin, Your Majesty. This is an abode of tigers and wolves—it is really unclear what will happen next. I have calculated how far you have to go and how long it will take to perform all the rituals and ceremonies at this meeting, and I reckon it cannot possibly take longer than thirty days. In the event that you don't come back by then, we will follow the precedent of Chu and establish the crown prince as king. That should put a stop to Qin's plans."

The king of Zhao agreed to this. When he arrived at Mianchi, it was to discover that the king of Qin was already there, and each of them went to the guesthouse where they were to stay. On the appointed day, the two kings greeted each other with all due ceremony and toasted one another in wine. When they had drunk enough to become a bit tipsy, the king of Qin said: "I have heard that you are an amateur musician, Your Majesty. I have a fine *se* zither here, and I would like you to play it."

The king of Zhao turned bright red, but he did not dare to refuse. Several servants from Qin brought in the instrument and put it down in front of the king of Zhao. He performed the song "The Spirit of the Xiang River," and the king of Qin praised his playing to the skies. When that was over, the king of Qin said: "I have heard that the founder of the

Zhao royal house was himself a fine musician. I can see that you have a great family tradition!"

He looked at his entourage as a signal that they were to summon his historian, indicating that he was to record his remarks. The court historian of Qin picked up his brush and a bamboo strip and wrote the following words: "On such and such a day, the king of Qin met the king of Zhao at Mianchi, and he ordered the king of Zhao to play the *se* for him."

Lin Xiangru stepped forward and said: "His Majesty has heard that you are good at performing Qin-style music. Let us bring in a cup and you can drum on it, so we can all enjoy the music!"

The king of Qin flushed bright red with anger, but he did not say anything. Lin Xiangru now picked up a cup full of wine. Kneeling in front of the king of Qin, he put it in place. Since the king of Qin was not willing to perform, Lin Xiangru said, "You are entirely reliant on Qin's military might. But I am now just five paces away from you and I could splash you with my blood if I were so inclined."

"This Xiangru is behaving disgracefully!" the king of Qin's servants screamed. They wanted to go forward and arrest him. Lin Xiangru opened his eyes wide as he bellowed at them, his hair standing on end and his beard bristling. The servants were shocked at the sight; unconsciously, they took several steps backwards. The king of Qin was furious, but he was afraid of Lin Xiangru, and so he forced himself to strike the cup once. Lin Xiangru got up from his seat and summoned the Zhao historian. He told him to write on a bamboo strip: "On such and such a day, the king of Zhao met the king of Qin at Mianchi, who ordered the king of Qin to drum on a cup for him."

The king of Qin's entourage was very unhappy about this. They got up from their seats and said to the king of Zhao, "Since we have welcomed you like this, please give the king of Qin fifteen cities as a birthday present!"

Lin Xiangru petitioned the king of Qin: "In ritual you both give and receive. If Zhao is going to give fifteen cities to Qin, you have to pay us back. Why don't you give Xianyang to the king of Zhao as his birthday present?"

"We are allies!" the king of Qin said. "I don't want anyone to say another word!"

He ordered his servants to bring in the wine, and everyone pretended to be enjoying themselves. The Qin minister without portfolio, Hu Shang, and a number of others secretly encouraged His Majesty to arrest the king of Zhao and Lin Xiangru, but the king of Qin said: "My spies have reported that Zhao has made careful preparations to deal with all eventualities. If anything were to go wrong, I would make myself a laughingstock."

He treated the king of Zhao with even greater respect. They agreed to a treaty in which they promised never to attack each other. He sent Yiren, the son of the crown prince, the Lord of Anguo, to Zhao as a hostage. His ministers all said: "You have made the alliance. Why do you have to give them a hostage?"

The king of Qin laughed and said: "Zhao is still too strong for us to have any hope of being able to conquer them. If we don't send them a hostage, Zhao will not trust us. As long as they trust us and our alliance with them holds firm, I can turn my attention to Han!" The Qin ministers were deeply impressed by His Majesty's plans.

There is a poem that testifies to this:

The meeting at Mianchi nearly ended in violence,
The king of Zhao was held in the palm of his hand.
But a single blow on the cup destroyed his authority,
And Lin Xiangru became famous for all time.

. . .

The king of Zhao said goodbye to the king of Qin and went home, arriving back just thirty days after he had left. "As long as I have Lin Xiangru," he said, "I am as secure as Mount Tai and my country stands as firm as the nine *dings*. Xiangru has done wonderfully well by me—none of my other ministers can compare." He appointed him to the office of Prime Minister of the Right, which he held in common with Lian Po.

"I have done great things in the service of my country," Lian Po said crossly, "attacking cities and fighting battles in the wilds. Xiangru has gotten where he is today merely by yapping, but his position is even higher than my own. He was just a member of a eunuch's household and his origins are humble indeed! How can I possibly accept being held inferior to such a man? The next time I see Xiangru I am going to kill him."

Lin Xiangru was informed of what Lian Po had said, and after that, every time the two of them were to hold open court, he would claim to be too ill to attend. This ensured he never met Lian Po face-to-face. The members of his household all thought that Lin Xiangru was a coward, and they discussed the matter in secret.

One day, Lin Xiangru happened to leave his house at the same time as Lian Po. In the distance Xiangru could see that Lian Po was driving forward, so he quickly ordered his own charioteer to pull into a narrow alleyway to hide, waiting for Lian Po's chariot to go past. His servants were more and more furious at the whole thing. They agreed that they would all go together to see Xiangru and remonstrate with him: "We have left home, abandoning our families, to come to seek positions in your household. We did this because we thought you were a remarkable man who may only come along once in a generation. We follow you because we admire you. But now you and Lian Po hold equivalent office; in fact you are the senior! He has said some nasty things to you, and not only do you not take revenge, you avoid him at court and hide from him in the city. Why are you so frightened? We are humiliated on your behalf. We have made up our minds to resign."

Lin Xiangru stopped them with the words: "There is a reason why I have been hiding from General Lian Po, but you have not been able to discover it."

"We are ignorant people lacking in foresight," his servants said. "Please explain your reasoning to us."

"Is Lian Po more important than the king of Qin?" Lin Xiangru asked.

"No," his servants all replied.

"With the power that the king of Qin commands, there is nobody in the world who dares to resist him. But I went to his court and shouted at him, humiliating his courtiers. If I were scared, why would that apply only to General Lian Po? The way I think about it, the only reason a country as powerful as Qin does not dare to attack Zhao is because of the two of us. When two tigers fight, only one of them survives. If Qin hears of that, they will take advantage of the situation to invade Zhao. The reason why I go to all of these lengths to avoid the man is because the security of the country is paramount: my own private enmity is comparatively unimportant."

The servants all sighed their admiration. Not long afterwards, Lin Xiangru's servants happened to bump into Lian Po's staff in a tavern. The two parties got into a fight over seats. One of Lin Xiangru's servants said, "Our master gives way to General Lian Po for the sake of the country. We should follow his example and give way to his clients." This made the victors even more arrogant.

. . .

There was a man named Yu Qing from east of the Yellow River who was traveling through Zhao and chanced to overhear what Lin Xiangru's servants said about him. He went to speak to the king of Zhao about this: "Are Lin Xiangru and Lian Po your only important ministers?"

"They are," the king agreed.

"I have heard that the ministers in previous administrations were much more numerous and that they respected each other and helped one another out," Yu Qing remarked. "This enabled them to govern the country well. However, today you have just two senior ministers, Your Majesty, and they get along together about as well as fire and water. This is not a matter that will bring good luck to the country. The more that Grandee Lin gives way, the more General Lian will push the matter. The more arrogant General Lian is, the more difficult Grandee Lin will find it to clip his wings without serious damage. They do not discuss matters together at court, and the longer this goes on the more intractable the problem will become. I am most worried about this and I think Your Majesty should be too! I think with a little help from Your Majesty I can make Grandee Lin and General Lian become friends."

"Wonderful!" the king of Zhao said.

Yu Qing then went to have an audience with Lian Po, at which he began by praising his military successes. Lian Po was very pleased. Yu Qing went on to say, "There is no one who can match you, General, when it comes to success in battle. However, when it comes to planning, I would have to give the palm to Lian Xiangru."

"That weakling is supposed to have achieved great things by yapping," Lian Po said crossly, "but I am not sure why you think he is so great."

"Lin Xiangru is no weakling," Yu Qing assured him. "He sees much deeper into things than you do." He explained to the general what Lin Xiangru had said to his servants and then continued: "This does not matter if you are trying to bring the kingdom of Zhao down. However, if you want to do your best for Zhao, with him giving way and you wrangling, I am afraid that when the day of reckoning comes, people will not be praising you."

Lian Po felt very ashamed of himself: "I had no idea of what you just told me. I really am far inferior to Lin Xiangru." He sent Yu Qing to present his apologies to Lin Xiangru and afterwards presented himself in person at the door of his house in a gesture of submission. "I am too stupid to have understood what you were doing," he said, "and I had no idea that you were so magnanimous. Death would not be enough to atone for my crime." He knelt down outside the main hall of his house.

Lin Xiangru rushed forward to help him to his feet. "Let us work together for the greater good of the country," he said. "I am delighted to know that you will help me, General; there is no need to apologize."

"I am a crude and violent man," Lian Po exclaimed. "Your forgiveness makes me feel even more humble." He wept as he took hold of the other. Lin Xiangru also burst into tears.

"From now on the two of us will be the closest of friends," Lian Po asserted. "Even if it costs me my life, I will never let you down."

He bowed and Lin Xiangru reciprocated. They held a banquet then and there, at which the two of them ate and drank in perfect harmony.

The Chinese expression for a deathless friendship is derived from these events.

There is an anonymous poem about this:

Drawing his chariot away to hide was a sign of his sincerity;
By his submission, the general showed that he was quite his equal.
As for the squabbling powerful families of today,
Which of them takes the greater good of the country to their hearts?

The king of Zhao presented Yu Qing with one hundred ingots of gold and appointed him as a senior minister.

. . .

At this time the Qin general Bai Qi attacked and defeated the Chu army, conquering the capital city, Ying, and establishing Nan Commandery. King Qingxiang of Chu fled, making a stand in Chen to the east. General Wei Ran then attacked and conquered Qianzhong, establishing Qianzhong Commandery. Chu was now in ever-increasing difficulties. His Majesty had no choice but to send Crown Prince Xiongwan, accompanied by Grand Tutor Huang Xie, to Qin as a hostage while begging for a peace treaty. Bai Qi now turned his attention to Wei, marching on Daliang. Wei sent their commander-in-chief, Bao Yuan, out to do battle, but he was defeated with the loss of forty thousand men. Wei presented three cities with their request for a peace treaty. Qin enfeoffed Bai Qi as Lord of Wu'an. Shortly afterwards, the minister without portfolio, Hu Shang, attacked Wei again, defeating their general Mang Mao, capturing Nanyang, and establishing Nanyang Commandery. The king of Qin enfeoffed Wei Ran as Marquis of Rang. After that, he sent Hu Shang in command of a force of two hundred thousand men to attack Han, laying siege to Yuyu.

King Li of Han sent an ambassador to request help from Zhao in this emergency. King Huiwen of Zhao summoned all his ministers to discuss the situation: should they rescue Han or not? Lin Xiangru, Lian Po, and Le Sheng all agreed: "Yuyu is located in a dangerous situation approached by narrow defiles. It will not be easy to rescue them."

The Lord of Pingyuan said: "The security of Han and Zhao is dependent upon each other—they are like the lips and the teeth. If we do not save them, weapons will be turned on us next!"

Zhao She sat silently. The king of Zhao asked him his opinion, and he answered: "It is true that Yuyu is located in a dangerous situation approached by narrow defiles. In that case it can be compared to two rats fighting in a hole—the bravest one will win."

The king of Zhao gave him fifty thousand picked men and told him to rescue Han. He marched thirty *li* out of the East Gate of the city of Handan before giving orders to build ramparts and make a camp. When they were well dug in, he issued the following command: "Anyone who speaks about military matters will be executed!" He had the gates of the camp closed and went off to sleep. His troops were stunned into silence. The Qin army sounded their battle drums with a thunderous racket—in the city of Yuyu, the very roof tiles were reverberating with the noise. A soldier came to report what the Qin army was up to, but Zhao She regarded this as a contravention of his express orders and had the man beheaded as an example to others. He stayed there for twenty-eight days without moving. Every day he had his men build the walls higher and dig the defensive trenches deeper, as if he were planning to hold this place forever.

The Qin general Hu Shang was informed that troops had arrived from Zhao to help, but he did not see them. He sent out spies to find out what was going on. They reported: "Zhao has indeed sent out an army to rescue Han, but the senior general, Zhao She, advanced just thirty *li* from Handan and made camp. He has not moved from there."

Hu Shang did not believe this, so he ordered some of his closest associates to go straight to the Zhao army and say: "Qin is attacking Yuyu, and it will fall at any moment. If you want to fight, come as quickly as you can!"

"The king of Zhao sent me here when his neighbor reported their emergency," Zhao She replied. "How could I dare to actually fight the Qin army?"

He treated his visitors with the utmost ceremony, holding a banquet in their honor. He also arranged for them to have a tour of his encampment. The Qin envoys went back to report this to Hu Shang, who said delightedly: "The Zhao troops have advanced just thirty *li* from their capital before settling down, not moving a step further. If they are spending their time improving their fortifications, it means they have no stomach for a fight. Yuyu will be mine!"

He launched in on an all-out attack on Han, making not the slightest preparations for defending against the possibility of an attack by Zhao.

Having seen off these visitors, Zhao She calculated that it would take him three days to reach the main Qin army. He gave orders that five thousand cavalry and trained archers should make up the vanguard, while the main body of the army advanced behind them. They were to travel day and night, making no noise at all. After traveling two days and one night, they arrived at the border with Han. They now built a second army camp just fifteen *li* from the city walls of Yuyu. Hu Shang was furious. Leaving one half of his army, he emptied the camp of everyone else and went off to fight the enemy.

There was an officer in the Zhao army named Xu Li who wrote the single word "Remonstrance" on a piece of bamboo and knelt down outside the camp. Zhao She was surprised at this and gave orders that his previous commands were now revoked. Then he summoned this man in and asked, "What do you have to say?"

"Qin was not expecting you to come here, and their morale is high," Xu Li replied. "You must strengthen your defenses lest you succumb to a surprise attack. Otherwise you are sure to be defeated."

"You are right!" Zhao She exclaimed. He gave orders for his troops to go into battle formation.

"According to *The Art of War*," Xu Li said, "the army that has the geographical advantage will win. In the vicinity of Yuyu, the mountains to the north are the only ones of any height, but the Qin army has made no arrangements to hold them. They have been left free for you, General, so you had better go and occupy them as soon as possible."

"You are right!" Zhao She shouted again.

He immediately ordered Xu Li to take command of ten thousand men and go to occupy the northern peaks, building fortifications there. As the Qin army marched forward, they could see exactly what they were up to. When Hu Shang's forces drew up, they had to fight for possession of these mountains. The occupied peaks were highly precipitous; a handful of brave soldiers on the Qin side attempted to scale them, but they were driven back, injured by a constant hail of rocks thrown down by the Zhao troops. Bellowing with rage, Hu Shang gave orders that his officers search in all directions for a better route. It was just at this moment that suddenly they heard the thunderous sound of drumming as Zhao She led his army forward to attack them. Hu Shang ordered that his troops split up to defend themselves. Zhao She had divided his ten thousand archers into two groups, five thousand on the right and five thousand on the left, and they now fired at will on the Qin army. Xu Li led his ten thousand men down the mountainside to attack them as well, in a screaming horde. Caught in front and behind, the Qin army was slaughtered. There was simply no place to hide.

Having sustained a terrible defeat, the survivors took to their heels. Hu Shang's horse stumbled and he fell to the ground. He was almost taken prisoner by a Zhao soldier, but it so happened that the Commandant Si Li arrived just in time with his troops, and he was saved. Zhao She chased the Qin army for fifty *li* so they could not return to camp— they just fled westward. The siege of Yuyu having been lifted, King Li of Han came in person to feast the army. He wrote a letter thanking the king of Zhao for his help. The king of Zhao enfeoffed Zhao She with the title of Lord of Mafu, and he held equivalent rank to Lin Xiangru or Lian Po. Zhao She recommended Xu Li as a man of ability, and he was appointed as Defender-in-Chief.

. . .

Zhao She's son, Zhao Kuo, had been very interested in military matters from the time that he was a small child; he learned the family copies of the *Six Secret Teachings* and the *Three Strategies* by heart after a single reading. He often discussed strategy with his father, winning one argument after the other. He thought he was the greatest military thinker of all time, and even Zhao She was not able to shake his supreme self-confidence. His wife said happily, "With a son like this, we have produced yet another fine general!"

"Kuo cannot become a general," Zhao She said irritably. "It would be a great blessing for the kingdom of Zhao should he take up some other profession!"

"Kuo has read all of your books," his wife chirruped, "and he says himself that there is not his equal as a strategist anywhere in the world. Now you say that he cannot become a general. Why is this?"

"Kuo thinks that nobody can better him," Zhao She said. "That is the very reason he is unsuited to a military career. A general has to go out on the field of battle and fight; he must always be thinking of what is best for his men. It is only someone who knows fear who will think carefully about what he is going to do—Kuo is only good at talking. If he were given command over the army, he'd take nobody's advice but his own. If he is impervious to loyal advice and good suggestions, he is sure to be defeated."

His wife told Kuo what his father had said. "Father is old and timid, that is why he speaks the way that he does," Zhao Kuo said confidently.

Two years after these events, Zhao She became seriously ill. On his deathbed, he told his son: "Weapons are evil things and warfare is dangerous; that is why our forefathers considered battle the last resort. I have been a general for many years, and I am lucky enough never to have suffered the humiliation of a defeat . . . I can rest in peace. You do not have the right character to be a good commander. Please do not try and take this office against my express wishes, for it will only lead to the ruin of our family."

He further instructed his wife: "If in the future the king of Zhao summons Kuo and wants to make him a general, you must refuse this in accordance with my last will and testament. It would be no minor matter if the army were to be butchered and the country humiliated!"

As soon as he had finished speaking, he breathed his last. In appreciation of all that Zhao She had done for the country, the king allowed Zhao Kuo to inherit his position as the Lord of Mafu.

If you don't know what happened next READ ON.

Chapter Ninety-seven

A "dead" Fan Ju plots his escape to the kingdom of Qin.

A false "Zhang Lu" openly humiliates the Wei ambassador.

In the city of Daliang there lived a man named Fan Ju, who could talk knowledgeably about every topic under the sun. It was his ambition to bring peace to his country. He wanted to seek office with the king of Wei, but his family was poor and he had no means to bring himself to His Majesty's attention. For this reason he joined the household of a mid-ranking grandee named Xu Jia, working as one of his retainers. In the past, King Min of Qi had behaved in a wickedly irresponsible manner, and so Le Yi had united four countries in a joint attack on Qi. Wei had been part of this, sending an army in support of Yan. When Tian Dan defeated Yan and restored Qi, Crown Prince Fazhang came to the throne as King Xiang. The king of Wei was worried lest he take revenge, so he discussed the situation with the prime minister, and they sent Grandee Xu Jia to Qi with instructions to restore the alliance between them. Xu Jia ordered Fan Ju to go with him. King Xiang of Qi asked Xu Jia: "In the past, when our former king joined with Wei in the coalition attack on Song, we were united. However, when the Yan army was sacking our country, Wei was on their side. When I think of what my father suffered, I have to grit my teeth to endure the pain! Now you turn up here trying to trick me with empty promises! Wei keeps changing sides without rhyme or reason; how can you expect me to trust you?" Xu Jia did not know how to reply.

Fan Ju, who was standing to one side, answered: "You are wrong, Your Majesty. When our former king participated in the campaign against Song, it was because he had been ordered to do so. The original agreement was that the kingdom of Song should be divided in three, but you ignored that, taking all its lands for yourself. After that, Qi treated its neighbors with even greater contempt. It is you who broke faith with us! The other kings were horrified by the arrogance and violence with which they were treated by Qi, and hence they ended up turning to Yan. At the battle of Jixi, you were defeated by an allied army from five different countries—not just Wei! Of course as far as you are concerned we did many bad things, but at least we did not dare to join Yan in the advance on Linzi; we treated Qi well in that regard! Now Your Majesty is in a position of great power and authority and you want to avenge the insult inflicted on your kingdom, having apparently learned nothing from the disaster that befell you. His Majesty was hoping that you might follow the example of Lord Huan of Qi, or indeed King Wei, and bring about a revival in your country's fortunes. This would put an end to the mistakes made by King Min, which would indeed be a great blessing. It is for this very reason that His Majesty sent Xu Jia here as an ambassador to restore treaty relations between our two countries. However, you seem to only be thinking of blaming other people without understanding the other side of the story. I am afraid that you are going to find yourself following in King Min's footsteps and repeating the mistakes of the past!"

King Xiang of Qi was startled. He got up from his seat and apologized: "I was wrong." He asked Xu Jia, "Who is this man?"

"He is one of my retainers: Fan Ju."

The king of Qi looked at him for a long time. Afterwards he escorted Xu Jia to the official guesthouse, where he made arrangements for him to be treated with lavish hospitality. He sent someone to visit Fan Ju in secret and say: "The king of Qi has been deeply impressed by your abilities, sir, and would like you to stay behind in Qi. He is prepared to give you the position of minister without portfolio. Please do not say no!"

"I came here with the ambassador, and I will leave with him," Fan Ju asserted. "How could I achieve anything in this life if I so clearly demonstrate my lack of faith and untrustworthiness?"

The king of Qi now redoubled his efforts. He sent someone back again with a gift of ten pounds of gold for Fan Ju, together with meat and wine. Fan Ju resolutely refused to accept this present. In accordance with the king of Qi's commands, the messenger urged him to take it half a dozen times, insisting that he could not possibly take His Majesty's presents back to him. Fan Ju now had no choice. He accepted the meat and the wine, but returned the gold. The messenger sighed and left.

Someone soon reported this development to Xu Jia. He summoned Fan Ju and asked him, "What did that messenger from the king of Qi want?"

"I don't know," Fan Ju replied. "Perhaps it is because I am a member of your staff, they thought that by making up to me, they would get into your good books."

"If they are giving presents to you and not to me, the official ambassador, it can only be because you are engaged in some kind of treasonous relationship with Qi!"

"A while back the king of Qi sent a messenger with an offer to let me stay behind and become a minister without portfolio here," Fan Ju retorted. "I refused. I have already ruined my career for the sake of loyalty and justice; how could I possibly be involved in a treasonous plot?"

This answer made Xu Jia even more suspicious.

. . .

When the embassy was over, Xu Jia and Fan Ju returned to Wei. Xu Jia spoke to the prime minister, Wei Qi: "The king of Qi wanted to keep my retainer, Fan Ju, and make him a minister without portfolio. To this end, he presented him with gold, meat, and wine. I suspect that from now on he will be acting as Qi's spy in our capital, and that is why he was given these gifts."

Wei Qi was furious. Summoning his guards, he ordered them to arrest Fan Ju because he intended to interrogate him personally. When Fan Ju arrived, he prostrated himself at the bottom of the steps. The prime minister asked him in a sharp voice, "Have you been in secret communication with the kingdom of Qi?"

"I would not dare to do such a thing!" Fan Ju replied.

"If you have not been involved in some underhanded dealings, why did the king of Qi want you to stay behind?"

"His Majesty did want me to stay, but I did not agree."

"Why did you accept the gift of gold, meat, and wine?" Wei Qi demanded.

"The messenger insisted over and over again that I do so, and I was afraid of offending the king of Qi. That is why I eventually agreed to take the meat and wine, but the ten pounds of gold I simply refused."

"Traitor!" Wei Qi screamed. "How dare you try to excuse your actions? You must have done something for them, that they wanted to give you food and wine!"

He shouted for his guards to tie the man up and beat him one hundred lashes. The torture would only stop when he had told all them everything about his dealings with Qi.

"I have done nothing wrong!" Fan Ju cried. "What do you want me to confess to?"

Wei Qi was now even more furious. "Beat this bastard to death!" he shouted. "If he lives he will only cause us trouble!" The guards whipped him all over his body. When they knocked out his teeth, Fan Ju's face was covered in his own blood. The pain was very difficult to bear. He kept protesting his innocence, but his torturers—seeing how angry the prime minister was—did not dare to stop. Wei Qi ordered his servants to bring in a big jug of wine, while at the same time he shouted at the guards to put their backs into their work. They tortured Fan Ju for hours until there was not a single whole piece of skin anywhere on his body and blood soaked the ground. When they broke his ribs with a horrible crunch, Fan Ju screamed once and stopped breathing.

> How sad that such a fine gentleman, loyal and brave,
> Should end up dead in a ditch!
> Xu Jia is supposed to have been a very great knight;
> How could he become involved in the torture of this good man?

The recluse of Qianyuan wrote the following poem:

> Why was Zhang Yi accused of stealing a jade disc in Chu?
> Why was Fan Ju said to have betrayed his country to Qi?
> Once suspicions have been aroused, they are difficult to allay.
> How many heroes have died, accused of crimes of which they were
>   innocent?

The guards reported: "Fan Ju has stopped breathing." Wei Qi inspected him in person. He saw that Fan Ju's rib cage had been broken and his teeth knocked out, while his body was covered in appalling wounds. He lay stretched out in the middle of a lake of blood. Pointing at him, Wei Qi said: "The traitor is dead! Good! Let this be a lesson to anyone thinking of doing the same thing!" He ordered the guards to wrap the body in a grass mat and throw it into a latrine. He wanted his men to piss on it, so that Fan Ju's defiled ghost would never rest in peace.

As it turned out, though, Fan Ju's story was not over yet. Although he had stopped breathing temporarily, he eventually returned to consciousness. Peering over the top of the grass mat in which he was wrapped, he saw that there was only one soldier on guard. Fan Ju sighed gently. The guard heard this and rushed over to him.

"I have suffered such severe injuries that I am going to die," Fan Ju said. "If you can help me to die at home and be buried in a proper coffin, I will give you a couple of gold ingots in thanks."

The soldier was tempted by the mention of the gold, and so he said, "You just stay there pretending to be dead. I will go in and see what I can do."

At that time Wei Qi and his retainers were all drunk. The guard entered and said, "The dead body in the latrine stinks to high heaven. I think it ought to be moved."

The retainers seconded the idea: "Although Fan Ju was a criminal, you have already punished him enough."

"Throw the body somewhere outside the suburbs where the wild animals can feast on his flesh," the prime minister said. When he had finished speaking, the party broke up. The retainers departed and Wei Qi went into the inner quarters. The guard waited until it was dark and everything was quiet. Then he secretly carried Fan Ju home on his back.

When Fan Ju's wife and children saw what had happened to him, they were absolutely horrified. Fan Ju ordered them to give the soldier some gold in thanks for his help. Freeing himself from the grass mat, he handed it to the soldier, so that he could throw it somewhere in the wilds, so that if someone showed an inclination to inquire into what had happened, it might mislead them. After the soldier had gone, his wife cleaned his wounds and bandaged them, as well as giving him something to eat and drink.

Fan Ju said calmly to his wife: "The prime minister hates me. Even though he thinks I am dead, he is very suspicious. The only reason I was able to escape from the latrine was because he was drunk. Tomorrow when he sends someone to look for my body, they will not be able to find it. After that, someone is sure to come here looking for me, and if they find me, they will kill me. I have a close friend called Zheng Anping who lives in a little alley by the West Gate. You must take me there under cover of darkness and, whatever happens, you must not tell anyone where I have gone. In about one month's time, when I have recovered enough from these injuries to leave, I will go into exile abroad. Once I have left the house, I want you to begin mourning, and you must carry on exactly as if I were genuinely dead. That may put an end to their suspicions."

His wife did exactly as he said. She sent a servant to inform Zheng Anping of what had happened. He immediately went to Fan Ju's house to see him. After that, Fan Ju's family carried him around to the other man's house.

The following day, just as Fan Ju had anticipated, Wei Qi started to become suspicious and he worried that his victim might perhaps have recovered consciousness. He ordered someone to go and find the body. The guards reported back: "The body was abandoned out in the wilds far from any human habitation. We found the grass mat, but the corpse must have been eaten by pigs or dogs."

Wei Qi sent someone to spy on Fan Ju's house. He discovered that they were all wearing mourning, so he felt he could relax and allow the matter to pass. All this time Fan Ju was lying in Zheng Anping's house, resting and taking his medicine and gradually returning to health. The two of them then went into hiding together at Mount Juzi. Fan Ju changed his name to Zhang Lu, and nobody else living there knew who he really was.

. . .

About six months later, Wang Ji came to the kingdom of Wei as an ambassador, in accordance with instructions that he had received from King Zhaoxiang of Qin. He took up residence in an official guesthouse. Zheng Anping dressed up like one of the people working there and wormed himself into Wang Ji's service. Since he was a very capable man, Wang Ji became extremely fond of him. One day he happened to ask in private conversation: "Do you know of any exceptionally talented man in this country who has not yet been recruited into government service?"

"Men of exceptional talent are rare!" Zheng Anping replied. "There was one man called Fan Ju who was very clever indeed, but he was beaten to death by the prime minister!"

Before he had even finished speaking, Wang Ji sighed and said, "How sad! If he had come to Qin, he would have had an arena in which to display his talents."

"There is a man living in my village called Zhang Lu whose talents are in no way inferior to those of Fan Ju. Would you like to meet him?"

"I would be delighted to meet this man," Wang Ji said. "Why don't you arrange it?"

"Zhang Lu has enemies in the capital," Zheng Anping said, "and hence he does not dare to move about in broad daylight. If it were not for these enemies, he would have been a senior official in Wei long before this!"

"I would be happy to meet him if he comes overnight," Wang Ji assured him. "I will stay up and wait for him."

Zheng Anping arranged for Zhang Lu to dress like someone working at the guesthouse, and in the middle of the night he smuggled him in to meet Wang Ji. Wang Ji began by mentioning various important matters of state, and Fan Ju explained one point after the other, showing a vast knowledge of the subject.

"You are clearly no ordinary man," Wang Ji said happily. "Would you be willing to go to Qin with me?"

"I have enemies here in Wei, and they do not give me any peace," Fan Ju explained. "If you set a date, I would be happy to join you."

Wang Ji crooked his finger and said, "I expect that it will take me another five days to finish the remaining business associated with my embassy. On that day you can wait for me in a deserted part of Santinggang, and we will head off together!"

Five days later, Wang Ji said goodbye to the king of Wei. The ministers of state held a banquet in his honor and escorted him out of the suburbs. Afterwards, they all said goodbye. Wang Ji rode his carriage to Santinggang. Suddenly he saw two men emerge from the forest. One was Zhang Lu and the other Zheng Anping. Wang Ji was as pleased as if someone had just given him a rare treasure. He rode back to Qin accompanied in the same carriage by Zhang Lu. The two of them ate and drank together throughout the journey and they slept in the same room. Talking of this and that, they became fast friends.

Within a couple of days, they had arrived at the Hu Pass on the Qin border. Looking into the distance, they could see a plume of dust rising opposite them as a line of carriages and cavalrymen approached from the west.

"Who is coming?" Fan Ju asked.

Wang Ji recognized the rider in front and said, "The chancellor, the Marquis of Rang, is on a tour of the eastern provinces."

The Marquis of Rang's personal name was Mi Weiran. He was the younger brother of Dowager Queen Xuan. The dowager queen was originally a member of a junior branch of the Chu royal family, and she was the mother of King Zhaoxiang of Qin. King Zhaoxiang came to the throne as a small child, and Dowager Queen Xuan took charge of the government during the regency. It was she who employed her younger brother as chancellor and gave him the title of Marquis of Rang. Later on she also appointed another younger brother, Mi Rong, as Lord of Huayang. The two of them controlled the government of the country.

When King Zhaoxiang grew up, he was afraid of the dowager queen, and so he enfeoffed his younger brother, Prince Kui, as Lord of Jingyang, and Prince Shi became the Lord of Gaoling. He was hoping by these means to clip the powers of the Mi family. The people of the capital called these men the "Four Aristocrats," but in fact none of them had anything approaching the power of the chancellor. Every year at this time the chancellor would go on a progress around the country representing the king. He would inspect the local officials, check in person on the maintenance of city walls and moats, inventory the number of chariots and horses present, and conduct a census of the populace. This was all done according to long-established rules.

Now the Marquis of Rang was going on his eastern progress and his train was so magnificent—how could Wang Ji fail to recognize him?

"I have heard that the Marquis of Rang monopolizes power in the government, and he is very jealous of the talents of other men," Fan Ju said. "He has a particular dislike for visitors from other countries because he is afraid that they will show him up. I had better hide in a trunk and escape notice."

A short time later, the Marquis of Rang arrived. Wang Ji got down from his carriage to greet him politely. The Marquis of Rang followed suit. "I see you have been working hard in the service of our country . . ." he said.

The two men stood in front of their carriages, chatting about various minor matters. "Was there any trouble around the eastern passes?" the marquis asked.

"None," Wang Ji said with a bow.

The Marquis of Rang looked inside the carriage. "I hope you have not brought back a foreign advisor! Those people go from country to country in search of fame and fortune, making wild assertions to rulers. In actual fact they are all useless."

"I wouldn't dare," Wang Ji assured him.

The Marquis of Rang then said goodbye and left. Fan Ju climbed out of the trunk and announced that this was where he would get off the carriage and continue on foot.

"The chancellor has already gone," Wang Ji said. "You can ride in the carriage with me."

"I caught a glimpse of the Marquis of Rang's face just now," Fan Ju remarked, "and I noticed that he has tiny pupils and a squint. A person like that is going to be suspicious but also a bit slow. He looked into the carriage—showing that he is definitely already suspicious—but he did not search it. Any minute now he is going to regret and come back to remedy his omission. I had better hide from him."

He called to Zheng Anping, and the two of them walked off. Wang Ji followed them in his carriage. When they had traveled about ten *li*, they could hear the sound of horses behind them. Just as Fan Ju had said, a group of twenty cavalry officers came from the east, riding like the wind. They halted by Wang Ji's carriage and said, "The chancellor has ordered us to come back and search your carriage. He is worried in case you have brought back a foreign advisor. I do hope you don't mind."

They searched every nook and cranny of the carriage, and when they had assured themselves that there was no foreigner concealed within it, they turned back. Wang Ji sighed and said, "Mr. Zhang is indeed a remarkably clever man. I simply cannot compare!"

He gave orders that his carriage should continue forward, and when they had advanced about five or six *li*, they caught up with Zhang Lu and Zheng Anping. He took them back into his carriage and they proceeded on their way to Xianyang.

An old man wrote a poem commemorating Fan Ju's departure from Wei:

> His skills in prognostication were truly amazing!
> Few in his generation could match his vast knowledge!
> What is the point of the Lord of Xinling keeping three thousand clients
> If he lets a man of such talent escape to the kingdom of Qin?

Wang Ji went to court to have an audience with King Zhaoxiang of Qin. When he had finished reporting about his embassy, he came forward and said: "There is a certain Mr. Zhang Lu in Wei who is amazingly brilliant—a man of truly remarkable talents. He told me that the situation in the kingdom of Qin is currently extremely precarious and suggested a plan for resolving our problems. However, he really needs to speak to Your Majesty in person, so I brought him back with me."

"Foreign advisors always like to talk big," the king of Qin declared. "However, I will let him stay in an official guesthouse."

He had him housed in one of the lesser guesthouses in order to summon him to the palace when needed. However, more than a year went by without a call. Suddenly one day it happened that Fan Ju was walking through the market and happened to see the Marquis of Rang going past, setting out on campaign with his army. Fan Ju quickly asked someone, "If the chancellor is going out on campaign, what country is he planning to attack?"

An old man replied: "He is going to attack Gangshou in Qi."

"Has the Qi army invaded Qin?" Fan Ju asked.

"No," the old man said.

"Qi and Qin balance each other to east and west; in between lie Han and Wei. If Qi has not attacked Qin in any way, why is Qin going so far to attack them?"

The old man dragged Fan Ju off to a quiet corner, then said, "The king of Qin doesn't want to attack Qi. However, the chancellor's fief is located at Mount Tao, and that is not too far from Gangshou. The chancellor wants the Lord of Wu'an to take command of the army and conquer it so that he can add it to his own territory!"

Fan Ju went back to the guesthouse and wrote a letter to the king of Qi, which said:

Your humble subject Zhang Lu has committed a crime deserving of the death penalty. I deserve to die! Let me explain. I have heard it said: "When an enlightened ruler governs the country, those who do great deeds in the service of the state will be rewarded, men of talent will be appointed to official positions, those who have worked hard will be given suitable emoluments, and those of great ability will receive noble titles." If these principles are applied, incapable men do not dare to occupy positions for which they are manifestly unqualified, while capable men do not find themselves neglected and unemployed. I have now spent one whole year here in this lesser guesthouse. If you believe I have something to contribute, then please give me a moment of your spare time and allow me to speak to you. If you think I do not have anything to offer, then why are you keeping me here? It is my job to speak; it is your job to listen. If I say something wrong, it will not be too late for you to punish me. You should not disregard the suggestion of the person who recommended me, even if you do not find me personally prepossessing.

The king of Qin had already forgotten all about Zhang Lu. When he read the letter, he sent someone in a chariot to bring him to the traveling palace for an audience. Fan Ju arrived before His Majesty. Seeing the king of Qin's carriage coming into view, he pretended not to have noticed it and deliberately walked down the road leading to the harem. One of the eunuchs ran after him and said, "His Majesty is here."

Fan Ju was deliberately insulting: "The only people who matter in the kingdom of Qin are the dowager queen and the Marquis of Rang. Who cares about the king?"

He kept on walking forward. Just as they were in the middle of their argument, the king of Qin arrived and asked the eunuch, "What is all the shouting about?"

The eunuch reported exactly what Fan Ju had said. The king of Qin was not angry at all, but greeted his guest and took him into the inner quarters. He treated him with all the respect due to an important visitor. Fan Ju made appropriate polite responses. The king of Qin sent all his servants away and then knelt down in front of him. "Please, can you tell me what to do?" he said.

"No . . . no!" Fan Ju replied.

A short time later, the king of Qin knelt down again and made the same request as before. Fan Ju continued to make polite noises of refusal. This happened another three times. "If you refuse to give me the benefits of your advice, sir," the king of Qin said, "is that because you think I am not worthy of listening to it?"

"How could that be?" Fan Ju replied. "In the past Lü Shang was fishing on the banks of the Wei River, where he happened to meet King Wen of Zhou; after one conversation, the king appointed Lü Shang as his chief advisor and always used his suggestions. Thus he was able to destroy the Shang dynasty and unite the world under his own control. The Viscount of Ji and Prince Bigan were members of the Shang royal family. They did everything they could think of to encourage His Majesty to listen to loyal advice, but the wicked King Zhou paid them no heed. He made one of them a slave and executed the other. As a result of this, the Shang dynasty perished. The crucial distinction here is about trust. Lü Shang was a complete stranger, but he was trusted by King Wen and thus he was able to found the Zhou dynasty. Lü Shang was rewarded with a noble title and fief that has been passed down from one generation to the next among his descendants. The Viscount of Ji and Prince Bigan were members of King Zhou's own family, but because His Majesty did not trust them, they both suffered humiliation and death without being able to do anything to save the country from its travails. Now, I am just a visitor to this country and I have no connections here. I want to talk about great plans to revive the fortunes of the country, but this means I must touch upon the actions of certain of Your Majesty's relatives. If I do not criticize them, then Qin cannot be saved. On the other hand, if I do criticize them, then I will suffer the same fate as the Viscount of Ji and Prince Bigan. That is the reason why I did not dare to agree even after Your Majesty requested me three times for advice. I am not yet sure if you trust me or not."

The king of Qin knelt down again and said, "What do you mean? I know that you are a very talented man, and that is why I sent away my entourage so that I could concentrate on hearing your advice. Normally people with things to say go either to the dowager queen or to the senior ministers. You can speak to me completely freely!" The king of Qin said this because of the argument that Fan Ju had become involved in with the eunuch when he tried to make his way to the harem area; the eunuch had reported him as saying, "The only people who matter in the kingdom of Qin are the dowager queen and the Marquis of Rang. Who cares about the king?" This had irritated him, and he was entirely sincere in wanting help to deal with the situation. For his part, Fan Ju was concerned lest if, at this first meeting, his words failed to reach the mark, he would never be given the opportunity to speak to His Majesty again. There were many people among the king's entourage who were flapping their ears—he was afraid that if they reported what he said, it would bring terrible consequences down upon his head. It was for that reason that he said what he did before entering the palace, in the hope that it would be like setting a spark to a pile of kindling.

"Since you have ordered me to speak, Your Majesty," he said, "I am happy to do so!" He bowed and the king of Qin returned his bow. Afterwards the two men sat down.

Fan Ju opened his remarks with the following words: "Qin's territory occupies a very advantageous situation, and your armies are so strong that no other kingdom in the world can match them. However, you have not brought about the unification of the country, and you have failed in your mission to become a great king. This can only be because the ministers at your disposal in Qin are not good enough!"

The king of Qin leaned forward in his seat. "Please explain why you say they are not good enough!"

"I have heard that the Marquis of Rang is going to attack Qi even though he has to cross Han and Wei to do so: this is simply stupid!" Fan Ju said. "Qi is located a very long way from Qin; Han and Wei lie between you. If you do not send out a large army, you cannot possibly inflict any damage on Qi. On the other hand, if you do send out a large army, it is Qin that will suffer first. In the past, Wei attacked Zhongshan in spite of the fact it was on the far side of Zhao—well, they conquered Zhongshan, but these lands ended up becoming part of Zhao. Why? It was because Zhongshan was close to Zhao and far from Wei. If you now attack Qi and do not defeat them, it will inflict a terrible humiliation on Qin. On the other hand, if you do succeed in defeating Qi, all that will happen is that you benefit Han and Wei. What good will that do Qin? In Your Majesty's position, it is most beneficial to forge alliances with kingdoms far away and attack your neighbors.

These alliances will please those distant monarchs while such attacks will expand Your Majesty's own territories. Thus you can proceed step by step, swallowing up all those that stand in your way just like a silk-worm munching at a mulberry leaf. In that case it will not be hard to unify the whole country."

The king of Qin now asked, "In what order should I proceed about allying with kingdoms far away and attacking my neighbors?"

"Your most important distant allies are Qi and Chu. The neighbors you should focus on attacking are Han and Wei. Once you have con-quered Han and Wei, how can Qi and Chu survive as independent king-doms?"

The king of Qin clapped his hands and exclaimed in delight. He immediately appointed Fan Ju to the position of minister without port-folio. Henceforth he was to be known as Minister Zhang. He decided to follow his advice and attack Han and Wei to the east. He also gave orders to halt Bai Qi's attack on Qi.

. . .

The chancellor, Mi Weiran, and General Bai Qi had both been involved in the government of the kingdom for a long time. Now they saw that Zhang Lu had suddenly obtained His Majesty's favor, and they were both unhappy about this. However, the king of Qin trusted him abso-lutely and his favor increased every day. He would summon him to discuss policy in private—even in the middle of the night—and did nothing without his approval. Fan Ju realized that the king of Qin had made up his mind, and so he asked for an audience. Having sent His Majesty's entourage away, he came forward and said: "Thanks to the fact that Your Majesty listens to my advice, I have become involved in the government of the country. Even if I were to be chopped to pieces, I could not repay all that you have done for me. I have a plan to bring peace to Qin, but I have never yet dared to present it to Your Majesty."

The king of Qin knelt down and said, "I have entrusted the country to you. If you have a plan to bring security to the kingdom and you don't tell me now . . . what are you waiting for?"

"I used to live on the Shandong peninsula, and at that time everyone knew about the Lord of Mengchang in Qi, but nobody had heard of the king. In the case of Qin, everyone knows about the dowager queen, the Marquis of Rang, and the lords of Huayang, Gaoling, and Jingyang, but nobody pays any attention to the king. The person who governs a country is called a king; he decides the life and death of his people, he gives and takes away—these are prerogatives that other people cannot take onto themselves. The dowager queen has relied upon the respect due to her as the Mother of the Country to govern Qin without considering anyone else for more than forty years. The Marquis of Rang is in sole charge of the kingdom of Qin; the Lord of Huayang just supports him. The lords of Gaoling and Jinyang have each established enormous households and great estates: they go around killing people just as they please. The wealth of these private families is ten times that of Your Majesty. However, if you were to accept being made a cipher, would that not be terribly dangerous? In the past Cui Shu monopolized power in Qi, and in the end he assassinated Lord Zhuang. Li Dui held ultimate power in Zhao and finally killed the Royal Father. The Marquis of Rang can rely upon the dowager queen's unhesitating support inside the palace and outside; he has long usurped the power and authority that ought to be Your Majesty's. If he uses troops, the other kings quake with fear; if he stands down his army, they admire his magnanimity. His eyes and ears are everywhere—they are here among your own entourage, Your Majesty! You have long been left without any supporters at court! I am afraid that with the fullness of time, it will not be Your Majesty's sons and grandsons who are sitting on the throne of Qin!"

When the king heard this, he could feel the hairs on the back of his neck prickling. He bowed twice and thanked Fan Ju, saying: "What you have said is nothing but the truth. This situation has been troubling me for a long time!"

The following day he gave orders to take back the seals of office from the Marquis of Rang, Mi Weiran, and demanded that he return to his estates. The Marquis of Rang borrowed more than one thousand oxcarts from other officials with which to move his possessions. A truly amazing collection of rare treasures was loaded onto these carts—things that you would not find even in the royal treasury of Qin. The following day, the king of Qin gave orders that the Lords of Huayang, Gaoling, and Jingyang were to leave the country for exile. He also arranged that the dowager queen should be placed under house arrest inside the harem, to prevent her from interfering in the government of the country again. He appointed Fan Ju as the chancellor and gave him the city of Ying as his fief. He was also granted the title of Marquis of Ying. Of course, the people of Qin all thought that their new chancellor was called Zhang Lu; with the exception of Zheng Anping, none of them knew that he was really Fan Ju. Fan Ju forbade him to mention this to anyone, and hence Zheng Anping did not dare to speak of it. These

events occurred in the forty-first year of the reign of King Zhaoxiang of
Qin, which was the forty-ninth year of the reign of King Nan of Zhou.

A historian wrote a poem, which reads:

The Four Aristocrats monopolized power in Qin,
They dominated the government for forty years.
Anyone who annoyed them ended up on the block,
Before they fell at the word of a minister without portfolio.

. . .

By this time King Zhao of Wei was already dead, and his son had come
to the throne as King Anli. When he discovered that the king of Qin was
following the advice of the newly appointed chancellor Zhang Lu, and
hence wanted to attack Wei, he quickly summoned all of his ministers
to discuss the situation. The Lord of Xinling said: "It has now been
many years since Qin last attacked the kingdom of Wei. If today they
raise an army against us for no good reason, then they are clearly trying
to take advantage of the fact that we cannot defend ourselves. We ought
to send our toughest soldiers to hold our key encampments and prepare
for a long defensive war."

"No," Wei Qi responded. "Qin is strong and Wei is weak; if we fight
them, we are going to lose. I have heard that Chancellor Zhang Lu of
Qin originally came from Wei. Surely he does not want his family and
friends to suffer in the coming war. Let us send an ambassador loaded
with lavish gifts to open communications with Zhang Lu. After that, he
can seek an audience with the king of Qin. If we agree to send hostages
to them, we ought to be able to remain safe."

King Anli had only just come to the throne and had no experience of
battle. He followed the prime minister's advice. He sent the mid-level
grandee Xu Jia to Qin as his ambassador. In accordance with his instructions, Xu Jia traveled to Qin and took up residence in a guesthouse. Fan
Ju was informed of this and said happily: "Xu Jia has come. Now is the
time for me to take revenge!"

He removed his fine garments and dressed himself like a servant.
Slipping out of the gate of his mansion in secret, he made his way to the
guesthouse, where he tottered in and asked to be allowed to see Xu Jia.
When Xu Jia caught sight of him, he was terribly shocked. "Are you
still alive, Fan Ju?" he exclaimed. "I thought that you had been beaten
to death by the prime minister! What are you doing living here?"

"They abandoned my body outside the suburbs, and after a couple
of days I came to," Fan Ju explained. "It so happened that a merchant

was passing by. Alerted by the sound of my moans, he felt sorry for me and rescued me. Although my life had been saved, I did not dare to go home. So I managed to make my way through the passes here to the kingdom of Qin. I was never expecting to see you here, sir!"

"Surely you don't hope to offer persuasion to the king of Qin?"

"That dream caused enough problems for me in the past in Wei," Fan Ju declared. "I barely escaped with my life! Having been lucky enough to survive that, how could I possibly hope to be involved in matters of state again?"

"How have you survived all this time in Qin?" Xu Jia asked.

"I have been living hand-to-mouth, earning a bit of money as a servant."

Xu Jia felt terribly sorry for him. He made him sit down and had food and wine brought in. Although it was winter, Fan Ju was just wearing thin clothing and seemed to be shivering with cold. Xu Jia sighed and said, "You have been chilled to the bone!" He ordered that a padded silk coat be brought and made him put it on.

"I could not possibly wear one of your garments, sir!" Fan Ju protested.

"We are old friends," Xu Jia declared. "There is no need to be so polite."

Fan Ju put the coat on, repeating his thanks over and over again. Then he asked, "What are you doing here, sir?"

"Chancellor Zhang Lu is now in charge of the government here, and I need to talk to him," Xu Jia explained. "It has proved more difficult than I expected to find someone to take a message to him. You have been living here in Qin for a long time. I don't suppose that you have an acquaintance who could put me in touch with this Zhang Lu, do you?"

"My master is a good friend of Chancellor Zhang Lu," Fan Ju replied. "I have often accompanied him to the chancellor's mansion. Zhang Lu likes a good debate, but my master is not particularly ready with his words and I always have to help him out. The chancellor has been impressed by some of my arguments and sometimes gives me meat and wine. You could say that I am acquainted with him myself. If you want to have an audience with Zhang Lu, I could go with you."

"If that is the case, then may I trouble you to pick a suitable day?"

"The chancellor is a busy man," Fan Ju said. "However, he is free today. Why don't we go now?"

"I came here in a great carriage drawn by a team of four horses," Xu Jia said. "One of my horses stumbled today and managed to break the axle on my carriage. I cannot go right away."

"My master has a suitable carriage that you could go in. I am sure that you could borrow it."

Fan Ju went back to his mansion and had his great carriage drawn by a team of four horses sent around to the guesthouse. He reported to Xu Jia: "The carriage and horses are ready. I will act as your charioteer."

Xu Jia got happily into the chariot, and Fan Ju picked up the reins. When they drove through the marketplace, people there spotted that it was the chancellor's carriage coming past. Either they stood to one side respectfully or they moved to get out of the way. Xu Jia thought that this was a gesture of respect to him—he had no idea that it was for Fan Ju. When they arrived at the mansion, Fan Ju said: "Please wait here, sir. I will go on ahead and communicate with the chancellor. If he agrees to see you, you will be able to have an audience with him immediately."

Fan Ju walked in through the gates to the mansion. Xu Jia got down from the carriage and stood outside the gate. He waited for ages, and then he heard the sound of drumming coming from inside the mansion. The gatekeepers shouted, "The chancellor is entering the main hall!" A whole host of underlings and retainers went rushing back and forth. He saw neither hide nor hair of Fan Ju. Xu Jia asked the guard at the gate, "A while back my old friend, Fan Ju, went in to see the chancellor, but he has not come out again; do you think you could take a message to him for me?"

"The man you want is called Fan Ju?" the guard said in puzzlement. "When did he enter the mansion?"

"He was the man who drove the chariot here just now . . ." Xu Jia said.

"The charioteer was Chancellor Zhang Lu himself. He was paying a private visit to an old friend staying in one of the guesthouses here; that is why he went out in plain clothes. Who is this Fan Ju that you mentioned?"

When Xu Jia heard this, it was as if he had been violently wrenched from his dreams. With his heart thumping wildly in his chest, he said, "I have been deceived by Fan Ju. He is going to kill me!"

As the saying goes: "A bride may not want to meet her in-laws, but she doesn't have a choice." He stripped off his robe and removed his belt, took of his hat and shoes, and knelt down in front of the gate. He asked the guards at the gate to take a message in. What he said was: "The criminal, Xu Jia, from the kingdom of Wei is awaiting death outside your gate!" After a long time, the servants announced that the chancellor had summoned him. Xu Jia was now even more terror-stricken than before. Hanging his head and walking forward on his knees, he went into the house through one of the side gates. When he arrived at the steps leading up to the main hall, he kowtowed over and over again, saying, "I deserve to die!"

Fan Ju was sitting in the hall, in full pomp and regalia. "Do you understand that you are guilty of a crime?" he asked.

Xu Jia prostrated himself and said: "I do."

"How many crimes are you guilty of?"

"Even if you were to pluck one hair out of my beard for every crime that I have committed, it would not be enough," Xu Jia declared.

"You are guilty of three crimes," Fan Ju announced. "My ancestors' graves are all in Wei, and that is the reason why I was not prepared to accept a government position in Qi, but you thought that I was engaged in some kind of treasonous commerce with them, and so you slandered me to the prime minister as a means of working off your anger. That is your first crime. When the prime minister was at the peak of his rage and ordered that I be beaten, nay, that I have my teeth knocked out and my ribs broken, you did not say a word to stop him. That is your second crime. When I was in a coma and lying helpless in the privy, you were the first of the prime minister's cronies to urinate on me. As Confucius said: 'Do unto others as you would have them do unto you.' Have you not been too cruel? That is your third crime. Now you are here, and I was originally thinking of having you executed to assuage my anger. The reason why I am not going to kill you is that you were kind enough to give me your silk coat—that shows that you still think of me as a friend. You should be grateful that you are going to survive!"

Xu Jia kowtowed and thanked him over and over again. Fan Ju waved him away, and he crawled out. It was now that the people of Qin discovered that Chancellor Zhang Lu was in fact Fan Ju from the kingdom of Wei, who had come to their country under an assumed name.

An old man wrote a poem that reads:

How much he suffered when his ribs were broken and his teeth knocked out!
Yet he went on to be appointed as chancellor and receive a marquisate.
His pain and anger were all there to be paid back,
Yet the gift of a silk coat was also weighed in the balance.

The next day, Fan Ju went to the palace and had an audience with the king of Qin. "The kingdom of Wei is so frightened they have sent an ambassador to beg for a peace treaty," he said. "There is no need to turn your troops against them. This is all thanks to Your Majesty's virtue and awe-inspiring presence."

The king of Qin was very pleased. After that, Fan Ju stepped forward and said, "I have been deceiving you, Your Majesty. If you promise not to punish me, I will tell you about it."

"I cannot imagine what you have been deceiving me about!" His Majesty said. "I am sure you have committed no crime against me!"

"In fact, my real name is not Zhang Lu—I am Fan Ju from the kingdom of Wei. I came from a poor family and was orphaned at a young age. I ended up joining the household of the mid-ranking grandee Xu Jia as one of his retainers. I went with Xu Jia on an embassy to Qi, and the king of Qi privately offered me a present of gold, which I refused to accept. Xu Jia slandered me to the prime minister, who had me beaten to within an inch of my life. I was lucky enough to survive everything that he did to me, and afterwards I changed my name to Zhang Lu and fled to Qin. There I was so fortunate as to be promoted by Your Majesty to my present position. Xu Jia came here as an ambassador and I revealed my true identity to him, since we knew each other of old. I hope that you will forgive me for my deception."

"I had no idea that you had suffered such an injustice!" the king of Qin exclaimed. "Since Xu Jia is here, I will behead him to avenge all that he did to you."

Fan Ju presented his opinion: "Xu Jia is here on a matter of state. Ever since ancient times it has been a rule that even in times of war, you do not behead an enemy ambassador—not to mention one that comes for a peace treaty! I would not dare to do harm to the public wheal in order to avenge a private enmity! The person who really wanted me dead is the prime minister of Wei; you cannot put all the blame on Xu Jia."

"That you are prepared to put the public good above your own personal concerns is a sign that you are truly loyal," the king exclaimed. "I will make sure that the prime minister of Wei pays for what he did to you. The ambassador will be free to go as you have suggested."

Fan Ju thanked His Majesty for his kindness and left the court. The king of Qin agreed to the peace treaty with Wei.

Xu Jia went to say goodbye to Fan Ju. "Since we are old acquaintances," Fan Ju said, "we should eat a meal together." He ordered his servants to keep Xu Jia standing by the gates while he ordered a great array of tables and seating mats to be brought in. Xu Jia was quietly thanking all the gods he knew: "What a wonderful man Fan Ju is! I feel so ashamed! If it were not for his enormous generosity and forgiveness, how could he treat me like this? He really is too kind!"

Fan Ju left the hall and Xu Jia entered all on his own. He now discovered that he was under armed guard and did not dare to move a muscle. He sat there for hour after hour, becoming hungrier and hungrier. Xu Jia thought to himself, "The other day at the hostel, I treated him to a meal. This is in return for that, since we are old friends. Why is he making it all so formal?"

A short time later, the arrangements for the banquet were completed. A long line of people walked in procession through the chancellor's mansion: these were ambassadors from foreign countries and the advisors attached to Fan Ju's own household. Xu Jia thought to himself, "These are all people whom he has invited to meet me. Since I don't know who they are, precedence is going to be a bit difficult. I don't want to make a mistake!"

While Xu Jia was hesitating, the ambassadors and advisors lined up and climbed the steps into the main hall. The butler checked them off and announced: "The guests are all here." Fan Ju came out to greet them. After he had completed this formal ceremony, cups were handed out and the guests were ordered to be seated. All the while, music was being played by an orchestra housed in the two side chambers. Fan Ju did not summon Xu Jia. By this time Xu Jia was hungry and thirsty, angry and upset, ashamed and humiliated, but he had no way to express his rage.

After the wine had circulated three times, Fan Ju said, "I have an old acquaintance visiting—I forgot his existence until this very moment."

The guests all got up from their seats and said, "If an old friend of the chancellor's is here, we should pay our respects."

"He is an old acquaintance," Fan Ju smiled, "but I would not like to impose his presence upon you."

He gave orders that a small table be brought in and placed at the foot of the main hall and had the visitor from Wei seated there, sandwiched between two tattooed felons. There was no meat or wine at this table— they were just given a kind of bean porridge. The two convicted criminals scooped it up with their bare hands and fed Xu Jia just as if they were feeding a horse. The other guests were rendered most uncomfortable and asked, "Do you really hate him that much, Chancellor?"

Fan Ju explained what had happened between them. "No wonder you are so angry," they said.

Even though Xu Jia was deeply humiliated, he did not dare to protest. He simply ate the bean porridge. When he had finished, he went so far as to kowtow and thank Fan Ju. The chancellor of Qin glared at him: "Even though the king of Qin has agreed to a peace treaty with Wei, I will still take revenge against the prime minister. The only reason I have spared your miserable life is so that you can go back and tell the king of Wei to behead the prime minister. I also want him to arrange for my family to come here safe and sound. If these two conditions are met, our countries will be at peace. Otherwise, I will take personal command of the army and put Daliang to the sword. By that time, it will be too late for regrets!"

Xu Jia was scared practically witless. He left, repeating polite words of agreement and acceptance.

Do you know whether the kingdom of Wei did indeed cut the head off their prime minister in order to make peace? READ ON.

Chapter Ninety-eight

*Having taken hostage the Lord of Pingyuan,
the king of Qin demands Wei Qi's head.*

*After the defeat at Changping, General Bai
Qi massacres the Zhao army.*

Having received this command, Xu Jia returned to Daliang, traveling
day and night. When he had an audience with the king of Wei, he
repeated the instructions he had received from Fan Ju. It would not be
at all difficult to make arrangements to send his family to join him; on
the other hand, the demand that the prime minister's head should be cut
off was very difficult, so he found it almost impossible to open his mouth
on the subject. The king of Wei hesitated, unable to make up his mind
what to do. When Wei Qi heard what had happened, he abandoned his
seals of office and fled to the kingdom of Zhao under cover of darkness
to throw in his lot with the Lord of Pingyuan. The king of Wei arranged
that Fan Ju's family should be sent to Xianyang with a panoply of horses
and chariots, together with a gift of one hundred ingots of gold and one
thousand lengths of silk. He also sent the following message: "The
prime minister heard of what was afoot and ran away. He is now living
in the mansion of the Lord of Pingyuan. This has nothing to do with the
kingdom of Wei."

Fan Ju reported this to the king of Qin.

"Zhao is one of our allies," His Majesty said. "At the meeting held
at Mianchi, we swore to maintain our close alliance, and so my grandson Yiren went to them as a hostage to affirm our good relationship.
When the Qin army attacked Han and laid siege to Yuyu, they sent
Zhao She to rescue Han, and he inflicted a terrible defeat on our army;
however, I did not punish them for that. Now they have seen fit to give

sanctuary to your great enemy. Your enemy, Chancellor, is my enemy! I am determined to attack Zhao. This is both to avenge the insult inflicted upon us at Yuyu and to capture the former prime minister of Wei."

He personally took command of an army of two hundred thousand men. He appointed Wang Yi as his senior general, and he promptly attacked and razed to the ground three cities in Zhao. By this time King Huiwen of Zhao was dead and his son, Crown Prince Dan, had come to the throne, taking the title of King Xiaocheng. King Xiaocheng was still a minor, so Dowager Queen Huiwen was regent. When she heard that the Qin army had penetrated deeply into their territory, she became very frightened.

. . .

At this time Lin Xiangru had retired on the grounds of old age, having become extremely sick, and Yu Qing had replaced him as prime minister. He sent Commander-in-Chief Lian Po to lead the army out to intercept the enemy; this simply resulted in a stalemate.

Yu Qing suggested to Dowager Queen Huiwen: "The matter is now at crisis point. I would like your permission to send the Lord of Chang'an to Qi as a hostage, to beg them for help." The dowager queen agreed to this.

It should be explained that the dowager queen was the daughter of King Min of Qi. King Xiang of Qi had died earlier that year, to be succeeded by his son, Crown Prince Jian. Since he too was only a small child, it was his mother, Dowager Queen Junwang, daughter of the Grand Astrologer, who governed the country. The two dowager queens (who were sisters-in-law) were very close friends and always got along well together. The Lord of Chang'an was Dowager Queen Huiwen's youngest and favorite son. Seeing him come to Qi as a hostage, how could Dowager Queen Junwang not be moved? She immediately appointed Tian Dan as the senior general and gave him an army of one hundred thousand men. He was to go to rescue Zhao.

The Qin general, Wang Yi, said to His Majesty: "Zhao has many fine generals, and the Lord of Pingyuan is an extremely clever man—they will not be easy to attack. Furthermore, reinforcements will arrive at any moment from Qi; we had better take our army home."

"If I have not captured his enemy," the king of Qin said, "how can I go back and face Fan Ju?" He had an envoy take the following message to the Lord of Pingyuan: "We have attacked Zhao because we want to lay hands on Wei Qi. If you are prepared to hand him over, we will withdraw our army."

"He is not with me," the Lord of Pingyuan replied. "You should not believe everything you hear."

Although three messengers were sent one after the other, the Lord of Pingyuan was unwilling to admit his involvement. The king of Qin now became very depressed. He wanted to advance his troops, but he was afraid that Qi and Zhao might join forces, in which case it would be very difficult to defeat them. He wanted to stand down his army, but if he did so, how could he hope to capture Wei Qi? He vacillated, but then suddenly he had a flash of inspiration. He wrote a letter to apologize to the king of Zhao, which read:

> You and I, Your Majesty, are allies. I was misled by malicious gossip into thinking that Wei Qi had found sanctuary in the household of the Lord of Pingyuan. That is why I raised an army and demanded that he be handed over to me. Otherwise, how could I have dared to cross the border with Zhao? I will return to you the three cities that I have captured. I would like to restore the alliance between our two countries and continue as before.

The king of Zhao sent a letter in response to this, thanking His Majesty for his suggestion of withdrawing his troops and returning the cities. When Tian Dan heard that the Qin army was on the retreat, he returned to Qi. When the king of Qin arrived at the Hangu Pass, he sent yet another message to the Lord of Pingyuan. When the Lord of Pingyuan opened it, this is what he read:

> I have heard much of your great sense of justice and I would like to be friends.
> If you would join me here, I will treat you to ten days of banqueting.

Having received this letter, the Lord of Pingyuan went to the palace to have an audience with the king of Zhao. His Majesty summoned his ministers to discuss the situation. The prime minister, Yu Qing, stepped forward and said: "Qin is a country of tigers and wolves. In the past the Lord of Mengchang went to Qin and almost did not make it out alive. Furthermore, they already suspect that Wei Qi is here in Zhao. The Lord of Pingyuan cannot go!"

"In the past Lin Xiangru was able to make it out of the kingdom of Qin on his own, having previously removed Bian He's jade disc from their clutches," Lian Po replied. "He came back safe and sound to Zhao, and Qin did nothing to try and punish us. If the Lord of Pingyuan does not go, it will give rise to more suspicion."

"I think that this is a nice gesture on the part of the king of Qin," the king of Zhao remarked. "We should not refuse."

Thus he ordered the Lord of Pingyuan to go to Xianyang in the company of the Qin ambassador. When he had an audience with the king of Qin, they got along very well together, and His Majesty held banquets every day in his honor. Having enjoyed themselves for several days in a row, the king of Qin was absolutely delighted by how things had gone. Raising his goblet, he toasted the Lord of Pingyuan: "I have a request to make. If you grant it, I will drain this cup to the dregs."

"Your Majesty can order me to do anything that you like . . . how could I refuse?" The Lord of Pingyuan also raised his cup and drank.

"In the past King Wen of Zhou obtained the services of Lü Shang and appointed him as the Great Lord, while Lord Huan of Qi found Guan Yiwu and made him Elder Zhong," the king of Qin said. "Fan Ju is my Great Lord or Elder Zhong. His greatest enemy is hiding in your house. I want you to send someone to cut his head off, to avenge everything that was done to Fan Ju. Then I will drink to you!"

"I have heard it said that you should make friends when you are in power, so you have someone to rely on when you are in trouble; and you should make friends when you are rich, so that you have someone to help you when you are poor," the Lord of Pingyuan said thoughtfully. "Wei Qi is my friend. Even if he really were in my mansion, I would not hand him over to you. Given that he is not, there is really nothing I can do!"

"If you do not hand him over, you will not be allowed to leave!" the king of Qin said angrily.

"It is up to Your Majesty whether I leave here or not. However, you brought me here for a banquet and now keep me here with threats of violence: everyone will know the rights and wrongs of this matter!"

The king of Qin understood that the Lord of Pingyuan had no intention of giving in. He took him back to Xianyang and lodged him in an official guesthouse. He ordered a messenger to take the following letter to the king of Zhao:

> I have Your Majesty's younger brother, the Lord of Pingyuan, here in Qin while Wei Qi is hiding in the Lord of Pingyuan's mansion. The moment his head arrives here, I will let the Lord of Pingyuan go. Otherwise, I will raise an army and attack Zhao, capturing the man myself. In that case I will not let the Lord of Pingyuan return home. You have been warned!

The king of Zhao was deeply shocked when he received this letter. He said to his ministers, "I am not going to put one of our own princes, a pillar of the kingdom, in danger simply in order to save a refugee from another country!" He ordered his troops to surround the Lord of Pingyuan's mansion and extract Wei Qi. There were a number of the Lord of Pingyuan's clients who had become very friendly with him; under cover of darkness they broke through the cordon and managed to escape together. Wei Qi went to throw in his lot with the prime minister, Yu Qing.

"The king of Zhao could not be more scared of Qin if it were a tiger or leopard," Yu Qing said. "This is not an argument that you can win. You had better go back to Daliang. The Lord of Xinling is always on the lookout for good men—there are many people in desperate circumstances who have given their allegiance to him. Besides, he is a good friend of the Lord of Pingyuan and will do his best to protect you. Of course, in your present plight, you cannot travel alone. I will go with you."

He immediately untied the prime minister's seal from his belt and wrote a letter of farewell to the king of Zhao. The two men disguised themselves and fled the kingdom of Zhao. When they arrived at Daliang, Yu Qing had his companion stay outside the suburbs in a place of concealment, consoling him with the words: "The Lord of Xinling is a man of great nobility of character. I will go and talk to him. I am sure that he will immediately come and collect you. You will not have long to wait!"

Yu Qing walked to the Lord of Xinling's mansion on foot and sent in a message asking for an audience. The majordomo went in to report this. The Lord of Xinling was bathing, and when he saw the chit, he said in amazement: "That is the prime minister of the kingdom of Zhao! What on earth is he doing here?" He ordered his majordomo to apologize on his behalf for being in the bath. He asked that Yu Qing wait for a moment, and inquired into his reasons for coming to Wei. Yu Qing was worried, but felt he had no choice but to explain exactly how Wei Qi had offended the authorities in Qin and how he had resigned his position in order to bring the man to safety in Wei. He gave the Lord of Xinling the general outlines of the situation. The majordomo went in to report this. The Lord of Xinling was frightened of offending Qin, so he did not want to give sanctuary to the former prime minister. However, it was very difficult to refuse since Yu Qing had come with him from so far away. Making a decision either way was troublesome and he hesitated, unable to make up his mind.

Yu Qing realized that the Lord of Xinling was feeling awkward and delaying having an audience with him, so he walked off in high dudgeon. The Lord of Xinling asked his chief advisor, "What kind of man is Yu Qing?"

At this time Hou Sheng was standing to one side. He laughed heartily and said, "Do you really not know? Yu Qing's brilliant rhetorical skills earned him the prime ministerial seals from the king of Zhao, not to mention a fief of ten thousand households. Now Wei Qi has gotten into trouble and thrown in his lot with Yu Qing; he responded by resigning his position and going with him, without begrudging the titles and emoluments that this cost him. There are not many people in the world who would behave like that! Are you still in any doubt that he is an amazing man?"

The Lord of Xinling felt very ashamed of himself. He quickly tied up his hair and put on a hat, ordering his charioteer to harness a carriage and head for the suburbs, chasing after him as quickly as he could.

Meanwhile Wei Qi was waiting on tenterhooks. After a very long time, during which nothing happened, he thought to himself: "Yu Qing said that the Lord of Xinling is a man of great nobility of character, and he was sure that he would immediately come and collect me. Nothing has happened for ages! Has something gone wrong?"

A short time later he saw Yu Qing return with tears in his eyes. He said, "The Lord of Xinling is not the man I thought him. He is scared of Qin and so he fobbed me off. I am afraid that we are going to have to go to Chu."

"Thanks to one mistake, I made a lifelong enemy in the form of Fan Ju," Wei Qi wailed. "I have already caused trouble for the Lord of Pingyuan and for you—how could I ask you to tramp from one country to another, going all the way to Chu, not knowing what reception is waiting for us there? Let me put an end to this!" He drew his sword and cut his own throat.

Yu Qing rushed forward to stop him, but it was too late. While Yu Qing was standing there horror-struck, the Lord of Xinling drove up in his carriage. Since Yu Qing spotted him while he was still some way away, he rushed off to hide, not wanting to see the man. When the Lord of Xinling caught sight of Wei Qi's body, he lifted it up and wept, saying, "This is all my fault!"

. . .

By this time the king of Zhao—having failed to arrest Wei Qi and discovering that Yu Qing had left the country—knew that the two men were together. They must have gone to either Han or Wei. He immediately sent envoys out in all directions to arrest them. When the envoy arrived at the suburbs of the Wei capital, he discovered that Wei Qi was dead. He presented his respects to the king of Wei and asked for his head, that they might ransom the Lord of Pingyuan and bring him home. The Lord of Xinling had given orders that the body be encoffined and could not bear the idea that the corpse would be desecrated.

"I know that you and the Lord of Pingyuan are very close and you would not like anything bad to happen to a mutual friend," the envoy said. "If Wei Qi were still alive, I would have nothing to say. But now he is dead and beyond all human cares, so what does it matter? Are you prepared to see the Lord of Pingyuan stay as a prisoner in Qin for the rest of his life?"

The Lord of Xinling had no choice. He took the head and placed it in a box. This he entrusted, sealed, to the Zhao envoy. The body was buried outside the suburbs of Daliang.

An old man wrote a poem about Wei Qi:

Having listened to Xu Jia, he tortured and humiliated a great man;
In the end his treatment of Fan Ju cost him his life.
Having destroyed other people's lives, he brought ruin to his own,
But when his head was carried to Xianyang, it was too late to learn this
   lesson!

Having resigned his position as prime minister and had enough of the troubles of government office, Yu Qing did not want to go back to his old life. Instead he lived at Mount Baiyun as a recluse, writing a book for his own amusement in which he criticized various aspects of contemporary society. This was titled *The Annals of Master Yu*.

An old man wrote another poem about this:

If he had not suffered a great deal, would he have written this book?
A thousand ages will remember the name of Yu Qing!
How sad that a man of such remarkable talents
Should have resigned his job to help someone like Wei Qi!

When the king of Zhao obtained possession of the head, he immediately sent it to Xianyang, with orders that the courier travel day and night. The king of Qin gave it to Fan Ju, who commanded that the skull be coated with lacquer so he could use it as a chamber pot. "You ordered your household to get drunk and urinate on me," he said. "Now that you are dead, I can urinate on you!"

The king of Qin sent the Lord of Pingyuan back to Zhao attended by every ceremony. Zhao appointed him as prime minister, replacing Yu Qing. Fan Ju now said to the king of Qin: "I was just a humble man of no account when I was lucky enough to be recognized by Your Majesty. Not only have you given me a senior position in the government, you have helped me to take revenge upon my enemy; nothing could have meant more to me! However, without Zheng Anping, I could never have survived in Wei; without Wang Ji, I would never have made it successfully to Qin. Please take my titles and emoluments, Your Majesty, and bestow them upon these two men, so I may repay them for everything that they have done for me. Even if I die, I will have no regrets!"

"If you had not reminded me, Chancellor, I would almost have forgotten!" the king exclaimed. He made Wang Ji magistrate in Hedong and appointed Zheng Anping as a junior general. From this time on, he took advice from nobody but Fan Ju and was determined to attack Han and Wei, sending ambassadors to confirm the alliance with Qi and Chu.

"I have heard that Dowager Queen Junwang of Qi is a most estimable and intelligent woman," Fan Ju said to the king of Qin. "I would like to find out whether this assertion is true."

He ordered an ambassador to take a chain made of linked jade discs and present it to Dowager Queen Junwang with the words: "If there is someone in the kingdom of Qi who can undo the links in this chain, the king of Qin will accept the junior place in this alliance."

Dowager Queen Junwang ordered someone to bring her a hammer and smashed the chain. She said to the ambassador, "Tell the king of Qin that I have already undone the links."

When the ambassador reported this, Fan Ju said, "Dowager Queen Junwang is indeed a remarkable woman. We should not offend her." He arranged that a blood covenant should be sworn with Qi, at which the two sides agreed not to invade each other. This brought peace to Qi for some years.

. . .

Let us now turn to the story of Crown Prince Xiongwan of Chu, who at this time was a hostage in the kingdom of Qin. He was kept there for sixteen years, not allowed to go home. When the Qin ambassador had concluded the alliance with Chu, an ambassador from Chu named Zhu Ying went back with him to Xianyang armed with diplomatic gifts. Zhu Ying reported that the king of Chu was terribly ill and not expected to recover. Grand Tutor Huang Xie said to Crown Prince Xiongwan, "His Majesty is dying while you are here in Qin. If the king of Chu does indeed pass away while you are not at his bedside, one of the other princes will come to the throne in your stead. In that case the kingdom of Chu will never be yours. I will go and speak to Fan Ju on your behalf."

"Good," the crown prince said.

Huang Xie went to the chancellor's mansion and spoke to Fan Ju. "Do you know that the king of Chu is ill?"

"I was informed of this by the ambassador."

"The crown prince of Chu has spent a long time here in Qin," Huang Xie continued, "and he has become close friends with many generals and senior ministers. If the king of Chu dies and the crown prince succeeds to the throne, he could support you in various ways. If you send him home at this critical moment, he will be very grateful to you. If you keep him here, Chu will enthrone one of the other princes. In that case the crown prince will remain in Qin, but he will be no different from an ordinary resident of Xianyang. Furthermore, the people of Chu are angry that their crown prince has been kept here for so many years—in the future they will not be sending any more hostages to Qin. I do not think it is a good idea to ruin the crown prince's prospects and become sworn enemies with such a powerful kingdom."

Fan Ju nodded his head in agreement. "You are absolutely right."

He reported to the king of Qin what Huang Xie had said. "Why don't we send the Grand Tutor back to Chu first and find out whether the king really is so very ill," His Majesty suggested. "Afterwards, if necessary, they can collect the crown prince."

When Huang Xie heard that the crown prince would not be allowed home, he secretly discussed the following plan with him: "The king of Qin is refusing to send you home because he is hoping to take advantage of the emergency situation to demand land from Chu, just as he did with King Huai. If the people from Chu do come here to try and collect you, they will simply be falling into Qin's trap. On the other hand, if they do not, you will be a prisoner here for the rest of your life."

The crown prince knelt down and asked, "What is your plan?"

"In my humble opinion, you had better disguise yourself and run away," Huang Xie said. "The Chu ambassador is about to return home: this opportunity must not be lost! I will stay behind on my own and make sure that you get away safely, even if it costs me my life!"

The crown prince wept and said, "If this comes off, I will share the kingdom of Chu with you."

Huang Xie went to visit Zhu Ying in secret and explained their plan. Zhu Ying agreed to play his part. Crown Prince Xiongwan dressed up like a charioteer and held the reins for the Chu ambassador. Thus he was able to make his way through the Hangu Pass without anyone being any the wiser. Huang Xie remained behind at their residence. When the king of Qin sent someone to inquire, Huang Xie said, "The crown prince is unwell and does not want to see anyone. When he is feeling a bit better, I will immediately report it to the court."

A couple of weeks later, having calculated that the crown prince must have crossed the border long ago, Huang Xie requested an audience with the king of Qin. He kowtowed and apologized: "I was afraid that if the king of Chu died, the crown prince would not come to the throne, in which case he would not be able to help you. Therefore I decided to send him home. By this time, he has already left the kingdom of Qin. I know that I have deceived you, Your Majesty, so please have me executed!"

The king of Qin said angrily, "Chu people are always so tricky!" He shouted at his guards to arrest Huang Xie because he was going to kill him.

Chancellor Fan Ju remonstrated: "Killing Huang Xie is not going to bring the crown prince back! All it will do is ruin your alliance with Chu. You had better reward his loyalty and send him home. When the king of Chu dies, the crown prince is sure to come to the throne and Huang Xie will become Grand Vizier. If both the king and the Grand Vizier feel that they have been well-treated by Qin, they will do what we want."

The king of Qin thought that this was good advice, and so he gave lavish gifts to Huang Xie and sent him home to Chu.

A historian wrote a poem about this:

A disguised prince grasped the reins, fleeing as fast as he could,
Otherwise he would have ended up a commoner in Xianyang.
If it were not for the far-sighted advice of the Lord of Chunshen,
The story of King Huai would simply have repeated itself.

Three months after Huang Xie arrived home, King Qingxiang of Chu died and Crown Prince Xiongwan succeeded to the throne, taking the title of King Kaolie. He appointed Grand Tutor Huang Xie as Grand Vizier and offered him twelve counties north of the Huai River as his fief. He took the title of the Lord of Chunshen.

"The area north of the Huai River borders on the kingdom of Qi," Huang Xie said. "You should make this into a commandery that will be easier to defend. I would rather be given a fief in the eastern Yangtze River delta region."

King Kaolie gave Huang Xie the territory of the former kingdom of Wu instead. Huang Xie restored the former capital of the kings of Wu and made it his headquarters. He had four north-south and five east-west canals dug inside the city walls, in order to give access to Lake Tai. He changed the name of the Defeating Chu Gate to the Glorious Gate. At this time, even though the Lord of Mengchang was dead, the Lord of Pingyuan in Zhao and the Lord of Xinling in Wei were both still maintaining large households of knights. Huang Xie admired them and accordingly started to recruit knights for himself, until he had a household of several thousand men. The Lord of Pingyuan often sent envoys to Huang Xie, who arranged that they be housed in the greatest luxury. The Zhao envoys constantly harped on the wonders of Chu: how the people there wore hairpins made of tortoiseshell and carried gem-encrusted swords. They felt very humiliated when they realized that Huang Xie had more than three thousand men in his household and his senior advisors all wore pearl-studded shoes. Thanks to the excellent advice of his knights, Huang Xie was able to conquer the lands of Zou and Lu to the north. He also appointed Xun Qing as the magistrate of Lanling. What is more, he presided over a revision of the law code and the restructuring of the army. This much strengthened the kingdom of Chu.

. . .

Let us now turn to another part of the story. When King Zhaoxiang of Qin had allied with Qi and Chu, he ordered the senior general, Wang He, to lead his army and attack Han. He moved grain along the Wei River, east into the Yellow River and the Luo, in order to provision his troops. They razed the city of Yewang. After this, the route by which Shangdang communicated with the capital was cut. The official in charge of the defense of Shangdang, Feng Ting, discussed the situation with his officers: "Since Qin has occupied Yuewang, Shangdang is no longer under Han control. However, rather than surrendering to Qin, it would be better if we turned to Zhao. Qin will be angry that Zhao has obtained this land and will move their armies to attack them—once Zhao is invaded, they will be forced to ally with Han. As long as Zhao and Han are allied, they can resist any attack by Qin."

He sent an envoy to present a letter of surrender, together with a map of the lands of Shangdang, to King Xiaocheng of Zhao. This occurred in the fourth year of the reign of King Xiaocheng, which was the fifty-third year of the reign of King Nan of Zhou.

The king of Zhao had a dream one night in which a man in a bicolored robe and a cloak came down from the sky riding on a dragon. The king got onto its back and the dragon soared off into the air. However, before he had reached Heaven, he had fallen off. He could see a gold mountain to one side and a jade mountain to the other, glittering and shining in a very attractive way. When the king woke up, he summoned Grandee Zhao Yu and told him of this dream.

"The multicolored robe must refer to our alliance," Zhao Yu said. "Riding on a dragon into the sky is an omen of success. The fact that you fell to the ground means that you will obtain land. The jade and gold piled up into mountains means that we will obtain great treasures. Your Majesty, in the immediate future you will expand your territories and acquire even greater wealth—this dream is very auspicious!"

The king of Zhao was very pleased. He summoned Astrologer Gan and had him perform a divination as well. Astrologer Gan announced: "The multicolored robe is a sign of division. Riding on the back of a dragon up into the skies and falling off before you reach it means that things will suddenly change for the worse: things that you have always believed will turn out not to be true. The gold and jade mountains are things that you could look at, but not actually use. This dream is inauspicious. Your Majesty must be very careful!"

The king of Zhao had much enjoyed the interpretation offered by Zhao Yu, and he did not think that Astrologer Gan could possibly be correct. Three days later, the envoy from Feng Ting, the official in charge of Shangdang, arrived in Zhao. The king of Zhao opened the letter that he had brought and read the following:

> Qin's campaign against Han has reached a critical point; Shangdang is about to be captured by them. The officials and people are unwilling to become part of Qin, so we would like to join Zhao. I would not dare to go against the wishes of the people, so I hereby take the seventeen cities in the Shangdang region and present them to Your Majesty with two bows. I hope that you will condescend to accept this gift.

The king of Zhao was delighted. "Zhao Yu said that I would be expanding my territory and become richer; today it has come true!"

"I have always thought that this kind of present comes with strings attached," Zhao Bao, the Lord of Pingyang, remonstrated. "Do not accept, Your Majesty!"

"They fear Qin and love us," His Majesty said. "That is why they want to be part of our kingdom. How can there possibly be any strings attached?"

"Qin is swallowing up Han," Zhao Bao retorted. "They have already taken Yewang, cutting off communications between Shangdang and the capital. They think of Shangdang as their own property, they just have not gotten around to collecting it. The moment that they discover that Shangdang now belongs to us, do you think that Qin will just let that go? Qin has put a lot of effort into this campaign, but apparently we are to enjoy the fruits of it. That is why I said that this must come with strings attached. The reason why Feng Ting is refusing to surrender to Qin, throwing in his lot with us instead, is that he is hoping to get us into trouble. He is hoping that we may draw Qin's fire and buy Han some breathing space. Why do you not see this, Your Majesty?"

The king of Zhao did not agree with this assessment at all. He summoned the Lord of Pingyuan to his side to help him decide the matter.

"We have sent out hundreds of thousands of soldiers," he said. "We have campaigned against many countries, we have fought year in and year out, but we have never been able to capture so much as a single city. Now without having to use even a single weapon or one ration of food, we have laid hands on seventeen cities. This is a wonderful opportunity that should not be lost!"

"I was hoping you would say that!" the king of Zhao replied. He ordered the Lord of Pingyuan to go to Shangdang to take control of this new territory at the head of an army of fifty thousand men. He enfeoffed Feng Ting with thirty thousand households and gave him the title of the Lord of Hualing—he remained in charge as the governor of Shangdang. The seventeen prefects of the cities were each given a fief of three thousand households and the hereditary title of marquis.

Feng Ting closed his gates and wept, refusing to see the Lord of Pingyuan. When the Lord of Pingyuan insisted, Feng Ting said, "I have made three terrible mistakes that mean that I do not deserve to see you. I did not die when I failed to preserve Shangdang for my own ruler: that was my first mistake. I handed over these lands to Zhao without an express order from my ruler: that was the second. Now my betrayal has been rewarded with a title and gift of land: that is the third thing I have done wrong."

The Lord of Pingyuan sighed and said, "What a loyal subject!" He waited by his gate, not leaving for three days. Feng Ting was impressed by his perseverance and finally came out to meet him. However, he was still crying. He decided to resign his position to allow for the appointment of another governor.

The Lord of Pingyuan repeatedly tried to cheer him up: "I understand how you feel. But if you do not continue as governor, we cannot hope to keep the other officials and people happy."

Feng Ting agreed to continue in office, but he absolutely refused to accept the fief.

When the Lord of Pingyuan said goodbye, Feng Ting said, "The reason why Shangdang surrendered to Zhao is that we cannot resist the might of Qin on our own. I hope that when you next have an audience with the king of Zhao, my lord, you will get him to send us a large army led by fine generals as quickly as possible, to prepare for an attack by Qin."

The Lord of Pingyuan returned and reported what had happened to the king of Zhao. His Majesty prepared wine for a congratulatory banquet to celebrate the acquisition of these new lands. There was some discussion of sending an army, but no decision was made. Meanwhile, the Qin general Wang He advanced his army and laid siege to Shangdang. Feng Ting held out for two months, but since no relief troops arrived from Zhao, he led his officials and many of the people to flee to Zhao. At this time, the king of Zhao appointed Lian Po as senior general and put him in command of two hundred thousand troops to rescue Shangdang. They had advanced as far as the Changping Pass when they met Feng Ting coming the other way. Then they realized that Shangdang was lost and that the Qin army would arrive at any moment. They built several dozen fortified encampments at the foot of Mount Jinmen, spread out like a constellation of stars. Ten thousand soldiers were handed over to Feng Ting, who was given orders to hold the city of Guanglang. Another twenty thousand men were given to the two commandants, Gai Fu and Gai Tong, who were to hold the cities of Eastern Zhang and Western Zhang. He also sent Assistant General Zhao Que far ahead in order to investigate the movements of the Qin army.

Zhao Que took five thousand men and searched a twenty *li* area outside the Changping Pass. There he ran into the Qin general, Sima Geng, who was spying out the land for his own side. Zhao Que decided to take advantage of the fact that Sima Geng did not have many men with him to launch an attack. It was just at that moment that the second wave of Qin's advance guard, under the command of Zhang Ting, arrived. Zhao Que hesitated and was lost—Sima Geng cut his head off with a single swipe, spreading panic among the Zhao forces. When Lian Po heard that his advance guard had run into trouble, he gave orders that everyone was to retreat behind the ramparts and remain on guard. They had strict orders not to do battle with the Qin army. He also sent some sappers out to dig a huge trench many feet deep and fill it with water. The soldiers had no idea what this was for.

When the main body of Wang He's army arrived, they made camp ten *li* from Mount Jinmen. He assigned some troops to attack the two cities of Eastern and Western Zhang. Gai Fu and Gai Tong went out to fight, only to be defeated. Having obtained this victory, Wang He turned his forces against the city of Guanglang. Sima Geng's troops were the first to climb the walls, followed by the rest of the army. Feng Ting suffered several defeats and was in the end forced to abandon the city; he fled to the main camp at Mount Jinmen, where Lian Po took him in. Now the Qin army came to attack these fortifications. Lian Po gave the following command: "Anyone who goes out to do battle will be executed, even if he wins."

Wang He attacked several times without being able to force a way in. After that, he moved his own encampment closer—just five *li* from the Zhao front line. He tried many times to provoke battle, but not a single Zhao soldier came out to fight.

"Lian Po is an experienced general and he manages his troops very well," Wang He declared. "We are not yet in a position to deal with him!"

One of the junior generals, Wang Ling, offered the following plan: "There is a river that flows at the foot of Mount Jinmen—it is called the Yanggu River. The Zhao and the Qin armies are both getting their water from the same source. The Zhao encampment is located to the south of this river and the Qin encampment to the west. The river rises in the west and flows in a southeasterly direction. If we dam this river, it will not flow along its old course, and the Zhao troops will have nothing to drink. Within a couple of days, the morale of their army will have collapsed and we can attack them. Victory is certain!"

Wang He thought this was a good idea and sent some troops to build a dam on the river.

Even today the Yanggu River is known as the Jue or "Stopped" River because of this.

They had no idea that Lian Po had already dug himself an enormous water tank, with more than enough supplies in it to manage their day-to-day requirements.

. . .

The stalemate between the Zhao and Qin armies lasted for more than four months. Since Wang He had not been able to make them fight so much as a single battle, he had no choice but to send someone back to Xianyang to report this to the king of Qin. His Majesty summoned Fan Ju and asked him to come up with a plan.

"Lian Po has been in charge of the army for a long time," Fan Ju said. "He knows exactly how strong the Qin army is, and so he is not prepared to fight unless he has to. He also knows that the Qin army has come a long way and that they cannot stay in the field for any great length of time. He is hoping to wear us out, waiting for the right moment to attack. If we do not get rid of him, we cannot defeat Zhao."

"Do you have a plan that will allow us to get rid of Lian Po?" His Majesty inquired.

Fan Ju sent away His Majesty's entourage. Then he said, "If you want to get rid of Lian Po, you are going to have to use a different kind of trick. You will have to do such-and-such . . . and it will cost you at least one thousand pieces of gold."

The king of Qin was delighted and immediately presented Fan Ju with the gold. Accordingly, the chancellor sent some of his most trusted men to sneak into Handan and use the money to bribe the king of Zhao's cronies. They were to spread the following rumor: "The Lord of Mafu was the finest of all the generals in Zhao, but his son, Zhao Kuo, is supposed to be even braver than his father. If he were to be appointed general, he would make short work of the Qin army. Lian Po is old and scared—he has been defeated time and again. He has lost thirty or forty thousand men, and the Qin forces are pressing ever closer. Any minute now he will have to surrender."

The king of Zhao had already heard of the death of Zhao Que and the loss of three cities in turn. He had sent someone to Changping to watch the progress of the battle and was aware of Lian Po's plan to sit behind his fortifications, refusing to do battle. Even the king of Zhao thought that he might be cowardly. When he heard what his entourage had to say, he believed it was true. He summoned Zhao Kuo and asked him, "Can you defeat the Qin army?"

"If Qin had sent the Lord of Wu'an here, it might have forced me to spend some time thinking," Zhao Kuo boasted. "However, Wang He is nothing."

"Why do you say that?"

"The Lord of Wu'an has been in charge of the Qin army in a number of important campaigns," Zhao Kuo explained. "He defeated Han and

Wei at Yique and killed two hundred and forty thousand of their soldiers. When he went back to attack Wei for a second time, he captured sixty-one cities, large and small. When he went south to attack Chu, he took the cities of Yan, Ying, Dingwu, and Qian. On his third campaign against Wei, he advanced as far as Mangmao and killed one hundred and thirty thousand enemy troops. He then attacked Han again and razed five cities to the ground, killing fifty thousand men. He even cut the head off the Zhao general Jia Yan and drowned twenty thousand of his men in the Yellow River. He is famous for having won every battle that he ever fought and conquered every city that he ever attacked. Our soldiers would be terrified at the mere mention of his name. If I were to fight him, I am really not sure that I could win . . . I would certainly have to think carefully. On the other hand, Wang He has only just been appointed as one of Qin's generals; he has dared to penetrate so deeply into our territory only because of Lian Po's cowardice. If he were to meet me, he would be like an autumn leaf blown in the wind—he'd be knocked straight to the ground!"

The king of Zhao was delighted. He appointed Zhao Kuo as the senior general and gave him a gift of gold and silk. He marched out to replace Lian Po, together with a further two hundred thousand troops.

. . .

When Zhao Kuo had completed his muster of the army, he went to see his mother, the gold and silk piled up in his chariot.

"When your father was dying," she said, "his last wish was that you should not become a general in Zhao. Why did you not refuse?"

"I wanted to refuse," Zhao Kuo assured her, "but there is nobody else for the job."

His mother wrote a letter to the king in which she remonstrated with him:

> Zhao Kuo has just read his father's books but knows nothing in practice about military matters. He will not make a good general. Please, Your Majesty, do not give him this office!

The king of Zhao summoned the old woman to explain in person. "My husband, Zhao She, was a general," she said, "and every single reward he ever received was shared among his men. On the day that he received the order to go into battle, he would spend the night with his troops, paying no attention to whatever was going on at home. He felt it his duty to live or die with his men. Every time a big decision had to be made he would discuss it with his officers—he never made up his mind without taking advice. However, when my son was appointed as a general, he made sure that he took the seat of honor at court, and his officers do not even dare to look him in the face. The gold and silk that you bestowed upon him was all taken home. Is this the way for a general to behave? When his father was dying, he warned me again and again: 'Do not let Kuo become a general; he will destroy the Zhao army!' I remember these words, and hence I ask Your Majesty to pick another person to command the troops. You must not give the job to Kuo."

"My mind is already made up!" His Majesty asserted.

"You have refused to listen to my advice, Your Majesty," she said. "If the army is defeated, I don't want my family to take any blame."

The king of Zhao agreed. Zhao Kuo led his troops out of Handan and set off in the direction of the Changping Pass.

There is a poem that testifies to this:

Lian Po may have been a coward, but he was strong in defense;
Zhao Kuo was good for nothing except running his mouth.
On this day he departed Handan trailing clouds of glory,
But all too soon he will be a corpse at Changping.

Fan Ju's spies were still in Handan, and they had been keeping their eyes and ears open. They knew every word that Zhao Kuo had spoken to His Majesty and that the king had appointed him to be the senior general. They selected a day to set off, and made their way back to Xianyang under cover of darkness to make their report. The king of Qin and Fan Ju discussed the situation: "We need the Lord of Wu'an to put an end to this." His Majesty appointed Bai Qi to be the new senior general, with Wang He as his deputy. The following orders were secretly issued to the army: "Anyone who leaks the information that the Lord of Wu'an is the new commander-in-chief will be executed."

Meanwhile, when Zhao Kuo arrived at Changping, Lian Po checked his tally and handed over all his paperwork to him. He took only his own private forces, just over a hundred men, back to Handan. Zhao Kuo immediately countermanded all of Lian Po's orders and had each of the small encampments massed into one huge fortified area. At this time Feng Ting was with the army. He remonstrated vehemently, but Zhao Kuo paid no attention. He replaced all the old generals with men he had brought with him from the capital. He gave them strict instructions: "If the Qin army comes, you are to attack them with everything you have. If you win, you are to follow up the victory by chasing them down. We are going to make sure that not even a single Qin soldier gets home alive."

When Bai Qi arrived at the Qin camp, he heard that Zhao Kuo had already changed all of Lian Po's orders. He began by sending three thousand men out of the encampment to provoke battle. Zhao Kuo immediately sent ten thousand men out to intercept them. The Qin army returned, having suffered a terrible defeat. Bai Qi was standing on the ramparts watching the Zhao army. "I know how we are going to win this," he said to Wang He.

Having won this first engagement, Zhao Kuo was so excited that he was jumping up and down, waving his arms. He sent an envoy to the Qin camp, requesting battle. Bai Qi told Wang He to reply: "We will fight tomorrow." He withdrew his army ten *li* and made camp again where Wang He's old encampments had been. Zhao Kuo said happily, "The Qin army is afraid of me." He had oxen killed to feast his officers, and then gave the following order: "In tomorrow's battle we need to capture Wang He alive, to make a laughingstock of him."

When Bai Qi had set up his camp and it was properly organized, he summoned all his generals and gave them their orders. Generals Wang Ben and Wang Ling were to take ten thousand men and put them into battle formation. They were going to fight Zhao Kuo's army. They were under instructions to lose—under no circumstances were they to defeat him. In the process they were to entice the Zhao army to attack the Qin encampment. If they succeeded, they would be heavily rewarded. The senior generals Sima Cuo and Sima Geng were each to take command of fifteen thousand troops. Their mission was to move around the back of the Zhao encampment and cut their supply route. The senior general Hu Shang was to take command of twenty thousand men and make camp nearby. He was to wait until the Zhao army broke through the ramparts and started attacking the Qin forces, and then lead his troops in the attack. The aim was to break the Zhao army into two pieces. The two senior generals, Meng Ao and Wang Jian, were each to take five thousand cavalry and wait out of sight until they were needed. Bai Qi and Wang He would command the defense of the encampment. As the saying goes: "The nets were spread with devilish cunning, waiting for the warriors to hurl themselves into the trap."

Zhao Kuo gave instructions to his soldiers that they would eat just before dawn and then get ready to fight. By full light his troops were advancing in formation. Before they had even gone five *li*, they encountered the Qin army. The two battle formations were exactly opposite each other. Zhao Kuo ordered the general in command of his vanguard, Fu Bao, to ride out and fight with the Qin general, Wang Ben. Having crossed swords thirty or more times, Wang Ben was defeated and ran away. Fu Bao chased after him. Zhao Kuo ordered Wang Rong to take his army out in support, and he ran straight into the Qin general, Wang Ling. Having crossed swords just a couple of times, Wang Ling was also defeated and ran away.

Seeing his army win victory after victory, Zhao Kuo decided to take his main army out to pursue them. Feng Ting remonstrated yet again: "The people of Qin are very deceitful. You cannot believe that they have been defeated so easily. Do not go after them!"

Zhao Kuo did not listen. He pursued the Qin troops for more than ten *li*, until he reached their encampment. Wang Ben and Wang Ling circled the camp and kept on going, since the gate was not opened for them. Zhao Kuo gave orders for a massive concerted attack. Even after fighting for several days, the Qin army held firm and they were not able to force their way in. Zhao Kuo sent someone to call for reinforcements, moving all of his men forward. It was at this moment that the Zhao general, Su She, came galloping forward on a lathered horse. He reported: "The Qin general, Hu Shang, took his army around to attack our rear camp. They cannot come in support."

Zhao Kuo bellowed with fury: "How dare Hu Shang do such a thing! I am going to deal with him myself!"

He sent someone to spy out the movements of the Qin army. They reported back: "There are chariots and horses moving in a constant stream on the western route, but there is nobody at all to the east."

Zhao Kuo signaled to his army to take the eastern approach. When they had advanced only two or three *li*, the senior general Meng Ao attacked them with his forces, cutting across their lines. "You have fallen into the Lord of Wu'an's trap, Zhao Kuo!" he shouted. "Why don't you surrender?"

Zhao Kuo was furious. Grabbing a spear, he went out to fight Meng Ao. The junior general, Wang Rong, stopped him with the words: "There is no need for you to go in person. Let me deal with him!"

Wang Rong went out to cross swords with Meng Ao. It was at this point that Wang Jian's army arrived too. The Zhao army now started to take serious casualties. Zhao Kuo decided it would be difficult for him to win this engagement, so he had the bells sounded to withdraw his troops. He ordered his scouts to find a place with good water and grass that would be suitable for them to make camp.

Feng Ting remonstrated yet again: "For your troops to stand a hope of winning their morale has to be high. Today our armies have suffered something of a setback, but they are still in a position to fight. If you were to withdraw back to our original encampment, you can resist the enemy with all your might. If we make camp here, we can be attacked from any direction . . . it will not be easy to get away."

Zhao Kuo did not listen to this either. He had his soldiers pile up earth to build high ramparts, which would serve to protect the camp. He sent an urgent dispatch to the king of Zhao asking for help, while at the same time ordering his rearguard to bring up as much food as possible. He was not expecting that by this time Sima Cuo and Sima Geng had already cut the route by which his grain supplies traveled. Bai Qi now moved his main army into position just in front of the Zhao army camp, while Hu Shang and Meng Ao had their forces at the back. Every day the Qin army repeated the Lord of Wu'an's command, demanding that Zhao Kuo surrender. By this time Zhao Kuo had realized that Bai Qi was indeed present and he was scared witless.

The king of Qin received a dispatch from Bai Qi, reporting that he had Zhao Kuo's army pinned down at Changping. He went in person to Henei, where His Majesty commanded every young man over the age of fifteen to join the army. They were sent out in different directions to steal and pillage as much food as they possibly could from the people of Zhao, while at the same time preventing the arrival of support troops. Zhao Kuo was kept under siege for forty-six days by the Qin army, by which time they had run out of food. The officers and men started killing and eating each other, and Zhao Kuo could do nothing to prevent it. He had his generals divide their forces into four groups. Fu Bao was in command of the group heading east, Su She would go west, Feng Ting would go south, and Wang Rong north. He ordered these four divisions to sound the drums at the same time and then rush out to try and force a passage through the attacking army. If one of them succeeded, Zhao Kuo would bring the remainder out along the same route. He had no idea that Bai Qi, the Lord of Wu'an, had arranged in advance for a group of archers to lie in ambush around the walls of the Zhao encampment. When anyone tried to leave the encampment, they simply shot them. The four divisions tried to break out three or four times, but each time they were turned back by a hail of arrows.

When another month had passed, Zhao Kuo was in a complete rage. He selected five thousand of his best men, dressed each of them in double armor, and gave each a fine horse to ride. Zhao Kuo himself took the lead, his spear in his hand. Fu Bao and Wang Rong were just behind him. They made a concerted attempt to break through the siege. Generals Wang Jian and Meng Ao attacked them. Zhao Kuo fought many rounds in this battle, but whatever he did he could not break through the encirclement. He turned around, wanting to make his way back to the walls, but it was just at this moment that his horse stumbled and fell. Zhao Kuo was killed by a single arrow. The Zhao army was now thrown into chaos. Fu Bao and Wang Rong were both killed as well, while Su She and Feng Ting managed to make good their escape.

"I remonstrated over and over again but he did not listen to me," Feng Ting said. "It is by Heaven's will that all this has happened! How can we escape?" He committed suicide by cutting his own throat. Su She continued his flight, heading for the territory of the northern nomads.

When Bai Qi ordered flags demanding surrender to be raised, the Zhao army all put down their weapons and took off their armor. Holding up their hands, they shouted, "Long live the king of Qin!" Bai Qi sent someone to collect Zhao Kuo's head and then went to the Zhao encampment to get them to surrender. When the two hundred thousand troops inside the camp saw that their commander-in-chief had been killed, they did not dare to fight any more. They were all now willing to put down their arms. Their weapons and armor were piled up into mountains—every item in the baggage of the Zhao army now belonged to Qin.

Bai Qi and Wang He discussed the situation: "When we captured Yewang, Shangdang should also have fallen to our army, but the people and officials there were not happy about the prospect of belonging to Qin, so they gave their allegiance to Zhao instead. From start to finish in this campaign, we have had about four hundred thousand Zhao soldiers surrender to us. If there is some kind of insurrection, how can we prevent it?"

They had the surrendered troops divided into ten camps, with ten generals ordered to command them. Two hundred thousand Qin troops were detailed off to guard them. Each was given meat and wine, with the following message: "Tomorrow the Lord of Wu'an will hold a muster of the Zhao army. The very best troops with the highest degree of experience and battle-readiness will be given weapons and taken back to Qin, to join the army and fight in future campaigns. The old and sick, or anyone who is incapable of further fighting, will be sent back to Zhao."

The Zhao troops were delighted. That evening Bai Qi sent a secret order to his ten generals: "When they wake up, tell everyone who wants to join the Qin army that they must tie a white rag around their heads. That way we will know that everyone who has a white rag on is a Zhao soldier. Every one of them must be killed."

The Qin forces followed these orders to the letter. The surrendered soldiers were completely unprepared and they had no weapons—they were butchered where they stood. Those who managed to escape from the camps were hunted down by troops commanded by Meng Ao and Wang Jian. The minute they were captured, they were beheaded. Within twenty-four hours, four hundred thousand men were dead. You could hear the blood trickling along the ground and the waters of the Yanggu River ran bright red.

Even today, this is known as the Red River.

The Lord of Wu'an ordered that the skulls of the Zhao troops be collected and piled inside the walls of the Qin encampment. He called this "Skull Mountain." He had a tower built there, which was very tall and precipitous—this was "Bai Qi's Tower." Its foundations reached to the bank of the Yanggu River.

Many centuries later, Emperor Xuanzong of the Tang dynasty visited this place on a progress and was deeply moved. He ordered three Tibetan monks to perform an exorcism ceremony lasting for seven days and nights to lay the ghosts of the dead soldiers. He renamed this place "Valley of Peaceful Ghosts." This happened much later on.

A historian wrote a poem about this:

> Below this great tower there are tens of thousands of skulls,
> Not whole skeletons—only the skulls!
> In the heat of battle an arrow or a chance stone may take your life
>   away,
> But how sad that surrendered troops were treated in such a heartless
>   way!

In the battle of Changping, four hundred and fifty thousand soldiers were either killed outright or executed later. Even the troops who had surrendered to Wang He were slain. Two hundred and forty child-soldiers were the only ones left alive. They were allowed to go home to Handan, where they could spread the word of the kingdom of Qin's awesome military might.

If you do not know whether the kingdom of Zhao survived, READ ON.

Chapter Ninety-nine

*Although innocent, the Lord of Wu'an dies
at Duyou.*

*Having hatched a cunning plan, Lü Buwei
sends Prince Yiren home.*

To begin with, when King Xiaocheng of Zhao received reports of Zhao Kuo's victories, he was absolutely thrilled. Later on he was informed that the Zhao army was under siege at Changping, and he was in the middle of discussing sending troops to rescue them when he received sudden news: "Zhao Kuo is dead and the entire Zhao army of more than four hundred thousand men surrendered to Qin. However, the Lord of Wu'an killed them all within twenty-four hours, and he has released just two hundred and forty children to return to Zhao."

The king of Zhao was horrified; indeed, all of his ministers were deeply appalled. Throughout the country there were children mourning the deaths of their fathers and parents mourning the deaths of their sons—older brothers cried at the news of their younger brothers' deaths, and younger brothers wept when they heard that their older brothers had perished. Grandparents bewailed the deaths of their grandsons and wives wept for their husbands. In every road and in every marketplace, you could hear the sounds of lamentation. The only person who did not cry was Zhao Kuo's mother. "Once he became a general," she said, "I knew I would not see him alive again."

Just as he had promised her, the king of Zhao did not punish Zhao Kuo's family in any way; instead, he gave her a gift of food and silk. He also sent someone to apologize to Lian Po. The kingdom of Zhao had been rocked to its very foundations, and then they received a report from the borders: "The Qin army has attacked and conquered Shangdang—these seventeen cities have already been incorporated into their territory. Now the Lord of Wu'an is leading his forces forward, and the word is that he is intending to lay siege to Handan."

"Who can stop the Qin army?" the king of Zhao asked his ministers, but none of his ministers responded. The Lord of Pingyuan went home and asked his clients; none of them responded either.

. . .

At this time Su Dai was one of the Lord of Pingyuan's clients, and he said to himself: "If I went to Xianyang, I am sure I could stop the Qin army from attacking Zhao." The Lord of Pingyuan reported this to the king of Zhao. His Majesty gave Su Dai large quantities of gold and silk to subsidize his trip to Qin. Su Dai went to have an audience with Fan Ju. The chancellor respectfully indicated that Su Dai could take the seat of honor, and asked: "Why have you come here, sir?"

"I have come to help you."

"What do you have to tell me?" Fan Ju asked.

"Has the Lord of Wu'an already killed Zhao Kuo?"

"Indeed he has."

"Is he at present laying siege to Handan?" Su Dai continued.

"Indeed he is," Fan Ju repeated.

"The Lord of Wu'an is a truly remarkable commander," Su Dai said. "During his time as a Qin general, he has conquered more than seventy cities and killed nearly one million enemy soldiers. These are achievements that not even Yi Yin or the Great Lord Lü Wang could match! Now he has raised an army and is laying siege to Handan—Zhao will be destroyed. If Zhao is destroyed, then Qin will become emperor. If Qin becomes emperor, the Lord of Wu'an will be by far the most important of the founding fathers of the empire. His position will be entirely comparable to that of Yi Yin in the founding of the Shang dynasty, or the Great Lord Lü Wang in the founding of the Zhou. Even though you hold high office, you will be subordinate to him."

Fan Ju got up hurriedly from his seat. "What can I do?" he asked.

"You had better agree to a peace treaty with Han and Zhao that is backed up by them giving Qin a parcel of land. If they present land to Qin, that will be ascribed to your merit. Furthermore, it will cause the Lord of Wu'an to lose power over the military. Your position will then be as stable as Mount Tai."

Fan Ju was thrilled. The next day he went to speak to the king of Qin. "Our armies have been long in the field; they are exhausted and need to rest. You had better send someone to Han and Zhao and ask them for a parcel of land, in which case we will agree to a peace treaty with them."

"As you wish," the king of Qin said.

Fan Ju gave Su Dai an enormous amount of silk and gold to pay for his journey and sent him to persuade Han and Zhao to follow this course of action. The two kings were petrified of Qin, and so they both agreed to Su Dai's suggestion. Han agreed to hand over the city of Huanyong, while Zhao promised to hand over six cities. They each sent an ambassador to request a peace treaty with Qin. The king of Qin was annoyed that Han was only giving one city, which he thought was too little, but the ambassador said, "The seventeen cities of Shangdang are also part of Han." The king of Qin laughed and agreed.

He now summoned the Lord of Wu'an home, ordering him to stand down his army. Bai Qi had won a series of battles and was just about to begin laying siege to Handan. Now he suddenly heard that he had to stand down his army, and he knew that this was all because of Fan Ju's machinations. He was very angry indeed. From this time on, Fan Ju and Bai Qi did not get along well at all.

Bai Qi spread the following message among the people: "After their defeat in the battle of Changbai, the inhabitants of Handan have been waking in a cold sweat ten times a night. If we had attacked them in the immediate wake of this victory, we could have captured the city in less than a month. It is such a shame that Fan Ju did not realize that he should take advantage of this, and instead decided to insist on standing down the army. He has lost us a great opportunity."

When the king of Qin heard this, he said with great regret: "If Bai Qi knew that Handan could be taken, why didn't he say so earlier?"

He again ordered Bai Qi to raise an army and attack Zhao. Bai Qi happened to be sick at this time, and so he could not go. Instead, His Majesty ordered the senior general, Wang Ling, to take an army of one hundred thousand men to attack Zhao, laying siege to the city of Handan. The king of Zhao ordered Lian Po to manage the defense, and he guarded the city with the greatest strictness. He used his family wealth to recruit suicide troops. From time to time they would be let down on ropes from the city walls at night to make surprise attacks on the Qin encampments. Wang Ling's forces suffered one defeat after another.

By this time the Lord of Wu'an had recovered his health, and the king of Qin wanted to send him to replace Wang Ling. Bai Qi presented his opinion: "At the present moment, Handan is not an easy city to attack. In the past, in the immediate wake of a terrible defeat when the inhabitants were extremely jittery, it would have been possible to take advantage of the situation. If they tried to defend the city, they would not have done so well; if they attacked us, they would not have used their full strength. At that time we could have taken the city. It is now two years later and they have recovered from the first shock of the blow. Furthermore, Lian Po is an extremely experienced general—you must not think of him as a second Zhao Kuo. Now the other rulers will look at us attacking Zhao again having made a peace treaty with them not long ago, and they will criticize us as being untrustworthy. They will revive the Vertical Alliance as a means of maintaining their own security. I cannot see Qin winning under any circumstances."

The king of Qin tried to insist that he go, but Bai Qi was resolute in his refusal. The king of Qin sent Fan Ju to make the same request. The Lord of Wu'an was still angry that Fan Ju had wrecked his previous campaign and declared he was unwell.

"Is the Lord of Wu'an really sick?" the king of Qin asked Fan Ju.

"I'm not sure if he is genuinely unwell," Fan Ju mused. "On the other hand, I am quite sure that he does not want to go."

"Does he imagine that we don't have any other generals and so we have to have him?" His Majesty demanded angrily. "In the victory at Changping, it was actually Wang He who fought the first engagements. In what way is he inferior to Bai Qi?"

He raised another one hundred thousand soldiers and ordered Wang He to go and replace Wang Ling. When Wang Ling returned to his country, he was stripped of all his offices. Wang He laid siege to Handan, but even after five months he was not able to take the city.

. . .

When the Lord of Wu'an heard this, he said to his clients, "I told His Majesty that Handan would not be easy to attack, but he did not listen to me. Now look what has happened!"

This client was a good friend of one of Fan Ju's advisors, and he mentioned this to him. Fan Ju reported it to the king of Qin. He was determined that Bai Qi should be sent out as a general. Bai Qi yet again pretended to be ill. The king of Qin was now absolutely furious. He stripped him of his titles and demoted him to be a mere captain in the army, sending him to serve in Yinmi. He was ordered to set out from Xianyang immediately without the slightest delay.

Bai Qi sighed and said: "As Fan Li once said, 'Once the cunning rabbit is dead, the dog used to chase it is killed.' I captured more than seventy cities for Qin, and now I am going to be killed."

He left Xianyang by the West Gate, and when he arrived at Duyou, he rested for a while, waiting for his luggage to catch up with him. Fan Ju said to the king of Qin: "When he set out on his journey, Bai Qi was absolutely furious and said many angry things. Every time he has claimed to be ill, it has been a lie. I am afraid that he will go to some other country and bring disaster down upon Qin."

His Majesty sent an envoy to present Bai Qi with a sword and order him to commit suicide. When the envoy arrived in Duyou, he informed him of the king of Qin's orders. Bai Qi took the sword in his hands and said with a sigh, "What crime have I committed that I should be reduced to this?" After a long time, he said: "I do deserve to die. After the battle of Changping, when more than four hundred thousand Zhao soldiers surrendered, I murdered them in the course of twenty-four hours. That is indeed a truly appalling crime! It is entirely appropriate that I should be put to death!" He killed himself by cutting his throat.

This occurred in the eleventh month of the fiftieth year of the reign of King Zhaoxiang of Qin. This was the fifty-eighth year of the reign of King Nan of Zhou. When the people of Qin heard that Bai Qi had been executed for no good reason, they all felt terribly sorry for him and built a shrine to his memory.

Later on, during the declining years of the Tang dynasty, there was an ox that was struck dead by lightning, and on its stomach were the words "Bai Qi." People who talked about this said that Bai Qi killed too many people, so even after many centuries had gone by, his reincarnated form was still being punished by being struck by lightning bolts. However, if this were the usual punishment for killing other people, what general could hope to escape?

Master Qianyuan wrote a poem:

He killed a million men as if butchering animals;
Leaving Xianyang, he had not a word to say.
If you really valued other lives as you value your own,
Would you allow innocent men to become vengeful ghosts?

Having killed Bai Qi, the king of Qin raised another fifty thousand experienced soldiers and put Zheng Anping in command. He was ordered to go and assist Wang He and not come back until Handan had been captured. When the king of Zhao heard that even more Qin troops had come to attack him, he was very frightened. He sent messengers in every direction, trying to get help from other rulers.

"The royal family of Wei is linked to us by a marriage alliance," the Lord of Pingyuan reminded him. "Our relationship with them is good, and they are sure to send troops to help us. Chu, on the other hand, is a huge country, but it is far away. The only way we can get their assistance is by reviving the Vertical Alliance. To achieve that, I will have to go in person."

He went and talked to his staff, for he wanted to obtain twenty excellent advisors skilled in both civil and military matters to go with him in his train. Well, of the more than three thousand men in his household, the ones who knew about civil matters knew nothing about the military, and vice versa. Having put them through a careful process of triage, he only found nineteen suitable men and not the round twenty that he had wanted. The Lord of Pingyuan sighed and said, "I have been maintaining this huge household for decades now. Why is obtaining one more good man so difficult?"

Among the junior members of his household, there was one man who stepped forward and said, "How about me? Wouldn't I be suitable to make up the numbers?"

The Lord of Pingyuan asked him his name.

"I am Mao Sui. I originally come from the city of Daliang. I have been a member of your household for three years."

The Lord of Pingyuan laughed and said, "Compared to the rest of his generation, a wise man is like an awl in a bag—he always sticks out. You have been part of my household for three years and yet I have not noticed you at all. This means that you know nothing about anything!"

"How about you try putting this particular 'awl' in a bag?" Mao Sui replied. "If you had tried it earlier, you would already have noticed me, because I would have stood out long before now!"

The Lord of Pingyuan was impressed by what he said and decided to make him the twentieth member of his party. The following day, he said goodbye to the king of Zhao and headed for the Chu capital.

When he arrived, the Lord of Pingyuan communicated first with Huang Xie, the Lord of Chunshen, since they had long been good friends. He asked that he speak to King Kaolie of Chu on his behalf. At dawn, the Lord of Pingyuan entered the court, and when the formalities of the audience had been completed, the two men were seated in the main hall. Mao Sui and the other nineteen men were lined up at the foot of the steps. The Lord of Pingyuan opened his remarks about reviving the Vertical Alliance to defend against Qin.

"It was Zhao who began the Vertical Alliance," the king of Chu said, "however, later on thanks to the persuasions of Zhang Yi, it did not hold firm. Our former monarch, King Huai, attacked Qin as Leader of the Vertical Alliance but was not victorious. King Min of Qi, the second Leader of the Vertical Alliance was betrayed by his allies. Now we all regard the Vertical Alliance as practically a matter of taboo. If you want to reconstitute this alliance, you are going to find it like trying to make bricks out of sand—it will be far from easy!"

"When Su Qin first created the Vertical Alliance, six kingdoms agreed to support each other, and they swore a blood covenant to this effect at the Huan River," the Lord of Pingyuan replied. "As a result, the Qin army did not dare to set foot outside the Hangu Pass for fifteen years. Later on, Qi and Wei were tricked by Qin, who wanted them to allow an attack on Zhao; furthermore, King Huai was taken prisoner by Zhang Yi, who wanted to be able to attack Qi. That is the reason why the Vertical Alliance eventually collapsed. Now, if our three kingdoms were to agree to keep to the covenant we swore at the Huan River and were not taken in by anything that Qin chose to tell us, what would they be able to do about it? King Min of Qi may have said that he wanted to affirm the Vertical Alliance, but in reality he did everything that he could to break it; that is the reason the other kings turned against him. Surely that has nothing to do with whether the Vertical Alliance is a good idea or not!"

"In the world today, Qin is strong and all the other kingdoms are weak," His Majesty returned. "The best we can do is to defend ourselves. What more can we hope for?"

"Even though Qin is strong," His Lordship said, "they are not in a position to be able to control all the six other kingdoms. Even though the six kingdoms are individually weak, joined together they would be more than strong enough to deal with Qin. If each is busy with defending its own territory and does not go to the aid of the others, then each battle will see one weak opponent pitted against one strong one. In that case, it is quite clear who will win! I am afraid that we will see the Qin army advance further forward with every day that passes!"

Now the king of Chu said: "In a single campaign, the Qin army captured seventeen cities in Shangdang and killed more than four hundred thousand Zhao troops—even the forces of Han and Zhao united were not enough to deal with the Lord of Wu'an on his own! Now they are pressing close on Handan, but the kingdom of Chu is located far away to the south. What do you think I can do to change anything?"

"His Majesty picked the wrong general, and that brought about the disaster that we suffered at Changping," the Lord of Pingyuan said. "Now Wang Ling and Wang He are camped at the foot of the city walls of Handan with an army of more than two hundred thousand men. All in all, they have been there for more than a year, and they have not been able to capture so much as an inch of land. If an army were to come to the rescue that could do something to blunt their ardor, we would win many years of peace!"

"We have recently signed a peace treaty with Qin, and yet you want me to go to the rescue of Zhao as the Leader of the Vertical Alliance," His Majesty replied. "In that case Qin is certain to take revenge on us. We will simply be the whipping boy for Zhao!"

"The reason Qin made peace with you was so that they could concentrate on the Three Jins," the Lord of Pingyuan pointed out. "If the Three Jins are conquered, do you think you will survive?"

From start to finish, the king of Chu was so terrified of Qin that he simply could not make up his mind what to do.

Mao Sui, standing with the others on the steps of the hall, was watching the sun climb in the sky. When it got to noon, he put his hand on the pommel of his sword and climbed up the steps. He said to the Lord of Pingyuan, "You could explain the reasons for His Majesty to join the Vertical Alliance in just two sentences. However, we got to court when the sun was rising, and now it is midday and you still have not yet concluded your discussion. What is going on?"

"Who are you?" the king of Chu demanded angrily.

"This is one of my clients: Mao Sui," the Lord of Pingyuan said soothingly.

"I am discussing matters of state with your lord. Don't interrupt!" The king of Chu shouted at him to go away.

Mao Sui came forward another couple of steps, his hand still on the pommel of his sword. "The Vertical Alliance is enormously important—this is something for everyone to discuss. Why are you shouting at me in front of my lord?"

The king of Chu calmed down a bit and asked, "What do you have to say?"

"The territories of Chu stretch for more than five thousand *li*, and since the time of Wen and Wu you have called yourselves kings," Mao Sui said. "Even today Chu is one of the most powerful countries in the world, and you have often served as the Master of Covenants. However, one fine day the Qin army suddenly rose up and defeated your armies in repeated battles, taking King Huai prisoner. Then Bai Qi fought a couple of campaigns and captured Yan and Ying, forcing you to move your capital. This is something that Chu should be deeply ashamed of. Even small children know that this is a source of national humiliation—do you, Your Majesty, really not care? We are talking about the Vertical Alliance to help you, not to help Zhao!"

"Oh yes! Indeed!" the king said.

"Have you made up your mind?" Mao Sui asked.

"I have made up my mind," His Majesty declared.

Mao Sui shouted at his entourage to bring forward a bowl of blood. Kneeling down in front of the king of Chu, he said: "Since you are the Leader of the Vertical Alliance, Your Majesty, you should smear your mouth with blood first, followed by His Lordship. After that, I too will smear my mouth."

It was in this way that the Vertical Alliance was renewed.

When Mao Sui had touched his lips with blood, he took the bowl in his left hand while with his right he gestured to the other nineteen men to join him. "You should join in swearing the oath," he said. "You are part of this too."

Having agreed to this alliance, the king of Chu ordered the Lord of Chunshen to take an army of eighty thousand men to rescue Zhao. The Lord of Pingyuan returned to his own country. He sighed and said: "Mao Sui's rhetoric can outweigh an army of one million men. I have seen many men, but never anyone like him. In the future, I will never claim to be able to weigh up anyone's abilities on sight!"

He appointed Mao Sui to be one of his senior advisors.

As the saying goes:

A shield may be huge, but it has to follow its master;
Although a hammer is small, it can crush a weight of one thousand
  pounds.
The sharp awl does not always find its way into the right bag,
Thus the Lord of Pingyuan was only able to find nineteen men.

At this time King Anli of Wei sent his senior general, Jin Bi, in command of an army of one hundred thousand men to rescue Zhao. When the king of Qin heard that other rulers had stepped in, he went in person to Handan to inspect the progress of the battle. He sent an ambassador to the king of Wei to say: "Qin is attacking Handan and it will fall at any moment. Anyone who dares to go to the rescue will find our troops turned against him next!" The king of Wei was horrified and sent an envoy rushing after General Jin Bi, warning him not to advance any further. Jin Bi made camp at Yexia. The Lord of Chunshen also made camp at the Wu Pass, keeping an eye on the progress of events but not advancing. Let us put this story aside for the moment.

. . .

After the meeting of Qin and Zhao at Mianchi, Royal Grandson Yiren was sent as a hostage to the Zhao court. He was one of the younger sons of the Lord of Anguo. The Lord of Anguo was better known as Prince Zhu, styled Zixi, King Zhaoxiang of Qin's crown prince. The Lord of Anguo had more than twenty sons, all of them the children of his concubines. Not a single one was born of the crown princess as his legitimate heir. His Lordship's favorite concubine, who originally came from Chu, held the title of Lady Huayang. She too had no children. Royal Grandson Yiren's mother was Lady Xia Ji, but the crown prince did not love her and she died young. It was for this reason that Royal Grandson Yiren was selected to go as a hostage to Zhao, without any communication with his family for a very long time. When the Zhao army was defeated in battle by Qin, the king decided to kill Yiren, venting his fury on his hostage.

One of his ministers remonstrated: "Yiren is not an important member of the royal family, so killing him won't change anything. It will just give Qin an excuse to attack us and make any peaceful resolution in the future impossible."

The king of Zhao had still not calmed down entirely from his anger, so he sent Yiren to live at the Zong Tower. He ordered Grandee Gongsun Qian to take charge of guarding him, keeping a close eye on his movements, while cutting down the emoluments he received. Not only did Royal Grandson Yiren not have a carriage to use, he found that he now did not even have enough money for his daily needs. This caused him to become sunk in depression.

It was at this time that he met a man named Lü Buwei from Yangdi. His father was a merchant, who spent his days traveling from one country to another, buying things cheap and selling them at a considerable markup, accumulating great reserves of wealth. Lü Buwei happened to be visiting Handan, where he caught sight of Royal Grandson Yiren on the road. He was a very striking-looking man—even when poor and friendless, he never lost his aristocratic air. Lü Buwei was impressed and asked one of the passers-by, "Who is that man?"

"That is the son of the crown prince of Qin, the Lord of Anguo," the man replied. "He is a hostage here in the kingdom of Zhao. Since the Qin army has repeatedly invaded our borders, the king wanted to kill him. Although he has escaped being put to death, he is now being held under close guard at the Zong Tower and they don't support him anymore, as a result of which he has become very poor."

Lü Buwei sighed and said to himself, "This is a remarkable business opportunity!"

He went home and asked his father, "What is the profit we expect from our agricultural investments?"

"Ten percent."

"What profit do we expect from our trade in pearls and precious stones?"

"One hundred percent."

"What kind of profit do you think we could expect if we established a king and took control of his country?"

His father laughed and asked, "Where could we find such a king? The profits would be one thousand percent, ten thousand percent—incalculable!"

Lü Buwei expended one hundred pieces of gold on making friends with Gongsun Qian. As the two of them became increasingly close, he was able to visit Royal Grandson Yiren. Pretending to know nothing about him, he asked who he was, and Gongsun Qian told him the truth.

One day, Gongsun Qian invited Lü Buwei to a drinks party. "Since you have invited no other guests and the Royal Grandson of Qin is here," Buwei said, "why don't you ask him to join us?"

Gongsun Qian followed his suggestion. He introduced Yiren to Lü Buwei, and they sat down on the same mat and started drinking. When they were all somewhat tipsy, Gongsun Qian got up in order to go to the privy. Lü Buwei now said in a low voice to the Royal Grandson: "The king of Qin is getting old. The crown prince loves Lady Huayang, but she does not have any children of her own. You have more than twenty other brothers, but there is none who is obviously more favored than the others. Why don't you ask to be allowed to return to the kingdom of Qin and, when you are there, seek to ingratiate yourself with Lady Huayang, maybe even become her adopted son? In that case, in the future, you might hope to become the king of Qin yourself!"

Yiren replied, almost in tears: "Do you think I don't want to go home? Every time I hear people talk about my home country, it is like my heart is being sliced open with a knife! I have no idea how I am going to get away from here!"

"Even though my family is poor," Buwei told him, "we can offer you one thousand pieces of gold towards the expenses of your journey to the west. Let me go and persuade the crown prince and Lady Huayang to rescue you and bring you home. How would that be?"

"If you can make that happen," Yiren said, "I will share my future wealth and honors with you."

When they had just finished speaking, Gongsun Qian came back. He asked, "What were you talking about?"

"I asked the Royal Grandson what the price of jade is like nowadays in Qin, and he was apologizing because he does not know," Lü Buwei said.

Gongsun Qian was not at all suspicious. He ordered that more wine be poured and, having enjoyed themselves heartily, the party finally broke up. After this, Lü Buwei and Royal Grandson Yiren often met one another, and he gave the latter five hundred gold pieces in secret, instructing him to buy some servants and make some useful friends. Yiren gave gold and silk to Gongsun Qian and his household, until they all felt they were practically like family and were not at all suspicious of what he might be up to.

Lü Buwei used another five hundred pieces of gold to buy various expensive jewels and other treasures. Having bade farewell to Gongsun Qian, he headed off to Xianyang. He discovered that Lady Huayang had an older sister who was also married in Qin, so he began by bribing some of her family servants to communicate the following message to her: "Royal Grandson Yiren is stuck in Zhao, but he very much misses Her Ladyship and asked me to bring her various presents to show his filial love. This little gift is from the Royal Grandson to his aunt." He presented her with a box of gold and pearls.

Lady Huayang's older sister was delighted and came out into the main hall of the house in person, where she had an audience with Lü Buwei from the far side of a curtain. "It is very kind of the Royal Grandson to send you all this way," she said. "Having spent all this time in Zhao, does he really miss his home so much?"

"I live opposite to the Royal Grandson and we often talk to one another," Lü Buwei explained. "I might say that I know him very well indeed. He misses Her Ladyship day and night. Having lost his own mother as a small child, he has come to feel that Lady Huayang is like his real mother. He would love to be able to come home to see her again, to fulfill the demands of his filial duty!"

"How has the Royal Grandson fared in Zhao?"

"The Qin army had repeatedly attacked the kingdom of Zhao," Lü Buwei replied. "Each time the king of Zhao has threatened to execute the Royal Grandson. Fortunately, he has been able to survive thanks to the representations of ministers and other people. That is the reason that he is so desperate to go home!"

"Why do the ministers and people of Zhao try and protect him?"

"The Royal Grandson is a remarkably filial and fine young man," Lü Buwei replied. "Every time that it is the birthday of the king of Qin, the crown prince, or Her Ladyship, or indeed New Year's Day or any other festival, the Royal Grandson performs full ritual lustrations and then burns incense while bowing to the west and praying for blessings for you all. Everyone in Zhao knows that he does this. He is also very studious and treats wise men with great respect—he has acquired many clients and advisors from other kingdoms. Wherever you go in the world, you would hear people talking about what a remarkable man he is. That is the reason why everyone has gone to such lengths to save his life!"

When he had finished speaking, Lü Buwei presented further rare items to the value of about five hundred pieces of gold: "Since the Royal Grandson cannot come back to serve Her Ladyship in person, he hopes that these little gifts will show his filial love for her. Please, would you give them to your sister on his behalf?"

Lady Huayang's older sister ordered a senior member of her household to entertain Lü Buwei with food and wine while she went to the palace to speak to Her Ladyship. When Lady Huayang saw these treasures, she thought that the Royal Grandson must really care about her, and she was very pleased. Her sister went back to report this to Lü Buwei, who asked, "How many children does Her Ladyship have?"

"She is childless."

"I have often heard people say that a woman who relies on her beauty for her position will find that love fades as she gets older," Lü Buwei remarked. "At the moment Her Ladyship is the crown prince's favorite, but she has no children of her own. In these circumstances she ought to select the most filial of his sons to adopt as her own. That way, in the fullness of time, he can become king and she will never lose power. Otherwise, if the crown prince's love does fade as she gets older, it will be too late! Now, Yiren is a very clever and filial young man, and he is deeply attached to Her Ladyship. He knows that as things stand, he has no hope of ever becoming king. However, were Her Ladyship to promote him to the position of heir apparent, would she not be loved in Qin from one generation to the next?"

Her sister again reported these words to Lady Huayang. "He is quite right," she said.

Accordingly one night, when she and the Lord of Anguo had been drinking together perfectly happily, she suddenly burst into tears. The crown prince was surprised and asked her what the matter was.

"Although I have been lucky enough to join your harem," Lady Huayang sobbed, "I have never been so fortunate as to have children. Of all your sons, Yiren is by far the most intelligent, and he is much admired by all the foreign ambassadors and advisors who come and go from Zhao—they cannot praise him enough. If I were to adopt him and he became your heir, I would have someone to rely on."

The crown prince agreed to her request.

"You have said yes now," Her Ladyship pouted. "But when your other concubines start nagging you, you will forget all about it."

"If you don't trust me, I will write my promise down," the crown prince told her.

He took a jade tablet and scratched four words upon it: "Yiren is my heir." He broke the tablet in half and they each kept one part of it as proof.

"Yiren is in Zhao," Lady Huayang said. "When will we bring him home?"

"I will find an opportunity to mention this to His Majesty," the crown prince assured her.

At this time King Zhaoxiang of Qin was furious with Zhao, so when the crown prince spoke to His Majesty, he did not listen. Lü Buwei knew that His Majesty was very fond of the queen's younger brother, the Lord of Yangquan, so he bribed his servants and asked to be allowed to have an audience with His Lordship. He began his persuasion as follows: "You, sir, have committed a crime deserving of the death penalty. Did you know that?"

The Lord of Yangquan was horrified. "What crime have I committed?" he asked.

"You have arranged for your entire household to receive important government posts," Lü Buwei said. "You enjoy rich emoluments, your stables are packed with the finest of horses, your harem is stuffed with the most beautiful of women—but where are the rich, noble, and powerful members of the crown prince's household? His Majesty is already an old man. When he passes away, the crown prince who will come to the throne and his household will certainly be filled with resentment towards you. Your situation will then be precarious indeed!"

"What should I do?" the Lord of Yangquan asked.

"I have a plan that could mean that you could live out your natural life span in complete security: as safe as Mount Tai," Lü Buwei declared. "Do you want to hear it?"

The Lord of Yangquan knelt down and invited him to speak. "His Majesty is getting on, and the crown prince does not have a legitimate heir," Lü Buwei continued. "Now, Royal Grandson Yiren is a wise and filial man whose conduct has won glowing praise from the other kings, and yet he is at present living as a hostage in Zhao, hoping day and night to be allowed to return home. You should ask the queen to speak to the king about bringing Yiren home, and have the crown prince appoint him as his heir. In that case Yiren will go from having nothing to being the future monarch; the crown prince's wife, Lady Huayang, will go from having no children to having a wonderful adopted son; the crown prince and the Royal Grandson will both be most grateful to the queen; and your own noble position will be preserved from one generation to the next without the slightest impairment!"

The Lord of Yangquan went down the steps and bowed to show his respect. "I am very grateful for your advice," he said.

He immediately reported what Lü Buwei had said to the queen. Her Majesty then spoke to the king of Qin about it. "When the people of Zhao beg for a peace treaty," he said, "I will bring my grandson home."

The crown prince summoned Lü Buwei and asked him, "I would like to bring Yiren home to Qin and make him my heir, but His Majesty will not allow it. Do you have a good plan to suggest?"

Lü Buwei kowtowed and said, "If you indeed intend to make him your heir, Crown Prince, I would not begrudge spending every penny I have. If I were to bribe the people in power in Zhao, I am sure I can save him."

The crown prince and Her Ladyship were both delighted and gave three hundred ingots of gold to Lü Buwei. This he was to hand over to Yiren, to pay for the expenses of his household. The queen gave him a further two hundred gold ingots. Lady Huayang also prepared a whole trunk of clothes for Yiren and gave Lü Buwei one hundred gold ingots to keep for himself, since she wanted to appoint him as the Grand Tutor. He was to take the following message to the Royal Grandson: "Any minute now we will get you out of there. Don't worry." Lü Buwei said goodbye and left.

There is a poem that testifies to this:

This idle merchant cared only about profit:
Now a few treasures bought him a Royal Grandson.
He was able to make a childless woman have her own son,
Convincing her to requite filial piety with an adoption.

When he arrived back in Handan, he went first to see his own father and tell him what had happened. His father was delighted. The following day he prepared presents and went to see Gongsun Qian. After that, he had an audience with Royal Grandson Yiren, at which he repeated exactly what the queen and Lady Huayang had said to him and presented him with the five hundred ingots of gold and the clothes. Yiren was very pleased. He said to Lü Buwei: "I will keep the clothes but you, sir, should take the gold. Even though I need money, I have put you to a lot of trouble and expense. If I ever get to go home, there is nothing I will not do for you."

. . .

It was about this time that Lü Buwei took a beautiful woman named Zhao Ji, who was good at singing and dancing, into his household. When he discovered that she was two months pregnant, he came up with a plan: "When Royal Grandson Yiren goes home, sooner or later he will become king. If I present this woman to him, she may give birth to a boy, who will be my own flesh and blood. If this boy eventually becomes king himself, then the Ying clan will be replaced on the throne by the Lü family. That is something that would be worth bankrupting us all to achieve!"

He invited Royal Grandson Yiren and Gongsun Qian to his house for drinks. The tables were groaning with the finest of delicacies, and the most delightful tunes were played by the musicians. When the wine circulated and they had become a little drunk, Lü Buwei announced: "I have recently acquired a new concubine who is good at singing and dancing. I would like her to come out and offer a toast; I hope you don't mind . . ." He commanded the maids to go and bring Zhao Ji out.

"Why don't you pay your respects to my honored guests?" Lü Buwei said.

Zhao Ji walked forward a couple of steps and then fell to her knees on the carpet and kowtowed. Royal Grandson Yiren and Gongsun Qian quickly made respectful bows in return. Lü Buwei ordered Zhao Ji to take a gold cup and toast each of the men in turn. When it came to

Yiren, he raised his head and looked at her, only to see that she was indeed very lovely.

How to describe her?

Her tresses billowed out, floating as lightly as a cicada's wing,
Her eyebrows were clearly marked in a beautiful wave-like curve.
Her lips were painted in a lovely cherry-red cupid's bow,
Her pearly teeth shone like brilliant white jade.
When she gave her seductive laugh:
You could imagine that she was Bao Si bewitching King You.
When she danced on her tiny feet:
You might think that this was Xi Shi beguiling the ruler of Wu.
You could never have enough of watching her enchanting ways,
You could paint her portrait a thousand times and never catch her
    charm.

When Zhao Ji had offered a toast to each of them, she shook loose the long sleeves of her gown. Taking up a position on the carpet, she began to dance. Her body moved with sinuous grace, and her sleeves arced through the air like rainbows. She spun like a feather being tossed on the wind, and she seemed so light as to be almost insubstantial, like mist or fog. It was all so delightful that Gongsun Qian and Yiren were completely bewitched. They sat there in a trance, their mouths agape, sighing with admiration. When Zhao Ji had finished dancing, Lü Buwei ordered her to pour large goblets of wine and toast everyone again. His two guests drained their cups in a single draft. When she had finished serving them wine, Zhao Ji withdrew into the women's quarters. The host and guests continued to drink, enjoying themselves very much.

Gongsun Qian got very drunk indeed and fell asleep where he sat. Royal Grandson Yiren was thinking about Zhao Ji. Pretending to be much drunker than he really was, he said to Lü Buwei, "I wish you would give her to me as my wife—after all, I am here as a hostage on my own and I spend my time alone. Having her would make me very happy. I don't know how much it would cost to buy her; I would refund you however much you spent on her in the first place . . ."

Lü Buwei pretended to be angry and said: "I invited you here and had my womenfolk come out to meet you because I wanted to show you my respect. How can you try and steal her from me?"

Yiren was very uncomfortable at the direction the conversation had taken. Falling to his knees, he said: "Since I am so lonely in my present situation, I was so desperate that I actually considered trying to take your concubine away from you! Treat it as drunken babbling . . . Please don't be angry!"

Lü Buwei rushed forward and helped him to his feet. He said: "In order to make it possible for you to go home, I have spent every penny of my family's wealth without regret. Why should I begrudge you a woman? However, she is very young and easily embarrassed, so I am afraid that she will not simply do your bidding. If she is willing, I will escort her to your residence so she can serve in your bedchamber."

Yiren bowed twice and expressed thanks. He waited until Gongsun Qian had woken from his drunken stupor and then the two of them went home in their carriage.

That night, Lü Buwei said to Zhao Ji, "The Royal Grandson from Qin loves you very much and would like to marry you. What do you think?"

"I have already lost my virginity to you," Zhao Ji said, "and I am carrying your baby—how could I leave you to marry someone else?"

"If you spend the rest of your life with me, you will never be more than the wife of a merchant," Lü Buwei hinted. "However, the Royal Grandson will be king of Qin one day. If you obtain his favor, you will certainly become his queen. If the baby you are carrying is a boy, he will naturally become crown prince. You and I will then be the father and mother of a future king of Qin, and we will be rich and powerful beyond our wildest dreams. If you have ever really loved me, then please follow my advice, but do not let anyone know what we are doing!"

"Your plan is indeed a great one," Zhao Ji said. "How could I dare to refuse to carry it out? However, given that we love each other, it is difficult indeed to be separated!" As she spoke she began to cry.

Lü Buwei soothed her: "As long as you love me, in the future when Qin is ours we can still be husband and wife, this time never to be parted. Would that not be wonderful?" The two of them then swore a solemn oath and spent the night together with redoubled affection, which does not need to be described.

. . .

The following day, Lü Buwei went to visit Gongsun Qian, to apologize for treating him rudely the night before.

"Actually," Gongsun Qian explained, "the Royal Grandson and I were just about to go to your residence to thank you for yesterday's entertainment. You really didn't need to come here in person." A short time later, Yiren came in and the two of them expressed their gratitude.

"Your Royal Highness was kind enough to mention that you did not think my concubine too ugly and that you would like her to serve you," Lü Buwei said. "I have spoken to her about it and she has already agreed. Today is a suitably auspicious day, and so I am going to escort her here immediately."

"Even if you ground my bones to powder," Yiren declared, "it would be difficult for me to repay you!"

"If there is going to be a marriage," Gongsun Qian said happily, "I will be the official matchmaker!" He ordered his servants to prepare a wedding banquet. Lü Buwei bade them farewell and left. That evening, he sent Zhao Ji around in a closed carriage, and she began her life with Royal Grandson Yiren.

An old man wrote a poem:

In an instant, a new fancy or an old love may be snuffed out;
When the candles in the bridal chamber gutter, it is time to enjoy
    oneself.
When this scion of the royal house stole the throne,
Who could have known it was for the son of Lü Buwei?

When Royal Grandson Yiren obtained Zhao Ji, he was extremely happy and loved her very much. After they had been together for about a month, Zhao Ji told him: "Since I have been lucky enough to serve you, I have become pregnant with your child." Yiren did not know the ins and outs of this and thought it was indeed his own child, so he was even more delighted. Zhao Ji married Yiren when she was two months pregnant, so she was expecting to give birth to the baby at nine months. However, time passed and nothing happened. Given that she was pregnant with the future First Emperor of China—a man who would change the destiny of the world—it is not surprising that his birth was heralded by unusual signs. So it was not until one year after she became pregnant that she finally gave birth to a baby boy. When he was born, a glowing red light filled the room and a myriad birds came flapping in to view the baby. At birth he had a prominent nose and large eyes, a square forehead, and double pupils. He had already cut a couple of teeth, and there was a pattern like the scales of a dragon on his back. When he began to scream, the sound was so loud that it could be heard throughout the entire city. He was born on New Year's Day in the forty-eighth year of the reign of his great-grandfather, King Zhaoxiang of Qin.

The Royal Grandson Yiren was thrilled and said: "I have heard that someone who will achieve remarkable things is always heralded by strange signs at the time of their birth. This child has a most unusual appearance and he is born on New Year's Day—in the future it will be he who rules a united China." He named the baby Zheng, or "United Rule." Later on, Zheng did indeed become the king of Qin. He unified the other six kingdoms and became the First Emperor of China. Of course, when Lü Buwei heard that Zhao Ji had given birth to a boy, he too was secretly delighted.

. . .

In the fiftieth year of the reign of King Zhaoxiang of Qin, Zheng turned three years old. At this time the Qin troops were pressing ever closer in their siege of Handan. Lü Buwei said to Yiren, "The king of Zhao might well try to take his anger out upon you again, Your Royal Highness! What are you going to do? You had better run away to the kingdom of Qin to get away from all of this."

"I will do whatever you suggest, sir," Royal Grandson Yiren said.

Lü Buwei collected a total of six hundred pounds of gold. He used three hundred pounds to bribe the general in command of guarding the South Gate. The following message was attached: "My family originally comes from Yangdi. We came here on business, but unluckily we got caught up in the siege by the Qin army, which has dragged on for many days. I really miss my home and I have now given you every last penny to distribute among your men. I hope you will help me by letting my family leave the city and go back to Yangdi. I will never forget this kindness!"

The general agreed to let him go. Lü Buwei presented another one hundred pounds of gold to Gongsun Qian and announced that he was going home to Yangdi. He said that he wanted Gongsun Qian to talk to the officers at the South Gate on his behalf. Since the general, officers, and men had already been bribed, they were happy to agree. Lü Buwei told Royal Grandson Yiren that he should secretly make arrangements to send Zhao Ji and the baby to live with her parents.

On the appointed day, he held a banquet for Gongsun Qian. He said, "I am going to be leaving the city in three days' time. I am holding this party to say goodbye!" He made sure that Gongsun Qian got so drunk that he could not move. The soldiers and guards present all ate and drank to their hearts' content until they were so stuffed that they simply went to sleep. At midnight, Royal Grandson Yiren mingled with the other servants, dressed in simple clothes, to follow Lü Buwei and his father as they walked out of the South Gate. The general there, not knowing what was really going on, unlocked the gate and let them out of the city. In actual fact, the Qin army's main camp was located outside the West Gate. However, because the road to Yangdi went via the South Gate and Lü Buwei was claiming that he wanted to go home, he had to leave that way. The three men and their servants raced through the night in a wide circle, trying to make their way over to the Qin army.

At dawn, they were taken prisoner by a party of Qin soldiers out on patrol. Lü Buwei pointed to Yiren and said, "This is Royal Grandson of Qin, who has been held hostage in Zhao. He has managed to escape from Handan and is on his way home. You had better do everything in your power to help him!"

The patrol got off their horses to let the three men ride and took them to the main camp. When the general there heard who they were, he invited them to come in and have an audience. He gave Yiren a suitable hat and robe to change into and held a banquet in his honor.

"His Majesty is here to view our progress in person," he said. "His traveling palace is not ten *li* from here." He prepared a carriage and horses and had them escorted there.

When King Zhaoxiang saw Yiren, he could not contain his delight. "The crown prince misses you day and night," he said. "Heaven has enabled you to escape from the tiger's jaws! You must go back to Xianyang immediately, so that your parents can stop worrying about you!"

Yiren said goodbye to the king of Qin. He got into a carriage with Lü Buwei and his father and headed for Xianyang.

Do you want to know how the meeting between father and son went? READ ON.

Chapter One Hundred

Lu Zhonglian refuses to allow Qin to become emperor.

The Lord of Xinling steals a tally to rescue Zhao.

As mentioned previously, Lü Buwei and Royal Grandson Yiren said goodbye to the king of Qin and headed for Xianyang. Someone had already reported this development to the crown prince, the Lord of Anguo. He said to Lady Huayang, "My son has arrived." The two of them took their seats in the main hall to wait for him.

"Lady Huayang is originally from the kingdom of Chu," Lü Buwei said to Yiren, "and you are just about to be adopted as her son. You must wear Chu dress when you go to see her, to show how affectionately you feel towards her."

Royal Grandson Yiren followed this advice and immediately changed his clothes. When he arrived at the East Palace, he first bowed to the Lord of Anguo and then to Her Ladyship. With tears running down his face, he said, "I feel deeply unfilial for having been separated so long from my family—I could do nothing to show my love and affection to you. I hope that you can forgive me!"

Her Ladyship noticed that Yiren was wearing a Chu hat on his head and boots made from wildcat fur, while his robe had short sleeves and his belt was made of leather. She was very surprised and exclaimed, "You have been living in Handan! Why are you dressed like someone from Chu?"

Yiren bowed and said: "I have missed you day and night, Mother, and that is why I had a set of Chu clothes made specially to represent my love for you."

"I am originally from the kingdom of Chu," Lady Huayang said happily. "Of course you are my son!"

"In the future, my boy," the Lord of Anguo said, "you can take the name of Prince Chu."

Yiren bowed and thanked him. The Lord of Anguo went on to ask, "How were you able to come home?"

The prince explained how the king of Zhao had wanted to execute him and how he had been saved by Lü Buwei spending his entire fortune on bribes. The Lord of Anguo summoned Lü Buwei and spoke kindly to him: "If it were not for you, sir, my wise and filial son might well have been killed! Let me reward you with two hundred acres of farmland from the estates attached to the East Palace, a mansion, and fifty ingots of gold to keep the wolf from the door. When His Majesty returns to his kingdom, I am sure that you will receive even greater titles and emoluments."

Lü Buwei thanked the crown prince for his kindness and withdrew. Afterwards, Prince Chu moved into Lady Huayang's palace. No more of this now.

. . .

On the morning after the party, Gongsun Qian awoke from his alcoholic stupor at dawn. His staff reported: "The Royal Grandson of Qin and his whole family have disappeared." He sent someone to ask Lü Buwei about this, but the messenger returned and said, "Lü Buwei has disappeared too!"

Gongsun Qian was deeply shocked: "Buwei said that he would be leaving in three days' time. Why should he suddenly depart overnight?"

He went to the South Gate to make inquiries, and the officer on guard there said: "Lü Buwei and his entire family are long gone now—he said this was in accordance with your orders."

"Was Royal Grandson Yiren with him?" Gongsun Qian asked.

"I just saw old Mr. Lü and his son with various servants and retainers," the officer reported. "The Royal Grandson was not with them."

Gongsun Qian stamped his foot and shouted: "One of them would have been Royal Grandson Yiren! I have fallen into those money-grubbers' trap!"

He reported this to the king of Zhao, saying: "I have failed to guard my charge as strictly as I should—the hostage, Royal Grandson Yiren, has been able to escape. This is an inexcusable crime!" He drew his sword and committed suicide by cutting his throat.

An old man wrote a poem to bewail these events:

A custodian has to be on guard day and night against every eventuality;
You cannot be greedy for food and drink, or even less for gold!
A drunken man allowed the Royal Grandson to escape to his home;
The sword-thrust shows that he took his regrets with him to the grave.

After his grandson had escaped and made his way home, the king of
Qin renewed his attacks on Zhao with redoubled vigor. The Zhao monarch sent messengers again to request military assistance from Wei.
General Xin Huanyan offered the following suggestion: "There is a reason why Qin is pressing the siege against Zhao so vigorously. In the past
His Majesty and King Min of Qi were each trying to become strong so
that they could declare themselves emperor; however, even though the
king of Qin assumed the title, he never actually used it. Now King Min
is dead and Qi is increasingly weak—Qin is the only strong country left.
They are unhappy that they have not yet formally been invested with
the title of emperor. They are sending wave after wave of troops out to
attack Zhao because they are going to use this campaign to establish
themselves. If Zhao were to send an ambassador to congratulate the
king of Qin on assuming the title, they would be delighted and withdraw their troops. By giving them this empty title, we can avoid a real
disaster."

The king of Wei was terrified of the consequences of going to the
rescue of Zhao, and he really thought this was an excellent idea. He
ordered Xin Huanyan to go with the messenger back to Handan and
repeat this suggestion to the king of Zhao. His Majesty discussed the
practicability of this plan with his ministers. They argued about it from
every angle but could not make up their minds. The Lord of Pingyuan
had lost his grip and simply could not offer any sensible recommendations.

. . .

As it happened, a certain man named Lu Zhonglian, originally from the
kingdom of Qi, was trapped in Handan by the siege. When he was
twelve years old, he had been sent to study with the rhetorician Tian Ba.
At that time everyone called him the "Child Prodigy."

"He isn't just a child prodigy," Tian Ba declared. "He's a genius!"

When he grew up, he did not take service with anyone, but spent his
time traveling around and helping people out of their difficulties. When
Lu Zhonglian heard that the Wei ambassador was recommending that

they refer to the ruler of Qin as the emperor, he was very angry. He asked for an audience with the Lord of Pingyuan and asked, "Everyone is saying that you are going to accept that Qin takes the title of emperor—is this true?"

"I feel like a wounded bird just waiting to die . . . how could I possibly become involved in such an important matter of state?" the Lord of Pingyuan replied. "This is just the message that Wei sent General Xin Huanyan to Zhao to deliver."

"You are supposed to be one of the cleverest princes in the world; do you really take orders from some lackey from Daliang?" Lu Zhonglian retorted. "Where is this General Xin Huanyan now? I am going to give him a right ticking-off and send him home with his tail between his legs!"

The Lord of Pingyuan called for Xin Huanyan. The general had already heard much of Lu Zhonglian and was afraid that, with the other man's skill in rhetoric, his own plans might be thrown into chaos. For this reason he refused to meet with him. The Lord of Pingyuan forced him to appear, ordering both him and Lu Zhonglian to be present at a meeting at the official guesthouse. When the two men met, Xin Huanyan raised his head to look at Lu Zhonglian. His eyes were so intelligent, so spirited and expressive that without quite realizing it, a powerful sense of awe was born in him.

"I am delighted to see you, sir, and I have a question," Xin Huanyan said. "If you don't want something from the Lord of Pingyuan, why have you stayed for so long in a city under siege, refusing to leave?"

"I have nothing to ask from the Lord of Pingyuan, but I do have something to ask of you," Lu Zhonglian replied.

"What do you have to ask, sir?"

"Please help Zhao without making Qin emperor!"

"What do you mean by asking me to help Zhao?" Xin Huanyan asked.

"I am going to make Wei and Yan save Zhao," Lu Zhonglian declared. "Once that happens, Qi and Chu will certainly also go to their assistance!"

Xin Huanyan laughed and said, "I know nothing about Yan. When it comes to Wei, well . . . I am a native of Daliang. Why do you want me to help Zhao?"

"Wei does not realize that it will be a disaster if Qin declares its king an emperor. If you understood how terrible it will be, you would certainly be ready to help Zhao!"

"Why would it be so bad for Qin to become emperor?"

"Qin is a country that has abandoned all the proper norms and customs," Lu Zhonglian explained, "and regards killing enemies in battle as the sole measure of merit. They use their power to bully and cheat everyone else, torturing and murdering countless innocent people. While their country is just one kingdom among many, they already behave in this terrible way . . . if they make their king an emperor, the situation will become even more brutal and violent. I would rather throw myself into the sea and drown than become one of their subjects. Would Wei be happy being ruled by them?"

"How could we be happy to be ruled by them?" Xin Huanyan screamed. "It would be like being a slave—kicked from pillar to post. Is it really the case that slaves are more stupid and unworthy than their master? They are just scared of him, which is why they behave the way they do!"

"So, does Wei see its situation as like that of a slave?" Lu Zhonglian sneered. "I guess it will be easy for me to get the king of Qin to butcher the king of Wei . . ."

"Why would you want the king of Qin to butcher His Majesty?" Xin Huanyan demanded angrily.

"In the past, the last king of the Shang dynasty had three senior ministers: the Marquis of Jiu, the Marquis of E, and the future King Wen of Zhou," Lu Zhonglian said. "The Marquis of Jiu's daughter was very lovely, and so he presented her to His Majesty. She disliked the debauched lifestyle of the Shang king and he became angry with her, as a result of which she was killed and her father turned into mincemeat. The Marquis of E remonstrated about this, and he was in turn boiled to death. When the future king Wen heard about these events, he lamented, and the Shang king had him imprisoned in Jiuli—he very nearly ended up being executed. Do you really think that these three senior ministers were inferior to the last Shang king? That is the way that the Son of Heaven treats his nobles and always has been. If Qin declares unilaterally that their king is now an emperor, they are going to demand that Wei pays court to them. If they want to punish your king the way that the Marquis of Jiu or the Marquis of E suffered, who is going to stop them?"

Xin Huanyan thought deeply about this and could not answer.

Lu Zhonglian continued: "And it gets worse. If Qin unilaterally declares that their ruler is now an emperor, they are going to want to turn the other kings into their vassals. They will get rid of the ones they don't like and try to increase the powers of the ones they do. With Qin princesses married into every ruling house, how does the king of Wei think that he is going to avoid their influence? How do you think you are going to keep your titles and emoluments?"

Xin Huanyan now jumped to his feet. He bowed twice and thanked him, saying: "You really are a remarkably brilliant man! I am going to go back and report this to His Majesty. I will never speak of making Qin the emperor again!"

When the king of Qin heard that the Wei ambassador had arrived to discuss making him an emperor, he was very pleased. He postponed his attack to await results. When he heard that the discussions had failed and the Wei ambassador had already gone back home, he sighed and said: "The people in this city under siege should not be underestimated!" He withdrew and made camp at the Fen River. He warned Wang He to make very careful preparations for defense.

. . .

After Xin Huanyan had departed, the Lord of Pingyuan sent yet another messenger to Yexia asking for help from Jin Bi, who refused to do anything on the grounds that he had not received an express order from His Majesty. The Lord of Pingyuan then wrote a letter of complaint to the Lord of Xinling:

> I agreed to a marriage alliance between our two families because I admire your sense of justice so much, going to the assistance of people in trouble. Any day now, Handan will fall to the Qin army, but Wei refuses to help us. Is this how our friendship will end? Your sister is very worried that the walls may be breached at any moment; she is in tears day and night. You may well not want to come and rescue me, but are you prepared to stand by and watch your sister suffer?

When the Lord of Xinling received this letter, he repeatedly requested permission from the king of Wei to order Jin Bi to advance his army.

"Zhao does not want to let Qin become emperor," His Majesty said. "Why should they drag us into the fight?" From beginning to end he refused to give permission. The Lord of Xinling sent various advisors to try and speak to His Majesty, but the king of Wei might as well have been deaf.

"I cannot let the Lord of Pingyuan down like this," the Lord of Xinling declared. "I am willing to go to Zhao alone, to die with him if I must."

He prepared more than one hundred chariots and agreed with his household that they would charge straight at the Qin army to fight with the Lord of Pingyuan in his hour of need. More than one thousand men in his household volunteered to go. When he passed through the Barbarian Gate, he said goodbye to Hou Sheng. The latter said: "There is no need, my lord. I am too old to go with you. I hope that you do not blame me . . ."

The Lord of Xinling looked at Hou Sheng a couple of times but did not say another word. His Lordship set off unhappily. When he had gone about ten *li*, he thought to himself: "I have always treated Hou Sheng with the utmost respect and ceremony. Today I am heading off on a suicide mission against the Qin army, and yet Hou Sheng did not make any suggestion or offer advice to me, nor did he try to prevent me from going. That is indeed most uncharacteristic."

He told the other men to carry on while he went back alone to find Hou Sheng. "He is half dead and completely useless," they said. "Why do you want to talk to him, my lord?" The Lord of Xinling paid no attention to them.

Hou Sheng had remained standing outside the gate. When he saw the Lord of Xinling drive up in his chariot, he laughed: "I knew you would be coming back!"

"How so?" His Lordship asked.

"You have always treated me well, and now you are going into terrible danger," Hou Sheng replied. "Since I made no effort to help you, you would become angry. That is why I knew you would be coming back."

The Lord of Xinling bowed twice and said, "To begin with, I was worried that I might have failed in some respect towards you and that was why you had given up on me. So I came back to ask you the reason for your behavior."

"I have been part of your household for several decades, and yet you have never asked me for any advice," Hou Sheng said. "Now you are proposing to hurl yourself against the lances of the mighty kingdom of Qin, which can be compared to throwing meat at a hungry tiger. What is the point of that?"

"I know it is useless," His Lordship replied, "but the Lord of Pingyuan and I have always been very close, and under the circumstances, I do not feel that I can simply leave him to die. Do you have some plan to offer?"

"Sit there," Hou Sheng said. "Let me have time to think . . ."

He sent away all of His Lordship's servants and then quietly asked, "I have heard that Lady Ru Ji is much favored by His Majesty—is this true?"

"It is."

"I have heard that when she was a child, Lady Ru Ji's father was murdered. Her Ladyship spoke to His Majesty about this, wanting him to avenge her father's death, and he tried to locate the murderer for three years without the slightest success. Later on it was a member of your household who cut off his head and presented it to Lady Ru Ji. Is that true?"

"Absolutely!" the Lord of Xinling replied.

"For a long time now, Lady Ru Ji has been looking for a way to pay you back for all that you have done; in fact, she would be willing to die for you," said Hou Sheng. "Jin Bi's military tally is kept in His Majesty's bedchamber. The only person who could possibly steal it is Lady Ru Ji. If you would be prepared to speak to her, she is sure to agree. If you obtain this tally, you can give orders to Jin Bi's army. In fact, you can use it to attack Qin and rescue Zhao. That is the kind of wonderful achievement to go down in history!"

The Lord of Xinling felt as if he had awoken from a dream. He bowed twice and thanked him for his advice. He gave orders that his forces should wait for him outside the suburbs while he went back home alone. He sent one of his most trusted servants, Yan En, to beg Lady Ru Ji to steal the tally.

"If it is by the prince's order . . .," Lady Ru Ji said. "If he wanted me to jump into a sea of flames, I would do that too, without hesitation!"

That very night, the king of Wei got drunk and fell asleep. Lady Ru Ji stole the tally and gave it to Yan En, who handed it over to the Lord of Xinling. He now went back to say goodbye to Hou Sheng. However, the latter reminded him: "When a general is out in the field, he does not necessarily have to obey his ruler's orders. Although you may have the tally, Jin Bi will not necessarily believe it, or he may delay by demanding further instructions and confirmation from the king of Wei. That will not help matters. I have a friend named Zhu Hai, who is an enormously strong warrior. You should take him with you. If Jin Bi follows your orders, that's fine. If he does not, order Zhu Hai to kill him."

At this point the Lord of Xinling started to cry. "What are you afraid of?" Hou Sheng asked.

"Jin Bi has done nothing wrong," the Lord of Xinling said, "but if he doesn't accept my orders I will have to kill him. I find that very upsetting. It is not that I am scared!"

After this, he and Hou Sheng went together to visit Zhu Hai. When they explained what was going on, Zhu Hai laughed and said: "I am just a butcher in the marketplace, and yet you have repeatedly visited me here, Your Royal Highness. The only reason I have done nothing to repay you is that I have not found anything suitably important. Now that you are in this critical position, it is time for me to put my life on the line!"

"I ought to be going with you," Hou Sheng said, "but I am far too old to be able to travel so far. Only my ghost will be able to accompany you, my prince!"

He cut his throat, right then and there in front of the chariot. The Lord of Xinling was deeply shocked and pained. He gave a generous gift of money to his family so that they could bury him with full ceremony. However, he did not dare to stay a moment longer himself. He rode north, traveling in the same chariot as Zhu Hai.

An old man wrote a poem:

> The king of Wei was so petrified of the enemy, he showed himself a
> coward.
> We can also bemoan the prince's stupid idea of simply killing himself.
> In a household of three thousand men, not one proved to be of the
> slightest use;
> Hou Sheng's plan had to be entrusted to Lady Ru Ji to carry out!

Although the king of Wei's tally had been stolen from his bedchamber, it was not until three days later that he noticed it was gone. He was absolutely appalled and questioned Lady Ru Ji. When she insisted that she knew nothing about it, the entire palace was searched, but without result. His Majesty ordered Yan En to torture all the palace servants, particularly anyone with direct access to his bedchamber. Although Yan En knew exactly what had happened, he had to pretend that he did not and carry on regardless. Having fretted himself for a whole day, the king of Wei suddenly bethought himself of Prince Wuji, the Lord of Xinling. He had repeatedly urged His Majesty to order Jin Bi to advance his troops, and in his household there were many thieves and villains— this must be his work! He sent someone to summon the Lord of Xinling. The messenger came back to report: "His Lordship left the city four or five days ago, in the company of about one thousand members of his household and one hundred or so chariots. The rumor is that he is going to rescue Zhao."

The king of Wei was absolutely furious. He ordered General Wey Qing to take three thousand soldiers and go in pursuit of the Lord of Xinling, traveling day and night.

. . .

The people in the city of Handan were hoping desperately for the arrival of relief troops, but when nobody came, the inhabitants became more and more demoralized and exhausted. Everywhere there was discussion of the possibility of surrender. The king of Zhao was deeply concerned. One of the officials in the Lord of Pingyuan's household, Li Tong, said to him: "Every day the people have to climb the walls of the city in order to defend them while you are sitting at home in the lap of luxury. Who would be willing to risk their life for you in such circumstances? You must order everyone from your wife downwards to join the defense forces, doing their best to help the city in its hour of need. Furthermore, every piece of silk in the house should be given to the officers organizing the defense. Given the desperate situation we are in, they will appreciate the gesture all the more. They will resist Qin with redoubled fervor."

The Lord of Pingyuan followed his advice and assembled a group of three thousand suicide troops to be led by none other than Li Tong. They let themselves down from the top of the city walls and raided the enemy encampments under cover of darkness. In this way they managed to kill more than one thousand Qin soldiers. Wang He was very shocked at this development and withdrew his forces thirty *li* before making camp again. This stabilized the situation inside the city. Li Tong suffered severe injuries and died shortly after coming back to the city. The Lord of Pingyuan wept at this news and had him buried with full honors.

. . .

Meanwhile, the Lord of Xinling arrived at Yexia. When he met with Jin Bi, he said: "His Majesty is concerned that you have spent so long in the field, General, that he sent me to replace you." He ordered Zhu Hai to present Jin Bi with the military tally and allow him to verify it. Jin Bi took the tally in his hands. He was feeling deeply uncomfortable, and thought to himself: "His Majesty entrusted me with command of one hundred thousand soldiers. Even though I have been stuck here in this remote spot, I have not been defeated in battle. The king of Wei hasn't sent me any message at all, but here is the prince with a tally, claiming that he has come to replace me. There is something fishy going on!"

Accordingly, he said to the Lord of Xinling: "I hope that you will not mind waiting a few days while I put my records in order before I hand them over to you?"

"Handan's fate is trembling in the balance!" the Lord of Xinling exclaimed. "I came here as quickly as I could to rescue them, traveling day and night. I am not prepared to wait another moment!"

"Let me tell you the truth," Jin Bi said. "Control over the army is a major matter. I will not hand over my troops until I have received a written confirmation of your command."

Before he had even finished speaking, Zhu Hai yelled: "The commander-in-chief is refusing to obey His Majesty's order! He is a traitor!"

Jin Bi turned to ask him: "Who are you?"

At that moment he saw Zhu Hai pull an iron hammer weighing quite forty pounds from his sleeve. He hit Jin Bi on the head with it, cracking his skull open and killing him instantly.

The Lord of Xinling showed the tally to the other generals. "His Majesty commanded me to take over from Jin Bi and lead our troops to rescue Zhao. Jin Bi refused to accept this command, and he has now been executed for his crime. In future you must obey my orders—do not do anything precipitate."

The entire encampment was shocked into silence. When Wey Qing arrived at Yexia, the Lord of Xinling had already killed Jin Bi and taken over his army. Realizing that His Lordship was quite determined to rescue Zhao from their predicament, he wanted to leave, but the Lord of Xinling said, "Since you are here, why don't you wait until after I have defeated the Qin army before going back to report to His Majesty?"

Wey Qing had no choice but to send a secret missive back to the king of Wei informing him of what had happened while he himself remained with the army. The Lord of Xinling held a great feast for his troops and then issued the following command: "If a father and his son are both present in the army, the father is allowed to go home. If there is an older brother and his younger brother present, the older brother may go home. If there is an only child here, he should go home and look after his parents. Anyone who is sick should stay here and receive treatment."

This resulted in about twenty percent of his army leaving. The eighty thousand men who remained were all fine soldiers. He divided them into infantry divisions of five men; this small grouping enabled him to instruct each division properly in military law.

There is a poem that testifies to this:

Having chosen eighty thousand men to rescue Handan,
He wanted to strike awe into the people of Qin.
Flags fluttered in the sky, spears glinted in the sun,
As he ascended the command platform to the shouts of his men.

The Lord of Xinling rode at the head of his troops, leading the members of his household to attack the Qin encampment. Wang He was not expecting to be attacked by the Wei army and had to assemble his forces to fight back in a great hurry. The Wei forces pressed forward, and as they did so, the Lord of Pingyuan led his troops out of the city in support. A huge battle was fought in which Wang He lost half his army—he had to flee back to the main encampment on the Fen River. The king of Qin gave orders to lift the siege and go back home. Zheng Anping was based in a separate encampment by the East Gate, together with twenty thousand men. Since he was caught by the Wei army, it was impossible for him to go home. He sighed and said, "Well, I was originally from Wei myself." He promptly surrendered to them. When the Lord of Chunshen heard that the Qin army had left, he too stood down his forces and went home. The king of Han took advantage of this opportunity to regain possession of Shangdang. This occurred in the fiftieth year of the reign of King Zhaoxiang of Qin, which was the fifty-eighth year of the reign of King Nan of Zhou.

An old man wrote a poem:

This fine army halted the Qin advance;
Let us praise the prince for rescuing his brother-in-law!
All of these great fortresses and huge encampments
Were filled with men trying to hide.

The king of Zhao personally took wine and meat out to feast the Wei army. He bowed twice to the Lord of Xinling and said: "It is all thanks to Your Royal Highness that the kingdom of Zhao has been rescued from the very brink of destruction. I do not think that any of the great sages of antiquity can match up to you."

The Lord of Pingyuan walked in front of him to clear the way, and the Lord of Xinling looked very pleased with himself. Zhu Hai stepped forward and said: "When other people help you, you must never forget it. However, when you help other people, you must forget it immediately. You lied about having an order from His Majesty, and you stole Jin Bi's army to rescue Zhao. You may have done great things for Zhao, but you have also committed many crimes against Wei. Why should you feel pleased with yourself?"

The Lord of Xinling felt ashamed. "I am very grateful for your advice."

When he arrived at the city of Handan, the king of Zhao moved out of his own quarters in the palace in order to allow the Lord of Xinling to move in—he treated him throughout with the utmost ceremony and respect. His Lordship kept apologizing: "I have done nothing for Zhao, and I am guilty of serious crimes against Wei."

When the feasting and banqueting was over and His Lordship returned to the official guesthouse, the king of Zhao said to the Lord of Pingyuan, "I would have liked to give five cities to the prince of Wei as a personal gift, but seeing how modest and retiring he is, it would have been too embarrassing to say anything. I would like to give the city of Hao to His Royal Highness as a gift, and I want you to convey this message to him."

As he had been ordered by the king of Zhao, the Lord of Pingyuan mentioned this to the prince of Wei. The Lord of Xinling refused this grant over and over again, before finally daring to accept it. His Lordship knew that he had offended the king of Wei, and so he did not dare to return home. He handed the tally over to General Wey Qing and had him take the army back to Wei, while he himself remained behind in the kingdom of Zhao. Those of his household who had stayed in Wei now fled to throw in their lot with the Lord of Xinling in Zhao. The king of Zhao also wanted to enfeoff Lu Zhonglian with a large city, but he simply refused. Then His Majesty tried to give him one thousand pieces of gold—he refused that also. "I do not want to have to truckle to someone for fame and fortune," he declared. "I would rather be poor and free."

The Lord of Xinling and the Lord of Pingyuan both wanted him to stay, but he refused. He drifted off in some new direction. What an amazing man he was!

A historian wrote in praise:

> Lu Zhonglian was a man of high principles,
> His virtues would be praised for a thousand generations!
> He was able to stop the powerful king of Qin from becoming emperor,
> He would rather throw himself into the sea to drown than see that!
> He saved people from danger but refused all reward,
> He traveled around the country as free as a bird.
> Think of Zhang Yi or Su Qin . . .
> This man was ten times greater than they were!

. . .

At this time there was a scholar named Master Mao in the kingdom of Zhao, a recluse living in Botu. There was also a certain Master Xue, who was resident in the household of a soy sauce seller. The Lord of Xinling had heard much of their wisdom, and so he sent Zhu Hai to visit them. Both men hid and refused to see him. Suddenly one day, the Lord of Xinling discovered from his servants that Master Mao was at Master Xue's house. Without even calling for his carriage and horses, His Lordship rushed there immediately, accompanied only by Zhu Hai. Since he was dressed in plain clothes and on foot, His Lordship was able to pretend that he wanted to buy some soy sauce. He went straight in and spoke to the two men. The two masters were holding cups and drinking together when the Lord of Xinling walked in on them and introduced himself, speaking and behaving in a very respectful manner.

When the Lord of Pingyuan heard about this, he said to his wife, "In the past I often heard people say that your little brother was a remarkable gentleman and that there was no other prince to beat him. Now he seems to be spending all his time with a soy sauce seller in Botu, making unsuitable friends. I am afraid that he is going to ruin his reputation if he carries on like this!"

Her Ladyship reported to the Lord of Xinling all that the Lord of Pingyuan had said. The Lord of Xinling replied: "I always thought that the Lord of Pingyuan was a clever man—that is why I was happy to turn against the king of Wei and steal an army to come and rescue him. Now I have discovered that in the Pingyuan mansion, all the clients and knights are separated by social status; he does not go out to look for wise men. Even when I was still living in the kingdom of Wei, I had heard of Master Mao and Master Xue in Zhao, and I very much wished to meet the pair of them. Now I am lucky enough to have been able to do a few minor services to them, but I am afraid that they will still never join my service. If the Lord of Pingyuan finds all of this embarrassing, how can he be said to enjoy the company of good knights? The Lord of Pingyuan is not a wise man, and so I am not willing to stay here a moment longer!"

He immediately ordered his household to gather their things because he intended to move abroad. When the Lord of Pingyuan heard that his brother-in-law was packing to leave, he was surprised and asked his wife, "I have always treated your younger brother with the utmost respect, so why is he suddenly leaving? Do you know the reason?"

"My brother thinks that you are not a wise man," she said, "and that is why he is not willing to stay." She repeated what the Lord of Xinling had told her.

The Lord of Pingyuan covered his face with his hands and sighed. "There were two great masters in the kingdom of Zhao, and the Lord of Xinling knew about them but I did not. I do not match up to him in any way! Really, when you think about it, I hardly qualify as human!"

He went in person to the official guesthouse, where he removed his hat and kowtowed to apologize for his nasty comments. Afterwards, the Lord of Xinling agreed to stay in Zhao. When the junior members of the Lord of Pingyuan's household heard what had happened, more than half of them left his service and went to join the Lord of Xinling. When knights from other realms visited Zhao, they all gave their allegiance to the Lord of Xinling; nobody so much as mentioned the Lord of Pingyuan again.

An old man wrote a poem:

A soy sauce seller can make many friends: why should you care that he's poor?
Sometimes a prince thinks nothing of power and is willing to seek out the humble.
How sad that the Lord of Pingyuan did not understand these points,
And tried to use his wealth and position to overawe clever men!

. . ..

Let us now turn to another part of the story. The king of Wei received a secret missive from General Wey Qing, which read: "Prince Wuji has indeed stolen the military tally and killed Jin Bi, taking command of his army. He is now advancing to rescue Zhao. He has forced me to stay with the army and I cannot go back home."

The king of Wei was deeply enraged. He thought of seizing all of the Lord of Xinling's land and possessions, or executing every member of his household who remained in the country. Lady Ru Ji knelt down and begged him: "This is not His Royal Highness's fault, but mine! I deserve to die!"

The king of Wei roared with anger: "So was it you who stole my military tally?"

"My father was murdered," Lady Ru Ji wailed. "Even though you are the king, you could not avenge his death. It was the prince who punished the killer. I deeply appreciate how much His Royal Highness has done for me, and I have long been hoping for a way to pay him back. The prince was so worried about the fate of his sister that he was crying day and night. I could not bear it! That is why I stole the tally that let him take control of General Jin Bi's army, so he could go to the rescue! I have heard it said that you should always go to the assistance of your treaty partners—and Zhao and Wei are partners. Your Majesty seemed to have forgotten that, but the prince was worried about the safety of our allies. If he is so lucky as to be able to force Qin to release their hold on Zhao, it is Your Majesty's glorious name that will be honored far and wide: you will be admired from sea to shining sea. If you were to cut my body into a thousand pieces, I would bear no resentment! But you want to confiscate all of the Lord of Xinling's property and execute his household! If he is defeated, I am sure he will accept whatever punishment you choose to mete out. But if he is victorious, do you really plan to deal with him in this brutal way?"

The king of Wei was sunk in silent thought for a long time as he gradually calmed down from his fit of rage.

"Even if it was you who stole the tally," His Majesty said, "you must have had some kind of go-between."

"The go-between was Yan En," Lady Ru Ji explained.

The king of Wei ordered Yan En to be brought before him in chains. "How dare you give my military tally to the Lord of Xinling!" he shouted.

"I have no idea what this military tally is that you are talking about," Yan En replied.

Lady Ru Ji glanced at Yan En and said, "The other day when I asked you to take a tiara as a present to the Lord of Xinling's wife, the box actually contained the military tally."

Yan En understood what she meant. Breaking down into tears, he said, "How could I possibly disobey one of Your Ladyship's orders? That day you just told me to take the tiara around, and the box was heavily sealed . . . How was I supposed to know what was inside? I am going to be killed for something that is not my fault!"

Lady Ru Ji was now crying too. "I have committed a crime and deserve to be punished for it," she said. "I don't want to see anyone else getting dragged in."

The king of Wei shouted for his guards to remove Yan En's chains. He was sent to prison, while Lady Ru Ji was incarcerated in the Cold Palace. At the same time he gave orders for people to find out whether the Lord of Xinling had won or not, for he was planning to deal with the situation accordingly. About two months later, Wey Qing arrived back with the army and came to court to return His Majesty's military tally. He reported: "Although the Lord of Xinling inflicted an enormous defeat on the Qin army, he does not dare to come back home, and so he remains in the Zhao capital. He wanted me to bow to Your Majesty and tell you that you will have to wait to punish him!"

The king of Wei asked about the battle, and Wey Qing explained exactly what had happened. The ministers present all bowed to His

Majesty and congratulated him, shouting: "Long live the king of Wei!" His Majesty was delighted. He sent his servants to summon Lady Ru Ji from the Cold Palace and release Yan En from prison, as both were pardoned.

When Lady Ru Ji had thanked His Majesty for his clemency, she said: "The rescue of Zhao has been enormously successful. Not only has the kingdom of Qin been deeply awed by your military might, the king of Zhao has also been very impressed by your virtues. You owe all of this to the Lord of Xinling. His Lordship is like a nation's Great Wall, or like a family's protective gods—how can he be abandoned in a foreign country? I beg that Your Majesty will send an ambassador to bring him back here. That will show you care about your family and appreciate what a clever man can do."

"Surely it is enough that I pardon him for the crime he has committed," the king of Wei said grudgingly. "Why do I have to reward him?"

Nevertheless, he gave the following instructions: "Appropriate fiefs and emoluments should be awarded to the Lord of Xinling and his former mansion, staff, and property should be restored to him, but no special efforts should be made to bring him back." From this time on, Wei and Zhao were at peace.

. . .

When King Zhaoxiang of Qin returned home with his defeated army, the crown prince, the Lord of Anguo, went out of the suburbs to meet him, accompanied by Prince Chu. They both praised Lü Buwei's actions to the skies. The king of Qin appointed him to the position of minister without portfolio and gave him a fief of one thousand households. When the king of Qin heard that Zheng Anping had surrendered to Wei, he was furious and had his entire family killed. Zheng Anping had been recommended for office by the chancellor, Fan Ju. According to Qin law, if a person recommended for office committed a crime, the person who made the original recommendation should also be punished. Zheng Anping had been punished by having his entire family executed for his crime in having surrendered to the enemy; now it was Fan Ju's turn. Fan Ju awaited His Majesty's judgment, seated penitently on a rush mat.

If you don't know whether he survived or not, READ ON.

Chapter One Hundred and One

The king of Qin destroys Zhou and moves the Nine Dings.

Lian Po defeats Yan and kills two of their generals.

After Zheng Anping surrendered to Wei with his entire army, according to the law, Fan Ju was guilty of a crime as well because he had recommended him. That is why he took his seat on a rush mat and waited to be punished. The king of Qin said, "Employing Zheng Anping was my idea; this has nothing to do with the chancellor." He spoke kindly to Fan Ju and ordered that he should be restored to office.

This was the subject of much debate among His Majesty's other ministers. The king of Qin was worried that Fan Ju might still be feeling unsure of his position, and so he issued the following edict to the capital: "Zheng Anping has committed a crime, and so his entire family has been executed. If anyone talks about this again, he will have his head cut off." The people in the capital did not dare to say another word. The king of Qin gave Fan Ju a gift of food and treated him much better than he had in the past. Fan Ju found it difficult to forget that he had suffered a very narrow squeak, so to ingratiate himself with the king, he suggested destroying Zhou and crowning himself as emperor. He appointed Zhang Tang as the senior general and ordered him to attack Han. The idea was to capture the city of Yang, which would allow them free access to the Three Rivers area—the region lying between the Jing, Wei, and Luo Rivers.

. . .

Let us turn now to another part of the story. When King Kaolie of Chu heard that the Lord of Xinling had inflicted a terrible defeat upon the

Qin army, while the Lord of Chunshen had stood down the army and returned without achieving anything at all, he sighed and said, "The Lord of Pingyuan was not wrong when he recommended the Vertical Alliance! I really regret not trusting the Lord of Xinling. After all, it is not like I am frightened of Qin!"

The Lord of Chunshen was feeling very ashamed of himself. He stepped forward and said, "In the past when the Vertical Alliance was first convened, the king of Chu was the Leader. Now the Qin army has recently been defeated and their morale is at low ebb. Why do you not send ambassadors to the other kingdoms, Your Majesty, and ask them to attend a meeting to join forces to attack Qin? You could also talk to the king of Zhou. If you show respect to him, you can use the name of the Son of Heaven. That will make your campaign a crusade. In the future, people will be talking about you and not the Five Hegemons!"

The king of Chu was thrilled with this idea. He sent an ambassador to Zhou to explain the idea of a campaign against Qin to King Nan. His Majesty was already aware that the king of Qin was planning his own campaign in the Three Rivers area with the intention of attacking Zhou. Now if there was an attack on Qin, this would be just what it says in *The Art of War*: "He who attacks first controls the situation." Why would he not agree? The king of Chu concluded an alliance with the other five kingdoms and set a date for their great campaign.

• • •

At this time King Nan of Zhou was in an extremely parlous situation. Even though he occupied the position of the Son of Heaven, this was just an empty title with no real authority attached. Nobody listened to his orders. The kingdoms of Han and Zhao had already divided the Royal Domain of the Zhou kings into two. The capital city of Luoyang south of the Yellow River was now Western Zhou, while the city of Chengzhou in the Gong region was Eastern Zhou. Each city was governed by a duke. When King Nan moved from Chengzhou to the royal capital, he found himself at the mercy of the Duke of Western Zhou, who showed him some respect in public but not much more. When it came to raising an army to attack Qin, he ordered the Duke of Western Zhou to inscribe his own forces into the army, which resulted in him obtaining some five or six thousand men. However, he could not afford the expense of buying any chariots or horses. He visited the wealthiest families in the city to borrow money from them to pay the army. His Majesty had to give them promissory notes. On the day that the army was stood down, he would repay them the principal and interest with his share of the captives and war booty. The Duke of Western Zhou commanded his own forces and went to camp at Yique, to wait for the arrival of forces from other countries.

At this moment Han was under attack, and so they were too busy trying to defend themselves to be able to respond. Zhao had just been released from a long siege and was still reeling from the effects. The kingdom of Qi was a longstanding ally of Qin, and they were not willing to join in this campaign. Only the Yan general, Le Xian, and the Chu general, Jing Yang, arrived with their troops. They made camp separately to await developments. When the king of Qin realized that the other kingdoms were not united against him and had no intention of actually attacking him, he sent even more troops to help Zhang Tang in his assault on the city of Yang. In addition to that, he had General Ying Jiu take one hundred thousand soldiers and make camp outside the Hangu Pass.

The Yan and Chu armies remained in camp for more than three months. When they realized that none of the other armies were coming, the soldiers' morale collapsed. In the end, both armies were stood down. The Duke of Western Zhou also led his troops back home. King Nan's campaign had cost a vast amount of money but had gained him nothing. The rich families all had promissory notes from him, and they wanted their money back. Every day they would gather at the gates to the palace, and the noise of their shouting could be heard even in the inner chambers. King Nan felt very humiliated by the whole thing, but he simply could not pay them back. Instead, he went to hide on top of a tower.

Later generations called this "Creditors' Tower."
There is an old song that testifies to this:

The whole world belongs to one man,
Every gem is his and every length of silk.
Yet the Nine Dings are nothing compared to the weight of his debts,
Alas! The glories of his ancestry mean little without an army.
How sad that he should be forced to borrow from his people;
A defaulting king takes refuge in a tower.
Military expenses have brought him to this pass,
But had the alliance against Qin held firm, would troops have been
    necessary?

When the king of Qin heard that the armies from Yan and Chu had withdrawn, he ordered Ying Jiu to join forces with Zhang Tang and proceed from the city of Yang to attack Western Zhou. King Nan had neither soldiers nor food—he simply could not make any kind of stand.

He decided to flee to the Three Jins. The Duke of Western Zhou stepped forward and said: "In the past, the Grand Astrologer Dan once said, 'In five hundred years' time Zhou and Qin will be united when a hegemon king appears.' That time has now come. Qin is determined to unify the warring kingdoms, and very soon the Three Jins will fall to their lot; there is no need for Your Majesty to suffer any more humiliation! You had better hand over your lands and pay allegiance to them, for that way at least you will retain some respect."

King Nan had no idea what he should do. He went with a group of ministers and clan members to weep and wail in the temples of Kings Wen and Wu for three days. After that, he collected all the maps and other documents and went in person to the Qin army to surrender. He announced that he would henceforth be paying his allegiance to Xianyang. Ying Jiu accepted the surrender, in which Qin gained thirty-six walled cities and thirty thousand new subjects. Once the territory of Western Zhou had been conquered, only Eastern Zhou remained.

Ying Jiu first ordered Zhang Tang to escort King Nan and his family to Qin to report their success, while he himself led the army to march on Luoyang, reorganizing the local administration and setting new boundaries as he went. King Nan requested an audience with the king of Qin, at which he kowtowed and apologized. The king of Qin felt very sorry for him and gave him the city of Liang as his fief. From this point onwards he would be known as the Duke of Zhou, a position comparable to the ruler of a subordinate territory. The Duke of Western Zhou was demoted to the status of a vassal. Meanwhile, the Duke of Eastern Zhou declared himself an independent ruler, the Lord of Eastern Zhou.

By this time King Nan was an old man, and the journey between Zhou and Qin was exhausting. Less than one month after his arrival in the city of Liang, he became ill and died. The king of Qin gave orders that his territory should revert to the crown. At the same time he commanded Ying Jiu to recruit the young men of Luoyang into his army, destroy the ancestral temples of the Zhou royal house, remove all the sacrificial vessels and other impedimenta—most importantly of all, he was to oversee the safe transport of the Nine Dings to Xianyang. Those people in Zhou who did not want to serve in the Qin army all ran away to Gong, where they joined the Lord of Eastern Zhou.

From this you can see that people were still not prepared to forget the Zhou dynasty!

On the day before the bronze *ding*-cauldrons were due to be moved, the people living nearby could hear the sound of crying proceeding from inside the vessels. When they were transported along the Si River, one *ding* suddenly flew from the boat and sank to the bottom of the river. Ying Jiu sent divers down to find it, but they could not see where the *ding* had gone. All they could see was a black dragon, its whiskers bristling with rage. In an instant the river was a mass of foaming waves. The people on the boats were terrified and did not dare to move.

That night, Ying Jiu dreamed that King Wu of Zhou was seated in his ancestral shrine and summoned him into his presence to upbraid him: "Why did you move my ceremonial vessels? Why did you destroy my temple?" He ordered his servants to whip Ying Jiu three hundred lashes. When Ying Jiu woke from his dream, he discovered his back was covered in ulcers. In spite of this, he managed to make his way back to Qin where he presented the eight remaining *ding*-cauldrons to the king of Qin and reported what had happened. When the king of Qin asked which *ding* had been lost, he was informed it was the one for Yuzhou—the region south of the Yellow River. The king of Qin sighed and said, "These lands all belong to me now. How is it that the *ding* is refusing to obey me?" He wanted to send even more soldiers out to recover this bronze vessel. Ying Jiu remonstrated with His Majesty: "This is a very special object with mystical powers all of its own. You will not be able to obtain possession of it." The king of Qin then stopped. In the end, Ying Jiu died of his ulcers.

The king of Qin put the eight *ding*-cauldrons and the other sacrificial bronze vessels on display in the temple dedicated to his ancestors. Furthermore, he performed the suburban sacrifices in honor of the High God at Yongzhou. He had this announced to the other kingdoms in order that they might come to court to present tribute and congratulate him. Those who did not come to present tribute would find themselves under attack. King Huanhui of Han was the first to arrive; he kowtowed and referred to himself as one of the king of Qin's "subjects." The kingdoms of Qi, Chu, Yan, and Zhao all sent their prime ministers to offer congratulations. It was only the kingdom of Wei that sent no ambassador. The king of Qin ordered the commander of his forces in Hedong, Wang Ji, to lead his army to make a surprise attack on Wei. Wang Ji was in private communication with Wei and had been well-bribed by them, so he leaked the news. The king of Wei was frightened into sending an ambassador to Xianyang to apologize. In addition, he offered his son, Crown Prince Zeng, as a hostage to Qin, announcing that henceforward he would be at their orders. From this time on, all six other kingdoms were in a subordinate relationship to Qin. This occurred in the fifty-second year of the reign of King Zhaoxiang of Qin.

His Majesty investigated the leak of information and summoned Wang Ji home for execution. Fan Ju was increasingly worried about his own position. One day, the king of Qin sighed when he was attending court. Fan Ju came forward and said: "I have heard that when a ruler feels sad, it is humiliating for his vassals; when a ruler is humiliated, his vassals should die to expunge the insult. Today Your Majesty has sighed while attending court, which means we must have failed in our duties in some respect. We have not been able to spare Your Majesty worry. If you must punish someone, let it be me!"

"It is unrealistic to expect everything to be perfect," the king of Qin said. "The Lord of Wu'an has been executed and Zheng Anping has betrayed me. We have many strong enemies, but I have no good generals. That is why I am worried."

Fan Ju was both ashamed and frightened. He did not dare reply and withdrew.

. . .

There was a man named Cai Ze from the kingdom of Yan, who was very learned and clever, as well as very ambitious. He rode in a chariot and traveled around the various countries of the world, visiting every part. When he arrived in Daliang, the capital of the kingdom of Wei, he happened to meet a famous fortune-teller named Tang Ju, who divined people's fates from the features on their faces. Cai Ze asked him, "I have heard that when you met the future prime minister of Zhao, Li Dui, you said, 'Within one hundred days you will be in charge of everything within the country.' Is this true?"

"It is."

"Well, what do you think of me?"

Tang Ju looked at him carefully before saying with a laugh: "Your nose snakes down the middle of your face . . . you have a humpback, protruding cheekbones and sunken eyes, as well as knock-knees. I have always been told that sages don't look like the rest of us. I guess here is living proof!"

Cai Ze knew that Tang Ju was making fun of him. "I know I am going to be rich and famous," he said. "I don't know how long I am going to live."

"You're going to live another forty-three years, sir," Tang Ju assured him.

Cai Ze laughed: "I will eat the finest of foods with meat at every meal; when I ride on my chariot, it will have the best of horses hitched in front;

the seal at my side will be made from pure gold, tied in place with a sash of purple silk; and I will be welcomed wherever I go by kings—another forty-three years of that is fine! What more could I ask for?"

He continued on his journey through Han and Zhao, but did not find anyone there prepared to give him high office. He traveled back to Wei, and outside the suburbs of the capital he was set upon by thieves who stole absolutely everything he owned, including his cooking pots, so he was not even able to make himself something to eat. While he was lying under a tree, Tang Ju happened to walk past. He joked, "I see you have not yet achieved fame and fortune . . ."

"I am still looking," Cai Ze said.

"Your face suggests that your fortune is to be found in the west," Tang Ju remarked. "At the moment the chancellor of Qin, Fan Ju, has recommended two men for office—Zheng Anping and Wang Ji—who both ended up committing serious crimes. He is a very worried man right now, and he needs someone to help him. Why don't you go to Qin instead of wasting your time here?"

"It is a long and difficult journey," Cai Ze said. "How am I supposed to make it?"

Tang Ju opened his bag and gave him a couple of pieces of silver. With this money, Cai Ze was able to go west and make his way to Xian-yang.

There, he said to the owner of the hostel he was staying in: "I want to be served only white rice, and the meat must have fat on it. When I become chancellor, I will reward you generously."

"Who on earth are you that you think you are going to become chancellor?" the hostel owner asked.

"My name is Cai Ze," he said. "I am one of the cleverest men in the world, and I have come here specially to seek an audience with the king of Qin. If His Majesty grants me an audience, he is sure to be delighted with what I have to say. He will then get rid of Fan Ju and employ me instead. The chancellor's seals will soon be hanging from my sash."

The owner of the hostel laughed at him, thinking he was quite mad. He told everyone he met what he had said. This story quickly came to the ears of a member of Fan Ju's household, who promptly reported it to his master.

"I know all the precedents of history and the teachings of each one of the major schools of philosophy," Fan Ju declared. "There is no master of rhetoric who has failed to be impressed by me. Who is this Cai Ze that he reckons he can persuade the king of Qin to strip me of office?"

He sent someone to the guesthouse to summon Cai Ze. When the owner heard this, he said, "This is a disaster for you! You have been talking about how you want to replace the chancellor, and now here he is summoning you! If you go, you are sure to meet some terrible fate!"

Cai Ze laughed: "If I meet Fan Ju, he is sure to resign his office in my favor. I don't even need to have an audience with the king of Qin!"

"You are totally insane," the hostel owner said. "Just try not to drag me into it."

Cai Ze went to meet Fan Ju dressed in ordinary plain clothing, with rush sandals on his feet. Fan Ju was sitting waiting for him, sprawled in an extremely disrespectful attitude. Cai Ze made a respectful gesture of his hands, but he did not bow. Fan Ju did not ask him to sit down, but shouted at him in a sharp tone of voice: "Everyone is saying that you are hoping to replace me as chancellor of Qin—is that correct?"

Cai Ze took his place to one side and said, "Yes."

"What do you have to say to justify your presumption that you can take away my office and titles?" Fan Ju demanded.

"Huh!" Cai Ze snorted. "It is already too late. It is the way of the world that a person who has had success must leave the stage to let new people take over. It is now your time to leave!"

"If I don't want to leave, who can make me?"

"Is it not the case that someone who is healthy and successful, not to mention extremely intelligent, and whose deeds are reported to every country in the world is the object of envy and admiration for every knight and man of ability?" Cai Ze asked.

"It is."

"Is it not the case that a man who achieves his ambitions and then goes on to enjoy his declining years in peace, passing his titles and emoluments on to his children and grandchildren, is greatly admired by one and all?"

"That is so," Fan Ju replied.

Now Cai Ze asked, "Would you be happy to follow the example of Shang Yang in the kingdom of Qin, or Wu Qi in the kingdom of Chu, or Grandee Zhong in the case of Yue, each one of whom was enormously successful and yet ended up getting killed?"

Fan Ju was startled and thought to himself: "This man is very tough. He is trying to force me into a corner. If I say that I am not willing to follow their example, I will have fallen into his trap."

So he lied and said: "Why not? Shang Yang served Lord Xiao without the slightest thought to selfish gain—he established the laws that brought good government to Qin and, as a general, he opened up thousands of *li* of new land. When Wu Qi served King Dao of Chu, he plundered the junior members of the royal family's coffers in order to be able to improve his army and thus was able to conquer the kingdoms of Wu and Yue in the south and threaten the Three Jins to the north. When Grandee Zhong served the king of Yue, he was able to turn weakness into strength, and thus they could conquer Wu and expunge the humiliation of their surrender at Mount Kuaiji. Even though they died in the end, they did so in a righteous cause. A man of such nobility of character looks on death as going home to rest. They have achieved great things and their fame will be handed down to later generations. Who would be unwilling to endure such a fate?"

Even though Fan Ju was not willing to admit defeat, he was squirming uneasily in his seat and now sat up straight to listen to what the other man had to say.

"It is a great blessing to any country to have a sagacious ruler and wise ministers," Cai Ze responded. "In just the same way, it is a blessing to any family to have a kind father and filial sons. A filial son would be happy to serve a kind father! A wise minister would be happy to serve a brilliant ruler! However, even Prince Bigan's loyalty was not able to save the Shang dynasty, and Scion Shensheng's filial piety could not prevent the state of Jin from collapsing into civil war. Though the pair of them both suffered terrible fates, how did that help their king or their father? What is worse, in the one case the king was wicked, and in the other the father was far from kind! Shang Yang, Wu Qi, and Grandee Zhong were unlucky, and hence they were killed. Surely they did not want to die in order to become famous among future generations. Prince Bigan was cut to pieces, and yet his equally virtuous contemporary, the Viscount of Wei, simply left the country. Or to cite another example, Shao Hu died a miserable death, and yet Guan Zhong remained alive. Are you telling me that the Viscount of Wei or Guan Zhong is any less famous than Prince Bigan or Shao Hu? Surely it is better to become famous for surviving rather than for dying? Besides which, if you die with your reputation ruined, haven't you lost everything?"

This really touched something deep in Fan Ju's heart. He got down from his seat and walked out into the hall. "How right you are!" he said.

"You have declared, sir, that you would be willing to emulate Shang Yang, Wu Qi, or Grandee Zhong in dying a righteous death," Cai Ze continued. "But how do these men match up to, say, Hong Yao, who served King Wen of Zhou, or the Duke of Zhou, who helped King Cheng to come to the throne?"

"Shang Yang and the others are not as important."

"Well then, how does the present king of Qin match up to Lord Xiao of Qin, or indeed King Dao of Chu, when it comes to trusting loyal men, giving employment to the wise, and treating old ministers with the respect that they deserve?"

Fan Ju was silent for a short time and then he said: "I don't know."

"Do you think that the things you have achieved in the service of the country, the plans that you have offered, can match up to those of Shang Yang, Wu Qi, or Grandee Zhong?"

"I don't know," Fan Ju said again.

"Even though His Majesty trusts the ministers who have done great things in his service, he does not match up to Lord Xiao of Qin, King Dao of Chu, or indeed King Goujian of Yue. What is more, your achievements are not as impressive as those of Shang Yang, Wu Qi, or Grandee Zhong. And yet your position and titles are much higher and your private fortune many times larger than of those three men. I do not understand why you do not resign in sheer self-defense. If the three of them could not prevent disaster from overtaking them, what do you think you can do? Kingfisher feathers and elephant ivory are so coveted that these creatures are in constant danger—what gets them killed is the fact that they cannot resist the bait that is used. Su Qin and the Earl of Zhi may have been clever, but that did not save them in the end! What got them killed was their greed . . . they did not know when to stop. You, sir, were a mere nobody when you met the king of Qin, and then overnight you were chancellor, having gained wealth and power beyond your wildest dreams. You were able to take revenge on your enemies and reward those who had helped you. However, you have still been greedy for yet more, and so you have refused to withdraw. I am afraid that the same fate as that suffered by Su Qin and the Earl of Zhi will soon overtake you! As the saying goes: 'When the sun is at its zenith, it must begin to set; when the moon has waxed, it will have to wane.' Why don't you take this opportunity to retire from your position as chancellor and select someone else to recommend for office? If the person you recommend is a good choice, it can only increase your consequence. You will appear to be resigning your position, but in fact you will be improving it. Then you can go and have fun visiting scenic spots and enjoying your declining years, secure in the knowledge that your title as the Marquis of Ying will be passed to your sons and grandsons in turn. Surely that is better than sticking to your present position through thick and thin, thereby running the risk of some terrible disaster?"

"You have claimed to be one of the cleverest men in the world, and it is naught but the truth!" Fan Ju exclaimed. "How could I refuse to accept your advice?"

He had the other man sit in the seat of honor while he himself performed the rituals of a guest. He arranged for Cai Ze to stay in an official guesthouse and feasted him with wine and meat.

The following day, Fan Ju went to court and presented the following memorial to the king of Qin: "I have recently encountered a man from the Shandong peninsular named Cai Ze. This man has truly remarkable talents—he will make you a hegemon king, Your Majesty! As we face the challenges of the future, he is the person we need to guide the government of the kingdom of Qin. I have met many men in my life, but never anybody like this! I know that I am not his equal. I would not dare to hide the presence of such a great man within our borders. and I sincerely recommend him to Your Majesty for office."

The king of Qin summoned Cai Ze for a meeting in one of the side halls and asked him for advice on how to unify the six kingdoms. He came up with a series of plans that delighted His Majesty. He was immediately appointed as minister without portfolio. Fan Ju announced that he was suffering from serious ill health and requested permission to resign his job as chancellor. The king of Qin refused to allow him to do this. Fan Ju then announced that he was dying. His Majesty was thus forced to appoint Cai Ze as the new chancellor, replacing Fan Ju. He was additionally granted the title of the Lord of Gangcheng. Fan Ju spent the rest of his life living in his fief at Ying.

A historian wrote the following poem:

Shang Yang was torn to pieces and the Lord of Wu'an was killed.
Given what they had achieved, how could they be innocent?
Do not think Cai Ze greedy for taking the position of chancellor,
He simply convinced the Marquis of Ying his hopes were fantasy!

. . .

Let us now turn to another part of the story. After King Zhao of Yan returned to his country, he ruled for thirty-three years, and then the throne passed to King Hui. He ruled for seven years, to be succeeded by King Wucheng. After fourteen years of rule, he was succeeded in turn by King Xiao, who reigned for only three years before the throne passed to

King Xi. When King Xi came to the throne, he appointed his son, Dan, as crown prince. The fourth year of the reign of King Xi of Yan was also the fifty-sixth year of the reign of King Zhaoxiang of Qin. It was in this same year that the Lord of Pingyuan died in Zhao. After this, Lian Po became prime minister and was granted the title of the Lord of Xinping. Since the lands of King Xi of Yan bordered upon the kingdom of Zhao, he sent his prime minister, Li Fu, to condole at the Lord of Pingyuan's funeral. He took this opportunity to give the king of Zhao five hundred gold pieces towards expenses, and the two of them affirmed the alliance between their countries. Li Fu was hoping to receive generous bribes from the king of Zhao, but instead His Majesty treated him with the same politeness that he would any other senior minister from a foreign state. Li Fu was not pleased.

He went home and reported to the king of Yan: "Ever since their defeat at the battle of Changping in which all their young men died, Zhao has been a country of orphaned children. The prime minister has just died, and Lian Po is already a tired old man. If you were to attack them when they are least expecting it, Zhao can be destroyed."

The king of Yan was stupid enough to agree. He summoned Le Xian, the Lord of Changguo, to discuss the matter. "Zhao is our neighbor to the east and their western border touches on Qin," Le Xian said. "To the south their lands stretch to join those of Han and Wei, while to the north they reach to the Hu and Mo nomadic peoples. Given that they have major enemies on all four sides, their people have long been accustomed to fighting. You shouldn't attack them unless you are very sure of what you are doing.

The king of Yan asked: "If we attack them with an army three times the size of theirs, can we defeat them?"

"No," Le Xian replied.

"Well, if we attack them with an army five times the size of theirs, can we defeat them?"

Le Xian did not respond. The king of Yan said crossly, "Is it because your father's grave is located in Zhao that you don't want to attack them?"

"If you don't believe me," Le Xian replied, "I can prove it to you."

The other ministers present, who were trying to please His Majesty, all said: "Has there ever been a battle anywhere where you needed five times the number of troops in order to win?"

Grandee Jiang Ju was the only person to try and remonstrate. "Your Majesty! Before we start talking about whether we have more soldiers than they do, how about we talk about the rights and wrongs of the matter? Yan and Zhao are allies, and you have just given the king of Zhao a present of five hundred gold pieces. You have decided to attack them purely on the basis of what your returning ambassador has reported to you. If you act in such an unjust way, the campaign cannot possibly go well!"

The king of Yan paid no attention to him. He appointed Li Fu as the senior general with Le Sheng as his deputy. They were to take an army of one hundred thousand men to attack the city of Hao. In addition, he appointed Qing Qin as the junior general with Le Xian as his deputy, and they too were given an army of one hundred thousand men and ordered to attack Dai. The king of Yan took personal command of the one hundred thousand men in the Central Army; he would follow on behind to provide support if necessary.

Just as he was about to climb into his chariot, Jiang Ju rushed forward and grabbed hold of the king's sleeve. Weeping, he said, "If you must attack Zhao, do not go in person, Your Majesty! I am afraid that it will be disastrous!"

The king of Yan was angry and kicked Jiang Ju away. He now grabbed hold of His Majesty's leg and said through his tears, "It is my loyalty to Your Majesty that makes me want to keep you here. If you do not listen, calamity will overtake the kingdom of Yan!"

The king of Yan was getting more and more furious. He gave orders that Jiang Ju should be thrown into prison. On the day that he returned in triumph, Jiang Ju would be executed.

The three armies advanced by different routes, their battle standards and banners spreading out through the wilderness, their martial spirit striking awe into all who saw them. They were looking forward to crushing the kingdom of Zhao and expanding Yan's territory enormously. Meanwhile, when the king of Zhao heard that the Yan army was on its way, he summoned his ministers to discuss the situation.

The prime minister, Lian Po, stepped forward and said: "Yan knows that we have suffered a terrible defeat in which many men died, hence our army is extremely small. If we were to hold a general muster and recruit every man over the age of fifteen into the army, so they all have to take up arms and help to fight, we should still be able to strike terror into the Yan forces. Li Fu is looking for an easy victory; he has no real strategy. Qing Qin is an idiot. Le Xian and Le Sheng, as relatives of the Lord of Changguo, have long been strong supporters of the alliance between us and Yan—they are not going to want to fight. The Yan army will be easy to defeat." He further recommended a man named Li Mu from Yanmen as a suitable general.

The king of Zhao promptly appointed Lian Po as the commander-in-chief. He was to take fifty thousand men and intercept Li Fu at Hao. Li Mu was appointed as the junior general. He was given command of fifty thousand troops and ordered to intercept Qing Qin at Dai.

When Lian Po's army arrived at the city of Fangzi, he discovered that Li Fu had already reached Hao. He therefore hid all of his best troops at Mount Tie, leaving just the old and weak to make camp. Li Fu's spies reported on the state of the Zhao encampment. "I knew that the Zhao army would be in no state to fight!" he said happily, and led all his troops in an all-out onslaught on the city of Hao. Since the people inside the city knew that their rescue forces had already arrived, they held the walls resolutely through fifteen days of battle. Lian Po led his troops forward. First he sent out a few thousand of his very worst troops to provoke battle. Li Fu told Le Sheng to stay behind and continue attacking the city while he went out to fight in person. After locking horns just once, the Zhao forces simply could not withstand his attack and they fled, having suffered serious losses. Li Fu signaled to his officers to pursue the Zhao army. When they had gone about six or seven *li*, the troops waiting in ambush rose up. A senior general rode out in his chariot at the head of his troops. He shouted, "I am Lian Po! Get off your chariot and surrender at once!"

Li Fu was furious. Brandishing his sword, he went forward to engage the enemy. Lian Po was a battle-hardened old campaigner and his troops were the very best that the country had to offer—any one of them was a match for one hundred men. After just a couple of engagements, the Yan army had sustained a terrible defeat. Lian Po captured Li Fu alive. When Lian Sheng heard that his senior general had been taken prisoner, he lifted the siege, intending to cut and run. Lian Po sent someone to take a message to him, which resulted in Lian Sheng surrendering to the Zhao army.

At the same time, Li Mu had successfully rescued the city of Dai, beheading Qing Qin. He sent someone to report his victory. Meanwhile, Le Xian led his remaining forces to make a stand at Mount Qingliang. Lian Po asked Le Sheng to write a letter to him encouraging him to surrender, after which he too submitted to Zhao. When the king of Yan heard that his two armies had both been destroyed, he fled back to his capital, traveling day and night. Lian Po sent his forces deep into enemy territory in pursuit, setting up a major siege. His Majesty now sent ambassadors to sue for peace.

Le Xian said to Le Sheng: "The person who really wanted this campaign against Zhao was Li Fu. Grandee Jiang Ju knew that it was going to be a disaster and remonstrated, but His Majesty would not listen to him, throwing him into prison. If they ask for a peace treaty, one of the conditions we should set is that the king of Yan must make Jiang Ju the prime minister. If it is he who comes to negotiate the peace treaty, we can agree."

Lian Po followed this advice. Since he had no other choice, the king of Yan ordered that Jiang Ju be released from prison and gave him the seals of office.

Jiang Ju refused to accept them, saying, "I am very sad that my predictions turned out to be correct. How could I possibly want to profit personally from the defeat of my country?"

"I brought humiliation down upon myself by failing to listen to your advice," the king of Yan said. "I need you to make peace with Zhao."

Jiang Ju then agreed to accept the seals. "Le Sheng and Le Xian have been forced to surrender to Zhao, but we should not forget the great things that the Le family did for Yan," he told the king. "You should send their wives and children to join them, to make sure they do not forget how much they owe to us. In that case, I imagine that the peace negotiations will be concluded pretty quickly." The king of Yan followed his advice.

Jiang Ju then went to the Zhao army to apologize for His Majesty's behavior and to escort Le Xian and Le Sheng's families to join them. Lian Po agreed to the peace treaty. He beheaded Li Fu and returned his body, and that of Qing Qin, to the kingdom of Yan. The next day he stood down his army and returned to Zhao.

The recluse of Qianyuan wrote a poem:

Their troops were battle-hardened thanks to enemies on all sides;
Old General Lian Po was also no pushover.
How sad that Li Fu had such a stupid plan,
That his king was left utterly helpless.

The king of Zhao enfeoffed Le Sheng as the Lord of Wuxiang, while Le Xian retained his old title of the Lord of Changguo. Li Mu became governor of Dai. At this time Ju Xin was the governor of Jizhou in the kingdom of Yan. His Majesty asked him to write to the Le family encouraging them to come back, since Ju Xin had earlier worked closely with Le Yi when they both served King Zhao of Yan. Le Sheng and Le Xian in the end decided to remain in Zhao, since neither of them liked the way the king of Yan did not seem to pay attention to loyal advice. Even though Jiang Ju was prime minister, this was something that had been forced on His Majesty. Less than six months later the situation became untenable, and Jiang Ju resigned his position on the grounds of ill health. The king of Yan appointed Ju Xin to replace him. Let us put this story to one side for the moment.

. . .

King Zhaoxiang of Qin ruled for fifty-six years. One autumn when he was nearly seventy, he got sick and died. His crown prince, the Lord of Anguo, succeeded to the throne and took the title of King Xiaowen. He established his wife, a Zhao princess, as queen, and Prince Chu as his crown prince. When the king of Han heard that the king of Qin was dead, he put on full mourning garb and went in person to attend the funeral, carrying out all the rituals of a subject. The other kings all sent their prime ministers or some other senior member of their administration to attend the obsequies. Three days after King Xiaowen had presided over his father's funeral, he held a huge banquet for all his ministers. When it was over, he went back to the palace and died. The people in the capital all suspected that the minister without portfolio, Lü Buwei, wanted to see Crown Prince Chu become king and therefore had bribed His Majesty's entourage with enormous amounts of money to have poison put into his wine. However, they were all much too frightened of Lü Buwei to say this openly. So it happened that Lü Buwei and the other ministers assisted Crown Prince Chu to succeed to the throne. He took the title of King Zhuangxiang.

His Majesty appointed Lady Huayang as the dowager queen and Zhao Ji as queen. His son, Zhaozheng, became crown prince, but at this time they took the word Zhao out of his name—he was just known as Prince Zheng. Cai Ze knew that King Zhuangxiang was very fond indeed of Lü Buwei and wanted him to become chancellor. He therefore announced that he was seriously sick and returned his seals of office. Thus Lü Buwei became chancellor of the kingdom of Qin, with the title of Marquis of Wenxin and a fief of one hundred thousand households in Luoyang in Henan. Lü Buwei had always nourished great admiration for the Lords of Mengchang, Xinling, Pingyuan, and Chunshen and felt himself humiliated by not being able to match them. He now built some guesthouses and began to recruit men to join his service, until he had accumulated more than three thousand clients.

When the Lord of Eastern Zhou heard that Qin had buried two monarchs in quick succession and the country was in turmoil, he sent ambassadors to the other kingdoms to talk about uniting in a Vertical Alliance to attack Qin. Chancellor Lü Buwei said to King Zhuangxiang, "Western Zhou has already been destroyed and Eastern Zhou is hanging by a thread. They are trying to cause a lot of trouble for us by claiming to represent the direct line of descent from the great Kings Wen and Wu of Zhou. We had better get rid of them to put a stop to this nonsense."

The king of Qin appointed Lü Buwei as the senior general, and he led an army of one hundred thousand men to attack Eastern Zhou. They captured the lord alive and took him back with them. In this campaign the Qin army conquered Gong and seven other cities. The Zhou dynasty received the Mandate of Heaven during the reign of King Wu. The dynasty collapsed in the reign of the Lord of Eastern Zhou—thirty-seven kings and eight hundred and seventy-three years later—when they were conquered by Qin.

There is a ditty that testifies to this:

Zhou flourished in the reigns of Kings Wu, Cheng, Kang, Zhao, Mu,
    and Gong,
Also in the reigns of Kings Yi, Xiao, Yee, Li, Xuan, and You.
These were the twelve kings that presided over Zhou's apogee,
A space of two hundred and fifty-two years.
After the move to the east came Kings Ping, Huan, Zhuang, Li, and Hui,
Followed by Kings Xiang, Qing, Kuang, Ding, Jian, and Ling.
After them came Kings Jing, Dao, Jìng, Yuan, Zhending, and Ai;
The line was continued by Kings Sikao, Weilie, and Anlie.
The dynasty collapsed with Kings Xian, Shenjing, and Nan:
The last of the twenty-six kings of the Eastern Zhou.
This family was descended from Hou Ji, the Millet God,
And established its powers under the founding ancestors: Tai,
    Ji, and Wen.
From start to finish there were thirty-eight rulers,
And the dynasty lasted for eight hundred and seventy-four years.
Whether you count the years or the number of generations,
There is no other dynasty in Chinese history comparable to this.

Taking advantage of his success in destroying Zhou, the king of Qin sent Meng Ao to attack Han, taking the cities of Chenggao and Rongyang and establishing Sanchuan Commandery. The borders of this region stretched almost to the city of Daliang. The king of Qin said, "In the past I was a hostage in Zhao, and His Majesty nearly had me killed. I am going to take revenge!" He ordered Meng Ao to attack Zhao again, whereupon he captured Yuci and another thirty-seven cities, creating Taiyuan Commandery. To the south, he occupied Shangdang.

Although the Qin army went on to attack the city of Gaodu in Wei, they could not capture it. His Majesty then sent Wang He in command of a further fifty thousand troops to assist in the battle. The Wei army suffered one defeat after another.

Lady Ru Ji said to the king of Wei: "The reason why the Qin army is attacking us so badly is because they are trying to bully us. The only reason that they dare to behave in this way is because the Lord of Xinling isn't here. The Lord of Xinling is famous throughout the entire world for his great wisdom and compassion . . . he would be able to obtain the support of the other kings in our hour of need. Why don't you send an ambassador to speak nicely to him and give him generous gifts so that he comes back from Zhao? If he could reconstruct the Vertical Alliance with other kings and we are united in our efforts to resist Qin's aggression, even if they had one hundred Meng Ao's they would not dare try and throw their weight around in Wei!"

The king of Wei understood that his situation was now very dangerous indeed and he had no choice but to follow her advice. He entrusted Yan En with the seals of the prime minister and a gift of gold and silk and sent him to Zhao to bring the Lord of Xinling back. He also sent the following letter:

> In the past you could not bear to see the dire straits to which the kingdom of Zhao had been reduced; are you happy to see Wei in danger today? We are in terrible trouble! I am awaiting your return to entrust matters of state to you. Please forget our past troubles.

Even though the Lord of Xinling was resident in Zhao, thanks to a constant stream of visitors, he was well-informed about the situation in Wei. When he heard that Wei was going to send an ambassador to bring him back, he said irritably, "The king of Wei has abandoned me in Zhao for more than a decade! Now that there is a crisis he wants me back, but this is clearly not because he genuinely misses me!"

He hung the following message from his gate: "Anyone who dares to communicate with the king of Wei will be killed!" His staff all took this warning very seriously, and there was no one who dared to encourage him to go home. Yan En spent two weeks in Zhao without being able to see the prince. The king of Wei sent a constant stream of messengers to him, ordering him to hurry up. Yan En begged the people at the gate to take in a letter for him, but they refused because they simply did not dare. Given this situation, Yan En decided to wait until the Lord of Xinling left the house and then try to intercept him. The Lord of Xinling decided that he would not even set foot outside his house, so as to avoid meeting the Wei ambassador. There was nothing that Yan En could do.

If you do not know whether the Lord of Xinling was willing to return to Wei in the end, READ ON.

Chapter One Hundred and Two

On the road to Huayin, the Lord of Xinling
defeats Meng Ao.

At the Hulu River, Pang Nuan beheads
Ju Xin.

Yan En was hoping to see the Lord of Xinling, but it was impossible, since his clients were not willing to take a message through. There was no other choice; he made contact with Master Mao and Master Xue, who had once lived in the household of a soy sauce seller. Yan En knew that they were senior advisors to the Lord of Xinling. Weeping, he told them of his problem. The two masters said: "In His Lordship's mansion, this is a forbidden subject. However, we will do our very best to talk to him."

"Whatever you can do," Yan En said. "Whatever you can do . . ."

The two masters went to see the Lord of Xinling and said: "We have heard that you are hitching your chariot up to go home, Your Lordship. We have come here specially to escort you."

"What are you talking about?" the Lord of Xinling demanded.

"The siege that the Qin army has inflicted on Wei is reaching crisis point," they replied. "Did you not know that?"

"I heard," the Lord of Xinling said. "But I said goodbye to Wei ten years ago and I am now a subject of Zhao. I have nothing to do with what is going on in Wei."

The two masters spoke in unison: "What do you mean, Your Lordship? The only reason that you are treated well in Zhao and famous among the kings is because of your position in Wei. The fact that you have been able to bring together all these great knights and establish so many brilliant men in your household is entirely due to Wei. Now Qin is attacking Wei, and they are in serious trouble. You seem to show no sympathy for them as if you actually want Qin to break into Daliang and destroy the tombs and shrines of your ancestors! Even if you don't care about your family, do you really not care about whether your ancestors continue to receive blood sacrifice? How do you think you will have the gall to demand your stipend from Zhao if that happens?"

Before they had even finished speaking, the Lord of Xinling leapt to his feet. Sweat was running down his face. He thanked them, saying, "You are absolutely right to complain of my behavior. I almost ended up doing something terribly wrong!"

He immediately ordered his household to pack up and went to court to say goodbye to the king of Zhao. His Majesty did not want to see the Lord of Xinling leave. Holding on to his arm, he wept and said: "Ever since I lost the Lord of Pingyuan, I have thought of you as my Great Wall. Now that you have decided to leave me, how can I protect my state altars?"

"I cannot bear to think of the temples of my ancestors being desecrated by the Qin armies," the Lord of Xinling replied. "I have to go home. If thanks to Your Majesty's blessings, my country can escape disaster, we are sure to meet again."

"In the past, you used the Wei army to rescue Zhao," His Majesty responded. "Now that you are going home in a time of national emergency, how could I refuse to send every soldier I can scrape together back with you?" He gave the seals of office of the senior general to the Lord of Xinling and appointed General Pang Nuan as his deputy. They were given an army of one hundred thousand men from Zhao to help them.

When the Lord of Xinling took control of these troops, he sent Yan En back to Wei to report this news first, and then he sent his clients with official letters to the other kings to request help. The three kingdoms of Yan, Han, and Chu were aware of the Lord of Xinling's brilliance, and when they heard that he had taken command of troops, they were delighted. They each sent a senior general in command of an army to go to Wei and serve under His Lordship's orders. Yan sent General Jiang Ju; Han sent Royal Grandson Ying; and Chu sent General Jing Yang. Only the kingdom of Qi refused to send anyone.

Just as the king of Wei was at the end of his tether, Yan En returned to report: "The Lord of Xinling is on his way to rescue us, assisted by armies from Yan, Zhao, Han, and Chu." The king of Wei felt like a thirsty man who has received water, or someone roasting in the fire who sees the flames quenched—he could not even begin to express how delighted he was. He ordered Wey Qing to mobilize all his forces and go out to meet His Lordship.

. . .

At this point, Meng Ao was laying siege to Jiazhou while Wang He was surrounding the city of Huazhou. "When the Qin army hears of my arrival," the Lord of Xinling commented, "their attacks will become even more ferocious. Jiazhou and Huazhou are located more than five hundred *li* apart to the east and west of our country. I am going to make a feint of moving against Meng Ao in Jiazhou, but in fact, we will be advancing our special forces as quickly as possible towards Huazhou. If Wang He's forces are defeated, Meng Ao will not be able to stay."

"That is true," his generals agreed.

He ordered Wey Qing to lead the armies of Wei and Chu off to build a series of encampments behind high ramparts to block any advance by Meng Ao. They were to fly the Lord of Xinling's personal banner there, but they had orders to stay safe behind the walls and not to fight. Meanwhile, he himself commanded the Zhao army of one hundred thousand men to travel to Huazhou at top speed, together with the soldiers from Yan and Han.

The Lord of Xinling discussed the situation with his generals: "The eastern end of the Shaohua mountain range touches on Huazhou. The Wei River is on the west side. Qin is using boats to transport grain to their troops, and these ships are all going down the Wei River. The Shaohua range is covered in thick forest cover and scrub, which is ideal for an ambush. If one of our armies goes off to the Wei River to steal the grain supplies, Wang He is going to have to mobilize all the forces at his disposal to go to the rescue. Our remaining troops will be waiting in ambush at Shaohua, which is where we will attack them. I am sure we will be victorious!"

He ordered the Zhao general Pang Nuan to take his army to the Wei River, to rob Qin's grain shipments. He ordered the Han general, Royal Grandson Ying, and the Yan general, Jiang Ju, to take their armies and pass the word that they were on their way to help the forces raiding the grain ships. In fact they were to march as far as Shaohua and then wait, ready to attack the Qin army in concert. The Lord of Xinling took personal command of a force of thirty thousand picked men. They lay in ambush in the foothills of the Shaohua mountain range. Pang Nuan was the first to set out. This move was immediately reported to Wang He's encampment by Qin soldiers whom he had left watching the main roads: "The Lord of Xinling is moving his troops in the direction of the Wei River."

Wang He was horrified. "The Lord of Xinling is a fine general. He has come here to rescue Huazhou, but he doesn't want to do battle. He is going to steal our grain at the Wei River. That means he wants to strike at our very hearts! I am going to have to go in person to prevent this!" He gave the following order: "One half of the army is to stay behind to continue the siege on the city, while the remainder will follow me to the Wei River."

When approaching the mountains, he suddenly caught sight of a huge army in the middle, with a banner reading "Jiang Ju, Prime Minister of the Kingdom of Yan" hoisted high in the sky. Wang He gave orders that his men should go into battle formation and then engage with Jiang Ju's vanguard. Before they had crossed swords more than a couple of times, another huge army turned up, this time bearing a banner reading "Royal Grandson Ying, Senior General of the Kingdom of Han." Wang He now divided his troops to counter the enemy.

The officers reported: "The grain ships on the Wei River have all been robbed by the Zhao general, Pang Nuan."

"In the circumstances," Wang He said, "this battle is the most important thing right now! If we can force the two armies of Yan and Han to retreat, we can make plans to deal with our other problems afterwards."

The three allied armies were now fighting as one, and battle raged the whole way through the afternoon without the sound of a bell being heard once to signal a retreat. Seeing that the Qin soldiers were becoming tired, the Lord of Xinling ordered his own troops waiting in ambush to rise up. He shouted: "The Lord of Xinling has come here in person with his own troops! Why don't you surrender now and spare us the trouble of soiling our battle-axes?"

Even though Wang He was a very experienced general, he did not have three heads and six arms—how could he possibly withstand this onslaught? Besides, the morale of the Qin army was shattered the moment they heard the name of the Lord of Xinling. The only thing they cared about now was surviving, and they started to flee. Wang He suffered a terrible defeat in which he lost more than fifty thousand men and all of his ships. He had no choice but to gather up his shattered forces and retreat by road to the south, heading for the Tong Pass. The Lord of Xinling ordered his victorious armies to march on Jiazhou by three different routes.

. . .

By this time, Meng Ao's spies had discovered that the Lord of Xinling's troops had gone to Huazhou. Leaving the older and weaker troops behind in camp, he had his own personal flag raised above it to trick the enemy. They were going to maintain the standoff with the Wei and Chu troops. Meng Ao himself advanced as quickly as he could in the direction of Huazhou, at the head of an army of picked men, moving at top speed and in silence. He was hoping that he would be able to join forces with Wang He. He had no idea that the Lord of Xinling had already defeated Wang He and put his troops to flight. He met the enemy at Huayang. The Lord of Xinling braved a hail of stones and arrows to charge the enemy at the head of his army. Royal Grandson Ying was to his left while Jiang Ju was on his right. The two sides launched into a terrible battle. Meng Ao lost over ten thousand men before sounding the bells to signal a retreat. He made camp and then mustered his soldiers and chariots, intending to work out the precise strength of his army before deciding his tactics for the next battle.

Meanwhile, back at his original encampment, the Wei general Wey Qing and the Chu general Jing Yang had been informed by their spies that Meng Ao was no longer present. They attacked and defeated the troops left behind in the Qin camp, thereby lifting the siege of Jiazhou. That done, they headed off towards Huazhou, hoping to be able to take the enemy by surprise and attack them again. This meant that Meng Ao now found himself under assault from two sides. Even though he was a very brave man, how could he possibly fight the forces of five kingdoms? He was facing attack on two flanks, and, having suffered a serious defeat, he retreated westward as quickly as he could. The Lord of Xinling led the allied forces as far as the Hangu Pass, where the armies of the five kingdoms established five huge encampments, showing off their military might. This continued for more than a month, as the Qin army kept the pass tightly closed and did not dare to go out to fight the enemy. The Lord of Xinling finally stood down his army. Each body of troops went home to their own country.

Historians, when talking about these events, would say that the Lord of Xinling's success was entirely down to Master Mao and Master Xue.
There is a poem about this:

When enemy soldiers threaten your city, who can lift the siege?
The Vertical Alliance would only obey the orders of the Lord of Xinling.
And when the time came, who was it that encouraged him into action?
Two old recluses from the humblest of circumstances!

When King Anli of Wei heard that the Lord of Xinling had inflicted a terrible defeat on the Qin army and was returning in triumph, he could not contain his joy. He went thirty *li* out of the city to meet him. The two brothers had by this time been estranged for a decade—when they met, happiness and sorrow were intermingled. They rode back to the palace together and discussed who had achieved great things in the service of the country and how they should be rewarded. The Lord of Xinling was appointed to the office of a senior minister and his fief was increased by five cities. At the same time, every matter of state, no matter how minor, came to him for approval. His Majesty pardoned Zhu Hai for the crime of killing Jin Bi and appointed him to the position of junior general. At this time the Lord of Xinling's reputation struck awe into the hearts of one and all. Each country sent him lavish gifts in the hope of learning his military strategies. In fact, the Lord of Xinling requested his clients to produce a book, which was edited down to twenty-one chapters with seven further scrolls of illustrations concerning battle formations. This was known as *The Prince of Wei's Art of War*.

. . .

Meng Ao and Wang He collected their defeated troops together in a single place. They went to have an audience with the king of Qin, at which they presented their opinion: "Ever since Prince Wuji of Wei revived the Vertical Alliance, he has been able to command a truly enormous army. That is the reason why we could not defeat him. However, having lost so many officers and men, we deserve the death penalty."

"You have won many battles and massively increased the territory of our country," the king of Qin reassured them. "Today's defeat comes from the fact that it was impossible for a few men to stand against so many. This is not your fault."

The Lord of Gangcheng, Cai Ze, stepped forward and said: "The reason the other kingdoms were prepared to join in this Vertical Alliance is entirely thanks to Prince Wuji. If Your Majesty were to send an ambassador to Wei to restore the alliance between your two countries, you could invite the prince here for a face-to-face meeting. We will wait until he has come through the passes and then arrest and kill him. That way we will have nothing to worry about in the future. Don't you think that would be a wonderful plan?"

The king of Qin followed this advice. He sent an ambassador to Wei to restore the alliance and invited the Lord of Xinling to his country.

"The Lords of Mengchang and Pingyuan were taken prisoner by Qin," Feng Huan warned him. "They were very lucky to be able to escape alive! I do not want to see Your Royal Highness following in their footsteps!"

The Lord of Xinling did not want to go either, so he reported to the king of Wei that Zhu Hai should go in the embassy in his stead. He sent a pair of jade discs to Qin to apologize for his nonappearance.

When the king of Qin realized that the Lord of Xinling would not be coming and his plan was not going to work, he was very angry indeed. Meng Ao secretly suggested to His Majesty: "This Zhu Hai who is coming here as an ambassador from Wei is the man who killed Jin Bi by hitting him with a hammer. He is one of the bravest knights in Wei—we ought to keep him here in Qin."

The king of Qin wanted to give Zhu Hai an official position, but he resolutely refused to accept it. The king of Qin was becoming more and more irritated, and so he ordered his entourage to throw Zhu Hai into his tiger pit. There was a huge stripy tiger in the pit, and when it saw that a man was approaching it wanted to pounce on him. Zhu Hai roared at the tiger: "What kind of animal would dare to be so rude!" He opened wide his eyes and stared until they practically popped out of his head and the blood vessels in them broke, spraying the tiger with blood. The tiger lay down on its haunches, and it was a long time before it dared to move. The king of Qin's servants had to let him out of the pit.

His Majesty sighed and said: "Not even Wu Huo or Ren Bi was that brave! If we release him and let him go back to Wei, he will only help the Lord of Xinling to cause more trouble to us!" He put much greater pressure on Zhu Hai to surrender to him.

Zhu Hai refused, and so he ordered him to be arrested and starved.

"The Lord of Xinling has treated me so well that only my death can requite his kindness!" Zhu Hai declared. He hurled himself against one of the pillars of the house. The pillar cracked, but his head remained unbroken. Instead, he put his hands around his throat and choked himself to death.

He really was a righteous knight!

When the king of Qin had killed Zhu Hai, he went on to plot with his ministers: "Even though Zhu Hai is dead, the Lord of Xinling is still flourishing and in power. We need to drive a wedge between him and his ruler. Does anybody have a good plan to suggest?"

Cai Ze, the Lord of Gangcheng, stepped forward and said, "In the past the Lord of Xinling stole a military tally in order to be able to rescue Zhao and hence committed a crime against the king of Wei. That is why the king of Wei left him in Zhao and refused to see him again. It is only because we laid siege to various key cities and he was in serious trouble that His Majesty was forced to summon him back again. Even though the Lord of Xinling was able to call four other kingdoms to his aid and achieved great things in the service of his country, it has put him in a position where he threatens the king's position. In such circumstances, how can the king avoid being suspicious of his brother's intentions? The Lord of Xinling was responsible for the hammer murder of Jin Bi. Since Jin Bi's death, his family and retainers loathe him down to the very marrow of their bones. If Your Majesty were prepared to invest ten thousand pounds of gold and send someone you really trust to Wei to make contact with Jin Bi's faction, with that kind of money you could buy enough people to spread a particular rumor. What we want them to say is: 'Other monarchs are so impressed by the Lord of Xinling that they would like him to become king of Wei. Any day now, the Lord of Xinling will usurp the throne.' In this way, the king will become increasingly alienated from his brother, and he will have to strip him of his powers. If the Lord of Xinling loses power, the other kings will certainly refuse to obey him. Even if we invade Wei, he will not be in a position to cause us any trouble!"

"That is an excellent plan," the king of Qin beamed. "Even though Wei has defeated our army, their Crown Prince Zeng is still here as a hostage. I want to arrest and execute him as a way of venting my anger. What do you think?"

"If you kill the crown prince," Cai Ze replied, "they will simply appoint another one. That will not trouble Wei at all. It would be much better to use the crown prince as an ambassador and send him back to Wei to work for us."

The king of Qin realized exactly what Cai Ze meant. He treated Crown Prince Zeng with great generosity while sending one of his most trusted men with ten thousand pounds of gold to go to the kingdom of Wei and get busy. At the same time, he arranged for some members of his retinue to become friendly with Crown Prince Zeng and "secretly" inform him: "The Lord of Xinling has been in exile for a decade during which time he became friendly with many other regnant monarchs; their prime ministers and generals all respect and fear him. At the moment he is commander-in-chief of the Wei army and has command of the allied forces—everyone has heard of the Lord of Xinling, and nobody cares a jot for the king of Wei. Even people in the kingdom of

Qin are terrified of the Lord of Xinling's military might. We want to make him king of Wei so as to be able to make peace with him. If the Lord of Xinling were to become king, he would certainly want Qin to kill you so you would not threaten his claim to the throne. Even if you escape death, you will have to spend the rest of your life here. What are you going to do?"

Crown Prince Zeng begged them for advice, tears pouring down his cheeks.

"Qin wants to make peace with Wei," they said. "Why don't you write a letter to His Majesty and get him to request your return home?"

"Even if His Majesty invites me home," Crown Prince Zeng cried, "will Qin release me and allow me to return?"

"The only reason that the king of Qin supports the Lord of Xinling's conspiracy to usurp the throne is because he is afraid of him—this is not what he really wants. If you promise to serve the interests of Qin when you go home, that is all that His Majesty could wish for. What would be the problem with letting you go home?"

Crown Prince Zeng wrote a secret missive that said that all the other kings were supporting the Lord of Xinling and Qin was encouraging him to usurp the throne. Afterwards he wrote of how he wanted to go home. This letter was given to a member of his household who conveyed it to the king of Wei. The king of Qin also wrote two letters. One was written to the king of Wei and was sent to him when Zhu Hai's body was returned for burial. According to this missive, he had become ill and died on his visit to Qin. The other letter was one of congratulation addressed to the Lord of Xinling, and it was accompanied by a gift of gold and silk.

. . .

By this time, the king of Wei had already become thoroughly alarmed by the rumors being circulated by Jin Bi's former retainers. Now an ambassador arrived from Qin with his credentials and a letter requesting a peace treaty with Wei. When His Majesty questioned this ambassador, he just rambled on about his respect for the Lord of Xinling. When this was followed up by the letter from the crown prince, he was even more concerned. When the Qin ambassador went on to visit the Lord of Xinling's mansion with a letter and the gifts, he made sure that news of this was widely known so that it would come to the ears of the king of Wei. On being informed that an ambassador had arrived from Qin to make peace, the Lord of Xinling said to his advisors: "There is nothing seriously wrong with the Qin army, so why are they asking for a peace treaty with Wei? There must be some trick here!" Before he had even finished speaking, his gatekeeper announced that the Qin ambassador was at the door: "The king of Qin offers you his congratulations by letter."

"As the minister of this country, I will not engage in any private communication with agents of a foreign power," the Lord of Xinling said firmly. "I will not accept the king of Qin's letter or his gifts."

The ambassador kept stressing that the king of Qin wanted him to have these things, but the Lord of Xinling simply refused. It was just at this moment that a messenger arrived from the king of Wei, who wanted him to read the letter from the king of Qin. The Lord of Xinling said, "His Majesty clearly knows all about this. If I say I never even read it, he won't believe me."

He immediately gave orders for his chariot to be harnessed. Commanding that the king of Qin's letters and gift items should be left with their original seals intact, he took them to the king of Wei and said: "I have already refused to have anything to do with all of this, so the seals are all unbroken. Seeing that you wanted to have a look at them, Your Majesty, I can only present them to you. Make of them what you will!"

"This letter must be some sort of invitation," His Majesty said. "If we don't open it, we won't know what it is." Accordingly, he broke open the seal and read the following missive:

Your fearsome reputation, Your Royal Highness, has made you feared far and wide. There is not a single ruler who does not admire you. Any day now you ought to formally take the throne and become the foremost monarch of our time. However, it is not yet clear when the king of Wei is going to abdicate. I hope it will be soon! I offer these meager gifts in congratulation. I do hope you don't mind.

When the king of Wei had finished reading this letter, he handed it to the Lord of Xinling to look at. The latter presented his opinion: "The people of Qin are notorious for their deviousness. This letter is designed to drive a wedge between Your Majesty and myself. The reason I refused to even open this letter was because I was worried that it might contain some treasonous suggestions and I would fall into their trap."

"Do not worry," the king of Wei said. "Why don't you write a reply here and now under my supervision?"

He ordered his servants to bring writing materials and told the Lord of Xinling to compose his reply. This is what he wrote:

I have been treated with such generosity by His Majesty that even the loss of my own life would not be enough to repay him! You should never speak to a minister about the kind of treason mentioned in your letter! I decline to accept your congratulations!

This letter was given to the Qin ambassador, and he was told to take back the gold and silk. The king of Wei also sent an envoy to thank Qin and say: "His Majesty is getting old and would like Crown Prince Zeng to return home." The king of Qin agreed to this and Crown Prince Zeng was allowed to return to Wei. Throughout these events, the Lord of Xinling remained in office. Although he knew that he had done nothing wrong, he was concerned about the king of Wei's attitude towards him, which never really warmed. Claiming to be ill, His Lordship ceased going to court. He returned his seals as prime minister and the military tallies to the king of Wei, spending his time drinking through the night with his retinue and having many affairs with women. It was as if he was trying to cram as much fun into every day as he could.

A historian wrote a poem about this:

His martial might brought a cold chill to his own time and to later
    generations;
His awe-inspiring reputation struck terror into the ghosts and spirits.
This one man was able to save both Zhao and Wei from danger;
In every battle he defeated the powerful kings of Qin.
In the defense of his country, he stood as strong as the Great Wall,
Until he was brought down by malicious gossip.
When heroes find no place to use their talents,
They waste their time with wine and women.

When King Zhuangxiang of Qin had been on the throne for three years, he became seriously ill. Chancellor Lü Buwei came to the palace to ask after his health, and ordered the palace servants to take a sealed message to the queen, reminding her of the oath that they once swore to be together forever. The queen was still very much in love with her former husband, and they began having an affair. Lü Buwei presented medicine to the king of Qin, and he died just one month later. Lü Buwei presided over the enthronement of the crown prince—at that time he was thirteen years old. Queen Zhuangxiang became the dowager queen and her younger brother, Zhao Chengqiao, became the Lord of Chang'an. All matters of state came to Lü Buwei to make the final decision. Since he liked to be compared to the Great Lord, he took the title of Shangfu. When Lü Buwei's father died, a huge number of officials from every corner of the country came to mourn him, and there were carriage jams on every road. There seemed to be even more people than for the burial of the king of Qin. As the saying goes: "He controlled everything inside the country and struck awe into the foreign kings." No more of this now.

. . .

In the first year of the reign of King Zheng of Qin, since Lü Buwei was aware that the Lord of Xinling had been dismissed, he began to discuss the possibility of launching another military campaign. He sent the senior generals Meng Ao and Zhang Tang to attack Zhao, whereupon they took the city of Jinyang. In the third year of His Majesty's reign, he sent Meng Ao and Wang He out again to attack Han. Han sent Royal Grandson Ying to organize the defense.

"I was defeated for the first time in Zhao and for the second time in Wei," Wang He said. "Fortunately, the king of Qin pardoned me and hence I was not killed, but if this mission fails, I am sure to end up on the execution ground."

He ordered his own private forces of one thousand men to launch an all-out assault on the Han encampment. Although Wang He himself died in the fighting, the Han troops were thrown into disorder. Meng Ao took advantage of this to inflict a terrible defeat on the Han forces. He killed Royal Grandson Ying and went home, having captured twelve cities.

Once the Lord of Xinling had been dismissed from office, the good relationship between Wei and Zhao was at an end. King Xiaocheng of Zhao ordered Lian Po to attack Wei, laying siege to Fanyang. Before the city had fallen, King Xiaocheng was dead. Crown Prince Yan succeeded to the throne, assuming the title of King Daoxiang. By this time Lian Po had succeeded in taking Fanyang, and, on the wings of this victory, he pressed on. Grandee Guo Kai was very jealous of Lian Po and often annoyed the old general by trying to slander him. As a result, when they met, Lian Po would shout at him in front of everyone else. Guo Kai was enormously resentful of this. He now poured his evil words into King Daoxiang's ear: "Lian Po is old and useless. He has spent ages on this campaign against Wei and achieved nothing." As a result, His Majesty sent the Lord of Wuxiang, Le Sheng, to replace Lian Po.

"Ever since King Huiwen first made me a general more than forty years ago, I have been a loyal servant of the state, never failing in any mission," Lian Po said crossly. "Who is this Le Sheng that he can replace me?"

He sent his troops to attack Sheng, who became frightened and fled homeward. Lian Po then went into exile in Wei. The king of Wei appointed him as a kind of guest general, but even though this was supposedly a great honor, he was not employed because His Majesty was suspicious of his loyalties. From this point on, Lian Po lived in Daliang.

. . .

In the tenth month of the fourth year of the reign of King Zheng of Qin, a plague of locusts arose in the east, covering the sky. After a very poor harvest, disease broke out. Lü Buwei and his advisors suggested creating a system whereby anyone giving one thousand bushels of grain to the state would be promoted one grade.

This was the beginning of a system much used in later dynasties.

In this same year, the Lord of Xinling became sick and died, his health ruined by alcohol. Feng Huan was so upset by his demise that he too died. More than one hundred of the Lord of Xinling's retainers committed suicide in the wake of his demise.

From this we can see how much they loved and respected him.

The following year, King Anli of Wei also died. Crown Prince Zeng inherited the throne, taking the title of King Jingmin.

The kingdom of Qin was aware of the fact that Wei had recently lost their monarch and that the Lord of Xinling had also died. They wanted to avenge the series of defeats inflicted on them, and so they sent the senior general, Meng Ao, to attack Wei. He captured twenty cities, including Suanzao, thereby creating Dong Commandery. Not long afterwards, he captured Chaoge and went on to attack Puyang. The Lord of Weiyuan, who was supposed to be guarding the place—and who also happened to be a son-in-law of the king of Wei—fled eastward to Yewang. There he took up residence in a mountain fastness.

King Jingmin of Wei sighed and said, "If only the Lord of Xinling were still alive, we would not be being ravaged by the Qin army like this!"

He sent an ambassador to Zhao to try and restore the alliance between their two countries. King Daoxiang was also very concerned about the constant attacks he was suffering at the hands of Qin, and so he wanted to send ambassadors out to each of the other kings, trying to replicate what the Lord of Xinling and the Lord of Pingyuan had achieved with their Vertical Alliance. It was at this point that he suddenly received word: "The kingdom of Yan has just appointed Ju Xin as their commander-in-chief, and he has invaded our northern border."

Ju Xin originally came from the kingdom of Zhao. When he was still living there, he had been a close friend of Pang Nuan. Later on, when Pang Nuan went to serve the king of Zhao, Ju Xin decided to throw in his lot with King Zhao of Yan. His Majesty appointed him as governor of Ji Commandery. When King Xi of Yan was forced to give Jiang Ju high office as part of the terms of the peace treaty forced upon him by the Zhao general Lian Po's siege, Ju Xin found it all deeply humiliating. Given that making Jiang Ju prime minister of Yan was all the doing of the people of Zhao and not at all what the king had in mind, there was no way for His Majesty to completely trust him, even though Jiang Ju had done great things in the service of the country in helping the Lord of Xinling defeat Qin. Therefore, having been prime minister for just over one year, Jiang Ju returned his seals of office on the pretext of ill health. The king of Yan summoned Ju Xin from Ji Commandery and appointed him as prime minister. Together they plotted their revenge on Zhao.

To begin with, they did not dare to do anything, because they were too frightened of Lian Po. Once he fled to Wei and Pang Nuan took over as general, Ju Xin decided that the time was ripe. Knowing that this was exactly what the king of Yan wanted to hear, he presented his opinion as follows: "Pang Nuan is a very mediocre commander, in no way to be compared to Lian Po. Given that the Qin army has just captured Jinyang, the Zhao army must be exhausted. If we were to take advantage of this moment to attack them, we would be able to expunge Li Fu's humiliating defeat."

"That's right!" the king of Yan said happily. "Can you do this for me?"

"I know the terrain well," Ju Xin asserted. "If you were to put me in charge, I promise to capture Pang Nuan alive and present him to Your Majesty!"

The king of Yan was thrilled and gave him one hundred thousand troops with which to attack Zhao. When the king of Zhao heard reports of what was afoot, he immediately summoned Pang Nuan for a consultation.

"Ju Xin is an arrogant man who is sure to underestimate the enemy," Pang Nuan said. "At the present moment Li Mu is the governor of Dai Commandery. Let him take his troops south along the road to Qingdu. That will cut off their retreat. I will take an army out to intercept them. With our forces in front and behind, Ju Xin will be easy to capture!"

The king of Zhao followed his advice.

. . .

Meanwhile, Ju Xin crossed the Yi River and headed for Zhongshan. He marched straight on Changshan, his army's morale at fever pitch. Pang Nuan had led the main body of his troops to make camp at Donghuan, where they waited for the arrival of the enemy behind huge ramparts and deep defensive trenches.

"Our army had penetrated deep into Zhao territory," Ju Xin remarked. "If they just sit there behind the walls and don't fight us, when are we ever going to win?" He asked his companions: "Which one of you dares to go out and provoke battle?"

The cavalry commander Li Yuan, the son of Li Fu, wanted to avenge the death of his father, so he was desperate to go. "It would be best if someone went with you in support," Ju Xin said.

The junior general, Wu Yangjing, asked permission to go. Ju Xin gave them ten thousand of his very finest soldiers and told them to charge the Zhao army. Pang Nuan ordered Le Shang and Le Xian to wait on the two wings. He himself led his troops out to fight. When the vanguards crossed swords, they had time for about twenty moves before the two wings advanced with a thunderous roar. They fired at will on the Yan army, using their powerful bows and crossbows. Wu Yangjing was hit by an arrow and died. Li Yuan could not possibly withstand such an onslaught, and he turned his chariot around to flee. At this point, Pang Nuan and his two other generals swept up from the rear. Only three thousand or so of the original ten thousand survived. Ju Xin was furious and immediately mobilized the main body of his troops, which he commanded himself. However, by the time they marched out, Pang Nuan had already returned to his encampment. Ju Xin attacked the ramparts but could not break through. He sent a letter to them, agreeing that they would meet—each in a single chariot—in front of their battle lines the following morning. Pang Nuan agreed to this, and so each side made its preparations.

The following day, the two armies both went into battle formation. They were given strict instructions: "Do not shoot any unless instructed!" Pang Nuan rode out in front of his lines in a single chariot and invited Ju Xin to join him. Ju Xin also rode out in a single chariot. Pang Nuan inclined and said, "I am glad to see you looking so well."

"It is sad that more than forty years have passed since we said good-bye when I left Zhao," Ju Xin said. "I am an old man now and so are you. Human life really is a fleeting moment between two great chasms."

"In the past you were tempted by the rewards that King Zhao of Yan offered to recruit knights into his service, and so you left Zhao to serve in Yan," Pang Nuan remarked. "A whole host of heroes went to join him, just like clouds following a dragon or wind following a tiger. However, now the Golden Tower is overgrown with weeds and the heroes of yesteryear have long been resting in their tombs. First Su Dai and then Zou Yan died one after the other and the Lord of Changguo returned to our country—from this we can know the situation that pertains in Yan! You are nearly sixty years old, so why do you alone remain at the court of this stupid king? Is it because you are still so greedy for power that you do such dangerous things with horrible weapons?"

"I have received great honors from three generations of the Yan royal family," Ju Xin replied. "Even if I were to be ground to dust, I could not repay all that they have done for me. I am planning to dedicate my remaining years to the task of expunging the humiliation inflicted on the country by the death of Li Fu!"

"Li Fu attacked Hao for no good reason," Pang Nuan stated. "He brought his defeat upon himself. That occasion saw Yan attacking Zhao, not Zhao attacking Yan!"

The two of them walked up and down in front of the army as they talked. Now Pang Nuan suddenly yelled: "Anyone who can take Ju Xin's head will be rewarded with three hundred pieces of gold!"

"Are you trying to annoy me?" Ju Xin demanded. "Do you really think I won't kill you?"

"My orders are clear!" Pang Nuan shouted. "Do your best, lads!"

Ju Xin was furious and waved his signal flag. Li Yuan led his army on the attack. Now Le Sheng and Le Xian came out to engage in battle, and the Yan army gradually lost their advantage. Ju Xin had advanced his own position too far, and so when Pang Nuan moved the main body of his army forward, the two sides met in a melee. The Yan army took much worse casualties than the Zhao army, and as night fell, they were forced to sound the bells to recall their troops.

Ju Xin returned to camp in a state of considerable depression. He wanted to retreat, but he had boasted so much in front of the king of Yan that it would be difficult. On the other hand, he knew it would be very hard for him to win if he remained. Just as he was hesitating, one of the officers guarding the camp suddenly came in to report: "An envoy from the kingdom of Zhao has brought a letter and is waiting outside the gates to the camp. He does not dare to bring it any further." Ju Xin ordered someone to collect the letter. It was sealed very securely in a couple of different places. He opened and read the letter, which said:

Li Mu, the governor of Dai Commandery, has led his army to make a surprise attack on Duhang, cutting your rear. You must retreat at once, or you will be in terrible danger. In memory of our old friendship, I feel that I ought to tell you this.

"Pang Nuan is just trying to disrupt our morale!" Ju Xin snarled. "Even if Li Mu's army does turn up, why should I be worried?"

He ordered that a letter be written in return, suggesting that they fight a decisive battle on the following day. When the envoy from the Zhao camp had left, Li Yuan stepped forward and said: "We cannot dismiss what Pang Nuan says lightly. If by some horrible mischance Li Mu does lead his army to make a surprise attack on our rear, we are going to find ourselves with the enemy in front and behind. How would we deal with that?"

Ju Xin laughed and said: "I have already thought about that possibility. Everything that I have said so far has been about trying to stabilize morale among our troops. You are going to give secret orders to abandon this encampment overnight and begin our retreat. I am going to be personally responsible for guarding our rear, to prevent anyone attacking us from behind."

Li Yuan went off to carry this out. What neither of them was expecting was that Pang Nuan's spies had discovered that the Yan encampment was in the process of being abandoned. He set off in pursuit with Le Sheng and Le Xian, each following a different route. Ju Xin fought every step of the retreat until he reached the Longquan River. There his spies reported: "There are a large number of battle standards blocking the road up ahead. Apparently it is the army from Dai Commandery."

Ju Xin said in a horrified voice, "So Pang Nuan didn't lie to me!" He did not dare to continue moving north, so instead he took his army east, hoping to be able to make it to Fucheng. From there, he was planning to go to Liaoyang. Pang Nuan caught up with him, and they fought a huge battle at the Hulu River. Ju Xin's army was defeated. He sighed and said, "How could I face being a prisoner of war in Zhao?" He committed suicide by cutting his own throat. This occurred in the thirteenth year of the reign of King Xi of Yan, which was also the fifth year of the reign of King Zheng of Qin.

An old man wrote a poem bewailing these events:

A host of heroes rushed to the Golden Tower, determined to make their
  names;
Together they helped King Zhao of Yan to restore his country to its old
  borders.

Does anyone today remember the Lord of Changguo and his brilliant deeds?

Or this one general, determined to fight even if it was all in vain?

Li Yuan was taken prisoner by Le Xian, who beheaded him. Twenty thousand men were killed, with the remainder of the army either running away or surrendering. The Zhao troops won a great victory. Pang Nuan agreed to advance in concert with Li Mu. They captured the lands of Wusui and Fangcheng. Meanwhile, the king of Yan went in person to Jiang Ju's door to ask him to act as ambassador and make peace with Zhao, apologizing for all their offenses. Since Pang Nuan decided to accept Jiang Ju's overtures, he stood down the army and they went home singing songs of triumph. Li Mu went back to his post as governor of Dai Commandery. King Daoxiang of Zhao welcomed Pang Nuan back to the capital and held a feast in his honor. "With your bravery and military prowess, general," he declared, "I feel that Lian Po and Lin Xiangru are alive and well in Zhao!"

"The people of Yan have already submitted to your authority," Pang Nuan said. "You should use this opportunity to rebuild the Vertical Alliance, uniting with other kings to defend against Qin, for that is the way to preserve our country intact."

Do you know what happened with the Vertical Alliance? READ ON.

Chapter One Hundred and Three

The king's uncle gets rid of the Lord of Chunshen in a power struggle.

Fan Yuqi circulates criticism in an attempt to punish the king of Qin.

Pang Nuan was hoping to be able to use the awe inspired by his victory over the Yan army to be able to rebuild the Vertical Alliance whereby everyone would unite to resist aggression by Qin. With the exception of Qi (which was by this time a staunch ally of the kingdom of Qin), Han, Wei, Chu, and Yan each contributed a fine army of well-trained troops. The larger armies were forty to fifty thousand men strong, but even the smallest comprised twenty to thirty thousand men. By mutual agreement, Huang Xie, the Lord of Chunshen, was appointed as commander-in-chief. Huang Xie discussed the situation with the other generals: "Many armies have been sent out to attack Qin, but they have all come to grief at the Hangu Pass. Qin guards that pass very strongly, and hence no other kingdom has succeeded in invading them. Since our troops know that we cannot attack Qin, they think that our only hope is to frighten them. However, if we were to take the road out of Puban and go west from Huazhou, we could make a surprise attack on Weinan. That would allow us to approach the Tong Pass instead. As *The Art of War* says: 'Go where the enemy least expects.'"

"You are right!" the generals declared. They divided their troops into five groups, and each headed for the Pu Pass. Marching along in the direction of Mount Li, they advanced and attacked Weinan. Since they were not successful, they laid siege to it. The chancellor of Qin, Lü Buwei, appointed generals Meng Ao, Wang Jian, Huan Yi, Li Xin, and Grand Astrologer Teng to command fifty thousand soldiers each, forming five armies, each of which would deal with one of the five countries invading them. Lü Buwei made himself the commander-in-chief. They all advanced and made five different camps just fifty *li* from the Tong Pass, just like a constellation of stars.

Wang Jian said to Lü Buwei: "With the forces that these five countries have at their disposal, for their finest troops to attack a city in concert and yet fail to take it shows that they are entirely useless! The Three Jins are all close to Qin, and they are used to fighting with us. Chu, on the other hand, comes from far to the south. Ever since Zhang Yi died, there have been thirty and more years of peace between our two countries. We should select the very best soldiers from the five armies at our disposal and send them all to attack Chu—they will not be able to withstand us. If the Chu army is defeated, the other four will collapse of their own accord."

Lü Buwei thought that this was a good idea. He ordered the five encampments to build their ramparts and erect their tents as usual, but in secret each camp was requested to select its best ten thousand men. They were told that at the fourth watch, they should get up and march on the Chu encampment to attack them by surprise. At this time the Qin army had its own problems, because Li Xin wanted to behead the junior general Gan Hui for delays in the arrival of the grain supplies. Thanks to the other generals pleading on his behalf, Gan Hui merely suffered a couple of hundred lashes. He was so angry that he fled that very night to the Chu encampment to inform them of Wang Jian's plan. The Lord of Chunshen was horrified. His first thought was to report this to the other armies, but then he realized that they might not arrive in time. Instead, he immediately gave orders to strike camp and retreat fifty *li* as quickly as they could. It was only when they had gone the set distance that they slowed down. By the time that the Qin army arrived, the Chu encampment was empty.

"If the Chu army has run away, it can only be because someone leaked my plan to them," Wang Jian snarled. "Even though I have not accomplished my original idea, since the army is here we might as well carry on."

He made a surprise attack on the Zhao army. The walls and ramparts of this camp held firm and they were not able to force an entry. Pang Nuan stood by the gate to the camp with a drawn sword and beheaded anyone who moved out of his place. They fought in one melee after another with the Qin army during the night. At dawn, reinforcements arrived in the form of troops from the Han, Wei, and Yan armies. Meng Ao and the other Qin generals now had no choice but to withdraw their troops in good order. Pang Nuan was surprised that the Chu army had not come to help, so he sent someone to find out what was going on. This was how he discovered that they had already retreated. He sighed and said, "The Vertical Alliance is dead!" The generals all requested permission to stand down their armies. Han and Wei were the first to go home. Pang Nuan was furious that Qi was still allied to Qin through thick and thin, so he joined forces with the Yan army to attack them. Having captured the city of Rao'an, they went back home.

. . .

When the Lord of Chunshen fled back to the capital city of Ying, the other four kingdoms each sent ambassadors to ask: "Chu is the leader of the Vertical Alliance. Why did you go home without saying a word to us? Can we know the reason?"

King Kaolie was furious with the Lord of Chunshen, who found his own humiliation virtually impossible to bear. At this time there was a man from Wei in the Lord of Chunshen's household—his name was Zhu Ying. He knew how deeply Chu feared Qin, and so he said to the Lord of Chunshen: "People all say that the kingdom of Chu was a strong country until you made it weak; I am the only one who seems to disagree with this assessment. In the reigns of previous kings, Qin was located far from Chu; to the west you were protected by the kingdoms of Ba and Shu, and between you was the Royal Domain: Western and Eastern Zhou. Furthermore, Han and Wei were constantly on the alert for any movement of their army. Thus there were fully thirty years when you did not have to fight with Qin: this was not because Chu was a powerful country, but because you were in an advantageous geographical position. Now the states of Western and Eastern Zhou have both been absorbed into Qin territory. They are now busy taking out their hatred on Wei, and it will fall at any moment now. In that case only Chen and Xu will lie between you; fighting between Qin and Chu will break out soon! Why don't you encourage His Majesty to move the capital east to Shouchun? It is much further away from Qin territory and is protected by the Yangtze and Huai Rivers. That would be much safer."

The Lord of Chunshen thought this was an excellent idea, and so he mentioned it to King Kaolie. His Majesty selected an auspicious day to move the capital.

The kingdom of Chu's first capital had been located in Ying. Then they moved it to Ruo and, after that, to Chen. Now they were again moving it to Shouchun—the fourth move.

A historian wrote a poem about this:

Zhou's move to the east brought about the collapse of the dynasty;
Thanks to their repeated changes of capital, the Chu kingdom was
  weakened.
Though avoiding the enemy may help you to survive a little longer,
You don't want to give an advantageous location to another royal house.

. . .

Although King Kaolie of Chu had been on the throne for many years, he
had no son to succeed him. Huang Xie, the Lord of Chunshen, sought
out all sorts of fertile women and presented them to His Majesty, but
none of them ever became pregnant. There was a man from Zhao named
Li Yuan who held a junior position in the Lord of Chunshen's household
with a very pretty younger sister named Li Yan. He wanted to present her
to the king of Chu, but he was worried lest her long-term relationship
with His Majesty be compromised if she too had no children. He vacillated, uncertain of what to do: "I should first present my sister to the
Lord of Chunshen and wait for him to get her pregnant. Then we should
offer her to His Majesty. If we are lucky and she gives birth to a son, in
the future he will become the king of Chu. In that case, I will be the king's
uncle." Then he thought: "If I simply give His Lordship my sister, he will
not treat her with any respect. I had better come up with a little scheme
to make sure that the Lord of Chunshen asks me for her himself."

To this end, he asked for five days' holiday to allow him to go home.
He deliberately stayed away longer than the leave he had been granted.
After ten days he came back. The Lord of Chunshen was surprised that
it had taken him so long, whereupon Li Yuan informed him: "I have a
younger sister named Yan who is very lovely. The king of Qi has heard
about her, and so he sent an ambassador to ask for her hand in marriage. I was feasting with the ambassador for a couple of days, and that
is why it all took longer than I was expecting."

Huang Xie thought: "If news of this woman has even reached the
kingdom of Qi, she must be superlatively beautiful." He asked, "Have
the betrothal gifts been exchanged yet?"

"We discussed this, but the formal gifts have not yet arrived," Li
Yuan said.

"Would it be possible for me to meet your sister?"

"I am a member of your household, and she is my younger sister," Li
Yuan assured him. "That makes her equivalent to one of your concubines or maidservants. How could I dare to refuse your request?"

He had his sister put on her finest clothes and jewels and escorted her to the Lord of Chunshen's mansion. Huang Xie fell in love with her at first sight. That very night he gave Li Yuan a pair of white jade discs and three hundred ingots of gold, and took Yan to bed. In less than three months, the girl was pregnant.

Li Yuan spoke privately to his younger sister. "Which is more important, a concubine or an official wife?"

She laughed and said, "How could a concubine compete with the main wife?"

"Well then, which is more important, a wife or a queen?"

Li Yan laughed again: "The queen is much more powerful."

"If you stay in the Lord of Chunshen's household, you will never be more than a favorite concubine. Now, the king of Chu has no children, but you are pregnant. If you are presented to His Majesty and in the future you give birth to a son, he will become the next king and, at the very least, you will become dowager queen. Wouldn't that be better than being a concubine?"

Having taught her exactly what she needed to say and do when she was in bed with His Lordship, he reminded her: "The Lord of Chunshen is going to do exactly what you tell him." Li Yan committed his script to memory.

That night when they were in bed together, she said to Huang Xie: "The king of Chu loves you and treats you with much more favor than any of his brothers. You have been Grand Vizier of Chu for more than twenty years now. Unfortunately, His Majesty has no sons, so when he dies the crown will have to pass to one of his brothers. They do not like you, and they all have favorites of their own. Do you think you will remain in power for long?"

When Huang Xie heard this, he became sunk in thought and did not reply. Li Yan continued: "I have been thinking deeply about this. You have occupied high office and for a very long time—there are many ways in which you have angered His Majesty's brothers. When they come to power, they are going to make you pay for this. I hope you do not think that your troubles will be limited to losing your fief east of the Yangtze River."

Huang Xie was shocked into saying, "You are absolutely right. I have been negligent. What should I do?"

"I have a plan that will not only save you from danger but bring you many blessings in the future," Li Yan said. "However, it scares me and I don't know if I can tell you my idea. It is only because I am frightened of how you will react that I don't dare to speak."

"You are doing this for my sake. Why should I react badly?"

"I am pregnant, but nobody knows this," Li Yan said. "Luckily, I haven't been with Your Lordship for any length of time. If you were to present me to the king of Chu, with your position at court, he would have to favor me. If I am fortunate enough to give birth to a son, in the future he will become His Majesty's heir. That means that your son will become the next king of Chu. In that case, the entire kingdom of Chu will be yours! Who would dare to cause trouble for you then?"

Huang Xie felt as though he had just woken from a deep sleep, or had his head become clear after drinking wine. He said happily: "I am sure that the saying 'clever women give birth to sons' was written for you!"

The following day, His Lordship summoned Li Yuan and informed him of his intentions. Li Yan was secretly moved out of the house to a different residence. Huang Xie then went to the palace and spoke to the king of Chu. "I have been informed that Li Yuan's younger sister, Li Yan, is of outstanding beauty, and a fortune-teller has announced that she is the kind of woman who will give birth to sons. What is more, she is very lovely; the king of Qi has already sent an ambassador to ask for her hand in marriage. You must get there first, Your Majesty!"

The king of Chu ordered his eunuchs to collect her and bring her back to the palace. She was indeed extremely beautiful, and the king of Chu loved and favored her. When the time came for her to give birth, she produced twin sons; the older was named Han, and the younger You. The king of Chu was even happier than he could express. He immediately appointed Li Yan as his queen and made the older of her sons, Prince Han, his crown prince. Li Yuan received special honors as the queen's brother—he was also increasingly involved in the government of the country, on a par with the Lord of Chunshen. Li Yuan was a very tricky man. Although he always seemed very respectful to the Lord of Chunshen, in actual fact he was deeply jealous of him. In the twenty-fifth year of the reign of King Kaolie of Chu, His Majesty became very ill, and even after much time, he showed no signs of getting better. Li Yuan was perfectly aware of the fact that the Lord of Chunshen knew the truth of his sister's pregnancy and it would be impossible to deal with him once the crown prince had become king. It was much better to kill him now and shut him up permanently. Therefore, he sent men out to all sorts of places to find brave knights. These he established in his household, feeding them well and giving them fine clothes to wear, to make sure that they would be loyal to him. When Zhu Ying heard about this development, he became suspicious: "If Li Yuan is recruiting assassins, it must be to deal with the Lord of Chunshen!"

He went to the mansion to have an audience with His Lordship, at which he said: "Did you know, my lord, that there are such things as unexpected disasters, unexpected blessings, and unexpected individuals?"

"What do you mean by unexpected blessings?"

"You have been Grand Vizier of Chu for more than twenty years," Zhu Ying replied. "Although your title is grand vizier, in actual fact you have been the real king of Chu. Now His Majesty is seriously sick and shows no signs of recovering, so one day soon he will die. In that case the little crown prince will succeed to the throne, and you will support him—just like Yi Yin or the Duke of Zhou, you will wait for His Majesty to grow up before handing over the government to him. In that case both Heaven and men will give their allegiance to him, and he will face south and rule as king. That is what is known as an unexpected blessing."

"What do you mean by unexpected disasters?"

"Li Yuan is the queen's brother, but you are much more powerful than he is," Zhu Ying replied. "Although he may appear to be friendly and accommodating, he hates his inferior position. As the saying goes: 'Two thieves who go to rob the same house are going to be jealous of one another.' This is natural to the situation in which you find yourselves. I have heard that he has been secretly recruiting assassins for a while now and he is going to use them to kill you once the king of Chu is dead. That way, he can seize power for himself. That is what is called an unexpected disaster."

"What do you mean by an unexpected person?"

"Thanks to his sister, Li Yuan is kept informed of everything that goes on in the palace the moment that it happens," Zhu Ying said. "You, my lord, live in a mansion outside the city walls, so you are always going to be late in reacting to events. If you spend all your time with other court officials, you can take charge and direct them. Li Yuan currently has the upper hand, and that is why I am going to kill him on your behalf. That is what is called an unexpected person."

Huang Xie tugged at his whiskers and laughed: "Li Yuan is a nobody, and he has always treated me with great respect—this cannot possibly be true! I am sure that you are reading far too much into this!"

"If you don't follow my advice today, by the time you regret it, it will be too late!" Zhu Ying replied.

"You can go now," Huang Xie declared. "I will investigate this. If I need your help, I will ask for it."

Zhu Ying left and waited for three days. When he did not see the slightest sign of the Lord of Chunshen doing anything, he knew that he had not really paid any attention to his advice. He sighed and said, "If I don't leave now, I am going to get caught up in this disaster too! I think I had better follow the example of Fan Li!" He departed without saying a word to anyone and headed for the Wu region to live as a recluse in the Five Lakes area.

An old man wrote a poem:

A beautiful woman entered the royal palace pregnant;
A wicked plan to usurp the throne was put in place.
There is every reason why the Lord of Chunshen should have been
    punished;
Why should Zhu Ying be allowed to kill his enemy?

Seventeen days after Zhu Ying left the country, King Kaolie of Chu passed away. Li Yuan had already made the following arrangements with the palace guard: "If there is any change in His Majesty's condition, report it to me first." When he got the news that the king was dead, he went straight to the palace. He gave secret instructions that mourning was not to begin and arranged that assassins should hide inside the palace gate. He waited until the sun went down and then sent someone to report what had happened to the Lord of Chunshen. He was very shocked and did not bother to stop to discuss the matter with his advisors but immediately leapt into his chariot and rode away. When he arrived at the palace gates, the assassins sprang out on both sides, shouting: "We have an edict from the queen. The Lord of Chunshen has been plotting treason and must be executed!" Huang Xie realized that a coup was in progress against him, and he tried to turn his chariot around as quickly as he could. His personal attendants were now either dead or fighting for their lives. Huang Xie's head was cut off and thrown out. Meanwhile, the city gates were all closed and the order to begin national mourning given.

Li Yuan arranged for Crown Prince Han to succeed to the throne, taking the title of King You of Chu. He was just six years old at the time. Li Yuan appointed himself as Grand Vizier and took sole control of the government, while Li Yan became dowager queen. This precious pair gave orders that the whole of the Lord of Chunshen's family should be killed and his lands confiscated. It was a real tragedy!

A historian wrote an encomium:

Huang Xie was a clever man who made Chu equal to Qin.
By finding a way to send the crown prince home, he made himself
  Grand Vizier.
He bedazzled the Zhao ambassadors from his fief in the kingdom of
  Wu,
But King Kaolie had no children and Li Yuan presented his sister.
The time to make decisions passed, and Zhu Ying was the only one to
  speak!

Once Li Yuan took over the country, the Lord of Chunshen's advisors all went elsewhere. The other princes of the royal house were alienated and without hope of government employment. With a child king and widowed queen in charge, the government of the country quickly fell into chaos. From this time on, Chu was in serious trouble.

. . .

Let us now turn to another part of the story. Lü Buwei was furious about having been attacked by the united forces of the five kingdoms and wanted revenge. He said, "The original architect of this plan was the Zhao general, Pang Nuan." He ordered Meng Ao and Zhang Tang to take an army of fifty thousand men to attack Zhao. Three days later, he ordered the Lord of Chang'an, Ying Chengqiao, and Fan Yuqi to take a further fifty thousand men in support. Lü Buwei's advisors were most concerned about this decision: "The Lord of Chang'an is still a very young man, and I am afraid that he will never make a good general."

Lü Buwei smiled and said, "You don't understand."

When Meng Ao marched his army out of the Hangu Pass, he took the road to Shangdang, where he proceeded to attack the city of Qingdu. He built a series of defensive encampments in the Du Mountains. The Lord of Chang'an made camp with the main body of the army at Tunliu, where he could be within call in case of need. Zhao appointed Prime Minister Pang Nuan as the commander-in-chief, with Hu Zhen as his deputy, and ordered him to take an army of one hundred thousand men to intercept the enemy. Pang Nuan was given permission by His Majesty to act as he saw fit according to conditions on the ground. Pang Nuan said: "North of Qingdu, Mount Yao is by far the tallest. Anyone who climbs Mount Yao will be able to keep a close eye on the Du Mountains. We ought to take possession of that peak."

He sent Hu Zhen to lead twenty thousand men to go on ahead. When they arrived at Mount Yao, they discovered that a force of ten thousand

Qin soldiers was already camped there. They were put to flight by Hu
Zhen's sudden onslaught. This enabled him to make camp right at the
peak. Meng Ao gave Zhang Tang twenty thousand men and told him to
recapture this fastness. However, Pang Nuan then arrived with the main
body of the army and the two sides drew up their forces in battle formation at the foot of the mountain. A terrible slaughter ensued. Hu Zhen,
from his vantage point at the top of the mountain, signaled the enemy
dispositions with red flags—when Zhang Tang moved east, the flags
immediately pointed east; when he moved west, the flags promptly signaled that he had changed direction. All the Zhao army had to do was
to follow the indications. Having surrounded the enemy forces, Pang
Nuan gave the following order: "Anyone who can take Zhang Tang
prisoner will be rewarded with one hundred *li* of land." The Zhao army
fought to the death. Even though Zhang Tang summoned up every last
vestige of his courage, he could not break through the lines encircling
him. It was just at this critical moment that Meng Ao arrived in support. The two of them were able to make their way back to their main
mountain encampment. Since the people of Qingdu knew that rescue
troops had arrived, they defended their city with redoubled vigor. Meng
Ao knew that they would not be able to defeat them, so he sent Zhang
Tang to Tunliu, to ask for reinforcements to be brought up as quickly as
possible.

At this time, Ying Chengqiao, the Lord of Chang'an, was seventeen
years old. He knew nothing about military matters, and so when the
order arrived, he summoned Fan Yuqi to discuss the matter. Fan Yuqi
loathed Lü Buwei for having seized control of the country by astutely
presenting a concubine to the king, so having sent away all the servants,
he told Ying Chengqiao all that had happened in considerable detail:
"His Present Majesty is not in fact the son of the late king—you are the
legitimate heir to the throne. If Lü Buwei has put you in command of
the army, it is because he harbors evil intentions towards you. No doubt
he is afraid that if the truth comes out, you will try and get rid of our
present monarch. That is why he pretends to favor and promote you,
when in fact what he is trying to do is to get rid of you. Lü Buwei goes
in and out of the place without any let or hindrance; he and the queen
dowager are continuing their adulterous relationship: the whole family
is in this together! The only person they are afraid of is you, my lord. If
you are lucky, you will merely find yourself stripped of all your honors.
If you are unlucky, you are going to be executed. Henceforward

the kingdom of Qin will be ruled by the Lü family! Everyone in the capital knows that this is true. You must make plans to deal with the situation!"

"If you had not told me," the Lord of Chang'an said, "I would not know anything about this. What should I do?"

"You have a fine army under your command," Fan Wuqi declared. "If you were to circulate placards proclaiming the crime committed by these wicked people and exposing the imposture practiced on His Late Majesty, what loyal subject of Qin would fail to support you as the rightful heir to the throne?"

His Lordship drew his sword, flushing bright red with excitement. "For a man death is nothing!" he exclaimed. "How can I bend the knee before the son of a mere merchant? I hope that you will help me get rid of these people!"

Fan Wuqi then drafted the text for these placards:

The Lord of Chang'an announces the following to the people: Within any monarchy a guaranteed succession within a single family is of paramount importance; any attempt to overthrow the ruling house is a crime of the blackest kind. The Marquis of Wenxin, Lü Buwei, was originally a merchant from Diyang, but now he is the uncrowned king in Xianyang—this is because our present king, Zheng, is not the son and heir of His Late Majesty but Lü Buwei's own child! He began by presenting a pregnant concubine to seduce the late king, and now we have ended up under the rule of a wicked impostor. The bloodline of our kings has been sullied! He has used his gold to buy his way into power, and his ultimate aim has always been to pervert the realm! There is a reason why two of our kings died before their time—are we going to let him get away with it? He has been in power now through the reign of three monarchs: who will stop him? The man currently presiding over the court is not the real king; a member of the Lü family has been imposed on us as a royal Ying! His Majesty has given his real father enormous power—although he is officially merely a minister, in fact he governs the country. The state is in danger! The gods are angry! As the real heir to the throne, I want to punish these wicked men! Any soldier is welcome to join my righteous cause. Any member of the public can throw in his lot with mine, secure in the knowledge that by doing so, they are supporting the Ying house. When you see this text, prepare your weapons, hitch up your chariots, and come and join me!

Fan Wuqi had the text circulated in all directions. There were many people in Qin who had heard the story of how Lü Buwei gained royal favor by presenting his concubine to His Majesty, but reading of how she had been pregnant at the time and given birth to an imposter prince, they believed that every word of it was true. The only reason they did not rise up was because they were too frightened of Lü Buwei. However, they were hoping that someone would get rid of him.

. . .

At this time a comet was sighted in the east, then it moved to the north, and finally to the west. Diviners said that this was an omen of a military uprising in the country. This caused people to become very nervous. Fan Wuqi recruited able-bodied young men from the counties close to Tunliu into his army and attacked the cities of Changzi and Huguan—his military might was visibly increasing. Zhang Tang realized that the Lord of Chang'an was now in open rebellion against the throne, and he rushed back to Xianyang under cover of darkness to report this uprising. When Zheng, king of Qin, saw the text of the placards, he was absolutely furious and summoned Lü Buwei to discuss the matter.

"The Lord of Chang'an is far too young to organize something like this," Lü Buwei pointed out. "It must be Fan Wuqi's doing. He is a brave man but pretty stupid. If you send the army out, Your Majesty, I am sure that you will be able to capture him alive. There is really nothing to worry about."

He appointed Wang Jian as the senior general, with Huan Yi and Wang Ben commanding the left and right vanguards. With a force of one hundred thousand men, they set off to put down the Lord of Chang'an's revolt. The Lord of Chang'an was terrified by this development.

"Your position today, my prince, is like a man riding a tiger," Fan Wuqi said. "Getting on is hard enough, but getting off is even worse. However, you have the forces of three cities at your disposal, an army of no fewer than one hundred and fifty thousand men. If they fight on home ground, it is not at all certain who will win and who will lose. There is nothing to be so frightened about!"

He arranged his troops into battle formation at the foot of the city walls and waited. Wang Jian put his troops into formation opposite him. He said to Fan Wuqi, "What has our country done to offend you that you incite the Lord of Chang'an to rebel?"

Fan Wuqi leaned out from his chariot and said, "The king of Qin is in actual fact the illegitimate son of Lü Buwei: everyone knows that! My family has worked for the government for generations—how can I just sit by and watch while everything that the Ying family built up with their own sweat and blood is stolen by the Lü family? The Lord of Chang'an is the true heir to our royal house, and that is why I am supporting him. If you still remember all that you owe to His Late Majesty, General, why don't you support this righteous cause and attack Xianyang, killing these wicked people and getting rid of the usurper? If you were to help the Lord of Chang'an to become king, you would certainly be enfeoffed as a marquis and enjoy great wealth and honor. Wouldn't that be wonderful?"

"The dowager queen was pregnant for an unusually long time when she gave birth to His Present Majesty, but he is certainly the son of our former king," Wang Jian retorted. "You have been spreading seditious rumors and illegally gathering troops—these are crimes that will see your entire family killed! Now you are trying to disturb the morale of my army with your wicked and baseless gossip. When I get my hands on you, I am going to rip you to pieces!"

Fan Wuqi was furious at this and opened his eyes wide as he bellowed with anger. Grabbing a long sword, he charged straight at the Qin army. When the soldiers saw his reckless courage, they simply could not withstand him. Fan Wuqi charged first to the left and then to the right, moving as if there were nobody else present on the field of battle. Wang Jian signaled to his troops to surround him. Although they did so on a number of occasions, each time Fan Wuqi was able to cut his way out. The Qin army suffered terrible losses.

In the evening, both sides recalled their troops. Wang Jian made camp at Mount Sangai. He thought to himself, "Fan Wuqi is a remarkably brave man and it will be extremely difficult to deal with him. We need a plan to destroy him." He asked the people present in his command tent, "Is anyone here acquainted with the Lord of Chang'an?"

The junior general, Yang Duanhe, originally a native of Tunliu, said, "I used to be a member of the Lord of Chang'an's household."

"I am going to write a letter and give it to you," Wang Jian said. "I want you to take it to the Lord of Chang'an. It will urge him to surrender to the court before he gets himself killed."

"How am I supposed to get into the city?" Yang Duanhe asked.

"You must wait until we are engaged in battle," Wang Jian instructed him. "You are to take advantage of the moment when they recall their troops to smuggle yourself into the city dressed as one of their soldiers. When the attack on the city has reached a critical point, you should go and ask for an audience with the Lord of Chang'an. That way, the situation will be sure to change in our favor."

Yang Duanhe agreed to follow this plan. Wang Jian then wrote out a letter in front of the assembled company and sealed it. This he handed over to Yang Duanhe for him to keep until the moment was ripe. Next he summoned Huan Yi and ordered him to take his army to attack the city of Changzi. Likewise, Wang Ben was commanded to lead his troops to attack the city of Huguan. Wang Jian himself would assault Tunliu, so that these three cities could be attacked simultaneously and one would not be able to go to the help of the others.

. . .

Fan Wuqi said to the Lord of Chang'an: "We must take advantage of the fact that they have divided their forces to win a decisive victory. Otherwise, if we lose Changzi and Huguan, the situation will move in favor of the Qin forces. In that case they will be much more difficult to defeat!"

The Lord of Chang'an was still little more than a child, and he was frightened. "You planned all of this, General," he sobbed, "and you are in charge. Please don't get me into trouble!"

Fan Wuqi selected an army of battle-hardened soldiers, one hundred thousand men strong. He opened the gates of the city and sent them out to fight. Wang Jian pretended to give way and withdrew ten *li*. He made camp at Mount Fulong. Fan Wuqi returned to the city in triumph. By this time Yang Duanhe had managed to mingle with his troops and marched back in with them. Given that he was originally a native of this city, it was easy for him to find a relative who would give him a place to stay. No more of this now.

. . .

On his return, the Lord of Chang'an asked Fan Wuqi, "If Wang Jian does not withdraw his army, what are we going to do?"

"Today's battle has already blunted their ardor," the general replied. "Tomorrow I am going to take my entire army out to fight, and our task will be to capture Wang Jian alive. Then we can march straight on Xianyang and put you on the throne. That is my greatest wish."

Do you want to know who won and who lost? READ ON.

Chapter One Hundred and Four

Gan Luo achieves high office at a young age.

*Ai Lao uses a faked castration to bring the
Qin palace to chaos.*

Having withdrawn his army ten *li*, Wang Jian instructed them to build
a huge rampart around the camp and dig deep ditches. Troops were
dispatched to defend any points of danger, and they were not allowed to
go out to fight under any circumstances. He sent twenty thousand soldiers to go and help Huan Yi and Wang Ben, to urge them to capture
their objectives as soon as possible. Fan Wuqi sent out his whole army
day after day, yet the Qin army simply did not respond. General Fan
decided that Wang Jian must be frightened. Just as he was debating the
possibility of dividing his army to go and rescue Changzi and Huguan,
suddenly one of his mounted spies reported: "The two cities have
already fallen to the Qin army!" Fan Wuqi was horrified. He immediately made camp outside the city, in order to encourage the Lord of
Chang'an to feel some confidence.

When Huan Yi and Wang Ben were informed that Wang Jian had
moved his camp to Mount Fulong, they took their troops there to join
him. They said: "The two cities have already returned to the fold. We
have left some of our soldiers there to guard them and maintain order."

"Tunliu is now isolated," Wang Jian said happily. "All we need to
do now is to capture Fan Wuqi alive, and that will put an end to this
matter."

Before he had even finished speaking, one of the soldiers guarding the
camp reported: "General Xin Sheng is outside the gates to the encampment with an order from the king of Qin."

Wang Jian escorted him back to the command tent and asked the general why he had come.

"First, His Majesty is very mindful of the suffering his armies have experienced on this campaign, so he sent me here with special rewards for everyone," Xin Sheng explained. "Secondly, the king of Qin hates Fan Wuqi and asked me to take the following message to you: 'You must capture this man alive because I want to behead him with my own sword, to assuage my anger!'"

"Since you are here, General," Wang Jian remarked, "you could be very useful!" He ordered the rewards to be distributed among his troops. Then he commanded Huan Yi and Wang Ben to each take their army and lie in ambush on either side. He instructed Xin Sheng to take five thousand cavalry and go forward to provoke battle, while he himself took the main body of the army to get ready to attack the city.

. . .

When the Lord of Chang'an heard that they had lost the cities of Changzi and Huguan, he sent someone to summon Fan Wuqi back to the city immediately to discuss the situation.

"Any minute now, we are going to have to fight the decisive battle," Fan Wuqi said. "If we lose, I will take you north to seek sanctuary in Zhao or Yan, creating an alliance among the other kings to launch a joint attack on Qin and execute the usurper! That way we can bring peace to the kingdom."

"Please be careful!" the Lord of Chang'an whimpered.

Fan Wuqi went back to his encampment. One of the mounted spies reported: "The king of Qin has recently appointed a new general, Xin Sheng, and he is on his way here to provoke battle."

"He is a poor strategist of no particular repute," Fan Wuqi sneered. "I will get rid of him straightaway."

He led his army out of the encampment and went forward to engage with Xin Sheng's troops. Having fought a couple of encounters, Xin Sheng started to pull back. Fan Wuqi charged forward recklessly. He had gone about five *li* when Huan Yi and Wang Ben ordered their ambushed troops into action. Fan Wuqi suffered a terrible defeat and turned his army back as quickly as he could. However, by that time Wang Jian's troops were already in position at the foot of the walls of Tunliu. Fan Wuqi hurled himself into battle, cutting a bloody swathe through the enemy forces. When the defenders on the city walls opened the gates to let him in, Wang Jian brought all his troops together to besiege the city, and the fighting reached a new peak of ferocity. Fan Wuqi patrolled the walls day and night, without the slightest sign of exhaustion.

At this time, Yang Duanhe was already in place inside the city. Realizing that the situation was now critical, he went under cover of darkness to ask for an audience with the Lord of Chang'an, saying: "I have something top secret to inform His Lordship."

When the Lord of Chang'an discovered that his visitor was a former member of his household, he happily called him in. Yang Duanhe had the servants sent away, and then he said: "You know how strong the Qin army is, my lord. Even the forces of the other six states combined cannot defeat them. If you are determined to fight them all on your own, you are bound to get into serious trouble!"

"Fan Wuqi says that His Majesty is not actually the son of the late king," the Lord of Chang'an said. "He got me into this. It was not my idea . . ."

"Fan Wuqi is very brave, but also very stupid, and he does not seem to care how many people he gets killed," Yang Duanhe said. "That is why he has dragged you into this mess. Although he has circulated his placards around every county and commandery, there has been no response. General Wang Jian is now attacking the city very fiercely. When the city falls, do you think you will be able to survive?"

"I was thinking of running away to Yan or Zhao and creating an alliance with them," the Lord of Chang'an explained. "Do you think that would work?"

"Tell me," Yang Duanhe demanded, "which of the six kingdoms is not afraid of Qin? Whichever country you go to, when Qin asks for you to be extradited, they will arrest you and hand you over. In such circumstances, how can you hope to stay alive?"

"What do you think I should do?" the Lord of Chang'an asked.

"General Wang knows that you have been led astray by Fan Wuqi. He wrote a secret missive and asked me to give it to you."

He presented this to His Lordship and Ying Chengjiao, the Lord of Chang'an, broke the seal, and read it:

Your Lordship is the brother of His Majesty the king, and you hold the title of Marquis of Qin. Why are you listening to malicious gossip and getting involved in matters that are much more serious than you can possibly understand? You have brought disaster down upon yourself, and I find this very regrettable. However, we all know that the architect of this misery is Fan Wuqi. If you can execute him and present his head to the army, while submitting to arrest yourself, I promise that I will speak up on your behalf to His Majesty. If you fail to do this immediately, the consequences will be on your own head!

When the Lord of Chang'an read this, he burst into tears. Weeping, he said, "Fan Wuqi is a loyal and upright gentleman. How could I bear to kill him?"

Yang Duanhe sighed and said, "That is what is known as being as weak as a woman. If you are not going to do what you are told, I am going to leave."

"I want you to stay with me for the time being," the Lord of Chang'an whimpered. "Do not go far away! You are going to have to wait for me to think about what you have said, and then we will speak again."

"Don't tell anyone what we have been talking about!" Yang Duanhe instructed him.

The next day, Fan Wuqi drove his chariot to the palace to have an audience with the Lord of Chang'an. "The Qin army is very powerful and the people are panicking," he explained. "The city will fall any day now. Let us go into exile in Yan or Zhao. Once we are in a place of safety, we can think about what to do next."

"My family is all in Xianyang," the Lord of Chang'an said. "If we now go far away to live in some foreign country, will they take us in?"

"Other countries have suffered a great deal from Qin's violent attacks," Fan Wuqi told him. "You do not need to worry about whether they will take us in or not!"

Just as they were talking, a report came in: "The Qin troops by the South Gate are trying to provoke battle!" Fan Wuqi tried repeatedly to make him hurry up: "If you don't go now, Your Highness, you will not be able to leave." The Lord of Chang'an hesitated, unable to make up his mind.

Fan Wuqi had no choice but to strap his sword to his side and get onto his chariot, speeding in the direction of the South Gate. There he fought yet another engagement with the Qin army. Yang Duanhe encouraged the Lord of Chang'an to climb up onto the city walls and watch the progress of the battle. All he could see was that Fan Wuqi was fighting desperately and the Qin army was pressing ever closer. Since General Fan could not resist the enemy onslaught, he raced back to the city, shouting, "Open the gates!" Yang Duanhe was standing next to the Lord of Chang'an, brandishing his sword. He shouted back, "His

Lordship has already surrendered the city! You are on your own now, General Fan! Anyone who dares to open the city gates will be beheaded!" He took a flag out of his sleeve—on it was the word "Surrender." Since His Lordship's servants were all old friends of Yang Duanhe, they immediately ran this flag up the pole, without so much as waiting for a sign of assent from the Lord of Chang'an. He just stood there weeping.

"There is no point in trying to help a weakling!" Fan Wuqi said with a sigh.

By this time, the Qin troops had encircled him in several concentric rings. As the king of Qin had specifically ordered them to capture him alive, they did not dare to simply shoot him full of arrows. Fan Wuqi hacked a bloodstained path through the surrounding soldiery and headed off for exile in Yan. Even though Wang Jian pursued him, he did not catch up with him. Yang Duanhe ordered the Lord of Chang'an to open the gates and allow the Qin army into the city. While His Lordship was held prisoner in the official guesthouse, Xin Sheng went back to Xianyang to report news of the victory to His Majesty and ask what he wanted done with the Lord of Chang'an. The Dowager Queen of Qin went to see His Majesty with her hair unbound, begging for clemency to be extended to His Lordship. She also pleaded with Lü Buwei to speak up for him.

"If this traitor is not punished," the king of Qin said crossly, "I am going to find my whole family plotting against me!"

He sent an envoy to order Wang Jian to have the Lord of Chang'an publicly beheaded at Tunliu. All the Qin soldiers and officials who had joined in his rebellion were to be executed. The entire population of the city was to be moved to Linzhao. He also put a price on Fan Wuqi's head—anyone who captured him alive would be rewarded with a fief of five cities. When the envoy arrived in Tunliu with the king of Qin's orders, the Lord of Chang'an heard that he would not be pardoned, so he hanged himself in the guesthouse. Wang Jian had his head cut off and suspended above the city gate. Tens of thousands of soldiers and officials were also executed. Then the inhabitants of the city were forced to move, leaving Tunliu entirely empty. This happened in the seventh year of the reign of Zheng, king of Qin.

An old man wrote a poem about this:

When your field is invaded by weeds, it is right to reach for the hoe,
Nevertheless, it is a good idea to consider the bigger picture.
The siege of Tunliu changed nothing for the better,
Yet the punishments meted out to those involved would fill a book.

By this time, King Zheng of Qin was all grown up. He was a tall and handsome young man, as well as being extremely clever and ambitious. He wanted to make his own decisions and would refuse to allow the queen dowager—or indeed Lü Buwei—to interfere. Having put an end to the trouble caused by the Lord of Chang'an, he was plotting how to avenge what had happened to Meng Ao. He gathered all his ministers to discuss an attack on Zhao.

Cai Ze, the Lord of Gangcheng, stepped forward and said: "Zhao has been the enemy of the kingdom of Yan for many generations; the alliance between these two states is far from being what they had in mind. I would like to send an ambassador to Yan and ask His Majesty for a hostage. That will leave Zhao completely isolated. If we then attack Zhao in concert with the Yan army, we will be able to extend our land holdings in the Hejian region. What could be more splendid?"

The king of Qin thought that this was a good idea and sent Cai Ze to Yan, where he persuaded the king of Yan: "You and Zhao are both states of ten thousand chariots. In your first battle against them, Li Fu was killed. In your second campaign, you lost Ju Xin. You seem to have forgotten the humiliation of those two defeats, Your Majesty, when you made your alliance with Zhao to resist the aggression of the powerful kingdom of Qin to the west. If this is successful, then Zhao will take all the credit. If it is unsuccessful, then Yan will suffer the consequences. I am afraid that your advisors have made a terrible miscalculation!"

"I am not happy about having to ally with Zhao either," the king of Yan returned. "However, I had no choice since we could not fight them."

"The king of Qin is determined to punish the people involved in the recent revival of the Vertical Alliance," Cai Ze said. "I think that since you and Zhao have long been enemies and you were forced to join by their forces, if you were to send your crown prince as a hostage to Qin as a token of good faith, and ask for a senior minister from their government to go to Yan as your prime minister, the alliance between our two countries would be as tight as glue and lacquer. If the two of us join forces, it will not be difficult to avenge the insults inflicted upon you by Zhao!"

The king of Yan followed his advice and sent Crown Prince Dan to Qin as a hostage and invited a senior minister from that country to become the prime minister of Yan. Lü Buwei wanted to send Zhang Tang and had the Grand Astrologer perform a divination about it. It was very auspicious. Zhang Tang announced that his health was so poor that he did not want to go. Lü Buwei went in a carriage to visit him in person. Zhang Tang refused the honor, saying: "I have repeatedly attacked Zhao and they really hate me. If I were to go to Yan, I would have to travel though Zhao territory. That is why I cannot go." Lü Buwei tried to force him to leave, but Zhang Tang resolutely refused.

When Lü Buwei returned home to his mansion, he sat alone in the main hall worrying about the situation. There was a member of his household named Gan Luo, the grandson of Gan Mao, who at that time was just twelve years of age. When he saw Lü Buwei looking so unhappy, he stepped forward and asked, "What is the problem, my lord?"

"You wouldn't understand it anyway, my boy," Lü Buwei said. "Why are you asking?"

"The reason why people value their retainers and advisors is because such people can help their masters solve the problems that beset them," Gan Luo said. "If you have a problem and don't tell anyone about it, how do you expect them to be able to help you?"

"I ordered the Lord of Gangcheng to go to Yan on an ambassadorial mission. Now Crown Prince Dan of Yan has already arrived here as a hostage, but Zhang Tang—whom I wanted to send to be the Yan prime minister, for which the auspices were entirely favorable—is refusing to go. That is the reason why I am upset."

"That is nothing," Gan Luo said. "Why didn't you tell me earlier? I can get him to go."

Lü Buwei got angry and shouted at him: "Go away! Go away! I went in person to get him go to and he refused. Surely he is not going to be willing to move for a child!"

"In the past, Xiang Tuo taught Confucius even though he was only seven years old at the time. I am twelve, which makes me five years old than Xiang Tuo. If you send me to have a go and I fail, you can shout at me then. Surely you are not the sort of person to measure someone purely on the basis of their appearance?"

Lü Buwei was impressed by these words, and so he apologized, looking much calmer: "If you can get Zhang Tang to go, you will be rewarded with a ministerial position."

Gan Luo said goodbye cheerfully and left to go and see Zhang Tang. Even though Zhang Tang knew that he was one of Lü Buwei's retainers, he did not take him at all seriously because he was so very young. "What do you want, brat?" he asked.

"I came specially to condole with you!"

"What has happened to me that you want to condole?"

"Well, how would you compare your achievements to those of Bai Qi, Lord of Wu'an?" Gan Luo inquired.

"The Lord of Wu'an fought the powerful kingdom of Chu to a standstill to the south, while striking awe into Zhao and Yan to the north. He fought countless successful battles and captured more cities than anyone can name. My achievements are not even one tenth of his!"

"When Fan Ju was prime minister in Qin," Gan Luo asked, "was he more powerful than Lü Buwei is today?"

"Oh no," Zhang Tang declared.

"So you would agree that Lü Buwei is a more significant figure than Fan Ju ever was?"

"How could I not agree?" Zhang Tang demanded.

"In the past, Fan Ju wanted the Lord of Wu'an to attack Zhao, and he was not willing to go. Fan Ju became angry and had him expelled from Xianyang, whereupon he died at Duyou. Now Lü Buwei wants you to go to Yan, and you don't want to go. This was the very reason that Fan Ju became irritated with the Lord of Wu'an, and it is exactly why Lü Buwei is angry with you! You are going to be sent to the execution ground any day now!"

Zhang Tang was appalled: "You are right to tell me about this." He asked Gan Luo to apologize to Lü Buwei for him, and immediately started packing.

When he was about to set off, Gan Luo said to Lü Buwei, "Zhang Tang listened to my advice and feels that he has no choice but to go to Yan. In the circumstances, it is not surprising he is worried about Zhao. Please lend me five chariots so that I can deal with Zhao on his behalf."

Lü Buwei was now aware of his talents, and so he went to the palace to have an audience with the king of Qin. He said: "There is a certain Gan Luo, the grandson of Gan Mao, who is very young but exceptionally intelligent, as befits a member of such a famous family. Recently Zhang Tang has been claiming to be ill because he did not want to go and be prime minister in Yan. When Gan Luo went and talked to him, he set off immediately. Now he is asking permission to go and speak to the king of Zhao. I think Your Majesty should grant his request."

The king of Qin summoned Gan Luo for an audience. He was a short boy, but very good-looking. The king of Qin thought him charming. He asked, "What are you going to say when you see the king of Zhao?"

Gan Luo responded: "I am going to see whether he is happy to see me or frightened and act accordingly. Words are like waves: they follow the winds. There is no set pattern."

The king of Qin gave him ten fine chariots and one hundred servants to escort him on this mission to Zhao.

King Daoxiang of Zhao was already aware that the alliance between Yan and Qin had been restored, and he was afraid that they would conspire together to attack him. When he was suddenly informed of the arrival of an ambassador from Qin, he could hardly contain his delight. He went twenty *li* outside the suburbs to meet Gan Luo. When he saw how young he was, he was very surprised and asked: "What relation are you, sir, to the member of the Gan family who captured the Sanchuan area for Qin?"

"That was my grandfather," Gan Luo answered.

"How old are you?" King Daoxiang asked,

"Twelve."

"Does the kingdom of Qin lack any suitable older person to send as ambassador?" the king of Zhao sneered. "Why are you here?"

"The king of Qin employs people in their rightful place," Gan Luo replied. "Older people are employed in serious matters of state while little things are entrusted to younger people. Since I am so very young, I was sent as an ambassador to Zhao."

The king of Zhao had by now caught the tenor of his remarks and was even more amazed. "Why have you come here?" he asked.

"Have you heard that Crown Prince Dan of Yan has gone to Qin as a hostage?"

"I am aware of that," King Daoxiang said.

"Do you know that Zhang Tang is to be the next prime minister of Yan?" Gan Luo asked again.

"I am aware of that too."

"Crown Prince Dan of Yan has gone as a hostage to Qin so that they cannot attack us," Gan Luo said. "Zhang Tang is going to Yan as prime minister to show that we will not attack them. If Yan and Qin are strong allies like this, then Zhao is in serious danger."

"What is the motive behind Qin's alliance with Yan?" the king asked.

"Qin has allied with Yan because they want to attack Zhao and expand their landholdings in the Hejian region," Gan Luo replied. "You had better select five cities from Hejian to give as a present to Qin. I will then speak to His Majesty and prevent Zhang Tang from making his journey, and that will put an end to our alliance with Yan. Instead we will ally with you. If you want to attack the weaker Yan, Qin will not go to their rescue. In that case, I am sure that you will gain much more than just five cities!"

The king of Yan was delighted by this and presented Gan Luo with one hundred ingots of gold and two pairs of white jade discs. He entrusted him with a map of the five cities and sent him back to report to the king of Qin.

"My lands in Hejian have been significantly increased by a child," the king said in admiration. "This kid's intelligence is much bigger than his body!"

He ordered Zhang Tang to stop his journey. Zhang Tang was deeply pleased by this development. When Zhao heard that he would not be going, they knew that Qin would not be helping Yan, so they ordered Pang Nuan and Li Mu to join forces and attack Yan, capturing thirty cities in the Shanggu region. Zhao took possession of nineteen of them, while the remaining eleven were made over to Qin. The king of Qin appointed Gan Luo as a senior minister and presented him with the houses and land that had previously been part of Gan Mao's fief.

There is a common saying that Gan Luo became chancellor when he was just twelve years old—it is derived from this story.

There is a poem that testifies to these events:

With just a few words he took possession of large areas of Hejian;
The borders of Shanggu were changed to the detriment of Yan.
Such remarkable achievements for such a young boy,
But inborn intelligence has never been a matter of years!

There is another poem, which reads:

The things that Gan Luo achieved when young took Ziya many years;
It is not a matter of their ages, but of meeting the right moment to act.
Look at the spring blossom, or the autumn-flowering chrysanthemum:
When the time comes, they appear without an instant's delay.

Crown Prince Dan of Yan was resident in Qin during these events. When he heard that Qin had turned its back on Yan and was now allied with Zhao, he felt as though he was sitting on a bed of nails. He wanted to escape and go home, but he was afraid that he would not be able to make his way through the passes. He made friends with Gan Luo because he wanted his advice about how to go home to Yan. Suddenly one night, Gan Luo dreamed that a messenger dressed in purple arrived holding a heavenly tally and said: "I have received an order from God on High to summon you to Heaven." After this, Gan Luo died without having experienced even a day's illness. How sad that such a remarkably intelligent boy should have died so young! After this, Crown Prince Dan had to stay in Qin.

. . .

Let us now turn to another part of the story. Thanks to his sexual prowess and military air, Lü Buwei was much loved by Dowager Queen Zhuangxiang. He came and went from the women's quarters of the palace without the slightest hindrance. When he realized that the king of Qin had grown up and was very clever, he started to get frightened. However, there was nothing that he could do about the fact that Dowager Queen Zhuangxiang was becoming more and more lecherous and would summon him at all hours of the day and night to come to the Sweet Springs Palace. Lü Buwei was worried that if one day their affair came to light he would be in serious trouble. He wanted to present someone to Her Majesty to replace himself, but finding someone who would satisfy her requirements was not so easy. He heard that there was a man working in the marketplace called Lao Da who was famous for the huge size of his penis. He was the object of much fighting among the lascivious local women. In the Qin language, a person who acted immorally was called "Ai," and so this man was known to everyone as Lao Ai. After he came to the attention of the authorities thanks to his adulterous affairs, Lü Buwei pardoned him and took him into his household as a retainer.

It was the custom in the kingdom of Qin to celebrate for three days after the end of the harvest, to mark the end of their labor. This was also a time when all kinds of different entertainers would ply their trade. Anyone with any skill, who could do something that others could not, would show it off during these three days. Lü Buwei had a wheel made of paulownia wood and ordered Lao Ai to stick his penis through the hole in the middle. Even though the chariot wheel spun around, his penis suffered no injury. This made the people in the marketplace fall about laughing. The dowager queen heard about it and made discreet inquiries of Lü Buwei—she seemed most interested.

"Would you like to meet this man, Your Majesty?" Lü Buwei asked. "I can make time to arrange it."

The dowager queen giggled and did not reply. Then after a long pause, she said, "Surely you are joking. How can an outsider possibly enter the palace?"

"I have a plan," Lü Buwei said. "I will get someone to rake up his old crimes and condemn him to castration. If you then bribe the executioner, Your Majesty, he will pretend to carry out the emasculation and, after that, Lao Ai can enter the palace as a eunuch working here. That way, you can enjoy him on a long-term basis."

"That is a wonderful idea!" the dowager queen exclaimed happily.

She gave Lü Buwei one hundred pieces of gold. He then secretly summoned Lao Ai and told him what was intended. Lao Ai was a man with strong sexual urges, who was naturally happy to pleasure a lady of such high rank. Lü Buwei ordered someone to accuse him of adultery yet again, and this time he was condemned to castration. The one hundred pieces of gold were given to the executioner and other officials who used a donkey's penis and its blood to pretend that the penalty had indeed been carried out. They plucked his beard to make him look like a eunuch. Meanwhile, the executioner arranged for the donkey's penis to be put on show so that everyone would believe that Lao Ai had indeed been castrated. Everyone who heard news of these events was most surprised. Having undergone this faked castration and had his appearance changed so that he looked like a eunuch, Lao Ai joined the other palace servants. The dowager queen had him allocated to her palace and ordered him to serve her overnight. She was very satisfied with the experience and thought him ten times better as a lover than Lü Buwei. The following day, she gave lavish rewards to Lü Buwei to thank him for all his hard work. He, on the other hand, was simply happy to have escaped.

The dowager queen lived with Lao Ai as if they were man and wife. When she got pregnant, she was afraid that she would not be able to keep it a secret, and so she announced that she was ill. She instructed Lao Ai to bribe a diviner with gold, and he said that the palace had become infested with evil spirits and the dowager queen needed to go at least two hundred *li* to the west to get away from them. The king of Qin was very unhappy about his mother's relationship with Lü Buwei, so he was delighted to see her gradually spending less and less time with him. He wanted to put a complete stop to their relationship, so he said: "Yongzhou is located two hundred *li* to the west of Xianyang. The palaces and halls are still well-maintained from when it was the capital of Qin. You can go and live there."

So it happened that the dowager queen traveled to Yongzhou in a carriage driven by Lao Ai. Having left Xianyang, they moved into the former royal palace known as the Dazheng Palace. Lao Ai and the dowager queen were now able to give free rein to their affection. In the space of two years, Her Majesty gave birth to two sons. She constructed a secret room where they were brought up. Her Majesty and Lao Ai agreed that when the king of Qin died, they would make one of their own children his successor. Although some people knew about this, they were too frightened to speak. The dowager queen claimed that Lao Ai had looked after her wonderfully when her son could not, and so he ought to be given an enfeoffment. The king of Qin could hardly refuse his mother's request, and so he invested Lao Ai as the Marquis of Changxin and gave him the lands of Shanyang.

Once Lao Ai had received this noble title, he became more and more arrogant and overbearing. Leaving on one side the gifts Her Majesty gave him every day, he went hunting or partying as the mood took him, using the palace, its contents, the chariots and horses as if they were his own personal belongings. Every matter, large or small, was decided by him. He had a household staff of several thousand people, not to mention the thousand and more men who had come to him in the hope of gaining an official position and agreed to remain as his retainers. He bribed many nobles and court officials to join his faction, and anyone who wanted to become powerful tried to gain his support. In many ways he was even more powerful than Lü Buwei himself.

In the ninth year of the reign of Zheng, king of Qin, a comet was seen in the heavens, its tail trailing halfway across the sky. The Grand Astrologer performed a divination about this and said, "There is going to be an armed uprising inside the country." Every year, the king of Qin had to carry out certain religious ceremonies. He had to perform the sacrifice to Baidi at Luzhi, which had first begun during the rule of Lord Xiang of Qin. Later on, when Lord De had moved the capital to Yongzhou, a suburban altar for the sacrifice to Heaven had been established at that city. In addition, His Majesty also had to sacrifice at the shrine to Lady Treasure, as mandated by Lord Mu of Qin. Although the capital had now moved to Xianyang, these sacrifices continued to be performed in their original location. Given that the dowager queen was living in Yongzhou, when the king went there for the suburban sacrifice, he would also go to see his mother. Once the ceremonies were over, he would stay at the Qi'nian Palace. Normally this sacrifice was performed in the spring, but this was changed because of the comet. When he was about to set off, His Majesty ordered General Wang Jian to make sure the army was highly visible for the next three days in Xianyang, since he and Lü Buwei would be in charge of maintaining order in the capital. Huan Yi led thirty thousand men to make camp at Mount Qi. After this was done, His Majesty got into his chariot and set off.

At this time the king of Qin was already twenty-two years old, but he had not yet held the official capping ceremony that would mark his assumption of adulthood. The dowager queen gave orders that this ceremony would be held in the temple dedicated to Lord De, and she presented His Majesty with a fine sword. This was followed by five days of feasting for all the officials. The dowager queen joined His Majesty in hosting an enormous banquet at the Dazheng Palace. Perhaps it was because Lao Ai had enjoyed too much power and honor for too long that he brought trouble down upon himself. He had been betting and drinking with some of his cronies, and, on the fourth day, it happened that he lost a whole series of bets, one after the other, with Grandee Yan Xie. He was drunk at the time and demanded that they start again from the beginning. Yan Xie—who was also drunk—refused. Lao Ai lunged forward and grabbed hold of him, punching him in the face. Yan Xie refused to budge and managed to rip Lao Ai's hat off his head.

Lao Ai was furious. Glaring at the man, he yelled: "I am His Majesty's stepfather! How dare you fight with me, you pestiferous peasant!"

Yan Xie was frightened and ran away. Purely by chance, he bumped straight into the king of Qin, who was leaving the palace after drinking a few toasts to his mother. Yan Xie threw himself on the ground and kowtowed, weeping and proclaiming that he deserved the death penalty. The king of Qin was not at all a stupid man. He did not say a word, but ordered his servants to pick him up and take him to the Qi'nian Palace where they could talk in private. Yan Xie informed His Majesty of how he had been punched in the face by Lao Ai, who had claimed to be the king's stepfather. He added: "Lao Ai is not really a eunuch. They pretended to castrate him, and then he went to serve the dowager queen. They have two children who are living here in the palace, and they have been plotting to usurp the throne."

When the king heard this, he was absolutely furious. He secretly sent someone with a military tally to summon Huan Yi, telling him to bring his troops to Yongzhou. However, the Palace Historian Si and Jie from the Palace Guard—two men who had received a great deal of money from Her Majesty and Lao Ai and hence were firm supporters of this precious pair—knew what was going on and rushed to Lao Ai's mansion to tell him all about it.

By this time Lao Ai had recovered from his drinking bout, and he was horrified. That night, he went to the Dazheng Palace to ask the dowager queen for an audience. He informed her of what had happened: "Under the circumstances, we had better assemble all our own guards and retainers to attack the Qi'nian Palace before Huan Yi arrives with his army. If we kill His Majesty, we will be able to survive this crisis."

"Will the palace guards obey my command?" she asked.

"Give me your seal!" Lao Ai demanded. "We can pretend that it is the proper royal one. Our excuse is going to be that the Qi'nian Palace has been attacked by rebels and His Majesty wants the palace guards to go and rescue him. They will have to obey."

The dowager queen was too flustered to understand quite what she was agreeing to. "Do so!" she said, handing her personal seal to Lao Ai.

He forged a document purporting to be from the king of Qin, to which he affixed the dowager queen's seal. Armed with this, he had the palace guards summoned. That his own retainers rushed to do his bidding goes without saying. The rebellion was set for the following day at noon. When everyone had assembled, Lao Ai, the Palace Historian Si, and Jie from the Palace Guard led their men to surround the Qi'nian Palace. The king of Qin climbed a tower and asked them what they were doing. They replied, "Lao Ai says that the palace is under attack by rebels. We came here to rescue Your Majesty."

"It is he who is the rebel," His Majesty retorted. "How could there be any trouble here at the palace?"

When the palace guards heard this, half of them simply went home. The other half showed their mettle by turning around and attacking Lao Ai and his retainers.

The king of Qin issued the following order: "Anyone who captures Lao Ai alive will be rewarded with one million pieces of gold. Anyone who kills him and brings me his head will be rewarded with five hundred thousand pieces of gold. Anyone who takes the head of a rebel will be promoted one grade. Whether you are commoner or slave, the rewards will be the same."

When this was announced, a number of eunuchs and stable boys rushed out to join the fray. When the people of Yongzhou heard that Lao Ai had rebelled, they too came running with whatever weapons they had at hand. Several hundred of Lao Ai's retainers were killed. When he realized that his men had been defeated, he forced his way out of the East Gate of the city, massacring anyone in his way. That meant that he ran straight into Huan Yi and his army coming the other way. Lao Ai was taken prisoner together with the Palace Historian and Jie of the Palace Guard. When they were thrown into prison, the truth quickly came out under interrogation. The king of Qin went in person to search the Dazheng Palace. He found the secret chamber in which Lao Ai's two illegitimate children lived, and he had his servants put them in a sack and beat them to death. The dowager queen was devastated, but she did not dare to try and save them—she just shut herself up in her own chambers and wept. The king of Qin did not attempt to see his mother, but returned to the Qi'nian palace.

The officials from the prison presented Lao Ai's confession: "Lao Ai entered the palace after a faked castration. This was all planned by the Marquis of Wenxin, Lü Buwei. Lao Ai had more than twenty coconspirators, including the Palace Historian Si and Jie from the Palace Guard . . ."

The king of Qin ordered that Lao Ai be pulled to pieces by chariots outside the East Gate to the city of Yongzhou. In addition, every member of his family to the third generation was put to death. The Palace Historian Si, Jie from the Palace Guard, and their ilk were all beheaded in public as a warning to others. Their retainers and everyone else who had fought for the rebels was to be executed. Those who had not actually participated personally in the rebellion but knew about it were exiled to Sichuan: that comprised some four thousand families. Since the dowager queen had allowed her personal seal to be used by the rebels, she could no longer remain the Mother of the Country. She was stripped of her titles and emoluments and sent to live at the Yuyang Palace. *This was the very smallest of the Qin traveling palaces.*

Three hundred soldiers were detailed to guard her, and if anyone entered or left the palace, they were subject to searching inquiries. From this time onwards, the dowager queen was a prisoner. What a terrible fate!

An anonymous poem describes this:

> For the Mother of the Country to have an affair is shocking enough;
> She flaunted the two children born from this second relationship.
> In spite of blatantly flouting the laws of Qin, she hoped to keep this a
>   secret;
> By keeping within the women's quarters, she thought nobody would
>   know.

When the king of Qin had put down Lao Ai's rebellion, he returned to Xianyang. Lü Buwei was afraid of being punished, so he pretended to be ill because he did not dare to go to court. The king wanted to execute him and asked his ministers for their opinion. Many of the ministers were close friends of Lü Buwei, and so they all said: "He played a crucial role in putting His Late Majesty on the throne, and he has done great things in the service of our country. Furthermore, there is no evidence to support Lao Ai's accusations. You cannot condemn him on the basis of mere gossip."

The king of Qin accordingly pardoned Lü Buwei and did not execute him, but he did strip him of his office as prime minister and took away his seal of office. Since Huan Yi had done so well in capturing the traitors alive, he was given a larger fief and promoted. In the fourth month of this year, it suddenly became very cold and snow fell, resulting in many people freezing to death. The people all said: "The king of Qin has disowned the dowager queen, which means that a son has turned against his own mother. That is why we are afflicted by such abnormal weather."

Grandee Chen Zhong stepped forward and remonstrated: "There is nobody in this world who does not have a mother. You should bring Her Majesty back to Xianyang and continue treating her with filial piety. Things will then return to normal in a couple of days."

The king of Qin was furious. He ordered that Chen Zhong be stripped of his clothes and thrown on top of a heap of brambles. There he was beaten to death. Finally, he had his body hung from one of the palace watchtowers with the following message attached: "If there is anyone else who wants to speak up for the dowager queen, look at this!" However, many ministers in the kingdom of Qin continued to remonstrate with His Majesty.

If you want to know whether the king of Qin was reconciled to his mother, READ ON.

Chapter One Hundred and Five

Mao Jiao removes his clothes to remonstrate with the king of Qin.

Li Mu retreats inside the walls of his encampment to stop Huan Yi's advance.

After Grandee Chen Zhong of Qin had been killed, a procession of other people wanting to remonstrate with His Majesty continued to arrive. The king of Qin immediately had all of them executed and put their bodies on display at the watchtower. In all, he had twenty-seven people killed in this way, and their corpses were piled up into a great heap. At this time, King Jian of Qi was visiting Qin to pay court to His Majesty—an official visit that coincided with that of King Daoxiang of Zhao. His Majesty held a banquet at the palace in Xianyang in their honor, and they all enjoyed themselves very much. However, when they saw the heap of corpses at the foot of the watchtower, they could not help sighing and privately criticizing His Majesty's lack of filial piety.

It just so happened that at this time there was a man named Mao Jiao, originally from Cangzhou, who was visiting Xianyang. He was staying in a hostel, and the other people residing there chatted about all this situation. Mao Jiao was appalled: "For a son to imprison his mother means that everything is topsy-turvy!"

He asked the owner of the hostel to heat some water. "I am going to have a bath, and then tomorrow morning, I will go to the palace to remonstrate with the king of Qin."

The other people staying at the same hostel laughed and said, "The twenty-seven men who died were all trusted ministers. The king of Qin wouldn't listen to them and so they were killed one after the other. What do you think a commoner like yourself can achieve?"

"If nobody goes to remonstrate," Mao Jiao retorted, "the king of Qin will certainly not listen. If somebody does go, even though his twenty-seven predecessors have failed, it does not mean that the king of Qin will refuse to listen to him." The other men all mocked his stupidity.

The following morning, Mao Jiao asked the hostel owner for a full meal. The man grabbed onto his clothes to try and stop him from going, but Mao Jiao wrenched himself free and left. The other residents were sure that he was going to get himself killed, so they stared dividing up his clothes and baggage among themselves. When Mao Jiao arrived at the watchtower, he threw himself down next to the pile of corpses and shouted: "My name is Mao Jiao and I come from the kingdom of Qi. I am here to remonstrate with His Majesty."

The king of Qin sent one of his eunuchs out to ask, "What do you want to remonstrate with His Majesty about? Is it something other than the dowager queen?"

"It is exactly about that matter that I have come," he declared. The eunuch went in to report: "It is another one come to remonstrate about the dowager queen."

"How about you warn him about the pile of corpses," the king of Qin said.

The eunuch said to Mao Jiao, "Do you not see all these dead bodies lying around the watchtower? Are you really not afraid to die?"

"I have heard that there are twenty-eight lunar lodges in the sky," Mao Jiao returned, "and when they are reborn on earth, they become righteous men. So far, His Majesty has killed twenty-seven of them, so he is still missing one. I have come here to make up the numbers. Everyone, saint and sinner, dies sooner or later, so what is there to be afraid of?"

The eunuch went back to report this. The king of Qin said angrily, "How dare this lunatic disobey my orders!" He looked at his entourage: "Why don't you boil up a cauldron of water in the courtyard and cook him alive? I am not going to let him leave a whole corpse to join the others at the foot of the watchtower! Why should he get to make up the numbers?"

The king of Qin sat down with his hand on his sword, looking deeply forbidding. The spittle flecked his mouth as he shouted with ungovernable rage: "Bring the madman in and cook him!" The eunuch went out to summon Mao Jiao. He deliberately adopted a very slow movement as he walked forward, showing not the slightest inclination to hurry. The eunuch tried to make him speed up, but Mao Jiao responded: "When I have audience with the king of Qin, he is going to kill me!

What is wrong with letting me delay that a bit?" The eunuch felt sorry for him and put a hand under his arm to help him along.

When Mao Jiao reached the steps, he bowed twice, kowtowed, and presented his opinion: "I have heard that every living thing must die sooner or later; every country will collapse at some point; and that once dead, you cannot return to life. An enlightened ruler thinks carefully about life and death, survival and collapse. I do not know whether Your Majesty is interested in this kind of subject or not."

The king of Qin was already looking somewhat calmer, and asked, "Do you have something that you want to say to me?"

"A loyal vassal does not fill his ruler's ears with empty flattery," Mao Jiao replied, "and an enlightened ruler does not do stupidly reckless things. If the ruler does something foolish and his vassals do not remonstrate, it means they have betrayed him. If his vassals give him loyal advice and the ruler does not listen, then he has let them down. You, Your Majesty, have done a terrible thing and yet you do not know it. I have loyal advice to give you but you don't want to hear. I am afraid that from this point onwards, the kingdom of Qin faces serious trouble!"

The king of Qin was silent for a long time. He was clearly calming down from his earlier rage. "What exactly are you talking about?" he said. "I would like you to explain."

"Do you want to conquer the whole world?" Mao Jiao asked.

"I do!" the king of Qin told him.

"Today, the reason why so many people respect Qin is not because you are so militarily powerful," Mao Jiao said, "but because Your Majesty is the finest ruler in the world. As a result, loyal vassals and brave knights have flocked to the Qin court. Now you have had your stepfather ripped to pieces by chariots, which is not benevolent. You had your two half-brothers put into sacks and beaten to death, which shows that you are lacking in fraternal love. You have forced your mother to go and live in the Yuyang Palace, which demonstrates that you are not filial. What is more, you have executed the men who tried to remonstrate with you and put their bodies on display at the foot of the watchtower. This is the kind of thing done by the evil last kings of the Xia and the Shang dynasties! You may want to conquer the world, but if you carry on like this, how can you expect anyone to give their allegiance to you? In the past the sage-king Shun served his wicked stepmother with exemplary filial love, and he ended up becoming the supreme ruler of the country. Evil King Jie killed Longguan Feng and wicked King Zhou tortured Prince Bigan to death, and so everyone rebelled against them.

Although I knew that I would die if I spoke out, I am even more afraid that after I am dead, there will be nobody else who dares to remonstrate with Your Majesty. In that case flattery and malicious gossip will increase day by day, the loyal will find they have no way to make their voices heard, you will become increasingly alienated from your people, and the other kings will rebel against your authority. How sad! Qin was on the point of unifying the entire country, and yet this great work failed because of you! Since I have now finished what I want to say, let me be boiled to death!"

At this point he stood up, took off his clothes, and ran towards the cauldron. The king of Qin rushed down into the courtyard and grabbed hold of Mao Jiao with his left hand. With his right hand, he waved to his entourage: "Take the cauldron away!"

"You have already circulated an order, Your Majesty, warning people not to remonstrate with you," Mao Jiao said. "If you don't kill me, you will be breaking your word."

The king of Qin ordered his staff to remove the warning notice and had his eunuchs assist Mao Jiao back into his clothes. He made him take a seat and apologized: "Those who remonstrated with me before just told me that I was wrong, they did not explain why it was important. Heaven sent you to me to clear my mind! How could I dare to refuse to listen to your advice?"

Mao Jiao bowed twice, stepped forward, and said: "If you have really paid attention to what I said, you ought to go and collect the queen dowager as quickly as you can. As for the bodies at the foot of the watchtower, these were all your loyal ministers. Please allow them to be given a decent burial."

The king of Qin immediately ordered his officials to collect the twenty-seven corpses. Afterwards, he had Mao Jiao drive him to Yongzhou.

Master Nan Ping wrote a historical poem about this:

As twenty-seven corpses lay in a heap,
Mao Jiao took off his clothes and ran towards the cauldron.
If the fates take a hand, however severe the crisis, you will not die;
His reputation for loyal advice will be honored for ten thousand
   generations.

When they arrived at the Yuyang Palace, His Majesty first gave orders that his presence be reported. Then, crawling forward on his knees, the king of Qin sought an audience with the dowager queen. He kowtowed and wept bitterly. His mother also burst into floods of tears. His Majesty presented Mao Jiao to the dowager queen. Pointing to him, he said: "This man is my Ying Kaoshu."

That evening, the king of Qin stayed overnight in the Yuyang Palace. The following day, he helped Her Majesty into a grand carriage and then set off in her wake, with an escort of one thousand chariots and ten thousand cavalrymen. A huge number of people followed on foot. Everyone who saw this procession praised His Majesty for his filial piety. When they returned to Xianyang, a banquet was held in the Sweet Springs Palace. The mother and son celebrated happily together. The dowager queen had wine served and toasted Mao Jiao. "It is entirely due to your efforts, sir," she said gratefully, "that I have been able to see my son again." The king of Qin appointed Mao Jiao as the Grand Tutor, with senior ministerial rank.

. . .

Zheng, king of Qin, remained concerned about the possibility that Lü Buwei would resume his affair with the dowager queen, so he made him leave the capital and sent him back to his original home country south of the Yellow River. When the various other kingdoms heard that he had returned, they each sent ambassadors to meet him and ask him to join their administrations as prime minister. These envoys formed a constant stream along the roads. The king of Qin then became worried that he might indeed be given high office in a foreign country, which would be disastrous for them, so he wrote the following letter and sent it to Lü Buwei:

> What did you achieve in the service of the Qin state that merited a fief of one hundred thousand households? What place did you hold in the Qin ruling house that you deserved the titles you received? Qin has been generous to you indeed! It is your fault that the Lao Ai rebellion ever happened; however, I could not bear to have you executed and allowed you to go back to your own country. You have failed to appreciate my gesture and opened communications with ambassadors of various foreign powers. Nevertheless, I am not proposing to mistreat you in any way. I am going to move you and your entire family to Sichuan, where the revenues of the city of Bei ought to be enough to support you in the style to which you have been accustomed for the rest of your life.

When Lü Buwei read this letter, he said angrily: "I bankrupted myself in order to put His Late Majesty on the throne—what service could be greater than that? The dowager queen was married to me before she ever served King Zhuangxiang, and I got her pregnant, so the present king of Qin is my son—who could be more closely related? Has His Majesty really completely turned against me?" A short time later, he sighed and said: "I put His Majesty on the throne in order to enrich myself, I plotted to usurp the throne for my son, I committed adultery with the king's wife, I murdered His Late Majesty, I put an end to the ancestral sacrifices of the Ying family—no wonder Heaven has decided that my time is at an end! I should have died years ago!"

He put poison in a cup of wine and drained it to the dregs. There were many members of his household who had been treated with great kindness by their master, so they secretly conveyed his body out of the house and buried it at the foot of Mount Beimang, in the same grave at his wife.

There is a large tomb west of Mount Beimang that is called the Grave of Madam Lü by the local people. It is likely that Lü Buwei's clients did not dare to tell anyone that he was buried there.

When the king of Qin heard that Lü Buwei was dead, he wanted to see the body but was informed that it had disappeared. He then expelled all of his former retainers from the country and gave orders for a major manhunt to be carried out inside the capital. All those who had come to Lü Buwei from abroad were told that they would not be allowed to remain resident in Xianyang. Those who had received official appointments were fired and ordered to leave the country within three days. Anyone who allowed them to stay would be punished, along with their entire family.

There was a certain Li Si from Shangcai in the kingdom of Chu who was a student of the famous Xun Qing—this man was remarkable for the breadth of his learning. He traveled to the kingdom of Qin, where he took office with Lü Buwei as one of his housemen. Lü Buwei recommended Li Si to the king of Qin for his abilities, and he was appointed to the position of a minister without portfolio. Now, when the order was given to remove the men who owed their positions to Lü Buwei, Li Si was among their number. He was forced to leave Xianyang by the administrator of public order. On his way to the border, Li Si wrote a memorial. With the excuse that his letter contained top-secret information of vital importance to the government, he persuaded a postal courier to take it to the king of Qin. It read:

> I have always understood that a mountain does not spurn the smallest clod of earth that could go towards making it higher; an ocean does not spurn the slightest rivulet that could go towards making it deeper. Similarly, a king does

not neglect even the meanest of his subjects who could make his virtue manifest. In the past, when Lord Mu of Qin was hegemon over the Central States, he took Yao Yu from the Rong nomadic people to the west and Baili Xi from Wan to the east. He brought in Jian Shu from Song, and Pi Bao and Noble Grandson Qi from Jin. Meanwhile, Lord Xiao employed Shang Yang to compose a law code for Qin and King Hui used Zhang Yi in order to disrupt the Vertical Alliance. King Zhao had Fan Ju develop the plans for unification. These four rulers were happy to use their foreign advisors to help them achieve their ambitions—in what way did these men betray the trust that these rulers placed in them? If you insist on getting rid of these foreigners, Your Majesty, they will leave Qin and go to work for your enemies. In the future, it will be impossible to find men prepared to serve Qin loyally!

When the king of Qin read this letter, he came to his senses. He immediately rescinded his order to have these men thrown out of the country and sent someone in a carriage to fetch Li Si. He caught up with him at Mount Li. When Li Si arrived back in Xianyang, the king of Qin restored him to his former office and trusted him as much as ever he had.

Li Si persuaded the king of Qin as follows: "In the past when Lord Mu of Qin became hegemon, there were still large numbers of other states and the virtue of the Zhou dynasty had not yet declined to the point of no return—it was impossible for him to try and unify the country. From the time of Lord Xiao, the Zhou royal house entered its final collapse and the lords fought one another to conquer each other's territory until only six kingdoms remained. It has now been a couple of generations since Qin was the most powerful of the lot. With Qin's military might and Your Majesty's great wisdom, it will be as easy for you to conquer these other kingdoms as sweeping dust from the floor. However, this is not the moment to allow your people to engage in infighting; that way you will find yourself delaying until the other kingdoms have recovered their strength and recreated the Vertical Alliance. If that occurs, it will be far too late for regrets!"

"I want to conquer the other six kingdoms," the king said. "What plan do you suggest I adopt?"

"Han is near to Qin and it is weak," Li Si replied. "I recommend that you conquer Han first and strike fear into the hearts of all the other kings!"

The king of Qin followed his advice and appointed the Palace Historian Teng as the senior general. He attacked Han with an army of one hundred thousand men.

. . .

At this time, King Huanhui of Han was dead and Crown Prince An had come to the throne. There was a certain Prince Fei who was interested in statecraft and legal matters. When he saw how Han was being carved up, he repeatedly wrote to the king, but the king was not bright enough to give him a government position. When the Qin army attacked Han, His Majesty was very frightened. Prince Fei was quite certain of his own talents and decided to seek office in Qin. He suggested to the king of Han that he should go as an ambassador to Qin and beg them to stop attacking. The king of Han followed this recommendation. Prince Fei went west to have an audience with the king of Qin, at which he announced that the king of Han was prepared to surrender his country to become a subordinate territory. The king of Qin was delighted.

Prince Fei went on to say: "I have a plan that would allow Qin to destroy the Vertical Alliance and unite the entire realm under Your Majesty's rule. If you use my plan and Han is not destroyed, Wei and Chu do not accept vassalage, and Qi and Yan do not submit, you can cut my head off as an example. Let me be a warning to any vassal contemplating disloyalty to his lord!"

He presented the king of Qin with his works: *On the Difficulty of Persuasion, Solitary Indignation, The Five Vermin, Collected Speeches,* and so on. His writings totaled five hundred thousand words. The king of Qin read them and was very impressed. He appointed Prince Fei as a minister without portfolio and would often discuss matters of state with him.

Li Si was very jealous of the prince's abilities and slandered him to the king of Qin, saying: "All the princes are close to their own families—surely they cannot really serve a foreign king. When Qin attacked Han, they quickly sent Prince Fei to us. Who knows whether this was part of a plan to ruin us, as it was with Su Qin? You must not trust him!"

"Do you think I should expel him then?" the king of Qin asked.

"Prince Wuji of Wei and the Lord of Pingyuan both spent time in Qin," Li Si said. "In the end we were not able to use them and allowed them to go back home. They both ended up causing terrible trouble to Qin. Prince Fei is a brilliantly clever man. You had better kill him in order to clip Han's wings!"

The king of Qin had Prince Fei imprisoned in Yunyang, where he was going to kill him. "What crime have I committed?" the prince asked.

"One mountain cannot accommodate two tigers," his guards replied. "With the way that the world is today, if you aren't useful they execute you. You don't need to actually have committed a crime."

In his misery, Prince Fei composed a poem:

"Persuasion" is indeed difficult,
But what does "Indignation" achieve?
"The Five Vermin" have not been eliminated,
So my "Collected Speeches" are pointless!
Aromatic plants have always been picked for their scent;
Deer have always been killed for their musk.

That night, Prince Fei committed suicide by hanging himself with the string to his hat.

An old man wrote a poem bewailing this:

From what it says in his book he already knew the difficulties of
    persuasion,
Yet he turned his back on his country and his clan to flatter Qin.
Who will feel sad about his corpse being left behind in Yunyang,
When we think about Qu Yuan throwing himself into the Yangtze
    River?

When the king of Han heard that Prince Fei was dead, he was even more frightened than before. He requested permission to hand over his kingdom and become a vassal of the king of Qin. After that, His Majesty ordered the Palace Historian Teng to withdraw his troops.

• • •

One day the king of Qin was discussing things with Li Si, praising Prince Fei's great intelligence and bemoaning his death. Li Si stepped forward and said, "I would like to recommend a man for office. His name is Wei Liao and he comes from Daliang. He is exceptionally learned in military matters, and his talents are ten times greater than those of Prince Fei!"

"Where is this man?" the king asked.

"He is already in Xianyang," Li Si replied. "But he is very proud, so you cannot treat him like an ordinary vassal."

The king of Qin summoned him with all the courtesy due to an honored guest. When Wei Liao had an audience with His Majesty, he made a respectful gesture with his hands but did not bow. The king of Qin, however, responded very courteously; offering him the seat of honor and addressing him as "sir."

Wei Liao then stepped forward and said: "The relationship of the other kingdoms to Qin can be compared to that a commandery and its counties—if you split them up, they are easily destroyed, but if you allow them to unite they are very difficult to attack. When the Three

Jins were united, it was easy for them to see off the Earl of Zhi; when five kingdoms were united, they could put King Min of Qi to flight. You must consider this very carefully."

"Do you have a plan to suggest," the king of Qin asked, "that will make them split up and prevent them from joining together in the future?"

"The governments of these countries are all in the hands of powerful ministers," Wei Liao replied. "These men are not likely to be either particularly loyal or very intelligent. However, they do enjoy their riches! Your Majesty, if you do not begrudge the treasures in your store-houses, you could give enormous bribes to these men and prevent them from plotting effectively against you. It would not cost you more than three hundred thousand pieces of gold and will guarantee that the other kings are destroyed!"

The king of Qin was delighted with this idea. He appointed Wei Liao to the position of a senior advisor. He treated him with the utmost cer-emony and ensured that his clothing, food, and drink were exactly the same as his own. From time to time His Majesty would go to Wei Liao's residence and ask for advice on his knees.

"I have carefully observed the character and appearance of the king of Qin," Wei Liao said thoughtfully. "He has a broad face and large eyes, sloping shoulders like an eagle, and a voice like the snarl of a leopard—his heart is that of a tiger or a wolf, and he lacks compassion for others. When he needs someone's help, he will treat them with great deference, but if he does not need them, he will simply toss them aside. Right now the world is not united, and so he is happy to be polite to a commoner. If he succeeds in his ambition, we will all be lambs to the slaughter!"

One night, Wei Liao left without giving notice to anyone. The offi-cials in charge of the hostel where he was staying rushed to report this to the king of Qin. His Majesty felt as though he had just lost an arm. He sent chariots out to search for him in all directions and bring him back. He swore an oath to Wei Liao, promising that he would hence-forth hold the title of defender-in-chief and be in sole charge of the army, not to mention that all his disciples would hold the rank of gran-dee. He also withdrew a large sum of money from his treasury and had this issued to ambassadors, who in turn traveled to various other for-eign countries. There they were to identify which ministers were in favor and held great power, and then bribe them lavishly to find out the key secrets of each state.

The king of Qin again asked Wei Liao for advice on the order of unification, and he replied: "Han is weak and easy to attack, so you should go after them first. After that you had better tackle Zhao and Wei. Once the Three Jins have been destroyed, you need to raise an army to attack Chu. Once Chu has been conquered, can Yan and Qi be far behind?"

"Han has already declared itself one of my subordinate territories, and the king of Zhao has attended banquets at the palace here in Xianyang," the king of Qin said. "I have no reason to attack either of them, so what am I to do?"

"Zhao is a large country with a strong army," Wei Liao explained. "If they have the help of Han and Wei, they will not be easy to conquer. With Han having declared itself one of our dependent territories, it means that Zhao has lost half their usual support. If you are concerned, Your Majesty, about the fact that you have no excuse for attacking Zhao, then turn your armies against Wei first. The king of Zhao has a favorite minister named Guo Kai—he is a man of immeasurable greed. If I were to send my disciple Wang Ao to initiate talks with the king of Wei, while also offering large bribes to Guo Kai to ask for military assistance from the king of Zhao, they will certainly send their armies out. We can move our forces to attack them on the grounds that Zhao will have violated the peace treaty between our two countries."

"Good!" the king of Qin replied.

His Majesty ordered the senior general Huan Yi to take command of an army of one hundred thousand men and go out of the Hangu Pass, making sure that everyone knew they were on their way to attack Wei. He also sent Wei Liao's disciple, Wang Ao, to Wei, armed with fifty thousand pounds of gold to cover his expenses.

. . .

When Wang Ao arrived in Wei, he had an audience with His Majesty, at which he said: "The reason why the Three Jins have been able to resist Qin is because they have a close defensive relationship. Now Han has agreed to become a dependent territory and the king of Zhao has been in person to visit Xianyang, where he was guest of honor at a banquet hosted by the king of Qin. Thus we can say that Han and Zhao are both determined to serve Qin's interests. The Qin army has already arrived on your borders—your kingdom is in danger! If you were prepared to offer the city of Ye as a bribe to Zhao, you would be in a position to ask them for help. Zhao would certainly send troops to garrison

Ye . . . you could say that they will be looking after the city on your behalf!"

"Do you think this will convince the king of Zhao?" His Majesty asked.

Wang Ao lied through his teeth: "Guo Kai is the most important minister in the kingdom of Zhao today. He and I are old friends, and he will certainly help us."

The king of Wei followed his advice and prepared a map showing Ye and three other cities, which he gave to Wang Ao to present to the kingdom of Zhao when asking for military assistance.

Wang Ao began by giving three thousand pounds of gold to Guo Kai, to ensure his good will. Afterwards, he talked about the Wei cities. Having taken the bribe, Guo Kai spoke to King Daoxiang of Zhao as follows: "Qin has attacked Wei because they are intending to conquer their territory. Once Wei is gone, it will be Zhao next. They have offered you Ye and three other cities in the hope that you will help them. You ought to listen to them, Your Majesty!"

King Daoxiang sent Hu Zhe in command of fifty thousand men to take control of these lands. The king of Qin immediately ordered Huan Yi to advance his troops to attack Ye. Hu Zhe moved his army to counter this, and they fought a huge battle at Mount Donggu. Hu Zhe was defeated, and Huan Yi followed up his victory by chasing after the defeated soldiers, taking the city of Ye. After this, he was able to conquer another nine cities. Hu Zhe's troops made their stand at Yi'an, while sending a messenger to report this emergency to the king of Zhao. His Majesty gathered all his ministers to discuss the situation, and they all said: "The only person in the past who could stop the Qin army's advance was Lian Po. Although the Pang and the Le families have given us many fine generals, Pang Nuan is dead now, and the Le family has left no descendants. We only have Lian Po, who is living in the kingdom of Wei at the moment. Why don't you summon him?"

Guo Kai loathed Lian Po and was afraid that he might yet again achieve high office. Therefore, he slandered him to the king of Zhao, saying: "Lian Po is now nearly seventy years of age, and he is not at all the man he used to be. Furthermore, he quarreled with Le Sheng in the past, so if you summon him and then do not employ him, he will be very angry with you. Why don't you send someone to spy on him and find out if he is up to the job? If you summon him once you know his state of health, you will still be in plenty of time."

The king of Zhao was thus tricked into sending the eunuch Tang Jiu to present the old general with a suit of rhinoceros-hide armor and a team of four horses. Ostensibly this was a memento from a grateful monarch, but in fact it was a test of his health. Guo Kai secretly invited Tang Jiu to his house, where he wined and dined him, presenting the eunuch with a gift of twenty ingots of gold. Tang Jiu was amazed by his generosity and said that he did not dare to accept so munificent a gift, having done nothing to deserve it.

"There is something that you can do for me," Guo Kai said, "but I wouldn't dare to mention it before you have agreed to take my present."

Tang Jiu took the gold and asked, "What can I do for you, sir?"

"General Lian Po and I have never been friends," Guo Kai explained. "If you go on this journey and discover that he is indeed failing in health, then there is nothing more to be said. But if it turns out he is completely well, I want you to return and describe him to the king of Zhao as being at death's door, to convince His Majesty not to recall him. If you do that, you have earned each and every one of those ingots." Tang Jiu agreed to do this.

When Tang Jiu arrived in the kingdom of Wei, he had an audience with Lian Po as he had been instructed by the king of Zhao. "Has the Qin army now invaded Zhao?" Lian Po asked.

"How did you know?" Tang Jiu demanded.

"I have been living in Wei for a couple of years now without a single word from the king of Zhao," Lian Po explained. "Now suddenly he sends me a suit of fine armor and a team of horses—he must be planning to employ me again. That is how I realized what is going on."

"Don't you hate the king of Zhao?" Tang Jiu asked.

"I have been thinking day and night of how to help the Zhao people," Lian Po returned. "How could I hate the king of Zhao?"

He had Tang Jiu stay with him and eat, deliberately making a show of his excellent spirits. In a single meal, Lian Po polished off nearly a peck of rice and more than ten pounds of meat, wolfing it all down until he was full. Taking off the armor that was the king of Zhao's gift, he leapt onto the back of a horse and galloped around, showing off his skill at twirling a spear. Then he jumped off the horse and said to Tang Jiu, "I don't think I am one whit inferior to what I was when young! Please go back and tell the king of Zhao I will spend the rest of my life in repaying his kindness to me."

Tang Jiu could clearly see that Lian Po was in fine fettle. However, since he had taken bribes from Guo Kai, he had to go back to Handan and tell the king of Zhao: "Even though General Lian Po is old, he still eats and drinks well. However, he appears to have some kind of bladder disease. When he was sitting with me, although we were not together for long, he had to go and relieve himself three times."

The king of Zhao sighed and said, "If you are fighting a battle, you can't be wetting yourself every five minutes. Lian Po is too old for this."

He decided not to summon him back and instead sent more troops to reinforce Hu Zhe. These events occurred in the ninth year of the reign of King Daoxiang of Zhao, which was the eleventh year of the reign of King Zheng of Qin. Later on, the king of Chu discovered that Lian Po was living in Wei and sent someone to invite him to come to his country. Lian Po took up office as a general in Chu. However, the Chu troops were far inferior to those of Zhao—Lian Po became depressed, and in the end he died. How sad!

A historian wrote a poem:

Lian Po became famous as a general only in old age;
How could anyone believe the malicious gossip that he suffered bladder
    disease?
Think of how Chancellor Bo Pi was killed once the kingdom of Wu fell,
Why did Guo Kai imagine that he would live to enjoy his golden bribes?

. . .

At this time Wang Ao was still in Zhao, and he said to Guo Kai: "Aren't you worried that the kingdom of Zhao may fall? Why don't you encourage His Majesty to recall Lian Po?"

"The survival or collapse of Zhao is a matter for the government," Guo Kai said. "Lian Po is my enemy, and I am not going to allow him to come back to Zhao again!"

From this, Wang Ao could understand that he had no intention of putting the interests of the country above his own. He pressed on: "If Zhao is indeed destroyed, what will you do?"

"We are located between Chu and Qi. I will pick one of them and go there."

"Qin is fully powerful enough to conquer all the other kingdoms," Wang Ao said. "Qi and Chu are no safer than Zhao or Wei. In my opinion, you would do better to throw in your lot with Qin. The king of Qin is a man of large ideas who is prepared to abase himself in order to recruit clever men into his administration. He is always happy to meet men of talent."

"You come from Wei," Guo Kai said in a puzzled voice. "How do you know so much about the king of Qin?"

"My master is Wei Liao, who is at present the defender-in-chief of Qin," Wang Ao explained. "In fact, I am a grandee of Qin myself. The king of Qin is aware of the fact that you hold a crucial position in the government of Zhao, and that is why he ordered me to come here and make friends with you. The gold I've given you was in fact a present from His Majesty. If Zhao is destroyed, you must come to Qin, where the position of a senior minister is waiting for you. We will reward you with the finest estates in all of Zhao."

"If you are willing to recommend me to the king of Qin," Guo Kai assured him, "I will do everything you say."

Wang Ao gave him another seven thousand pounds of gold and said, "The king of Qin entrusted me with ten thousand pounds of gold, to be divided among the senior ministers and generals in Zhao. I have now given it all to you. In the future when we need help, I hope that you will come to our assistance."

"Since the king of Qin has been so generous to me," Guo Kai said happily, "if I did not do my very best to repay him, I really would be less than human!"

Wang Ao accordingly said goodbye to Guo Kai and returned to Qin. He handed back the remaining forty thousand pounds of gold to His Majesty and said, "I have used ten thousand pounds to deal with Guo Kai, and he will give us Zhao."

When the king of Qin realized that Zhao had no intention of recalling Lian Po, he ordered Huan Yi to advance his troops. King Daoxiang of Zhao was so horrified, he became sick and died.

. . .

King Daoxiang of Zhao had a son born of his queen whose name was Prince Jia. Later on, there was a courtesan in Zhao who was famous for her singing and dancing. King Daoxiang fell in love with her and had her move into the palace, whereupon she gave birth to a son: Prince Qian. King Daoxiang loved the courtesan and her son so much that he ignored Prince Jia's legal rights and appointed Prince Qian as the crown prince. His Majesty appointed Guo Kai to the position of Grand Tutor. Crown Prince Qian was not interested in studying, and Guo Kai soon learned to restrict his conversation to matters of sex, dogs, and horses, as a result of which the two of them got along very well. When King Daoxiang died, Guo Kai helped Crown Prince Qian to ascend the throne. Prince Jia was given a fief of three hundred households and ordered to remain resident in the capital. Guo Kai now took the position of prime minister. Huan Yi took advantage of the period of national mourning in Zhao to make a surprise attack on their army at Yi'an. In this battle, he beheaded General Hu Zhe and killed nearly one hundred thousand Zhao soldiers. Then he pressed close to Handan.

When Qian, king of Zhao, was still just the crown prince, he heard much of the abilities of Li Mu, the governor of Dai. He now sent someone to report this emergency and give him the seals of the commander-in-chief. In Dai, Li Mu had an army of one thousand five hundred chariots, thirteen thousand cavalrymen, and fifty thousand foot-soldiers—all the best of their kind. Leaving behind three hundred chariots, three thousand cavalrymen, and ten thousand infantry soldiers to guard Dai, he set off with the remainder and made camp outside the walls of Handan. He went into the city alone to have an audience with the king of Zhao.

The king of Zhao asked how the Qin army was to be stopped. Li Mu presented his opinion: "The Qin army has a fearsome reputation as a result of the many victories that they have won and their vanguard is extremely tough—it will not be easy to defeat them. I will only accept your order to fight if you are prepared to give me full authority to act, without requiring endless permissions."

The king of Zhao agreed to this and then asked: "Do you have enough soldiers from Dai for this battle?"

"I don't have enough soldiers to fight an offensive campaign," Li Mu replied. "But there are more than enough for defense."

"Our entire army is one hundred thousand men," His Majesty said. "I am going to give you the generals Zhao Cong and Yan Ju, each with fifty thousand soldiers under their command."

Li Mu bowed and accepted His Majesty's command. He advanced to make camp at Feilei, where he constructed stockades with very strong defenses. His troops stayed inside, not coming out to fight. Every day he would hold a party for his officers, as well as having them divide their forces into teams to practice their archery. The officers enjoyed the parties, but when they wanted to go out to fight, Li Mu refused to allow it.

. . .

The Qin general, Huan Yi, said, "In the past Lian Po prevented Wang He from attacking any further by retreating behind strong encampments. Li Mu is using exactly the same strategy." He divided his army in half and sent them to make a surprise attack on the city of Ganquan. Zhao Cong asked permission to go to the rescue, but Li Mu said: "If they attack and we go to the rescue, it means that we are always on the back foot. This is something that no military strategist would countenance. We had better go and attack their camp while they are busy at Ganquan. Their camp is sure to be pretty much empty, and they have watched us sit behind our walls for so long that they will be unprepared. If we make a surprise attack and take their camp, that should cramp Huan Yi's ambitions."

He divided his troops into three groups and had them advance on the enemy encampment under cover of darkness. Since they were not expecting an attack by the Zhao army, they suffered a terrible defeat. More than ten junior generals were killed in this one engagement, not to mention countless officers and men. The defeated troops fled to Ganquan to report this disaster to Huan Yi, who was furious. He gathered up his entire army and advanced to do battle. Li Mu was waiting for him, his army drawn up in two wings. The troops from Dai advanced bravely and clashed with the vanguard of the Qin army. Now the left and right wings advanced too. Huan Yi could not withstand their onslaught and fled back to Xianyang, having suffered another terrible defeat. When the king of Zhao heard of Li Mu's success in stopping Qin, he declared: "Li Mu is my Bai Qi!" He granted him the title of Lord of Wu'an and enfeoffed him with ten thousand households. King Zheng of Qin was so furious at Huan Yi's defeat that he demoted him to the status of a commoner. He ordered the senior generals Wang Jian and Yang Duanhe to march on Zhao with their respective armies.

If you want to know who won and who lost, READ ON.

Chapter One Hundred and Six

Wang Ao comes up with a plan to get Li Mu killed.

Tian Guang cuts his throat after recommending Jing Ke.

In the fifth year of the reign of Qian, king of Zhao, there was an earthquake in the Dai region, in which more than half the houses collapsed and a rent opened up on a flat plain that was more than one hundred and thirty paces long. In the wake of this, Handan suffered a terrible drought. A children's song circulated widely among the people:

> The Qin people laugh,
> The Zhao people cry.
> If you don't believe me,
> Look at the hairs on the ground.

The following year, long white hair-like substances more than a foot long were observed emerging from the ground. Guo Kai kept this a secret since he did not want the king of Zhao to know about it. At this precise moment, the king of Qin sent the senior generals Wang Jian and Yang Duanhe to invade Zhao again, proceeding along different routes. Wang Jian advanced his army from Taiyuan, while Yang Duanhe marched from Mount Chang. His Majesty also sent Palace Historian Teng in command of one hundred thousand men to make camp at Shangdang and move to assist if required. Crown Prince Dan of Yan was still a hostage in Qin, and he knew that once they had mobilized such a huge army to attack Zhao, the disaster would also affect Yan. He secretly sent someone to take a message to the king of Yan for him, alerting him to the need to prepare for war. He also told the king of Yan that he should pretend to be ill and request the return of the crown prince from Xianyang. The king of Yan did indeed do exactly as requested and sent an ambassador to Qin.

"Until the king of Yan is actually dead," the king of Qin said, "the crown prince is not going to be allowed to return. Only when crows' heads turn white and horses grow horns will the crown prince be allowed to go home early!"

Crown Prince Dan looked up to the sky and screamed his resentment. His anger reached the cerulean Heavens and the crows' heads all turned white. The king of Qin still refused to let him go. Crown Prince Dan now had no choice but to change his clothes and alter his appearance to pretend that he was just a servant. Thus he was able to smuggle himself out through the Hangu Pass and escape to Yan, traveling day and night.

To this day in the southern part of Dingzhou city in Zhending Prefecture, there is a tower called the Cockcrow Tower. When Crown Prince Dan of Yan was escaping from Qin, this is where he heard the cocks' crowing early in the morning and set off on his journey home.

The king of Qin was so caught up in his campaigns against Han and Zhao that he simply did not have time to punish Crown Prince Dan for his escape.

. . .

Let us now turn to another part of the story. Li Mu, the Lord of Wu'an, had his main army make camp at Mount Huiquan. He had a series of camps constructed, located just a couple of *li* apart from one another. When the Qin army arrived by their two separate routes, they did not dare to advance. As soon as the king of Qin got wind of this news, he sent Wang Ao to join Wang Jian's camp.

"Li Mu is one of the most famous generals in the north, and it will not be easy to defeat him," Wang Ao declared. "You must go to him and ask for a peace treaty. You do not actually need to conclude such a treaty, you just need to set up traffic between our two camps. I will do the rest."

Wang Jian did indeed send someone to the Zhao encampment to request a peace treaty, and Li Mu sent a messenger back to reply to these overtures. Meanwhile, Wang Ao went to Zhao and informed Guo Kai: "Li Mu has secretly agreed with the Qin army that on the day that the kingdom of Zhao falls, he will receive Dai Commandery as his fief. You must inform the king of Zhao of these developments and get him to replace Li Mu with one of his other generals. I will speak to the king of Qin, and you will have your reward."

Guo Kai understood exactly what was required of him. He went to have a private audience with the king of Zhao, at which he simply repeated what Wang Ao had told him. His Majesty ordered his servants to investigate the truth of this, and they discovered that Li Mu had indeed been in communication with Wang Jian, with letters traveling back and forth. His Majesty now believed that everything he had been told was true, and so he discussed his plans with Guo Kai.

Guo Kai presented his opinion: "Zhao Cong and Yan Ju are at present out with the army. If you were to send an envoy armed with your military tally out there, you could have Zhao Cong appointed as commander-in-chief on the spot to replace Li Mu. You can say that you are planning to make Li Mu the prime minister. He will not be suspicious of that."

The king of Zhao followed this advice and sent Sima Shang to the encampment at Mount Huiquan, with the military tally, to announce His Majesty's new orders.

"Our two armies are lined up against each other," Li Mu said, "and the fate of the country is trembling in the balance. You cannot dismiss me now! Even though this is His Majesty's order, I refuse to obey!"

Sima Shang secretly informed Li Mu: "Guo Kai has slandered you to His Majesty, accusing you of treason. The king of Zhao believes every word that he says, and that is why he wants to recall you. He may say that he is intending to appoint you to be the next prime minister, but that is all lies!"

"Guo Kai has already lied through his teeth about Lian Po, and now he is busy slandering me!" Li Mu said angrily. "I ought to march my troops on the capital and begin by removing this wicked creature from His Majesty's orbit: after that, I can go and fight Qin!"

"If you turn your troops against the capital," Sima Shang said, "everyone who knows you will understand that you are completely loyal, but those who do not will say that you are a traitor. All you will do is give further credence to these horrible rumors. With your remarkable talents, General, you will achieve great things wherever you go; why should you have to stay in Zhao?"

Li Mu sighed and said: "I have often criticized Le Yi and Lian Po for failing to serve the Zhao government to the end. I never expected that I would end up in the same situation!" Then he continued: "Zhao Cong cannot control the officers from Dai. I will refuse to give him my seals of office."

He left the seals hanging in his tent and fled into the night, dressed in plain clothes, heading for the kingdom of Wei. Zhao Cong was very pleased because Guo Kai had recommended him for promotion, and he was furious with Li Mu for refusing to hand over his seals of office. He sent a group of strong knights out to track down and arrest Li Mu. They caught up with him in a hostel. Taking advantage of the fact that he was drunk, they tied him up and cut his head off. When they returned, they presented his head. Li Mu was perhaps the finest general of his day, and yet he ended up being killed by Guo Kai—is that not terrible?

A historian wrote a poem about this:

> He made his reputation by stopping Qin's invasion of Dai,
> The security of the entire kingdom of Zhao rested on his shoulders!
> Guo Kai was so greedy for the gold of a foreign power
> That he was prepared to destroy his country for a moment's
> gratification!

Sima Shang did not dare to go back to court, so he secretly collected his wife and family and fled to the coast. Once he had possession of Li Mu's seals, Zhao Cong took control of the army as commander-in-chief; Yan Ju was his deputy. The troops from Dai were very loyal to Li Mu, and they were furious when they discovered he had been murdered. They abandoned the rest of the Zhao army overnight, slipping away through the mountain valleys. Zhao Cong could do nothing to prevent this.

When the Qin army heard that Li Mu was dead, they held a huge banquet in the middle of the camp. Afterwards, Wang Jian and Yang Duanhe advanced their troops in concert. Zhao Cong and Yan Ju discussed the situation—the former wanted to divide their forces to go and rescue Taiyuan and Changshan.

"You have only just been appointed as the new commander-in-chief, and the situation within the army has not yet been stabilized," Yan Ju said. "If you keep your troops together, they will be fine in defense. If you split them up, they will be severely weakened!"

Before he had even finished speaking, a mounted sentry reported: "Wang Jian is attacking the city of Langmeng with great ferocity. It will fall at any moment."

"If they take Langmeng," Zhao Cong squawked, "that will open up the route to the Jinjing Pass. The two halves of the Qin army will then be able to attack Changshan together. That would make the position of Handan untenable. We have no choice but to go to the rescue!" Ignoring Yan Ju's remonstrance, he gave orders to strike camp.

Wang Jian was immediately informed of this development by his spies. He had troops waiting in ambush at the valley and scouts stationed on high land. They waited until one half of Zhao Cong's army had passed and then fired the siege engines, whereupon the troops waiting in ambush rose up as one man and attacked. The Zhao army was cut in half by their assault so that they were unable to help each other. Wang Jian led the main body of his army forward in an attack that crushed all that stood in their way. Zhao Cong moved to intercept the enemy, but his troops were defeated and he himself killed. Yan Ju collected the battered remains of the Zhao army and fled back to Handan. The Qin army captured Langmeng and then advanced on the Jinjing Pass. There they proceeded to attack and capture the city of Xiayi. Meanwhile, Yang Duanhe had successfully concluded his campaign, capturing Changshan and the surrounding area. He marched on Handan and laid siege to the city.

When the king of Qin heard that his two armies had both been victorious, he ordered the Palace Historian Teng to move his army to Han to take over their territory. King An of Han was so panic-stricken that he simply handed over all his cities and became a vassal of the Qin king. From this point onwards, the lands of Han were Yingchuan Commandery in the kingdom of Qin. This occurred in the ninth year of the reign of An, king of Han, which was the seventeenth year of the reign of Zheng, king of Qin.

The state of Han was founded when Viscount Wu received these lands as a fief from Jin. Three generations later, Viscount Xian had taken over the government of Jin, and then, three generations after that, Viscount Kang had killed the Earl of Zhi. Viscount Kang of Han's son had been the first marquis—Lord Jing—and he was the first ruler of Han to be accounted independent of Jin's authority. Six generations later, King Xuanhui was the first to take the title of monarch of this kingdom. Four generations after him, King An handed his country over to Qin. From the sixth year of the rule of Viscount Kang to the ninth year of the reign of King Xuanhui, Han was an independent state for eighty years. From the tenth year of King Xuanhui's reign to the ninth year of King An, when the country was finally destroyed, Han was a monarchy for ninety-four years. After this, the number of Qin's enemies had been reduced to five.

A historian wrote of these events:

> Han Yuan was the founder of the family, enfeoffed with ten thousand
>   households.
> The finest of his many descendants was the brilliant Han Jue.
> It was thanks to this man that the orphan of the Zhao clan survived;
> He accumulated much merit by his virtuous actions.
> To begin with, the Han family was one of the six ministerial clans;
> In the end, they divided the state of Jin together with Wei and Zhao.
> When the Vertical Alliance failed to hold them together,
> It was Han who kowtowed to Qin and became a vassal state.
> Not even all the remarkable talents of their ambassador, Prince Fei,
> Could save the kingdom from destruction then!

. . .

When the Qin army laid siege to Handan, Yan Ju mobilized all his
forces to defend the city. The king of Zhao was terrified and wanted to
send ambassadors to neighboring countries to ask for help. Guo Kai
stepped forward and said: "The king of Han is now a vassal of Qin. Yan
and Wei are so busy defending themselves that they have no time to
spare for anyone else. Whom are we going to ask to come to our aid? In
my humble opinion, given the enormous military might that Qin can
bring to bear, you had better simply hand over your country to them
and accept a fief as a marquis."

Qian, king of Zhao, wanted to follow his advice. Prince Jia threw
himself to the ground and wept bitterly: "How can you abandon the
lands and ancestral temples entrusted to your care by our former kings?
I am going to fight to the death with Yan Ju. If by some horrible mischance the city does fall, we still have several hundred *li* of land in Dai
Commandery. You could establish an independent country there. Why
should you stretch out your hands for them to put you in chains?"

"If the city falls," Guo Kai returned, "His Majesty will be taken prisoner. How can he possibly make it as far as Dai?"

Prince Jia drew his sword and pointed it at Guo Kai. "How dare you
talk like this? Are you trying to bring the country to its knees by your
malicious and evil murmurings? I am going to kill you."

The king of Zhao urged them to calm down and the meeting broke
up. King Qian returned to his palace, and having no idea what else to
do, he spent his time in getting drunk.

Guo Kai wanted to meet the Qin army to arrange for a schedule to
hand over the city, but there was nothing he could do about the fact
that Prince Jia had taken all his retainers and every member of his fam-

ily out to help Yan Ju guard the walls. Not so much as a drop of water could leave the city unnoticed, and so Guo Kai had no way to make contact with the attacking army. At this time the kingdom of Zhao had suffered famine for several years in a row. The population that had once lived outside the city walls had now fled, and the Qin army found they could get nothing to eat in the wilds. There was a considerable amount of grain stored inside the city, whose inhabitants had more than enough to eat. No matter how fiercely they were attacked, the city of Handan stood firm. Wang Jian discussed the situation with Yang Duanhe, and they agreed to temporarily withdraw their forces fifty *li*, to facilitate the transport of food. When the people inside the city saw that the Qin forces had withdrawn, they gradually slackened their defenses. They agreed to open the city gates once a day, to allow people to go in and out. Guo Kai took advantage of this to send one of his most trusted servants out of Handan with a secret missive that he was to take to the Qin encampment. The letter said:

> I want to surrender the city to you, but I have not been able to do so due to circumstances beyond my control. The king of Zhao is already in a complete panic. If the king of Qin would agree to come here in person, I will do my very best to persuade the king of Zhao to give you everything that you want.

When Wang Jian received this missive, he immediately sent someone to communicate its contents to the king of Qin. Zheng, king of Qin, took personal command of an army of thirty thousand picked men and ordered the senior general Li Xin to escort him. Traveling by way of Taiyuan, they arrived at Handan and joined the siege of the city. The attackers were now under orders to advance day and night. When the people on the city walls saw in the distance a new huge banner reading "The King of Qin," they rushed to report this development to King Qian. His Majesty was now even more petrified with fright.

"If the king of Qin is here in person," Guo Kai remarked, "it is a sign that this time he is determined to capture Handan. You cannot put your trust in people like Prince Jia and Yan Ju. I hope that you will make your own decision about how to deal with this crisis, Your Majesty."

"I want to surrender to Qin," the king said, "but I am afraid that they will kill me."

"Qin did not kill the king of Han after he surrendered, so why should they kill Your Majesty?" Guo Kai asked. "If you present the king of Qin with Bian He's jade disc and a map of the lands of Handan, I am sure that he will be delighted."

"I am sure that you are right. Please draft a document of surrender for me."

Guo Kai wrote out the text and again presented his opinion to His Majesty: "Even though I have now prepared this document of surrender for you, Prince Jia will try and stop you. I have been informed that the king of Qin has his main camp by the West Gate. You must go there under the pretext of patrolling the walls. If you were to open the gates and present these tokens, I am sure that you wouldn't need to worry that they might be refused."

The king of Zhao was now so overwhelmed that he was not prepared to listen to anyone except Guo Kai. In this critical situation, he found he had no resources of his own to call upon, so he was reduced to doing what someone else told him.

Yan Ju was inspecting his forces at the North Gate when he heard that the king of Zhao had left the West Gate with presents for the Qin army. He was absolutely horrified. Prince Jia arrived on a lathered horse and said, "The people on the walls have hoisted the flag of surrender as ordered by the king of Zhao. Any moment now, the Qin army will enter the city."

"I am going to hold the North Gate even if it kills me," Yan Ju proclaimed. "Go and collect your family, my prince, and bring them here as quickly as you possibly can. We will go to Dai together and plan the restoration of the kingdom of Zhao from there."

Prince Jia followed this advice and led several hundred members of his family and household out of the North Gate together with Yan Ju himself. They fled to Dai under cover of darkness. Yan Ju encouraged Prince Jia to crown himself king of Dai, so that he would be able to take command of the people there. To show his recognition of all that Li Mu had done in the service of the state, King Jia restored his titles and built a shrine to his memory, thereby gaining the gratitude of the people of Dai. He sent an ambassador east with instructions to make peace with Yan. At the same time he stationed his army in Shanggu, to prevent any invasion by the Qin army. This did much to stabilize the situation in the kingdom of Dai. No more of this now.

. . .

After Zheng, king of Qin, had agreed to accept the king of Zhao's surrender, he traveled to Handan as quickly as he could, taking up residence in the Zhao royal palace. The king of Zhao had audience with His Majesty using the ceremonies appropriate to a vassal, and the king of Qin accepted this—there were many old ministers in tears during the proceedings. The following day, the king of Qin took possession of Bian He's jade disc. Laughing, he said to his assembled ministers, "My ancestor gave fifteen cities for this and still did not get it." Afterwards, the king of Qin gave orders that the lands of Zhao would be reorganized as Julu Commandery and established a garrison there. He sent the king of Zhao to live in Fangling and appointed Guo Kai to be a senior minister. The king of Zhao now realized how he and his country had been betrayed by Guo Kai. Sighing, he said: "If Li Mu was still here, the people of Qin would never have been able to capture Handan."

At Fangling, people lived inside caves, which were otherwise just like regular houses. The king of Zhao moved into one of these, and promptly noticed the sound of trickling water. He asked his entourage about this.

"There are four rivers in Chu," they replied, "the Yangtze, the Han, the Ju, and the Zhang. This is the Ju River, which flows from Mount Fang to join the Han and the Yangtze."

The king of Zhao sighed sadly: "A river is a heartless thing. It can go and join the Han and the Yangtze, but I am cooped up here. No matter how much I may long for my hometown a thousand *li* away, I will never see it again!"

Thus he composed the "Lament of the Mountain River":

> The caves of Mount Fang are now my palace,
> The waters of the Ju River have become my wine.
> I will never again hear the music of the zither and the flute,
> My ears will henceforth be filled by the sounds of bubbling water!
> The river is a heartless thing!
> It wends its own way to join the Han and the Yangtze.
> Though I was once the lord of a kingdom of ten thousand chariots,
> It is only in my dreams that I can return to my old home.
> What brought me to these dire straits?
> The malicious gossip of a wicked man.
> My loyal ministers have all been killed,
> The altars of soil and grain have been desecrated.
> I was told of this but I did not listen . . .
> How can I blame the king of Qin for my fate?

His Majesty was bored to tears during the long nights; every time he sang this song, his servants were moved by how much he suffered. In the end he became sick and bedridden. When Jia, king of Dai, heard that the king of Zhao was dead, he gave him the posthumous title of King Youmiu—meaning "Deluded."

There is a poem that testifies to this:

> King Fuchai of Wu was killed by the wicked flattery of Bo Pi;
> Qian, king of Zhao, died as a result of Guo Kai's greed.
> If you keep your distance from greedy flatterers,
> You will keep your blessings for ten thousand years.

The king of Qin stood down his army and returned to Xianyang, allowing his army to rest and recuperate for a while. Guo Kai had amassed so much gold that he could not possibly carry it with him; instead, he hid it all in the cellars of his mansion at Handan. When everything was over, he spoke to the king of Qin and asked for time off to return to Zhao to collect his property. The king of Qin laughed and gave him permission. On arrival in Handan, he opened the cellars and recovered all his gold, which filled several carts. However, on his way back to Xianyang, he was killed by bandits on the road and they stole the gold. Some people said, "This was the work of Li Mu's retainers!" Alas! He betrayed his country for money and all it brought him was death. Is this not stupid?

. . .

Let us now turn to another part of the story. After Crown Prince Dan of Yan returned home, his hatred of the king of Qin was so great that he spent every coin in his coffers to gain a great number of retainers, hoping to plot his revenge against him. He obtained the services of brave knights like Xia Fu and Song Yi, and he treated these men with the greatest generosity. There was also a man named Qin Wuyang. At the age of thirteen, he had killed an enemy in the marketplace in broad daylight, and nobody present had dared to move a muscle. The crown prince pardoned him for his crime and had him join his household. After the Qin general Fan Wuqi had angered His Majesty, he had fled for his life to Yan, hiding deep in the mountains. When he heard how much the crown prince appreciated men of honor, he came out and gave his allegiance to him. Crown Prince Dan treated him as a senior retainer. He built a castle east of the Yi River in which the general could reside: this was called the Fan Mansion.

The Grand Tutor, Ju Wu, remonstrated as follows: "Qin is a country of wolves and tigers. They are gulping down one kingdom after another. Even if you are one of their allies they may still attack you, not to mention if you harbor one of their most wanted criminals! What you are doing is like stroking a dragon the wrong way—you are sure to get hurt! Why don't you send General Fan to attack the Xiongnu and put him out of the way? Then you can ally with the Three Jins to the west, Chu and Qi to the south, and the Xiongnu to the north. In that case you might be able to withstand Qin."

"The plan that you have suggested, Grand Tutor, is one that would take years to bring into effect," Crown Prince Dan exclaimed. "I am in a hurry and cannot wait that long! Furthermore, General Fan came to me when he was at the very end of his tether—I helped him because I felt sorry for him. I am not proposing to abandon General Fan somewhere out in the desert because I am afraid of Qin's military might! Even if this decision brings about my own demise, I am not going to change my mind. I hope that you can come up with some other plan to help me."

"For a weak country like Yan to fight the mighty Qin is like throwing a feather onto a stove," Ju Wu declared. "Of course it is going to get burned up! Or you could say it is like throwing an egg against a rock— it is going to smash! I am a stupid and ignorant man and cannot possibly help Your Royal Highness come up with a sensible plan. However, I am acquainted with a certain Master Tian Guang. He is exceptionally clever and extremely brave, not to mention being a man of great learning. If you are determined to take on Qin, my prince, you could not do better than ask Master Tian for help."

"I have never been introduced to Master Tian," the crown prince said. "I would like you to arrange a meeting for me."

"Your wish is my command," Ju Wu said.

He immediately drove his carriage to Tian Guang's house and announced: "Crown Prince Dan feels great admiration for you, sir, and he would very much appreciate your advice. Please do not refuse!"

"The crown prince is a member of the royal family," Tian Guang said, "so I would not expect him to come here in person. However, if he does not mind the fact that I am of humble status and would still like to receive the benefits of my advice, I will go and see him. How could I dare to refuse?"

"The crown prince is very lucky that you are prepared to meet him!" Ju Wu said. He and Tian Guang then rode in the same carriage as they traveled to the crown prince's palace. When Crown Prince Dan heard that Tian Guang had arrived, he went out in person to greet him. Seizing the reins, His Royal Highness helped Tian Guang down from the chariot; retreating backwards before him, he bowed twice as a sign of respect. Kneeling down, he brushed off the seat where the master was to sit. Tian Guang was now an old man and so hobbled forward to the seat of honor. Those watching were all trying to stifle their laughter.

The crown prince sent his servants away and then stood up from his seat to speak: "In the situation in which we find ourselves today, Qin and Yan cannot coexist. I have heard that you are a wise and brave man, capable of developing unusual plans to deal with any crisis—can you save Yan from disaster?"

"I have heard it said that when a blood-horse is in the peak of condition it can gallop one thousand *li* in a single day, but once it gets old, even a mule can overtake it," Tian Guang replied. "Grand Tutor Ju Wu knew what I was like in my prime, but he does not seem to realize that I have grown old."

"I know that you have spent a great deal of time traveling, sir, so do you know of some person whose wisdom and bravery is the equivalent of what you had when you were young?" Crown Prince Dan inquired. "Perhaps you could recommend such a man to us instead?"

Tian Guang shook his head. "That is very difficult . . . very difficult indeed. However, you have a number of fine retainers in your household, Your Highness. Perhaps I might be permitted to meet them?"

The crown prince immediately summoned Xia Fu, Song Yi, and Qin Wuyang and introduced them to Tian Guang, who looked at them one by one, asking their names. He then said to the crown prince, "I have inspected all of your retainers, Your Royal Highness, and not one of them is suitable. Xia Fu is a brave man, but the moment he gets angry his face turns red. Song Yi likewise is brave, but the moment he gets angry his face becomes set. Qin Wuyang is brave too, but when he gets angry he goes pale. If you show your temper on your face and other people notice it, how can you ever hope to achieve anything? I know of a man called Master Jing, who is extremely brave but never shows his emotions by even the slightest sign. He would seem to be better than anyone you can call upon."

"What is this Master Jing's name?" Crown Prince Dan asked. "Where does he come from?"

"Master Jing's full name is Jing Ke," Tian Guang explained. "Originally his surname was Qing—he is a descendant of Grandee Qing Feng of Qi. When Qing Feng fled to Wu, his family settled in Zhufang. When Chu executed him, his family fled to Wey and took up residence there. Jing Ke himself tried to seek service with Lord Yuan of Wey on the basis of his swordcraft, but Lord Yuan did not want to employ him. When Qin captured these lands and established the Dong Commandery, Jing Ke fled to Yan. It was at that point that he changed his surname to Jing.

Everyone calls him Master Jing. He is a great drinker and has become very friendly with the musician Gao Jianli. They go drinking together in the marketplace of the Yan capital. When they are drunk, Gao Jianli plays his lute and Jing Ke sings in harmony with his melody. When he has finished his song, he bursts into tears because he thinks there is no place for him in the world. This man is both clever and cunning—I could never have been his equal!"

"I have never had any dealings with this Master Jing," Crown Prince Dan said. "Please introduce me to him."

"Jing Ke is poor, and I pay for his wine," Tian Guang said. "He ought to listen to what I say."

Crown Prince Dan escorted Tian Guang to the gate of the palace and helped him into the carriage that he normally rode in himself. He ordered one of the palace eunuchs to act as charioteer. When Tian Guang got into the carriage, the crown prince instructed him: "What we have been discussing is an important matter of state. Do not mention it to anyone else."

Tian Guang laughed and said, "I would not dream of it!"

Tian Guang rode in his carriage to the wine shop where Jing Ke was drinking. Jing Ke and Gao Jianli were there together, half-drunk. Gao Jianli was playing his lute. When Tian Guang heard the sound, he got down from his carriage and walked straight in, calling for Master Jing. Gao Jianli removed himself and his instrument. When Tian Guang and Jing Ke met, he invited the latter to come to his house and then said: "You always complain that there is nobody who understands your true worth. I have always agreed with you. However, I am old now and there is little that I can do about it. I cannot help you to achieve the things of which you are capable. You are a young man—do you intend to try your own strength?"

"I would love to prove what I can do," Jing Ke declared. "I have never met the right person to help me."

"Crown Prince Dan economizes on his own expenses in order to maintain the knights in his service," Tian Guang said. "Everyone in the kingdom of Yan knows that! Since His Royal Highness did not know of my age and poor state of health, he summoned me today to discuss matters of state. Since we are friends and I know just what you are capable of, I recommended you to His Royal Highness in my place. I hope that you will go immediately to the crown prince's palace."

"Since you have commanded me to do so, sir," Jing Ke said, "how could I refuse?"

Tian Guang wanted to give a spur to Jing Ke's ambitions, so he picked up his sword and said with a sigh: "I have heard it said that when a man has things to do, nothing and nobody should be allowed to stand in his way! Today, the crown prince discussed various matters with me that touch upon issues of national security and warned me not to mention them to anyone else. That means he suspects me. I could do nothing to help His Royal Highness with his troubles and instead find myself the object of his suspicions. I am going to use my death to absolve myself from blame. Please go at once to inform His Royal Highness of this." He then drew his sword to commit suicide by cutting his own throat.

Jing Ke wept at this tragedy. However, just at that moment a messenger arrived from the crown prince to ask if Master Jing was coming or not. Jing Ke realized that the crown prince was sincere in seeking his assistance and got into the carriage that Tian Guang had just used, heading for the crown prince's palace. The crown prince greeted Jing Ke just exactly as he had Tian Guang, but then he looked around and asked, "Has Master Tian not come with you?"

"Having heard your instructions," Jing Ke explained, "the master wanted to use his death to show that he would never divulge your secrets. He has committed suicide."

The crown prince threw up his hands in horror. Weeping, he exclaimed: "It is my fault that he is dead! How could I kill an innocent man?" It was a long time before he stopped crying. He asked Jing Ke to take the seat of honor and then, standing before him, he dropped to his knees to kowtow. Jing Ke hastily responded. "Master Tian Guang did me the honor of recommending you to my service," Crown Prince Dan said. "This may be said to be a blessing from Heaven. I hope that you will not refuse to come to my assistance."

"Why are you so frightened of Qin?" Jing Ke asked.

"Qin can be compared to a tiger or a wolf," Crown Prince Dan said. "No matter how much they eat, they are hungry for more. The king of Qin will not be satisfied until he has conquered every inch of land within the four seas and made every king submit to him in vassalage. Now the king of Han has already handed over all his lands and they have become a commandery of Qin, after which Wang Jian moved his armies to attack Zhao, taking their king prisoner. Now that Zhao is gone, Yan is going to be next. This is why I cannot sleep at night and why my food turns to ashes in my mouth."

"Is it your plan to raise the largest army that you can and fight to see who can win," Jing Ke asked, "or do you have some other intention?"

"Yan is a small and weak country," he replied, "which has repeatedly suffered incursions from enemy armies. Now Prince Jia of Zhao has declared himself King of Dai and wants us to join him in an alliance to defend against Qin. However, I am worried that even if I mobilize every single able-bodied man in the country, they will not be able to withstand just one of Qin's armies. Furthermore, although we are nominally allied to the king of Dai, we have yet to see whether he is as powerful as he says. Wei and Qi are now allied to Qin, and Chu is far too far away to help. Everyone is terrified of Qin's military might, and they are not prepared to ally against them. In my humble opinion, the only thing left to do is to obtain the services of some brave knight and send him on a mission to Qin armed with lavish gifts. Driven by his greed, the king of Qin will let the ambassador get close to him and he can then take advantage of that moment to take him hostage. With the king of Qin as a hostage, he can be forced to disgorge all the land that he has conquered from other kingdoms. That would be the best plan, I think. Of course, the other option is to assassinate the king of Qin. Each of his generals has many troops under his command, and they will not be prepared to take orders from one another. Once the king of Qin is gone, his country will be ripped apart by civil war. That is a country where everyone is suspicious of everyone else. After the king is dead, we can join with Chu and Wei to reestablish Han and Zhao; united, we can destroy Qin. In that case, everything will go back to normal. It is up to you to say if you are willing to join in!"

Jing Ke was sunk in thought for a long time. Then he replied: "This is an important matter of state. I am afraid that I come from far too low a social level to be able to complete such a mission!"

Crown Prince Dan kowtowed and said, "My life is in your hands. Please do not refuse!"

Jing Ke insisted again that he was unworthy of such trust, but in the end he was forced to agree. The crown prince appointed Jing Ke as a senior minister and built him a mansion to one side of that which he had previously erected for Fan Wuqi. This place was known as Jing Castle. Crown Prince Dan visited him every day, holding a grand feast in his honor. He gave him chariots and horses, not to mention beautiful women and anything else he had set his heart on. He was always afraid of not doing enough for Jing Ke.

One day the two men were at the crown prince's palace and wandered around, admiring the lakes and other water features. There was a large turtle sitting by the water, and Jing Ke happened to shoot it with a clay shot—the crown prince promptly presented him with a shot of solid gold to replace the clay one. On another occasion, they were out riding together and the crown prince was riding a fine horse, capable of galloping a thousand *li* in a day. Jing Ke happened to mention that he thought horse liver delicious. A short time later, the palace cooks presented him with a dish of liver; the horse that had been killed was Crown Prince Dan's mount. His Royal Highness told Jing Ke about how Fan Wuqi had offended the king of Qin and come to the kingdom of Yan. Jing Ke wanted to meet him, so the crown prince held a banquet on the Huayang Tower, which the two men were invited to attend. He had his own concubine serve wine and then ordered her to play the *qin* to entertain his guests. Jing Ke caught sight of her beautiful pale hands and exclaimed, "How lovely!" When the banquet was over, His Highness had a eunuch present a jade box to Jing Ke. When he opened it and looked inside, he discovered the concubine's hands. This was done to make it clear to Jing Ke that the crown prince begrudged him nothing. Jing Ke sighed and said, "How generously His Highness has treated me! Only my death can repay him!"

Do you know what Jing Ke did next? READ ON.

Chapter One Hundred and Seven

On presenting a map, Jing Ke's assassination attempt throws the Qin palace into chaos.

After a discussion of military strategy, Wang Jian replaces Li Xin.

Jing Ke was always interested in discussing swordcraft with other people, but very rarely found anyone who knew more than he did. However, he greatly admired Ge Nie from Yuci, whom he believed to be a much finer swordsman than himself. The two men were extremely close friends. Now that Jing Ke had been treated with such kindness by Crown Prince Dan of Yan, he decided he should go west to take the king of Qin hostage. Therefore, he sent someone to ask Ge Nie if he would come to Yan to discuss the situation with him. Unfortunately, Ge Nie was out traveling and nobody knew exactly where he had gone; certainly he was not expected back in the near future. Crown Prince Dan knew that Jing Ke was a great knight, and so he always treated him with the utmost respect, not daring to suggest that it was time he was on his way. Then border officials suddenly reported: "The king of Qin has sent his senior general, Wang Jian, north to invade Yan. Jia, king of Dai, has sent an ambassador here to suggest that we join forces to guard Shanggu and prevent Qin from advancing any further."

Crown Prince Dan was horrified. He said to Jing Ke, "Any moment now, the Qin army will cross the Yi River. I know you want to help us, but at that point, will you be able to do anything to change the situation?"

"I have considered the matter deeply," Jing Ke replied. "If I embark on this mission without some special thing to put the king of Qin off guard, he will not let me get close to him. General Fan has deeply offended His Majesty, so the king of Qin put a price on his head of one thousand pounds of gold and a fief of ten thousand households. Qin is also desperate to lay hands on the lands of Dukang, which are so very rich. If I had the head of General Fan and a map of Dukang, I could present them to the king of Qin. He would certainly be delighted and grant me an audience. That would give me an opportunity to repay Your Highness for all your kindness to me."

Crown Prince Dan demurred: "General Fan came to me when he was in dire straits; how could I possibly kill him? The map of Dukang, though, I do not begrudge you."

Jing Ke knew that Crown Prince Dan could not bear to contemplate executing the general, so he went in private to see Fan Wuqi. "You have suffered much from the king of Qin," he said. "Your father and mother were tortured to death by him, together with the rest of your clan. Now he has offered a price on your head of one thousand pounds of gold and a fief of ten thousand households. How do you plan to avenge this, General?"

Fan Wuqi looked up at the sky and sighed deeply. With tears streaming down his face, he said: "Every time I think of Zheng of Qin, the pain penetrates into the very marrow of my bones. But even though I want to kill him, I would never be able to get even close."

"I have a suggestion," Jing Ke said, "which would at one and the same time resolve the political difficulties of the kingdom of Yan and allow you to take revenge on your enemy. Would you be prepared to hear it?"

Fan Wuqi immediately asked: "If you have a suggestion, why don't you tell me?"

Jing Ke hesitated, not saying a word.

"Why don't you speak?" Fan Wuqi demanded.

"I have a plan, but it is hard to put into words."

"If it will allow me to take revenge upon Qin, I do not care if your plan calls for my bones to be ground to dust," Fan Wuqi declared. "Why is it so difficult to tell me what you have in mind?"

"It is my plan to assassinate the king of Qin," Jing Ke explained, "but I am afraid that he will not let me approach. If I could present your head to Qin, the king would be delighted and grant me an audience. I can then grab hold of him with one hand and stab him in the chest with the other. That way, you can have your revenge, General, and Yan can escape destruction. What do you think?"

Fan Wuqi threw off his jacket. Then, waving his arms and stamping his feet, he shouted: "Day and night I have been racking my brains and never come up with a decent plan. Now I have finally heard something sensible!"

He drew the sword that hung by his side and cut his own throat. Although his neck was severed, his head was still attached to his body. Jing Ke picked up the sword and hacked through the spine.

There is a poem that testifies to this:

> When he heard this cunning plan, he was like a man possessed,
> His soul had already hastened off towards Xianyang.
> If Jing Ke had succeeded in his strategy to kill the king of Qin,
> Fan Wuqi would have had no reason to regret his violent death.

Jing Ke immediately sent someone to report to Crown Prince Dan: "I have the head of General Fan Wuqi."

When the prince got this news, he came as quickly as he could. Throwing himself across the body, he wept with great sadness. He gave orders that the general's corpse be buried with full honors. His head, however, was enclosed inside a wooden box.

"Have you found me a good dagger yet?" Jing Ke asked.

"For one hundred pieces of gold," Crown Prince Dan said, "I have bought a very sharp dagger, one foot eight inches long, from a Zhao person named Xu Furen. An artisan has treated the blade with poison. This has been tested, and anyone cut with this dagger suffers a hemorrhage, immediately bleeding to death. This weapon has been ready and waiting for you for ages, but I don't know when you plan to set off."

"My friend, Ge Nie, has not yet arrived," Jing Ke said. "I am waiting for him because I need him in support."

"Your friend seems to be very elusive, like a piece of seaweed floating on the ocean," the crown prince responded. "I have a number of brave knights in my household, of whom Qin Wuyang is by far the best. Perhaps he could go with you as your deputy?"

Jing Ke understood that the prince was desperate. He sighed and said, "If I am to go and attack the king of such a powerful country as Qin armed only with a dagger, I will not come back alive. The reason why I have been delaying is because I wanted to wait for my friend, who will ensure the success of our plan. However, since Your Highness is in a fever of impatience, I had better be on my way!"

Crown Prince Dan wrote out a letter of credentials. Then he gave him the map of Dukang and Fan Wuqi's head, together with a thousand pieces of gold to cover the expenses of the journey. Qin Wuyang was to go with him as his deputy. On the day that they were to set out, Crown

Prince Dan and all his retainers who knew what was afoot dressed in white robes and plain hats and congregated above the Yi River to hold a banquet in his honor. When Gao Jianli heard that Jing Ke was going to Qin, he came too, bringing a shoulder of pork and a large pot of wine. Jing Ke introduced him to Crown Prince Dan, and His Highness gave orders that they should all sit together. When the wine had circulated several times, Gao Jianli began to play his lute and Jing Ke sang. The music played was a sorrowful tune. The words of the song ran:

> The wind soughs and the waters of the Yi River run cold,
> The hero leaves but he will not return!

The melody was extremely sad and all the men who had come there began to weep, as if they were attending a funeral. Jing Ke looked up at the sky and sighed. His breath came out in a puff; as it floated into the heavens, it transformed into a rainbow, piercing the sun. Everyone who saw this was absolutely amazed. Jing Ke now began to sing a martial air:

> He who enters the tiger's lair or the haunts of dragons
> Has breath that will transform into rainbows in the air.

This song was very stirring and the company felt themselves excited, as if they were about to engage in battle. Now Crown Prince Dan poured more wine into a goblet, and kneeling in front of Jing Ke, he presented it to him. Jing Ke drained the cup in a single draft. Grabbing hold of Qin Wuyang's arm, he jumped into a chariot. Whipping up his horses, he sped away and never turned back to look at those left behind. Crown Prince Dan climbed onto a hill so that he could watch them leave. He did not move until they were out of sight, as sad as if he had lost something. He returned to his companions in tears.

In the Jin dynasty, the recluse Tao Yuanming wrote a poem about this:

> Crown Prince Dan of Yan built up a stable of knights,
> In order to take revenge upon the powerful kingdom of Qin.
> Having brought together hundreds of good men,
> In the end fate brought him Jing Ke.
> A gentleman is prepared to die for the sake of the man who understands him,
> Thus Jing Ke took his sword and left the Yan capital.
> As his horse neighed on the broad road,
> Unhappy men came to see him off.
> Beneath his hat, his hair bristled with energy,

His official garb masked his heroic bravery.
The farewell banquet was held by the Yi River,
The finest of heroes were seated there—
On one side, Gao Jianli played a sorrowful song on his lute,
On the other side, Jing Ke sang at the top of his voice.
The trees soughed as a tragic wind blew through their branches,
The waters crashed as cold waves were whipped up.
The first song moved everyone present to tears;
With the second song, brave knights leapt to their feet.
Although he knew that he would not return,
He left a great name for later generations.

. . .

When Jing Ke arrived in Xianyang, he discovered that the king of Qin was very fond of one of the cadets in the Palace Guard, a man named Meng Jia. Thus, Jing Ke began by bribing this man with one thousand pieces of gold to put in a good word for him with the king of Qin. Meng Jia went to the palace, where he presented his opinion to His Majesty: "The king of Yan is so much in awe of Your Majesty's military might that he does not dare to so much as raise an army, in case it offended you. He would like to have his country incorporated into Qin by peaceful means, accepting a position comparable to a feudal lord under the Zhou dynasty. He will offer you tribute and accept his territory being divided into Qin-style commanderies and counties, providing that he is allowed to continue the sacrifices at the temples dedicated to his ancestors. However, he is too much frightened to come here in person, so he has sent an ambassador here, armed with the head of Fan Wuqi, a map of the lands of Dukang, and a letter with the personal seal of the king of Yan affixed. This ambassador, Jing Ke, is waiting even as we speak in an official guesthouse. Please give the command, Your Majesty."

When the king of Qin heard that Fan Wuqi had been beheaded, he was delighted. He put on full court dress and arranged for the most lavish ceremonies to be performed. Then he had the ambassador summoned to the palace at Xianyang for an audience. Jing Ke came forward with the dagger in his sleeve, holding the box that contained Fan Wuqi's head. Qin Wuyang held the box containing the map of Dukang. As they walked up the steps, Qin Wuyang was deadly pale and seemed to be shaking with fear. One of the servants asked, "Why are you so frightened?"

Jing Ke turned his head to look at Qin Wuyang and smiled. Stepping forward, he kowtowed and apologized to the king: "This man is Qin

Wuyang, a barbarian from the remote northern regions. He has never in his life seen the Son of Heaven before, so he cannot help feeling nervous and behaving differently from normal. I do hope that Your Majesty will not be offended. Please let him complete his mission."

The king of Qin gave orders that only the chief ambassador from Yan should ascend to the main hall. His entourage shouted at Qin Wuyang to go down the steps. His Majesty gave orders that the head-box be opened so that he could inspect the contents: it was indeed Fan Wuqi's head.

"Why didn't you kill this traitor years ago?" he demanded.

"After Fan Wuqi committed his crime against Your Majesty," Jing Ke replied respectfully, "he went and hid in the Gobi Desert. The king of Yan offered a reward of one thousand pieces of gold to get him. His original intention was to present him to Your Majesty alive, but being afraid that it might prove difficult to transport him all that way, he had his head cut off. Nevertheless, he hopes in some small way to assuage Your Majesty's anger." Jing Ke's voice was calm and his appearance friendly, so the king of Qin felt no alarm.

It was now time for Qin Wuyang to present the map. He bowed and knelt at the bottom of the steps. The king of Qin said to Jing Ke: "Get the map that this Qin Wuyang is holding and let me see it!"

Jing Ke took the box containing the map from Qin Wuyang's hands and personally presented it to the king. His Majesty spread the map open and began to study it. It was at this moment that Jing Ke's dagger fell into view, and he could not hide it. In a panic, Jing Ke grabbed the king of Qin's sleeve with one hand while, with the other, he stabbed at his chest. Before the point of the dagger had pierced his skin, His Majesty wrenched himself free with a strength born from terror, tearing his sleeve.

It was the first week in the fifth month, so the weather was already quite warm. His Majesty was wearing an unlined fine silk jacket, which tore easily.

To one side of His Majesty's throne was a screen some eight feet in height. His Majesty leapt behind it and the screen came crashing to the ground. Jing Ke chased after him, the dagger gripped in his hand. The king of Qin could not escape him, so he ran around and around the pillars of the room. By Qin law, it was illegal for anyone to enter the audience hall with a weapon. All the palace guards and military officials were arrayed outside the building, but without a direct order from the king, they did not dare to enter. Now an assassination attempt was underway, His Majesty did not have time to call for his guards—his retinue had to fight Jing Ke off with their bare hands.

Jing Ke fought bravely, stabbing at all the men who came near him. The royal physician, Xia Wuju, used his medicine bag to swing at Jing Ke. He lifted his arm to ward off the blow, cutting the medicine bag in two. Even though Jing Ke fought ferociously and the people trying to defend the king of Qin could not deal with him, there were many of them and only one of him. This enabled the king of Qin to keep running from one side of the hall to the other, and Jing Ke could not get close to him.

The king of Qin was wearing a sword, a fine blade called *Ripple*, but when he wanted to draw his sword to fight back, it got stuck in the scabbard because it was so very long. A young eunuch screamed, "Why don't you put the sword behind you, Your Majesty, and then try to draw it?" The king of Qin realized the good sense of this and did what he suggested. When the sword was behind him, it came out perfectly easily. Jing Ke was quite as brave as the king of Qin, but the former was armed with a dagger useful only for stabbing at close quarters, whereas the sword, being much longer, could be used at a greater distance. With the sword in his hand, the king of Qin felt much more confident. He charged forward and slashed at Jing Ke, inflicting a deep cut in his left thigh. Jing Ke fell back against one of the bronze pillars of the palace, unable to get up. All he could do was to throw his dagger at the king of Qin. The king leapt to one side, and the dagger flew past his ear to imbed itself in the bronze pillar with a shower of sparks.

The king of Qin attacked Jing Ke again. Jing Ke grabbed hold of the blade of the sword, losing three fingers in the process. Having been stabbed eight times, he leaned against the pillars and laughed, then he cursed the king of Qin, his legs splayed out in front of him: "You are a lucky man! I wanted to just hold you hostage, forcing you to give back the lands that you have conquered from the other kings. Now the whole thing has gone wrong and you have been able to escape. This must be the will of Heaven! Since Qin is so strong, you will soon conquer all the other kingdoms, but how long will you enjoy your own?"

The king of Qin's retainers forced their way forward to beat him to death. Qin Wuyang, standing outside the hall, realized that Jing Ke had launched his assassination attempt and tried to join in. He was immediately killed by the palace guards. This occurred in the twentieth year of the reign of Zheng, king of Qin.

How sad it is that, after Crown Prince Dan had done so much for Jing Ke and sent him on this special mission to Qin, he failed completely. Not only did he bring about his own death, but this also cost the lives of Tian Guang, Fan Wuqi, and Qin Wuyang. He even got the king of Yan and Crown Prince Dan killed too. Can it be that his swordsmanship was not as good as everyone thought it?

An old man wrote a poem:

> Armed only with a dagger, he entered the capital of Qin.
> Although brave, his swordsmanship failed him.
> This hero did not return, the conspiracy collapsed;
> Fan Wuqi should never have entrusted him with his head!

When it was all over, the king of Qin sat still for a long time, his eyes staring into space. Having recovered somewhat from the shock, he went over to look at Jing Ke. His eyes were wide open, staring, and filled with rage. The king of Qin was horrified. He ordered that the bodies of Jing Ke and Qin Wuyang be removed and burned in the marketplace, together with Fan Wuqi's head. Every member of this embassy from Yan was killed, and their heads were suspended from the city gates. Afterwards, His Majesty got into a carriage and drove to the inner palace. His womenfolk had by this time heard that an assassination had been attempted, and they all rushed forward to make inquiries. They had wine served to celebrate His Majesty's survival and help him recover from the shock.

There was a certain Lady Hu Ji, who had originally been a maid in the royal palace at Zhao, who had been selected to come to Qin when Zhao was conquered. She was much favored by His Majesty because of her skill as a musician, which saw her elevated to the position of a junior wife. The king of Qin ordered her to play to cheer him up. Lady Hu Ji strummed her *qin* and sang:

> A fine silk jacket is good to tear,
> A palace screen is good to hide behind,
> The *Ripple* sword is good to wear,
> A wicked man is good to kill!

The king of Qin was very pleased by her composition and rewarded her with a box of silk. That night he enjoyed himself to the utmost, spending the night in Lady Hu Ji's chamber. Later on Lady Hu Ji gave birth to a son: Prince Huhai, who eventually became the Second Emperor of Qin. This all happened much later on.

. . .

The following morning the king of Qin held court, at which rewards were distributed for the actions of the previous day. In the first rank was

Xia Wuju, who was presented with two hundred gold ingots. His Majesty said: "Xia Wuju must love me, because he used his medicine bag to hit Jing Ke!" Next he summoned the eunuch, Zhao Gao, and said: "It was you who told me to put the sword behind me." He was rewarded with one hundred ingots. The members of the king's retinue who had fought Jing Ke off with their bare hands were rewarded according to the severity of the injuries that they had suffered. The members of the Palace Guard who had killed Qin Wuyang were also given rewards. Meng Jia had made the mistake of recommending that His Majesty meet Jing Ke, so he was executed together with his entire family. By this time Meng Ao was already dead, and his son, Meng Wu, was serving in the army. Given that he could have had nothing to do with all of this, he was given a special pardon. These orders did not entirely assuage the king of Qin's rage. He commanded that more troops would be sent to join those already attacking Yan under the command of Wang Jian. These men were to be commanded by Wang Ben, the latter's son.

Crown Prince Dan of Yan was infuriated by this move. He took out his entire army and did battle west of the Yi River. The Yan army suffered a terrible defeat, in which Xia Fu and Song Yi were both killed. Crown Prince Dan fled back to the city of Ji—this was when Ju Wu was killed. Wang Jian joined forces with his son to besiege the city, and in the tenth month the city wall was breached.

"It is all your fault that our country is going to be conquered!" Xi, King of Yan, complained to his son.

"So is the fall of Han and Zhao my fault too?" Crown Prince Dan snapped. "We have twenty thousand fine soldiers inside the city—if you can make it to Liaodong, you can make your stand there, protected by the mountains and rivers. You must leave immediately, Your Majesty!"

King Xi had no choice. He climbed into his chariot, opened the East Gate of the city, and fled. Crown Prince Dan sent all of his finest soldiers out with the king, guarding the rear himself. He escorted His Majesty safely to the east, to Liaodong, where they took up residence in Pingrang, the new capital of Yan. Wang Jian captured the city of Ji and reported his victory to Xianyang. At the same time, the general announced that he wished to retire, having become ill as a result of the stress of prolonged campaigning.

"My hatred for Crown Prince Dan is such that I can never forget it even for a moment!" the king of Qin declared. "But it is true that Wang Jian is too old for this!"

He ordered General Li Xin to take over, leading his troops in pursuit of the king of Yan and his son. Meanwhile Wang Jian was summoned home, where he was loaded with generous rewards. Wang Jian then retired to Pinyang on the grounds of ill health.

. . .

When the king of Yan heard that Li Xin had arrived at the head of his army, he sent an ambassador to ask for help from Jia, king of Dai. He wrote the following reply to the king of Yan:

> The reason that Qin is prosecuting their attack upon Yan so vigorously is that they hate Crown Prince Dan. If you would be prepared to kill Dan and apologize to Qin, they will become less enraged with you. In that case the state altars of Yan may continue to enjoy blood sacrifice.

Xi, king of Yan, hesitated, unable to make up his mind about killing his own son. However, the crown prince became frightened that he might indeed be executed, so he and his retainers fled to hide on Taohua Island. Li Xin had his army make camp at Mount Shou, while he sent a messenger to take a letter to the king of Yan, listing the crown prince's crimes. The king of Yan was now very frightened indeed. On the pretense of needing to discuss matters of state, he tricked his son into coming back and got him drunk. Having garroted Crown Prince Dan, he had his head cut off, weeping bitterly throughout. Although it was then the fifth month, there was a sudden fall of snow that covered the ground to the depth of two feet and five inches, and it became as cold as if it were the depths of winter. Everyone said this was caused by the unjust death of Crown Prince Dan. The king of Yan had his son's head placed in a box and sent to Li Xin's encampment, together with a letter of apology. Li Xin immediately reported this to the king of Qin and said: "There has been heavy snow here in the fifth month, and my troops are suffering greatly from the cold. Please allow me to stand down my army temporarily."

The king of Qin discussed this with Wei Liao. Wei Liao presented his opinion: "The kingdom of Yan has now been reduced to a last hideout in Liaodong, while the kingdom of Zhao is now down to a little piece of land in Dai. Their situation is no better than that of lost souls; sooner rather than later, they will disappear forever. It would be best to conquer Wei first and then turn your armies against Chu. Once those two kingdoms have gone, Yan and Dai will fall without a fight."

"Good," said the king of Qin. He ordered Li Xin to collect his troops and bring them home. Meanwhile, he appointed Wang Ben as general, and he led an army of one hundred thousand men out of the Hangu Pass to attack Wei.

• • •

By this time, King Jingmin of Wei was already dead and his son, Crown Prince Jia, had been on the throne for three years. When Qin attacked Yan, Jia, king of Wei, had the walls of Daliang reinforced, with huge trenches dug on both sides of the defenses, to prepare for future attacks. He also sent an ambassador to try and make an alliance with the king of Qi. Persuading him of the benefits of doing so, he said: "The fates of Wei and Qi are like the lips and the teeth—once the lips are gone, the teeth feel cold. If Wei is conquered, Qi will be next. We ought to help each other and defend each other in times of need."

In Qi, ever since the death of Queen Junwang, it was her younger brother, Hou Sheng, who took charge of the government in his capacity as prime minister. He had received a great deal of gold from Qin. He therefore insisted to His Majesty: "Qin will never betray their alliance with Qi. If you join in this Vertical Alliance with Wei, you will only make them angry." King Jian of Qi was misled by his advice into refusing the overtures of the Wei ambassador.

Wang Ben, having won one battle after another, advanced and laid siege to Daliang. This occurred during the rainy season. Wang Ben rode in a carriage roofed in waterproof oiled cloth to inspect the local rivers. Thus he discovered that the Yellow River flowed just to the northwest of the city. The Bian River rose at Yingyang, flowing past the west side of the city. Wang Ben ordered his men to dig a canal from the northwest corner of the city, which would channel the waters from these two rivers. He constructed a dam to contain the flow. The men went out in the rain to carry out this work—Wang Ben himself joined them with a spade to speed them on. When the canal was constructed, it promptly rained for ten days without stopping. When the power of the waters was at its height, Wang Ben ordered the dam to be breached to allow the flood to pour into the channel they had prepared. In an instant, the trenches inside and outside the city were overflowing. Once the city walls had been battered by the floodwaters for three days, they were breached at several points. The Qin army was able to enter the city through these holes. Jia, king of Wei, was taken prisoner by Wang Ben just as he was in the middle of discussing the possibility of surrender with his ministers. His Majesty was loaded into a prison wagon with the rest of his family and escorted to Xianyang. En route, King Jia got sick and died. Wang Ben took possession of all the lands of Wei and created Sanchuan Commandery. At the same time, he captured the lands of Yewang, reducing the Jiao, Lord of Wey, to the status of a commoner.

The history of Wei begins in the reign of Lord Xian of Jin, when he enfeoffed Wei Biwan. Wei Biwan's son was called Mangji and his grandson was Wei Chou, who held the title of Viscount Wu. It was in large part thanks to Wei Chou that Lord Wen of Jin became hegemon. Four generations later, Viscount Huan of Wei destroyed the Fan, Zhonghang, and Zhi clans. Viscount Huan's son took the title of Marquis Wen of Wei—it was he who divided the state of Jin into three parts, in concert with Han and Zhao. Seven generations later, in the time of King Jia, the country was destroyed. This kingdom lasted for just two hundred years.

A historian wrote in commemoration:

The descendants of Wei Biwan
Took his surname as the name of their kingdom.
His heirs flourished and brought their country much glory,
From one generation to the next they were loyal and upright.
Lord Wen was the first ruler to be numbered among the aristocrats of
    Zhou,
Lord Wu made the country increasingly powerful.
King Hui was a man who loved warfare,
And Daliang knew no peace.
The Lord of Xinling kept a house full of brave knights,
His remarkable qualities were known to all the world.
In the reign of King Jingmin, the government began to fail;
A generation later, everything collapsed.

This occurred in the twenty-second year of the reign of Zheng, king of Qin. In that same year, in accordance with Wei Liao's advice, the king of Qin began to plan his attack on Chu. He asked Li Xin: "How many people will I need for a successful attack on Chu?"

"No more than two hundred thousand men," Li Xin replied.

His Majesty summoned the old general, Wang Jian, and asked him the same question.

"Li Xin may think he can attack Chu with just two hundred thousand soldiers, but he is sure to be defeated," Wang Jian said. "For this, you need at least six hundred thousand men."

The king of Qin said to himself, "Old people often become more cautious and frightened—Wang Jian is no longer as brave as Li Xin." He told Wang Jian that he would not be needed and appointed Li Xin to be

Chapter 107 | 437

the commander-in-chief, with Meng Wu as his deputy. They led two hundred thousand men to attack Chu. Li Xin proceeded against Pingyu, while Meng Wu assaulted the city of Qinqiu. Li Xin was a young and positively foolhardy young man. Having succeeded in taking Pingyu at his first attack, he advanced his army westward, to take the city of Shen. He sent someone to take a letter to Meng Wu, telling him that they would meet at Chengfu, since he wanted to join forces with him to attack the city of Zhu.

. . .

Let us now turn to another part of the story. In the kingdom of Chu, after Li Yuan had murdered Huang Xie, Lord of Chunshen, he put Crown Prince Han on the throne—he took the title of King You. Crown Prince Han was, of course, the son of the Lord of Chunshen and Queen Li. King You died without any children in the tenth year of his reign. By this time, Li Yuan was also dead. The ministers decided to establish Prince You as the next king—he took the title of King Ai. In just the second month after King Ai's coronation, he was taken by surprise and murdered by his half-brother, Prince Fuzou. This prince now established himself as king.

In the third year of the reign of King Fuzou, he heard that the Qin army had penetrated deep into Chu territory. Appointing Xiang Yan as the commander-in-chief, he took command of an army of more than two hundred thousand men, advancing by water and overland to intercept the Qin forces. When his spies discovered that Li Xin's army had already set out from Shen, he led the main army in person to intercept the enemy at Xiling. He ordered his junior general, Qu Ding, to set seven ambushes at various points around Mount Lutai. Li Xin advanced bravely, and when he encountered Xiang Yan, the two armies began to fight. At the height of the battle, the soldiers in ambush at the seven key points rose up. Li Xin simply could not withstand the enemy onslaught and fled, having sustained a bad defeat. Xiang Yan pursued him for three days and three nights without cease, killing seven commandants and countless Qin officers and men. Li Xin withdrew the battered remnants of his army to the fortress at Ming'e. Xiang Yan attacked again and defeated them. Li Xin abandoned the fortifications and fled. Xiang Yan chased him all the way back to Pingyu, taking the conquered cities back.

Before Meng Wu had even arrived at Chengfu, he was informed of Li Xin's defeat. He withdrew to the border, sending a messenger back to Xianyang to report the emergency. The king of Qin was absolutely furious. He stripped Li Xin of his honors and official titles and went in person to visit Wang Jian at Pinyang. "You said that you reckoned that Li Xin would certainly be defeated if he attacked Chu with only two hundred thousand men," His Majesty said. "Now events have proved you right and our army has been humiliated. I know that you suffer from poor health, General, but do you think you would be well enough to rejoin the army for a time?"

Wang Jian bowed twice and apologized to the king, saying, "I am now extremely unwell and my powers are definitely failing. Your Majesty must choose some other good general."

"I am afraid that I need you to go in person," the king said. "Please do not refuse."

"If you insist on giving me this job, then I must demand an army of six hundred thousand men from you."

"I have heard it said that in antiquity, the largest countries had three armies, the ones of middling size had two, while little countries had just one army. It was unheard of for the entire army to be sent out in any single campaign, to ensure that there would always be more soldiers. When the Five Hegemons exercised their powers over the other lords, they never had an army of more than one thousand chariots. If you calculate from the fact that each chariot had seventy-five infantry attached to it: that would mean they did not have an army of even one hundred thousand men. Now you are insisting on being given six hundred thousand men, which is unprecedented."

"In antiquity," Wang Jian said, "the two sides would agree on a day to put their troops into battle formation, and then they would fight. There were set ways in which infantry soldiers were used—they were often there to show military might and would not actually be put into positions where they might be wounded or killed. These campaigns were conducted to punish crimes by rulers and not to conquer territory, so even though weapons were brandished, warfare was still conducted on the principles of proper ritual and ceremony. Therefore, when the sage-kings of antiquity fought a battle, they never used many troops. When Lord Huan of Qi was hegemon, he was victorious with armies smaller than thirty thousand men, but that was still more than enough for him to bring peace to the borders. When we fight today, the strong kill the weak, the many butcher the few. If you encounter enemy soldiers, then you kill them; if you see an opportunity, you attack. The records of heads taken in modern battles show that tens of thousands of men may die in a single campaign; when cities are besieged, the siege may last for many years. Every farmer knows how to use a halberd and a sword, and even small children find themselves conscripted into the army. Power comes from how many men you can put in the field on the day: this is a situation where skimping is not an option. Furthermore, Chu occupies the entire southeast—once the king of Chu gives his command, as many as one million men will find themselves under arms. The six hundred thousand I have asked for may well not be enough! You cannot possibly provide less."

The king of Qin sighed and said, "You are speaking from years of experience, sir. I will listen to your advice!"

He returned to court with Wang Jian riding in one of the carriages at the rear of his train. He immediately appointed him to the position of senior general, with six hundred thousand men under his command, and Meng Wu as his deputy.

When the army was about to set off, the king of Qin went in person to Bashang to hold a banquet in the old general's honor. Wang Jian lifted his cup and toasted His Majesty: "Please drink this, for I have a request to make."

The king of Qin drained the cup in a single draft and then asked, "What do you want to say?"

Wang Jian pulled a bamboo document from his sleeve. It contained a list of the finest lands and best houses in the vicinity of Xianyang: "Please give these to me."

"If you return victorious," the king of Qin said, "I will reward you with wealth and honors—why should you worry about being poor?"

"I am an old man," Wang Jian replied. "Even if you were to give me the title of a marquis or some such as a reward, my position would still be like that of a candle in the wind—having flared for a moment, it is gone forever. Why don't you give me these things when I am still alive to enjoy them? Then I can hand them on to my sons and grandsons, who will bless Your Majesty from one generation to the next." The king of Qin cackled with laughter and agreed.

When Wang Jian arrived at the Hangu Pass, he sent a messenger to the king to ask for yet more orchards and wetlands.

"Aren't you asking for too much?" Meng Wu asked.

Wang Jian whispered to him: "The king of Qin is a forceful character, but he is very suspicious. He has entrusted me with six hundred thousand men—this campaign has left the country empty. The more fields and houses, orchards and wetlands that I ask for, the more I talk about wanting to help my children and grandchildren, the happier the king of Qin is going to be about giving me such power."

"That is very clever," Meng Wu said admiringly. "I really am no match for you."

If you do not know how Wang Jian's campaign against Chu fared, READ ON.

Chapter One Hundred and Eight

Having united six kingdoms, a fresh plan of the country is drawn.

After taking the title of First Emperor, Zheng of Qin establishes a new order.

When Wang Jian replaced Li Xin as commander-in-chief, he took an army of six hundred thousand men and announced that he was marching on Chu. Xiang Yan organized the defense of the city of Donggang, with the intention of blocking his advance. When he realized quite how enormous the Qin army was, he sent someone to report this as quickly as possible to the king of Chu, requesting auxiliary troops and additional generals. The king of Chu raised a further two hundred thousand soldiers and appointed General Jing Qi to command them, in support of Xiang Yan. At this time Wang Jian's troops were camped at Mount Tianzhong. The various encampments stretched for a dozen *li*, each one entrenched behind high ramparts. Every day Xiang Yan sent his troops out to provoke battle, but the enemy never responded. Xiang Yan said: "Old General Wang Jian must be too scared to fight!"

Wang Jian gave his officers time off to go and bathe, then every day he killed oxen to allow them to eat their fill. He always ate exactly the same food as the men. His soldiers appreciated this very much and wanted to do their best for him. Repeatedly they asked permission to go out and fight, but he would simply order them to drink more wine. This situation continued for several months in a row. Since the soldiers had nothing else to do with their time, they amused themselves by various stone-throwing and high-jumping competitions. This was all done according to the rules laid out in *Fan Li's Art of War*: When throwing stones, the weight of each ball had to be twelve pounds, and they used a wooden scoop to hurl them into the air. Anyone who threw more than three hundred paces was accounted a winner; anyone who failed to throw that distance lost. Someone very strong would be able to throw with their bare hands, and that was regarded as an even finer victory. When doing the high-jump, they would put the bar at seven or eight feet and compete as to who could jump over it—that was how they judged success. Wang Jian asked officials in each of the camps to make a note of who won what each day, so he would know who were the strongest of his men. Apart from that, he made sure that his soldiers stayed ready to defend themselves, while making sure that they did not cause trouble by demanding provisions from the local people. If his troops captured any Chu people, he would give them wine and food before sending them back home. This stalemate endured for more than a year. Since Xiang Yan did not see his enemy fight even once during this time, he decided that even though Wang Jian was supposed to be attacking Chu, he actually had no intention of doing so. Hence, he made no preparations for war.

Suddenly one day, Wang Jian held a great feast for all his officers and announced: "Today we are going to conquer Chu." The generals all clapped their hands and punched the air with their fists—they each wanted to be the first to go into action. He selected twenty thousand men for their bravery and strength, and made them into a separate army of great warriors: they would form the vanguard. The remainder of his forces he divided into a number of separate units; he ordered that once they received news that the Chu army had been defeated, they were to fan out through the country, occupying as much territory as they could. Since Xiang Yan was not expecting an attack by Wang Jian, he was taken completely by surprise. When he rushed out to do battle, the vanguard warriors screamed and hurled themselves into the fray—each man was the equal of one hundred. All the practice that they had put in paid off on the day. The Chu army suffered a bad defeat. Qu Ding was killed in battle, while Xiang Yan and Jing Qi gathered up the shattered remnants of their forces and retreated to the east. Wang Jian took advantage of his victory and chased after them; a second battle was fought at the city of Yong'an. Again the Chu forces sustained a terrible defeat. Next they attacked and took the city of Xiling. The kingdom of Chu was now terror-struck. Wang Jian ordered Meng Wu to take half the army, making camp at E'zhu, while circulating placards around every region in Hunan, proclaiming the virtue and might of the king of Qin. He himself commanded the rest of the army to go at all speed to the Huainan area, marching on the city of Shouchun. At this point, Wang Jian sent an envoy to Xianyang to announce his victories. Since Xiang Yan was out in the Huaishang region, trying to muster troops, Wang Jian took advantage of his absence to make a surprise attack on the city. When the walls were breached, Jing Qi cut his own throat at one of the watchtowers, while King Fuchu of Chu was taken prisoner. The king of Qin went in person to Fankou to collect his prisoner—he upbraided King Fuchu for his crime of assassinating the former monarch and demoted him to the status of a commoner. He ordered Wang Jian to gather all his forces at E'zhu to facilitate the conquest of the rest of the kingdom. Every county in the Hu and Xiang region was watching the development of events nervously.

Xiang Yan succeeded in mustering an army of twenty-five thousand men. When he arrived at the city of Xu, he happened to meet the king of Chu's younger brother, the Lord of Changping, who had fled from the fighting. "Shouchun has fallen," he said, "and the king of Chu is a prisoner. I do not know if he is alive or dead."

"We still have more than a thousand square *li* of land south of the Yangtze River in the former kingdoms of Wu and Yue," Xiang Yan said. "This would make a perfectly good independent country."

He led his forces across the river, where he crowned the Lord of Changping as the new king of Chu. Having established his capital at Lanling, he ordered his troops to guard the city.

• • •

Once Wang Jian had pacified the region north and south of the Huai River, he went to meet the king of Qin at E'zhu. His Majesty praised his many successes, after which he said: "Xiang Yan has already crowned a new king of Chu south of the Yangtze. What are we going to do about this?"

"The kingdom of Chu has traditionally been sited along the Huai and Yangtze Rivers," Wang Jian replied. "Now the whole of the Huai River region is in our hands, so they really are at their last gasp. Once the main body of the army arrives, they will quickly mop up any opposition. There is nothing for you to worry about."

"Although you are an old man, general," the king of Qin said, "you are still very ambitious!"

The following day, the king of Qin got into his carriage to begin the journey back to Xianyang. Wang Jian remained behind with his army, with orders to pacify the area south of the Yangtze River. Wang Jian ordered Meng Wu to take charge of boat-building operations on Parrot Island, where he constructed ships for more than a year. When they were ready, he sailed down the river, and none of the soldiers stationed in forts along the way were able to withstand them. When the Qin army regained dry land, they left one hundred thousand men stationed at Mount Huang, to secure access along the Yangtze River. The main body of the army advanced from Zhufang to lay siege to Lanling. They made camp on all four sides of the city, their battle cries shaking the heavens. Soldiers occupied the whole area between Mount Fujiao, Mount Jun, and Mount Jingnan to prevent any attempt to move in reinforcements from Yuezhong. Xiang Yan mobilized every single soldier within the city to fight a final battle at the foot of the walls.

When the battle began, the Qin army found itself at a slight disadvantage. Wang Jian divided his very best troops into two columns and armed them with swords for hand-to-hand fighting. Screaming battle cries, they hurled themselves against the enemy positions. Meng Wu personally beheaded one enemy commander and took another general prisoner. This increased the morale of the Qin forces tenfold. Xiang Yan sustained yet another bad defeat and fled back to the city, where he barricaded the gates and prepared for a long, drawn-out siege. Wang Jian had ladders prepared and resumed the attack; Xiang Yan responded with fire-arrows, which burned the ladders to a crisp.

"Xiang Yan is like a lobster in a pot," Meng Wu said. "If we build ramparts on all sides of the city level with the tops of the walls and attack simultaneously, they will not be able to withstand us, because we are many and they are few. Within a month, the city will fall."

Wang Jian followed his advice and attacked the city with redoubled vigor. The Lord of Changping was on patrol around the city walls when he was struck by a stray arrow—although his guards carried him back to the palace, he died that night. Xiang Yan wept and said, "The only reason why I am still alive today was that I thought it my duty to support the last member of the Mi royal family. What hope is left now?"

He looked up at the sky and shouted three times, then committed suicide by cutting his throat with his sword. The city was now thrown into complete chaos. The Qin army climbed up the walls and opened the gates, allowing Wang Jian to enter the city at the head of his forces. He made sure that the inhabitants of the city were pacified and then led the main army south as far as Mount Xi. The soldiers dug pits in which to put their cooking pots, and thus they discovered an ancient stone stele. There were some words carved on its surface:

As long as tin is mined here, it will be made into weapons,
And the world will be riven by warfare.
Once the tin is exhausted, there will be an end,
And the world will be at peace.

Wang Jian summoned a local man and asked him about it. "This is the eastern peak of Mount Hui," he said. "At the time when King Ping of Zhou moved the capital east to Luoyang, this mountain was mined for tin and lead. That is why it is called Xi or 'Tin' Mountain. However, within the last forty years, the veins of metal have been exhausted and, in recent times, the amount recovered has been significantly reduced. I do not know who put up this stele, though."

Wang Jian sighed and said: "Now that this stele has appeared, it means that the world will soon be at peace. Some person in ancient times must have foreseen this and set up this stele in order to instruct later generations. In the future, this place should be known as Wuxi, or 'No Tin.'"

The name of modern-day Wuxi County came from this.

Wang Jian's troops advanced past Gusu, and the officials responsible for guarding the city simply surrendered. Afterwards, they crossed the Zhe River to pacify the lands of Yue. After the fall of the kingdom of Yue, the junior members of the royal house had scattered throughout the region between the Yongjiang River and Mount Tiantai, living by the sea. Although they assumed titles suggesting that they were rulers or headmen, in fact they were completely disunited. Now, hearing of the military might and virtue of the king of Qin, they all came to surrender. Wang Jian received maps and census information from them, immediately reporting this development to His Majesty. Thus he was able to pacify the Yuzhang region and establish the commanderies of Jiujiang and Kuaiji, putting an end to the royal line descended from King Zhurong of Chu. This occurred in the twenty-fourth year of the reign of King Zheng of Qin.

It was in the sixteenth year of King Huan of Zhou that the ruler of Chu, Xiongtong, first felt himself to be powerful enough to declare himself a king; he took the title of King Wu. From this point onwards, year by year, the rulers of Chu conquered smaller states. Five generations later, King Zhuang of Chu took the title of hegemon. Afterwards, in the time of King Zhao of Chu, his kingdom was nearly destroyed by Wu. Six generations later, in the time of King Wei, the lands of both Wu and Yue were incorporated into Chu, and thus the entire region between the Huai and the Yangtze Rivers was governed by this one kingdom that occupied nearly half the known world. King Huai made the mistake of trusting the wicked minister, Jin Shang, and ended up being kicked around by Qin, which marked the beginning of Chu's decline. Five generations later, in the time of King Fuchu, the entire country was conquered by Qin.

A historian wrote a poem of commemoration:

> The descendants of Yuxiong
> Were initially enfeoffed in Chu.
> First they became kings and then they became hegemons,
> Opening up vast stretches of land in the south.
> King Cheng usurped the throne, displacing the rightful monarch;
> His son, King Mu, murdered his father.
> Not realizing that they were bringing down disaster upon themselves,
> They conspired against their own family members and butchered one
>   another.
> King Zhao was forced to abandon the capital and flee,
> King Huai suffered the humiliation of dying a prisoner in a foreign land.
> Kings Xiang and Kaolie presided over a further decline,
> Thus King Fuchu ended his reign as a captive of Qin.

Having destroyed the kingdom of Chu, Wang Jian stood down his army and returned to Xianyang. The king of Qin rewarded him with one thousand ingots of gold. Wang Jian announced that he was now too old to continue in office any longer, so he moved back to live in his hometown of Pinyang. The king of Qin appointed Wang Jian's son, Wang Ben, to the position of commander-in-chief. He attacked the king of Yan at Liaodong. His orders from the king of Qin were as follows: "If you can pacify the Liaodong region, you should take advantage of Dai being isolated to conquer them, thus saving yourself the trouble of having to engage in two separate campaigns."

Wang Ben took his army across the Yalu River and laid siege to the city of Pingrang. When he captured the city, he took Xi, king of Yan, prisoner. His Majesty was sent to Xianyang, where he was demoted to become a commoner. The kings of Yan were descended from the Duke of Shao, who was the first to be enfeoffed here. Nine generations later, Lord Hui was in power when King Li of Zhou was forced to flee to Zhi. Eight generations later, in the time of Lord Zhuang of Yan, Lord Huan of Qi attacked the Mountain Rong and gave the five hundred *li* of land he had conquered to Yan. This is when Yan first became an important and powerful country. A further nineteen generations later, when Su Qin created the Vertical Alliance, it was Lord Wen who was in power.

It was his son, Yi, who first adopted the title of king, and Yan was numbered among the seven great kingdoms of the Warring States era. King Yi's son, King Kuai, was killed by Qi, and his son, King Zhao, restored the kingdom. Four generations later, in the time of King Xi, the country was finally destroyed.

A historian wrote in commemoration:

The Duke of Shao brought order to this remote region;
The song "The Sweet Pear Tree" records his great virtue.
King Yi of Yan usurped the title of a monarch,
Joining the other six kingdoms of the Warring States era.
King Kuai was killed thanks to his weakness;
It was his son, King Zhao, who restored the prestige of the kingdom.
However, when Crown Prince Dan's plot failed,
The whole of the Liaodong peninsula was lost.
The ruling house endured for forty-three generations,
They remained in power for eight or nine centuries.
This was the last branch of the Zhou royal family to be killed,
Thanks to the enormous blessings Heaven gave to the great Duke of
Shao.

When Wang Ben had conquered Yan, he moved his troops westward to attack Dai. The armies of Jia, king of Dai, were defeated. He intended to flee to the Xiongnu nomadic people, but Wang Ben caught up with him at Mao'er Village, taking him prisoner. King Jia committed suicide, and Qin gained control of all the lands of Yunzhong and Yanmen. These events occurred in the twenty-fifth year of the reign of Zheng, King of Qin.

Zhao Zaofu had served one of the early Zhou kings, and his descendants were hereditary grandees of the Royal Domain. When King You behaved with such wickedness, Zhao Shudai fled to Jin, where he took office with the first Lord Wen of Jin. It was at this time that the Zhao clan was founded. Five generations later, Zhao Su served Lord Xian of Jin; and his son, Zhao Cui, served the second Lord Wen. It was Zhao Cui's son, Zhao Dun, who served three rulers of Jin in turn: Lord Xiang, Lord Cheng, and Lord Jing. The rulers of Jin at this time held the title of hegemon, and the Zhao family stood at their right hand. Although Zhao Dun's son, Shuo, was murdered, Shuo's son, Zhao Wu, returned to power. Two generations later, we come to Viscount Jian of Zhao—it was his son, Lord Xiang, who divided the state of Jin with Han and Wei. Lord Xiang was succeeded by his nephew, who was in turn succeeded by his son, the first to take the title of marquis: he was Lord Lie of Zhao. Six generations later, in the time of King Wuling of Zhao, the Hu nomads submitted to their authority. Four generations after that, Qian, king of Zhao, was taken prisoner by Qin, which meant Prince Jia established himself as king of Dai. He preserved the sacrifices to the ancestors of the Zhao family, but in the sixth year of his reign, Dai was destroyed. Five of the six kingdoms of the Warring States era were now gone—only Qi remained.

A historian wrote in commemoration:

> The ruling house of the kingdom of Zhao
> Was a branch of the royal family of Qin.
> When King Mu of Zhou pacified the state of Xu,
> He enfeoffed Zaofu, the ancestor of this family.
> Zhao Shudai was the first to serve in the government of Jin;
> His descendent, Zhao Su, was the first to be granted land.
> From the time of Zhao Wu onwards, they were hereditary ministers,
> Their title was Lord of Zhao.
> The surrender of the Hu nomads made this country strong,
> But internal troubles brought them ill fame abroad.
> Unable to understand the merits of Lian Po and Li Mu,
> Qian of Zhao ended up a prisoner.
> For six years Jia held out in Yunzhong,
> The last flicker of a dying light.

Wang Ben wrote a letter to Xianyang to report his victory. The king of Qin was very pleased and wrote back in person. The letter read:

> In a single campaign, you have succeeded in pacifying both Yan and Dai, bringing us more than two thousand *li* of new territory. You are every bit as brilliant as your father and, like him, you will receive no less a reward. However, since it is easy to travel from Yan to Qi, I would like you to continue your campaign to the southeast. As long as Qi survives, I will feel like I am missing an arm. I hope that with your awe-inspiring reputation in battle, General, you can descend upon them like a clap of thunder. You and your father will then have done more for Qin than anyone else in history!

When Wang Ben received this letter, he advanced his army to capture Mount Yan. From there he could survey the region south of the Yellow River, and prepare to move south.

. . .

On the advice of his prime minister, Hou Sheng, Jian, king of Qi, made no attempt to rescue Han or Wei. Instead, as each kingdom was destroyed in turn, he sent an ambassador to Qin to offer his congratulations. Qin made sure that this ambassador was always heavily bribed with gold so that when he went back home, he would praise how generously he had been treated by the king of Qin. King Jian was quite convinced that the alliance between their two kingdoms was strong, and so he made no preparations for war. When he heard that all the other five kingdoms had been destroyed, King Jian became uneasy. He discussed the situation with Hou Sheng, and began to move troops to guard the western frontier to prevent a surprise attack by the Qin army. This did not prevent Wang Ben's troops from crossing the Wu Bridge and marching straight on Ji'nan.

By this time, the king of Qi had been in power for forty-four years. He had never so much as fought a single battle; his people were so used to peace that they had never even engaged in any military exercises. Besides, the Qin army was so very powerful; by common account they had hundreds of thousands of men under arms. They fell on their victims with all the crushing weight of a toppling Mount Tai, so how could the people of Qi not be frightened at the mere thought? Who would dare to resist them?

Wang Ben marched on Linzi, having taken the cities of Lixia and Zichuan en route. As they advanced on the capital, the soldiers were struck by the fact that the countryside seemed to be entirely deserted. Within Linzi itself, people were running around trying to find places to hide; there was no attempt made even to guard the gates. Hou Sheng had no idea what to do—he suggested to King Jian that he simply surrender. Within the space of two months, Wang Ben's armies conquered the whole of the Shangdong peninsula without fighting a single battle. When the king of Qin heard the news of his forces' victory, he gave the following orders: "Jian, king of Qi, refused the overtures of the Qin ambassador under Hou Sheng's orders because he was hoping to cause trouble. Now, fortunately, my soldiers have been victorious and the kingdom of Qi has been swept into history. Originally, it was my intention to have both ruler and ministers put to death, but bearing in mind that King Jian was a loyal ally for more than forty years, I have decided to spare him the death penalty. He and his wife will be moved to the city of Gong, where their living expenses will be paid from the public purse. There they can spend the rest of their lives in peace. Hou Sheng is to be beheaded on the spot."

Wang Ben carried out the execution of Hou Sheng as he had been commanded to do. At the same time, he sent a platoon of soldiers to escort the former king of Qi to Gong and make sure that he was settled there. The residence allocated to him turned out to be a tiny thatched cottage located at the foot of Mount Taihang. Nobody else lived nearby—the place was surrounded by cypress and pine trees. Even though the palace staff had mostly left, he still had a couple of dozen people with him. The allowance he received was not enough to feed all these mouths, and the official in charge was often late in handing it over. His Majesty had one son with him, who was still a child. In the middle of the night the boy started crying with hunger. Jian woke up with a start; he could hear the sound of the wind soughing in the branches of the cypress and pine trees. The former king of Qi thought to himself, "When I was living in Linzi, I was unbelievably powerful and rich! I lost my kingdom because I made the mistake of listening to the wicked Hou Sheng's advice. Here I am, starving slowly on a remote mountainside, and all my regrets are to no avail!"

He wept and wailed ceaselessly, and within a couple of days he was dead. The last remaining palace servants all fled, and the fate of his young son is not known.

There is a tradition that says that Jian, king of Qi, starved to death. When his people heard this, they were deeply upset and composed this song to commemorate him:

> Oh cypress tree! Oh pine!
> I am hungry but I cannot eat.
> What brought King Jian to these dire straits?
> He trusted the wrong man!

Later generations called this the "Cypress and Pine Song"; it bewails the way in which Hou Sheng betrayed his country.

The royal family of Qi was descended from Chen Ding, the son of Lord Li of Chen. In the fifteenth year of the reign of King Zhuang of Zhou, this man fled from trouble to find sanctuary in Qi. When he took office in Qi, he changed his surname from Chen to Tian. A couple of generations later we come to Viscount Huan of Tian, the architect of the family fortunes. His descendant, Lord Xi, disbursed much of the family property in order to obtain popular support. The Tian family became stronger day by day. It was Lord Xi's son who assassinated the Marquis of Qi. Three generations later, this family usurped the marquisate. Another three generations after that, in the time of King Wei of Qi, the country became very strong and they assumed the title of king. Four generations later, in the time of King Jian, the kingdom was destroyed.

A historian wrote in commemoration:

> The Honorable Wan of Chen fled from troubles in his own country,
> And sought sanctuary with the Jiang family in Qi.

It is impossible that two families should share one kingdom,
Thus the Gui clan replaced the Jiangs and the house of Tian flourished.
Tian He was the first to seize power in this state,
Wei then took the title of king.
The Lord of Mengchang assembled many retainers,
While Tian Dan saved a kingdom in peril.
Prime Minister Hou Sheng was so delighted with his bribes
That he thought of the men who would kill him as his friends.
How sad that Jian, king of Qi,
Died in the forests of cypress trees and pines!

In the twenty-sixth year of the reign of Zheng, king of Qin, the whole world was unified as the other six kingdoms had been conquered. The king of Qin was mindful of the fact that the six rulers whose lands he had conquered all had the title of king, and so he decided that this was not sufficiently exalted—he wanted to assume the title of emperor. In the past this title had existed, but it had not been passed down to later generations, nor had it struck awe into the four barbarians. When thinking about the titles of rulers in high antiquity, there were the three sage-kings and five emperors, whose achievements and virtue were far superior to the founding monarchs of the three dynasties. Since Qin's virtue was equal to that of the three sage-kings and his achievements were parallel to those of the five emperors, he took the combined title of Sagacious Emperor. He began by giving his father—the late King Zhuangxiang—the title of Supreme Emperor. His Majesty also decided that he did not like the system of posthumous titles first introduced by the Duke of Zhou; he thought this type of honorific title used by sons to criticize their late fathers, or subjects to criticize their late rulers, to be extremely rude. Thus, he abolished this system: "I will take the title of First Emperor, and later generations will be numbered Second Emperor, Third Emperor, and so on, up to the hundredth or the thousandth generation, for my descendants will rule this realm forever."

The First Emperor assumed the royal we, as befitted the Son of Heaven, and ordered that his subjects refer to him as "Your Imperial Majesty." He summoned the finest of craftsmen to carve the jade disc of Bian He into the new imperial seal. The text on the seal read: "Having Received the Mandate of Heaven, the Empire will Flourish Forever." Thinking about the cycle of the Five Phases, he decided that since the Zhou dynasty represented the element Fire, and Water quenches Fire, this would be the symbol of the Qin Empire. He commanded that all uniforms, battle standards, and flags should be made in the color black.

Since the element Water in this system corresponds to the number six, all weights and measures associated with the Qin Empire were divisible by six. The First Emperor decided that he would officially begin his reign on the first day of the tenth month, and the entire court congratulated him at this time. The personal name of the First Emperor was to be taboo, but unfortunately, the word "Zheng," meaning "straight" or "correct," had exactly the same pronunciation. To get around the taboo, another character of similar pronunciation was used instead. The original meaning of this new character was "to levy taxes" and hence was not very auspicious, but since this was the word that the First Emperor wanted them to use instead, nobody dared to complain.

. . .

When Wei Liao saw how arrogant and self-satisfied the First Emperor had become, not to mention his relentless determination to reform every minute detail of the administration, he secretly sighed and said: "Although Qin has now brought the empire together, the process of decline has already begun. How can this endure forever?"

One night he and his disciple, Wang Ao, fled, never to be seen again.

The First Emperor asked his ministers, "Why has Wei Liao abandoned me?"

"Wei Liao helped Your Imperial Majesty pacify the lands within the four seas, and his contribution to this great work was enormous," they replied. "No doubt he was hoping to be given a large land grant, comparable to that which the Great Earl of Wu or the Duke of Zhou received from the founders of that dynasty. Now you have decided upon your own title, Your Imperial Majesty, and yet failed to reward any of your followers. Wei Liao was disappointed and that is why he left."

"The Zhou dynasty was a feudal system," the First Emperor said. "Is that still what we want?"

"The lands that you have conquered from Yan, Qi, Chu, and Dai are all far from Xianyang and hard to govern well at such a remove," the ministers replied. "If you do not impose a feudal system, how will you keep control over them?"

"The Zhou dynasty established several hundred feudal states under their auspices; the majority were governed by relatives of the Zhou royal family," Li Si remarked. "However, later on their descendants fought amongst themselves and butchered each other mercilessly. Now you, Your Imperial Majesty, have united all the lands within the four seas and established a large number of counties and commanderies.

Even though you have a number of subjects whom you want to reward, you could just give them generous emoluments, with no rights over lands or people. That way, you can prevent further bloodshed in the future. Is this not the way to maintain peace for many generations to come?"

The First Emperor followed his advice and divided the empire into thirty-six commanderies. These were as follows:

Neishi, Hanzhong, Beidi, Longxi,
Shang, Taiyuan, Hedong, Shangdang,
Yunzhong, Yanmen, Dai, Sanchuan,
Handan, Nanyang, Yingchuan, Qi (also known as Langya),
Xue (otherwise known as Sishui), Dong, Liaoxi, Liaodong,
Shanggu, Yuyang, Julu, Youbeiping,
Jiujiang, Kuaiji, Zhang, Minzhong,
Nanhai, Xiang, Guilin, Ba,
Shu, Nianzhong, Nan, and Changsha.

At this time, the northern borders of the empire suffered much from raids by the Hu nomads, hence the commanderies located there, Yuyang, Shanggu, and so on, were by far the smallest. These commanderies were built around military encampments and fortifications. In the south, where the lands were fertile and at peace, the commanderies were extremely large—this can be seen in Jiujiang and Kuaiji. They were in fact much bigger than the kind of administrative division that Li Si had originally intended. Each commandery had a military governor and a supervisory censor. The First Emperor collected weapons from all over the empire and had them brought to Xianyang to be melted down and cast into twelve enormous bronze figures, each weighing a thousand pounds. These he had set up in the courtyard of his palace that they might correspond to the omen of the giants appearing in Lintao. His Imperial Majesty also ordered that the richest and most powerful families in the empire would henceforth have to live in the capital: this resulted in two hundred thousand households moving to Xianyang.

On the northern outskirts of the city, he built six palaces that replicated exactly the royal palaces of the kingdoms that he had conquered. In addition to that, he also constructed the famous E'pang Palace. Li Si was appointed as chancellor of the Qin Empire, while Zhao Gao became the new chamberlain for attendants. Those military commanders who had achieved great success in the service of the country, such as Wang Ben and Meng Wu, were each enfeoffed with ten thousand households, while their junior commanders were given one thousand households.

However, that merely meant that they received the tax revenue from such households—the money was handed over to them by a government official. The First Emperor went on to burn the texts of the classics and bury Confucian scholars alive, not to mention wasting time and money on progresses around the empire. He constructed the Great Wall of China in order to prevent incursions by the Hu nomads, which caused much grumbling among the people: in many cases they lost their livelihood because of this. In the time of the Second Emperor, the government was even more violent and cruel than under his father. Thus, Chen Sheng and Wu Guang were able to gather a crowd of supporters and launch the rebellion that finally brought down the dynasty.

A historian wrote the "Song of the Kingdoms in Peril," which goes as follows:

> After the move of the capital to the east, Qi and Zheng were the
>   strongest states.
> Chu began its rise to power in the reigns of Kings Huan and Wen.
> King Zhuang of Chu, Lord Xiang of Song, and Lord Mu of Qin
> All competed to succeed to the position of hegemon.
> Although Lords Xiang, Jing, and Dao of Jin claimed this title as their due,
> Later generations did not match up to the standards of their forebears.
> Once Jin and Chu began to fail, Wu and Yue filled the vacuum.
> How to choose which was stronger: Helü or Goujian?
> In the Spring and Autumn era there were too many states to be counted,
> Nevertheless a number of important family lines died out at this time.
> Lu, Wey, Jin, Yan, Cao, Zheng, and Cai
> Were allied with the kingdom of Wu, like them a branch of the Zhou
>   royal house.
> Qi was ruled by the Jiang family and Song by the descendants of the
>   Shang kings,
> Sage-king Yu's posterity ruled in Yue and Zhuanxu's offspring in Chu.
> Qin's rulers were also descended from Zhuanxu, Chen's from the
>   sage-king Shun,
> Xu's ruling family was descended from Taiyue—yet each went their
>   separate way.
> The Warring States era saw seven kingdoms competing for supremacy;
> Between them Han, Wei, and Zhao ripped the state of Jin in three.
> Although Wei and Han were both branches of the Zhou royal house,
> The rulers of Zhao were descended from the same family as Qin.
> The Jiangs of Qi was displaced by the Tians, descended from the lords
>   of Chen;
> Thanks to the Lord of Chunshen, the royal line of the Chu kings was
>   usurped.
> After the destruction of Song, their territory was partitioned by Qi
>   and Lu;

Wu and Yue, having fought each other for generations, lost their lands
 to Chu.
Once the *dings* of the Zhou kings moved and the Vertical Alliance
 collapsed,
It was only a matter of time before the six kingdoms were conquered by
 Qin.

An old man, having read *Kingdoms in Peril*, wrote the following
poem:

The Zhou dynasty lasted for nearly eight hundred years:
Half their history was created by their own hands, the other half was
 the will of Heaven.
In the long march of history, we can see the records of the noble and the
 brave,
Countries rise and states fall in an endless cycle through time.
The other six kingdoms willingly surrendered to powerful Qin,
The Zhou dynasty owed its collapse to the decision to move to the east.
What we learn from the fates endured by these ancient kingdoms in
 peril
Is that everything rests on the quality of those serving at court!

Founded in 1893,
UNIVERSITY OF CALIFORNIA PRESS
publishes bold, progressive books and journals
on topics in the arts, humanities, social sciences,
and natural sciences—with a focus on social
justice issues—that inspire thought and action
among readers worldwide.

The UC PRESS FOUNDATION
raises funds to uphold the press's vital role
as an independent, nonprofit publisher, and
receives philanthropic support from a wide
range of individuals and institutions—and from
committed readers like you. To learn more, visit
ucpress.edu/supportus.